Testimonials for the Dynamicist Trilogy

For *Herald*

"The searching, surprising second volume of Hunt's Dynamicist Trilogy (after *Dynamicist*) finds the stakes higher, the pacing more assured, and Hunt's challenges to the orthodoxies of fantasy storytelling more provocative.

He renders scenes of action with crisp power and the action sequences are winningly varied. Readers will enjoy a tavern brawl, a fracas at an underground cult meeting, a confrontation with a legendary magician, and a desperate battle against monstrous "skolves," in which Robert and his classmates must cooperate with everyday soldiers who are understandably skeptical of magic schoolboys. The most memorable elements of the series remain Hunt's philosophical provocations and his vividly detailed magical system. It's a joy to see the characters dig into the study and theory of magic as well as the cultural consequences of its use. Engaging deeply with how heroes' actions affect the lives of everyone else, this sequel finds Robert discovering the complex truths about why his world fears change. Even the cultists, he realizes, have their reasons. This is an exciting, expansive, and ultimately satisfying exploration of the meaning of heroism, the economics of magic, and the role of innovation in society."

—*Booklife Reviews*

"This has deep relevance to life in the early 21st century, and reaching out to readers is a noble endeavor. A bold fantasy sequel that delivers on the first volume's call to action."

—*Kirkus Reviews*

For *Dynamicist*

"A philosophically minded series opener that deftly merges science, fantasy, and college life. Hunt's series starter offers a grounded, scientifically detailed answer to the Harry Potter universe."

—Kirkus Reviews

"Mathematics matter as much as magic in Hunt's inventive adult fantasy, a modern take on the wizarding school. Concerned with economics, architecture, and its protagonist's philosophical musings, the novel moves deliberately, caught up in mind and milieu rather than plot. Readers eager for a thoughtful challenge to genre conventions will appreciate Hunt's rigorous reimagining of how a society with access to magic might endeavor to train and regulate its users. This is a compelling story for readers who crave complex worldbuilding."

—Booklife Reviews

LEE HUNT

KNIGHT IN RETROGRADE

THE DYNAMICIST TRILOGY

BOOK THREE

FIRST EDITION
Knight in Retrograde © 2020 Lee Hunt
Cover art by Jeff Brown
Interior design & typesetting © 2019 Jared Shapiro

Distributed by
Ingram Spark, and IslandBlue Book Printing
P.O.D.

Library and Archives Canada Cataloguing in Publication

ISBN Softcover Book: 978-1-9990935-4-9

ISBN Electronic Book: 978-1-9990935-5-6

Edited & Proofread by: John McAllister

Novels by Lee Hunt

Dynamicist Series

Dynamicist
Herald
Knight in Retrograde

KNIGHT IN RETROGRADE

For the dead mathematicians.

Chapter One

Breakthrough, Part 1

How many people does it take to commit suicide?

One.

That's the best answer.

Looking down from the high stone wall at the unending column of approaching maniacs, it looked like the great mathematician thought the right answer was *everyone*. He had certainly brought everyone with him. I wished he had come alone. That way, when he died, he wouldn't take so much unnecessary company with him.

Including me.

I sighed. *Including them.*

Only one person makes the breakthrough. Only one person cracks the inventive barrier. Only one person really needs to die. But that wasn't going to be what would happen here. The *great* professor, Rodryck Cornell, great-grandson of the greater and oh-so-much deader mathematician Breyton Cornell, inventor of the Cornell Kernel, had brought along others to die with him.

Or rather *for* him.

Supposedly, Rodryck Cornell had come here to invent another shiny new transform, together with its inversion. His plan, supposedly, was to make this inventive breakthrough and somehow survive the inevitable arrival of the punishing demon, Nimrheal. All these accompanying knights—some of them even big-K knights—would, again supposedly, protect him from Nimrheal. This had all been thought through by the brightest, most optimistic minds, the best of those Nimrheal had not already murdered. Supposedly.

Straining my eyes in a vain attempt to make out the end of the approaching column, it hit me just how seriously those brightest minds were taking this latest attempt. They had clearly decided to reinforce quality with quantity this time. Behind the two big-K, plate-clad, shining wonders who led Cornell strode five full eights dressed in mail, swords at hip, crossbows strapped to their backs.

Not loaded, I hope. Hate to see someone get a haircut.

Two officers with painted breastplates and two-handed swords marched at a break in the formation near the rear of the eights, looking proud and cocky, as if swinging a bigger sword had anything to do with sound leadership.

What happens if you don't want to carry such a monstrous big sword? Do you get demoted?

One of the officers flickered in the empyreal sky, reminding me momentarily of a Deladieyr Knight.

Perhaps he really has been demoted.

Cornell did not lack for other kinds of help. Behind the officers, a troop of carpenters hauled the mathematician's long, flat boards on a wagon. They would recreate the great man's laboratory high up within the castle. His assistant walked beside him, notebook in hand as always, ready catch his every command or insight. A gaggle of academics waddled along behind him, carrying their big leather books and packs full of ink and feather pens. Cornell could not leave home without his students, scribes, and mathematical sycophants. They were there to take notes during the momentous event. Nothing would be missed; no act of suicidal genius would go unrecorded. Everyone would be there, ready for the big moment of discovery, and for the arrival of the transcendental punisher. Cornell had even commandeered two wizards to be on hand to jump into the fray. I was one of them.

Could he succeed? Could he create the new transform? Could he make its inverse? Could any of us survive?

The only "inversion" I thought likely to manifest lay in who would die. The purpose of a shield, after all, was to be struck. Mortality *might* be turned on its head in one way though. Cornell's new mathematical transformation could result in all of *us* dead while *he* skipped away without paying the price.

He is so knights-damned selfish.

"What do you think of our great experiment, Luciena?"

I turned to answer Lord Auvigne, who stood beside me on the wall with his wife. They looked like two straight-backed, tall, dark-skinned gods, their green eyes setting off the urbane faces of the true aristocracy of Engevelen. These tall flowers might have been twins, they were so similar in their effortless poise, their commanding presence, their generous nature. I felt unworthy to stand in their shadows, they were so glorious.

Too bad they had chosen to patronize this debacle. Even worse that I had failed to talk them out of it. Without their influence and wealth, and their castle, the whole mad experiment might never have come to be. Staring into the umbra of their beauty, I realized that they infuriated me most of all. They were most responsible for what was about to happen. They also had the most to lose. This was their home, after all.

"I can hardly think of a greater and more important undertaking, my lord," I replied, trying to keep my true feelings from betraying my voice.

Two pairs of penetrating green eyes bore down on me. I was known to them as a poor liar. I looked away. The two shining, big-K knights had marched ahead and were approaching the gate now. I could see the empyreal medium warp and bend around them in a halo. Great crowds of townsfolk lined the way and kneeled as the knights passed, hands outstretched toward the Elysium-sent saviors, tears no doubt streaming down their faces. I could hear the crowd beseeching the knights as they approached the castle gate, cheering them, glorifying the insane undertaking they had come here to protect.

The shorter Methueyn Knight had no helm and carried an enormous, long-handled hammer. *Darday'l.* Two long, brown braids of hair swayed gracefully behind her. She paused to help one of the kneeling supplicants, who had stumbled onto all fours. She patted the old woman on the shoulder and continued her smooth passage toward us. Then she looked up at me. I was transfixed, and a moment passed between us before she passed under the gate. What was that look on her face, that wry smile? Did she also know I was lying? Why did she also have to be so generous with me?

"Come, Luciena, we have to try." Lady Auvigne's voice was softer than a goose-down pillow and just as comforting.

"This dark age has gone on long enough, dear." The great Prince of Engevelen put his arm around my shoulders. "We must fight it. You have said so yourself, dozens of times." His voice dropped lower, to reassure me. "It will be okay."

They were both smiling at me with that encouraging, supremely confident air they seemed to inhabit whatever the circumstances. It made me want to be as brave as them, as upright, as supportive, as good. It almost made me want to scream and throttle them.

"Perhaps we will find a way," I allowed, smiling back, thinking I was more likely to solve the last digit for pi than we were to stop Nimrheal from finger-painting the mathematician's chalkboard with our blood. But what could I do? I had argued enough with them already. The crop was already planted, and my misgivings would not see the sprouts tilled over. The hordes of awe-struck onlookers already lined the road, the troops were already pouring in through the gate, and the mathematician was already imagining the feel of a stick of chalk in his fingers. I'm a wizard. I have an instinct for everything, especially for these things. The sword had been poured. Everyone here, everyone still pouring in under the gate, had already decided, already committed themselves, already imagined themselves as either heroes or dead. Or both.

This lunatic party was not going to be cancelled because of anything rational I could say. I would have to think of some other way for this grand endeavor to roll the one-one of Nimrheal and discover nothing worth dying for.

"I can't work under these conditions!" Cornell screamed, his face red, the ligaments in his neck jumping to attention. "They're pissing in the sink! Where I wash my hands! How am I supposed to handle the chalk after that?"

"That does sound wrong, Professor," Lady Auvigne said, keeping a straight face with difficulty. "But I am sure it was just one or two bad stalks. I will speak to them."

"Speak to them? Just one or two? They were lined up for the sink! Lined. Up." His voice lowered to strangulation level and his eyes bulged like a frog's. "To *urinate.*"

Perfect. Perhaps he would expire from apoplexy. Or quit the whole project. Or at least take a nap. Any delay was a good delay. I turned away from Cornell's tantrum—who hasn't had to pee in a sink, after all, though it is harder for some to pull off than others, especially with a line of gawkers right behind you—and tried to hide my joy by examining the organized chaos around me. Even though I wanted nothing more than the whole project to fall into the null hypothesis, I had to admit the setup was impressive.

Our headquarters were on the top floor of the great circular tower of the observatory. The room was at least eighty feet in diameter and had the only retractable roof in the known world. Through this, the telescope had been removed by a crane and placed on the roof of one of the four adjacent towers. The observatory was the reason Lord and Lady Auvigne—and the committee, of course—had chosen Ardvaser Castle for the experiment instead of their summer home at Auvigne or their seat in Engevelen City. Supposedly, the castle's wondrous ambience would aid Cornell's process of mathematical invention. I hoped not. I hoped it would rain and the roof get stuck open.

Perhaps I can ensure that.

"What are you thinking so hard about, Luciena?"

Gil Harbinger's voice startled me so badly that I almost jumped out of my knickers. Good luck keeping this crowd of soldiers in line if that happened. Those knights-damned sink-pissers were rude enough without the encouragement of seeing my underthings. I turned ninety degrees to face the old wizard. "I was just admiring all the wonderful … carpentry, Gil," I said. The carpenters had almost finished building the supports for all three eight-foot-wide chalkboards and facing tables. Cornell's amanuensis, Eydith, was riding herd on the woodworking, making sure everything was solid, square, and precisely level. Cornell's tantrums could be provoked by the tiniest irregularity.

Eydith needed to look out for everything concerned with Cornell's work, from the alignment of the chalkboards to the protocols for the academics and recorders, to the backup recorders, to the positions of the guards and their schedules, to the lighting arrangements. She buzzed between Cornell, Lord and Lady Auvigne, the carpenters, the other academics, the miscellaneous sycophants, and the milling troop of sink urinators. I wondered how Eydith managed to look so lively and young despite what I knew to be her age, pulled between so many people, working for a man so petulant and demanding. But she looked after him well, never complaining or flustered, and her back was still straight, her black hair still absent any grey, and she smiled constantly despite the chaos around her.

"Luciena? Are you all right?"

It was Gil Harbinger again, still staring at me with his large brown eyes, looking worried. Perhaps he was also trying to figure out how to make something go wrong. With this much chaos, opportunities abounded, or would until Eydith and Lord and Lady Auvigne had sorted things out.

"I'm not an animal!" Cornell whined.

I walked farther away from the mathematician. He continued bellyaching to the indescribably patient Lady Auvigne, both circled by the still buzzing, busy Eydith, as Harbinger kept pace with me. He was a true man of South Harkness, brown skinned and bulbous nosed, with thinning hair and a love of fat, drawn-out conversations. He was not much for accomplishing tasks, however. Intelligent, polite—jovial even—he was a man with an extensive list of achievements in his past, and a most perplexing way of never getting anything done in the present. Perhaps I needed to draw on his talents.

"Do you really think this is going to work, Gil?" It was a question I had not meant to ask.

"Are you serious, Luciena?" Gil Harbinger responded, smiling his easy smile, making his potato nose widen, its dark pores shifting. "After investing so much time on this, you're afraid it will fail?"

He nodded his head and slowly, pointedly turned, inviting me to turn with him. We made a full circle, taking in the room. "We have five full eights, forty elite soldiers of Engevelen, and their leader, the inestimable Guard Captain Veygard, veteran of a dozen battles with Novgoreyl up on the ley line at Arsenault. Veygard, you know, was considered by the Council of Knights for the Ceremony of Rising. He was rejected, I hear, on ... philosophical grounds."

He looked at me conspiratorially. "After that, ah ... incident with Sir Seygis ten years back—I'm sure you remember us talking about it, since it was so unusual—they are much more careful about who they let Rise and who goes near the Methueyn Bridge. Ninth Methueyn Angel indeed! Don't tell the Steel Castle I said that. But all the same, no one doubts Captain Veygard has some power in him. Plenty of it, and as I mentioned, he did not come alone. All those forty-odd armor-cased heroes are right here too. And that doesn't include the five hundred other soldiers spread around the rest of the castle and its environs." He waved a hand generously, vaguely, in the direction of the soldiers who were milling about, trying to find something useful to do with themselves but mostly just getting in the way of the carpenters.

"All those men and women, watching, making sure nothing goes wrong, ensuring everything goes right. It's a knights-damned marvel!"

Harbinger slapped a heavy palm onto my shoulder, puffing as if this was the best day of his life. "And they aren't even the big trebuchets at the siege. We have a full Methueyn Knight, Darday'l, and her squire— sorry, I shouldn't have said that, don't tell on me, okay—the Deladieyr Knight Sir Hasconeyt. Either of those ladies could probably punch a hole in most armies."

Harbinger stepped closer. "Can you feel them?" He nudged his big spheroidal nose up toward the edge of the rolling roof, where the two gleaming women stood. If you could really still call them women. I was not sure. Sir Darday'l shone in the empyreal sky, a brilliant sun beside the bonfire that was Hasconeyt, both singularities piped into Elysium. I had to release the empyreal sky because of the tears their blazing luminescence brought forth. Through the liquid refraction of my full and blinking eyes, I thought I made out Sir Darday'l staring at me again, her eyes transfixing me like twin monochromatic rays from heaven.

"What could go wrong while two such angels watch over us?" Harbinger asked, lowering his voice conspiratorially. I heard him, but I couldn't stop gazing at the two knights standing on the edge of the roof above us, staring down at the things we did, at the things we would attempt to do. *Judging us too, maybe.*

Maybe. I blinked again, trying to clear my mind, wondering what it would be like to touch heaven, what it would be like to touch *her.*

"If that doesn't do it for this project, consider the mathematicians. I know you've always had some funny ideas about mathematics, Luciena, so you will enjoy this. Take Eydith, working away so busily over there." He pointed to the small spritely woman, who was holding a level to one of the tables, shaking her head. "As you know, Eydith is an accomplished mathematician in her own right. She will help Rodryck. She'll do more than just take notes on every step of the work. She can even challenge the great man, if it comes to that, get him back on track. Eydith has also made sure that all the students, the academics, the sycophants—or scribes, if you prefer—are good at their jobs and do exactly as they're told. Anything Cornell puts on any of the chalkboards will instantly be written into a dozen notebooks. Anything he says, as well. He won't be able to so much as whisper to himself without them capturing it for the future. Nothing paid for can afford to be lost, you know." Harbinger winked at me.

"We will have some influence on the outcome as well, Luciena," he added, nodding his lumpy head at me. "Two wizards, one a master— that's me of course—the other of undeniable promise despite being barely more than a girl."

He put up two hands in mock surrender. "I know, you're seventeen already, practically a full-grown woman. But everyone knows you're destined for greatness." He grinned, his face seeming to fold in two.

"Everyone loves you, Luciena. Lord and Lady Auvigne want to keep you as their own despite your lack of a single drop of the blood of Engevelen." He followed my eyes up toward the two glorious women on the roof. "Even the holy knights follow you with their gaze like sunflowers following the sun. Do you think Cornell doesn't feel it?"

"Stop making fun of me," I said, looking down, trying not to look back up at the two beautiful knights on the open roof. "This is serious."

"I know it is, Luciena. I know. This is just how I talk. To you." I could feel him staring at the back of my head. "Do you know what Lord Auvigne said to me just the other day?" Harbinger asked, drawing the question out.

I shook my head at the floor, feeling my face heat up.

"He said I should watch Cornell, of course, but if Nimrheal was to come, I should protect you first. Save his little girl."

I am not a little girl!

"And Lady Auvigne pulled me aside later and told me the same thing."

No!

"Do you really think we can win, then?" I blurted this out, shot it out by the pressure of my fear that we could not possibly win.

"Win?" He looked confused.

"When we fight Nimrheal."

"Fight Nimrheal? Why would we fight Nimrheal?"

"Yes, Nimrheal!" I exclaimed, exasperated. "When he comes."

Gil Harbinger, one of the great wizards of our time, laughed now, hands on his legs, bent over, finally wheezing. "Nimrheal isn't coming, Luciena," he almost shouted as he straightened up, pulled a handkerchief out of some hidden pocket in his robes, and wiped his eyes and his great protuberant nose. "If Nimrheal were to punch his way into this realm, I would be the first to run away. But see?" he spread his arms. "I'm not running anywhere."

I tried not to roll my eyes or gnash my teeth. I tried not to imagine kicking him in the shins. It was difficult. "Then why," I said through gritted teeth, my eyes wet again, "are you going on and on about all our preparations, Eydith, the soldiers, mathematicians, knights?"

Why are you saying all the things I have been thinking about, enunciating my fears, announcing our doom?

"Why are you pointing out," I asked, jabbing at him with my index finger, "all the people who are going to try to make this experiment work?"

Harbinger laughed again, though not for as long or with such abandon. "You don't understand, Luciena. And please don't tell this story to anyone else once you *do* fully understand me. This is just for *you*. As far as everyone *else* is concerned, I think this little experiment is the best thing since we invented the harrow." He put his handkerchief away and stood up straighter.

"I point all these others out because they are part of the reason this whole thing is destined to fail. All this effort, these soldiers, these two sublime, shining goddesses, Eydith and all her fellow mathematicians, all these great people, not to mention us, we are all reasons. They—we—are not why we will *succeed*, but why we will certainly *fail*."

"Are you out of your mind?" I had just about had enough of his never-ending chatter. If I had liked him more, I would have wanted to throttle him.

"No, Luciena, I'm not." Harbinger's smile evaporated, and he looked straight at me, serious now, trying to tell me something important. "His mathematical greatness, Lord Rodryck Cornell, can't even take a piss—sorry, urinate—with someone standing behind him. Do you think he's really going to be able to do something truly creative with the pressure of all of us watching him? He is going to have so much performance anxiety that there is no chance at all that he can ... perform. He won't invent a new way to do anything. No one creates on demand or in committee, no human, anyway." He pulled me into a hug I was in no mood for. "This whole venture is doomed," he said, releasing me with a kiss on the top of my head, then whispered, "You'll be okay. There will be lots of time to satisfy your curiosity after this whole debacle plays itself out."

"We'll see about that," I declared, turning away from him, hoping he was right.

"Luciena!" Gil hissed from behind me, trying not to be overheard, "You won't be blamed when this fails. Don't worry so much."

If this works out, I'll blame myself.

I knew that much.

I strode hurriedly away from the old man, shot through the shadows cast by the two angels, shouldered my way through a knot of startled soldiers, ignored the bearded, breastplated Captain Veygard, who looked like he wanted to say something to me, leapt over a sawhorse, the hem of my dress making it wobble as I passed, dodged Eydith's attempt to intercept me, and planted myself directly in front of Cornell and Lady Auvigne.

"Lucy!" Lady Auvigne cried, flinching almost imperceptibly, her hands reaching for my face.

Ignoring her, I opened myself to the empyreal sky, looking deep into Rodryck Cornell, trying to see if he was the kind of man who really might break through the inventive barrier. There was *something*, something in him, something that could make all the difference. *Yes.* I reached out across the sky and touched it, made the tiniest adjustment.

Suddenly I felt like a dam had burst inside me, like my heart had either broken or abruptly stilled, felt relief that *they* could be saved even if it meant *I* would be damned.

Lady Auvigne moved closer. I smiled as she wiped the tears from my cheeks. I was done crying. According to Harbinger, creativity can only be tapped by a single person working in isolation. An audience spoils the process. I am not sure if he is right, but I take no chances. I have an instinct for these things, and it had been screaming at me for days. Now I have taken matters into my own hands. I have seen into Cornell and done what needed to be done. The smallest change, the smallest thing, can make the biggest difference.

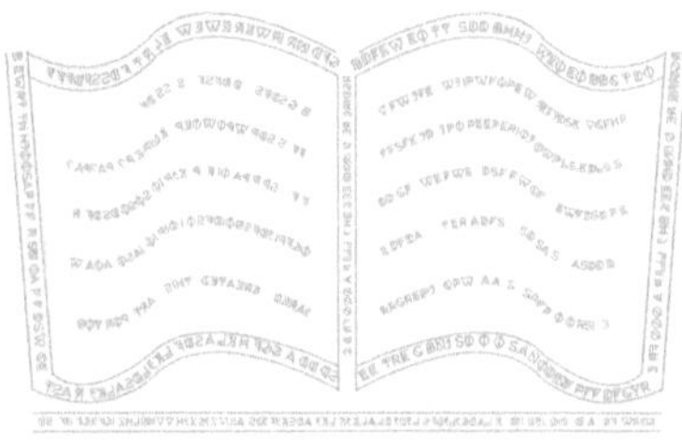

Breach

"PUSH, KORIA, YOU'RE ALMOST THERE." BETHYN'S VOICE WAS AS ENCOURAGING AS Koria had ever heard it. From Bethyn, such a soft and caring tone was beyond unusual. Only Robert had ever managed to break through Bethyn's thick layer of cynicism and only on the odd occasion. But perhaps, in this case, it was the occasion that worked the miracle.

Or perhaps Bethyn was afraid.

"Just push a little harder, you're so close." She squeezed Koria's hand gently.

Bethyn sat behind the stone tub, one hand resting on Koria's head, the other reaching over her shoulder and holding Koria's right hand. Trying to give her strength. "How is the water? Is it hot enough?"

"It's fine, Bethyn."

"How's the light. Dim enough?"

"Perfect." It was dim indeed. Only a single candle lit the room, casting more shadow than light. The lanterns had been hooded, the towels had been piled within reach, and everyone but the two matronly attendants at the back had been ordered from the room. There were no distractions from the process at hand, from this transformation of Koria's life as she attempted her own miracle. The only thing that could have made it better would have been to have her husband, Robert, there. He did not know that her labor had started. Koria did not want him distracted on the night before the most important expedition of his career. He had *his* life-changing mission; she had hers.

"Are you scared?"

Koria took a big, deep breath and pushed, opening herself further. This moment had been planned for well in advance, of course. It had been long awaited. It was welcome and, when done, it would be celebrated as its own little miracle. "A little." Koria *was* a little scared. Life progressed, plans progressed, actions were taken that became—by their nature—commitments. Some of them were dangerous. It was only natural to feel apprehensive, even if she was on the cusp of being part of such a wonderful thing. And she had never done this before. It was one thing to speak about it hypothetically, to theorize. It was quite another to experience it, to live it in the moment.

"Still willing to go through with this?"

Koria craned her head to look back at Bethyn, making the hot water splash gently. "A little late now for second thoughts," she replied archly.

"Well, quit fooling around then. Let's get this wagon on the road. I've got things to do tonight other than play nursemaid." *There* was the old Bethyn asperity.

Koria squeezed her friend's sweat-slick hand and bore down. She needed to focus. She had achieved the first breakdown with ease, ignored the greater breakdown, and was an infinitesimal leap of imagination away from pushing through the third breakdown, the extradimensional barrier. She had seen Robert do it four years ago on the terrible night when, desperate and enraged, he had torn a hole into Elysium. It had nearly killed him.

A stab of fear shot through her, sharp, causing her to tighten up. But Koria Valcourt, daughter of one of the oldest surviving houses of Engevelen, was not a victim of her emotions, however appropriate they might be. She marshalled her courage and ordered her thoughts. She reminded herself that she had gone to great lengths to ensure that this attempt would be different. Trial runs had been made and backed off from at lesser milestones. They had set up the experiment in one of the few hot pools within the castle. The heat sink from the water was a surety against adverse hypothermic effects; the dim lights, expert assistants, and hushed atmosphere were all designed to aid her mental concentration. And Koria brought her own deep sense of discipline to the task as well.

I'm not going to smash through the breakdown, but I shall look through the window. I am not going to borrow a hurricane full of energy. I shall learn something. I am not going into battle; I am going to school.

Yearning to be right, Koria pushed almost imperceptibly harder, drawing asymptotically closer to the energy required for an extradimensional breakdown of the Huygens modulus. She felt a pressure somewhere near her sinus cavities. It built steadily like a vise being screwed tighter and tighter. She began to feel the pressure on her arms and legs, then on her abdomen. She wondered if she was shaking; the medium seemed to spasm and spasm again. Shockwaves arrived in powerful, arrhythmic waves. *I'm skipping off the surface of the medium.*

Koria adjusted her effort. Opening eyes she had not realized were closed, she saw through the dim light that she was not moving at all, that the hot water of the huge tub was not being flung all around the dark room, that the shaking was all in the empyreal sky now.

"Temperature down by two degrees," Bethyn reported, craning her head forward to view the thermometer in Koria's mouth. "Thirty-six point five."

"Okay." That was expected.

"What can you see?" asked Bethyn gently, leaning close to Koria's ear, stroking her hair.

"Nothing. Yet," said Koria, gritting her teeth against the sharpening pain.

"Can you get there?" Bethyn had no hope of making the same attempt. Her affinity was abnormally high, even for a dynamicist, but Koria's natural ability was an order of magnitude higher. Koria could go to the place where the angels used to come from, but being Koria, she would go carefully. She would not *crack the sky* like Robert had done. She would only glide up to the window and peer subtly through into the world beyond.

Another violent wave shot invisibly through her. It felt as if it had lifted her into the air, but in the visible world she lay still.

"Yes. Now. I can just perceive a kind of luminescence."

"Thirty-five degrees."

Koria was right at the point of achieving extradimensional breakdown, and at exactly the same temperature as the last time. The two silent matrons were undoubtedly writing down everything that was said. They would confirm the temperature data later. The initial perception of luminescence had ended the previous test. Not this time. Ignoring the violent, rocking, unpredictable pain, she pushed smoothly, almost gently, through the last nanoscopic step and opened a window into heaven. She held it open.

Women don't have the same difficulty peeing in the middle of the night as old men do.

Koria was in too much pain to laugh at the random thought. Her abdomen felt pinned by a crushing load, but Robert's comparison of opening a heraldic window to an old man struggling to pee had always amused her. It was how his grandfather had first explained the technique to him, and it did capture the strange mix of effort and repose that was required. The extradimensional heraldry she was now attempting called for a similar mix but was much, much more difficult. Koria had gradually developed a deft hand for finding and then sustaining just the right amount of pressure to keep a window open without breaking anything. She did not want to have to start over and have to approach the energy of breakdown again, and she definitely did not want to fall through the window. She had no idea what would happen if she did. *Nothing good.*

"Thirty-four degrees." Bethyn's voice was muted now, its higher frequencies attenuated as if by some vast distance.

There was something beyond the light. A shape! Koria spoke her thoughts aloud for the benefit of the matrons as she wondered if it was a cloud or a mountain. The image sharpened. Was it an enormous, building-sized face? *If this is where the Methueyn Angels came from, the spirit partners of the Methueyn Knights, perhaps I should expect to see a god.* The Steel Castle preached that the eight sacred angels were the gods of heaven, the only gods there were. Others said they were not like humans at all, that the angels were pure *idea.* If so, what would an idea look like?

Those questions were part of the purpose of the test. The most powerful dynamicists could—at harrowing risk—borrow energy from Elysium, but could heaven be communicated with? Could it be done without the lost Methueyn Bridge? And if this one, profound step could be taken, what else could be accomplished? Could they fully understand, at last, what Nehring Ardgour had done when he changed the Huygens modulus?

"Koria, are you okay?" Bethyn's voice seemed to come from farther and farther away. "You're shaking. Thirty-three degrees now. Keep talking."

If it's going to hurt this much, it's strangely comforting to know the pain is real. It was worrying, though, that the arrhythmic waves were manifesting physically now. The pain was excruciating. Her left foot spasmed, the toes curling of their own accord, and her medial longitudinal arch tightened as if trying to bend at a right angle through itself. She had to make a conscious effort to breathe. Her core was locked tight from the stress.

"You should stop. You're below thirty-two degrees."

"Not yet." Koria focused on the enormous face, struggling to make out its strange geometry, but as soon as she tried to quantify what she was seeing, it changed, blurring as if a thin onion skin had been overlain. And now there was another shape, orthogonal to the first but occupying the same space. Gasping for breath, Koria fought to make sense of what she was seeing and describe it for Bethyn and the matrons, but even as she made the attempt, another blurring overwrote the tableau, a new shape overlaying it at another right angle.

"Ahhh, knights!" Koria panted.

"Let it go!" shouted Bethyn.

Koria could not do so. She understood the accumulation of consequence and feared what would happen if she failed in her mission, what would happen to Lighthouse and, eventually, to Robert. She held on as another onionskin layer fell across the scene, and then another and another, each somehow orthogonal, each creating a new, impossible geometry that Koria's mind recoiled from. The image felt infinitely compressed and incomprehensibly complex.

"Let it go, Koria!" Bethyn screamed again, from an eternity away.

Koria's responding scream made no sound, took up no space in the complex geometry of her extradimensional heraldry. It went, apparently, unheard. Possibly for the best. She let go. Or was shaken loose. She said nothing more, shaking in the hot water, feeling the waves of pain slowly fade.

"I think you might have crushed my hand," Bethyn gasped. Koria felt her hair move as Bethyn lifted her head and addressed the matrons. "Unhood the lanterns and bring up the light."

"Raising the hoods," replied a calm female voice as one of the matrons fiddled with a lantern and the light slowly increased.

"What an amazing grip you have, Koria," Bethyn said over the soft rustling of the other attendant, who must have been lighting another lantern. "I thought Robert was the blacksmith in the family. Just stay there. We can add more hot water now that the experiment is done. Your core temperature is way down."

Koria's abdomen was still cramped, though nowhere near as badly as before, but she smiled up at her friend. Bethyn's griping meant that her hand could not actually be crushed. Everything was okay. The lights came up further, bringing color back into the room.

"Well, that was interesting," Koria said, feeling euphoric now as the pain continued to ease. She closed her eyes contentedly, thinking ahead to what would have to be done on the next trial.

"Oh, dear knights, Koria! You're bleeding," Bethyn cried. The horrified words brought Koria's eyes open again. The huge tub of water was red with blood.

Koria quickly opened herself to the empyreal sky, surveying the damage. A new pain rolled over her, not physical this time, yet worse than any of the pain she had experienced in her attempt to breach heaven.

"Is it your baby?" asked one of the attendants. "Is she okay?"

Koria already knew the answer. She could see that the spark of life was absent. "No."

Our baby is dead.

Until a moment ago, she had thought the experiment a failure only of a transient kind. A setback to be recovered from on the next, better-informed attempt. Until that moment, Koria had thought she could try again on another day. She had always prided herself on her ability to avoid irreversible consequences through planning and foresight. That had not been true here. She had woefully underestimated the risks and the depth of her own ignorance. There was no going back from this kind of failure, no analysis of data that would reverse time and bring life back to her womb.

This is what failure really is. The answer bore down on her, massive and gray. *Unrecoverable loss.*

"Leyla's light," exclaimed the matron, scrambling toward Koria from the back of the room. "Did you give birth in the pool?"

"No. She's still … inside." *Still.*

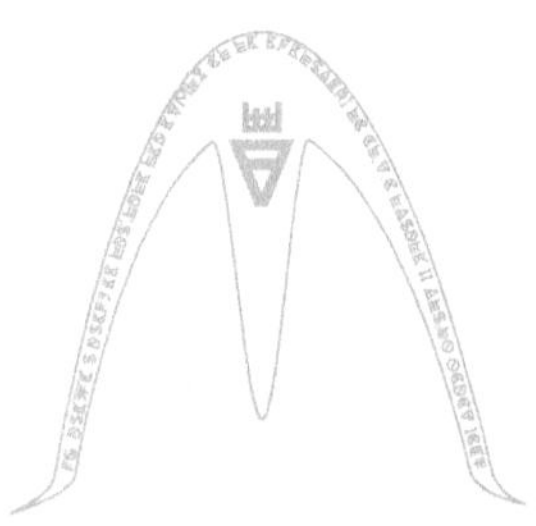

Chapter Three

On the Wall

"HOW FAR CAN YOU THROW AN IDEA?" SIR CHRISTENSEN GAZED OUT ACROSS THE Castlereagh Line at the endless rows of wheat shifting in the breeze. Corporal Rhysheart did not seem to hear him. The young soldier had been watching for Ida Yseult before Christensen ascended the wall, longing to see her striding through the wheat, returning. He had been looking for her all week, growing more and more anxious.

"What?" the young man finally asked, embarrassed to have drifted so far away.

"I asked how far an idea can be thrown."

When Rhysheart hesitated to answer, looking confused, but probably intimidated as well, Christensen continued his rumination. "How far do you think Sir Robert will throw Gerveault's great javelin? Once it's thrown, will it propagate like the wheat out there, spreading and spreading, infiltrating and conquering, overwhelming everything in its path?" He turned to look at the man beside him.

Rhysheart shrugged diffidently. "I don't know, sir. There's only one javelin right now."

Christensen looked down at the open notebook in the palm of his left hand. "Right now, that's true. One you can throw, that is. It is a thing, Rhysheart, but Javelin is also an idea. These things provoke. They propagate … ideas, thoughts. Fears too."

Eight knights, no. Skoll and Hati burning the New School, Skolves at their backs. A row of dark knights following even closer.

Christensen suppressed the images from his dream and tried to remember where he was. On the wall, on the line, standing sentry to other plans and dreams, watching for the return of missing soldiers. Four years into Lighthouse and the wheat went out a long way. Miles and miles. How many teams were out there right now, surveying, planting, evaluating? Some of them were way out on the edge of the wheat line, on the ragged periphery of the plan, pushing the idea just a little further, trying to achieve the next milestone. Some had been lost, having pushed too far.

How far will it go?

Rhysheart had no answers. His thoughts were undoubtedly bent toward the wheat line too, expectant, dreading. Christensen stifled a sigh, aware that he was out of sorts, lacking in certainty, vacillating between his plans and his fears. Since when did he have fears? Since when did he vacillate about anything? He knew the answer. He knew what had changed, and when.

I am no Hemdale. I am no Keith Euyn, thank the knights. I am no longer even myself as I once was. The thought spun his perspective around. New questions, more inspiring ones, leapt to mind.

"You know Sir Robert, don't you, Rhysheart? You were with him in the tower?"

The young soldier straightened up, happy to speak about something that did not confuse him, perhaps happy, too, for the distraction from Ida and her failure to appear. "Yes sir, I do. I was there."

"I knew him in those days too." Christensen remembered the optimistic young man on that day when Robert had first been knighted. He remembered grasping the superb Endicott sword that Robert's grandfather had made. He remembered, months later, seeing the carnage at the Bifrost and not being able to line it up with that sunny young man. Robert Endicott had changed that day, and even more the next day, when they had faced the great Keith Euyn. Christensen frowned. None of those changes could compare to the cataclysm that was the embassy siege.

I should never have asked Robert to come with me. Not then, not with the duchess dying, not with Armadale's ambassador choosing that moment to taunt everyone from inside his estate, and certainly not after Sir Hemdale's sudden appearance. Everyone had thought Hemdale was still at the Line. So many things had gone wrong so quickly.

"What was he like?" *What was he like before we changed him?*

"Robert?" Rhysheart replied. "Smart. He got us into the tower. We'd have been overrun otherwise. Nothing could have been done if we hadn't managed that first." Christensen gazed at the soldier. Blondie, he was called, though his hair was not very blond at all.

"He was scared, though. Like the rest of us," Rhysheart continued. "But determined."

"Hmm." Christensen knew Robert Endicott was determined, as determined as anyone he had ever met. "Do you think that was what made the difference?"

"Being determined always helps," Rhysheart said. "But three of our friends died that day, soldiers who I always thought were pretty determined. Sir Robert had more than just determination going for him. A whole heap more."

"What else?"

Rhysheart frowned.

Instinct told Christensen this was important. "What was in that heap, Blondie?"

"I don't think I know how to put it into words, sir."

"I understand," Christensen nodded genially. "It's okay. Take a step back. Why don't you just tell me what you remember."

Rhysheart had not been fully present for days. His eyes had often been vacant, his thoughts out there, across the line. Christensen could see the young soldier defocus once more, thinking, trying to remember.

Rhysheart came out of his reverie. "That night in the tower … made my greatest and my worst memories." He looked at Christensen, begging for understanding. The knight smiled encouragingly.

"That night contained the most fear but also the most camaraderie of my life. It opened my eyes to so much." Rhysheart closed his eyes. "I'll remember the rotten-meat stench of the skolves forever. I'll hear their howls and the … indescribable sound of Sir Gregory's shield as it deflected their rocks and spears. I'll see the lightning Sir Robert called down and feel the shockwaves as they rolled over us, rocking the whole tower." He smiled, eyes still closed. "It was chaos, it was hell, and it was *transcendent*. Robert was happy. Not scared but certain. We cheered him as he went off, but we thought he was going off to die. I haven't cheered for anyone like that since. I remember our words echoing off the walls of the tower. Redoubt Empyrean! But what did Sir Robert *have*? I don't know. Something special … something beautiful."

Rhysheart trailed off, opening his eyes as he emerged from the memory. Under Sir Christensen's expectant stare, he could not reduce what was in his head to any easy answer. Certainly not an answer he could speak with words. He could not say what had made the difference for Sir Robert under all that stress. He had no conception of what the young man had used to hold himself together.

There is no answer he can give. Explanations of the ineffable become so many clichés when put into words, separated from the rich truth of experience by the narrow dimension of speech.

Christensen snapped his notebook shut and fastened it tightly with two leather straps. "Did you know that all Deladieyr Knights used to journey across the Castlereagh Line after their Ceremony of Rising? It was a rite the Council of Knights enacted after the Methueyn War. Do you know why?"

"Uh, no," Rhysheart stammered, surprised by the shift in conversation. "To fight Skoll and Hati?"

"No. Not to fight, *to find, to seek.*" Christensen held the bound book in his hands and looked out across the rampart to the north. "They—we—were sent, sent ourselves really, to find the Bifrost, the Methueyn Bridge." He smiled ruefully. "We cannot become Methueyns without it."

Rhysheart nodded, catching up. "I *did* know that, but I thought it was an anachronism." He blanched. "I shouldn't have said that. I apologize. I thought it was no longer done because it has been so long and, well, no one thinks the Bifrost can be found anymore …" He trailed off, face turning red, embarrassingly in the moment now.

Christensen did not smile, but his voice was gentle. "Well, no one has found it, not in a quarter millennium. Hmff." He made a sound like a choked-off laugh. "I long harbored the suspicion that Keith Euyn had found it and left it there without telling anyone." His voice trailed away, down to a whisper. "Keith never did like the Methueyn Knights." He shook his head. "No one will ever know now, so I suppose it doesn't matter. The Bifrost is still lost, either way. No Bridge, no Methueyn Knights, corporal. And with this last generation, there haven't been enough of us alive to keep looking, especially with Armadale's knights closed to us. The quest has fallen by the wayside. But Skoll and Hati are still out there, and other things too."

"Yes, they are," Rhysheart said with an uncharacteristic flatness.

Sir Christensen frowned. "I'm sorry to remind you after what happened to Heylor and Ida's eight."

The young man nodded and looking searchingly out across the line again. "What does it have to do with Sir Robert? Do you think he could Rise? Do you think he could have been a Methueyn Knight if we had the Bridge?"

"Í don't know." After the Battle of the Bifrost, probably yes, Christensen thought. But after the embassy siege, he doubted it. Doubts had made their unwelcome introduction to his life on that day. "Perhaps. Maybe if he could find again whatever power it was he found in the tower four years ago."

I must give it a chance.

Christensen thrust the notebook to Rhysheart. "Do something for me, corporal. Take this to Emyr Wynn and ask her to have it couriered at once to Sir Robert."

"Will do." Rhysheart smiled, clearly delighted to be doing a favor for the knight. Walking down the stairs, Rhysheart suddenly stopped. "I should thank you for reminding me again of that ordeal in the tower. It brings to mind my first real look at Ida. I had seen her before, of course, plenty of times, but I had never appreciated her properly for who she was." He smiled rapturously. "Ida was there, standing tall despite her injured hand, smiling despite the pain. She was transcendent. Thinking about her almost makes me cry."

He shook his head. "She is still out there across the line. Alive? If Heylor could suddenly appear in the hall last week, why not Ida? I need her to be alive, Sir Christensen. Ida shines. She has always shone for me since that night in the tower. I fell in love with her then and there."

"Oh, knights." Rhysheart cursed, looking back up at the rampart, in the grip of some epiphany. "I remember!" he announced in a louder voice. "Sir Robert said he *was* love. Not *in* love, *was* love. Sounds like nonsense now, perhaps, but it seemed to make sense at the time." Of their own volition, his eyes slid upward to the heavens. "You had to be there, in the flickering light in the tower, with skolves and an enormous thunderstorm closing in. The word suddenly had a ... weight that I think I understand now, talking with you. He said he could triumph through his fear because of *love*."

There was no reply. "Sir Christensen?" Rhysheart dropped his gaze back to the parapet. Sir Christensen was gone. Rhysheart trotted back up the stairs, but the walkway was empty.

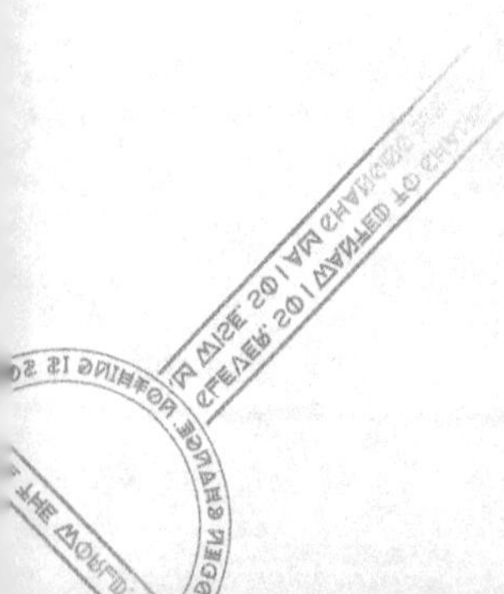

Chapter Four

Act of Worship

"Do you see this- Eloise?" She looked up at the colossal form of her great-uncle. His armor was gone. For the longest time, pieces of the plate and chain had hung from his long limbs, broken, dented, cracked, like ripped clothes but made of metal, ruined in the brittle ways that only hard things can be. Finally, the last of the armor had fallen away. Blood streamed down his face, down his arms, off the ends of his fingers, but he held the sword up to show her the hilt. "Do you see it?"

"Do you see this, Eloise?" Gregory held up a dark cylindrical object.

"I am very disappointed in you, dear," Eloise said, shaking her head, recoiling internally from the intersection of past and present. "It used to be that you'd worship me with dazzling things like this shield." She raised the huge, amorphous, shimmering aegis with her left hand. Light rippled along its glassy surface. Even painted black to make it less conspicuous, the shield shone like the moon.

It would deflect almost any assault that her arms could hold it against, but it could do nothing to correct the unbalancing effect of remembering that day she longed to forget. Eloise continued talking, some gentler part of her mind attempting to deflect memory with more banter. "Nowadays all you seem to have for me is skolve shit. I recognize it from all the other times you've held it up and uttered some deep comment or cautionary maxim." She winked at Eoyan March as he watched, thankfully quiet for the moment. "It's not like I need presents from you. I'm my own woman."

"The best of them," Eoyan interjected, not able to stay out of it after all.

"The best of them," she agreed.

"With the biggest—"

Eloise whirled on the idiot before he could finish. She had assumed he was about to make another stupid joke about her breasts, but he was pointing at his nose with one long finger. Eloise had a *prominent* nose. And somewhat bent, it had to be said.

Whumf!

She connected with Eoyan's nose, bending it sideways with her shield. "Gahk!" He stumbled backward, nearly falling before recovering his balance. He blinked at Eloise through blurry, startled, tear-filled eyes, but did not complain. He knew better. Honor must be upheld.

"Can we all just please grow up? It's a little too early in the morning—and much too far past the Line—for this kind of foolishness." Gregory put a little bit of the lord in his tone, then took a breath. "We don't want our charges to see us behaving this way *anywhere* out here." He looked backwards, but the rest of the team was still out of sight.

Gregory was as tall as Eoyan, though shorter than his wife, like almost everyone. He was also very serious, usually. He brandished the turd at them. "This is indeed skolve feces. Skolves have been here. Recently."

"Let me see that," said Eoyan, reaching for the spoor. He held it up close, blinking the last of the tears out of his eyes as he examined Gregory's find. He was a man who pretended to be a fool and thought this masked who he really was. "This is a month old at least," he said, tossing it into the stalks of wheat. "And by itself it only tells us that they still come through here from time to time." His nostrils flared as he breathed slowly in through his nose. "Let the survey team do their job." He touched the hilt of his sword, eyes scanning the horizon.

Eloise had learned to read both men easily. Gregory was not as concerned as he wanted to appear, at least not about the feces. What really worried him was the bickering that Eloise and Eoyan were engaging in, even if it was mostly ironic. He thought it distracted them from the matter at hand. And Eoyan, Eloise knew, was always more actor than idiot. He might have tossed the turd away as if it was nothing, but he would remember it. They had both seen Heylor the night before they had left on this mission. His screams at the feast would not soon be forgotten by anyone who had been there.

"Fine," she said, knowing the time for jokes was long past. *This is no place for fooling around.* The childhood memory had made her foolish. Standing in the endless field of wheat, anyone might be fooled into thinking it was safe. But it was not. The wheat was an invader. *They* were invaders. The air of safety produced by the familiar crop was a lie. It said that people lived in this place and belonged in it, but neither claim was true. Not yet. Gregory had held up the truth and shown it to her.

This internal admission was as far as she would allow herself to feel embarrassed. Embarrassment, like the jokes, like bashing Eoyan in the face—even if honor called for it—was an indulgence that Eloise had learned she could not afford. "Let's gather everyone in and go over the procedure once more. The wheat line isn't far off."

The team that gathered under the shade of a tall, heavily leafed tree was a large group. Vyrnus Hedt, a dynamicist from the third class of the Duchess's Program, had fifteen agricultural students under his watch, all loaded with notebooks, sample bags, and provision packs. Vern, as everyone called him, was unlikely to say much during the short meeting. Ever since he had foolishly called Eloise a "man with tits" and gotten beaten up in front of everyone, he had been reserved around her, to put it mildly. Eloise did not care why he had made the stupid remark, even if it had been prompted by misplaced animosity toward her uncle, as Gregory had suggested later. It could also have been that Vern, not only older but also a more senior dynamicist than Gregory or her, was their subordinate. Both Eloise and Gregory were Knights of Vercors, trained at the military school as well as in dynamics, and even Gregory was probably a more skilled dynamicist than Vern. Honor was honor, and everyone guarded theirs jealously. Whether the joke had been a response to a perceived slight against his honor or simply reflected his flawed character could be left an open question as far as Eloise was concerned. Short, squat Vern had always acted the big smelly turd from time to time. Only someone with an agenda asked what kind of woman you were; it was only ever a pejorative question.

He cried louder than I ever did. Despite herself, the memories kept returning, this time from even further back. It was the day her uncle had come to rescue the family, to take them out of Armadale. She had not cried then, not even when her father had given his life to stay behind and guard their way, nor when her mother had frozen to death, nor when the last piece of shattered armor had fallen, ruined, from Hemdale's body and two score of knights still blocked their way. "Do you see it?" he had said, showing her the one thing he had that was more resilient even than himself. She had seen it, and she had not cried. *Only the deepest truths are written in steel. Crying over them is not what a woman should do.*

Truths written in steel, the deep truths of womanhood, or of the human condition in general, were not subjects Eloise wanted to share with most people, especially Vyrnus Hedt. Truths could not be communicated. They had to be experienced to be known. And so she had beaten Vern up. That experience would have taught him at least one truth he needed to know. Violence was not the last refuge of the incompetent, as Robert and Gregory liked to say. It was the right response if you were in a hurry, dealing with a fool, or when honor had been besmirched. *Violence is not a refuge; it is simply what most people deserve and respond to. Talk is only for the best.*

Along with Vern and his crew of students, Eloise had five soldiers under her joint command with Gregory. It was her command, really, since that beautiful stupe would damned well do what she told him. Except in the very rare cases when she agreed that her temper could lead her astray. At those times, Gregory's even-handed approach could be useful. Together with the irascible Eoyan, the armed members made up her eight, organized to match the number of the extinct line of Methueyn Knights and the angels in Elysium. "We are going over today's protocol again," she declared to the assembly.

There was some grumbling from the aggies. "Preparation, not inspiration," declared Gregory, frowning prettily. "That's what will keep the skolves from finding you."

A few students grumbled, "What skolves?" because they had not seen any yet.

"We're not dynamicists," added Ellis, a little louder than the rest. He was a thick-bodied, second-year aggie. He had a normal-sized upper lip, but his lower one belonged to a man three sizes his size and tended to pout as if he was an idiot who had misplaced his village. Ellis had his uses, though. He liked to talk, and he often said what the rest of the crew were thinking. He provided an opportunity to correct them all.

"You shut your loaf-hole," commanded Eoyan. "You don't need to be a dynamicist, you need to listen. No one besides Sir Robert Endicott himself has survived more skolves than Sir Gregory."

This was not, strictly speaking, true. Keith Euyn certainly had seen and killed far more skolves, and Sir Hemdale probably had too, back when he was younger and went out searching the Ardgour Wilderness for the Methueyn Bridge. But Eloise was not about to correct Eoyan. She was proud of her husband. He had braved the wilderness for her, as the price to be paid for the materials needed to make her entropic shield. And he had gone through hell out there, and more hell when he made it back in time to fight and nearly die in the Battle of the Bifrost. She looked over at him. He was dark haired, straight backed, earnest. He was so serious, such a believer, so sincerely trying to be a *good* man nearly every waking moment of his life. *Such a romantic idiot.*

"Just because you haven't seen any doesn't mean they aren't out there," Eoyan continued. "I shouldn't have to tell you this again, you've heard it enough. Be *glad* you haven't seen any skolves, Ellis. Yet. Guillaume's team never came back. They had aggies with them just like you lot, probably complaining at their last process-and-protocol meeting too. No one knows what happened to them. Nothing has been found. And look at what happened to Heylor Style." He visibly winced. "Knights! We don't need any more of that. So pay attention to what people who know better than you have to say."

"I'm sorry," Ellis mumbled, big blubbery lower lip hanging down.

"Don't be sorry. Be smart and live."

"As you know, we will soon be separating into two groups," Gregory said evenly, to balance out Eoyan's drama. "One to work on the survey and the other to go out past the wheat line." He looked at Vern, who stood silent, arms crossed. "We've already seen Skolve feces, so the separation of forces is even more important. Vyrnus, if you see or feel any sign we are in trouble, retreat to your rally point. Don't hesitate or second-guess. End your work immediately and leave silently. No fires. Don't look to help us."

"Oh, I won't," Vern replied, putting on an air of confidence and looking anywhere but at Eloise.

No, he won't. No surprises there. Offended or not, Vyrnus wanted no part of a fight with skolves, or with Skoll and Hati. Eloise did not blame him for that, though it did not make her like him or respect him. Whatever Vern was, he was consistent. He might not have understood what kind of woman Eloise was, but that hardly mattered. Vern knew what kind of man *he* was and stuck with it. "Good." She nodded to him cordially, and he managed not to flinch, even if he still could not hold her eyes. "If we do run into a problem, we will retreat to our secondary cache so as to avoid bringing any skolves your way." Eloise turned to Sergeant Brayburn, who had been standing quietly with the other four soldiers.

"You will be in charge of bringing them out past the Castlereagh Line if that happens. Anything to add?"

Brayburn touched his long moustache and studied the aggies before replying. "Keep it quiet out there. There's no outrunning skolves, not this far out. Make your notes quietly. Pretend you're in the Steel Castle, listening to a sermon. Keep calm, breathe deep and even. Let's not have any fear-sweat out there. A skolve can smell it from a mile away. Literally."

Someone made a choking sound, and Ellis took it upon himself to translate. "You're scaring us now."

"Yup. Probably." Brayburn winked at him. "Take a few deep breaths and remember your jobs. Think about that. You New School types tend to lose yourselves in your work. So do your work, do it quietly, and leave the security to us."

†

THEY WERE FIVE MILES FROM THE REST OF THE TEAM AND OVER FORTY MILES PAST THE Castlereagh Line when they hit the wheat line. It was not a line as such, more a thinning out of the New School's invasive breed of triticale and a thickening of older, wild grasses and scrub. It did not happen all at once, but when Eloise paused at the last stalk of wheat, she knew she stood at the current true border of the wilderness. The special triticale had spread at a rate that amazed even Gerveault, the New School's head of dynamics, and Kennyth Brice, Duke of Vercors. It was poisonous to skolves and pushed them out with it, perhaps was even reducing their overall population. It had almost pushed them as far as today's objective, a lonely castle sitting on a wide and gentle hill. Gregory held up another skolve turd. This one was significantly fresher, moist enough for bits of it to stick to the tall man's fingers. Gregory said nothing this time. No further admonition was required. Preparing to step past the last new stalk and cross the wheat line required the solemnity of an act of worship. It was an act that required acceptance of unquantifiable risks.

Eoyan loosened the heavy spear he had taken from Brayburn and turned his head slowly one way and then the other. Gregory locked eyes with Eloise for a moment, then checked the straps on his shield. It, too, was a gift from Robert, though a much less advanced one than hers. He loosened his entropic sword,

Justice, in its sheath. He would not draw it, not yet, but he wanted it ready. In the entire known world, only a handful of blades were as sharp and hard as Justice, and almost all of them had been smithed dynamically by Robert Endicott's family.

Robert's grandfather had made Justice, and Gregory acted with near religious reverence whenever he thought it might be needed. Eloise had a sword much like it, made by the same man, originally for Robert. After his first heraldic dream, Robert had given the superlative blade to Eloise, and except for using it during the final combat with Keith Euyn, he had refused to take it back when the events of that dream had finally played out. *He loves me.* Of that, Eloise had no doubt. Robert loved her. *He has good sense that way.*

She checked her shield first, just as Gregory had, then grasped the hilt of her sword. It was comfortable in her hand. Unlike Justice, it had no name, though many had encouraged her to give it one. Sir Hemdale, the rare possessor of another Endicott masterpiece, had named his, but he refused—except on one dimly remembered occasion—to utter that name in anyone's hearing. When no one was looking, the old knight would speak to his sword with a reverence exceeding even Gregory's treatment of Justice. When Robert had fulfilled his promise to Heylor and made him a blade as fine as his grandfather's best, his fidgety young friend had given the weapon his family name, "Style," as he had always vowed he would if he ever had a sword that deserved the name. But Eloise resisted trying to come up with the perfect name for hers. *If a name has value, it will come to me.*

She looked out toward the castle in the near distance, squatting lonely on its knoll. It was as if it had been waiting for them, unoccupied and solitary, since the Methueyn War. What was a castle without a people to shelter and protect? But apart from Eloise, Gregory, and Eoyan, no human beings had ventured so far past the Castlereagh Line for centuries. The castle had received no human visitors at all, only skolves. And the two demons, Skoll and Hati.

A more sentimental or more easily frightened person might have trembled to look at that pile of stone, but Eloise seldom felt fear, and she was sentimental even more rarely. Practicality had been stamped into her soul at an early age. To her, this wilderness was purely a practical problem. Far from stirring any deep emotions, it put her into an even more pragmatic frame of mind.

My sword's name hardly matters.

She stepped out past the last stalk of wheat, crouched low, and jogged swiftly up the hill, trying to keep her long, lean body as near as possible to the level of the grasses, hoping not to make an obvious silhouette. Gregory and Eoyan silently flanked her, crouching too, panting from the exertion. Eloise did not breathe as hard as the men. She rarely felt overtaxed, physically or mentally. She did sometimes run out of patience with people, as Eoyan's recently bent nose could attest. Even with those she loved. Gregory's endless moralizing had sometimes driven her to anger. He was a good man, one of the best, but why did he always have to make being fair-minded such arduous work?

Robert had been even worse before the embassy siege, always second-guessing himself, always worrying his conscience, trying to take responsibility for everyone and everything, thinking he could save the world. He had toughened up in that first year at the New School, thanks in no small part to Eloise's excellent advice. The embassy siege had nearly completed the process, though not in a way Eloise completely approved of. *He should never have fought Keith Euyn without me. Or gone to the embassy siege afterward.* She huffed silently, remembering that was *after* he and Gregory had run off across the line without her.

Men. They never learned. They were all stupes. But these men were *her* stupes.

Eloise entered the shadow of the castle's wall. Large stones littered the approach, not unusually for the old fortresses of the Ardgour Wilderness. For centuries, no one had been there to care for them. Not since the Methueyn War. And no one had ever found the place that Skoll and Hati called home. Did *they* keep a fortress? They were an unknown, but they were only two. The skolves were another matter. There were thousands of them, and it was apparent from early in the Lighthouse plan that skolves did not bother to maintain any of the old structures in the wilderness. Sometimes they would take shelter in an old tower or storehouse, but they had never improved any building that any team had found so far.

The castle was made of granitoid blocks. Andesite, Eloise thought. The walls were thick and massive, close to thirty feet high and, unlike many of the other towers they had examined, there was an inner keep of some kind and a barbican complete with what looked like two portcullises.

This might be the one.

If so, it would be an amazing stroke of luck. Eloise knelt down beside a pile of twisted, rusted metal that had to be what was left of the outer portcullis.

Grasses had pushed their way up through the reddish knots of iron, obscuring most of the original, intricate design. Something had ripped the entire gate away from the enormous stone gatehouse. She looked over at Gregory, whose right hand had released his sword hilt and then gone to the inside of his jacket, unconsciously reaching for his notebook. She glared at him, silently ordering him to stay on task, to do one thing at a time.

No such worries with Eoyan, whose eyes were in constant motion, looking unnaturally big as he consciously tried to take in all the details of the scene. Eloise doubted he would attempt even one joke until they were well back on the south side of the wheat line. He nodded to her and Gregory and scooted forward, low and fast, toward the barbican. Eloise drew her sword and followed him, not stopping until she stood under the outer arch of the gatehouse. On her right, the grooves for the portcullis were ruined, the outer edge having failed from shin to chest height. The left set of grooves were not in much better shape. A peppering of skolve spoor decorated the pieces of stone that lay all about the arch, scattered about as if sprayed there.

Skoll or Hati did this. One of them ripped the portcullis free of its grooves. A big team of oxen could possibly have done the same, if rigged up cleverly enough, but that is not what had happened all those years ago. No, the demons had come here. This could be the castle the team were looking for, closer in by miles of travel and years of grain invasion than they had expected. She stood watch over Gregory as he leaned his shield against the arch and measured the width and height of the gate, noting down their dimensions and no doubt detailing the damage to the grooves. Eoyan had passed through the second portcullis and must have found the inside stairs to the second level of the barbican. She could hear him moving above them, examining whatever remained of the winch and pulley system.

When Gregory put his right hand on her shoulder, she moved on to the second, inner portcullis, which was still down and in position. The mechanism, at least all that she could see of it, was in decent shape. Except for a colossal, man-shaped hole cut through the center of the iron bars. It was as if an eight-foot shadow had been cast on the portcullis and then burned the iron away. Eloise waited to step through the hole until Gregory finished making his notes on its state of repair.

"I'd love to test it," Gregory whispered, his hand back on her shoulder.

Eloise scowled. "But you won't," she replied just as sub-audibly. She could imagine too easily the clatter the portcullis would make if they dropped it during a test, how the sharp sound of rusty colliding metal and hard andesite would echo out across the wilderness. Nothing natural could groan in the same way as tortured iron. Taking a risk like that was against process for a reason. "Whether it moves or not," she whispered, eyes looking out through the arch, "we need a functioning smithy onsite to make repairs first."

"Or Robert."

"He has Javelin to worry about." Eloise thought even Robert would need a smithy for this one. They would also need to mix cement for the grooves and have a wagonful of good, unweathered iron to work with in case they failed to find enough inside the castle. The list of tools and materials necessary to effect repairs would have to be tallied by committee in the post-mission review and filed for either phase two or four of Lighthouse.

Eoyan appeared on the far side of the arch and gestured them through. "Kind of a strange- looking keep," he said, nodding at the curved building.

Gregory's brows rose fractionally as he got his first unobstructed view of the inner keep. "Is that an observatory on the roof?"

"Might be," allowed Eoyan, studying the same feature Eloise and Gregory were staring at, a small round structure at the center of the keep's roof.

Gregory blinked. "Checking that out should be a priority."

"Yes," whispered Eloise, way ahead of him.

"Well, you're the boss," Eoyan quipped, a smile tugging at his lips.

Gregory hefted his shield. "Great. I'll—"

Eloise planted a hand on Gregory's chest. "He didn't mean you, dear. You test Huygens while we find out what they built up there on the roof. Testing takes a while."

Gregory shook his head but said nothing. He would argue with her when he thought it was worthwhile. But not here, not past the wheat line. In this place, ego had to be stowed, posturing skipped, and the correct procedures followed without hesitation. They had been trained to act this way. It was their process, and Gregory had taken to process training earnestly. He liked it, perhaps because he had spent years learning *not* to act like a lord. He also knew that he was the best choice to test Huygens. He had the weakest affinity, which made for a shorter and more accurate test. Eloise nodded, satisfied, and left him there to prepare the experiment.

She looked over her shoulder intermittently as she and Eoyan walked away, searching for a route into the round keep and onto the roof. A shadowy hole stood right across from the barbican. It turned out to be an eight-foot-wide double doorway, thoroughly rotted and far too inviting to be ignored. Glancing back again, Eloise saw that her husband had already put his shield aside and found the handful of dice, carefully packed thermometer, and sand clock that he carried for this crucial experiment. The last thing she saw as she entered the doorway was Gregory pulling his jacket over his head to mitigate the effect of the noon hour sun on the test. *Why doesn't he just move to the shade in the gatehouse so he can see properly?*

Squeezing in beside Eoyan as her eyes adjusted to the dim interior, Eloise realized she knew why. Gregory had trouble concentrating. He needed to shut out the world. She had seen him contrive similar setups before. He was the weakest of their class at dynamics, even if that was rather like being the worst of the best, but he had enough of the lord in him for this to bother him a little. It bothered her a little leaving him there, unprotected except for a jacket.

Stepping into the dark keep, Eloise both felt and smelled moisture. The unusual quality of the architecture went unobserved. It was irrelevant to her, not part of the process. The design of the structure only mattered if it meant the gates were a non-standard width or used non-standard mechanics. It mattered if the walls were insecure or a water source was lacking. Being able to refortify and hold key structures within the Ardgour Wilderness was crucial to Lighthouse phases two, four and six. The fine carvings inlaid on the door arches or the once-dazzling tapestries, largely rotted away after two hundred years of neglect, were immaterial to Eloise's purpose. She kept her eyes on what mattered practically. "There's spoor here," she said flatly. She had spotted some in the barbican as well.

"And water too," Eoyan replied in an even more hushed tone. He must have felt the moisture as well. "Maybe they come in here to drink. Infrequently, I hope."

Eloise bit down on the comment that leapt into her mind about the naivety of hopes that rise unbidden and, without replying, passed further into the keep. Reflexively, she opened herself to the empyreal sky, careful to avoid heralding. Technically speaking, using the empyreal sky as a device to see in the dark meant hovering on or just through the first breakdown of the Huygens modulus. All her classmates could do it as easily as breathing, even Gregory now, but there was still some risk in performing even that level of dynamics out here in the wilderness. No one knew for sure what Skoll and Hati could detect. They could certainly detect *heraldry*, as Heylor had confirmed in typically disastrous fashion.

Any competent dynamicist could use the empyreal sky to see in the dark, even up to the absence of almost all light. Some, like Eloise, could see through walls or focus down to microscopic levels. Robert and Koria were both masters of the art, able to effortlessly resolve an order of magnitude finer than anyone besides Gerveault. Robert used it in his smithing as a key part of the complex, horrendously difficult, highly dangerous work of creating entropic weapons and armor. His fine control also made anything he did that much more effective, even if it was destruction. Koria reserved her skill for more constructive purposes to do with knowledge and the assessment of knowledge. Knowledge was what Eloise wanted now. She needed to see in the dark and, with dynamics, she could.

How Eoyan kept from stumbling about in the dusty, debris-filled gloom, she had no idea. A thick layer of fine dirt carpeted the floor. Eloise could feel it as she walked and taste it as she breathed. The dust made a soft swooshing sound as they trod through it, ignoring nearly everything it could tell them of the keep's former occupants, their attention fixed solely on answering one question. *Is this the place we've been looking for? Is it here?*

Eoyan's voice, muted as it was, echoed in the stone-bound keep, little more than an abandoned crypt now. "More spore."

Eloise did not reply. There was no need. She could not miss feeling the skolve shit as it crunched under her feet, or fail to see it in the empyreal sky. It lay all about them, telling a story, reminding her that too much sand was falling through the sand clock and that the risk assessment they had each unconsciously made was misjudged. She refocused, searching for the source of the water, trying to sense where the microdroplets were densest. *There.* She led Eoyan to a central room, where she stepped heedlessly over broken wood, possibly a smashed bench, and approached a vast curving wall that rose from floor to ceiling. Water sweated from microcracks all over it.

"Uncle Eoyan thinks it's one big, long shaft," Eoyan whispered, making a joke after all. Calling himself "Uncle Eoyan" was expressly against process. He had been told often enough, had been swatted for it even more. Eloise did not have time to discipline him now. In any case, she knew that Eoyan was giving the situation his full attention, that even in the poor light his eyes were darting everywhere. Necessary or not, such discipline would itself be against process anyway, and she was busy refocusing within the empyreal sky. *Where does this cylinder go?*

"Come on," Eloise ordered, "the stairs are over here." Uncle Eoyan kept his mouth shut and his hands tight around his spear shaft as he followed her through the detritus and into a narrow circular stairwell. It went up through three levels of the keep, the open doorways of which they ignored until they emerged into a shaft of sunlight and ascended the last few steps onto the roof. It was blindingly bright on the stone paving. Eloise sighed, looking up gratefully at the sun and incongruously shading her eyes with her right hand as she welcomed the warm rays. Emerging straight from a perceptual midnight into the prime hours of daylight was reinvigorating.

She jogged over to edge of the keep to check on her husband. Gregory still sat in the courtyard near the barbican, jacket draped over himself, no doubt rolling his dice and taking his temperature. She smiled.

The roof was covered in skolve scat. "Let's go, March. Now," she ordered, wheeling on her heels and jogging away from the edge toward the small structure in the center of the roof.

It lacked its own roof, had only waist-high andesite walls with regular four-foot-wide gaps, and from the outside, did look like some kind of observatory. Row upon row of two-foot-high stacks of bones lay in front of one of the walls. Each was a femur—or the skolve equivalent—longer and heavier than any human bone. The bones were clean, and the stacks were neat, which was decidedly odd. Skolves seldom spent energy organizing anything. Eloise frowned. She could not imagine what these strange, neat piles of bones might portend.

Eloise set thoughts of the bones aside. There were more urgent, more practical matters to think about. Stepping gingerly into a gap between the walls, she noticed a ball of coarse, wire-like skolve fur caught on an edge. Silently, she pointed the tangle of hairs out to Eoyan, whose eyes had grown wide again, his body language taut. He nodded. Eloise took another step and passed into the large, open space framed by the building's arcuate walls. There was no trace of a telescope, but the sun shone down directly into the space. At night the stars would as well. But there was no sign of any equipment ever having been here, only the twenty-foot-wide open stone cylinder. It was filled with clear, clean-looking water. She looked down through the depths to a stony bottom far below, and nothing else. *Where is it?* Eloise opened herself to the empyreal sky again, looking for a resonance in the Huygens medium. Something, anything. *Nothing. This is not the place.*

"Have you ever seen so many beads?" Eoyan's whispered question interrupted her feeling of disappointment. Inside the short walls of the central structure there was no skolve scat. Instead, the rock was covered in glass beads. There were thousands of them, some blue, others green or pink. Someone else might have asked where skolves could possibly have obtained thousands of round glass beads, or why. Eloise did not. She remembered the only place she had ever heard of skolves leaving beads. It was in the story *The Lonely Wizard*, when the eponymous wizard himself had found the body of a Methueyn Knight, Volsang, seemingly murdered by Nimrheal during the Methueyn War. Skolves had come to the site and seemed to have paid homage to the angel's corpse with offerings of glass beads. The behavior of skolves in most ways resisted any anthropomorphic interpretation, but Eloise thought Keith Euyn had been correct in concluding that the offering had been an act of worship.

"We have to go," Eloise declared, heart thumping hard.

Chapter Five

Domains and Desserts

"Sir Robert. You are here at last." Kennyth Brice, Duke of Vercors spoke warmly, in his most sonorous tones, and more warmly still, gripped both of Robert Endicott's shoulders. The duke, dark-haired, smooth-faced, a youthful, elegant man in his thirties, was ever so slightly taller than Robert. Their eyes were almost level as they met each other's frank gaze. "We have been looking forward to seeing you again," the duke said.

Endicott took in the elegant, warm, and now nearly full private dining room. Only two middle seats remained open, and a strangely diverse group stared back at him. Massive, heavily muscled Bat Merrett scowled from the near end of the huge oak table, his grotesquely wrinkled ears glowing pinkly in the soft lantern light of the room. As Endicott and the duke passed him on the way to their seats, all the big man said by way of greeting was, "Blouse." No answer was required. It was an old blend of insult and joke.

Tall, lanky, thoughtful Jeyn Lindseth smiled softly from his place beside Merrett. He and Merrett made a pair as usual. They had followed Endicott from his first year at the New School and were now the only ones he ever entered the Ardgour Wilderness with. Merrett would object to the idea that he *followed* Robert Endicott. For this stoic soldier, it had simply been his job to keep the schoolboy out of trouble.

Lindseth said nothing as Endicott and the duke passed him. The tall, laconic soldier rarely spoke only for the sake of speaking. Nor did he speak to insult; he was too constructive for that. Jeyn Lindseth most often spoke to satisfy a calm and surprisingly gentle curiosity, to satisfy a philosophical turn of mind.

Neither soldier had really changed in the four years Endicott had known them. Endicott, on the contrary, was scarcely recognizable from the sunny young man of those early days. The young Robert Endicott had gone to the New School hoping to change the world but had endured nerve-shattering heraldic dreams of a terrible future and ended up in a desperate, ruthless struggle to avert the dreams' dreaded outcome. The dangers and cruelties of attempting to change that outcome had changed *him* almost beyond recognition.

No one can alter the future without paying the future's price.

Farther down the table sat a man who was a walking event. Sir Hemdale. The big, old, wild-eyed Deladieyr Knight looked distinctly out of place in this elegant room with its oiled-wood bookshelves and polished oak table. Sir Hemdale was more rock than man, scarred, ugly, obdurate, and prone to damaging whatever he came into contact with. *He does not belong with smooth, polished wood and fine things.*

Endicott groaned inwardly as he recalled that day at the Armadale embassy siege four years in the past. The situation had seemed intractable. An unprecedented siege of a foreign embassy, with full-scale war likely to follow. Yet that was the least of it. The duke and duchess were dead, and that dreadful news was enough to cause a war by itself, but more fuel was being added to the diplomatic fire every moment. First came the ambassador's ill-timed taunts aimed at Kennyth's grief. And then Sir Hemdale had arrived from the Castlereagh Line to hurl kerosene on the flames. When he heard about the taunts on top of Keith Euyn's murder of the duke and duchess, he raced toward the embassy wall, mad and alone, shouting ancient oaths and imprecations. His insane fury seemed to release some parallel emotion in Kennyth. He followed Hemdale, and Endicott had no choice but to follow in turn. He had to protect the heir to the throne. And so the metaphorical fire became an actual conflagration. When the fire finally burned out—and all but one survivor from the embassy had been slaughtered—Endicott had lost another layer of optimism, perhaps the final layer.

Looking at Sir Hemdale now made him almost physically sick.

Despite the feelings of revulsion that Endicott could not prevent his face from betraying, the old knight grinned back at him, his homely, scarred face displaying an unequivocal, incongruous affection. "Nephew," he said cordially, though Endicott was no relation of his.

Opposite Hemdale sat Gerveault, just as old, but not so given to life-changing violence. *The last dynamicist of his generation now that grandpa is dead.* Gerveault sat ramrod straight and simply nodded at Endicott. The old professor had always preferred objective truth to subjective pleasantries, though he was unfailingly proper. Gerveault's ebony skin and blue eyes gave away his heritage as a survivor of fallen Engevelen and a member of its nobility. His uprightness would have told as quickly as his skin and eyes what rare blood ran through his veins. Gerveault was a distant cousin to Koria's Valcourt family, and on seeing him erect and unmoving in his seat, Endicott's emotional temperature veered strongly toward respect and affection, but he only nodded back at his mentor.

Another child of Engevelen sat beside Hemdale. This was Marielle Engel, a tall, dark-skinned, green-eyed young woman. Her face was almost as absent of expression as Gerveault's, but Endicott knew she was carefully evaluating the scene. He also sensed the magnetism in her, though it was a quality she never seemed to use consciously. It was an antumbral glow that shone from her and that everyone who met her either saw or felt. Engel was the green-eyed girl, the chosen one, thought by all to be destined for the ranks of the Deladieyr Knights. Endicott smiled her way. She reminded him of a much taller Koria, and the similarity brought an unconscious affection with it.

"I am sorry to keep everyone waiting," Endicott said when he and the duke reached their chairs at the center of the table.

Kennyth Brice smiled urbanely. "We would have waited longer, Sir Robert. Happily." He clasped the younger man's shoulders again. "You are like a brother to me."

We both loved your mother. That's enough for me to make you my brother. This thought was connected to the real reason that Endicott had charged the embassy that day. He had been bone-tired from fighting Keith Euyn barely an hour before, and from the Battle of the Bifrost the day before, and at the tower across the Castlereagh Line just days before that and the frantic ride back to Vercors City immediately after. Endicott had had nothing left that day. All his strength and love, abundant as they were, had been rubbed raw already, but he had joined the charge so that he could protect Kennyth.

"Is Lady Koria not coming?" Lindseth's soft voice was absent any presumption that may have gone with the question.

"No," Endicott responded evenly, thinking about his wife and her ambitious plans. "Koria has a vital experiment to conduct tonight." She had not said which experiment, even to him. "She said it's a big one and that she may not be done with the write-up before morning." He might not even see her before he left.

Lindseth's face sang sadness. "She can't leave the experiment even for a moment to say goodbye?"

"That's process for you." No one was allowed to leave an experiment of the kind Koria was doing until the full report was complete. It was a protocol inspired by the old days when vengeful Nimrheal might come at any moment. The knowledge had to be captured before the experimenter was murdered and the results lost forever. And though there was no Nimrheal now, no one ever tired of recreating customs from fabled, fallen Engevelen. A few years back, Heylor Style had taken a day off after some minor experiment, and when he returned to the work, was unable to find his data. It had disappeared into the ether. Gerveault had severely criticized the mistake and reminded them all, at great length, about how things had been done in the old days of his former country. Since then, everyone was required to complete their work to the last letter before they so much as left the room.

Heylor.

He hoped his friend was recovering. When he had appeared, blood-soaked and covered in frost in the dining hall, screaming in pain, a vast gray hand attached to his face, Endicott had doubted he would survive. *He was so cold. As cold as I have ever been.*

"I will be participating in the after-experiment review later tonight," Gerveault said evenly. The old man was so proper and old-fashioned that he even refused to use the customary acronym, AER. "If you have left anything unsaid, I can pass it along to Lady Koria."

"Do it after dinner," instructed Merrett pointedly, "I don't want to hear any love poetry before I go into the wilderness."

"No poetry required," Endicott returned, deadpan, "I told her I love her just moments ago."

"Knights, stop!" Merrett held his rough hands in front of his face. "You and your love. We are about to eat here, you know."

My love. Endicott knew he did not say it as much as he used to, except to Koria. *When did the count of people I've killed grow larger than the number of those I love?* But he knew when that had happened. Seeing the ghastly Sir Hemdale grinning across the table at him reminded him of exactly when.

Kennyth Brice smiled tolerantly at the repartee. "Perhaps Lieutenant Merrett is correct. We really should eat. This is our pre-experiment ceremony." He raised a hand and four waiters walked softly into the room, bearing steaming platters of food. The sight and smell of roast beef made Endicott salivate. Heaping plates of potatoes, carrots, and turnips added to the cornucopia, which was swiftly and quietly laid out before the group. Other waiters brought in wine, water, and tea. Endicott was happy to find that Engel, along with Gerveault and Lindseth, joined him in drinking tea instead of wine. It saved him further sparring with Merrett, who knew better than to insult Marielle Engel.

As soon as Kennyth Brice saw that everyone had dished up and was happily eating, he signaled the serving staff to leave the room. That subtle action brought Endicott to full attention. His mind had been occupied by thoughts of Koria and of which particular experiment she might be running out of the many possible on the docket. He was thinking, too, of his own dangerous mission, of Heylor and his slow recovery, and of Gregory, Eoyan, and Eloise, who were still away on their own survey mission. His classmates had been scattered by dangerous winds, the winds of the Lighthouse project.

To resettle the Ardgour Wilderness, to control what's out there, to drive out the skolves with dynamically manipulated grain, and eventually, eventually, do two additional things even more important and dangerous.

Kennyth raised his glass of dark wine. "Let us toast this latest and most important mission." He held his glass up until everyone had joined him with their own, even if theirs held tea. "The Javelin mission. We have waited a long time to make this attempt, this throw. But now all the pieces are in place. Javelin has been perfected," Kennyth concluded, nodding to Gerveault.

The old wizard nodded back, but added, still holding his tea up, "Lady Koria was of major help in sharpening it."

"Yes, she was, indeed," replied the young duke. "We also have our best team ready to wield it, led by Sir Robert here, and we have Marielle Engel ready to do her part." He smiled and nodded at Engel. "She is like the first incarnation of Sendeyl since the Methueyn War, ready to travel any distance at speed and meet our team." He thrust his wine glass higher. "Redoubt Empyrean." They all responded, "Redoubt Empyrean," and drank to the success of the mission.

"What difference do you think it will make?" Lindseth's question followed the toast without a pause. It produced an abrupt silence. Merrett shook his head almost imperceptibly at his tall companion, Sir Hemdale frowned, and Gerveault looked perplexed, though his narrowing eyes suggested he was on the edge of taking offence. Engel's expression revealed nothing. Her jade eyes seemed to gaze into infinity. Endicott was neither surprised nor offended. He knew Jeyn Lindseth too well. Kennyth Brice did not know Lindseth nearly so well, but he did not seem put off, not visibly at least.

"You mean Javelin, of course." The young duke stood up and moved to stand near the servants' door. "It is a good question." His eyebrows went up. "It borders on why, which I like." He smiled broadly. "I have an opinion, which is implied, I suppose, in my decision to approve the mission. But I am not going to say what it is specifically. Out in court or in the square, I project my policy, sometimes forcefully. I must. But here, privately, I would like to hear your opinions. You will be on the sharp end of Javelin after all." He clapped his hands sharply together, once. "Let's go around the table and see what everyone thinks. Fear no judgement from me. Bat Merrett, you lead off."

Merrett's mouth was full of roast beef. "Mmff. I don't—mmff—ask that question." He paused, chewed, then swallowed loudly. "I am at a table full of dreamers. Someone has to pay attention and see that the mission works out."

"That's all?" Kennyth asked, a twinkle in his eyes.

Merrett speared a potato with his fork. "It needs to be all. We have my partner Jeyn, who wants to philosophize about it. Fine. We also have Mister Love himself, Sir Robert Endicott. He's going to take all that love and angst and sudden furies and dreams or nightmares of the future out there and roll everything into a ball." The big man poured a big dollop of viscous gravy over his potato. "After that ball festers for a while, he's going to wrap the mission in significance. I don't need to add to that mess. I need to keep things simple and make sure we all come back alive."

"Stick to that, it *is* your job," said Gerveault. He raised his index finger toward the ceiling. "Going out is one thing." He raised another finger. "Meeting at point B and accomplishing the mission is another." He raised a third finger. "But there is no real success until you are all back safe." He made a fist and held it high.

"Here, here," approved Brice. "Anything more to add, Professor Gerveault?"

"Objectively? I invented the javelin. I know its properties. You and I designed the mission, and so we know what we are trying to do, at least in the short term. What will happen in the far post-mission future, who can say? How do I feel about it all?" The old man shook his head slowly. "That those things are too unknowable, imprecise, or subjective for me to comment upon."

The duke laughed softly. "Perhaps you're right, but what you said still feels a little … uncharitable."

"Ha!" Gerveault waggled a finger at Kennyth. "*Not* saying—that is the real charity. Reach too far into the future and you lose your anchor of hard information. Eventually, you become isolated from other ideas and possibilities except for what you have taken with you. Finally, you close yourself within your own bell chamber where your ideas, fears, and ambitions are amplified. The far heralds have all left us—only Sir Robert's grandfather with any dignity—and I know better than to try to be one." He paused and looked slowly around the table with a glowering intensity. "Someday you may all understand this."

"It may be, *maybe*," Kennyth held his hands up in mock surrender. "I think Professor Gerveault may have just killed your question, Jeyn."

Lindseth's brows rose in little pyramids. "There is a middle ground between the straight mission objectives as written and the far future goals. There must be. From where else come our hopes and dreams? Surely there is value in examining them before their hopefulness is so attenuated that it vanishes into madness." He smiled around his eyes. "I did not myself wish to answer the question, I wanted only that it be asked. Like Bat, my job is to keep the mission safe. I especially want to know what Sir Robert thinks. Bat may tease, but from all I have seen since the terrible night, Sir Robert is the compass to what comes."

"I don't know what that even means," responded Endicott, frowning. He felt he was no compass, no Deladieyr Knight. There had been no flashes of supernal strength in four years. His strength and certainty had been attenuated in the embassy siege.

Certainty is dangerous.

As discouraged in some ways as Endicott was, some optimism remained in him. Despite part of him doubting that his moral arrow could be a guiding compass for anything, Endicott still had ideas he believed in. He had always been complex and changeable—contradictory in many ways—and as he sat and thought, the optimistic part of him came to the fore. "Perhaps I can address the question in a roundabout way."

"You mean a long, rambling story," interrupted Merrett.

"Quiet, Bat," rumbled Sir Hemdale, eyes bulging dangerously. "He saved your life at the Bifrost. The least you could do is show some respect."

Caught up in the moment, Endicott forgot how much Hemdale sickened him. It was not the sickness of hate, still less of spite or any childish petulance. It was a sickness of disappointment, and not just in Hemdale. It was a sadness so deep it made him ill. "To be fair, saving Merrett's butt was incidental. I was trying to help Koria and Eloise." He looked at the old man. It hurt him to look at the knight's ravaged face, but it also hurt to feel so negatively toward the ancient warrior. Playing along and making a joke reminded him that he had once felt close to Hemdale. Even though he hated what they had done together in the embassy on that pitiless day four years ago, he could never forget someone who had fought beside him. His knotted emotions told Endicott he might still love Hemdale, but the love was buried under the weight of events. For the first time in the evening, Endicott nodded Hemdale's way.

Kennyth Brice may have seen the nod, for he nodded to himself. "Tell us your long, rambling story, Sir Robert."

Endicott took a deep breath. "You might think that the javelin is just a weapon, but it doesn't take a lot of thought to see that it is much more than a tool for killing skolves. It will change us. It will add a new dimension to our capability. It will be transformational for the world." He looked at Bat Merrett. "You may shrug and say, 'so what?' It is okay to think about the here and now, to be in the present." He smiled. "Someone has to. But the future hurls back toward us in the present at speeds we cannot predict. We are called to unexpected, *kairotic* moments when we are unprepared, often to the point of disaster. For that reason, others *do* have to think about the future, and to risk Lindseth and Professor Gerveault's vanishing point into autoregressive madness. This much I know from experience."

"But I'm wandering from the point." He took a sip of tea and looked around. "The point I am trying to make shows up in mathematics all the time. We find ourselves with an impossible problem, an equation we just cannot solve, that it seems no one can with any amount of time or effort. It simply cannot be done. But then we find the right transform. The transform becomes the way; we *change* the problem to solve the problem. Let me give you an example. We make a forward Lessingham transform of the equation into Lessingham space and find that the impossible problem is immediately solved. *Easily* solved. Then we apply the inverse transform and bring our solution out of Lessingham space with us. Koria—I really wish she were here—Koria and I spent the last three years working on finding the best domains to solve some of our most intransigent problems. And we have some big, impossible-seeming problems ahead of us. In phase seven of Lighthouse, we have to kill Skoll and Hati. That is something eight Methueyn Knights failed to do in the Methueyn War. More recently, Heylor showed us what a monumental task that is going to be. Koria, Professor Gerveault, and I have worked hard to find the right transformational domain for it. One approach we have, called exact shaping, may be just that. It—"

Gerveault interrupted him. "Do not even think about it, Robert. Exact shaping is too dangerous. It is something the *old* you might have tried—and probably killed all of us in the process."

"Well," whispered Robert, "you need not worry, the old me is gone." He raised his voice slightly. "The main point is that nothing is impossible if you find the right space, the right perspective. With the right transform and the right domain, I would not need Elysium. We would not need Methueyn Knights. I could have stopped Keith Euyn. He would never have been able to kill E-Eleanor."

Endicott's voice broke up. The room was silent, faces clearly shocked at the sudden mention of the duchess and the young knight's use of her first name. Kennyth Brice's eyes were locked on Endicott's, unreadable, while the other man fought the hot, angry feeling that had suddenly possessed him. "Put aside the mathematics now. With a javelin, we could have avoided ever having to go to the embassy that day. There would have been no need. If we had *only* had it back then, we would have been able to save Eleanor, of that I'm certain. That's how important Javelin is."

"Thank you, my brother," Kennyth breathed out as the room went still. But he was never silent for long, and a moment later he looked around the silent room. "Does anyone object to that long story?" He caught Merrett's eye. "What about you, Bat?"

"No."

Endicott did not know what Bat Merrett was thinking, but the soldier's face betrayed neither humor or disdain. If Endicott had to guess, he would have said Merrett's face betrayed only mourning.

Kennyth sighed. "Eleanor is missed."

"I—" Lindseth hesitated, looking at his plate, then back at Kennyth. "I-I wonder what she would have said if she were with us today."

The duke smiled. "Oh, she would have been pleased to sit with us, but what would she have said? Something encouraging, I think." He swallowed. "When I was young, she gave me a book, *The Fall of Engevelen in Four Acts*. Did you know the first act happened over seven hundred years ago right here in Ardvaser? Well, the castle was rebuilt later, but the death of the Auvignes was a bigger blow than the hole in the old walls. Engevelen was never the same after that, and over the many years between then and now there were three more acts until, finally, there was no Engevelen at all." He smiled at Gerveault and Engel. "Except in the few of her people that remain. My mother wanted Engevelen to return." He blinked. "Perhaps she would have spoken of that were she here."

"Thank you," Lindseth said in his soft voice.

Kennyth Brice nodded. "I have said too much. I wanted to hear from *you*, not tell you about my memories or my mother's dreams." He stood taller. "What about you, Sir Hemdale? What do you think about the Javelin project?"

Sir Hemdale's eyebrows curled, nearly closing on each other. "I miss her as well. The duchess was a visionary. She loved ideas. They are at the core of what it is to be a Methueyn Knight." He thumped his chest. "The core of *my* beliefs. She understood that better than all the bishops of the Steel Castle. I also supported Javelin for historical reasons. The past is important in making a future. I think of how Javelin will affect the Methueyn Treaty. Robert's mathematics? Duchess Eleanor would have been interested, but mathematics never crosses my mind. What do I know of it? Those aren't the ideas I have spent my life pondering. Doesn't matter. I respect what Sir Robert said even if I don't understand it, though I hope he does not speak out of guilt over what happened in the past."

He locked his eyes on Endicott. "He always did think too much. Regret is the poison of self-hate. The old Robert fought hard. I liked him. The new Robert lacks his knightly strength—we've seen that, sadly—but I think he is wiser. I like him too." The big man's scarred face seemed to crack under the smile he attempted to deliver. "I cannot add to what has been said. Instead, I want to remind everyone here about the role of Marielle Engel—a daughter of Engevelen—in the mission." He thumped a hand on her shoulder. She did not react in any visible way, despite the heavy, uninvited hand. Her body did not move or flinch. It was as if she was made of dark, polished marble. Engel had said nothing during the proceedings. Her thoughts, as usual, were a mystery.

Hemdale beamed at her, the smile on his broken face somehow both beautiful and terrifying at once. "She is going out alone, at least until point B. When she comes back, we are going to have her Ceremony of Rising." He thumped the table heavily with his right hand, making the dishes rattle. "The Methueyn Treaty will be here, waiting for her. I've called in all the brothers and sisters of our order to approve the Rising. They will all be here. Even Sir Kaimari from Neahon across the sea will attend. We haven't seen all the Deladieyr Knights together in one place in ten years. We will see change from the Javelin project, and stability from the Treaty, all at the same time."

Lindseth shifted in his seat, staring at the tall, enigmatic woman beside Hemdale. "Do you feel a sense of pressure, Marielle, from what Sir Hemdale just said?"

"No." Engel's voice was even, showing little emotion. Her face was calm—gentle even—but she did not smile.

"Surely you can say more, Marielle," Kennyth said encouragingly, winking at her.

For a moment it seemed Engel would add nothing, but finally she gazed back at him before her green eyes slid slowly toward Lindseth. "What is it that you want, Jeyn? Do you want me to step into the bell chamber that Professor Gerveault described? Should I speak of the weight and drag of history and sentiment, or of the hopes for the holy orders of knights? Sir Hemdale has not told you all of his mind, you know. He hopes for more. But if I spoke of those things, it would not be *my* bell chamber, would it? I would be repeating someone else's dream." Engel tapped her spoon against her unused wine glass. It hummed a high-pitched tone that lasted a moment and faded away.

She placed the spoon carefully on the table. "To speak so would go against my integrity. I hear only the voice inside *my* head. I hear it *once* and I act upon it. There is no reverberation, no debate or escalation in my mind." She locked eyes on Kennyth Brice, who was still standing near the servant's door. "I want people to be free. Though I appreciate your mother's good intentions, the name of the country they live in does not concern me." She turned to look at Endicott. "I hear a poetry in your words of transformation, Sir Robert. There is something beautiful in your appreciation of mathematics. But I do not seek *transformational* change." She switched her gaze to Sir Hemdale. "Ultimately, we will find what we are looking for, or we will not. I will Rise, or I will not. I will become a Deladieyr Knight, or it is likely that I will die alone in the wilderness. This will happen not because of an exterior ambition I am reaching for but because of intrinsic properties I already have. I am going out on the Javelin mission because I have decided it is the right thing to do. That decision is my present state of mind."

Bat Merrett's fork fell and hit the table with a clang that echoed around the room. "Is there dessert?"

Chapter Six.

Relegated

"HERE HE IS, HEYLOR STYLE HIMSELF." GAEL GUISE SPOKE WITH AN ENTHUSIASM that Heylor did not reciprocate. She also waved a hand theatrically toward Constable Lynwen as if she was passing a baton to the other woman. "Fresh from his … work across the Castlereagh Line."

Lynwen looked confused.

Like the constables normally do, as I recall.

Heylor smothered the uncharitable thought. He barely knew Lynwen, and he had other people to flagellate, people that deserved it more. Himself, chiefly. *Actually, sad to say, the list starts and ends with me.* Still, she did look as confused as he remembered her four years back when the cloaked man—cloaked *men*, it turned out—were busy murdering at will on the New School campus. Lynwen was tall, perhaps his height, maybe a hair taller in her polished boots. The patent leather footwear set off her trim uniform—and her trimmer, athletic profile—very nicely indeed. She was still young, and still glowed with the energy of youth. Aside from her baffled expression, which gave her face a vacant look, Lynwen would have been a welcome sight to most young men, and not a few young women, coming back from the wilderness. But not Heylor. Not today. Not after what had happened. Maybe not ever again.

I killed them all.

Sadly, he could not even self-correct the thought. It was a fact. As surely as Lynwen looked clueless, with her big grey eyes open just a little too wide and her pink-lipped mouth open just a bit too slackly, he had definitely and surely killed all seven of his teammates. And left their bodies behind to be torn to pieces, eaten by scavengers or decorating the limbs of trees.

"This might explain a few things," Gael said, facing Lynwen but watching Heylor stew through the corner of her eyes. She handed Lynwen the sealed envelope, pupils still turned sideways on Heylor. *She's scared of me, scared to take her eyes off the murderer. Who knows what I'll skolve up next?*

Lynwen had taken a letter opener from the desk behind her. Carefully, slowly, she sliced the envelope along the top seam and pulled a crisp, thick, cream-colored paper out. She read the document, frowning, at a glacial speed, drawing out the suspense. Heylor resisted the urge to climb the wall as the constable continued reading at the approximate pace of a frozen slug. He stopped his right hand from involuntarily tugging at her sleeve to make her stop and just listen while he explained what he had done and what the inevitable consequences must be. He squeezed the hand into a tight fist, painfully digging the nails into his palm, shaking the fist by his thigh to remind himself how he needed to be if he were to avoid making the same mistakes again. If he ever got the chance.

Process, process, process. I must *slow down. I* must *be careful and follow the process. Or everyone dies.*

Finally, Lynwen concluded her minute examination of the letter and peered at him over the top of the paper. "It is our pleasure to welcome you back to the city, Mr. Style—"

"Heylor. Only my professors call me Mr. Style."

"Heylor it is, then." She glanced quickly toward the door. "Um. I just need to talk to the vice-constable for a moment. Wait here." With tight lips and a nervous clatter, she pushed past her own chair, out the door of the office, and disappeared down the hallway of the constabulary building. Alone again with Gael Guise, Heylor nervously studied her tanned and wind-burned face. She had a network of fine white lines on her forehead and around her eyes from squinting at the horizon. They were the furrows the sun and the wind had not been able to reach while she had gazed across fields, down roads, into the perilous future. She had guided him all the way back from Ardvaser Castle after the duke had sent him away, banished him for what he had done, and failed to do, across the line.

"Your bruises have passed into green, Heylor." Gael was pointing at the mass of dark, multicolored bruises mottling his neck and the lower half of his face. "Normally, I might tell a young man like yourself that women like bruises, but on the face? Not so much." She smiled at him. "What is your mom gonna say?"

Heylor looked down. "What is there to say? I skolved up. I'm a coward."

Again.

Still.

Smack!

Heylor winced from the sharp, open-handed blow Gael had delivered.

"Hey! My face hurts enough already."

Heylor's left hand went to his face, but Gael knocked it away and lunged forward, grabbing him by the blood-encrusted lapels of his jacket. "That's not all that's gonna hurt if you don't stop talking skolve-scat," she hissed in a faint voice, just for him. She pulled him close and locked eyes with him, almost like a lover. Or an enemy. The intimacy made the young man listen hard. One should listen carefully to enemies and lovers, but that was not why he wanted to hear every word she was about to say. Her closeness made him feel less alone.

"You *survived*, Heylor. That's more than Guillaume's team can say. None of them came back. You took off Skoll's whole *arm*, which is more than anyone, anywhere, has *ever* done."

With that, Gael released Heylor's collar and straightened his jacket on his shoulders, still holding him fast with her eyes. "Stop indulging your guilt. Stop feeling sorry for yourself and start the *process* of moving on to what's next."

"Yes," he mumbled. "Yes. I know." He had to agree with her, even if his eyes were red, even if he felt something hot and painful in his throat. She was not entirely correct, but she was also not entirely wrong. He did need process. Among other things.

Process. No more shortcuts.

His predicament reminded him of the day after the Battle of the Bifrost, another fight from which he had run away. Robert had similarly reassured him afterward, though without slapping him upside the head. *Oh, Robert.* If only he could have stayed to help Robert with the Javelin mission. But, yes, now he had to move on. Plucking up what courage he could, he ventured a question. "What's next, do you think? Now that I've been relegated back here."

Gael laughed, her face softening. "You get to relax, Heylor." She clapped his shoulder. "Take a break. Recover. Help out the constabulary where you can. Nothing much is going on here, so life should be easy." She pointed out the door. "Here comes Lynwen. I'd best be off. You aren't the only hero I've got to escort, you know."

Т

"Are you my babysitter?" Heylor knew he was being peevish, but that did not stop him. Awareness just added another thin layer of guilt to the guilt already there.

"Are you a child?"

"No."

"Then no."

"Then why are you following me home?" Heylor asked Lynwen, trying to keep the whining tone to a minimum.

"I'm not *following you home*, Heylor." Lynwen adjusted the baton and short sword on her hips as she walked. They sat uncomfortably, Heylor guessed. He knew how a sword on the hip could disrupt the stride, how it had felt tripping on Style, the entropic sword Robert had made for him after they had killed Keith Euyn together. The empty scabbard was still on his hip. "You're my partner for the next few weeks," she continued. "My instructions are to pick you up for patrol every morning. So I need to know where you live."

Where I live.

Heylor suppressed a shiver. He had not been home in what seemed like a very long time. He wondered if he would even recognize the place. *What will Lynwen think when she sees it?* She did not look so stunned now as she had when she had read the letter. She had a stern— even determined—look about her. No slack jaw anymore. Her eyes ... maybe she just had unusually big, round eyes. Really, very round.

"What?" She had caught him staring.

"Nothing." *I need to learn how to do that sideways, corner-of-the-eye thing Gael does.* "Just wondering what was in that letter."

I should have stolen it.

"Well," Lynwen said, puffing herself up and thrusting her chest out just enough for Heylor to get a very good look at her breasts before good manners ordered his gaze to safer, more polite places. "Lord Kennyth Brice, the Duke of Vercors, remembers how helpful working with the constabulary was for Sir Robert back in the day, and he thought you might enjoy doing the same while your injuries heal."

Heylor started coughing—choking, really. He remembered the constabulary being of no real help to Robert whatsoever. Always late, their help never very helpful, their equipment—such as the defective whistle they had given Robert—of dubious quality. Thinking of the constabulary's incompetence started to make him feel better. *I am being punished after all.*

"Are you okay?" Lynwen asked.

"Fine." She looked like she might even care. Those big, round eyes were pointed right at him.

She doesn't know her true role!

Injuries?

"What injuries?" He felt fine.

"Heydron herself, Heylor," Lynwen exclaimed, turning on him. "Have you looked in the mirror? You look like you've been painted green, yellow, and purple, but by a hand three times the size of any hand I ever saw. How did you manage to keep your head attached to your body?"

"Good luck?"

No, bad decisions. Abandonment of process

"Those bruises have got to hurt."

Only when I think about them.

But now that she had brought the subject up, they did hurt. When he talked. When he turned his head. When he looked up. Swallowing was agony.

"Not really."

But thanks for reminding me.

He started walking again, brushing past her, forcing her to keep up. "So what are we *partners* working on come tomorrow morning?"

Lynwen ignored the sarcasm. "I think we should start by taking a look around the New School campus." She smiled self-consciously as if hoping this might cheer Heylor up. "There's not much going on there lately, but we can take a look at your old haunts."

"Great."

Knights damn it.

When trying to forget your past, trawling back through it was the opposite of what you should do.

ᛏ

"I'm not sure you should come in."

Lynwen looked hurt. Her mouth was open again. "Is it because I'm a … constable?" She looked down. "Some people hate us coming into their houses."

Save me softly, Heydron. Heylor did not know whether to feel bad that he had seemed to hurt her feelings or annoyed that she was so sensitive. Her feelings were interfering with his own self-centered journey. "I doubt anyone *hates* you, Lynwen."

Except me.

Not really.

Maybe a little.

Liar!

I am slightly *put out.*

Nope, that's not it either.

I'm embarrassed.

Heylor was more than embarrassed. He was worried. Davyn had once hypothesized that Heylor's family had been alcoholic, but that was not it. Yes, he had known—and lost—friends and relatives to drinking, but the truth about his background was worse. He did not know precisely what horrors awaited them behind the door to his parents' house, only that the experience would be horrific. Of that, he was certain. The door itself was deceptive. It looked fine. It was handcrafted from oak and iron, and fairly new. And it was attached to a fine, big stone house in a rich part of the city. Heylor's family were not peasants anymore, not since the end of first year at the New School, when Heylor's name had become widely known and employers had come looking to hire from his family line.

Despite heraldry being the easiest of the dynamic arts, heralds were still exceedingly rare, and so they had become enormous strategic assets in commerce after the grain futures market started up. The old duke and duchess—Eleanor especially—had made extensive use of Keith Euyn's incredible facility for heraldry. They had been able to stay a step ahead of all the other heralds thanks to the Lonely Wizard, though the Banker's Ban and other legislation protecting farm ownership had also helped when grain prices exploded. But like many tools, heraldry proved to have an additional sharp edge, one that could easily cut the user. Keith Euyn had gone mad. Age and a terrible heraldic dream had driven him to treason and murder. No one knew what it was the great man had dreamt, only that it had destroyed his mind.

No one knows. Except for me.

As soon as Eloise's blade had impaled the old man, Robert had run off to see what had happened to Eleanor and Koria. Only Heylor had stayed to hear the last words of the Lonely Wizard. They had been coughed out haltingly in a mist of blood droplets that had soaked the younger man's face and chest.

And now, with Keith Euyn gone, Operation Lighthouse on the way, and grain more valuable than ever, heralds were paid a small fortune. Heylor put his hand on the door. *Not that money makes a difference for what we are about to see.*

He knocked. It was his own family's house, but he did not feel at home here. Or anywhere for that matter. He had skolved up. He was an outcast.

The door swung open in an artless and energetic sweep, the only warning to take a defensive step back having been the thump, thump of heavy steps rushing toward it from somewhere inside. "It's my big brother!" a young woman exclaimed, one hand on the open door. She was almost Heylor's height, but heavier, with straight, shoulder-length brown hair and lively brown eyes. Her clothes were loose and cheap, worn in a slovenly fashion, the shirt billowing out, a blotchy stain of unknown provenance decorating the lower hem.

"Shelley." Heylor said the name like you might say "dead fish," perhaps because he was feeling like one himself.

"Well, what are you doing just standing there? Get your skinny butt in here." Shelley Style did not have quite the volume of the sorely missed Davyn Daley, but she came a close second. Heylor hesitated just long enough for Shelley to take matters into her own fleshy hands. She yanked her whip-lean brother across the threshold and engulfed him in a hug. After a long moment, she pushed him back out to arm's length. "What in Urieyn's urn happened to your face, Heylor? Who'd you get in a fight with, a giant?"

"I'm fine," Heylor said without conviction. Eager to forestall Shelley's interrogation, he turned to wave one arm at Lynwen. "This is Constable Lynwen."

"You're pretty!" Shelley blurted to Lynwen. "Are you Heylor's girlfriend?" Heylor missed seeing the constable's face turn several shades of red as he pushed past his sister into the house.

Oh no.

It was palatial. Shelley barged past him, yanking on Lynwen's hand to show her what was inside. She bragged that there were no less than three fireplaces on the ground floor alone, done in the newest style. Then with a flourish, she waved a floppy arm, showing Lynwen the six by twelve-foot dining table that had been cut from one enormous slab of glazed dolostone and elaborately carved by hand. She danced artlessly by the wood burning stove with its eight burners and two interior roasting spaces, spun a circle and flapped a meaty hand at the floor-to-ceiling bookshelves lining the enormous den. They were made of rare cherrywood from Harkness. The place was beautiful. Or it would have been if only his family did not live there.

Knights-damned hoarders.

The bookshelves were crammed with books, papers stolen from posts, the rusted-out blade from an old garden hoe, various tools (mostly broken), forty-three mismatched beer steins (mostly unbroken), some with old beer still in them, judging from the smell lingering in the room, a post maul, a large ornate copper sextant, three dented telescopes—one of them suspiciously familiar— in various diameters, about seventeen oversized drawing books, metal hoops of several sizes, some so big they overhung the shelves and teetered on the edge of falling, and a variety of other junk gathered apparently from abandoned farms and back alleys.

A yellow, striped cat lay high on the top shelf, burrowed in a pile of cotton place settings, its tail trailing upwards toward the ceiling. The stove was covered in dirty dishes and one cracked kerosene lamp. The dining table was piled with dice, dishes, and doilies, and an old, dented, rusty wheelbarrow was crammed into the closest fireplace. Another cat peered out from that, eyes shining. All this was only what Heylor could see from the doorway. He knew there must be a lot more junk just out of sight.

"This place is a sty," Heylor hissed, barely audible, disgusted.

"Come give your mother a hug," boomed a deep, husky voice from behind. The speaker, Heylor's mother Jesteyn, was a little taller than him, about twice his weight, and every bit as loud as her daughter. The sound of her voice plunged Heylor into despair. He was disgusted by the filth, the cats—he knew there were many more lurking about the house—the old tools and instruments, all the unnecessariness of it. This hoarding and chaos had been his life before escaping to the New School, but it seemed utterly foreign now. It felt wrong in much the same way that Heylor felt that he himself was wrong, especially after his latest failure, the disaster he had supervised in the wilderness. As his mother pulled him in for a smothering, odoriferous hug, another feeling spiked. Guilt. He felt bad about being ashamed of his family, no matter how much they deserved it

They're good people.

Just really, really messy. Skolved up, like me.

The hug went on for far too long. Heylor could hardly breathe, he was pulled in so tight by his mother's soft yet crushing embrace. "Okay, Mom, let me go!" he finally gasped, pushing away from her, mortified, ashamed of his own mother and ashamed of himself for feeling that way.

"Hello, son. It's nice to see you." This was Heylor's father, Herevor, his quiet voice and subdued manner in startling contrast to those of his wife and daughter. As rail thin as his son, he was his spitting image in features as well, except for being twice the younger man's age and missing several teeth. He took Heylor's hand in his, shaking it hard and fast.

As their eyes met, Heylor found himself abruptly pulled away from the handshake and whirled around by the strong hands of his mother on his shoulder. "What in Leylah's long night happened to your face, Heylor?"

This again.

"It looks like he got trampled across the gizzard by a team of oxen," said Herevor in a deadpan voice, rubbing his long narrow jaw with his right hand. His fingernails were black with dirt.

"He wouldn't tell me what happened!" Shelley yelled from the kitchen table.

I don't want to talk about it.

"Who's there?" came a new voice from the couch. It was grandma's broken, warbly twitter. Heylor peered into the den again and saw her slouched low on the half-collapsed couch. Beside her, perched primly with a straight back, sat Constable Lynwen, hands on lap. Heylor had not seen the young woman cross the room and sit down. He had forgotten about her completely, and now there she was beside his grandma.

"It's me, Grandma. Heylor."

The old lady squinted at him. She seemed little more than a bundle of thin, wrinkled skin and microfractured bones, looking as if she had lost another two inches of height in the months since Heylor last saw her. Looking at her, spine hunched like a question mark and eyes rheumy and clouded with cataracts, felt like a stab in the gut.

"I thought you were out there across the line. Playing in the wheat."

"I was." Heylor looked at Lynwen again, sitting beside his grandma. *What is she thinking?* "I'm back. Where are Heyden, Scrandeyn, and Helloise?"

Jesteyn crossed her arms. "They're out farm-handing, Heylor. We told you that at the beginning of the season."

Shelley could not resist jumping in. "And I'm only here because I'm in school and campus isn't far away."

"Sorry, I forgot about the farm work," Heylor mumbled, ignoring his sister. "It's probably a good thing they're not here."

"Why's that?" Jesteyn asked, eyes narrowing. "They'd love to see you. You know that."

"Why would they?" Heylor spread his arms wide in a surge of frustration. "They must be glad to be away from here. I can't believe all the junk you have here."

Herevor flinched for a microsecond before breaking into a mad grin that exposed every one of his missing teeth. "One knight's junk is another knight's armor."

"Oh, for knights' sake," Heylor exclaimed, "why is there a wheelbarrow full of cats in the fireplace? What knight is going to make plate out of that? The *cat* would be better armor! And isn't that Shelley's sextant on the bookshelf? She lives in the orchid now. I *do* remember that. And isn't that my old cooper's kit spread out on the shelf yonder? I gave that away to cousin Heygard a year ago. And why do we have three busted telescopes? I'm sure I threw away the bronze one after second year. What *is* all this stuff doing here?"

"I needed a place to store my spare things," Shelley replied evenly. "My room in the Orchid isn't big enough."

"Those rooms are huge!"

"Nope." Shelley was not flustered in the least.

Heylor clenched both fists so hard his face hurt where Skoll had gripped it. "What about the cooper's kit?"

"Heygard thought we should hold on to it for him until harvest is done," his father answered nonchalantly

"Oh, of course," Heylor whispered. "What about the telescope I know I threw away?"

"I think I can fix that," Grandma piped up.

You? You can barely stand up!

"Well, that accounts for one telescope. How about the other two?"

"That's me," jumped in Herevor. "I thought I would see if I could make a small version of an Eindarch Eye."

Heylor blinked. "Did you succeed?"

"Nope."

Heylor shook his head. *Of course you didn't.* "How about the old wheelbarrow?"

Herevor rubbed his jaw again. "Scrandeyn didn't want it anymore. I figured it could come in handy. Someday."

"Of course! Of course it could. Someday," Heylor almost shouted, angrier than ever. Everything about his family reminded him of himself, of his own failings, of killing his friends. In that moment, he despised them like he despised himself. "It's come in handy for the cat at least. Whose cat is that anyway? No, don't answer, I know it came from a cousin or was thrown away by someone somewhere. Everything is useful, everything comes back. From everyone. Nothing is trash. It's all worth something. My hand-me-down clothes probably got handed back and used for another cat's nest." He whirled around. "You know what this family is? Sick, crazy hoarders. It's an illness. You're so bad that, even when one of you finally throws something out, it gets thrown back by some other member of the family. When they throw something out, you take it. It's a circle, a circle of junk, a knights-damned hoarding circle! We should study it in the New School. It's a mathematical singularity for trash. Nothing ever leaves that doesn't re-enter. There's no escape from the entropic pull of the Style family's hoarding circle vortex! No junk is abandoned, no mistakes are left behind, nothing is forgotten or moved on from." Heylor held his hands up and whirled slowly around. "This might be a big new house, but we're still just the same old peasants."

Smack!

Heylor's jaw rung for the second time that day, this time from the big hand of his own mother.

"My face already hurts, Mom! Don't hit me."

"I love you, boy, but I know that hurts less than what you're carrying." Jesteyn had hit him, but she did not look angry. Her liquid eyes betrayed a different emotion. "What mistakes aren't you leaving behind? What pain are *you* hoarding? What happened to your face? It's your family here. The only way yer gonna get rid of whatever it is, is to share it."

Heylor started laughing. "That's so clever, Mom." He kept laughing and didn't stop until his nose started running because he really was crying. Through blurry eyes, he looked over at Lynwen, sitting silently, watching. "I'm sure you want to leave now, Constable."

"Nope." Lynwen smiled slightly.

Was that sympathy on her face? Did she have her own crazy family? Were all families crazy if you got to know them? Heylor could not answer any of those questions. He did not know Lynwen. He could not guess why she apparently wanted to sit and watch the embarrassing spectacle of his messy family dynamic, but he did know he needed to say something after his rant. "My face? It's the reason I've been relegated back here. Sent home to get better." He laughed again. "Shelley guessed it exactly. I got in a fight with a giant."

"Did you win?" Grandma's warbly voice.

Do I look like I skolving won?

"I lost. We all lost."

There was silence. But silence never lasted long in the Style household. Jesteyn broke it. "Are your friends okay? How is Ida?"

Heylor looked down, throat tight, eyes hot and wet. "L-lost." He could barely push out the word.

Jesteyn tried to pull Heylor in for another embrace, but he wanted no comfort and pushed her off, feeling another layer of guilt on top of his sorrow and shame. The guilt was self-reinforcing. Heylor thought he deserved to feel bad, and everything he did to make it worse felt deserved.

"What about Ildrys?" Herevor asked hopefully. "That canny lad got you out of it, didn't he?"

"No." Heylor screwed his eyes shut, trying to block out the image of Ildrys's bloody foot flying through the air. "No one got out."

"No one?" Shelley did not sound like she believed him. Her voice had lost its hale heartiness.

"Only me."

"How?" Herevor asked. "I mean, I'm glad, but how did you manage when they couldn't?"

How do you think?

I ran away. Like always.

Unexpectedly, Lynwen spoke up. "It doesn't matter how. Heylor made it back to you."

"You're so right, Helloise," said Grandma, smiling at Lynwen. The constable's perplexed frown at being mistaken for Heylor's sister lasted only a heartbeat. She put her hand gently on Grandma's.

"We're glad, Heylor," added Jesteyn at the same moment his dad said the same thing.

Shelley was nodding along, but her eyes suddenly widened in alarm. "Oh, dear knights! Where is *Style?* Where is your sword?"

Heylor looked down at the empty scabbard on his hip. Where indeed was the magnificent entropic sword that Robert had made for him, a sword so sharp and tough that it was hard to know whether to call it a masterpiece of metallurgic art or of magic?

"I lost that too."

The most valuable thing I owned or ever will own. Yet it was the least of what was abandoned out there.

Chapter Seven

Make it Rain Grain

WHAT KIND OF WOMAN AM I?

Most others asked the wrong questions about her. To outsiders, Eloise's nature—what kind of woman she truly was—was irrelevant. *They don't need to know. They will* never *need to know. They will never be close enough for it to matter.* Even for Eloise, the question was not at the top of her list. Not right now anyway. Right now, Eloise cared more about the question of how fast she could move.

"Forget about the knights-damned test, stupe!" she hissed, roughly pulling the coat off Gregory's back, catching it in a tangle on the bottom of her shield. "We don't have time for that."

"What?" Somehow the thermometer did not fall out of Gregory's half-open mouth. It hung, forgotten, from his lower lip. His eyes were as big as teacups, his dice scattered on the stone, and his notebook fallen from his lap. He had clearly not even heard the others running back from the roof of the keep and across the courtyard toward him. He had been concentrating totally on his work. *Typical.*

Eoyan crouched low beside him, eyes up, voice low and calm between puffy breaths. "There are beads, bones, and balls of fur here. This place is loaded with skolve-sign."

Gregory nodded earnestly and scrambled to pick up his jacket, dice, and other paraphernalia. "Forget them, stupe!" Eloise pushed his notebook into his hands and booted his dice away. They skipped and rolled chaotically away over the stones. One bounced off Eoyan's knee and onto Gregory's shield. Her foot connected with the sand clock as well. It flipped end over end through the air and shattered on the cobbles between the gatehouse and the keep, sand and glass flying everywhere.

Gregory was aghast. He stared up at Eloise as if he were seeing an alien species. *Is he like Vern now, wondering what kind of a woman I really am?* Eloise stared back at him for an instant. *I'm sure as hell not the kind of woman who orphans her daughters because I don't know when to move my arse!* "We have to go. Now!" She shoved him, knocking him off balance, hoping to penetrate his shock. *Why is no one ever fast enough when it's time to run?*

Eloise grasped the hilt of her sword as she remembered again that day with Hemdale years ago. The old memory had been on her mind off and on since morning. *Maybe it's trying to tell me something.* No one had been quite fast enough that day either. There had been plenty of warnings, all of them ignored until it was too late. The bad people—bad *things*—had not been diabolically intelligent. That is not why she and Hemdale and the others were outsmarted. The bad guys were not *geniuses.* They just did what their opponents did not imagine they would do, things that their opponents recoiled from thinking about, possibilities that lay outside their moral boundaries. Bad people succeeded because they were *allowed* to, were enabled to through the willful or naive ignorance of their victims. They achieved their goals because that ignorance yielded the initiative to them. Eloise had learned that day that hiding from the realities of the world did nobody any good.

Hiding from the fact that this castle was some kind of unimaginably perverse skolve church was one of those things. They could not afford to ignore this for one second longer. They would only survive by kicking away the unimportant and hanging on to what was left, by either preparing to fight for their lives or getting the hell out of here before anything started.

That is the kind of woman I am. I am the kind who keeps my loved ones alive. By whatever means necessary.

Releasing the hilt of her sword, she reached down, yanked the thermometer out of Gregory's mouth, and tossed it over her shoulder. "Now!" she ordered, hauling him to his feet and into motion. He gave up on his pack but managed to grab his shield as Eloise dragged him across the courtyard. She was tempted to try some impromptu heraldry to see which direction of flight was best, but as she leapt through the gap burned into the inner portcullis, still clasping her startled husband, she thought better of it. Skoll or Hati, one or both, would be enough to undo them all. Heylor had proven that to everyone. He had shown the price to be paid for forgetting it was still a wilderness out past the Castlereagh Line.

I'm not a tenth the herald Koria is anyway. In that first year at the New School, it had seemed that was all Koria did: worry, herald, stalk Robert, and have the most horrific heraldic dreams imaginable. As far as Eloise could tell, heraldry was an invitation to pain, a road to madness, a formula for making memories of the future that could only haunt you. It was better to live in the moment and take your chances. She would let her fighter's instincts guide her. "Left!" she called as they emerged from the barbican, turning them in that direction to approach the wheat line at an angle.

Eloise knew that without heraldry, without sampling the other outcomes, it was impossible to know if her choice would turn out to be the best one or the worst. There was no way to know if any skolves were nearby, but no one questioned the need to exfiltrate immediately back across the wheat line. Process called for it, and too much had happened to other missions recently that had been less than scrupulous about process. "Quicker," she shouted at Eoyan and Gregory. She glanced back. They were two or three steps behind her. She raced through the grasses and undergrowth, following game trails when she could, breathing as evenly as she could. A quick glance up reminded her there was still plenty of light left in the day.

She jumped a black, rotted log, a difficult feat with a heavy pack on her back and her sword and shield strapped and scabbarded.

CRRRRRRAAAK.

Eoyan had connected with the log and snapped it. She turned her head to see him career wildly but catch his balance, wincing at the noise. Gregory, a step behind him, ran straight through the debris, scattering it on all sides. It was a flagrant but situationally understandable breach of process. Even running like this was technically against process, but it was unavoidable now. *You have to know when to abandon one set of rules and take up another.* Eloise saw the low pastel wall of wheat ahead. They were already among the few isolated stalks of forerunners. An immature spike brushed her leg as she passed.

A rancid smell assaulted her nostrils. *Rotten meat.* "Stop!" she commanded. "They're here." She spun, feeling the breeze on her face, quickly ascertaining where the wind—and the foul stink—were coming from. Not behind them. To the right. West. Eloise pushed through the first breakdown, not to herald, only to able to see the skolves flying through the mixed shrubs, trees, and wheat toward them. *Thirteen. Too many.*

"Thirteen incoming west."

She only heard Eoyan shrug his pack to the ground and take the big, heavy spear in both hands. He drew up close on her right. Gregory was on her left, Justice ringing as he drew it. Eloise drew her unnamed sword. It sang a tune as well, one she liked hearing. Beneath that autonomic excitement—almost a kind of joy—at the prospect of imminent combat, lay a fathomless depth of fear and frustration. She knew that no matter how well they fought, the three of them would never survive thirteen skolves in the open. Without cover, not even their entropic swords and shields could make enough of a difference. Skolves were physically superior in every respect—bigger, stronger, faster, more flexible, keener of sight and smell. With only a very few reported exceptions, they fought without any thought of retreat. In all the stories Eloise had heard, only Keith Euyn—the Lonely Wizard himself—had ever forced skolves to flee. Not even Robert had been able to scare them off on that prodigious night four years ago, and he had brought a thunderstorm's worth of lightning to the fight.

Every dynamicist who passed the Castlereagh Line was required to take Robert's course on dynamic combat. Eoyan and Gregory helped teach it, but only Robert had truly mastered the art of deploying dynamics in real-time hostilities. Keith Euyn was dead, Gerveault claimed to be too old for fighting, and all the other mature dynamicists were either too specialized, too weak, or too risk averse to learn. Of their class, Koria could have become adept at it, Eloise knew. Koria had an even finer touch than her husband, but she had chosen a different path. Gregory's weak affinity made dynamic combat as dangerous to himself as to his opponents. Bethyn was a cranky narcissist who always made everything difficult. She only ever did what Bethyn wanted to do, and burning her enemies alive was apparently not one of those things. *She just cannot be easy and get along, like me.* Heylor was not a bad hand at dynamic combat, but he was erratic and unpredictable, unlikely to follow process and protocol consistently, given to poor choices, and unlikely to think through the consequences of his choices. *And look at what just happened to him.*

Eloise was no master of dynamic combat, but she enjoyed destroying her enemies in each and any way available to her. In any case, thirteen skolves made dynamics imperative. They were moving through the scrub in a wedge, faster than a V-formation of geese, shooting toward them like a flight of arrows. Without the empyreal sky, Eloise would never even have seen the charging skolves in time, would never have enjoyed the single sharp instant to think these thoughts and decide what she had to do.

There was no more time. "Calculating!" she called out. Her hands were full, so she could not make the agreed visual gesture, but she had to warn Gregory and Eoyan not to move. In truth, she was not actually calculating anything. She did not even attempt to model the heat energy in the ground as Robert and Koria would. She lacked their memory or skill and could not hope to innovate at their fine-grained level of support. All her calculating was in the past. Her solution had been to memorize a few big transformations during the combat course and keep their mathematical operators ready. The efficiency of these canned innovations, as she thought of them, would suffer, the error or operator artefacts would be greater, there would be none of the accurate, fine modeling that mattered so much to Robert and Koria, but the trade-off was something that could work, at least for Eloise, in a pinch. Her method was lightning fast, and it could only be used like a bludgeon. But up to now, nothing she had tried in practice had burned quite hot enough. The skolves' shocking speed contributed to the current dilemma. The limitations of her method might well convert dilemma to disaster, but there was no other option. She could not avoid those shortcomings, but she knew, as surely as she remembered that awful day as a child with Hemdale, that she needed to overcome them. Otherwise they would all die.

Eloise took the largest safe heat transfer she had ever used in the equation and heedlessly doubled it. "Innovating," she announced again, crashing though the breakdown, reaching for the heat energy within a broad circle of the earth, and using her canned transform to place it in the air the skolves would have to pass through.

Whoomph!

An enormous circle of scrub ignited, its southern perimeter not more than fifteen yards in front of Eloise and her companions. It caught the skolves just as they shot out of the undergrowth. The eight rearmost burst into flames as they tried to pass through the circle, but the five in the lead shot through before suffering any lethal damage. A violent error wave preceded them, hot-cold-hot-cold, not so much rolling over Eloise, Gregory, and Eoyan as hammering them. The pain overwhelmed Eloise in a flash, from her toes to her scalp, so cold it burned. Her muscles locked tight in a powerful cramp.

I can't raise my shield! Eloise was locked up, and the skolves were right on top of her and her men.

With a roar, Gregory leapt in front of her, blocking a skolve as it swung a heavy rusted bar overhead at her. Its short gray fur was smoking, and it was screaming at an ear-piercing volume.

Bwaaaa!

The bar exploded against Gregory's raised shield and the skolve tripped, colliding with Eloise's lowered shield.

Thwack!

Another skolve veered around the first one and swung a thick tree branch low into Gregor's left shin. He had no chance to block the blow.

CRAAACK.

Gregory collapsed, howling in pain.

Gregory! Eloise's cramp gave way to rage, and she was suddenly able to move again. She raised her shield and smashed it into the skolve who had connected with it a moment before, hurling the beast back several feet despite its size. Then she rushed toward Gregory, swinging her sword at the skolve that had wounded him. Like the others, Eloise had been thoroughly educated about skolves, but she had never encountered a live one. Now she was learning just how accurate the classroom descriptions had been.

They looked like a cross between men and bipedal wolves, with long snouts and even longer six-fingered paws that resembled, grotesquely, the hands of a human being, but terminated in enormous, sharp talons. At just over seven feet tall, the skolve she now advanced against had well over a hand of height on her. Her entropic sword came whistling down. Its unnaturally sharp edge cut the skolve's snout in two before the beast had a chance to dodge the blade. The snout end, spraying blood, fell directly on Gregory, who was writhing on the ground, clutching at his lower leg. Before her husband could register this new horror, Eloise had swung her sword around again and cut straight down through the top of the skolve's head to its neck. As she pulled her sword out, the rest of the beast collapsed onto Gregory.

She instinctively turned to the first skolve, who was still on the ground, and stabbed her blade straight through the spot that on a human would be the space between the eyebrows. Still smoking from passing through the circle of fire, it spasmed sharply as the blade penetrated. It had still, she realized, been screaming. Between the fire, the thermal hammer of operator artefact, the sharp, painful, hypothermic consequences of her doubled innovation, Gregory's roar as he tried to protect her, and his scream when he went down, she had not noticed that the skolve had continued its high, keening wail.

Probably the fire. It was one thing to run through a suddenly burning land-scape and quite another to be unaffected by it. *All* the skolves had been badly hurt, not just the trailing eight, who continued to stagger about wildly, still on fire. A scalded-red skolve charged her with a raised hammer from Eoyan's side but crashed into one of its burning comrades. They both went down, thrashing, instinctively lashing out at each other. Eloise leapt over the roiling mess to help Eoyan, who with his spear was facing off against a chain-wielding skolve. As the beast swung the chain around its head, Eloise put her entire body into a ferocious lateral strike that cut the skolve in half at the waist. The heavy chain just missed Eoyan as it flew off into the grass.

Whirling to see if there were any other threats, Eloise saw another fire-con-torted skolve collide with a tree, screaming, and then collapse. She and Eoyan set to work stabbing the two skolves that were still rolling on the ground, frenetically snapping at each other, now perilously close to Gregory, who was struggling out from under the skolve that Eloise had killed. He was covered in blood and a gray-white goo that may have been brain matter. He tried to stand up, but his left leg gave out and he plopped awkwardly down on pieces of dead skolve.

"Gross!" Eoyan declared, wheezing for breath, bent over his spear, his own coat soaked in blood. "You should get that leg looked at, Lord Justice." He sniffed loudly. "Knights, they smell even worse roasted." He straightened up and wiped a trickle of blood away from his eyes. "I had hoped never to smell that stench again." He blew another heavy breath out of his lips and spun around in an effort to account for all the skolves. "Hey, look at this, Eloise." He pointed his spear at a cadaver that was visibly less roasted than the others, presumably the leader. There was a red hole where its right eye used to be. "I got him right on the instant of contact. That lucky thrust may have saved all our lives."

From his position on the ground, Gregory craned his head sideways and tried to open his eyes wider through the sticky gore that gummed them up. The effort appeared owlish. "Congratulations."

"Yep, you got one, Eoyan. You're the hero here, all right," added Eloise with a superhuman bite of sarcasm. She was thinking about what had happened to her at the moment of contact. She had been locked in a hypothermic muscle spasm, unable to move. In another instant, she would have died, if not for her husband. *Why am I not cold now?* She knew she should still be hypothermic. Her reckless dynamics might well have been instantly fatal. *I'm not cold at all.*

The same could not be said for the grass, wheat, and shrubs around them. Outside the circular area that was still weakly burning, a repeating pattern of arcuate scars marked the ground, frosted strips alternating with scorched. It was a wasteland. Eloise realized that the muck on Gregory and Eoyan was not entirely tissue and bodily fluids from the skolves. The skolve filth was mixed with melted frost and condensation from the error wave. She shook her head and knew that the ends of her long blond hair were still frozen solid. Yet her core temperature was fine, and she did not *feel* cold at all. What had happened to the hypothermic cost?

We were lucky. Strangely so. She looked down at Gregory, who had not come through the fight so well. Opening herself to the empyreal sky again, she examined his leg. *He shouldn't have tried to help me.* "Your shin is broken," Eloise announced bluntly, crouching next to Gregory but looking away from him, hiding her eyes. "Bleeding internally and externally too. I'll bind it so we don't leave a blood trail." She tried to reach for her backpack, then tried to shrug it off, but it was impossible with her shield strapped to her left arm. She had forgotten about that. A wave of frustration rolled through her, starting at her head and ending at her feet. She wanted to scream or hit something. She felt suddenly hot and her eyes began to burn and sting. She was unable to say anything intelligible.

Eloise jumped to her feet, keeping her back to Gregory, clawed at the buckles on her forearm, and tossed her shield roughly to one side. She pulled her backpack off and tore through it, looking for a rolled cloth and string. Gregory said nothing when she crouched down beside him again and began working on his leg. He only stared at her. She could feel his eyes on her face as she worked. Eoyan was wise enough to say nothing, silently keeping guard while she worked. A few moments later, Eloise was satisfied that Gregory would not paint the wheat they passed through with his blood.

"Climb up on my back. I'll carry you." It had only been a few moments since she had last spoken, but her voice felt coarse in her throat and in her ears. "We need to get some distance away from all this smoke."

He was hurt for me.

Again.

Eloise remembered other people being hurt, dying, for her.

Look at this, Eloise.

✝

"AUGH," GREGORY GRUNTED AS ELOISE RAN AND HE BOUNCED ON HER SHOULDER. "DON'T you ever get tired?"

She felt no exhaustion at all. She was the kind of woman who could carry her husband when she had to. Eoyan jogged alongside, carrying her shield and Gregory's as well, so that Eloise only had to manage the weight of her husband. All in, he could not have been more than a hundred and eighty or ninety pounds. Still, her pace was reduced to something between a trot and a fast walk. "You're welcome," she whispered, not slowing down.

"I—ow," he winced as he bounced again, "owe you again."

"Nope. You took one for me," Eloise returned barely audibly, eyes ahead. "I owe *you.*" She had her emotions under control again. Luckily no one had noticed her eyes earlier or commented on those tears if they had seen them. She could still be who she had to be. Even in her normal state of conscious-locked indifference, Eloise never forgot a debt. *Never.* She still owed a bigger debt to Robert, possibly unpayable. Koria may have foreseen his arrival, four years earlier, at the New School with her frequent, harrowing heraldic dreams, but Eloise had made sure she was also there to greet him that morning. She had taken it as fate that he was joining her class, and Koria had provided her with the perfect excuse to go meet him when he arrived in Vercors. As much as she had followed Robert to support Koria's need, she had stalked him for her own ends. Keeping that idiot alive had the added benefit of being fun. He was always up to something interesting—always driven—and while they were in school, Gregory went with him. She also owed Robert a debt for showing her Gregory's quality. *That puts me even further in hock.* And now here she was carrying Gregory after he had thrust himself between her and certain death. She patted his firm behind as she ran, smiling at the romantic payback she planned to deliver for his chivalric gesture.

†

"Bury this, Eoyan," Eloise ordered, passing the wrapped bundle of bloody clothes and soaked cloth out through the front entrance of the low tent. They had made it back, eventually, by an elaborately circuitous route, passing through streams as if attempting to tie knots in water, building geometries of entry and re-entry to watercourses that could not be cut by any knife or pulled apart by any hands. They had hopped over rocks, and stepped under a few, doubled and tripled back, pissed in false directions and dropped three small packages of mustard powder in directions they were not going in. It was a puzzle meant to spoil the skolves' preternatural sense of smell and tracking skills, to confuse and lose any of them that might try to follow. Eloise had been careful not to drop Gregory during any of this, and doubly careful not to leave any of her husband's blood behind. The sun was approaching the horizon when they finally arrived at their secondary, retreat cache, and Eloise and Eoyan immediately set to work on Gregory's broken tibia. With Eoyan's help, Eloise set the bone, sewed the torn skin back into one piece, and splinted the leg with parts taken from Eoyan's tent. The shin was not the most painful place on the human body to take a wound, but the work hurt quite enough, and Gregory had nearly busted a tooth from the pain, despite biting down on his own leather belt throughout the ordeal.

Eoyan took the bundle without a word and walked away, making a gentle rustle in the thick wheat. When Eloise turned back to Gregory, his eyes were on her. They were red from the ordeal. "Is the pain very bad?"

Gregory smiled tightly, his teeth showing. "It hurts a little." He winced. "A lot."

Eloise smiled. The fight was over, and she had done something for her injured husband. "I am feeling really good," she purred, crouching on her hands and knees. She always felt good after a fight. Intensely alive. "Let me just tuck you in." Careful to pass over Gregory's lower leg without touching it, Eloise straddled him, reaching around to make sure his head was cushioned on a bag of their cached clothes. She had cut his pants off to work on his leg. Eoyan was off somewhere disposing of them, but there was another pair in the bag. Still straddling Gregory, she grabbed their blanket and held it up. "Ready to sleep?"

"I don't know if I'll be able to."

"That's pain for you," Eloise smiled again, lowering herself gently onto his lap, her arms on either side of his head, holding herself steady above him. Her heavy, blond hair, thawed now and soft, spilled across his face.

"Aahg!" he said, though the strands of hair.

Eloise realized she had inadvertently put pressure on the bad leg. "Knights damn it, you're right," she whispered, taking her weight off him. "We've got to do this right."

"Do what?"

"I think you know." She got up on her knees, again careful of his leg, and shimmied out of her shirt and then her pants and knickers. "This will be much more comfortable." She crouched over him again. "And effective."

"Really?"

"Yes, husband," she purred, "your dreams have come true."

Gregory winced. "Again?"

There had been an … incident in the military school infirmary a few days after the Battle of the Bifrost. Bat Merrett had left the infirmary in the middle of it and never returned even though his ear was still more attached by thread than skin. Eloise had thought the big man was asleep, but you could never tell with Merrett.

"I'll be more careful this time."

"Aahg!"

"Sorry," she breathed, adjusting herself, trying not to put weight anywhere near his injured shin. "This is for your own good, you know."

Gregory looked like he did not know if he should laugh, cry, or moan as Eloise brushed herself gently against him. She was always euphoric after battle. Sometimes it manifested itself as a kind of friendly and uncritical relaxation, which was such an unusual state of mind for her that it had been remarked upon by just about everyone who knew her and had witnessed it. At other times it lifted her into another kind of excitement. And Gregory had taken his injury for her. Most warriors felt close after the stress of battle, but with Gregory now, Eloise needed a purer and much more intense, an indivisible, form of closeness. She wanted to reward him and make him feel better, but she also wanted him closer to her, inside her, feeling the same physical pleasure, the same emotional closeness, the same intense happiness at just being alive that she did.

"Uhh," Gregory whimpered, "I may not be at my best right now."

"I'll be the judge of that," Eloise whispered back. She lowered herself further, brushing Gregory's face with her left nipple. "Do something with that, would you?"

"O-kay," Gregory replied in a hesitant tone.

Slowly and carefully, she lowered herself onto him.

"Aahg!"

Not carefully enough, apparently. Gregory had turned away from her breast and was trying to make eye contact through the strands of her long, blond hair piled on his face and chest. "Sorry dear," she said.

"It's okay with me," came Eoyan March's voice from outside the tent. "Carry on."

Eloise frowned, raising herself a few inches above Gregory. "Shut up and go away, you perv!"

"I can't!" Eoyan's voice was plaintive. "First, I don't really want to, and second, I have to stand guard with you both so … preoccupied."

Eloise tried to forget about Eoyan and returned her attention to her husband. He was practically drowning in her hair, and there was one other detail that she had missed. "Oh. I forgot something. Don't move." Eloise carefully maneuvered herself off Gregory and started working his underwear off. It was hard to do so since he could not put pressure on the bad leg to lift himself, but Eloise kept at the task, doing all the work.

"Aahg!" The ginch had snagged on Gregory's splint.

"Oh dear," she said to herself, trying to unsnag the cotton shorts without ripping them or pulling too hard on his broken leg. "There!"

Eoyan's voice floated through the thin canvas wall of the tent again. "Do you need a hand in there?"

"No!"

Eloise repositioned and lowered herself, ever so gently, again. Gregory's hands rested lightly on her hips and began their own smooth motions. She kept her face propped up and smiled at him as she began rocking back and forth very slowly, keeping her full weight off him. *He's already broken. I must be careful.* "How's that?"

Gregory nodded. It was impossible to tell if his open-mouthed expression was one of pain or pleasure. Both, probably.

"What Uncle Eoyan can't believe," Eoyan's voice floated in from outside again, "is that you are ravishing a man with a broken leg. Be careful you don't break the other one."

"I'm being careful, stupe!"

"Well, that's no way to have sex."

"Didn't I tell you to shut the hell up?"

"Maybe I should come in and help. I'll do whatever. Up, down, sideways, it's all knightly. Uncle Eoyan is fine whichever way the wind blows."

"We know that, Eoyan. *Everyone* knows it. Just stay on guard. Out there!"

"Aahg!"

"Sorry, dear." Eloise slowed down and oriented herself at a shallower angle to his pelvis, rubbing herself slowly back and forth against him. She throbbed in time with her heartbeat, with her own motion, with her emotion. She craned her neck so she could kiss him.

"Aahg!"

"Stop struggling, dear," she breathed, face inches from his. "This will go better for you if you just let me do the work."

"I think you're hurting him."

Eloise looked over her shoulder at the canvas wall of the tent in the direction of Eoyan's voice. "This is good for him, stupe."

"How?"

Eloise rocked more urgently against Gregory who had now closed his eyes, accepting what was happening, letting Eloise do it her way. "I am breaking the pain cycle. You can't feel two acute sensations at the same time. His leg's broken, you know."

"Huh."

"Just relax, dear." Eloise rocked harder. Gregory pushed back, trying to arch his pelvis despite the possibility of putting pressure on the broken leg. At the same time, he pulled her hips harder against himself. He was not complaining. He was beyond pain now. The tent was shaking.

"You know, you're knocking the grain kernels off the rachises. It's raining grain out here." After a brief moment, his voice came again. "I think it's metaphorical."

They ignored him.

"You know, Uncle Eoyan broke his leg once too. No one straddled me and offered to make it all better. In fact, I remember being abandoned at some little outpost on the Line while my friends, including you, Gregory, ran off to have fun. Knights damn it, you're lucky, Justice!"

Eloise and Gregory were well past being distractible now, but Eoyan kept talking. "If the skolves have managed to track us and show up now, we're pretty much done for." He paused as if narrating a cliffhanger. "Oh, wait, I know. I can negotiate. Give them something." The tent continued to shake as Eoyan continued. "Sir Gregory's smooth skin will be my offering. Even though it's never been done before, the skolves have got to want something. I think negotiation is possible..."

No one was listening to Eoyan. He was no longer even background noise.

Eloise's mouth was open. She smiled down on her husband, pushing on him firmly. "Ingrid and Egyl told me they want a little brother." He smiled back, his eyes wet, though not red.

If she could have swallowed her husband up, she would have, such was her euphoria. She wanted him, she was having him, she was one with him. It was a perfect moment. If the moment could have played over and over again like the infinite worlds of a heralding, she would have kissed him everywhere, touched him everywhere, sucked on him everywhere, bit him, tongued him, teased him, breathed gently upon him, held him. She would have done it all. She would gladly have participated in every possible scenario. But life was not heraldry, and love and sex were not probabilistic exercises in cosmology and potentiality. There was no infinite multitude of variations to be played over and over again. As she orgasmed, she pulled herself hard onto him, closer, burrowing, wrapping her arms around him, engulfing the man she loved, holding him for everything their love was worth, unequivocally satisfied and alive. There was only one life, and Eloise was the kind of woman who lived it fully and in the moment.

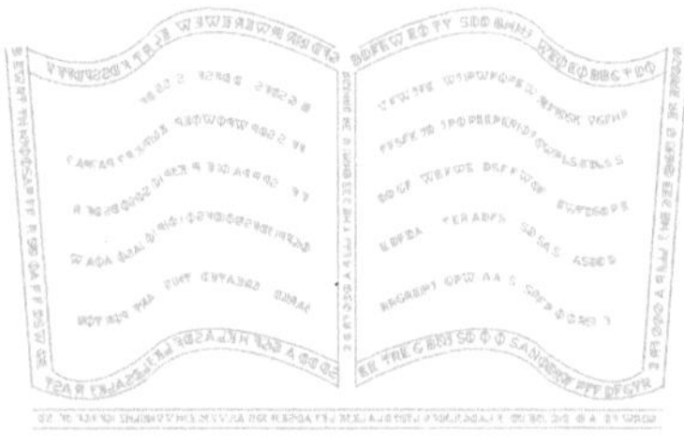

Chapter Eight

More Knights

*T*HERE ARE FUNDAMENTAL MODULI THAT CONTROL THE WORKINGS OF EACH WORLD. *THEY ARE connected but are also different in ways we do not yet understand.*

—Huygens, *The Measure of Worlds*

"I AM WORRIED ABOUT THE PLAN, BETHYN," KORIA SAID, REMOVING THE THERMOMETER from her former classmate's mouth and jotting down the data in her notebook. She handed Bethyn a clean, white handkerchief. "Lighthouse makes assumptions about our capabilities that we may not be able to live up to."

Bethyn dabbed her mouth and looked at her friend caustically. "You think?" She tossed the handkerchief aside. "I can tell you I wouldn't be volunteering to try that experiment again if I was you." She moved closer to Koria until her face was less than a foot from the darker-skinned girl's. "In fact," she hissed, "*I* won't be assisting again if that's how it's going to be." She sat back. "You should be in bed. You lost your baby. You could have died." She gestured sharply at Koria with her right hand. "You look like cobbled skolve shit. If Robert sees you, he isn't going to go anywhere."

Koria reached across the distance between them and gently placed the palm of her hand against Bethyn's cheek. She *did* feel tired. Faint and weak. It was difficult to sit up straight. "I love you too, Bethyn."

Bethyn reached up for Koria's hand and held it for a moment before releasing it and standing up. "Now you sound just like him." Bethyn put her hands on her hips and shook her head. "One maniac in the family is enough, don't you think?"

Koria did not want to continue discussing it, did not want to think about it again so soon after suffering through the awful, drawn-out process. She had hoped to learn something new, to create knowledge. She had failed. Worse, the failure was not complete until she had labored for hours to eject her lifeless daughter.

Instead of a triumphant act of creation, Koria had given birth to something dead. That was why, instead of looking backwards or responding to Bethyn, she looked down at her notes. "Some of this post hoc data is strange. I don't know whether to cull or residualize."

Bethyn walked to the door of the small meeting room. "You don't know when to stop."

"Could you get me some spinach juice, please? It will be a while before I can reduce this data, let alone write it up."

Щ

"Are you really planning not to see Sir Robert before he leaves?" Gerveault asked. They had been going over the data for some time, elements of it scrawled across the chalkboard. Bethyn had finally left for good, announcing that the sun was up and that it was past time to sleep.

"I was going to herald him." Koria was a master at this. She could herald her husband's activities as long as she was within a mile or so of him. Not only could she see what he was doing but, within a probabilistic framework, what he was about to do. She had been doing it for four years now, and more extensively than anyone knew except Eloise.

"That is not right, you know. Especially now, Lady Koria, after what just happened to you." Gerveault's shaggy brows narrowed. He had no intention of letting the matter lie regardless of how much she said she did not wish to discuss it, no matter how much she wanted to bury herself more deeply in her work. "You should not herald for three days at least after this." He closed his eyes in an uncharacteristic show of feeling. "We cannot be losing any more children of Engevelen."

Koria knew Gerveault was speaking of both her and her unborn baby—now never to be born. A spasm went through her. It had no physical cause, but it nevertheless felt intensely physical. *My daughter is gone.* Her abdomen hurt with a phantom pain where the baby should be, where life should be dawning, where love should be growing. The absence was a knife, the withdrawing of which was a horror. It was a terrible price to pay for the experiment, and not one that she had in any way agreed to. What happened had been an enormous, appalling surprise. It was the reason Gerveault and Bethyn had been up for hours with her. They both wanted her to stop, to take a break, to recover, to never again attempt the fatal experiment. But if Koria did not learn what they needed to know, who would?

I won't have my husband die next.

Koria's stomach unclenched enough for her to respond to the old man without giving voice to her pain. "A strange prescription when the post hoc protocol is to perform a standard heraldry calibration." She forced a smile. "Which I did, and with no abnormalities."

Gerveault was unimpressed. "You are as driven as any Deladieyr Knight, Lady Koria. Worse, because what drives you is too subtle for most to appreciate. You are worse than Sir Hemdale and his endless quest for the Bridge, as bad as Sir Robert after his first heraldic dream. You seem calm but act in hidden ways. That subtlety fools many. You are as inexorable a person as I have ever known. Just because you do not shout and fight with a sword does not mean you do not fight." He raised his right index finger and pointed it at the ceiling. "And there *was* an abnormality in your post hoc test!"

I must choose my battles carefully. Koria did not bother pointing out that everyone's memories of Robert after his heraldic dream—everyone's but hers—had softened with time. To Koria, no one was more driven, reckless, or brave than her husband. Anyone who was would have become a monster. Or be dead. *That's why I must keep my heraldic eyes on him.* That and the fact that she loved him. She had loved him since the first night she had dreamt of him and seen him die. The rest of what the old man had said she would not bother disputing. What Gerveault had claimed might well be true, except for something so far unspoken. "The test abnormality wasn't me; it was the modulus."

"The modulus!" Gerveault held a second finger in the air, then seemed to think better of it. He lowered his arm and hand altogether. "Prove that to me."

Koria opened her notebook to the temperature-accuracy versus time-heraldry graph. One line showed the number of predictive errors for each act of heraldry, while the other showed Koria's temperature after each event. The temperature data showed a smooth, steady curve, except for two blips where Koria's temperature did not change at all but she had made predictive errors. Except for those two blips, Koria had made no other errors. Two dice out of thirty-six had been incorrect on the first occasion and three out of thirty-six on the second. "I have not made a mistake with thirty-six dice in seventeen months. I made two here, and my temperature almost rose instead of dropping."

Gerveault looked down before making eye contact with her again. "Lady Koria. You were just tired, that is all. The temperature change, or lack of it, was within normal experimental error range. It is difficult to measure a temperature change at all under such a slight load, but this data *does* show that you need to rest. You have not made a mistake like this in over a year. It happened because you are exhausted. Your skin is more gray than black. Your eyes are as red as coals. You. Need. Rest."

Tired or not, Koria could always smile when she knew she was right. "That argument would not be *completely* unreasonable," she replied, "except for the second experiment." She flipped several pages in the notebook until she found another, similar graph. It also had a smooth curve, but with three strange blips. "This is Bethyn's post hoc test. When we saw my results, I asked Bethyn to perform one for control against the medium."

Gerveault's eye widened. "What made you think to do that?"

Koria shrugged. "We do it as a matter of course out past the Castlereagh Line."

"That is for an entirely different reason!" Gerveault expelled a big breath. "However, if the modulus is unstable, we have a big problem." He frowned at her. "This should have been among the first things we discussed, not the last! The Bridge could be failing."

Koria's smile was subtle and more intellectual than emotional. It touched her eyes more than her lips. "Possibly."

A trickle of sweat appeared on the old man's forehead. "If the Bridge fails before we find it, the duchy will fall."

"Now you know where my mind has been," she said primly. "Still want me to take a three-day nap?"

"I need to think, Lady Koria." Gerveault stood up and began pacing around the room. Koria resisted the urge to slump forward onto the table. It was … difficult, but she had learned that outward composure helped with inner composure. She was not going to let herself wilt, not when there were urgent problems to solve. Not on the morning that Robert was leaving on the Javelin mission.

"Okay," Gerveault announced at last, sitting down. "I have some ideas, but since you arrived at this uncomfortable crossroads before me, let us discuss yours first."

Koria pursed her lips. "Action plans or questions and implications?"

"The latter, please."

I agree.

Koria liked the *why* best. "Does this instability really mean the Bridge is failing? If so, at what rate? Will Skoll and Hati sense this? Have they already? What adjustments should we make to Lighthouse to compensate? If we don't have the fifteen additional years we planned for, what can we do?"

Gerveault nodded. "Those are good questions, Koria. They are also on my list. Anything else?"

"Yes," she said, quickly. "Are Skoll and Hati our only enemies here? Did Novgoreyl agree to give us back the Ardgour Wilderness because they knew?" Thinking back to Novgoreyl and the treaty that had spawned Lighthouse, Koria had another thought. *Could this even be some part of what Keith dreamed about four years ago? Too late to find the answer to that.* "Does Armadale know the Bridge is failing, and what would they do if they did know?" She found her jaw involuntarily clenching. "Most important of all, will Nimrheal return if and when the Bridge fails? If Nimrheal comes back before we have learned what we need to, if he comes back before phase seven is complete and both Skoll and Hati are dead, how will we possibly learn what we need to? How will we survive?"

"Yes," Gerveault agreed, "this could be a non-linear situation." He stood up and began pacing again, this time as if he were addressing a class in the New School. "Once Nimrheal is back, our knowledge growth will essentially be over. We will have very little time. There will be no more experiments with the greenstone, no investigations of decay and Huygens, and certainly no chance of completing our understanding of what Nehring did, or coming up with an independent, dynamic solution." He raised his index finger. "Action plans, then. We either need to figure out how much time we have left, or we need to find the Bridge before it fails regardless of the time. To address the former, we will put our classes at the New School to work. I'll send a message to them to begin comprehensive, daily heraldry calibration tests. All classes will do this, only excepting the medical research team and you and me. Meredeth Callum and her students can work on reducing and analyzing the data. If there is a predictive trend, Meredeth will find it. Deryn Endicott is sending a shipment of hardened arrowheads to Ardvaser soon. If he personally delivers them, I will speak with him. Perhaps Robert's uncle knows some Endicott family secret we need to hear." He raised another finger. "I will also speak to the duke about mobilizing additional armed forces. Perhaps the emperor can be persuaded to send help."

The old professor stopped pacing and fixed Koria with one of his famous penetrating looks. "What am I missing here, Lady Koria?"

"The location of the Bridge."

Gerveault raised a third finger. "We have not found it in over two centuries, so how are we going to find it now?" He gazed expectantly at her.

"With data," she replied.

"Yes," he affirmed crisply. "Let's residualize everything we have from the field and see if we can find a new clue. Bethyn has a good head for that."

"And our enemies?"

Gerveault lowered his hand and chuckled mirthlessly. "I have some news about them that I've been saving. You are aware of Sir Hemdale's long preparation for a Ceremony of Rising for Marielle Engel? Well, it is happening here, and soon. Moreover, Armadale has sent a messenger. They are coming, and not just Sir Jormundheim and Sir Valcryst. Armadale is sending their political arm. They are sending the new ambassador!" He smiled wolfishly. "Our enemies are coming to us. We will *sift* them."

Koria stood up a little too quickly. She was still lightheaded from loss of blood. "I will attempt a far heraldry."

"No. Do not." Gerveault held up both hands, palms facing her. It was the strongest gesture of negation he permitted himself. "There is a locus out there, and you do not need to butt heads with it in your condition. I meant what I said about rest."

"What should I do, then?" Koria asked irritably. "I can't just sit on my hands?"

"You should, but you will not." Gerveault looked at her appraisingly. "I imagine you will spy on your husband before he leaves … which will be quite soon. After that, if you do not simply pass out, how about reviewing the old texts for new clues on Nehring Ardgour's apparatus or how to fight Nimrheal?"

"I found something interesting, as a matter of fact," Koria said evenly. "It's an alternate account of the first act in the fall of Engevelen. This one wasn't written by the Steel Castle, so it might have some unsullied information."

"Sounds interesting. Do read that. Excellent." Gerveault suddenly went still. "Who wrote this account?"

Koria did not miss the change in Gerveault's manner. "It's the journal of a young wizard from the time. Luciena was her name."

Gerveault's eyes narrowed. "I may have heard of it. A long time ago, from Keith." He began pacing again. Koria was too tired to interrupt him while he went back and forth. Then suddenly, the old man stopped as if yanked by a rope. "I remember now," he said in a distant tone. "Yes," he added more confidently. "Keith said it had inspired him back when he was just beginning to put together the nascent ideas for dynamics. Definitely read that one carefully."

Interesting. Koria nodded. "I'll pass it along to you when I've finished."

"I will look forward to that."

"But Professor Gerveault," Koria said in a smaller voice.

"Yes?"

"We really are in a lot of trouble. I have no idea why extradimensional observation should have had the ... the effect on me that it did." Without thinking, Koria looked down at her flattening belly.

Gerveault did not reply for a long moment. Looking up again, Koria noticed his eyelids fluttering. She had never seen that in him before. Gerveault had often seemed cold and calculating, not perhaps as bloodless or logical as Keith Euyn, though almost on some days. Not today. Perhaps he caught her staring, for the fluttering suddenly stopped.

"Neither do I," he said, eyes flickering to her abdomen. "Perhaps we should abandon that line of research."

"How can we learn how to stop Nimrheal if we do?" She found herself in tears for the first time since realizing she had lost her baby. Pushing through her tears, she continued speaking. "If we cannot understand where he comes from, or how to harness those energies, we are unlikely to find a way to stop him. We do not know what we need to know, and now we may never know. It may simply be beyond our comprehension."

"Perhaps, after all, it is beyond our ability to survive," Gerveault said.

"Or both," Koria agreed. "Nimrheal might as well be here now." The loss of her baby had the lead weight of finality. It felt as heavy, flat, and endless as the sea. It was non-linear and it could not be reversed. The death carried with it a hopelessness that was cousin to the hopelessness of a fight against

Nimrheal without any deeper comprehension of what that being really was. It was a hopelessness that portended only more deaths.

"Sleep on it, Lady Koria."

Щ

There he goes- off on his adventure. Koria stood on the roof of the cardinal tower of Ardvaser Castle, the central tower, the tallest one. Both before and after Ardvaser was rebuilt, it had housed an observatory. Koria still used it to observe. She had seen, not long before, Sir Hemdale standing guard on the floating bridge to the Steel Tower when the service for members of the Javelin mission had been held in the great octagonal room. Robert had not attended, which was no surprise. The rest of his team, and a good number of those off duty that day, had gone to hear the words of the bishop. Many of the attendees, on opening the great iron door and seeing Sir Hemdale waiting on the narrow stone walkway, rigged out for war, had flinched visibly enough for Koria to notice from the tower. Koria wondered if Marielle Engel had felt any trepidation at the sight of Sir Hemdale standing there with his sword drawn. *Didn't look like it.* In her body language at least, Engel had betrayed nothing of her feelings.

It was an ancient custom for a renowned knight to stand guard over the service. The custom had been an offshoot of similar but more important ceremonies in the past. Since the time of Sir Seygis, the Council of Knights had jealously defended their right to approve any candidates who sought to cross the Methueyn Bridge. The legend of Seygis, called the ninth knight by some and the cannibal knight by others, was a horrific story. In its time, the grisly incident had even threatened the cosmological authority of the Steel Castle. Luckily for the church, other crises had since arisen to make most forget the lessons that Seygis had taught.

There are more than eight ideas and not every idea should be given voice.

The approval process was almost moot now, however. The Bridge had been lost.

And wherever it is, it is failing. Koria was sure of that now. The data would prove it, she was certain, and perhaps, as Gerveault suggested, it might even give some indication of *when*. It was probably too much to hope that the data could also show *where*. Only data from way out past the wheat line had the potential to reveal that, but so far it had only yielded clues. Could Robert now find the data they needed?

He was gone now. It would happen or it would not. The great throngs had seen him off, cheering and shouting:

"Shout, shout.
Redoubt, redoubt
Redoubt Empyrean!
It's echoed, echoed
In the halls of Elysium!"

The massed voices shouting to the heavens had an effect even as far away as the tower where Koria listened. *Goosebumps.* And a certain awe, to be sure. Yet the mob always made her nervous too, and did so now, even though the throngs below were bellowing in support of her husband. Koria wondered how many of them knew they might never see him again except in Elysium.

Watching Robert don his armor, speak to Arthur Wolverton and to Lindseth's short, wizened mother and a few others, and take one last look around—probably hoping to see her—Koria had longed to run down to see him off. She wanted to feel his love and return that feeling to him before he left. But she knew better. First of all, she was still in no condition to run, and anyway she could not let him see her, feeling as she did. It would necessitate an extended conversation that would undo him. Neither of them had time now for the grief that Koria felt.

Now he was gone, and it felt as final as the loss of their daughter, a loss he could not be allowed to know about.

Exhausted or not, melancholy or not, Koria had work to do. *I have my mission, and it cannot wait any longer.* She had climbed the tower to watch Robert leave, and she had. Now she needed a moment alone in the garden of the old rooftop observatory to think about their situation. She had been discouraged but not defeated. Koria did not give up. *I will fight in my way. Perhaps we will still see each other again on earth rather than Elysium.*

"Ah, Lady Koria, it is so nice to find you here."

Koria did not think so, though she did not speak her thoughts. The short, stooped, slightly overweight man before her was the Bishop of Ardvaser, the priest responsible for the Steel Castle in this northernmost fortress of Vercors.

"But no surprise, surely," she replied. No one climbed the cardinal tower by accident.

His smile was not as brief as hers had been on seeing him. His smile had to last long enough to appear beneficent. *Now he will ask for something, saying he is trying to do me a favor. But it will really be for something in* his *favor.*

"No," he agreed. "We held the service for your husband's mission not long ago. I was sad to see that he did not attend."

Koria said nothing. She knew the bishop intended his remark as a question. *If he wants a favor, I am not starting by giving him any for free.*

His munificent smile faltered after a moment, but he managed to resurrect it before taking a breath to speak again. "Why do you suppose he did not join us?"

"Probably for the same reason I did not join *him*, good bishop." Koria kept a close eye on the smiling man. "He was busy. A man heading off into the wilderness on a quest requiring more skill and knowledge than any mission in Lighthouse might reasonably choose to spend the spare time he had left to … study his maps." She had no doubt that Robert had, though she also knew he had committed most of the maps to memory.

"I can see that," the bishop breathed, frowning ever so slightly. "It makes sense, of course. That is good. I was worried I might have offended him."

"Surely not."

"No." he smiled again. "This is a time of big events, Lady Koria. The biggest Council of Deladieyr Knights in decades has been called. We will have a new Ceremony of Rising for Marielle Engel when she and Sir Robert return from across the Line."

"Yes."

"Do you think …" His voice trailed off. For a moment he seemed uncharacteristically at a loss for words before recovering himself. "Do you think that Sir Robert would submit himself for consideration to Rise? It would be so heartening to the faithful if we had *two* new Deladieyr Knights."

He is wondering if Robert still has his power. In the fight with Keith Euyn, the younger man had held his own against the greatest knight in modern history with the possible exception of Sir Hemdale. Despite being over eighty years old, Keith had demolished Sir Christensen even while holding off Gerveault's dynamics. In the embassy siege, Robert had done incredible things as well, but things that had harmed him. Since then, he had avoided all fighting. He had even avoided sparring in public. His reputation, however, remained as sharp as Likelihood, the entropic sword he now kept on his hip. Keith's sword.

"I too would like to see my husband Rise," Koria said, feigning a smile of her own while feeling viscerally ill again. *If I am right, we will have to win in the worst way: by fighting again. We will need more knights. A lot more.*

Щ

KORIA FELT NO BETTER AFTER THE SLOW WALK TO HER AND ROBERT'S APARTMENT. AS SHE fumbled with her keys, a page in yellow and blue livery rushed enthusiastically to intercept her at the door. "Lady Koria!" he called out in a bright voice.

"Yes," she answered as evenly as she could, her back as straight as it could be, with as much poise as she could summon to disguise her weariness.

The young man, a boy really, smiled and held out a small package wrapped in brown paper and tied with a string. "An urgent package for Sir Robert. From Sir Christensen."

It felt like a book.

Chapter Nine.

Hung Jury

"THAT IS REVOLTING," HEYLOR CHOKED OUT, LOOKING FIRST AT THE HANGING BODY and then at the liquids that had accumulated underneath it, a viscous, immiscible conglomeration of yellow and white fluid. Some of the foul brew trailed from the dead man's left pant leg. His neck had been twisted so that he hung lopsided, and the gruesome solution had therefore run down the lower leg. A reddish brown, blood-like trail emanated from his nose.

"That's what happens when you get hanged." Constable Lynwen's voice was matter of fact. "You should be glad he doesn't seem to have eaten beforehand."

Heylor stifled a gallows chuckle and looked at her. She really was quite pretty. And smart too, though in unexpected ways. His family loved how she had made herself at home in their house and happily joined in the rowdy scrum that defined the household. Grandma thought she *was* one of the family. Heylor could not believe that just a day or two ago he had considered her a tedious pest. Yet today here he was, eyeing her trim, pert figure and enjoying her peculiar, flat speaking voice while examining a dead body. He suddenly wanted to reach out and touch her despite the starched uniform she wore, despite the shocking sight and terrible smell of the dead body. It seemed like they had been together for months rather than for less than two days.

How did we get here?

T

"I KEEP HAVING THESE NIGHTMARES, SON," HEREVOR STYLE, HEYLOR'S DAD, COMPLAINED for at least the third time.

Heylor shook his head. "That's great dad, but for knight's sake, can you put some pants on?" He ran to the window and peered out the curtains. "Lynwen is going to be here any minute. I don't want her to see you in your ginch."

"Okay, okay." Herevor disappeared down the wide hallway toward his room. A fat orange cat watched his retreating back, then sprawled in the hallway and turned its fickle, lazy attention to watching Heylor pace back and forth. The young man wore a smart new set of clothes, including the gold cape that Eleanor had given him only a few days before her death. *That was back when my biggest mistakes only went so far as almost destroying a town's water supply.*

Robert had saved him from that one. Well, Bethyn had saved him from hypothermic death, and Robert had repaired the water reservoir in an act of dynamics that bordered on the full-on wizardry that Gerveault abhorred. How many times had Robert stepped in between Heylor and disaster, acting as his own personal Heydron? *More than he should have had to. I just never learn. What is so hard about making good decisions?* But Heylor knew the answer. Being patient and following process was something that went fundamentally against his nature.

Perhaps it would have been okay if the consequences of his mistakes had not kept getting worse.

I never used to kill people before.

I killed Keith Euyn.

Well, Robert did all the work. I just ran in at the last minute.

Still.

That doesn't count anyway. Killing the great man wasn't an accident.

Heylor sighed so loudly that the orange cat raised its head and gave him its full attention for at least a second before resuming its usual indifference. Heylor had apologized for his outburst of the night before, but no apology could make him forget the fact that he had killed his comrades-in-arms. This was a burden he was never going to get used to carrying. Other mistakes would have been forgotten by now. He would have moved on to some other escapade. But there was no getting over this disaster. His friends' bodies had been left far past the Castlereagh Line, past even the wheat line. There was no apologizing to them, no making this right.

Maybe I'm apologizing to the wrong people.

But what can I do?

Heylor heard a sound, and his head swiveled instinctively toward the window. *Lynwen!* A feeling had been building in him, and it had to do with the attractive young constable. He had disliked her at first, but over the course of a single day this had changed dramatically. There was, after all, *something* about her. Was it the way she had sat so comfortably beside Grandma? Or the way she had accepted his impossible family? Or was it just that she had stuck up for him when he had gone on his rant? *Is this just vanity? No, there's something more.*

Heylor *was* certainly infatuated with the constable, but as he watched her stepping briskly toward the heavy door, a deeper instinct sang to him. He was going to help her, and somehow that would help him.

Moving quickly and impulsively, as he always did, he bounded to the door and swung it open in Lynwen's face, startling her just as she raised her hand to knock. Her pupils dilated and her mouth opened in that cute way she had when surprised. She wore her baton and short sword just as she had the day before, but she also carried a large leather bag in her left hand.

"What's in the bag, Lynwen?" Heylor asked artlessly, then winced. "Sorry. I mean, good morning, Constable Lynwen. Nice to see you."

Lynwen's mouth moved from a startled 'O' into a sweet smile. "Nice to see you too, Heylor Style. This," she raised the bag and shook it at him, "is makeup. We need to conceal those bruises. They really are quite something. And not what people expect to see on an agent of the law. Have a seat and I'll go to work. We can, uh … discuss where we are going to patrol today. I also have a uniform for you."

Heylor pulled out a heavy wooden kitchen chair. "I thought we were going to the New School."

"I thought you didn't want to go there."

"That was the self-pity talking."

Lynwen did not look at him as she pushed a pile of debris across the large, polished surface of the table and set her bag on it. "There's really nothing going on there. I don't want you to be bored."

"You'll be there to entertain me."

"I could show you how we run the Office of the Constabulary."

Boring.

"I'd rather Nimrheal rode a thunderhead from hell and disemboweled me."

"How about a trip to the Registered Seed Office?"

"And watch seeds germinating in a bin? Perhaps I could go back across the Line and let Skoll finish tearing my head off." Heylor stood up, put his hands on Lynwen's strong shoulders, and looked her in her big gray eyes. "What aren't you telling me, constable?"

"Sit down, Heylor Style. I have to tell you the truth."

He sat down, a wide smile spreading across his face.

"I may have exaggerated something." Lynwen dug in the bag, pulled out the shirt, pants, belt, and jacket of a constable's uniform. She dug further and produced a small, fine brush and several minute tins.

"You lied to me?" Heylor was smiling so hard his face hurt.

"Lying is a subjective term," Lynwen replied, unscrewing the lids from the tins. "Last night, when I said nothing was going on at the New School, I was telling the truth as I knew it then. But this morning there has been word of a new protest." She held up one of the tins in his direction and looked from it to him. "I think this is the right one."

"For what?"

Lynwen put the tin down and mushed the brush around in it. "I told you, for covering up those horrific bruises. Now loosen your collar and tell me all about what happened with Skoll."

Heylor was not about to tell her what happened with the demon, but he still could not get the grin off his face. The hallway cat had fallen asleep, but Heylor felt jumpier—and more alive—than ever. The strange thrill of being lied to by Lynwen and then having her apply make-up to his neck and face made him feel happy again for the first time since his discovery that Skoll actually existed.

Ψ

"I can't wear this uniform."

Her eyes widened. Hurt. "Why not?"

"I haven't earned it." Heylor had never had much respect for the constables. When he was a kid in the poor part of town—the peasant quarter, as it was known—the constables had been a dim-witted annoyance. Later, during the time when the cloaked figure had menaced the New School, they had just seemed incompetent. But looking at Lynwen, an undoubtedly clever young woman—and a real human being who would lie to him for his own good—he could no longer brush the constabulary off quite so easily. As changeable and resilient as he usually was, he also felt shame. He had let his eight down. They were gone. He could not pretend he was a trustworthy servant of the public now.

His hand reached out of its own accord and took Lynwen's. "Maybe I could go undercover." He looked down at her hand. Holding it gave him an electric thrill. "Uh, sorry." He let it go.

"Are you two running off to join the street performers?" It was Herevor, dressed for work now. That meant a blue cloak and a top hat. His black leather boots were, to Heylor's astonishment, clean as a whistle and polished to a high sheen.

Lynwen jumped, face flushed, mouth open. Again.

Herevor crossed the distance between them in a heartbeat, leaned down, and squinted at his son. "Not a bad job, constable. It almost covers the mangle-marks." It irritated Heylor to watch his father's quick, restless movements. They were too much like his own.

That top hat is never going to stay on his head.

"So where *are* you two off to?"

Lynwen collected herself. "Apparently we're going to the New School."

"Oh," Herevor said, eyes distant, momentarily still. "I wish I had gone there." He shrugged, walking toward the door. "I would have liked to learn to herald properly, like you, Heylor. The Duchess's Program didn't exist in my day." He smiled, but it came and went quick as a wink. "There was no way I could have afforded it without that help." He swung the door open and paused, looking back. "Hey, do you think you could borrow the Eindarch Eye for me, son?"

"No," Heylor answered automatically, knowing the Eye was in high demand, not thinking. He did a double take, remembering his father mentioning the Eye the night before. "Why?"

"Ever hear of a locus?"

"Y-yes." Heylor remembered reading about one in *The Lonely Wizard*. It had also come up in third year, but only as a theoretical oddity. *A knot in probability through which heraldry is impossible. Or was it something about an event that ties a knot in probability? Something that heraldry cannot escape from? That heralds cannot escape from? Something like that. I should have paid more attention.* "You've encountered one?" *Would you even know what it looked like if you did?*

Herevor raised his eyebrows. "I'm no far herald, son—none of us are—but yes, a locus is the current consensus among my peers."

The door closed behind him.

"Why can't you get this Rudolph Eye, whatever it is, for your dad?"

"Hmm?" Heylor turned back to Lynwen, who was staring at him. "*Eindarch* Eye. There's only one, and the last thing the New School would want is for it to fall into the hands of the Rawles Trading Company. Dad shouldn't even have asked. He knows better." It irritated Heylor that his father was so impulsive. "Let's go." He started toward the door, but Lynwen put a hand on his chest, stopping him.

"I understand why you won't wear the uniform, but you should carry a baton at least." Lynwen pulled her baton out and tried to pass it to Heylor, who backed away from her.

"Only constables wear a baton."

"You should have something."

Heylor knew she was right, but he was too impatient to listen. It was like a heat that had built in him, the need to get moving, to do *something*. "Let's just go." He walked to the door and pulled it open. Then he suddenly stopped, causing Lynwen to crash into him.

"What?" she asked.

"Knights damn it. You're right. I always do this!" Heylor turned, practically nose to nose with her. "I need to follow process. Don't—don't let me get away with this kind of skolve shit, Lynwen. I need to do things right. Excuse me." He stepped around the young constable, crossed through the entry way and kitchen, and started rifling through the den's enormous bookshelf.

Hammer? No. Iron hoop? No. Cat? Umm, no. Washers? No. Books? Nah. Nails? No. With the hammer? Interesting ... but no. Magnifying glass? No. Wait—yes!

He pocketed the magnifying glass.

Hat? Definitely.

He put the hat on. It was a nondescript merchant's hat, tan in color. Remembering his dad's ostentatious cape, he set his golden cape on the shelf where the hat had been. *Too conspicuous.* He returned to his search.

Hoe? No. Waxed rope? No. Second cat? Nope. Ahh, there it is.

Heylor pulled a heavy wooden cane out from under a stack of bags and some kind of unidentified iron triangle and whirled it around. "How does that look?"

"Fetching." Lynwen's brows were inched up in a frown.

"What?"

"You said I should stop you from making mistakes."

"Yes."

"How?"

"Just *tell* me, Lynwen. Why are you making this so hard?"

"You don't always listen. I think we can agree on that."

"Nope, I won't agree. Just stop me. Let's go." Heylor was still impatient. He started walking toward the door again but was brought up short by the end of Lynwen's baton in his sternum. "Ow." He glared at her in shock, but then broke out in a grin. "That's it! Just use your baton!"

"Hit you?"

"Sure." He absently leaned the cane against the doorframe.

"But that's abuse."

"You don't know my former roommate, Sir Eloise Kyre, do you?"

"You're right, I don't know her. Well, I've heard of her, and I've seen her once or twice. She's kind of mean."

"It sounds like you know Eloise well enough." Heylor rubbed his jaw thoughtfully, then stepped around the baton, surprising Lynwen with his speed, and grasped her by the shoulders again. He probably should not have done this, he knew, but he liked touching her. Oddly, this just made his feelings more urgent. But his emotional makeup was about as well ordered and sensible as his parents' den. Suddenly it seemed crucially important to explain something to Lynwen.

Her mouth was hanging open again. "Are you okay?"

"No, I'm not. Definitely not." Unable to control himself any longer, he wrapped Lynwen in a hug. She squeaked in surprise like a squeeze toy. "My friends are dead because of my impulsiveness," Heylor whispered into her ear. He pulled back a little and looked her in the eyes. "Now you're stuck with me, and I'm just not ... right, Lynwen. I've always been like this, at least a little. But now ... it's worse than ever, worse even than Robert after his dream, and I can't seem to get on an even keel." Heylor rubbed her back with one of his hands. "I don't always respond to conventional methods, you've seen that for yourself, so go ahead and use the baton if you have to." He released her from the hug and stepped back. "I would rather you hit me than I did something that got you hurt."

"That's really sweet." Lynwen's eyes shone. "No one's ever asked me to hit them before."

Τ

"Well, that's just strange," Heylor whispered, peering around the corner. "Where did this come from?"

Lynwen squeezed against him to get her head around the corner too. Her cheek was against his, and she placed a hand lightly on the back of his belt to keep her balance. "A few people from Apple Square came down with the goose fever. It's scared people, and some of them decided to blame the New School."

Heylor could feel the inside of her hip against his. He struggled to resist the urge to reach behind and wrap an arm around her waist. He feared his hand might act of its own volition, that it would irresistibly creep around her waist and betray the gentleman he was trying to be, and that Lynwen might think this a step too far and refuse to work with him any longer. It surprised him that she had put up with him so far. *She's too good for me, too pretty, too smart. She'd probably really use that baton on me too, if I went any further. Or maybe she'd escalate straight to her sword.*

Lynwen moved back around the corner and Heylor's crisis of will subsided. He was able to think non-Lynwen thoughts again. He frowned at the crowd of protestors, perhaps forty of them, marching along the street. Consistent with Heylor's memory of protests past, they spanned all social and economic classes, although the majority looked poor enough. They were pacing slowly back and forth along a small section of the campus Ring Road. A few held up signs painted in bold, aggressive colors. One read:

"Poison Not Enough!

Dooke's Wizards Cause

Goose Fever!!!

Bad."

Another advised:

"Kant Leave Well

Enuff Alone.

Respect The

Old Ways."

Heylor slid back around the corner, out of sight of the protestors. "I should go talk to them." *That's what Robert would do.*

Lynwen's hand went to the handle of her baton, veins and tendons jumping against the thin skin of her pale hand. "I don't know if that's a good idea, Heylor Style."

"Wait!" Heylor held his hands up in surrender. "Did you notice that other group just standing and watching. Gawkers, right?"

"Right." Lynwen's hand relaxed on her baton, the tendons standing down. "Gawkers always show up once one of these protests gets going properly."

"I'll just saunter over there and see what they have to say."

Lynwen frowned at him, her hand reflexively squeezing and relaxing on the baton handle.

"Oh, for knights' sake," Heylor exclaimed, "Did you notice one lady with her very tiny—maybe four-year-old—daughter with her. I'll talk *only* to her."

Lynwen drew her baton and held the end out threateningly toward Heylor. "That kid is five," she growled.

"Okay, five-year-old daughter." Heylor thought about fighting her off with his cane, then realized he had forgotten it back at his parents' house. *Knights damn it!*

"And that's the only person you'll talk to?"

"I promise."

Lynwen's smile was radiant.

It could be that she's really enjoying this. Heylor walked as casually as he could across the Ring Road. He crossed a full block north of the protest so he could walk naturally up to the edge of the scrum. He knew Lynwen was watching him, so he did not dawdle too much. The woman was still there, holding her daughter by the hand, crouching low and whispering to her. They both had dark hair, almost black, and freckly faces. Heylor slowed down and stood near them, waiting for his chance.

A long moment passed. Heylor's thin layer of patience began to fray.

She's watching me.

The thought of Lynwen's stern gaze and his promise to be careful bought him another sixty seconds of standing around, enough time, he decided, to have blended in with the gawkers. He defocused and his mind flashed to the encounter with Skoll. He had killed his friends because he could not master his impulses. The memory was a shot of adrenaline that bought him another sixty seconds, but it was hard to just stand there.

"Are you okay, mithster?" the little girl said.

Heylor looked down at her. She had sweet, innocent brown eyes to complement the lisp. *She is so only four.* He turned his gaze to her mother, who seemed only now to notice him. "Oh, I'm fine," he said to mother and daughter equally. "This is just kind of upsetting."

"It is," replied the mother crisply and swept her gaze back to the protestors.

"My sister has the goose fever," Heylor added to keep the conversation going.

"Oh, no!" exclaimed the little girl. "Her brains are gonntha boil!" She made a little two-handed, finger-wiggling gesture that might have been meant to depict an explosion.

Heylor swallowed.

Children can be creepy, even the cutest ones.

Mom's lips tightened. "Tessa! I told you how you should talk to other people." She smiled wanly at Heylor. "I'm sorry, sir. Children can be so direct. I've been trying to teach her discretion, but she's still so young. She just blurts out whatever comes to mind!"

Creeps often do. Heylor gave the lady the most unctuous expression he could muster. "That's quite all right ma'am. Children often do. We have to be honest about the situation, so little Tessa here has not said anything we haven't discussed, er … in different language, of course." Before the lady could turn away from him again, Heylor asked, "But why have you come, ma'am?"

She smiled genially at him. "I wanted to show my daughter what evil looks like."

ℑ

"She really thinks the New School is causing the fever?" Lynwen could not seem to believe it. "That lady and her five-year-old daughter?"

"Tessa is four." Heylor and Lynwen had retreated several blocks away from the Ring Road and spent several hours patrolling—walking, talking, and looking around the streets just off the academic plateau. By lunchtime, Heylor had steered the two of them north to the Lord's Commons, where he produced the old Duchess's Program medallion and secured them a free lunch.

"What *is* the New School doing?"

Heylor speared a carrot off his plate. "Well, that is interesting, but also highly secret." He shook his head theatrically. "I don't know if I can tell you."

Lynwen drew her baton and placed it on the table. Her index finger tapped on the hilt.

Heylor beamed at her. "How was it so easy to make a monster out of you?"

Lynwen looked back at him, her face blank. "You only just met me, Heylor Style. For all you know I—"

"It's my big brother!"

It's my loud-voiced sister. Shelley was dressed in the New School tartan, as were many of the other students in the Commons. The skirt ended just above her knees.

She sat down heavily beside Heylor, smiling ingenuously. "This is my classmate Camille." She waved toward a similarly dressed, tall young woman with the distinctive, dark coloring of Engevelen who had come up behind her. Camille had blue rather than the much-coveted green eyes of the old aristocracy, but she moved with the fluid grace everyone expected of her people.

"You are Heylor Style," she said with such elegance that the redundancy of the statement felt almost chic. "I have heard so much about you."

Her words sounded like silk to Heylor's ears, but all the same, he was annoyed that his flirting with Lynwen had been interrupted. He looked across at the plainer, lighter, common-colored constable who some might have said would be lucky to be Camille's servant. Heylor was not one of those people. He barely resisted the impulse to put his chin in his hands and stare at Lynwen. *She had been about to say she might be a monster.*

"Camille is Marielle Engel's sister," Shelley said, snapping the young man back to attention.

They've probably left on the Javelin mission already. Marielle is probably alone in the wilderness by now. Heylor shivered. Alone was not good.

"The new Deladieyr Knight?" Lynwen asked.

"Not yet," Camille said easily, hand reaching out to pat Lynwen's arm. "She has to seek approval from the council, and more importantly, she has to Rise."

Hang, you mean. Heylor shivered for the second time.

"But I don't know when that might happen." Camille smiled. "Marielle does not often speak about the future."

"Well, I hate the past," declared Heylor without thinking. As soon as he spoke, he wanted to take the words back, though they were true. All his mistakes lived on in the past.

"Why?" Shelley asked, incredulously. "Look at all you've done!" She made big eyes at Camille, who had sat down now and was listening carefully. "You survived the Battle of the Bifrost."

I ran away and jumped in the river.

"That was a total meat grinder!" Shelley almost shouted. "And then you fought side by side with Sir Robert himself in the throne room."

Mostly I just lay on the floor, convulsing.

Heylor struggled to keep his composure, but Lynwen may have caught the distressed look behind his eyes. Certainly, such subtleties were lost on skolve-in-a-pottery-shop Shelley. "Maybe we should skip past and future and speak of the present," Lynwen interjected.

"Yes," Camille agreed, smiling slightly. "You are a constable." It was her second recitation of the obvious, eerily similar to her first in its cool poise, and somehow just as soothing. Lynwen nodded, and Camille continued in her cultivated voice. "I wanted to alert the constabulary about something. Last night I was followed from Ring Road to Cobbler Street."

"Followed?" Lynwen's face took on its bland, wide-eyed look. "How can you be sure—no, never mind that. Tell me what he looked like."

Camille's posture was beautifully upright, her neck straight and long, but she did at least frown as she replied. "Yes, it probably was a man. He was quite big. Taller than me, and he looked bulky in his cloak."

A cloaked man.

Heylor shivered for the third time.

ᛏ

"The cloaked man is one of the most common stalking complaints that we get since Professor Euyn died. Most come from around campus, but there have been sightings in every district of the city." Lynwen walked easily next to Heylor, occasionally nudging the handles of her short sword and baton to keep from being tripped by them.

They were almost at the Ring Road. Heylor could not believe how quickly the time was going by. "I had no idea."

"Right," Lynwen nodded. "The constabulary has tried to keep it out of the posts to avoid panicking anyone."

"Has he killed people?"

Lynwen looked at him incredulously. "No!"

"None?"

"None."

"So are these sightings genuine or not?"

"You know, Heylor Style, we have a lot fewer murders than perhaps you imagine." Her slightly upturned lip was coy. "I cannot say for sure if all the complaints are … mistaken." Her avoidance of a simple answer was vaguely annoying. "Many of them are, let's say, unresolved."

"What about the ones you did manage to sort out?"

Lynwen's eyes narrowed. "One turned out to be a man with too much interest in girls of a certain age." Her expression turned arch. "Some men like the New School skirt, especially on girls with some Engevelen in them."

"Really?" Heylor pretended he did not know what she was on about. "Who would have thought? Not me." He smiled at her with his most winning grin.

"Good," she nodded, hand back on her baton. "Several other complaints turned out to be caused by arts students performing what they described as an experiment. Later we found out they thought the cloaked man had been doing something that needed to be done. They were expelled."

"*Arts* students?" Heylor could not believe it. He thought students would have been the last to protest the innovations of the New School.

"Yes, they were stalking aggies."

Just south of them on the Ring Road, three men were loading garbage onto a horse-drawn cart from the wooden bins bordering campus.

Students stalking students. Over the new grain. "So what do you think is going on in this case, constable?" Heylor looked down the Ring Road, thinking they should cross. One of the workmen hobbled strangely. He had a short, scraggly brown beard and a ruddy complexion.

No!

Whatever Lynwen was about to say was cut off when Heylor grabbed her by the shoulders and swung around to her far side, slouching slightly and pulling his hat down low.

"What are you doing now, Heylor Style?" Lynwen's voice was somewhere between amused and annoyed.

"It's Sackelly-belly-full-of-jelly!" he kept low, partially hidden by her, and pointed at the gimpy man in faded overalls loading the garbage cart. The man was looking at them now. All three of the men were looking. Heylor put an arm around Lynwen's waist and began hurrying her across the Ring Road.

"Who?" Her head whirled around even as he pushed her along.

Can't I get away with anything? "Sackelly-belly-full-of-jelly. He's the one with the skolvish beard."

"But he does not have a jelly-b—"

"It's an old nickname. He was chubby as a kid."

"So he doesn't like you because you were mean to him as a child?"

"No! Well—maybe. No." *There was that one time.* The more he thought about it, the more times he could remember. "I don't know. He's volatile."

They had made it across Ring Road and quickly passed out of sight of the workmen. Lynwen stopped. He realized she was looking pointedly down at his arm, which was still around her waist. It was even possible that some of his hand had strayed onto her shapely behind. It had. It was definitely on her arse. "Oh! Sorry!"

It did that on its own!

She'll never believe me.

Heydron's tits!

Don't you mean, Heydron's arse?

Shut up!

Forgetting something, are we?

What?

It's still there!

Heylor hastily pulled his arm away, mortified for the second time that day and for the same reason.

Lynwen smiled at him. "Later, when I'm out of uniform. But ask me first if you can put your arm back then."

Heylor felt his face redden. "I certainly will. I promise."

"And close your mouth, Heylor. It's hanging open."

When did the shoe get on the other hand, er, foot? They continued walking, aiming for Cobbler Street and the building into which Camille said the cloaked man had disappeared when she had made it clear to him that she knew she was being followed.

"You know, you could just talk to him, Heylor. Work it out."

"I don't want to."

"Why not?"

Heylor stopped. He was embarrassed in a very different way now. It was the paralyzing kind. In fact, it was shame. And it was not just about Sackelly-belly-full-of-jelly. He admired the unpredictable young constable, and that was enough to make him own up. "I don't like the past, Lynwen. Every time I think about it, all I see are the mistakes I made. My dad says his mistakes made him the man he is today. Eloise has killed more people than I have siblings, but she says she has no regrets. Only Robert has the true sense of it. He knows how hard it is to change. But I'm not half the man he is, I'm not a quarter. When you make as many mistakes as I do, you had *better* regret them. I am *full* of regrets, and I only hope my mistakes don't determine who I can be today."

"It's okay, Heylor—"

"No, it isn't!" he cried. "Every day I wake up and tell myself that today I am going to start fresh and not skolve anything up, but I *do* skolve something up. Always. A fresh mistake every time, and each new mistake worse than the old ones. I need to get away from myself, Lynwen. I don't want to relive the old Sackelly years. He probably still hates me, and maybe he's right to. I just hope he didn't see me."

"Oh, he saw you all right, Heylor Style. No doubt about that. Recognize, I'm not so sure of."

Heylor started laughing.

Lynwen watched him appraisingly. "You don't like the past. Marielle Engel apparently doesn't like the future. Those New School protestors want to *return* to the past as if it was somehow better." She shook her head. "Their memories aren't very good, and your memory is too good. They forgive the past too much, and you don't forgive your past mistakes enough."

"I think I love you."

Lynwen's mouth opened in the biggest 'O' yet, but only for a split second before it shaped itself into a broad smile. "Saying *that* wasn't a mistake, Heylor Style." She clapped him on the shoulder. "Now, let's go find this cloaked man."

T

"Constable!" A bent old man in a heavily stained shopkeeper's apron was calling after them. "Constable, please. Over here!"

After two hours of enquiries in the building the cloaked figure had entered, and then up and down the rest of Cobbler Street, they had failed to come up with any leads. No one else had seen the man, and the building Camille had identified was associated with no other reported crime or complaint. They were on their way back, feeling more than a little dejected, when the old man called to them.

Lynwen waved to him and prepared to head his way, then spoke to Heylor first, her expression blank. "Remember, no love talk now, not in front of a civilian." When he pretended to scowl back at this, she added, "And definitely not in front of other constables if we meet any."

"You know, I only said I *think* I love you."

The old man took them into the back of his small butcher's shop and down some stairs into a cold room. It was surprisingly large, but there was not much beef hanging in it. Only one hanging man.

"Fattening season is still on," the old man explained incongruously.

"So how much does the dead guy go for?" Heylor asked, nearly earning himself a kiss from Lynwen's baton. Luckily, the old man did not seem to hear him properly.

"No, he is not one of mine." Bent as he was, the man turned his stiff neck up to stare myopically at the slowly hanging man. "I mean he's not employed here. I've never seen him before. I only just found him now. Not much reason to come down here until I get more stock. I was heading to the constabulary when I saw you passing."

It's got to be a suicide. Heylor briefly scanned the room in the empyreal sky, not sure what he was looking for but finding nothing he could not see conventionally. The most noticeable—and sickening—things in the room were the man's pooling bodily fluids. But then there was Constable Lynwen. The sight of one made him feel sick, the other happy and excited despite the horror of the hanging body.

How did we get here?

Did I really say I thought I love her? The impulsiveness had not been out of character, but he had never actually told anyone that he loved them before this. He had *fancied* Bethyn, and still did a little, though he had come to realize that Bethyn was not attracted to men. Except perhaps for one. He looked again at Lynwen, her mouth unconsciously open again, but her eyes busy.

I'm not taking it back.

"Other than being hung, no signs of violence," Lynwen said, bringing Heylor out of his reverie. "No bruising, other than his neck." She pointed at the system of crossbeams, chains, and hooks on the cold room's ceiling. "I wonder why he brought his own rope instead of just using one of these chains and hooks."

"Why didn't he tie it to the beam?" Heylor asked. The rope had been slung over a crossbeam and then tied to an enormous iron trolley. The trolley had a narrow, circular iron rail front and back, presumably used to push it along. This had provided a handy place to tie off the rope.

Lynwen shrugged "He might have stood on that rail and then kicked himself off it."

"Huh. Where is his suicide note?"

"Ah!" Lynwen responded, eyes shining. "Let's not assume, my dear Heylor. We don't know it was a suicide. And suicides don't always leave convenient notes."

"Don't most people want some kind of closure before they make their own closing?" Heylor hissed.

"Most of the time."

"So it's not suicide, then?"

"No, I think it probably is. His clothes are handmade, no labels. His fingernails are clean, his shoes also. Standard men's shoes, unremarkable."

Lynwen had been carefully, gingerly but without any apparent repugnance, going through the corpse's pockets. "Nothing to identify him so far. We will somehow have to figure out who this man was and speak to his family."

"To let them know."

"Yes, of course, but also to see if the suicide hypothesis holds up." Lynwen gave him a sad look. "It probably will. All this talk of mistakes and regret, Heylor. This is a mistake you cannot undo."

Looking at the pathetic mess that violent death and the fluids it releases had made of the cadaver reinforced the wisdom of Lynwen's comments. "This guy needed a shorter, more forgiving memory. He needed to judge himself less harshly." What Lynwen said earlier had not been lost on him. He had declared his possible love for her after she had said it, after all.

"Yes, Heylor Style." She patted his shoulder and left her hand there. "When people kill themselves, they are enacting the ultimate, irreversible judgement on their past." She looked at him. "And closing off the future forever."

Chapter Ten

Gerveault's Javelin

"I REALLY DON'T NEED TO DIE OUT HERE, BLOUSE, SO LET'S JUST GO EASY."

Merrett's admonishment was difficult to take seriously with the big man stuffed in a rain barrel while saying it. They were at a mobile station a day and a half across the Castlereagh Line and less than a day from the wheat line. Besides food and equipment, the station provided fresh, clean, scent-free clothes—and rain barrels. The idea, among other things, was to provide temporary odor invisibility to soldiers venturing into skolve territory. It was an expensive precaution used only on the most important missions.

"You can stay here if you want, Bat." Endicott spoke without rancor. He knew his man. "But it's time to be about it." He threw Merrett a towel. The big man caught it with his right hand and stared back at him, saying nothing.

"I think our large friend needs help getting out of the barrel," suggested Lindseth in a hoarse, early-morning voice. He had already bathed and was almost finished donning a new, scent-free outfit. Now he was bending over his pack, but he spared a look and a smile for Endicott. "It's a difficult feat to do gracefully, especially for someone plus-sized."

Endicott remembered Merrett stuffing him into a heated rain barrel at Aignen. Apparently it was easier tossing someone in than getting out.

"You gentlemen are terrible," declared Sergeant Brianna Caithonayt. "I'll help him." She was a stout brunette with a confident, energetic manner. She speed-marched over to Merrett. "Put one hand on my shoulder, big man, and the other on the rim of the barrel." A few more instructions and Merrett was out and toweling off. Brianna, never shy, continued lecturing him. "Get yourself thoroughly dry, lieutenant. Rub well," she said slyly, "It's cold out here. You don't want to come down with something."

"You'll come down with the back of my hand if you don't ease off, sergeant," he growled back.

I don't recall ever seeing Merrett hit anyone outside the sparring fence. Unless it was to kill them.

Brianna evidently did not believe the threat either. She laughed at him. "Promises, promises," she sighed. "Well, since you are all in such a charming mood, I'll give you the report now. A few messages came in last night." She reached into her slightly wet jacket and pulled out a stack of papers. "Sir Kyre and Sir Justice came back across the wheat line two days ago, about …" Her lips moved as she made some calculations. "Ten miles west of here. They found some kind of apparatus to the north at Site 127 and were pursued by skolves."

"And?" Endicott asked, worried but working to keep it out of his voice.

"And nothing," Brianna answered. "That's good news, right?"

"No news is good news," grunted Merrett.

Lindseth put his pack down and looked up. "Deaths are always reported." He gestured with his head for the sergeant to continue.

"Commander Arthur Wolverton wishes to remind you once more that the mission is not successful until you return safely." Brianna flipped to a new page. "Lord Gerveault says no exact shaping." Brianna shrugged and moved on to the next paper. She frowned as she read it. "Sir Hemdale has sent a message as well. He says that the Via is awaiting more than just Marielle Engel. He says that a true Rising doesn't take a ceremony or a sword." She scratched her head theatrically. "Sorry, I don't know what that means."

I do. Robert caught Lindseth looking at him quizzically and shook his head at the taller man. *Not now.* "Thank you, sergeant," Endicott said crisply. "Let's get our packs squared, gentlemen, and then let's go find our knight."

Squaring away the packs was no simple matter. Each pack needed to be tight, every strap tied down securely. They needed to be silent when moving. Their entire ensemble—packs, clothes, even weapons—needed to move as quietly as possible. Endicott's group had settled on a leather armor protocol that included light wool shirts, soft three-quarter length leather coats, thicker pants, and leather gloves, greaves, and vambraces along the lines of the equipment Koria had procured for him on his first trip across the Line four years ago. Water cans needed to be full, and weapons needed to be handy but not to rattle around. Merrett's bow was kept strung and in hand, with all but one of his arrows tied in a tight bundle that nevertheless had to be easy to open. His sword was strapped to his pack and would take a moment to get to. Jeyn Lindseth kept one sword within easy reach and the other strapped like Merrett's. Endicott strapped Likelihood, Keith Euyn's magnificent longsword that he had inherited, in a breakaway scabbard on his back. All he had to do was pull hard enough on the hilt and the sword would cut sideways and come free.

When Brianna had no more reminders about loose ties or rattles, Robert called Merrett and Lindseth close. "Huddle up." Without a word, they formed up on either side, making a close circle with their arms over each other's shoulders. Brianna stood off to the side, watching. "We are going to be quiet. We are going to be careful. We aren't going to argue, but if something needs to be said, it shall be said. Above all, we are going to look out for each other, and we are going to bring each other out of the wilderness. No one will be left behind. We are going to test the javelin." The device had been stowed most carefully in the pack. It would not be used until its time came. "And we are going to find Marielle at point B and come back out with her." He took a breath, remembering how he used to be when he had first come to the New School. "I love you."

"I love you both as well," replied Lindseth confidently.

"Fuck you two," Merrett finished, contracting both of his arms on their shoulders.

"Good," Endicott nodded. "Let's go."

▽

"Does it feel to you that this test is unnecessary?" Lindseth's voice was soft and low, permissible by process, but only just.

Merrett, walking directly in front of Endicott, shook his head. "That's not quite what you asked at dinner the other night."

"But is it?" Lindseth persisted. "It worked in the lab well enough."

"Operations are different," Merrett replied tersely, left hand holding his bow, right hand holding an arrow. "Things get damaged, people make mistakes."

"That's it," agreed Endicott quietly. "We have to make sure we can use it in battle. Having a weapon is one thing, using it as intended is another. We are going to learn something—even if we don't yet know what—and whatever it is will help everyone else later on when we mass-produce the thing."

Lindseth's voice floated forward again. "Is that what Marielle is doing too?"

Merrett's voice was not as soft. More annoyed. "You lost me again."

"She's the best anyone has seen in years," Lindseth supplied, keeping his voice down. "The strongest and quickest in sparring. She's reliable and knows what she's doing." He paused for a moment. "In the lab."

She is beautiful and perfect. Like an angel. But also unknowable and untouchable.

Marielle Engel was the best all-rounder Endicott had ever seen. Strong like Eloise and Hemdale, wise and intelligent like Koria. She was a goddess of fallen Engevelen. People stopped and stared when she walked by. They knew she was something that had long been lost. She gave them hope that Engevelen could rise again. Even among those who did not idolize what had been destroyed, who did not give a damn about Engevelen, Engel was a symbol. *She makes them think not only that there will be a new Deladieyr Knight, but that the Methueyns might walk again.*

Endicott admired Engel, but he did not feel for her what he did for Koria or Eloise. He did not *quite* love her. She was too remote, too refined, for his imperfect love. He did not truly know her and knew he probably never would. *Well, one can never truly know god either.*

"But she still needs a field test," Lindseth continued, "Marielle may be perfect, but she needs to know the imperfect and unpredictable world out here before Rising."

Endicott felt a wave of irritation. "I like a philosophical conversation as much as most people, Lind—"

"Way *more* than most people."

"More than you anyway, Bat," Endicott said. "And I know you just like to ask questions, Lindseth, but we are talking about a comrade here. It seems wrong, a little dehumanizing in fact, to say Engel needs a field test. She's not a machine."

Lindseth did not appear chastened. He smiled easily. "But we are all field-tested every day, gentlemen. Usually in small ways about unimportant things." He looked at Merrett. "Like manners. Marielle is being tested in a more significant way for a far more serious purpose. And it is a test she is putting *herself* to."

Merrett scowled. "You are some kind of special, Jeyn."

Endicott had no doubt Engel would survive the mission even if the rest of them did not. *So I had better focus on us surviving. There is no need to worry about Marielle.*

There was no wheat ahead of them. "Hold up," he whispered. "The wheat line should still be at least two miles off." He reached carefully into his jacket's inner pocket and pulled out a notebook. Opening it confirmed what his memory was telling him. *Talk about imperfect.*

Merrett strung his one available arrow but did not draw. He stood in front of Endicott and watched the horizon. "What's wrong?" he whispered without turning his head.

"The maps," Endicott replied. "All the maps are wrong."

"I think we are just on a whaleback," Lindseth said, right sword drawn now, pacing a small perimeter around Merrett and Endicott. "The seeds never blew up here, and the aggies never sampled this finely."

Merrett's hand made his bow creak. "Are you sure we are where you think we are?"

"I'm sure." *Whaleback.* Endicott realized they were making a silhouette. "Crawl!"

As quietly as possible, they got on their stomachs and crawled laboriously to the steeper side of the small hill they had just climbed. Below and just ahead, rows of wheat waved their pastel stems and spikes.

"Just goes to show we don't know everything," Lindseth whispered.

When they had descended the hill and could stand in the grain again, Endicott scanned the golden fields carefully. Whatever the maps said, however inaccurate they were, he knew the point of change could not be far off. Cautiously he led the small troop forward and a half hour later saw that the wheat was once more growing ragged. They were close. Endicott paused at a stalk and asked himself if he could see any more wheat ahead or any more to the side. *None.* He stopped and lowered himself to one knee. "We are here," he said.

He always felt something spiritual when entering the wilderness. *Gods and monsters, the Lonely Wizard said.* Endicott had experienced the same complex emotion, a mix of fear, excitement, curiosity, and awe, when he had first crossed the Castlereagh Line, but the border of the wilderness was here at the edge of the wheat now. They could not cross that line without pause or thought. It needed to be respected.

Set aside thoughts of knowing everything. We cannot even be sure we know anything. It was a lesson Endicott had learned in his first year at the New School. Lighthouse had been going so well that some had grown confident that momentum was on their side and that their progress would always exceed their plans, that the skolves and demons would be pushed back as easily as the wheat seemed to push forward, ever northward. But those people had never endured Endicott's heraldic dreams or fought the two cloaked men. Those people had never seen friends killed or embassies burn. *They do not understand that sometimes we know nothing.*

There is a fear to the unknown, but there is also excitement and awe. Admitting we know nothing is even, in some ways, liberating. A person who truly understands their ignorance is released to be honest about what they see and hear. New information is freed from the burden of fitting any prior hypothesis. Ego is uncoupled from understanding. Endicott relished this freedom. It was like a fresh starting point. It was also a place where every conceivable effort to be careful made clear sense. *We will take no unnecessary chances.*

Endicott felt one other emotion as he knelt beside the last stalk of wheat: an almost melancholy feeling of inevitability, an elegiac sense that he *deserved* to be out there nearly alone.

Do I deserve to be punished for killing so many people?

Or is this just a necessary process after so much death?

His thoughts were not clear. As he looked out into the wild brambles past the wheat line, he could only acknowledge that he felt this mix of emotions as deeply as he had ever felt anything. They mixed in his gut, difficult to unravel or discriminate from each other.

"Let's go," he said, and stood up.

▽

"What do you think, Blouse?" Merrett whispered like a bull on tiptoe.

They were three days across the wheat line now, and Endicott did not mind stopping and considering their position. The small river in front of them was not particularly wide, though too wide to jump. Leaning out over the tall grass, Endicott could see far enough into the clear water to know that it was also too deep to wade across. Morning dew had soaked his pant legs. There was a cool, fresh edge in the air, but the sky was brightening. The day would be warm. *No need to hurry this decision.* He pulled a map out of his jacket and retreated from the waters' edge to the shade of a tree.

"Let's see if this bridge is still standing," he said, pointing at a small symbol on the map.

"We aren't using that bridge," Merrett growled.

Endicott's smile came and went in a heartbeat. He folded up his map. "No. But we are going to see if it's still standing. Take the lead, Bat."

They set off, moving quietly through the grass along the riverbank. However carefully the three young men avoided stepping on fallen trees and trying not to disturb the undergrowth, it was impossible to leave no traces behind. The grass was too tall and thick. Sometimes brambles and rosebushes could be avoided, but not always, not if any forward progress was to be made. Even paying minute attention to their steps could not insure against every hazard. At a bend in the river, Merrett stumbled over an old stone archway that had sunk into a low spot, a victim of time and hydrodynamics. The stone, which must once have been a dazzling white, was gray now, and the keep it had once proudly announced was entirely down, its stonework scattered and overgrown. The old broken things of the Ardgour Wilderness were dangerous. Lindseth led their retreat. They all knew how easily the hidden holes of these overgrown ruins could translate into sprained ankles or trapped feet.

Back on an animal track, Lindseth trailed close behind Endicott, close enough to whisper. "What are the odds that bridge is still standing?"

Endicott did not take the question as a challenge. Mission protocol put mapping of local bridges low on the priority list, but it was still useful information. Endicott was not a defensive person, and Lindseth had a way of asking questions without the appearance of presupposition. The tall, graceful man was a curious, thoughtful person. Endicott considered the question seriously. He tallied up the other bridges that had been mapped in the four years of Lighthouse, then he reflected on the broad valley they had been following, how the watershed would probably act, whether the river was likely to have been subject to flooding. "I think perhaps one chance in ten." He looked back at his friend. "But there might be a ford not too far past it. Or was. It will depend on how much the river has migrated."

"The things we build don't last."

"Not when we aren't around to maintain them," Endicott replied. "Nature is a relentless entropic force."

"No doubt about that." Lindseth's voice rolled forward, tones easy, volume low. "But we've helped her, haven't we? First Novgoreyl overruns Engevelen. Wrecks what they'd built right down to the Castlereagh Line. It gets mostly rebuilt. In the style of the Novs, of course. Then Nehring Ardgour brings Skoll, Hati, and the skolves from hell, and they take the place down to the bare stones. If it weren't for all those choices, made by *people*, things would be very different here. I wond—"

He was interrupted by an urgent hand signal from Merrett. The three men went down on hands and knees at once. They crawled through the still wet grass until they came to a line of rounded, skull-sized stones just off the riverbank. The bridge lay about forty yards off. It had been made of enormous blocks of hewn granite and was partially intact, though the center had collapsed. Blocks fallen from the bridge had caused the river to pool all the way back to where the three men crouched.

"Should be an easy rebuild," Endicott observed. "Most of the damage looks recent." He rolled onto his back and pulled a map and notebook out of his jacket. After scribbling a quick note, he rose cautiously to his feet, gesturing to the others to follow suit. "We better find that ford, if it exists. The highlands are only fifteen miles north of us."

▽

"ARE WE ABOUT READY TO TEST THIS JAVELIN?" MERRETT ASKED, SCOWLING. THEY HAD reached the highlands by late afternoon and set up camp in a semicircle of man-sized boulders. All day they had seen skolve scat, but none of it recent, and they had avoided wild oat and barley patches. Detouring around these skolve food sources had added time and distance to their journey, but no one had complained. It was not even worth commenting on. As they set up camp, the conversation alternated between tactical issues related to the protocol of the mission and more philosophical topics. Merrett's tolerance for the former was limitless, but it quickly evaporated for the latter.

"It is not yet time," Endicott replied. Despite this, he had begun assembling the device.

Lindseth's tolerance for philosophy was far from exhausted. "Don't you think it was sad—beyond sad, really—how Sir Hemdale went on and on after dessert about Marielle becoming a Deladieyr Knight, especially after what she said earlier?" Lindseth looked toward Merrett and then at Endicott, making eye contact with each before continuing. "He is obsessed."

Seeing Hemdale again had made Endicott sick, but hearing him spoken of like that made him sicker. He looked up from his work on the javelin. "It was a *celebration*, Jeyn. Kennyth—the duke—asked us to express ourselves. *You* asked us leading questions. Why don't we give the old man a break?"

Lindseth smiled brightly. "I'm glad you said that, Robert. It's nice that you still have some sympathy for him. After all, you disappointed him second."

"Second?" Endicott asked.

Merrett shook his head. "Make sense, philosopher. You mean *first*. And I'm sure Robert has disappointed lots of people."

"No," Jeyn shook his head in a slow, exaggerated display. "Second. Eloise was his first disappointment."

Eloise? In Endicott's experience, few people were more themselves than Eloise. A person could only be disappointed by Eloise if they did not know who she was. Anyone else could see what was coming from miles away.

Merrett knew this too. "Just say what you mean, man," he said wearily.

"Fine." Lindseth nodded slowly. "Sir Hemdale brought her out of Armadale when she was a little girl. People think she was five years old, but they were fooled by her size. She was only three. He rescued her before the old king could misuse her. That song *The March of Hemdale* tells what came of that and what happened to the king even if it neglects to mention Eloise."

"You said disappointment," Merrett persisted.

"Not a word safely used with reference to Eloise," Endicott added, his eyes on the task of fitting a joint together on the javelin.

"Sir Hemdale brought her out for love, I don't doubt," Lindseth said. "But she was in danger because her mother was such a powerful wizard, and her father's line—Hemdale's side of the family—was famous for their Deladieyr Knights. Eloise's dad was something to behold, apparently. It was assumed that Eloise would be a Deladieyr Knight one day too." Lindseth pointedly raised his eyebrows. "But she is no knight."

Endicott remembered Eloise stopping the two rapists, Vard and Lynal, with just a heavy bottle, killing one of them in the process. "She's knight enough for me," he said. "And she *is* a Knight of Vercors."

"True." Lindseth raised both hands in submission. "But Sir Hemdale is obsessed with the *holy* knights—the knights of the Empyrean—the Deladieyr and Methueyn. He wants the Methueyns to return."

"That can't happen," Endicott said flatly.

"And yet here we are," Lindseth replied, gesturing at the endless expanse around them.

"Methueyn Knights are *not* why we are here."

Lindseth blanched at something he saw in Endicott's face or heard in his voice. "Okay, not exactly."

Merrett scowled, reaching a new level of strained patience. "Do you have a point?"

"Yes, I do actually," Lindseth said to Merrett. "Sir Hemdale thought Robert could become a Deladieyr Knight. He wasn't the only one who thought so. Everyone across the Line at the tower thought so. At the battle of the Bifrost, *I* thought so. It even occurred to you, Merrett. And then the throne room and the embassy. Everyone hoped Robert would be the next Deladieyr, and Hemdale hoped the most. But now, for reasons I don't presume to understand, it looks like the sun has set on that idea." Lindseth's gaze swept back to Endicott. "So somehow you disappointed Sir Hemdale, Robert. Now his hopes are set on Marielle instead. But you were there before her. So, yes, second."

Endicott had no response. *I have to focus on the javelin now.* But he would have to think about what Lindseth had said. Later.

"You disgust me," Merrett said, shaking his head. "You too, Robert. All your hopes and all your transforms. Everyone has been putting way too much on this Javelin project. We need to calm down and stop with all the plans and schemes."

Lindseth was not put off. "But shouldn't we be discussing this? Javelin is going to change everything. It would be irresponsible not to plan ahead."

"Knights!" Merrett spat. The sky was beginning to darken. The sun was almost at the horizon. "Then I'm even more scared. Don't you see? Things might change in ways we don't expect. And if all our plans depend on Javelin, then where will we be?"

Endicott looked up from his work. The device, at last, was ready. "Change is inevitable, Bat. The javelin is here. It can't be uninvented. There's no going back." He opened himself to the empyreal sky. "Quiet now. I'm activating it." He cracked through the second breakdown with ease and moved an infinitesimal bolt of lightning. "This is Captain Robert Endicott reporting in. Do you receive me?"

A crackly noise emanated from the small metal box. Endicott had attached several metal rods to the javelin, one of which telescoped vertically toward the sky, and fitted an iron slider to a terminal on the front, but other than that, the box was outwardly unremarkable. "This is Gerveault, Sir Robert." The voice was unmistakably that of the old dynamicist. "It is nice to hear your voice from so far away."

Chapter Eleven

Crutches

"*D*o you see this- Eloise?"

"What did you say?" Eloise asked, stopping in full stride. Gregory and Eoyan had already passed through the doorway, ready to give testimony at the after-experiment review, but Koria had pulled Eloise aside.

Koria squinted at her. "I said that Huygens might be changing."

"Yah, so? That's why we test it." *To find the Bridge.* Eloise barely managed to keep from calling Koria a stupe. It was not a term that went with her green-eyed friend. Plus, Koria looked three-quarters of the way to dead. She might not have a broken leg like Gregory, but something was seriously wrong. It was impossible even for Eloise not to feel sorry for her. Her eyes were hooded and her dark skin an unhealthy gray. And were her hands shaking just a little?

"In time, not space."

✝

"So you used dynamics to detect Sir Justice's fracture. Do you think that might have brought the skolves?"

Lord Latimer was the secretary for this AER. On his right at the long table were Kennyth Brice, who attended as many AER meetings as he could, and Arthur Wolverton, who sat like a statue next to Brice. He attended *every* AER. On the other side of Latimer sat Professor Gerveault, not looking very happy at all, and Koria, looking unhealthier with every passing moment. Eloise did not think Koria's condition was only due to the miscarriage and the problem with Huygens.

She's been heralding.

Eloise knew the effects of that from their days at the New School. Given how badly Koria looked, Eloise suspected that she may even have had a heraldic dream, a vision of the future so vivid that it was like the memory of a real event, usually a terrible one. It was said that heraldic dreams were psychologically indistinguishable from fact, with all the traumatic power that implied. Looking at her old friend, watching the signs of trauma and distress, Eloise felt pride.

Koria does battle.

Thinking about Koria's struggles was a relief. The AER had been going on for hours, and Latimer's repetitive questioning had become vexatious.

He can't change my mind. "You need to pay closer attention. I have answered that question already, Lord Latimer."

"Five times," interjected Koria, looking sideways at Latimer.

"The facts will not change," continued Eloise, enjoying working with her small friend as they had in their school days, "in the next five times. I'm not the kind of woman who lies."

"I do apologize," Latimer said, looking distinctly unapologetic. "After Heylor Style's mission, we have had to become more…sensitive about the use of dynamics out past the wheat line."

"If anyone brought them on, it was me," said Gregory, perched uncomfortably with his splinted leg stuck out straight from his chair and supported by a footstool. "I performed the Huygens calibration at Site 127."

Professor Gerveault sighed. "Skolves do not react to dynamics." He sat as straight as Wolverton, the two of them in stark contrast to weary-looking Koria, who seemed to slump down further in her chair every time Latimer launched into another question. Seeing three persons from old Engevelen at one table was unusual. They were every bit as lordly looking as the duke, even Koria, slumped and half dead, retained something special. Gerveault may have appeared apathetic throughout much of the review, but he showed none of that now as he continued speaking. "Except, of course, when they are set on fire. Only Skoll and Hati react to dynamics. And since neither Skoll nor Hati were seen, this particular avenue of discussion is a waste of time."

"Agreed," said Wolverton. "Repeating a question invites bias." He added, "We should be satisfied with one answer." He looked meaningfully at Brice, who nodded back. "I would like to discuss the mysterious cylinder in more detail."

Gerveault raised a finger to the ceiling. "We also need to reconsider the Huygens data."

Eoyan described as precisely as he could the large vertical cylinder they had discovered at the tower. Brice wanted to know how sure Eoyan and Eloise were that it was, in fact, full of water.

Eloise let Eoyan talk. A chill had run through her when Gerveault had brought up Huygens again. Koria had given her a quick rundown of the problem before the meeting, but Eloise had not appreciated the implications until now. Koria had not spoken yet about whatever it was that nearly killed her—and *had* killed her unborn baby—but she had mentioned the modulus. Eloise was not the kind of woman to get excited over the technical details, but if Huygens was changing, other, bigger changes might be coming. And soon.

†

Bang, bang, bang.

Bang, bang, bang.

Whoever was hammering on the door was hammering hard, pounding impatiently. Gregory, in a chair with his fractured, splinted leg elevated over the back of another, smaller chair, looked at the rattling wooden door and then back at Eloise. This annoyed her. Eloise's initial reaction was that everyone should handle their own business; Gregory should get off his butt and attend to the door. Then she remembered why that would not be easy for him, and then the details of how he had got himself broken and how they had escaped a situation that could have killed them all.

"I'll get it, dear," she said in a sweet voice that for some reason made Gregory blanch. She rose statuesquely from her chair beside his, strode across the big, rectangular area rug and onto the cold stone of the castle floor, and approached the massive, iron-bound oak door.

Bang, bang, bang.

Whoever was on the other side was certainly strong. *Hemdale?* Eloise flung the door open just as the big brute on the other side was about to pound on it again. He was not as tall as her, but he was as broad as Merrett and as hairy as a bear.

"What do you want?" he demanded.

His incongruous question did not put Eloise off her stride for a second. "You're the one knocking away on our door, idiot!"

"What do you want?" the big, hirsute stupe repeated more stridently than before.

"I want you to go stuff yourself in a privy."

"So I can look like you did when you finally dragged yourselves back across the Line?" he shot back. Looking past her and into the room, he added, "And you brought some of your broken toys back too."

"They break as easily as you will if you don't stop your yammering."

"Don't hurt yourself."

"Are you coming in or not, Arrayn?" Gregory called. Eloise stepped back so that Robert's uncle could stamp his way through the doorway. It never ceased to amaze her that this man was so closely related to her Robert. Everything about him was different. He was bigger and immensely coarser in his bone structure, his musculature, and his manners. At least, that was how he appeared on the outside, and he usually acted as if he was nothing but outside. Arrayn strode confidently over to a couch and dropped heavily into it. His face was smeared with dirt. *He hasn't washed since coming in off the road.*

"I heard you used your leg as a shield, Justice," he said, looking at a smiling Gregory. "Don't you like the one Robert made for you?"

Gregory's shield was the cheaper prototype that he and Robert had created as a trial of the process for the superior shields they had then made for Eloise and Kennyth Brice. It had been through a lot already and had never let him down. It might only be the less expensive prototype, but it was still better than just about any shield in existence.

"There are more important things than my leg." Gregory turned his puppy dog eyes on Eloise as he spoke.

Arrayn started fishing in his pockets for his cigar, taper, and metal striker. His complicated, annoying procedure for lighting the cigar thankfully diverted Eloise from deciding whether Gregory's sentimental assertion had pissed her off or inspired her to carry him off to bed. She watched the other big idiot until he finally got his cigar lit, took an enormous puff, leaned forward, and exhaled the stinking blue smoke into Gregory's face.

Eloise was on her feet in an instant, fists bunched, veins standing out in her neck. Gregory had not even started coughing before Eloise remembered how Arrayn had behaved at Robert's wedding and Finlay Endicott's funeral. If Eoyan March was a pretend fool, Arrayn Endicott might be a pretend asshole. Perhaps he was halfway to being a real one, but she had learned that his intentions were not always as cruel as his manners. With some difficulty, she stopped short of jumping on the brute and resorted to words instead of her fists. "Do you want to end up on your arse, stupe?"

Arrayn sat back, unperturbed by the threat. "And here I came to do you a favor."

"Would you like some tea?" Gregory asked with exaggerated politeness before Eloise could say or do anything more.

"I'd take some."

Moments later, the big man had a little cup in his big paw, prepared and delivered with great reluctance by Eloise, and was grumbling on about the shop his brother Deryn had opened in Vercors. It was some kind of smithy, but also did fine metalwork, including precision parts for stitching engines. Arrayn had just come from the shop with a load of razor-sharp, extra-heavy arrow and crossbow quarrel heads. He boasted that they could punch a hole in Armadale plate armor when shot from standard arms at close range.

Gregory's face grew animated. "Does Deryn do what Robert does when he smiths?"

Arrayn drained his cup in one long gulp. "I don't know what you mean."

The hairy man's answer was unsurprising. The common thinking among friends of the family was that Deryn Endicott had the same talent as Robert and Finlay Endicott, though Deryn never spoke of it or revealed what he could do. Arrayn's boast about the quality of Deryn's work—and the innuendo about Deryn's powers it perhaps conveyed—may have intrigued Gregory, who had little else to occupy him, but Eloise had no patience for games. "Why are you here, Arrayn?"

"How long before Lord Justice here will be able to walk to the outhouse by himself?"

"Hey," objected Gregory, seemingly not sure whether he should be angry or amused. "It's not so bad as that. Yes, our eight is off the Line while I get better, but in another few days we should be ready to travel to my family's estate. Ingrid and Egyl will be wondering what has happened to us. And I'll have you know I can hobble to the privy without any assistance."

"Congratulations. But if I remember your daughters, they won't be impressed. Face it, you're not good for much right now. You won't be for at least six weeks." The big man scowled at Eloise. "Probably longer the way you mother him, Kyre."

"You don't seem to be good for anything right now yourself," she shot back.

Her riposte had no effect. "A lot is going to happen in the next few weeks," Arrayn replied.

The locus. Eloise felt a cold knot in her gut. *Huygens!* Her stomach felt tied in a knot. Arrayn was an oaf, but she could not ignore what this statement might imply. The change in Huygens' stability might not lead anywhere important, but Eloise's clenched stomach said otherwise. She knew the subtle history of the Endicotts too well, and she had learned too young what happened when risks were ignored. All the same, she did not want to give Robert's loudmouthed uncle the satisfaction of knowing he had rattled her. She was determined not to betray her concern. "So?"

Arrayn shrugged. "Deryn sent me to fetch you. I brought the good carriage. The one that rides easy and doesn't hurt broken bones. While you're sitting here babying your invalid husband, Deryn's making a leg brace that will have him back in fighting trim in days."

Eloise would have laughed in Arrayn's face if not for her gut and the lessons of her childhood. And Koria's gray-faced warning. It was past time to go home and see her daughters, not to run off to Vercors City, but here was Arrayn Endicott, sent by Deryn Endicott, covered in road dust and implying that matters had become urgent. *What kind of woman am I?*

 Declaration

"**C**OME ON, HEYLOR STYLE, YOU PROMISED TO SHOW ME THE FACE OF TRUE EVIL."

I did promise but ...

Looking down on Lynwen lying below him, Heylor had no desire to go anywhere, promise or not. Her purring voice and naked midriff did nothing to change his mind either. Lynwen was on her back, wearing only her form-fitting constable's pants and a silky shirt that barely reached her navel. Currently, it had ridden up just high enough to expose the round base of her breasts. His quick, busy mind had been fully occupied in a tense internal debate over whether to go for her belly button or the nipples that were so outstandingly silhouetted through the thin fabric of her undershirt.

"Now."

"Fine," he said, getting off her. "Though I don't know if you'll look at me the same afterwards. Some things can't be unseen." He knew *that* from experience. But he also knew it was almost time to start the day's patrol. Lynwen had been arriving earlier and earlier to pick him up. It seemed to be permissible to fraternize with him before their shift started—he was disinclined to ask—but all his attempts to fraternize *after* a shift started had been met with threats of batoning.

"Good," she said, rolling off his bed. "We just have to make that one stop at the constabulary first." She must have seen Heylor's horrified expression. "I told you," she added, "it's just a form we use to make sure no one is being taken advantage of." She frowned at him. "It is *not* a marriage application."

T

"GET LEYLAH OUT OF THE TREE," WHINED THE SKINNY, DOPEY-LOOKING CHILD. IT WAS hard to tell if the words were a question or a statement.

Who names their cat after a Methueyn Knight?

The lean, angular boy could not have been older than seven. Beyond the dumb name for his cat, one other thing made Heylor doubt the kid's mental development.

Who puts their cats in a tree? Everyone knows they go in bookshelves or wheelbarrows.

They were not even *close* to the constabulary office yet. There they would "declare their relationship," a ridiculous bit of bureaucracy as far as Heylor was concerned. And a scary one too. He was not looking forward to the mockery he anticipated from the other constables, and besides, he expected word to get around town instantly. Only grandma could have known that Lynwen was arriving earlier and earlier each morning, but she was too purblind to notice how handsy they were getting, too confused to realize Lynwen was not Helloise, and too deaf to hear the goings-on in his bedroom. Everyone else was usually out already when the young constable arrived, and his other sister, Shelley, lived mostly at the Orchid. The only times Heylor ever saw her now was when she wanted to tell him about new sightings of the cloaked man.

Word was all over the Lords' Commons about the legendary stalker, but as terrified as Heylor was by the idea of the cloaked man, he was more afraid of the relationship with Lynwen being discovered by his shameless, gossipy family. He had kept it from them so far, but if word hit the street, they would all know soon enough. Then there would be no end of rude, intrusive questions, vulgar jokes, and unsolicited advice directed at both of them.

How can she love me? And even if she does, how can her love possibly survive my family's antics once they know about us?

Not that she had ever said she loved him. Not that Heylor felt lovable. He was a coward who could not follow simple protocols. He had killed his friends and left their limbs as tree ornaments. What was there to love in someone like that? Looking at Lynwen and her adorable, slack-jawed expression as she considered the cat up the tree, he wished he was lovable, for he surely did love *her*.

Somehow he had to keep Lynwen from realizing just how wrong he was for her. Saving Leylah, this ridiculous feline namesake of the angel of night, was at least a distraction from that doomed project. Anything that allowed him to spend more time with Lynwen before it all ended was welcome.

"Save Leylah?" the kid asked again. His eyes were all watery and red now.

"I think we need a ladder," Lynwen suggested, still looking up, mouth still open in that cute way she had.

The cat was a good twenty feet up a coniferous tree whose branches had been trimmed away from the bottom ten feet or so. Someone had made the tree only climbable by cats, and apparently only in one direction. *Cats! What kind of animal can only go in one direction? Up the tree but not down. Fixated and unable to change with the circumstances.* Heylor stood there projecting his hatred of himself onto cats. They had been on his mind since returning to his parents' house and finding the place full of them. He was not growing into a love for felines any more than for himself.

Heylor looked at Lynwen. "Where can we find a ladder?"

She shrugged. "At the nearest fire hall, I would think." She crouched down to reassure the tearful child. "We'll be back with a ladder just as soon as we can. Stay here and keep an eye on Leylah for us, okay."

As the boy turned his attention back to the high branch where Leylah squatted, casting a baleful glare back down at her tiny owner, Lynwen whispered. "The nearest fire station is not close, and there will be some paperwork when we get there. It could take us an hour to get back with the ladder. I hope the kid—and the cat— can wait that long."

An hour? So two hours by the time we get the ladder back and do whatever tedious paperwork is required to sign it in again. Knights! I'll never last two hours on cat duty.

It was out of the question. It was under-stimulating. A moment ago, he had been happy to waste all the time in the world just as long as he did so with Lynwen. He loved her, but he lacked the patience and attention to devote two hours of his life to one stranded cat. He needed more stimulus than that. *We have evil and declarations to get to.*

"Hey!" Heylor yelled, "Look at that!" He pointed theatrically in the opposite direction to the cat and its unidirectional climbing tree. Distraction could be a tool as well as a weakness. It worked mostly through enthusiasm and volume. He had noticed that many things worked that way. When he was a boy, he had used the technique to get the better of Sackelly-belly-full-of-jelly.

While Lynwen and the boy looked the wrong way, Heylor did the one trick of dynamics he could do better than anyone else. Outside his family, in fact, Heylor had never met anyone who could do it at all. It was the first bit of dynamics he had learned, though it was more a matter of wizard-like instinct than calculated science. With no more thought that most people put into blinking their eyes, Heylor performed his trick. One second the cat was in the tree, and the next it was in his arms, hissing with ingratitude and scratching at his face.

Yeeooow!

Cats apparently did not enjoy being dynamically tunneled.

"What?" the boy and Lynwen simultaneously shouted as they turned back and saw the unappreciative feline pinwheeling its claws and yowling at Heylor.

"Here!" Heylor threw the cat at the stupefied child in a decisively, question-ending move. It snarled and began to claw at its new victim. "Job done, let's go!" He seized Lynwen's hand and pulled her along the street away from the furious cat and the yowling child, now shedding tears of pain rather than of worry.

"What just happened?" Lynwen asked.

"We just saved the day." Heylor avoided her eyes.

"But how?"

"The cat jumped out of the tree." Heylor paused dramatically. "As they often do."

Lynwen pulled her hand out of his. "Not *that* cat." She stopped in her tracks, which compelled Heylor to stop almost as abruptly.

"Look," he said, knowing the jig was up, "I'll explain later, I promise, but right now I need to show you the true face of evil like I said I would earlier."

Lynwen's face was an open-mouthed picture of skepticism. "Okay," she said, fingers playing over the handle of her baton. "I'll hold you to that. But it had better be *really* evil."

T

No evil was to be immediately had. It was a day of more distractions. First came the case of the stolen broom, which turned out to be a delusion of its ancient owner. The back of the broom closet had of course been the last place they looked for it. The old lady seemed to want them to stay and talk all morning.

"I think she just wanted some company," Heylor complained when they finally managed to get out the door.

"It's not that unusual," Lynwen agreed. "Some people invent a crime only because they have no one to talk to."

Heylor no longer trusted old people much, not after the murderous rampage of the mad octogenarian Keith Euyn. Only his grandma was more or less exempt from suspicion, and he kept his eyes on her. "That was wasting constabulary resources," he declared pretentiously.

Lynwen smiled. "I'll check the logs back at the constabulary when we get there. We can see if she has done this kind of thing before."

And then what? If she did this again and again, it could indicate dementia or some other mental problem. *But who could change that?* Heylor shivered, not liking where his thinking was going.

Similarly fruitless was the case of the meat smoker who stopped them to complain that someone was stealing his bacon. The thieves turned out to be rats in his walls. Heylor found them immediately in the empyreal sky but wished he had not. Hidden, nesting rats was not an image he would soon forget. He did not need the Eindarch Eye to deduce that they came out at night and carried off what meat they could.

Lynwen took a harder line with the bacon maker than she had with the old woman and pressed him with some sharp questions. Would rats only carry away the meat? Wouldn't they also have eaten some as it lay in the cold room. Would they not have left spoor behind? Had the man not noticed rat droppings when he cleaned the room? Had he not said anything because rat poo was bad for business licenses? She made a note to send a report to the health inspector when they got back to the office.

It seemed like they were waylaid on every block by someone with a case that looked serious and turned out to be trivial or non-existent. In each alleged crime, the supposed victim had played a role in their own little drama. Heylor began to wonder what the real job of the constabulary was. And what the cumulative effect of all these red herrings would be on those charged with investigating them. What was this doing to Lynwen's attitude? Would she become a better, more open-minded investigator, or would she eventually be ground down into a sullen state of cynicism and come to view each self-described victim as a likely faker? Watching the bounce in Lynwen's step, Heylor hoped for the former. He wanted that open-mouthed lack of preconceptions to stay.

Of all the complaints that interrupted their journey to the office, only the case of the broken horn seemed genuine. This prized object, a mock-up of Hervor's famous horn, had disappeared from its mount behind the bar of the tavern named after it. Someone had apparently stolen it the night before, but no doors have been forced or windows broken. It was a mystery until the meticulous Lynwen found traces of the paste with which the back door's locking mechanism had been gummed up, allowing the ingenious thief to creep into the establishment after hours.

Even so, Heylor had trouble taking the case seriously. "Hervor's horn indeed! We need to get to these important crime scenes more quickly, my dear constable," he said with a wink as they continued on their way. "If we'd been here quicker, I could have heralded retrograde and seen exactly what was done and by whom. We would have solved the case and caught the evildoers immediately." He shook his head dramatically and made as if to wipe away a tear. "I only wish to live in such a world."

"I wonder, if you heralded retrograde now, how many of your little jokes would be found to deserve a batoning in the future," rejoined Lynwen, "and could thereby be avoided. It would be as if they never were. That's the world *I* want to live in."

"Damn it!" Heylor said. "There's Sackelly-belly-full-of-jelly again!"

"Who?" Lynwen's head darted around as she tried to spot the cause of Heylor's theatrics.

"There," Heylor whispered, pointing with his hand pressed to his chest, trying and failing to be subtle. Sackelly and two other men were loading their horse-drawn refuse wagon on the other side of the road. It was the same setup as before. Sackelly still hobbled in the same strange way as he had the first time they encountered him.

Lynwen squinted at the workmen as Heylor tried to speed-walk inconspicuously past them. "He doesn't look *that*—"

"Fat?" Heylor hissed. "I said he was fat when he was a boy. He had less of a beard then too."

"No, I mean he doesn't look all that—"

Heylor was still speed-walking, but it was too late. Sackelly-belly-full-of-jelly had seen them. His eyes widened under his furiously bushy eyebrows, betraying the recognition that had been absent the last time Heylor had scuttled past. "Heylor Style?" he called from across the road. He chewed at something in his mouth. "Is that you?"

"No!" replied Heylor, trying to push Lynwen along with a hand on the small of her back. "I'm—I'm someone else. I mean, who's Heylor Pyle? Never heard of him." He turned away as they left the workmen behind. "Off to business now. Lots to do. See you." *Not.*

Sackelly began hobbling diagonally across the street in lame and noisy pursuit. He practically lurched with each awkward stride. His coworkers stared aghast at the unlikely chase. "That is so you, Heylor! I know you. And don't think I've forgotten what you did!"

"I didn't do it!" Heylor shouted, head still twisted backward. He winced. "I mean *anything.* I didn't do anything." He put on a sympathetic face. "Did something happen to you?"

But he did not wait for an answer. They kept up their speed walk, Lynwen's face unreadable now. They rounded a corner by the New School and narrowly missed running into a small, freckle-faced boy about twelve years old with a large, hand-lettered sign on his shoulder. It read:

"Bring back the old ways!

We used to know what

The truth was!"

Which ones, which truths? Heylor was unclear on what the sign meant or why someone so young would want to carry that cryptic message to the New School. *The credibility gap is astounding.* He glanced nervously behind again. His pursuer had finally stopped. Hunched over his gimpy leg, giving up now, Sackelly-belly-full-of-jelly called out, "I'll catch you one day, Style!"

No, you won't.

They were at the north edge of campus now. "I think we're good," Heylor said, satisfied that the chase was over. "Perhaps we can turn diagonal and go by the medical research buildings. That's where the ev—"

"What did you do to this Sackelly-jelly-belly anyway, Heylor Style?" Lynwen interrupted, breaking free of him and planting her hands on her hips. "From the way he came after us, I doubt it was something small."

What didn't I do? There were so many things. He shook his head. *So many.* "I can't remember."

Nothing in Lynwen's face suggested she believed him. He frowned at her. *She thinks she's my conscience.*

Suddenly his frown turned to a smile. *She* does *love me.* Then he frowned again. Lynwen did not really know him yet. He still had not told her what happened out past the wheat line, let alone any of his many childhood transgressions, like the ones Sackelly had obviously never gotten over. *For now. She loves me only for now.*

Some of these thoughts must have showed on his face. "What is *wrong* with you, Heylor Style?" Lynwen sounded exasperated now.

"Me?" he exclaimed, trying to steer the constable to a different line of enquiry. "I just got threatened, and you did nothing to help. Nah. Thing."

"Really?" Lynwen almost stood on her toes in her frustration. "I was too busy being bustled off to do anything." She shook her head and smiled ruefully. "It was barely even a threat. Actually, it wasn't at all." Lynwen shrugged. "And I don't see how that qualifies as *evil*, Heylor. You really aren't keeping any of your promises today. Usually that kind of negligence only happens in a relationship *after* the papers are signed."

What are *these papers?* Heylor knew Lynwen was teasing him, but part of him was starting to wonder if there might not be more to this relationship declaration than she was saying.

"Come quick! A hanging!" The woman's voice cut right through the equanimity that had begun to return to Heylor's jumpy, inconstant mind. He looked up to see a stout woman in a woodworking apron. Her short arms, which she was waving vigorously toward Lynwen, were thick with muscle. Lynwen left him and jogged quickly over to the woman. Heylor followed more slowly, thinking about how quickly Lynwen could have fled from Sackelly if she had wanted to.

As he approached the two women, Heylor thought he heard a kettle boiling over, then realized it was the aproned woman trying to speak. Her excited voice rose and fell in high-pitched, breathless fragments. "Just swinging there." A pause. "Turning round and round … Slowly … Terrible." She paused longer to build up new steam. "I went in … With the lantern … There she was." Her voice reached a new pitch. "Dead!"

"Hung?" Heylor asked unnecessarily, desperate now to insert himself into a more interesting investigation than those of cats, brooms, and rats. Or the festering grievances of childhood friends.

T

THE WOMAN'S NAME WAS DIEDRE. SHE WAS THE STAGE MANAGER OF THE EIGHT KNIGHTS Playhouse, a theatre company that worked out of a large brick building not far down the street. Being just off campus, it attracted the better-off and artsier students along with theatergoers from the town. She explained that they were rehearsing a new production of Ardgour's Folly, not a comedy, she was careful to point out, despite the name. "So we really need to clean this up before the troupe arrives," she insisted in a much cooler voice than she had first used. "Actors are *so* sensitive, you know. They won't be able to work if they see her hanging there." She shot Lynwen a pleading look. "Can't we get her out of here quickly?"

Lynwen gave Heylor a look that stopped just short of an eye roll. "Let's take a look first," she told the woman in a flat, patient tone.

It did not look good.

The woman had been hanged from a beam right in the middle of the stage. As if giving a final performance, she was revolving slowly from the imaginary audience to her non-existent fellow players and back again.

This makes a little too much sense. Heylor saw at once why a theatre was a perfect place to hang yourself. First, you would certainly be found fairly quickly. Second, theatres were built to hang all sorts of things—curtains, props, false walls, doors. Why not a person too? This theatre even had an enormous workbench that had been used to anchor the rope. Finally, the lighting was excellent. There were sconces everywhere, and the hanging body cast a long, dramatic shadow as it slowly rotated. When all the sconces were lit, the shadow could even be adjusted for artistic effect.

Heylor sat down in the front row, nursing these morbid reflections and watching Lynwen secure the scene. Diedre's stagehands were put to work as they arrived. Some were sent as runners to the constabulary, while others used spare rope to cordon off the area under the hanging woman and around the big workbench. Not the same thick rope as the woman had hanged herself with, but a smaller gauge. Lynwen also did the preliminary questioning of Diedre, her assistants and—as they arrived—the startled actors.

Time seemed to move slowly, and Heylor soon felt bored. He had already seen what a hanged body looked like. Even an attractive woman, which this lady looked like she must have been before putting the rope around her neck, was not pretty at the end of a rope. Man or woman, the eyes bulged out, the fluids dripped, and the same smell began to waft as the body dangled.

Seen one hanging, seen them all.

He caught Lynwen staring at him. She gave him a look that had to be a request for patience. His restlessness must be obvious. Or she already knew him better than he had thought.

Why am I here?

Heylor remembered how the others used to ask the same question at night out across the wheat line. *Why are we here?* No one in his eight except him had known what Lighthouse was really about, or why he was always rolling the dice and testing Huygens. But they had protected him while he did so and trusted him when he told them where to go. They should not have trusted his vague answers about why they were there in the wilderness, his platitudes about settling a new county. Above all, they should never have trusted him to follow protocol or make good decisions. They should never have trusted that he could master himself.

I must do better.

He told himself that a thousand times a day, in between doing worse.

I am unstable.

Lynwen was stable. She was good at protocol. She even seemed to enjoy it. Heylor watched her as she questioned the assistants and later the actors and took her careful, precise notes of what they said and what she observed. She had patience and method. If he were more like her, Ildrys would have kept all his limbs. Ida would still be alive.

Ida.

The tall, hanging woman reminded him of Ida when Skoll had fastened its massive hand on her neck. Her eyes had also bulged. He had said in the AER that she might have survived, but having also had Skoll's giant hand around his neck, the bruises only just now fading, he doubted it.

Ida.

Heylor closed his eyes.

I must do better.

When he opened his eyes, he looked at the scene with a new determination. He had promised himself that he would help Lynwen, and in doing so, that he would help himself. Looking at the dead woman, he realized there were more than himself to be helped. He brought his strong but erratic powers of concentration to bear on the problem of what had happened. He looked again, taking more care this time, stifling the impulse to distort the scene with his own feelings.

As Heylor focused, a constabulary sergeant rushed in. A large, hard-angled man composed of muscle, protruding bone, and spidery blue veins, he spoke with Lynwen for a moment before shaking his head and scanning the expansive room. His eyes settled on the group of actors who were now huddled in several rows of seats off to the side of where Heylor sat. True to Diedre's word, they had reacted with an abundance of emotion to the shocking sight of the woman hanging above their stage. Some had cried, and others had cried out; most did some of both. They cried out to Heydron for protection, to Volsang for vengeance, to Darday'l to find out why such a tragedy had occurred, and to Michael to join Volsang and make war on whoever had hanged the poor woman. One young man even called on Nimrheal to set things right.

Funny they never cried out the dead woman's name.

"You're Heylor Style, aren't you?" It was the sergeant. He did not bother to introduce himself, but a badge above his breast pocket announced his name. Kayne. He spoke in a soft voice for such a hard-looking man. While Heylor had been thinking about the actors, Kayne must have approached him almost silently, too silently for such a large man.

"Yes."

"You survived the Battle of the Bifrost."

"Yes." *I ran away.*

"I saw you in the Citadel," Kayne continued. He was eying Heylor strangely now. "After Keith Euyn wiped out the ducal guard."

And the duke. And the duchess. Heylor nodded, not trusting himself to speak about those days. He thought about them more than enough.

Kayne nodded back, gazing off into a shadowy corner of the expansive room as if examining some memory of his own that Heylor could not guess at. "This kind of thing—suicide, most likely—has got to seem pretty boring to you after all that."

Heylor looked from the big man to the big bench on the stage. "There's always something to be learned," he said, then nodded toward the actors. "None of them knew her, did they?"

"So says Constable Lynwen." Kayne's eyes were unreadable. He nodded a good-bye and approached the actors while Heylor got up to rejoin his beloved.

Lynwen confirmed Heylor's guess. No one at the theatre had known the dead woman. Or would admit to having known her.

"So why pick this place to hang herself? For attention?"

"Perhaps, but no note," Lynwen said. "Like the hanging we found by Cobbler Street."

"But do you see the anomaly?" Heylor asked, vibrating with excitement and almost smirking.

Lynwen smiled back at him, a gleam in her eyes. "She could not have moved that heavy bench by herself. It must weigh twice what she does. I doubt if she could even have pushed it. Anyway, there are no scuff marks."

"I love you." Heylor did not prevaricate this time.

"Woah!" The exclamation came from behind him. He turned and found Kayne staring at him, the big man's heavy eyebrows raised ironically. He had returned from interviewing the actors as silently as he had sneaked up on Heylor earlier. "You two had better fill out a relationship declaration." He shook his head in a self-satisfied way. The expression was incongruous on a man with such hard, granitic features. "I have to be off. Let me know anything else you find out, constable. If you're right about the bench, it's a murder or some kind of conspiracy. Keep me in the loop, but it will be your case. You two seem to be enjoying it so much that I don't want to take it away from you." His face, so affable during most of the discussion, hardened again. "But don't forget that declaration."

T

It was evening before Lynwen was satisfied that the actors and crew had told her everything they could or would. She let them go but warned them not to speak about the case. There was probably little hope they would cooperate, but it was protocol. Lynwen and Heylor stayed to wait for a wagon from the Vercors Ice Company to collect the body. They sat in the first row, stage right, facing the dead woman at an angle as she continued to rotate ever more slowly.

I almost missed it. I almost fell victim to myself, got bored, got restless, stopped observing, stopped being careful. I almost missed that one moment when I needed to care enough to master myself and make a difference.

"Do you ever feel like the days are repeating?" Heylor asked, staring at the woman's bulging eyes. "That you never quite learn your lesson, that you just keep repeating the mistakes of the past instead of learning from them and moving on, not even holding your own, going retrograde." It was like something Robert had once said to him in their first year. He had not understood why Robert had said it back then, but he recognized the feeling in himself now.

Lynwen had stopped looking at the dead woman. She was gazing right into Heylor's eyes. "Are you thinking about that belly-jelly fellow? About how we ran, well, walked very quickly, away from him a second time, like we were little kids?" She put her hand on his. "I see that kind of thing all the time. People regress in the strangest ways when they're around family or childhood friends, when they are confronted with past trauma."

If only that was what I meant. Heylor was tempted to go along with Lynwen's plausible narrative, except that it was not true. "No, not Sackelly. I mean the pro-testors objecting to the New School all over again. I mean the cloaked man, or maybe men, stalking students again. Every time we set foot on campus, someone reports a new sighting."

He stood up suddenly, unable to sit still any longer, and jumped up on the stage. Lynwen stayed where she was, watching him intently.

"No, even that isn't what I really meant," he boomed from the stage like an actor, "as worrying as those things are. I mean *me*. I skolved up so badly out there, Lynwen. My eight *died!*"

He strode to the edge of the stage and looked straight down at her. "Dear Lynwen, I think about it every day. I know I told you all this yesterday and the day before and the day before that. I get up and get excited about today, but I keep remembering yesterday." He shook his head. "Remembering doesn't make me learn from it, so what's the point?" He clutched at his hair dramatically with both hands. "Why do you even *like* me? How can you stand the boredom of all my mistakes and complaints?"

Lynwen stood up, drew her baton, and in one smooth motion, hurled it toward him. His right hand shot up to catch it, but if catching it was all he could do, he would have missed. The baton was aimed a good foot to the right of where he could reach. As it was about to fly by, it vanished and reappeared in his hand, giving his palm a sharp thwack as it made contact.

"You didn't do *that* yesterday," she said, then grinned at him. "Heylor Style I've watched you for four years." She walked up the stairs and joined him on stage. "I remember you sticking up for Sir Robert after the Battle of the Bifrost." She smiled at him. "You really gave it to the vice-constable. You were loyal to your friend. I liked that."

"Loyalty to Robert is easy. He deserves your love, not me. You know what *I* did in that battle? I ran away. Robert had to execute those two knights in order to send Lindseth to pull me out of the river, where I had jumped rather than stay and fight with my friends."

Lynwen's eyebrows rose skeptically. "Sir Robert scares me. People like him are so sure, so driven, they don't make sense to me. He's like one of those Methueyn Knights from the old stories. He has no restraint when he thinks he is doing what he should. And he always thinks that. He barely seems human. Being with a man like Sir Robert would be as strange as partnering with an angel like the Methueyns used to do." She shook her head. "His wife is no better. Think she's approachable? Why did she even bring you all there in the middle of the night? Jumping in the river makes a lot more sense to me."

"Oh, I'm some hero all right." Heylor wished it were true, but he was so sure it was not that the words coming out of his mouth barely hurt. It made no sense that warm tears ran down his face.

"You are," Lynwen said, taking her baton from his hand and dropping it on the floor. "Not many people walked out of the Bifrost that night, and fewer still walked out of the Citadel's throne room the next day. *None* of them killed Keith Euyn."

"It was a trick," Heylor said looking down at the baton on the stage floor. The shadow of the hanged woman swayed over it.

Lynwen stepped closer to him, her body leaning forward, almost touching him. "A trick only you could do, cat-catcher."

"I was lying on the floor the whole time Robert fought him, you know. At first, I couldn't even move. I had been electrocuted. But later, after my muscles released, I just stayed there. Scared. Frozen with fear."

"You didn't stay there forever, Heylor." Lynwen pressed up close to him. "Just like you do eventually learn. Look at what we figured out today. That was solid, patient detective work." The shadow of the dead woman passed slowly over them. Lynwen leaned in. In a softer voice, she whispered in his ear, setting him tingling,

"Today you declared your absolute love for me out loud. Not so long ago, you just *imagined* you felt that way."

Heylor did a sudden pirouette, but not because of Lynwen's encouragement of his love talk. An idea had, from nowhere, seized him. He seized Lynwen's shoulders. "What was that you said about Methueyn Knights?"

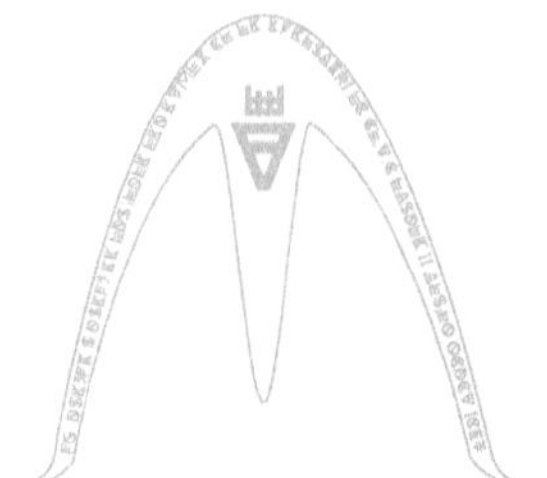

Chapter Thirteen

Knights Alone, Armor Brittle or Strong

MARIELLE ENGEL GAVE NO THOUGHT TO BEING ALONE IN THE WILDERNESS. She ghosted through the grass, quiet and quick. She did not sneak; she simply moved well. Strongly, subtly. She had passed the wheat line days ago but had not paused there to review old memories or make new promises. She knew what the wheat line was. She accepted its meaning and significance and left it at that.

She was where she meant to be. What she was doing was what she meant to do. She held few opinions on morality or ethics; she *knew* what she should do. Her certainty was not a brittle thing. It was not riddled with the flaws, cracks, and gaps that, if she were a sword or shield, would fatigue metal and end in sudden, cataclysmic failure. Her certainty was not a mask for insecurity. If questioned, she did not react with anger. Questions from others were fine. Ideas from others were often interesting but never threatening. Her certainty was not a fraud that threatened holy war if challenged. How could there be offense in questioning something certain and unassailable. She did not need others to agree with her. She did not need them to understand. She was not going to change for anyone else, and she had no desire to change others, to infect them, like a virus, with her certainty. That was for the insecure. The need to be assured by others betrayed a lack of confidence. Like everything else about Marielle Engel, her certainty simply was.

Others might see how fast she was and how strong. They might see the incredible things that she could do, and feel awe, for she was awesomely capable. When Marielle Engel chose to do a thing, it was done. What she was capable of doing could change the world, but Marielle Engel was not herself dynamic. She was constant, steady, unaffected. Only someone like that could make the world revolve around her. When she transformed the world, it would be done without thought or debate, tears or anger. No animal in the wild thought to interfere with her as she passed so quickly and thoughtlessly by. They also acted on instinct.

Δ

What is the mistake that starts it all?

Sir Christensen crouched low in the shadows of the great needled tree. He was downwind of the skolves, but their ears were almost as keen as their snouts. He kept still. There were fourteen of the beasts, not too many, perhaps, for a knight of his caliber to defeat in a fight if no more came, but Sir Christensen never sought unnecessary combat, and even he could be killed. His bright, heavy plate had been left behind, and his skin was not as good an armor as it used to be. He squatted lower to improve his sightline. He needed to see his target.

It was a slim stone tower rising out of a valley shaped like a bowl, a valley that had been shaped by a massive engineering project in Nehring Ardgour's time, a fact apparent even now, centuries later. The lake at the center had been deepened by an expensive reshaping of the valley's natural synclinal topography. Thrusted rock had been augmented, reinforced, and waterproofed by many years of meticulous stone masonry. Sir Racheyl Stirling, also known as Sir Ameleyn Forteys in *The Lonely Wizard*, had examined the lake from another vantage point during her search for Keith Euyn. Although she had never approached closer than the ridge from which she had first spied it, she had made special mention of the valley's evidently man-made features in her notes.

The lake, with its reshaped valley, was yet another previously unknown, monumental engineering project by Nehring Ardgour. It was so far past the Castlereagh Line that only Keith and Racheyl had seen it until now. Until the invasion of the wheat had brought everything in the wilderness so much closer. Being closer made investigation feasible, at least for Sir Christensen. But it did not make decision-making any easier.

What do I do now that I've found it?

Sir Christensen had lost his former certainty. Facing Keith Euyn had started the process. What a horror it had been to draw steel against the greatest knight in history. Even at eighty years of age, deranged by heraldic dreams, Keith's power—*his* certainty—had dwarfed Christensen's. Robert had done better. He could have become a better Deladieyr Knight than Keith if not for what came after at the embassy. There was still something about the young man, something Christensen could not define, but he knew it existed.

Christensen had sent his notebook to Robert out of a sense of hope, but also because he thought the young man would understand his own dilemma. Robert knew what it was like to be disappointed in himself. It was a certainty killer.

The search for the Methueyn Bridge was an immemorial quest. Rhysheart was right about that. He was wrong that it had been abandoned. Many newly Risen knights, and even some candidates, still went out in search of it. Christensen thought that it could be argued that Marielle Engel was doing that now, or was about to do it, depending on when the Javelin mission actually started.

Is it Javelin?

Christensen had been plagued by his dream of the destruction of Vercors since he first had it. Images of Skoll and Hati and a group of dark knights burning Vercors and the New School played again and again through his mind. Deladieyr Knights could have heraldic dreams, though they could not consciously herald. They were not wizards or dynamicists, but sometimes the future reached back for them too.

Javelins would change the world. He knew that. To be able to communicate instantly over vast distances would have immediate and tremendous consequences. The military ones would be momentous and come first, but the social and cultural ramifications would undoubtedly be even greater. It would be world changing. In the old days, Nimrheal would surely have come for the javelin's inventor, for Gerveault.

I don't think the *Javelin project is responsible.*

Unlike his former self, the new Sir Christensen did not know, he only thought. His instincts now were compromised by uncertainty. He did not now *think* it could have been Javelin that caused the events that led to his dream. Not directly. The dream unfolded something that would happen very soon, but the effects of Javelin more likely belonged to the long term. Ultimately, certainty is reductive. In logic, certainty only comes about once the criterion of adequacy is achieved—a process that is often long and arduous but usually ends in the simplicity of a problem conclusively solved. Christensen suspected his journey would become very reductive very soon.

If I find the Bridge, what will I do? What will happen? Will I recover my sense of certainty and my former resolve? Will it still be possible to cross?

Is something perfect that is broken always broken? When it breaks, does it shatter, or can it be restored?

If I restore the Methueyn Knights, will I restore myself?

Chapter Fourteen

Point B

"WE WILL GET NOWHERE IF WE GO ALONE."

"Yes, Blouse, I've heard that before," Merrett replied. He was too busy scanning the low scrubby bushes and tall grasses to scowl at Endicott.

Some conversations never end. It would be uncharitable to say they get recycled and repeated like dogma, though that did happen. A lot.

Endicott made a conscious effort to take in more of the terrain, widen his eyes, and look around at where they were passing through. He wanted to expand his perception, to step away from inward-oriented thoughts. The intrinsic was important, but here, this far out, it was the extrinsic that could kill you. He felt no need to respond to Merrett immediately. The same conversation would continue in fits and starts all though their efforts to enlarge awareness of the wilderness.

Should a conversation ever end? Endicott was not sure. Yes, for some things. For the trivial, always. For the operational—sometimes. Maybe. Conversations born of frustration, looking for easy answers or prejudicial targets, should never happen at all, except that people were human and flawed. Conversations should end for things that were known or certain. But most of the world was unknown or uncertain, much of it only guessed at. Even heraldry was just a guess at the future, and often a biased one.

Ideas. Ideas were endless. Conversations about ideas should endure. The Methueyn Knights had been living embodiments of ideas. Protection, righteous retribution, curiosity, love, and all the rest. In the old days, before the Methueyn War ended and the Huygens modulus changed, a Deladieyr Knight could cross a metaphysical bridge and join with an angel who embodied one of the eight immortal ideas. It only worked if the Deladieyr was single-mindedly concerned with the same idea as the angel. They had to be compatible.

I wonder if knight and angel exist together in a perpetual conversation about their idea? Endicott spared a quick glance at Merrett. The big man walked with great care through the grasses, placing his feet with a conscientiousness that would surprise someone who did not know the ways of the wilderness. Endicott knew that he and Merrett were not ideally compatible. Merrett and Lindseth, on the other hand, were complementary. Tall, lanky Lindseth's cool, philosophical attitude was a useful counterpoint to stocky Merrett's grouchy pragmatism. *Their differences make the combination interesting.* Endicott wondered if the perfect compatibility of knight and angel would logically end their conversation over the shared idea. Would they be too much in accord? Would your Methueyn Knight be a bore to have to dinner?

"It's too bad you only *heard* it before, but never understood it," whispered Lindseth, restarting the debate. Endicott refused to look round, but he knew the tall man was smiling. There was no malice in Lindseth, but he took the odd shot to keep his partner honest.

"We're close now gentlemen," Endicott said. "She can't be far." He saw a jumble of stones on a hill through a stand of low trees. He hoped Engel was there. They needed her. They needed to combine forces. He wanted them to be a microcosm of the larger forces that would combine and cooperate in further phases of Lighthouse. They would need to learn to work together in very large, coordinated numbers to defeat or drive off Skoll and Hati and find the lost Methueyn Bridge, the original Bifrost.

Endicott also wanted to be sure that Marielle Engel was safe. He knew she was one of the persons in the world least in need of his protection, but that did not lessen his anxiety. A few days earlier it had occurred to him that he did not—quite—love her, but that did not matter. In the wilderness everyone was equally important, and *almost* loving someone was nearly an infinite distance from not caring about them at all.

Lindseth passed by on Endicott's left, moving quickly and gracefully toward the rocky hill. As Endicott started up the hill behind him, he noticed that many of the boulders were squared. He stopped suddenly. Merrett, behind him now, also stopped.

This used to be a tower.

Endicott closed his eyes and reimagined what he had seen. A roughness on the hill, conical in shape. It had been a tower, and something had blown it down, scattering the stones of its walls down the hill on the side they were climbing. Some of the rock had been thrown for over three hundred yards.

What could do that?

"Robert." It was Lindseth's voice, not far ahead. He stood near a clump of rocks and straggly rosebushes. "She's here."

Marielle Engel stepped out of the shadows beside him, her tan leather clothes and partial armor blending in well with the surroundings. Endicott only just managed to keep himself from rushing forward and hugging her, then checked himself, feeling a wave of fear. He was not afraid to expose his feelings; he was worried he had lost his concentration in a wilderness where beings that could knock over stone castles still lived.

What is the idea that defines Skoll or Hati?

▽

"Ulsrud?" Lindseth said, squinting. "Northwest of the Roache Guyon Highlands. That is a stretch. A big one. No one will be able to help us that far out."

They had activated the javelin again. This time Koria had answered and given them their next location. It had been wonderful to hear her voice, though there had been something in it he did not like. Worry? It was difficult to know with Koria. She still liked to keep a few secrets.

Merrett looked at Lindseth like he would have looked at a squashed turd pasted onto his boot. "If we're in over our heads already, what's the difference? No one can help us here either."

As far as they knew, Ulsrud was the farthest out that anyone had ever been, at least since the war. Even Heylor Style's ill-fated mission had met its end a good two days closer to civilization. Ulsrud was a destination at least two years too early in the Lighthouse timetable by Endicott's calculations. Even though the Javelin mission parameters called for the second objective to be a surprise, Endicott was certain that Ulsrud was not what had originally been planned.

Why are they accelerating matters so recklessly?

"Merrett, my friend," Lindseth said, obviously struggling to be patient, "Ulsrud is so far past the Line that no one will even find our bodies."

"Who cares?"

"Lindseth's mother, for one," Endicott chimed in, coming out of his thoughts and getting back to the present. That ancient lady always made a point of asking him to look after her son. "Be sure to bring Jeyn back to me," she would always say. She seemed to think he could because of what had happened with Syriol Lindseth on the terrible night.

"Well, isn't that a tomato?" huffed Merrett. He was staring at the hardtack in his hand as he said it. He started chewing on it, his jaw working hard. "What do you think, Marielle?"

She had been quiet since they had met. Perhaps she had become used to being alone. "Ulsrud used to have a different name back in the days of Engevelen, before Novgoreyl came and changed things." Her voice was soft. "It was called Nuage."

Merrett had a sick look on his face as if he wanted to say something caustic but thought better of it. He swallowed his mouthful of half-chewed biscuit and looked even sicker. In a move that only strengthened the impression of some stifled sarcasm, he swallowed the hardtack loudly. "Huh," he said instead of whatever he had been thinking.

"A lot of things have changed since then," said Lindseth. "Can we just acknowledge that this new objective is significant?"

"Will that shut you up?" Merrett shot back, then answered his own question. "Doubtful. But sure, I agree, for all that it matters."

"We are going, regardless." Engel's emotionless certainty put an end to the conversation.

Robert had already begun laying out the maps. He had not worked out scenarios for Ulsrud, or Nuage, before. It had been beyond contemplation during their mission preparation. "Let's discuss our route, then," he said, pointing at Ulsrud on the map. It was on a lone mountain overlooking a long, flat plain. A geographic anomaly, and one of the locations that Nehring Ardgour had been suspected of using for certain mysterious research. He held up a finger in unconscious imitation of Gerveault. "Potential hazards."

Mostly unknown.

He held up a second finger. "Meal plans."

Not enough food. We will have to hunt on the way back.

He held up a third finger. "Anything else." *Everything we can think of without properly preparing.* Endicott smiled grimly to himself. Not having all the information was a situation he did not enjoy, but one that he had survived in the past. *We must take whatever initiative we can.*

"Let's talk before we walk."

$$\nabla$$

WHAT DO YOU SEE WHEN YOU WALK THROUGH THE RUINS OF AN OLD CIVILIZATION?

Endicott had hoped to see the little things, the remaining traces of humanity. He found it strange that a man as closed off as the Lonely Wizard would find a whistle and think of children, would find the remains of a silage pit and imagine a farmer turning lyrics while she worked. After nearly a quarter millennium, whistles would not be easily found. Perhaps in some submerged vault or preserved trunk, a whistle lurked. In some of the other ruined castles, small things had remained—Endicott had seen and left many—but not out in the plains. Not away from the preserving strength of rock. In the spaces between towers, there was almost nothing at all. Wooden roofs were rotted and fell and were buried by new life. The old silage pits were overgrown too. All that remained was broken stone.

How is it we do not mourn them?

No one mourned the loss of Nehring Ardgour. He had made the mistake, committed the folly, that had nearly ended everything. Those of his people who survived the Methueyn War had fled north to Novgoreyl rather than be absorbed into the remains of Engevelen or the growing power of Vercors and the empire to which it belonged. The few latter-day survivors of Engevelen, a country four times ruined, *did* mourn the loss of most of their homeland. But those from Novgoreyl did not mourn at all. They had given the land back, broken, useless.

"What pile is this?" asked Lindseth, standing at the foot of a conical mound. It had been colonized by alfalfa, but Endicott did not need a bird's perspective to see it had been made by man. Just beyond it lay a pond, and adjacent to that, a dark rock wall.

"It's a mine," said Endicott, just barely avoiding opening himself to the empyreal sky to find the cave mouth. No such mine was on his maps.

Lindseth stayed rooted to where he was. "For what, do you suppose?"

Endicott came up to stand beside his tall friend. Curious as well, he decided to make a better survey of the environs. Merrett and Engel were given sentry duty while he and Lindseth went to work. Cautious observation and a climb around the cliffs eventually revealed a broken system of aqueducts and the remains of a giant tank that might have been used for some kind of hydraulic mining. Back down near the enormous conical pile, Endicott made careful notes on his map.

Pffft.

Even closed to the empyreal sky, the young man felt it. He had been hit by something very small and fast, and perhaps he was no longer ever *completely* closed to the sky anymore. "Stay here," he said to Lindseth and approached the cliff wall. He had noted earlier that it was either a granitoid or possibly some kind of metamorphic rock. He had not identified it more specifically; it was covered in lichen. With a renewed sense of motivation now, he brushed furiously at the lichen, which gradually gave way. The rock looked familiar. Going against protocol for a bare instant, Endicott opened himself and looked at it through the empyreal sky. What he saw was astounding. The rock was radically unstable, spitting out energy and pieces of itself, constantly changing. Changing dangerously.

Knights in heaven. It's greenstone.

It had often been discussed in Vercors, the puzzle of how Nehring Ardgour had made his great discovery. The initial steps, the missteps, the groping for a suitable source of power, the mind-twisting, mostly unknown, possibly unknowable physics that connected worlds, that affected the universal moduli. No one knew precisely how Ardgour had learned to affect Huygens, or how he had avoided a fatal visit from Nimrheal while doing so, but there were plenty of guesses. Greenstone and the strange, mutable element it contained was one possibility.

This mine held rock of amazing purity, but even so the amount of the transformational element relative to that of other, more mundane elements was vanishingly low. Ardgour had likely mined thousands of tons of the rock to get what he wanted. Endicott bore down on the empyreal sky, braving hypothermia. Nearly shouting with the effort, he attempted to push the resolution of his vision to the limits of his capability, trying to see the moment when a single atom would change. The image fuzzed when he approached that ultimate resolution, fighting his comprehension. In the lab, he had measured empirically the probability field that governed the breakdown of a statistical sample of the material. He and Koria had tried to match it with a mathematical function. Behavior could be observed, some of it at least, but reason escaped like the particles of lightning that burst free when the element changed. He had seen the other, quicker, even less definable effects of the change, watched a very few of these flashes of light hurl across the interdimensional barrier, there and gone again. He had even, once, used their limited understanding of probability to play at effecting the transformation of a minuscule sample, unleashing a raw and poisonous lightning in the lab from a power source beyond any he had ever seen in its strength. It was a harrowing, chaotic, perilous experiment that he had been forbidden to attempt a second time by both Gerveault and Koria.

Curiosity made the young man want to try again, to feel the probabilistic dance of the strange matter, hear it as a song, hum to its beauty—a beauty he could feel in a way that transcended the mathematical functions they had used to describe it—to bridge probabilities and pull the power out of those atoms and let them fly. But shivering out here in the old abandoned mine, it was not hard to see the folly of this impulse. Whatever the greenstone had been used for had hastened the end of Ardgour, and understanding how it all worked was likely decades or more in the future. The twenty-year deadline on Lighthouse never seemed shorter than when viewed against all that they did not yet understand.

They stayed to survey the mine for several hours, but Endicott did not allow anyone to enter the cave. In the end they learned nothing more than the evident fact that Ardgour had once mined this primordial rock.

As old as the earth, yet still transforming. It can wait a little longer.

We have our own job to do.

To make up time, they travelled late into the day. Soon after setting out again, they passed the ruins of an enormous castle not far from the mine. *Castle 197.* Its outer walls still mostly stood, relatively unblemished, but the inner keep had been smashed as if a hundred-foot-wide fist from heaven had punched it into the earth. A rocky pit—now a pond—was all that remained. It had been hit so hard and so precisely that the shards of the once-massive stone blocks of the keep were half submerged in water. Lindseth had remarked, with no trace of humour, that moats usually went on the outside of castles.

As strange as the site was, it had at least been on Endicott's maps, though with nothing to indicate the unique and awesome destruction of the inner keep. Even Merrett was impressed enough to comment. "It isn't a ruin, it's a wreck. This whole county is wrecked." He left unsaid the question of whether it was wise to attempt to reinhabit something so devastated, but his face had turned gray when they passed the blasted castle. Endicott feared to imagine how powerful the beings were that could wreak such havoc.

"But Ardgour and his people had such grandiose ideas," Lindseth whispered later, after they had made camp for the night and were quietly setting themselves up in a grove of broad oak trees. Everyone turned to look at him. No one seemed to understand what he meant at first. "It makes it all sadder for me," he explained.

"Wait," Merrett said, holding a big paw up. "Are you saying you feel bad about the destruction because Nehring Ardgour mobilized so many of his people to build the engines that brought us Skoll and Hati? You feel bad that all those mines, or whatever they were, and all the other things we are spending years investigating were destroyed?" His eyes hardened. "You feel bad that the means by which he brought the skolves to us are gone?" Merrett sat down on a fallen tree. "Are you out of your mind, Jeyn?"

"Maybe," Lindseth said, "but think of the ambition of those projects. To touch heaven, to bridge it *materially*, not just spiritually as the Methueyn Knights did. The whole nation must have been involved. And all their dreams and efforts were wasted."

Even Endicott understood why Merrett was turning a dark shade of red. "That is a curiously detached way of looking at the morality of the consequences, Jeyn," he said.

"I don't know," Lindseth replied, looking genuinely sad. "Most of them also died for their efforts."

Bat Merrett ignored his comrade's mournful expression. "Well, maybe they shouldn't have helped Ardgour with his crazy schemes."

As if they could have refused to work.

Endicott did not bother saying this out loud. He knew Merrett understood it as well as he. Lindseth should have too. There would have been no choice in the matter.

Lindseth surveyed his two male companions, then turned to Engel, who had sat quietly, listening but giving no indication of her feelings, if any. "What do you think, Marielle? Do you really think the people would have had a choice at the time?" It always amazed Endicott how calmly Lindseth could argue. His voice betrayed not the least trace of defensiveness or aggression.

"We always have a choice," Engel replied.

"Come on, Marielle," Lindseth said, smiling easily. "Most of what most people do is done as a matter of course."

"You mean it is amoral," Endicott supplied.

"Right," Lindseth nodded. "How can people be held responsible for doing what they are told to do if they want to put food on the table?"

Engel neither smiled like Lindseth or frowned like Merrett. "Look at our people," she said.

"Huh?" grunted Merrett. "I want you to win this argument, Marielle, because I think Jeyn here has finally, fully, become a lunatic. But what?"

"I don't *want* to win," Engel replied. "Nor do I wish to sit in judgement of the past. I do not enjoy telling people what to do or what they should have done."

"But if we are to learn from the past," Lindseth said, "we must." He held out his arms, as if to take in the scene around them. "How many days have we spent walking through the ruins of the past? How many stones have we seen broken on the ground? How many dead are represented by each lifeless rock?" He nudged his jaw toward Engel. "I understand that Marielle, who likes to journey, prefers her travels to be inward. But she is a clear thinker. Please continue."

"I will," she said firmly. "Consider the protestors that were such a problem a few years back. Think about what they were doing. Set aside the fact that they were misinformed."

"And manipulated by Armadale and by Lord Glynnis, don't forget," Endicott added.

"Yes," Engel said, "for the moment, set both those factors aside. The act of protesting was—for them—an exercise of morality. That they failed to obtain the correct facts was a failing on their part, but they were attempting an act of responsibility. As far as they were concerned, they were speaking out against an unjust power."

Lindseth rubbed his chin. "So those people in Vercors deserved what they got because they protested, but Ardgour's people got what they deserved because they went along? Then I guess everyone gets what they deserve."

Engel smiled for the first time. "Instead of *deserve*, let's just agree that everyone has some degree of accountability."

No, that doesn't seem quite right.

Endicott did not voice this doubt immediately. He thought about some of the choices he had made and the circumstances in which he had made them. Then he spoke. "The argument is reductive. Sometimes people simply do not have a choice."

"Like you didn't?" Lindseth asked.

"No, not me. *People.* How can we make some poor miner in Ardgour's time responsible for what happened?"

Endicott sighed. The issue was too big. Nothing he said was going to capture all its nuances. But something made him keep talking. "The poor miner would be unlikely to know what the plan was for the ore they mined, let alone for the Huygens modulus and everything that followed. Finding out about those things, for someone in that position, might well have been impossible. In which case, the responsibility for the consequences would all be on the leader." Endicott grimaced. "It would be much the same for the soldiers too."

"Like the soldiers of Armadale that you killed at the embassy siege?" Engel asked, as if she had read Endicott's mind. "You think those soldiers had no choice? Yet you still feel regret over that."

"Yes," Endicott replied, feeling as if he had been punched in the stomach, wishing the conversation had not turned so suddenly in his direction, surprised the question had even been on Engel's mind. "Of course I do. I killed … A lot of people died there, Marielle." Endicott gazed at her perfect face, her dark green eyes, and felt nothing but sorrow. "I'm glad you have never had to kill anyone. You may find that things do not seem so simple afterward."

Without warning, Engel crouched down right in front of Endicott and placed one hand on his knee. The sudden move astonished him, and probably everyone else. "It had better seem just as simple, Robert, or I will have made a mistake." She tightened her hand on his knee. "If you had to do it all over, if the circumstances were the same, would you kill again?"

Eloise had asked him the same question after the Battle of the Bifrost. It was not a question Endicott had ever wanted to hear again. He did not rush into a response. That would only reveal to himself that he had learned nothing the first time, that he had made no progress.

But have *I made any progress? Would I do it all again, knowing I might never fully process my feelings, never get over it, never recover?*

Perhaps it was fitting that some things could not be recovered from. In any case, he did not wish to answer Engel's question. He did not wish to speak of the thing at all, yet she reminded him too much of Koria not to be answered. When he did speak, it was barely a whisper. "Yes."

"Then you acted righteously, Sir Robert." Her green eyes bored into him. "If you choose to take a life, you must accept your choice." She stood up. "This will continue to unbalance you until you learn … grace."

Chapter Fifteen

Of Heaven and Hell

"**Y**OU AND MY BIG BROTHER ARE GOING TO THE STEEL CASTLE TOGETHER!" SHELLEY blurted out, as loudly as she always did. And as always, her bellowing mortified Heylor. "Are you two getting married?" she yelled. All conversation in the Lords' Commons seemed to stop. All eyes seemed to stare at Heylor and Lynwen.

"No," Lynwen said in a low voice. "Not yet, anyway." Her eyes narrowed. "But let's go with that for now, Shelley." She winked at Heylor's grinning sister and announced in a louder voice, "Yes, we thought we would scout out the church to see if it would work for our wedding." With the loudest sound yet, she enthusiastically kissed the side of Heylor's hot, red face.

The relationship declaration had been signed, Heylor had declared his love, and both he and Lynwen were going to the cathedral. And everyone knew it. Heylor was surprised the saliva from Lynwen's wet, smacking kiss was not boiling off his heated face. Perhaps it was. He could barely hear a thing over the ringing in his ears. It was a nightmare. It was not that his love for Lynwen was false or had diminished. Quite the opposite. He was embarrassed because thieves and the guilty do not like everyone looking at them.

I wish something would happen, I don't care what, just to end this moment.

"Heylor Style." The silky, precise intonations of Camille Engel cut easily through the sound of overheated blood throbbing in Heylor's ears. Tall, graceful, darkly beautiful, Camille effortlessly stole all the attention from Heylor and Lynwen's fictitious nuptials simply by speaking. It hardly mattered what she said. At least that is what Heylor thought until she spoke again. "A man in a cloak followed me last night. I had to duck into the Apprentice's Library to rid myself of him."

A cloaked man.

Heylor's blood roared through his ears again.

"Was anyone with you?" Lynwen asked.

"Yes, Gyselle Eckels was there too. She saw him before he ran off."

Lynwen had her notebook out. "Did anyone else?"

"No one else was there."

"What time was this?" Heylor asked.

"About eight."

"Hati's hell! If we had a javelin in everyone's hands, we could coordinate in real time and catch him!" Heylor exclaimed, proving that Shelley was not the only Style who blurted out things best kept discreet. He did, however, instantly regret the lapse. It took all his self-awareness to keep from covering his mouth with both hands.

"What are you talking about?" Shelley did not, of course, ask the question discreetly. She roared it as loudly as his old friend Davyn would have.

Lighthouse insiders and a select few military planners knew what Javelin was, but information about the project had not been disseminated outside that small circle yet. The story would leak out, almost certainly had leaked out of Ardvaser already, but it had yet to hit the New School. Given that Gerveault had invented the device at a lab on campus and that an enormous early model was under guard and being monitored for secret messages from the duke in the basement of the mathematics and physics building, this was a considerable feat of information management, but that only made Heylor's blunder seem worse to him. "Uh, never mind," Heylor said lamely. "Forget it. I didn't say anything." All three women stared at him with narrowed eyes.

"What? I misspoke, that's all."

"You're such a liar!" Shelley said, standing up, big fists bunched.

"Yes, I am." Heylor put both hands up in surrender, lips pursed. A moment of silence went by in which the three women looked expectantly at him.

Lynwen was the first to realize that Heylor intended his silence to be permanent. She shook her head. "Wow. Nice apology. I may have to reconsider our engagement."

Already? He knew this moment would have come sooner or later, though he had hoped it would be later, much later. He rallied his courage, such as it was, and stood up.

"Hold off on that decision, dear." He detected a smile tugging at Lynwen's lips. "Let me take you somewhere that will change your mind." Then, turning to

Camille Engel and his sister, he added, "I do have an idea that might help catch the cloaked man."

"Oh, really?" Camille asked, her skepticism incongruously attractive.

"Really. Maybe."

"I think he's telling the truth," Shelley boomed. "He's not overselling it."

Heylor did not know where that bit of character assassination came from. "Look," he said to both Camille and Shelley, "for the time being, just don't go anywhere in groups smaller than three, okay? Pass that around. I don't think *every single person* on campus is eavesdropping on our conversation." He glanced around and confirmed that their group was still the center of attention. "This could take a couple of tries. Come on, constable, we have an overdue date with evil."

"It better really happen this time, or you're gonna have a date with my baton," Lynwen whispered, not unsweetly, into his ear as they left the table.

"A couple of tries?" Shelley yelled at his back as he and Lynwen crossed the Lords' Commons. "Don't you mean a couple of days?"

T

"The first thing you need to know is that the grain is not poisonous. To people. Mostly."

Lynwen stopped in the middle of a pathway by a corner of the math and physics building. "The baton is right here, Heylor Style. Make sense, prevaricator."

"No, no, no," Heylor said with a smile. He loved it when Lynwen threatened him. *She still loves me.* He also loved that her mean side seemed reserved for him alone. With everyone else she was a study in professionalism. "I didn't ... er, prevaricate. I didn't lie to *you*. I lied to *them*. To you it's just a truth deferred." He unleashed his goofiest expression, though he thought he was being debonair. "Besides, I *love* you. I wouldn't *permanently* lie to you."

"You lied to your own sister. You love *her*."

"Like a *sister*! I don't think of you like a sister at all."

"Should I feel relieved?"

"I love you ... differently."

"Differently how?"

"I love you like a ... *partner*."

Her gray eyes did not soften. Neither did her tone. "Partner?"

"Someone I never, ever want to be parted from."

Lynwen nodded, looking satisfied, at least for now. "Okay. Punishment also is deferred. For a period inversely proportional to the time it takes you to tell me what's going on in that strange mind of yours."

Heylor looked around. They were close to where they needed to be. He could hear the protestors though he couldn't yet see them. "Do you remember way back when people used to protest the new grain, calling it poison?"

"They still call it poison."

"Yes," Heylor's grin turned sickly. "I suppose some of them do. But back when it all started, the allegation really bothered Robert. He even asked Kennyth Brice to fund medical research to investigate possible long-term effects of the grain. And you know our duke. He'd do anything for Sir Robert. He treats him like he's his own brother. So a special department was created in the New School. One that combined medical research and dynamics."

"Combined them?"

"Sure," said Heylor. "What most people don't know, probably because most people who don't attend the New School will never in their whole life meet someone who can perform the least bit of dynamics, is how much a dynamicist can actually see. When people gossip about dynamics, they usually only focus on the techniques used to *change* things. Breed grain, throw fire and lightning. The dramatic stuff." He shivered, remembering Keith Euyn effortlessly throwing sheets of blue-white electrical fire across the throne room, immolating the guards before they knew what hit them.

"As remarkable as those things are, as horrific as they can sometimes be, they may not be the most useful things we can do." Heylor motioned Lynwen to walk with him, but he proceeded slowly between the buildings, trying to pinpoint the sounds of the protestors.

Lynwen could also hear the protestors somewhere ahead. It was visible in the way her eyes moved from suspicion of him to concern for what lay ahead. "And what are those most useful things, my deferred truth-teller?" she asked.

They rounded a corner. Not far ahead, the protestors marched in front of a multistory, tan-colored dolostone building. "A dynamicist can see into the nature of things. She can read the Book of Nature. Changing the book, yes that is spectacular, though risky. But being able to *understand*, to see what's what, what lies behind those changes, that's fundamentally a more important ability." Heylor stopped. "Marry that understanding with the methods of science and you can learn an awful lot."

"Why aren't we going to the medical building?" Lynwen pointed at the besieged edifice. "That's where the protestors seem to think that evil resides."

And indeed they did. Heylor spotted some new placards waving from the crowd of protestors. One of them, in bold red paint, stood out. It read:

"BETTER YOU WERE KILLED

BY NIMRHEAL

THAN TRANSGRESS

AGAINST NATURE."

Another, in black paint, was more direct:

"STOP

KILLING

OUR CHILDREN!"

A third sign capped off the trilogy. Evidently directed personally to the researchers inside, it read:

"WHO NEEDS

NIMRHEAL?

WE HAVE

YOU."

It's a good thing Robert isn't here to see this. Heylor could easily imagine the fury and intolerance that would boil up in his heroic friend. *It's no wonder he prefers the quiet of the wild.* Shaking his head, Heylor motioned Lynwen toward the iron-bound oak door in the nondescript brick building they had paused beside. He smiled. "We aren't going there because they are protesting at the wrong building."

Her mouth opened in an "O," which made him smile more broadly. "After the Battle of the Bifrost, we decentralized our research. We even change buildings from time to time." He used both arms to slowly swing open the door and, turning back to Lynwen, added, "This is an even bigger secret than the one I deferred telling you about in the Commons. Just follow my lead when we get in there. I'll explain everything later." He winked at her. "That's what *deferred* means."

They proceeded through the massive door and down a short corridor to another door, this one made of some dark metal, and new, with no scuffs or other markings on it. Two men in chain mail, armed with swords, stood by this barrier. Heylor produced his medallion, and the men pulled open the heavy door. Another door, this one made of narrowly spaced metal bars, now confronted them. Heylor could see through the spaces, but only just. Not even an expert archer would be able to put an arrow into anything on the other side.

There was no one outside this door and no sign of anyone lurking behind it, but Heylor brandished his medallion once again, said his name, and after a long delay the door opened as if by itself, revealing two guards inside, also armored heavily. Their hands were on the hilts of their swords. Looking back, Heylor saw that the first set of guards had closed and barred the outer set of doors, and with swords drawn, were inside now, guarding the exit.

"There's a book on the table there, sir," said the smaller of the two inner guards, a lady by her voice and the slight curve of her chest and legs. "Sign and print your name. The constable as well."

After they had signed in, another delay followed while the book was taken through yet another door by the female guard. This lasted several minutes, but the two guards behind did not relax, put their swords away, or make any move to unbar the door. The remaining guard in front kept his eyes fixed on Heylor and Lynwen.

"Okay, Heylor Style and guest from the constabulary. You may proceed," said the female guard as she returned with the book.

"I bet you think that there is just one more door left, and it leads to the outside," said Heylor with a smirk once the door closed behind them.

"You read my mind," replied Lynwen, eyes still big. "I was trying to calculate how much of the building was being used up just by doors and guards." An archway loomed ahead of them, but it had no words written on its curve.

Heylor proceeded through the arch into a large, lantern-lit workroom. The floor and walls were stone, and a series of stone basins filled with water were arrayed down the entire length of the room. In front of each basin sat a metal table with a collection of trays, bottles, notebooks, microscopes, and other instruments. Against one wall was a huge cabinet made of some dark metal. A thick glass door on the other side of the room was closed. *The door to the cold room.* Behind this, Heylor knew, was where the ice and samples were stored.

"Heylor? I can't believe it," Deleske said, though not in tones of true surprise. "What are you doing here?" He sounded more bored than curious, and what smile of welcome there was on his face had a sour glint to it. "Where's Style? Didn't they let you bring it in here?"

Heylor was not wearing any weapon at all. Every day he and Lynwen argued about this, and every day he managed to find a way to forget to bring a sword or even a cane with him. He knew it would have felt wrong to wear anything but the sword Robert had made him.

"I left it at home," he lied.

Or more accurately, lying on the ground in the wilderness where I dropped it as I ran away.

Deleske shrugged. "Swords are for idiots anyway."

To stop himself from throttling Deleske, Heylor looked around the room again. Two women were consulting at one of the nearer tables. Sitting between them was the Eindarch Eye, a cylindrical object about eighteen inches long. It resembled a telescope but was clamped to a device that held it nearly vertical. Heylor turned his attention from the Eye to the women. One of them was short, angular, and visibly well-muscled despite her long white coat. When she saw Heylor, her eyes shone with real enthusiasm, unlike Deleske's. "It really is you, Heylor," Lil Hilliard exclaimed, leaving her colleague and approaching the two visitors. "I hardly ever see you anymore." Lil was well into her thirties but retained the physical presence of a much younger woman.

We hardly ever saw each other before.

All the same, Heylor could never forget Lil. She had been at the Battle of the Bifrost and had almost been carried off by soldiers of Armadale, probably in an effort to learn what she knew about the New School's grain. "This is my partner, Constable Lynwen," Heylor said. The two women shook hands. Lynwen, taller than Lil by half a foot or more, made stern eye contact with Heylor over the other woman's head.

Right. His deferral of some of the information Lynwen needed—almost all of it—left her at a loss for something to say to Lil. He jumped in. "The constable and I were concerned about the protestors outside and thought we would come and speak with you for a moment." Heylor cleared his throat. "Is the protest affecting you at all?"

"They're skolve-damned irritating," grumbled Deleske. "As if they knew the first thing about what we do here."

"They are frightened," said Lil's colleague. She had remained standing by the table. Around Lil's age, but looking it, and about average height, she had dark hair and also wore a white coat. "I would like to speak with them."

Deleske's response dripped with sarcasm. "Well, *that* would be a good idea." He tilted his head toward Heylor. "Others have tried. Nothing good has come of it."

"You cannot reason with a mob," Lynwen said, surprising Heylor. "But you can speak with people as individuals. Consider time and place. Find a setting to engage positively with them, one on one or in a small group."

Huh.

The woman at the table smiled broadly at Lynwen and stepped away from her work. Coming up to them, she extended her hand to the tall constable. "I'm Ailis Ellis." After a round of introductions, she took up Lynwen's notion again. "We *could* try another presentation at the New School square, followed by a question and answer session this time."

"You should," said Lynwen. "Let them be a part of the process."

Lil Hilliard nodded. "I'm willing to try. This is *for* them, after all."

An air of optimism was rising from the three women. Heylor could practically see it, though he wondered how far Lynwen could truly share the feeling, given how little she knew of the work being done in the lab. Yet her eyes were just as wet and just as shiny as Lil's and Ailis's. When he felt their enthusiastic gazes turn to him, he hastily added, "That might work."

You might get murdered.

Their gazes swung to Deleske. "I'm busy that night." Deleske was generally impervious to others' enthusiasms and rarely felt any need to go along with anyone. Neither Lil nor Ailis seemed to care about his lack of faith. They just turned ever so slightly away from him.

"What would you lead with when you do make the presentation?" Lynwen asked.

Ailis put a hand on Lil's shoulder. "Thanks to dynamics and our new understanding of infectious disease, we have cured goose fever."

T

"Does that really work?" Lynwen asked, sitting on a bench in the math and physics square.

"Apparently," said Heylor. "Kill what kills you and put it into you."

"It just sounds … gross," Lynwen persisted. "What if it infects you?"

Heylor pursed his lips. "It's dead. It can't infect you. But your body reacts as if it could, so if you come into contact with the live disease later, it can fight it off."

"And how does the Rudolph Eye fit into it?"

"*Eindarch* Eye, constable." He scowled at her, knowing she was having fun with him. Heylor was glad for it. Lynwen had been shocked at the vaccination story. Even though the goose fever vaccine had been discussed in the posts and distributed to hospitals, it was still new, and the science behind it was revolutionary.

So new that a lot of people don't believe it. They think we're trying to kill their kids. They think we are evil.

"Right. Aardvark Eye. I saw you gesturing at the thing every time it got mentioned, but what is it?"

Heylor laughed. "I'm going to kiss you, Aardvark."

"No. We're deferring all that until your truth deferral is over."

"Hmm. Okay then. The *Eindarch* Eye helps a dynamicist to see through the empyreal sky with a very fine degree of control." Heylor looked off into the distance. "It's the same as with normal vision. Objects too far away or too small get blurred, right? But some people have sharper vision than others. It's the same with dynamics, except that we are perceiving a kind of energy with our minds."

"Energy?"

Not for the first time, Heylor wished that Koria or Robert were around to explain the technical details. *I should have paid better attention in class!* "Yes, it's a different kind of wave that you see with, but—"

"What are you talking about? I see with my eyes, Heylor, not with a *wave*," Lynwen said patronizingly.

"You see *waves* with your eyes, dear." Heylor held up a hand to forestall further objections. "Anyway, the Eindarch Eye allows a dynamicist to see smaller or farther objects than they normally could, and at a very small cost. With the Eye, even a mediocre talent like Deleske can easily observe objects at the scale Robert or Koria can without it. And with the Eye, Deleske can do it for hours without danger."

"So?"

"So," Heylor said, "the goose fever is caused by a tiny creature. An infinitesimal little monster. Now *I* can see it without the Eye. I can actually see much smaller things, but at great thermodynamic cost. I need to be at a forge or a hot bath or something like that to survive even a few minutes of looking so hard."

"A hot pool?" Lynwen said incredulously. "I've heard stories about what happened in your hot pools."

I wish. "With the Eye," Heylor continued, ignoring Lynwen's cynical expression, "I could observe the tiny fever monster for as long as I want without freezing. And with the Eye, I could see when I've killed it."

Lynwen stood up, suddenly serious again. "I understand. I do. Now. It's amazing. This Eye is a tool that has allowed Ailis Ellis, through the services of Lil Hilliard and Deleske Lachlan, to perform her experiments. It enabled her to develop the vaccine."

"Yes," Heylor said, also jumping to his feet. He was too excited to stay on his butt. "And more than that, it enabled Ailis to be sure the vaccine would work as theorized and not kill her patients before she injected it into anyone."

"How?"

Heylor grinned. "Why, *heraldry*, my dear Lynwen, heraldry. Which is why all the heralds working for the Rawles Trading Company, like my dad, want access to the Eye so badly. They know it will help them predict the grain futures more accurately. It will also help *us* catch the cloaked man."

Lynwen narrowed her eyes at him. "You may be enjoying this too much."

"No, I'm not. The Eindarch Eye makes heraldry much easier and safer. Ailis, using the Eye and the talents of her dynamicists, could predict the outcome of her experiments *before* they happened. Heraldry through the eye is a thousand times easier than without it. A thousand times more accurate."

"So we are going to be able to see the cloaked man even before he comes?"

Heylor shook his head. "I'm not Robert or Koria. Open-ended questions are still difficult. Only the far heralds attempt them, even with the Eye."

Lynwen's face contorted skeptically. "I thought dynamics was a science. If the Eye is as powerful as you say, why can't you far-herald with it? A *thousand* times better, you said."

Heylor laughed, searching furiously for the right words to answer her. He knew what he wanted to say, but the concept was difficult to verbalize.

"Dynamics *is* a science," he said at last. "At least it follows the methodology of science to test its theories. It's a subjective experience, but it looks for *objective* truth." His smile faded. "But it's also a lie in a sense. It has not been able to answer any of the really deep, fundamental questions. Dynamics is this structure—like my cloak—that we put around this talent—wizardry—that we don't understand. It's dangerous, but the cloak makes it safer and makes it look like something we can understand. Many, many things about dynamics are … effective … but even so, some things are not reproducible from one dynamicist to another. Heraldry is the easiest and most common skill we have, but to follow a single line of reality far into the future, like Koria Valcourt does, I just cannot do."

He remembered Keith Euyn, driven mad by heraldic dreams and old age, and shivered. *I don't dare to even try.* "I only see probabilities, and even then they have to be right in front of me. I cannot … search reality for unknown people or events. Not for one second. No magnification through the Eye can improve what, without it, I can't do at all."

"So what are we going to do about the cloaked man, then?"

"You really should have been a dynamicist," Heylor said. "You're smarter than me." Lynwen raised her eyebrows again. "No, really, I could never sit through a whole lecture," he hastily added.

"That I believe."

"I always tell you the truth, constable. Eventually. So what I am going to do is called heralding retrograde. Looking into the past is something I *can* do. As soon as we hear about the next solid sighting of the cloaked man, we are going to go to where he was and use the Eye to see what happened."

"And where he went afterward."

"Yes."

Lynwen slowly turned a circle, clearly trying to process what she had just learned. "You still have to tell me about that … thingamajig you mentioned in the Commons, the jumble thing?"

"Javelin. I'll tell you right now," Heylor replied with a shrug. "Deferral over. Kissing about to begin."

"We're still on duty."

"Just one?"

Lynwen seemed to reflect for a moment, then pulled him close and whispered, "Just one." She leaned in, her lips slowly approaching his, then suddenly stopped. "So they're just going to loan you the Eye?"

Heylor pulled her to him and kissed her deeply. When the long seconds had passed, he leaned back just far enough to see all of her face. "Hervor's horn, no. The Eye is loaned out to no one. Ever. We're stealing it!"

As her mouth opened in shock, he kissed her again.

T

"We aren't going to steal the Methueyn Treaty next, are we?" Lynwen asked.

Heylor looked sideways at her. She had chosen a pretty blue dress for this mission rather than her constable's uniform. He liked looking at her in it. She had very long legs, and the play of the silky fabric over her bare skin mesmerized him.

"Heylor."

"Huh. No," he said making a heroic effort to look away from Lynwen's legs. "It's too big to steal. Where would I put it? And besides, Sir Hemdale had it taken to Ardvaser Castle a week ago."

"Hold on a second, dear," Lynwen said. She stepped up to the young man and straightened the gold cloak around his neck, running her long fingers over his shoulders for just long enough to capture his absolute attention. "You know I am an officer of the law, don't you?" she asked quietly.

"This isn't going to be theft. Not really," Heylor said, thrilling at her touch and enjoying the attention even if he was not certain how much was play and how much was serious. "It's going to be a deferred return."

Lynwen raised her right eyebrow and started walking again.

"Also, two days ago I sent a letter north to Kennyth Brice requesting his permission to borrow it," Heylor added. "Hopefully, we will hear back from him with a yes before the cloaked man reappears."

"Good," she said crisply. "Perhaps you really have changed, Heylor Style. Your recklessness is becoming almost responsible. Are you ready to get married?"

"Yes." Heylor felt such an overwhelming jumble of emotions that he just wanted to burrow into her. But they were too close to the Steel Castle for any physical display of his powerful, transcendental feelings for Lynwen. The Vercors Steel

Castle was one of the grandest in the empire, possibly the world. Not that Heylor had seen very much of the world, but that is what he had heard.

Built of polished limestone, it was an eight-sided, eight-apse fortress with an entryway shaped like the hilt of a sword and a high, soaring dome in the exact center of the edifice. Throngs of people surged through the doors. As Heylor and Lynwen approached, the crowd felt like a tide pulling them in.

He reached for her hand as they edged into the press of people. It had been years since Heylor had entered a church. Robert's aversion to the Steel Castle had perhaps influenced him, but Heylor thought it just as likely that the unwavering focus on logic and science of the Duchess's Program was mainly responsible. Though none of the professors had ever spoken against the Steel Castle, they had also made it clear that the beliefs of the church had nothing to do with the work of the classroom. Bethyn had summed it up best. He could almost hear her cynical voice again. *"Dynamics uses science to put structures we can understand around what we don't. The Steel Castle uses faith to put confidence we can't doubt around what we should."*

Heylor had liked Bethyn, but he *loved* Lynwen. His tall constable had revealed an unexpected combination of qualities, not the least surprising having been the discovery that her public professionalism and reserve hid a secret acuity and a wicked sense of humor. There was something else, too, and it had nothing to do with her gorgeous legs or strong, trim figure.

She believes in something.

As they got to within a few paces of the church doors, Heylor resolved that he would find out some day what it was Lynwen had faith in. The last things his eyes caught sight of before they entered the church were the aspirational sigils of the Methueyn Knights. Darday'l's scroll on maul caught his eye first. She was the patron angel of the New School, and her scroll displayed a fitting motto. It read,

"Curiosity before frustration,

Debate before proclamation,

Questions before judgement."

Heylor almost choked on the irony. He was not expecting any sort of conversation or call for questions inside a church. *Well, I am curious about several things. Let's see what we discover.*

"Heylor!" The familiar voice startled him. He looked around for its source and saw Shelley with his mom, dad, and grandmother in a pew near the front, waving theatrically to him. Well, not his grandma. She was basically blind, but Shelley was waving enough to make up for her. But they were only miming their greeting. The voice had originated elsewhere.

"Stupe!" came the harsh voice once more, apparently unembarrassed to use such a profane word in such a sacred place. Heylor whirled, barely keeping hold of Lynwen's hand, and saw Eloise and Gregory in formal dress a few rows behind his family. He would have seen Eloise sooner, but he had not been looking high enough. Her incredible size always surprised him when he had been away from her for any length of time. Gregory stood at the open end of the row and Heylor could see a shiny metal contraption covering each of his legs. It looked like it was made of the same dynamic alloy that Robert forged.

Heylor pointed to his family but drew closer to Eloise and Gregory, pulling a startled Lynwen after him. "We'll talk with you afterward," he stage-whispered.

Gregory smiled warmly. "You look better," he said, putting a hand toward his throat in pantomime of the terrible bruises Heylor had sported when he had materialized in Ardvaser.

"Not half as dead as before," Eloise added, not bothering to whisper. Her voice echoed off the high ceiling.

"One day you are going to tell me what really happened out past the wheat line, aren't you, dear?" Lynwen whispered into his ear as they maneuvered their way to the seats Shelley had saved for them.

Thinking about confessing the horrific incident to Lynwen instantly damped the joy of seeing Gregory and Eloise again. "Definitely," he said, trying to hide the shame he felt. "Certainly. Before we get married, I promise." *Because you might not want to be married to me after you hear the truth.*

Shelley for once was dressed in clean, well-pressed clothes. His mom, dad, and grandma had all made a special effort too, though with typically mixed results. For all they knew, he and Lynwen really were planning an imminent marriage ceremony, not just using their developing relationship as an excuse to investigate the Steel Castle, and they seemed to be trying not to scare the young constable off. The young man had feared that their crude manners, compulsive hoarding, and collection of random unpleasant cats might end his relationship with Lynwen, but the honest part of him knew it was his own character flaws that he needed to worry about. Heylor kept a tight grip on

Lynwen's hand. He knew the truth might cause her to leave him, but he was not going to let go easily.

Grandma, wearing a dark shawl, took Lynwen's other hand as they squeezed into the pew. Almost simultaneously, the Bishop of Vercors entered the church and walked once around the perimeter of the vast room, pausing at each of the eight great apses to pay respect to the Methueyn Knight depicted at each of them. Heydron was shown shielding children against either Skoll or Hati, Heylor could not be sure which from where he was sitting, craning his neck to see. Michael and Volsang were attacking Nimrheal in their separate apses. The angels always seemed to act alone. Heylor was curious to see how Darday'l would be depicted. Curiosity was a difficult concept to illustrate with an image, but he could not see past the people to make out what the church had that particular knight doing. At last, the priest completed her solitary circular procession and ascended the great floating bridge in the center of the cathedral. The bridge hung high above the crowd, and even further above that rose the great central tower, its many-windowed dome casting an ethereal light on the silhouetted figure of the bishop. The bishop stood there for a long time, silently gazing up at the light of the dome. Finally, she gazed down upon the congregation. "Hear the words of Elysium," she intoned, her voice reverberating in the dome.

"We hear the words of heaven," two thousand and more voices chanted back to her.

"For these are the words of the angels," the bishop said in her rich, echoing voice.

"Tell us the truth, oh speaker for God," the congregation replied in a ragged singsong.

On and on it went. Parts of it were sung beautifully. Parts of it were poetic and uplifting. Some of it was even haunting. But despite the grandeur and solemnity, Heylor was quickly bored and fidgety. It was all memorized, all canned, as unchanging as the School of Statics. The audience participated with apparent devotion, but their role could have been squawked out by a goose for all that it mattered. What they said was always the same, and of course needed to be always the same. The Steel Castle claimed to speak for the Methueyn Knights, but for two hundred and fifty years there had been no knights to dispute what the priests repeated. *No new Methueyn Knights, no new messages.*

Heylor tried not to twitch, but the struggle grew increasingly arduous. *I wonder if there ever were new messages.* Perhaps the words from on high had never changed. To distract himself from the urge to jump up and run out of the building, he forced his mind back to things he really was curious about. He looked around the cathedral, studying the iconography. Each of the eight apses was filled with representations of its titular knight, but the rest of the cathedral was also steeped in symbolism. Most impressive were the huge, high, stained-glass windows between the apses that showed the Three Vias of the Methueyn Knights.

The first Via, the first of the bridges to heaven, was the sacrament known as Build. In this window, a child was depicted rising into adulthood in a series of transformations. Heylor had no idea what the sequence really meant, but he knew that the first Via had nothing to do with *physical* maturity. The second Via held his attention longer. The Middle Bridge involved an ordeal. Being hanged but not dying. This was the Ceremony of Rising. In this great sunlit window, a woman was shown hanging by her neck, the thick rope thrown over the branch of a great tree and attached on the other side by the gargantuan sword of the Methueyn Treaty. A solemn group of women and men watched the proceedings. *Creepy.* Heylor could not help thinking they really should help her out, maybe try to lift up her legs, but at the same time he understood that the point of the exercise was for the hanged woman to prove heavier than the massive sword. *If the Treaty is not available, perhaps a large table will do. Or an iron meat trolley.*

He gestured toward the window of the Middle Bridge and whispered softly to Lynwen, "Is that not what we just saw? Twice."

"Yes," she whispered back. "Although in our version they weren't smiling beatifically. Keep looking."

The third Via, the Crossing, was all about the Methueyn Bridge, which was depicted as a large diamond-shaped stone in one part of the third great window but was also shown later as a physical bridge that the knight walked upon to heaven. It looked much like the hanging bridge the priest stood upon. With a start, Heylor remembered the words Keith Euyn had coughed out as he lay dying. They had been about the Bridge and how it hung in the air: "I saw. The furthest herald sees a different war."

The great man had coughed bloody droplets directly into Heylor's face then, making him flinch and blink his eyes. The coughing went on and on. The young man had thought the Lonely Wizard was done, that he would cough until he choked on his own blood.

I punctured his lung.

But he had more to say. It came out wetly, slurred imprecisely in a way the great man would never have tolerated in his classroom: "I saw the Bridge, only it is not a bridge. It hangs in the air. It is a circle in the sky, floating on the mountain. Skolves gather on the margins, worshipping. Skoll and Hati come. Vercors City burns. The New School burns."

He had said more after that, but it had made even less sense. Perhaps if the great man had lived longer, he could have connected his ravings into something more coherent. But perhaps if he had lived longer, he would have killed them all.

Could Keith Euyn really have found it? Heylor had not taken the dying man's words literally. The old lunatic had been insane. He had killed dozens of guards. He had killed the duke and duchess. He had killed Davyn Daly, and for *that* Heylor had made sure the great man's final words went unrecorded.

Only a few yards from the priest and her pulpit at the edge of the bridge hung the end of an actual rope. Heylor had missed it the first few times he had looked. He had been focused on the priest, on the bridge, the light, the height of the dome above, and had missed the noose. Looking hard now, he could see that the other side of the rope hung down only a few feet from the first side. *What is it attached to?* Whatever it hung from was not visible from Heylor's angle. *Some crossbeam hidden in the dome?* The end of the rope closest to the ground was tied to a six-foot replica of the Methueyn Treaty that Heylor had not noticed earlier in the press of humanity and distraction of friends and family. The noose ended at bridge level, where it was attached to a much smaller rope that would have been difficult for any of the congregation to see.

Lynwen nudged his arm and gestured with her jaw toward the rope. Heylor wondered if she was thinking the same thing he was.

Why not just hang yourself here? At least you would die closer to Elysium.

Chapter Sixteen

Inventive Breakthrough Part 2

Five days into the great experiment and no one had been killed. Yet. The sky had not broken open, split by lightning or torn by hell. There had been no loss, no blood, no mourning. But there had also been no inspiration, no breakthrough. Nothing new had been learned.

Just as I planned it.

Every day the guards became more bored and Rodryck Cornell more frustrated. I had with some satisfaction watched the great mathematician leave many times to go to the privy and come back so very much later and not so much relieved. If Eydith was bothered by his lack of focus or success, she did not show it. That lady appeared to be completely imperturbable. She kept her thoughts and feelings under tight control, but I suspected her of a secret intelligence that went beyond riding herd on a grumpy, pretentious, discomfited would-be inventor. I would need to keep an eye on her.

Gil Harbinger was also imperturbable, but for different reasons. He just chuckled and told the soldiers to "Keep on alert, you never know." To me he said, "Things like this have been tried before and have never worked, Luciena." This, I knew, was not precisely true, but it was close enough for him. He did not care anyway, provided nothing happened, and he seemed sure that would continue to be the case. Certainly nothing was going to change because he had taken the initiative or done anything unexpected. Unlike Eydith, Harbinger was lazy, content with the world as it was.

Lord and Lady Auvigne were too poised to betray their concern, but I knew them well. They were hoping that a little more time would allow Cornell to find his moment of genius and were loath to add to the pressure he must surely be under. They were the careful, loving parents, hoping their children could pull something off, wise enough to leave them alone to try, brave enough to allow them to fail. Sometimes they watched me, worried. Their constant love might have been irritating if not for the other set of eyes that bore into me.

For five days I endured the direct, transcendent gaze of the Methueyn Knight Darday'l. In physical presence, she is not remarkable. Her hair, a plain brown, is done up in two long braids, and her complexion is a common tan color. She is not tall either. She does not look like a hero from the stories. The long, heavy-headed hammer she carries is as tall as she is. No one who could not raise the Methueyn Treaty while hanging by the neck could carry such a thing without being overbalanced, but she lifts it with ease. The incongruity of her monstrous weapon is not what makes the hairs on my neck tingle every time I see her. Darday'l's eyes—angels in heaven!—her eyes ... they pierce. Her regard is a fathomless sea, a window to an infinite and unknowable depth.

She must know what I did to Cornell. But why hasn't she said something?

Those eyes are electric. They made me feel guilt; they excited me. They reached in and saw everything. Everywhere I went, her eyes followed me. Whatever she saw must have interested her, for she stared at me more and more as the days passed. More than anything, more than some animal magnetism, more powerful than the pull of gravity, Darday'l's gaze attracted me. It sent thrills of curiosity through me.

She sees me. Why hasn't she judged me?

The door opened before my hand struck the wood. She stood there in a long, white shift, smiling in flickering candlelight.

"I had hoped you would come sooner." She smiled fearlessly as she said this, showing me all her teeth. Then, without another word, she turned and walked slowly away from the door toward the couch where, I presumed, she had been lounging. I stayed where I was and watched the play of fabric over her curves. With my empyreal sight, clothing held no mystery to me, but I did not use it, for fear of spoiling the anticipation. The play of shadow and light across her thin shift, half revealing some of the delights beneath and leaving others to my imagination, was too enticing to be ruined by my peculiar talent. I did not stop looking or close the door until she turned again and picked up the book that she had left on one of the soft cushions.

"I should have," I said, meaning it. *I should have.* Watching her walk away in the soft candlelight had been worth the trip to her tower by itself. The sight reached out toward a bottomless curiosity.

"How did you know?" I asked.

"That you wanted to speak with me?" She lay back against the cushions but curled her legs to leave room for me to sit near her feet. I did so, smoothing my dress, and trying to sit still despite the excitement I felt at being alone with her. "Perhaps for the same reason that I want to speak with you." She arched her back as she turned slightly against the arm of the couch to face me better. "I want to *know* you, Lucy."

She lifted her legs and draped them over my thighs. Her left calf lay below the hem line of my dress. It felt deliciously smooth. It was cool, but from it an urgent, powerful, visceral heat spread upwards below my dress. I shivered. My heartbeat sounded in my ears. "But you're a Methueyn Knight, joined with a god. You know everything."

Darday'l laughed easily at this. "Not a god, Luciena, and I don't know everything, though I wish I did. It is my curiosity, in fact, that makes it possible to merge with the ... angel."

She did not feel like a god. She felt and looked like a beautiful, flesh-and-blood woman in a flimsy nightgown. I slipped reflexively into the empyreal sky and saw how she glowed in empyreal space, how she was connected to the elsewhere of Elysium. Looking into her eyes, I shivered again, excited, more than a little scared. There was a unique fascination in seeing this beautiful creature both as an alluring woman in yellow candlelight and, through the luminescence of her connection to heaven, as something far greater. I could not parse what attracted me more at that moment. I wanted to know the secrets of both the woman and the angel, and to know them separately and together.

Still, what she said did not seem right. "I thought—no, I am sure, the Steel Castle has said—that you know everything, that your words are the words of heaven."

"You know better than that, Lucy," she said in a relaxed, familiar tone. "The Steel Castle simplifies something they don't understand into words that they do. They build a structure of language and ceremony around a phenomenon that is beyond their ability to comprehend."

I had worked with physicists and had attempted to apply mathematical models to real things. Other wizards laughed about this, calling it a dead end, but I knew the effort was worthwhile. My interest in such things was one of the reasons the Auvignes had so strongly supported Rodryck Cornell's project. They thought it would please me. And so it would, if they had only agreed to leave the castle while the experiment was being conducted. If Nimrheal came, they would die because they loved me and wanted to indulge me. Never mind that somewhere along the line they had fallen in love with the idea of a better world too. When my dream became theirs, it had transformed into a nightmare.

One thing all that—at the time—unpopular work taught me was that, in the wrong mouths, simplification was another word for deception. Most of the time, the simplifications a physicist made were necessary steps, temporary ones along the road to a verifiable, more complex truth. When priests or politicians simplified, experience had taught me they did it to manipulate. "They're liars!" I exclaimed, not caring that, in this, I also oversimplified.

Darday'l curled up and forward to reach me. The motion pulled the fabric of her shift higher on her thighs, but what made me gasp was the kiss she breathed out onto my neck. My whole body seemed to vibrate, and I found myself leaning sideways into her. "You are so beautifully honest in your passions, Lucy." She let go and lay back against the arm of the couch. I almost went with her. I had, incongruously, first stiffened and then, an instant later, nearly melted at the brief contact.

"From time to time, one of us must act to straighten out the priests and right the Castle. When they go too far." She shrugged, "Mostly they try their best and we leave them to it."

I wanted her lips on my neck again, the rest of her closer, within my grasp. But I also had questions. I had never spoken to a Methueyn Knight before, never been really near one. I might never have this opportunity again in all my life. I wanted to touch her, but first I needed to know.

Eyes fastened on hers, I asked, "What *is* the truth then?"

"About what, Lucy? About you? About us? About what you did to Rodryck Cornell?" Her eyes seemed more amused than judgmental.

I should have been afraid. Methueyn Knights, when they act, tend to act decisively. She could strike me down in an instant. "Can we come back to that later?" I asked.

"Yes." Her legs once again rested overtop of mine.

"Thank you," I said, meaning the words in two ways. "If you are connected to an angel in Elysium, why don't you know everything? Don't you know what your angel knows?"

"I do not. My angel, right now, does not know what she normally knows."

"I don't understand."

Darday'l smiled impishly. I never thought a Methueyn Knight would have such a naughty expression in her arsenal. "Nor do I. Imagine an indefinably vast being that has forced itself into an infinitesimally tiny space. Imagine a ball trying to fit into a line or a point. Darday'l in Elysium is an infinite being, an infinite *idea*, I believe. That idea—the love of knowledge, the curiosity to find it—is the only thing of Darday'l that has anything in common with human beings, or with me in particular. *I* am also curious." Her smile faded away. "In crossing the Bridge and marrying me, Darday'l has limited itself, made itself finite. The angel does not speak; it is only an idea in my mind, and the power to pursue that idea."

"It doesn't speak at all?"

"Only twice," she sighed. "The second time was when I thought I would die in battle, when the end seemed inevitable even with the angel inside me."

"And the first?"

"The first time was a bigger surprise. I had never experienced the *idea* of my name. It was a word, but it wasn't. It was also a picture of me, a feeling, a concept of my inner being." She seemed to look off into memory. "I heard my name for the first time just before I crossed the Bridge."

"That is beautiful," I said, meaning it. I ran my hand along her calf and up onto her thigh. "What does Darday'l think of sex?"

She laughed heartily. "Who knows? Darday'l is ever curious, but I doubt it knows what sex is."

"Or gender?" I had only been with men before; well, *a* man, and young like me.

"Hmm," Darday'l said. "An infinite being ... I am sure it does not care about gender or age." Her own eyes looked infinite as they swept over my body. "But it does enjoy discovery."

Me too. I needed to know things. I needed to experience them. The only way to get there would be to deal with what I had done. Without further hesitation, I jumped into it. "Rodryck had a hard, mineral formation, a very small one, in one of his kidneys."

"I have heard of such a thing," Darday'l said.

"I mobilized it." She said nothing, so I said more. "It is small enough for him to pass, but it makes him think he needs to urinate all the time. It also makes it difficult for him to urinate. In a few days, it will be gone from his body, but he will be gone from this castle too."

All she said was, "Wicked," with a glint in her eyes.

That's it? That's all?

"Why aren't you punishing me for what I did to Cornell?"

Darday'l sat up again, close to me, bringing one arm over my shoulder and revealing a tantalizing glimpse of the inside of her thighs and a flash of white knickers. "Or tell on you?" she said, her lips not far from my ears. "Lucy, you only changed the timing of things. If Rodryck had a stone in his kidney, it's better if it moves sooner than later." She smiled. "You may have saved his life. For now. Those stones can be dangerous if they grow too large."

She eased away from me, her face more serious. "You only hurt yourself, Lucy, when you fight who you are. If Rodryck is going to solve his transformational equation, he will do it sooner or later. Please don't do anything to stop him again. I'm here, and my whole purpose is to learn or to help make learning possible. *I will protect your Lord and Lady, if I can.*"

"What about you?" I asked.

"Me?" She smiled in a way she had never done so far. Sadly. "Few Methueyn Knights live long in opposition to Nimrheal. Heydron and I fight the demon more often than all the other knights combined. At most I have only a few years."

"I don't want you to die." It sounded childish in my ears, but I did not care. I wanted her to live and never leave.

"We are both doomed, Lucy," she said. I must have looked aghast, but she only pursed her lips. "Do you know what attracts me to you, what pulls my attention inexorably toward you, what captures my mind every time you are nearby? Do you know why I *want* you?"

She had barely finished speaking before I got up on my knees on the couch and ran my hands over her shift, ending at her hips. I gently pulled those curves forward and then slid in between and along her legs, pushing my hips and chest into hers. My lips met Darday'l's. I lost connection to time and thought.

After some time, a long time but not nearly long enough, she pushed me back. "You should know," she breathed. "You are different, Lucy. Everyone sees it. Everyone is attracted to you. Me most of all."

"Why?" My voice was small, like a child's again. I looked away.

"Because you shine with potential, Luciena. With love and wit, and sometimes with selfish scheming. At every moment your mind gives off a creative impulse. You are *dynamic* and beautiful. You will make new discoveries. You cannot help it. That is what you are. That is why you must not stop Rodryck. It goes against your being." Her hand glided over my breast. "You are a shining star. Your incessant curiosity pulls me— and my angel—into your orbit. But eventually, you too will summon Nimrheal."

When that happens, I will die.

I had never truly considered my own mortality before.

I looked once more at Darday'l. She glowed, monochromatic with her single idea. She was a god, crackling with potential, plumbed into heaven, bottomless, immeasurable. I could *see* her in the empyreal sky. She was a unique singularity, but as much as she was tied into elsewhere, another part of her was rooted in humanity. Her idea was divine, but she was a woman, and I appreciated her womanliness in a way that only the finite tasting the infinite could. I could see all that with my eyes and with my talent. I could understand ... some of what she was with my mind. But I needed to feel her with my body. I needed to do more than kiss her, as intoxicating as that had been. My blood sang with the need to touch her, to know her, and to feel all of what she was. I was a wizard. I was used to acting and moving on instinct, allowing powers I could never speak of, let alone understand, work through me and be worked by me in turn.

I had best live fully. If my life was destined to end so abruptly, I wanted it to also be sweet. I would *know* Darday'l.

I glided over her, not knowing precisely what to do but happy to try new hypotheses, enjoying the question and answer of new sensations. Her skin was impossibly soft and smooth and at the same time hard and taut. She was both cold, everlasting perfection and lively, exigent heat. When I kissed her, I felt what I had never felt before, tasted what I had never tasted, breathed air and swam in water with an electric potential I could never have imagined to exist. I tasted her infinite beauty, appreciating her in a way only someone with my flaws could. For the first time, I experienced transcendent love and understood its transcendence, gasped and flailed in its tidal power, its visceral urgency, arching into it with all of my being.

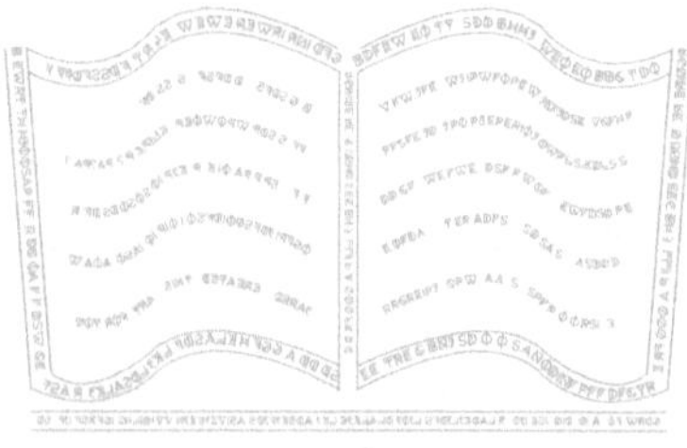

Chapter Seventeen.

Locus

THERE IS ONLY ONE WORLD INTO WHICH THE SUCCESSFUL WIZARD REACHES WHEN SHE BREAKS *through the barriers of this one. Heaven and hell, and all the worlds visited or stolen from, are the same. Thieves and visitors alike return with gifts and stories according to their nature and their narrative.*

—Esthauer, moments before she was killed by Nimrheal.

KORIA CLOSED THE OLD TEXT AND SLID IT TO THE FAR SIDE OF THE TABLE. MANY PEOPLE had espoused cosmological theories, many of which were quite different. A few of those theoreticians had been killed by Nimrheal, but some of the murdered scientists had disagreed vehemently with each other.

You don't have to be right to be murdered by Nimrheal. You only have to be sufficiently creative.

It was a chilling thought. When Nimrheal killed an artist or a poet, their work was assumed to have been original and innovative. When Nimrheal murdered a scientist, their theories were assumed to true. But that was not the case. It did not pass inspection. The more Koria studied, the less she felt she knew about Nimrheal's motives, and the more she was convinced that those who said they knew were either liars or fools. Nimrheal was not summoned by truth. No one knew if the demon understood or cared what was true and what was a lie, or even if those terms held any meaning at all for the vengeful creature. No, Nimrheal came because of something else. Keith Euyn had called it the euphonic wave of creation.

"Esthauer is interesting, but she doesn't go anywhere," said Bethyn from the big chair where she sat. "No evidence. No hypothesis to test." She shrugged. "No solution for us."

Koria's eyes scanned the pile of books in front of her. Bethyn was spending most of her time working on the calibration data now, which left Koria with the bulk of the historical research. "I might try Verinath next."

Bethyn scowled. "Oh joy." She made a note in the ledger she was working on, seemed to think better of it, and then closed the book entirely. "It would be better if the texts were at least fun," she complained. "This is like second year at the New School. Nothing much seemed to happen after all the excitement of the first. It almost drove me to drink."

No almost about it. As far as Koria had seen, Bethyn found most conditions conducive to drinking.

"I cannot claim to have found a solution to our big problem," said Koria, "but I may have come across something to relieve the boredom." She reached over to a stack of books on her left and retrieved a thin leather volume. "I almost had to resort to Heylor Style's services to get this particular book. It's very rare. I think the Steel Castle would rather it was lost altogether."

Bethyn's expression shifted between skeptical and curious. "What's it called?"

"It doesn't have a title," Koria replied with the barest hint of a smile. "It's a journal. Take it for now, but I'll need it back later. I need to reread the last two sections. I was too upset on the first read-through to analyze them objectively."

Bethyn's eyes blazed. She slapped her hand down on the table in her best theatrical manner. "I don't want to be upset, woman!"

"Trust me," Koria said, "you'll find the second act worth your while." She slid the book toward Bethyn. "You should … consider having Ethelyn come read it with you." Her smile turned impish. "Some of it is quite stimulating."

Where is Robert when I need him?

Bethyn took the book in both her hands, and narrowing her eyes, said, "So you don't mind if it comes back soggy?"

Koria sometimes imagined she was worldly, but this question almost made her choke, and then she did blush. Bethyn laughed and placed the book carefully on top of her take-home pile.

"What did I miss, ladies?"

They both jumped. Neither had heard Gerveault open the door to the private library. Koria blushed even more deeply, and Bethyn's wicked smile broadened. "Nothing you can help us with, professor," she said, exaggerating her impish expression.

The old man was clearly suspicious, but he let it go. "We need to talk about the locus."

Щ

HEYLOR AND A TALL, FIT WOMAN STAND UNDER THE SWINGING BODY OF A MAN IN EXPENSIVE robes. The dead body turns slowly, A rope hangs from its twisted neck.

Is that the young constable from first year? She showed up at the murder of Konrad and Rendell and the Battle of the Bifrost as well as for Keith Euyn's manic slaughter at the Citadel on the worst day of all. Strange that she always seemed to be there, staring at Heylor.

The unfolding scene is lost in a painful flash of white. It is a jarring disruption, and an unusual one for Koria, whose mastery of heraldic dreams has taken the emotional and physical sting from most of them. Most of the time.

Gregory stands tall, holding his entropic sword and shield, his mouth open in horror.

Another flash of painful, jarring white light.

What is happening?

Koria struggles for calm, for control, but fails.

A spear emerges from Gregory's face. Blood and teeth litter the ground behind him.

Knights, no!

It is a pain beyond words. If Koria had been stabbed in her own face, it might have hurt less. She struggles to exert control over the dream, to see what came before, but the white light flashes again, and she loses the fate of her friend to a tide she can neither see nor control.

A little girl stands beside her mother. She clutches a sign in her tiny hands. It says:

"I WOULD RATHER DIE

OF THE GOOSE FEVER

THAN BE POISONED

BY THE DUKE'S WIZARDS."

Seeing the little girl makes Koria feel sick in a different way than seeing Gregory did, more hopeless than visceral. The light flashes with the gentleness of epilepsy.

Heylor rushes across a busy road. A bearded man waits in the shadows of an alley. A cudgel rests on his shoulder.

Heylor!

Try as she might, Koria cannot shout into the infinite worlds of probability or send a message through uncharted time to warn her friend of the ambush. The light makes Koria shudder painfully. The spasm reminds her of what it felt like to lose her baby.

A line of plate-armored knights face the more lightly armored soldiers of Vercors in a field.

Where?

Like the twitch of electricity circling the edge of sleep, Koria loses her grip on the image.

Eloise weeps as she sticks her head into a noose and jumps from a stony ledge.

El!

The flash of light is jarring, unexpected, uncontrollable. Despite being blindingly white, it feels like being pushed backwards down a set of stairs in the dark.

Hemdale fights an enormous man in a desolate ruin. His adversary stands at least a foot taller than him. The stone floor cracks under the giant's feet.

Koria fights the dream, struggles to wake up, but only manages to thrash toward a new and more terrifying image.

Robert stands beside a wooden bridge while a meteor streaks down across the sky toward him. It approaches at an impossible speed, disturbing the air with fire and heat. Then its contents become visible for a moment. It is not a heavenly rock but an enormous, cloaked figure holding a gleaming, black spear. It dives toward her love with a deafening roar.

Robert!

Щ

"My dreams were just as disjointed," Gerveault said, grimacing. "And just as upsetting." His hand reached for Koria's shoulder. "But everyone's are unique."

Koria's eyes stung as if knuckles were being pressed into them. "It's been years since I've had so little control." She took a deep breath and exhaled slowly, attempting to release tension. "I don't think my heraldic dreams have ever been so out of control. They've never jumped around like this."

The old man's hand never quite made it to Koria's shoulder. It hung in the air for a moment, then fell diffidently away. "Do you at least see the same things every time?"

"No. Not at all." In Koria's experience, it was unusual for dreams of such apparent urgency not to repeat. "It is as if all probability is perturbed."

Bethyn scowled. "It's a locus," she pronounced sagely. Gerveault stared at her. All she could know about loci was what he had told her and the others in class.

A locus was a point of extreme instability in probability. That is what the old man had told them. The lecture had touched on the various different, yet outcome-equivalent interpretations of the phenomenon before closing with what must have seemed to most of those in the class like hyperbole. "History changes on the cusp of the locus," Gerveault had pronounced, finger raised to the ceiling of the Lott.

"Yes, it must be a locus," Koria said, evidently remembering that moment. "History may dance around its probabilistic whaleback, but can't we find a way to balance on its cusp?" she added, thinking aloud. "What if we tried to … walk into it? Have you ever attempted a heraldic trance? Perhaps that would constrain the results."

"I tried that yesterday," Gerveault said, pinching his nose. "The headache has still not entirely abated."

"Have a drink," Bethyn chirped with a smirk. "That works for me in those situations." To Gerveault's answering scowl, she whispered, "You're welcome."

The old man stiffened, clearly in no mood for Bethyn's sarcasm.

"Can we take stock of our situation, please?" Koria said, trying to de-escalate the rising tension. "What exactly are our problems? What have we learned?"

"Well, let's see," Bethyn mused, then added unhelpfully, "Everything and nothing. Respectively."

Gerveault ignored her this time. "We are taking in the calibration data from Vercors now. The duke ordered Rawles to have their heralds perform the tests as well, so we will have comparative data soon."

Bethyn crossed her arms. "Their data won't be as stable. Apart from Elyze, their most senior herald, the rest don't have a deep background."

They're uneducated, to put it less diplomatically.

"Correct, Miss Trail." The old man nodded. "They lack a heraldic passport." He raised his index finger to the ceiling. "But they may make up for the lack of quality with quantity." He shrugged in a distinctly un-Gerveault-like fashion. "This was always a statistical exercise."

"Good," affirmed Koria. "That should at least help us address the timing of the potential Huygens failure. What else?"

Gerveault looked at his hand, minutely wiggling his fingers as he made some mental tally. It spoke to his disturbed state of mind that he felt the need to resort to such a crude device. "Meredeth Callum's analysis of the Huygens failure will follow that data by only a few days at most. Her analysis should be excellent, probably better than our own. Meanwhile, we should stop worrying about Kennyth Brice's military preparations. I have spoken to him. He is doing everything he can—moving Elysium, one might say—to bring more soldiers up as quickly as possible." He looked at Bethyn. "The best way we can make a difference now is with the field data on the possible location of the Bridge."

"Right," Bethyn agreed, all business now. "There is definitely something there. I just want to try a few more residualizations before showing you. Heylor's data point is significant, but because it is so far out there, the results vary wildly."

"I will ask Robert to perform a calibration tonight. He should be able to collate the data and send the results before dark," Koria said. "I think that takes us back to the locus itself and what we are seeing."

"But everybody's seeing something different, and differently each time," Bethyn complained.

Koria felt goosebumps on her arms. "Why don't we collect and organize the information comprehensively?"

"Yes," Gerveault agreed. "We need to catalogue *everyone's* dreams. All the heralds in Vercors."

"What a party that'll be," observed Bethyn flatly. "We can serve broken glass and rotten fish to go with it."

Koria and Gerveault looked sharply at Bethyn. She shrugged. "Well, what did you do at the last locus party?"

"Even I," hissed Gerveault, "was not alive then."

"Well, do we know anything about it?" Bethyn asked. "Maybe we can learn something from what happened then."

"There were several loci during the Methueyn War, the biggest one just before the Bridge disappeared and Huygens changed."

Bethyn smirked. "We know that the Bridge didn't just disappear. The Methueyns took it."

"We know it wasn't a coincidence," Koria interjected. "Huygens, the Bridge, the Ardgour Wilderness."

"It wasn't a wilderness back then," Bethyn added.

Gerveault's eyebrows shot up. "But it became one right after the loci broke."

"That is my point," Koria said. "Correlation and causality. We can't defeat the locus with *dynamics*." Bethyn and Gerveault stared at her.

Don't you see?" she continued. "We are too married to our particular specialization. It has made us look at this all wrong. History doesn't change on the cusp of the locus *because* of the locus. The locus exists because *history* is macroscopically uncertain."

"You are right!" Gerveault almost shouted, seizing eagerly on Koria's point. "We need to consider how to stabilize outcome space."

Bethyn shook her head and laughed. An outsider might have thought the mousy-haired woman did not care, but Koria knew better. She heard an edge in Bethyn's laughter that suggested something very different. Through an uncomfortably long moment, Bethyn's cackling approached closer and closer to the edge of hysteria. "Outcome space!" she shrieked at last.

"We are not in the classroom anymore," she bellowed. "This is real. Koria lost her baby over this exercise. When they return Robert's body, with the horse caparisoned backwards, are we going to speak about conditional probability, soft constraints, the null hypothesis?"

Bethyn paused for breath. Koria and Gerveault stared at her, speechless. She pointed heavenward with one long finger, raised her chin, and assumed a cranky expression. It was a grotesque but unmistakable imitation of Gerveault. "Oh my," she went on in a pedantic voice, "the outcome space really has turned to poop. Everyone we love is dead. Oh well, it used to be death for the old mathematicians, you know. Let us all return to the lab and our books now. Tomorrow's prediction will surely be more accurate." She dropped her hand, and her tone abruptly turned acidic. "Because we will have a new data point."

Bethyn punctuated this last word with a table-clearing sweep with both arms. Books flew across the room, flaps open, pages fluttering like panicked pigeons.

Luciena's journal landed, open, on Gerveault's left foot. He reached down and picked it up, pausing and frowning as he closed the damaged cover. "I think you had plans for this later, Bethyn." He held the book out to her. "Happier ones, I trust."

Instead of laughing again, Bethyn burst into tears. She was a messy crier. Her hair wilted, her face turned ashen and her eyes red. Her snub nose poured tears of clear snot into her mouth. "What on earth are we going to do?" she slobbered, sniffing loudly.

"I am truly sorry, Bethyn," Gerveault said in a low voice.

"For what?"

"For not knowing."

Acting on instinct, Koria reached for her leather satchel. *Data. We need every data point we can get.* She began pulling books and papers out of it. *There.* Sir Christensen's bound book lay in her hands. She untied the strings with trembling fingers. The Deladieyr Knight had been missing now for almost two weeks. His unexplained departure from the wall had caused endless, futile speculation. Disappearing without any warning could have been expected of passionate, egotistic Sir Hemdale, but not Christensen. He had always been upright, proper, predictable. Above all, careful. He always explained what he was doing, and what he did had always had a clear rationale. Until now.

Sir Christensen had left nothing behind to explain his disappearance. Only this book, addressed to Robert's eyes only. The courier had missed her husband, but the book lay in her hands now. She had considered opening it many times, but common politeness—and an upbringing that stressed the virtue of discretion—had stopped her. Until now.

To understand the present, we need the data of the past. To affect the future, we must understand the present. Past, present, and data—all together—shape the direction and magnitude of history.

She opened the book, mind opening to whatever vectors it might reveal.

Chapter Eighteen

Advice

CLACK, CLACK, CLACK-CLACK-CLACK, CLACK.

The metal on metal of swords in opposition was sweet music to Eloise's ears. It was an *honest* sound. If it was often harsh, it was always vital and decisive, always in the service of things mortal. It put the young woman in the proper state of mind for action, removed her from the gray area of thought, debate, and theory. It brought Eloise, a woman always brimming with energy, to even greater life. It had always done so.

"Hati's hell, Eoyan, be careful." Gregory's voice was another sound that brought Eloise to life. "Son of a skolve, that hurts," he said, though she knew he was not as upset as his words suggested. From his position on the stones of the courtyard, he looked up at his towering wife. "Did you see that, Eloise?"

"I saw you get knocked down, stupe," she replied lovingly. He had been sparring with Eoyan March. "You need to improve your footwork."

Gregory was back on his feet, dusting off his pants with a little extra theatricality. "It's a wonder we are even talking about my footwork." Eloise guessed that he was thinking of the shining metal apparatus that Robert's Uncle Deryn had made for him, and the curious way in which his broken shin had improved after being examined by the man.

"Ha!" exclaimed Eoyan. "Did I ever tell you about the time one of my arms and one of legs were both broken?"

"Yes!" both Eloise and Gregory said together.

†

"BE CAREFUL GETTING DOWN OR YOU'LL END UP WITH ANOTHER BROKEN LEG. WHAT GOOD will you be then?"

Arrayn Endicott, the big grumpy bear of Robert's family, had not grown any more personable during the four-day trip from Ardvaser to Vercors. He seemed to enjoy being grumpy and rude. Whenever Eloise began to wonder if it might all be just an act hiding a sweet, cuddly man, he would raise the bar a little more. Everything about his behavior, from his off-putting greetings to his smoke-blowing, his pernicious flatulence, and his gruff, unsympathetic jokes, to his clearly intentional driving over ruts and potholes spoke to a deliberate, if casual, brutality. And yet he had driven his horses to exhaustion to get to Ardvaser and pick up Eloise, Gregory, and Eoyan as quickly as possible.

He had also cried like a baby at Finlay Endicott's funeral, but such vulnerability had yet to resurface. Arrayn seemed to enjoy picking on Gregory especially.

"If you grab my horse's tail again, I'm going to give you two broken arms to match your legs!" This basso threat had been heard before. Arrayn may not have been kind to people, but he was very protective of his six-horse hitch.

"I have never grabbed *anyone's* tail," Gregory objected, leaning against the big wagon to keep his balance and stay well away from equine hooves. Arrayn's threats and mockery, no matter how harsh, seemed to roll off him, perhaps because of who Arrayn's nephew was. Gregory may have felt he had adopted the whole Endicott family when he called Robert his brother. Eloise assumed this was the case because that was how she felt.

Eoyan could not resist the temptation. "Well, that's not true," he said with a goofy smirk. "Aargh," he added after Eloise shouldered him into the hitching post.

On entering Deryn's cobblestone courtyard, they had passed through a wide gate and arrived in an imposing compound consisting of a central fountain, an elaborate piping system to and from a three-story water tower, a waterwheel, the sprawling main house, a barn for the horses, wagons, and associated sundries, a big forge with huge whirlybird fans on its roof, a stitching machine factory, and a machine shop. Over the next few hours, Deryn and Ellys Endicott had been only too happy showing them around and describing the operations of the workshops in minute detail. Ellys had done most of the actual describing. Deryn was a quiet man, perhaps like his father Finlay Endicott had been.

When they first arrived, Eloise could only wonder at the purpose of the various buildings and their complicated apparatus. Deryn had stood on the porch of the main house, leaning against a post. He said nothing as they climbed off Arrayn's big rig, and after shouldering Eoyan, Eloise lost track of him, but a moment later, he emerged from the main house with two padded, wooden crutches. Still saying nothing, he crossed the courtyard and approached where Gregory was leaning against Arrayn's wagon.

"Are those for me?" Gregory asked, knowing they were but feeling that he should say something.

"Hopefully not for long," was all Deryn replied.

Gregory slid the crutches under his arms and gave them a test hobble. They fit the tall young man perfectly. "I don't know how to thank you," Gregory said.

"Don't, then." The terse words were friendly enough, but Deryn was as laconic as he had been at the funeral. He looked a lot like Robert, especially in his lean, rawboned body. They were the same height, but Deryn had a slight stoop. His serious, thoughtful eyes, though not his short beard, were so much like Robert's that Eloise skipped a breath when they fell upon her.

"How's my armor coming?" Arrayn asked his brother by way of greeting.

"Coming," Deryn said. "Staying the night?"

"I have to," Arrayn replied. "Tired my horses out carrying these three. I really should say four. This giant," he grunted, nodding toward Eloise, "is as heavy as two normal people."

"Ha!" Eloise snorted. "Look who's talking, stupe."

"It's her saddlebags," Eoyan stage-whispered, pointing at Eloise's buttocks.

"Keep talking if you want a new story to tell about how your finger got snapped in two."

Deryn ignored this less than sparkling repartee, only giving his guests a good looking over. "It's broken all right," he said, after only a glance at Gregory's left shin.

"How was the ride in?" Ellys asked. Robert's aunt had joined the group while Gregory tested his crutches. She was of average height, with sandy-colored hair and a somewhat dumpy figure. "You must be tired out."

"No," Eloise said. Her two stupes said nothing, trapped by her quick answer. Gregory at least was clearly exhausted. Having his leg broken and then getting it bumped around on the long journey had not been a restful experience.

"Well, let's get you cleaned up, anyway," Ellys said. "You've had a long trip, and the boys have some plans for you. How about some hot water to wash up with and then some tea and scones?"

"Yes, *please!*" Eoyan barked, hurrying after Ellys toward the main house. "It was hungry work carrying Lord Justice across half the wilderness and almost as much of the duchy."

The liar had not carried Gregory even once, but for a change Eloise opted not to straighten him out. If she called her men on all of their skolve-shit, she would be calling them out all day, every day. *Luckily for them, I am exceedingly tolerant.*

Entering the house and feeling its cool, shaded air, Eloise realized she might actually enjoy an opportunity to rest. She suddenly noticed that Gregory was missing. *Where's that stupe now?* Craning her head back toward the door, she saw that he was still hobbling across the courtyard. His crutches may have fit well, but he was not likely to win any races with them. Noticing that Gregory had fallen behind everyone else, Arrayn hung his head out the door and yelled, "Hurry up, Justice! Do you have an anvil tied to your leg?"

†

"Stay still," Deryn said as he tightened the bolt on a sliding piece of housing, only one of many parts of the elaborate leg brace he had crafted for Gregory. "Almost done." Deryn slid the housing until it was hidden from sight.

Is it a brace or is it armor?

It could have been sold, at a very high price, as either. The metal reminded Eloise of the Justice family sword, and of her own sword and shield. It was glassy and liquid-like, reflecting and seeming to intensify any light that hit it. When Eloise looked at the brace in the empyreal sky, she saw five elements arrayed in the distinctive entropic pattern she had seen with other Endicott family work and almost nowhere else.

"It looks like a fancy greave," Eoyan mused, fascinated. The outer face was almost indistinguishable from that piece of armor except for the articulated knee covering. The structural support—the brace for Gregory's shin—was hidden inside.

"Try taking a step," Deryn commanded, adding, "Just one."

Gregory's craned his head back toward Eloise before he did anything. His eyes were wide. Eloise was not sure what they showed.

Arrayn's deep voice cut through the moment. "What are you afraid of Justice? Hop to it."

"I'm not afraid," he said, eyes still on Eloise.

It is some kind of fear. She knew her husband to be studiously fair-minded, conscientious, and utterly loyal. He had also shown an amazing tolerance of Arrayn, whether he viewed the crude oaf as part of some horrific extended family or not. And while Gregory did feel fear, she had never seen it stop him from doing what he thought he should. He had kept Robert from destroying himself all that first year. *He helped Koria and me protect Robert,* Eloise amended in her mind. Spending any extended period of time with Robert Endicott required bravery. *Look where the man is now.*

They were in Deryn's machine shop, which was nothing like the Ardgour Wilderness. It was a place of forges and gears, placed adjacent to the waterwheel, which drove the metal lathe. The building was spotlessly neat. No gods or monsters hid behind the big drills or rows of hammers.

Still looking at his wife, Gregory pushed himself up from the fitting chair. He took one hesitant step and smiled. "It feels as good as new!" he exclaimed. Unable to contain himself, he executed a delighted pirouette.

"Stop!" Deryn growled. Gregory obeyed at once, his joy barely suppressed, and waited while Deryn made some minute adjustments to the device. "One more step." Gregory obeyed again. Deryn pointed at the chair again and Eloise pushed it forward. Gregory sat back down.

"Is it okay?" Eoyan asked. "What now?"

Deryn said nothing. He walked over to a large wooden trunk and opened it. Arrayn crossed his big hairy arms, a strange look on his face. "Just wait," he said in an uncharacteristically mild voice. For a moment he sounded almost kind.

Deryn closed the trunk. He had another shining, greave-like device in his arms. "It's easy to make two."

Once you figure out how to make one. This was what Robert had said, according to Gregory, after making a shield for Eloise and another for Kennyth Brice. With Gregory's help, he had made a prototype first, not quite as complex, not quite as hard, but it taught the young men how to make the two masterpieces that came next. Gregory had put the prototype to good use. He carried it still. Everyone that had been in the tower with them that night four years back had called it magic.

"They're light, incredibly light," Gregory exclaimed, strutting around the courtyard a little later, both braces now precisely adjusted and operating to plan. It was as if his shin had never been broken at all.

"How strong are they?" Eloise asked.

"Hmmf," snorted Arrayn. "You could stop a boulder thrown from a catapult with those."

"But don't try," Deryn hastily added.

"What I want to know," said Eoyan, "is where is *my* magic armor?" He lifted both hands, palms up. "You know, I suffered both a broken arm and a broken leg defending Robert and Gregory. After walking out of a perfectly good tower to face a herd of skolves. For *them*."

Eloise shook her head in disgust. "Do you have to bring this up every knight's-damned, fucking time, March? Every skolving angel-damned time."

"Ha!" Eoyan shot back, then turned to the Endicott brothers. Both of them were smiling at his antics. "I got nothing. Abandoned in fact." He pointed dramatically at Gregory. "He gets everything. Do you know what he got the day his leg was broken?"

Eloise made a fist at the goofy moron. "I'm going to give you something all right."

"No, he's right," Gregory said. He had been on the verge of laughing, but his mood had abruptly done a one-eighty. "These are worth a duke's ransom. More, in fact. No duke anywhere has anything like them. What can I do to repay you, Deryn?"

The quiet man's tolerant grin fell away. He looked at Gregory for a moment, then turned and walked away.

What?

Arrayn Endicott, big bear of a man that he was, walked up to Gregory until they were nose to nose. They were about the same height, but Arrayn was at least eighty pounds heavier. Gregory somehow avoided flinching when Arrayn's giant hands came down hard on both his shoulders.

"Do what you do, Justice. That's good enough for us." Then he too walked wordlessly away.

It was only after both Endicotts had left them in the courtyard that Eloise looked at Gregory again through the empyreal sky and swore that the big fracture in his shin was already partially healed.

†

IN THE DAYS THAT FOLLOWED, ELOISE, ARRAYN, AND EOYAN HELPED GREGORY BEGIN TO rehabilitate his atrophied leg muscles. This involved a fair amount of corporal punishment in the form of sparring. Eloise also decided that she and Gregory should make the long walk to the great campus Steel Castle.

Perhaps we will see our daughters in a day or two if he keeps getting stronger so quickly.

The trip would also be a bit of a special occasion, a chance to be part of the world again after so much time in the Ardgour Wilderness. They both wore their Knight of Vercors cloaks. Gregory was forced to borrow a bright vest of chainmail to offset his greaves, but Eloise donned her old New School tartan, something she never got to do anymore. Certainly not on a horse, a wagon, or in the wilderness.

The Castle was busier than Eloise remembered it ever having been. Streams of people came and went, some in their best rags, others in their best silk. None were prevented from entering. Eloise's eyes scanned the vast interior, illuminated by stained-glass windows that filtered the bright light of the late morning into hues of blue, gold, and red. She noted the martial aspect of the Methueyn Knights depicted in their eight apses. For all their swords, axes, and shields, there was a spiritual thread connecting them. A great horn hung suspended in the air, only reachable by a nearly invisible spiral staircase. The organ's array of pipes was arranged in the shape of a rising sun, while the choir's drums resembled shields and their drumsticks hammers and axes.

There were so many doctrines of the faith embedded in the iconography of this, the greatest church in the duchy, that Eloise, fascinated by it all, would have missed seeing Heylor Style enter with a young woman if Gregory had not pointed them out. The woman, about Heylor's height, was fit-looking in her breezy dress, with mousy hair and a naive, open-mouthed expression. She held Heylor's hand in what looked like a tight, proprietary grip. Eloise was dumbfounded. It was not that Heylor was unattractive. At least he was not quite the coatrack-thin teenager he had once been. There was some muscle on his still lean frame now, and while he was much, much shorter than Eloise, he was about average height for a man. As far as she was concerned, he would always be a runty little brother: smelly, dirty, fidgety, and annoying. It was good to see him, all the same. The woman with him though ... did she seem familiar?

Where have I seen that dopey expression before?

"Heylor!" Eloise called out, not caring that she was in the most sacred space in the duchy. The stupe's head darted around with the nervous alarm Heylor was known for.

"Stupe!" Eloise called again. This time he saw her and Gregory. His eyes grew as large as those of the young woman beside him. Then he smirked, whispered something at her and Gregory that she could not hear, and made an awkward waving motion to indicate, Eloise assumed, that they would meet up after the service. This seemed about to begin, so Eloise was content to wait.

The overdressed woman intoning her liturgy from the bridge was more annoying than Heylor had ever been. She did not stare at Eloise in Heylor's gormless way. Her gaze from so high on the floating bridge was something else, something much more formidable. She did not dynamically steal anything either, not that Eloise could tell. She talked a lot, though, just like Heylor used to, and she obviously enjoyed telling everyone what to do, something Heylor had never tried to do.

After going on and on about being the word of the gods, the liturgy started prescribing how people ought to behave. When "we hear the words of heaven" changed to "this is what you must do," the proceedings lost Eloise completely. Moralistic prescriptions irritated her. Meekly accepting such prescriptions, which everyone there seemed to be doing, irritated her even more. The point of the liturgy, she realized, was to train them to take all these instructions on faith. Their singsong responses, beautiful as they were, only underscored the conformity that bothered Eloise so much. She was not the kind of woman who liked to be told what to do.

Eloise did have a real interest in looking at the eight apses and their depictions of each of the knights, but she had not come early enough to study them properly, and it looked like the priest was not going to say anything interesting about them in her sermon. Except that they would come back soon. *Hemdale would like that.* The only part of the sermon that Eloise did not mind was the priest's proclamation that, "The Methueyn Knights would return soon to lead the people through this most troubling time." It was a fantasy, of course, but a nice one. The proceedings ended with the *Hymn of the Knights*, sung by the choir and the whole congregation and supported by horns, pipe organ, and drums. It went,

"I saw the sun,
Burn with music.
Topping a hill,
I followed the wind.
I lifted a sword,
And made war.
To protect the small,
I raised a shield.
I hurled a question,
Into the void.
With an axe,
I made it right.
I called our eight,
With a broken horn.
For everyone,
Night someday comes.

But after night,
Day comes again,
And with it,
The sun.
After every night,
The Knights Rise again.
They Rise again,
They Rise."

†

"AND SO THAT'S WHY I'M GOING TO STEAL THE AARDV—EINDARCH EYE," HEYLOR FINISHED. Sitting in a deserted corner of the Apprentice's Library over beer and biscuits, he had told them all about his being partnered up with Lynwen, the medical protestors, and the hangings. He had also explained, in excruciating detail, his plans to steal the Eindarch Eye and use it to capture the cloaked man, or men.

His account of the scheme was elaborate. It was unlike Heylor. The whole project was, including his theory about the hangings.

He has changed. It was incongruous, sitting amid the books of the Library, reminded of the days when they had sat in the same strangely styled public house, to face the possibility that Heylor could have transformed himself—even if only a little.

"He's not *stealing* anything," said Constable Lynwen, shaking her head with some exasperation at Heylor. "We are going to borrow it."

"Good luck with that," said Gregory. "The Eye is one of the most closely guarded secrets in the duchy."

"No," said Lynwen in some sort of denial. "He wrote a letter to the duke."

Gregory looked at her with a kind of generous pity. "Lord Kennyth Brice is sympathetic to Heylor, but he isn't going to loan the Eye out for something like this." He reflexively tried to scratch his leg through the armored brace. Since his fingernails were not made of entropic steel, he got nowhere, then smiled to himself at his folly. "Not unless your name is Robert Endicott, and even then, I'm not sure he'd agree."

"I'll get it one way or another," Heylor said absently.

Lynwen pulled out her baton and put it down on the table with the tip pointing toward Heylor. "You aren't stealing anything, dear."

"You do know the stupe you've hitched your wagon to, don't you?" Eloise asked her, thinking, not unsympathetically, of all the disappointment the young woman was going to experience if she really had fallen in love with Heylor Style.

"I have to do it," Heylor said under his breath.

Eloise did not miss this, and neither did the young constable. "But why?" asked Lynwen, fingers playing over the hilt of the baton. "Why are you so obsessed about this?"

"Yah, why?" added Eloise. Both women glared at Gregory.

"I am curious as well, Heylor." Gregory took a sip of beer, eyes moving between Heylor and the two women.

"You know why," Heylor said, trying to glare back at Lynwen. "I've told you every day." His face had suddenly gone red. He turned his gaze to Eloise. She saw the anguish in his eyes. "And you *saw* why, Eloise. All my eight are dead because of me. I need to do *something* right for once. This is going to be it.

I'm going to catch this new cloaked man and see if he's as tough as the Lonely Wizard was."

Whoever he is, he won't be one hundredth as dangerous as Keith Euyn was.

Eloise did not voice the thought. Heylor had started crying, and Lynwen had forgotten about her baton. With an arm around his shoulders, she was whispering in her young lover's ear. Gregory sat silently, looking uncomfortable, not knowing how to help, surely not thinking that assisting Heylor in an outrageous heist was a rational thing to do. The few other nearby patrons of the dark and atmospheric Apprentice's Library seemed content to ignore the situation. A few buried their noses ostentatiously in their books. Crying students may not have been that unusual. Eloise considered the situation. She had seen Heylor cry before. She had *made* him cry before, but he had deserved it on those occasions. This time it was not as much fun. It was not fun at all.

The last time she had seen him cry was on that awful night at Ardvaser, when he had appeared out of thin air in the dining hall, covered in blood, howling with grief and distress. He had been so distraught that Robert and Christensen together had struggled to keep him from hurting himself as he thrashed wildly around. The sight was so harrowing that the colossal arm that had appeared with him was momentarily forgotten. His eight had died. Heylor had only survived by doing the impossible and stepping across space from far out across the wheat line to Ardvaser in a blink. It was his old familiar trick, but played out on a vaster scale than anyone imagined was possible. That was the only reason he was alive now to feel so sorry for himself.

He hasn't changed in that respect.

Except that he was also sorry for his teammates.

"Okay, stupe. Enough," Eloise commanded. This had no effect. "Heylor!" she shouted. The entire room froze. Heads looked up and conversations stopped. Heylor poked his head out from Lynwen's sheltering embrace, and Eloise added, a little more quietly, "It's your fault, all right, idiot."

Gregory gawped at her, and Lynwen closed her mouth and frowned. Heylor sat up straighter and wiped his nose on a cloth napkin.

"I told you it was."

"Yes," Eloise agreed. "It is knights-damned surely your fault that you're *crying*. But it isn't your fault that your eight are dead."

"You weren't there," Heylor said quietly.

"I didn't need to be," Eloise said. "Did you summon the skolves across reality into our world? Did you bring in Skoll and Hati? No, you didn't. You didn't plan Lighthouse either or sign up your eight. People made decisions all up and down the line, across time and circumstances." She reached over and swatted him across the top of his head. "All you did was bravely try to help."

"But I ran away."

Eloise smiled. It was good to see Heylor again. "Never feel bad for surviving."

"But—"

"—enough!" Eloise stood up. "You know what your problem is, Heylor Style? You think you're responsible for everything." She leaned forward and down, so she could look him in the eyes. "But what you *need* to take responsibility for is *what* you take responsibility for."

It was a strange piece of advice, but it seemed to fit.

After these wise words, Eloise expected her fidgety friend to perk up. But he continued sniveling, his face a mess now, red, botched, and snotty. Even though, a moment ago, she had felt happy to see him again, his incurable self-pity suddenly enraged her. *I bet he's been inflicting the same self-indulgent scene on this poor Lynwen every day.* People who could not get over their issues really pissed her off. They made her furious, and she refused to move on from it.

Nevertheless, Eloise made an effort to control herself. "Okay, we've had a good talk, Heylor, and you've had a good cry. Now let's move on," she said, hoping a straightforward command delivered in a calm voice would stop his mewling.

Heylor settled down a little but continued crying in tiny fits and starts, like hiccups.

"Knights damn, you, Heylor, can't you get past anything like a normal person?"

"Look at this, Eloise."

Hearing those words jarred Eloise. She snapped her head to Gregory. "What?"

He pursed his lips and tried to look reasonable. "I said, *look* Eloise."

Somewhere in her head, she still heard her uncle Hemdale saying, *"Look at this, Eloise."* Why did that strange moment keep coming back to her?

"Just ease off," Gregory continued, some steel in his voice now. "He heard you."

But had he really? Heylor needed to do more than listen. He had to *change*, and he was not the only one.

Robert.

He and Heylor had always been a little alike. Heylor *was* Robert, if Robert had been less poised, less massively talented, a little smaller, way less mature, significantly less intelligent, and if he had been raised by someone other than Finlay Endicott. Those were actually a lot of differences, she had to admit, but other than all those, the two young men really were quite similar. Robert needed to hear that advice too.

Eloise realized that the idea of stopping off at the family estate and seeing the girls was going to have to be put off again. The world was changing. *Huygens* was changing. Deryn Endicott had never explained why he had made the leg braces for Gregory in such a hurry—he was taciturn Finlay Endicott's son in that way too—but he would only have worked that fast for a compelling reason. No one at the New School, not even Gerveault, knew when the locus was going to hit, but Deryn clearly thought it would be soon. *We need to get back to Ardvaser.*

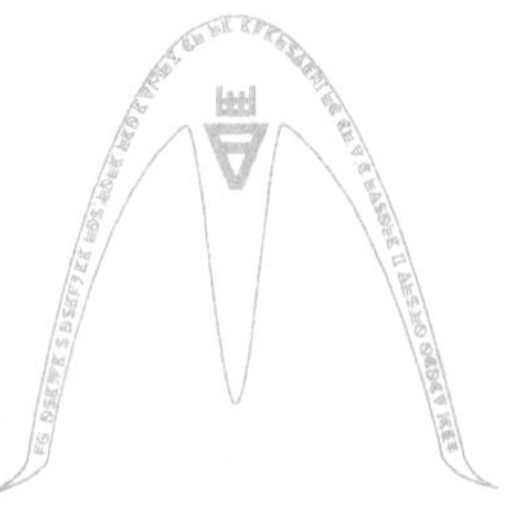

Chapter Nineteen

Entropic Potential

CHRISTENSEN SQUINTED INTO THE RISING SUN. HE HAD BEEN WALKING SINCE THE MOON came up. The night before, he had sensed the electric potential in the air and suspected he was getting close. He knew he was at last nearly there when he reached the grotesquely mounted remains of the Methueyn Knight described in *The Lonely Wizard*. Keith Euyn's poem had been carved into the knight's breastplate, just as the book had described it. Glass beads adorned the whole eerie scene.

Sir Christensen was no dynamicist, no wizard, yet he felt the resonance. As he crossed the first suspension bridge, his teeth were chattering from it. He could not see the fundamental particles of reality, the electrons and packets of light energy as Gerveault had described them, but he felt them with the hairs on his body. Every single hair seemed to be standing up.

The feeling that something must come of this, that something must be made from all this potential, only increased as he passed through the castle and along the narrow roadway that led from it to the next suspension bridge. Even with electricity crackling along the hairs on his arm, Sir Christensen could not resist stopping, awestruck, when he reached the center of the bridge. It spanned a powerful, violent river that tumbled and roared between two andesite cliff faces, sheer and high. Such was the river's power that curtains of mist rose from the water a hundred feet below to swirl and undulate over the whole span of the bridge. The scene was magnificent, but something else caught Christensen's eye. It confirmed that, at last, he was approaching the Bifrost, the legendary Methueyn Bridge.

The bridge floating in air.

He could see the image of the floating bridge in the mist above him, fluttering, white and arcuate, one end hanging free to the sky. Sir Christensen involuntarily grasped for it, though he knew it was out of his reach and immaterial.

Now where is that reflection coming from?

Through the churning mist, he could just make out, somewhere beyond the far side of the bridge, a bowl in the mountain. It must be there, hidden in the bowl. He would have missed it if not for the reflective sheen of the mist. It was captured there like a mirage or a dream, ephemeral and hovering, a sight he had both desired and dreaded. He still did not know what he would do when he ascended it.

The old rope and wood plank bridge he was on now was rotted and slippery. That it had held together this long was a miracle. Perhaps the wood had been treated with a resin. The rope had to have been, even though much of it was gone. Nothing man-made can withstand two and a half centuries of sun, water, and entropy unharmed without some shield. But whatever protective sealant it was that had kept the bridge together, more or less, had by now degraded to nothing. The foot-thick planks were gray and crumbling. The ten-inch-thick ropes had unwound and hung on as tufts, bunched here and there but not everywhere they needed to be. Only a thin metal cable held the planks together now.

Nothing stays the same forever.

Perhaps nothing should.

As he was about to step off the other end of the bridge, Christensen felt a tremor run through the length of it. He looked back from where he had come. A man in dark, heavy armor was following him across the bridge. The dark knight's steps were confident yet cautious. Whether his movements were so carefully considered because he had been trying to creep up on the Deladieyr Knight or because he feared breaking through the time-ruined steps was yet to be known. Christensen stepped past the posts at the end of the bridge and moved a few paces away from the edge of the cliff.

He watched the plate-armored figure wend his slow, circumspect way along the trembling bridge. When the man was perhaps twenty steps from the end, Christensen saw the stylized sword hilt poking up from behind his head. Even through the mist he could see that it was shaped in the distinctive style of Neahon, the sunrise lands across the sea.

Sir Christensen drew his own sword. It hummed just loudly enough for him to hear over the thunder of the river below. It was not a full entropic sword, but Sir Robert had worked on it, making the fine blade that was there even better than it had been. Whatever the brilliant young man had done made it shine in the moonlight. Christensen took two steps backward, careful of the glass beads underfoot, watching the approaching man.

The knight had been watching his own steps, but as he neared the end of the bridge, he looked up and smiled at Christensen. He was only average in height, though thick and stocky-looking in his heavy black plate armor. He wore no helm. He should have. The left corner of his head above his temple had been sliced open. The hair was missing there, and the scar was raw and pink. His nose was broken and had not healed yet. On his breastplate glowed the Armadalian symbol for nine. Christensen did not know the man, but he knew where he came from and what he would now try to do.

Christensen had dreamed of a group of dark knights who marched with the demons Skoll and Hati. They had burned Vercors. This knight was one of them.

"Hello there," the dark knight shouted incongruously, as if greeting an old friend. "Sir Christensen of Vercors, is it not?" His voice was rough and heavily accented like Hemdale's. "Why have you drawn such beautiful steel on me?" He reached back with his right hand and touched the hilt of the Neahon sword on his back. "I too have beautiful steel."

"When did you murder Sir Kaimari?" Christensen saw no reason to delay the inevitable with pleasantries, but he *did* want to know what had happened to Kaimari.

"Murder?" the knight said, hands out palm up. "It was a duel, the price for crossing Armadale."

So Armadale has broken the Methueyn Treaty again. Despite the lesson that Sir Hemdale had delivered to Armadale last time, Christensen could still believe it, reckless and terrible as doing so would be. He did not, however, believe this man had defeated Sir Kaimari in a fair fight. "How many duels did he have to fight before you finally wore him down?"

The knight laughed. "Enough. There are many of us, you know." He shook his head in apparent satisfaction. "He fought well." He again held a palm up and out toward Christensen. "Wait. We need not fight yet."

"Why should I suspend what must be, even for a moment?"

"Because I want to thank you."

"For what?"

"Forgive my manners, I am Sir Penrod. Of the Seygis Knights."

Sir Seygis had been a Deladieyr Knight seven centuries in the past. He was the reason the Council of Knights still screened Deladieyr candidates so carefully. When Seygis had crossed the Methueyn Bridge, he had found an idea outside the eight knights.

The ninth knight.

Christensen could guess the rationale behind Armadale creating such an order. There had always been some born with the gifts and single-mindedness to develop Deladieyr-like powers, but they were not always honorable, kind, protective, or intellectually curious. Probably just as many were greedy and evil as virtuous and noble. It was a reality that the true order of Deladieyr Knights had always dealt with firmly. But now it appeared to be something Armadale had found a use for.

"I must kill you, Penrod."

"*Sir* Penrod," came the haughty response, along with the admonitory shaking of a gauntleted finger. "Not very polite for a Deladieyr. First allow me to give you my thanks."

Sir Christensen looked inward. He knew he had not been himself since the embassy siege. He was aware that he had become indecisive, melancholy. His strength had ebbed. But he also knew why Penrod had come.

I must not allow this monster to retrieve the Bifrost. That prospect was what led to my dream.

He was certain of it.

"You see," Sir Penrod said, "I had run out of places to look for the Methueyn Bridge. I was at the limit of our research. But then I found *your* trail. You knew more than me, that was obvious. How many of Ardgour's old sites have you found? There must have been so many. Knights, what an expense it must have been to build all those places, what a tremendous investment in humanity." The words felt incongruous, spoken on this barren, rocky slope, next to the ruined castle, by a man Christensen was sure had very little humanity in him.

Penrod tutted, as if to himself. "So sad. I think, in the end, you found all of them. And you were so driven too. At first, I didn't want to catch you. I needed your guidance. But then I found it difficult to keep up. You went from sunup to sundown and sometimes through the night. We eventually ran out of food."

The man smiled, showing all his teeth. "There was no time to hunt, not with your obsessive pace. I had to eat my squires. The second one struggled so. But I needed to do it to keep up my strength, and the poor lads couldn't sustain the pace anymore." He gestured dismissively at Christensen. "I mean, I didn't want to starve like you have." He shook his head and pouted sympathetically. "Why, you look all worn down, Sir Christensen. Not half the man you used to be." With a screech, he drew Sir Kaimari's straight blade. "And you left all your armor behind too." Penrod dipped the end of his sword in salute to Sir Christensen. "Please accept my thanks."

Christensen knew Penrod was right. He *was* worn down. He *was* starving. He had walked hundreds of miles in a relentless, compulsive, solo search for the Bridge. Now, after all that suffering, it looked like he had found it.

He hoped he had also found his certainty and optimism once more. No sacrifice was too great to use against the Seygis Knight. Christensen did not react to Penrod's monstrous confession. Whether the cannibalism was a lie or not was immaterial. Christensen's own degraded physical condition would not improve with any further delay. He knew what he must do, and he knew that he must do it now.

Wordlessly, he charged Penrod, his feet cracking the rock beneath him. Even without his beautiful, gleaming armor, Christensen seemed to shine. Electrons crackled around him as he hurtled toward his enemy. At the last moment, he threw his sword to the side. A blue-white electrical discharge briefly maintained the connection of the hilt to his hand as the blade flew off into the mist. Penrod's eyes widened as Christensen collided with him, carrying them both over the cliff, through the obscure reflection of the bridge hanging in the air, toward the turbid water.

Moments later, Christensen struggled out of the river, ascended the sheer rock walls, and found his sword again.

Penrod did not swim well in that heavy armor.

Christensen had made sure of that.

He stumbled toward the bowl and the bridge in the sky, leaving bloody tracks behind. When he coughed, he sprayed microscopic droplets of blood that reminded him of Keith Euyn's last moments in the throne room of the Citadel. Penrod's sword had cut through his ribs and into his lung.

Dying, he felt like he had at last truly Risen.

Δ

The long, limping walk to the mountain bowl was an exercise in voluntary agony. Christensen left clouds of bloody mist in the air as he wheezed along. He was hurt too badly to heal without help, perhaps to heal *with* help, despite being a Deladieyr Knight. He had been thoroughly depleted by his long, circuitous quest, but it was more than exhaustion that weakened him now. His empyreal powers were sapped, and they were growing feebler with every step he took toward the bowl. When at last he saw the great broken torus, he knew that no dynamicist would need a calibration test to realize that the Bifrost was there.

It is sucking the life from me.

This is not what the Methueyn Bridge should do. And yet it was Gerveault who had said it likely *would* do that when he briefed the Lighthouse insiders. Ardgour had changed it, the professor said, with the cooperation of the Methueyn Knights of the time. He had taken this stupendous gift from Elysium and combined it with whatever apparatus his decades of research had produced. The alliance had been a desperate move on the part of the Council of Knights, but Skoll and Hati had proven too powerful. Sacrifices had to be made. Terrible sacrifices.

Christensen had been doubtful of the story Gerveault told. The Council of Knights had not left a proper record, only a few cryptic words. He saw now—he could feel the Bridge's effects—that Gerveault was right. The Bifrost was no longer a bridge. It was a closed door.

As Christensen overtopped a small ridge, he got his first full view of the construct. What he had thought was a bridge hanging in the air when glimpsed through the river's misty mirage was the broken edge of a great toroidal aqueduct supported by enormous stone columns. In the center of the vast construct was a tower. He hobbled toward the colossal structure.

Just outside the perimeter of the toroid, Christensen found more beads. They lay near another pile of bones, skolve bones this time. He thought about how the skolves had carried out some rite for the dead Methueyn Knight he had seen earlier in the day. *What about* their *bones?* He did not know if skolves even had death rites. All he could do was pass by. Once under the shadow of the towering aqueduct, he saw no further signs of them. The skolves, it seemed, feared the structure and what it did.

Neither Skoll nor Hati will come closer either. This started as a guess, but as he strode closer into the strange, buzzing energy field, he became almost certain.

His own connection to the empyrean was choked to almost nothing, barely a trickle. Neither demon could tolerate such an environment. The electric potential in the air continued to increase, and Christensen thought he could hear it now as a continuous bright hum in the background. Christensen could live without his connection to the empyreal sky, normally he could, but now, with his horrible wound, it was all that was keeping him upright.

Just over a line of broken rock lay the armored remains of a woman. Her breastplate and small size were all that spoke of her gender now. From helm to gauntlets to sabatons, she was a miniature plate-armored wonder. Or had been. The armor—except for one missing part—still looked in good condition, but she was only bones. Her weapons, whatever they might have been, were gone. As was her left leg, which had been sheared off, nowhere to be seen.

Who was this?

Leylah? Darday'l? Heydron? Yes … Yeyncie Greene. It must be her. Christensen wished he could have spoken to Yeyncie. He had always dreamed of speaking to someone in communion with Elysium, and that young girl had been legendary. Just to speak to her for a moment would have been enough! Christensen had always known he would never himself cross the Bridge even if he found it. Conversation was all he could hope for. "I'm sorry I never knew you," he said to her. "I'll come back and bury you properly."

He had to make that promise four more times within the shadow of the mountain bowl and its great, broken hoop. Four more sets of remains lay scattered in the rubble. The first of them was perhaps Michael. The second had to be Darday'l. A shattered maul lay by her arm, its iron head smashed into pebble-sized pieces by an unimaginably powerful blow.

Why did Sir Racheyl Stirling not bury you?

He answered his own question. The answer was obvious. Racheyl had never approached closer than the first suspension bridge. She had probably not even crossed it. She had certainly never entered the castle and felt the resonance's power increase so dramatically. Once she was certain that Keith had doubled back, she would have turned about, as fixed on her purpose of recovering the great man as he had been fixed, at the time, on being lost. Shaking his head at fate, luck, and the things so easily missed when the mind was focused elsewhere, Christensen trudged on.

I should be thankful she noted the location at all.

As he struggled up the narrow interior stairs of the tower, Christensen felt the particles bombarding him. He could sense the damage being done to his body, the breakdown of tissue, and the warping of the Book of Nature that had spelled out his existence until now. His impending dissolution did not sadden him. Since seeing Penrod make his careful way across the suspension bridge, Christensen had known he would not return alive from this mission.

No. I knew before then. He had known even before he had left the walls of the Castlereagh Line behind him on this last, solitary quest. *I have known since the embassy siege that I was doomed. That I have doomed myself.*

Only now, he thought he might also have redeemed himself.

I have found it.

Sir Christensen had trouble seeing where he was going. His vision had grown blurry, but he had stopped paying attention anyway. He passed instruments and paraphernalia of every kind, intent only on the end. Eventually he found himself in a room with no further stairs, only doors and floating walkways leading, like spokes, out to the aqueduct. The room hummed and crackled. A sharp blue light flickered everywhere.

Whether it was an effect of the blue light or of the electric charge in the air, Christensen's degraded vision sharpened suddenly. The Bifrost, glowing in the center of the room, was an oval crystal, glassy in appearance, about eight inches across. It sat nested within a seven-foot-wide greenstone toroid, standing on end, rotating slowly in some unnatural pattern, off axis to his perception. There was something preternatural about the greenstone of the torus. *Purified somehow?* It had certainly been smoothed and worked. It was quite different from anything he had seen in a natural outcrop. The crystal was in the middle of this rotating torus, sitting on an intricate bed of metal wire. Christensen had no idea what the bird's nest of metal filaments was meant to do, but it had to be something important. Too much trouble had been taken for the elaborate design to be merely decorative.

Some parts of the apparatus appeared to have become powdered and gray. A few feet away from the Bridge lay another plate-armored figure. The armor was deeply pitted and worn away here and there in a manner Christensen had never seen. Sparks danced across the metal surface. This knight had been of unremarkable height, but it was impossible to guess the sex. The figure lay stomach down, head toward the Methueyn Bridge. The body of another, smaller person lay under the armored form.

Who?

As Christensen watched, the spinning torus suddenly stopped, screeching as it did so. The metal bed the crystal rested on collapsed, and the Bridge fell free of the now motionless torus, landing on the stone floor with a sharp, high-pitched report.

***

Sitting beside the line of graves, Christensen at last rested. He had buried six Methueyn Knights with the shovel he had found in one of the lower rooms. Thinking of the poem that Keith Euyn had written in steel for the other knight, Christensen had kept one breastplate aside. *They deserve some memorial, if I live long enough to write it in this steel.* He was surprised to find that he might yet have time. When the crystal fell free of the torus, he had felt the suppression of his empyreal connection disappear. He could not be sure, as damaged as he was, but he felt stronger in some ways than he ever had. He had also stopped coughing blood.

I am still dying, only slower.

There was a poison in him. He did not know if it was only from his wound. The marrow from his own ribs had been leaking into him for hours. The green-stone had also done something to him which he did not think would heal. He had vomited twice since returning from the tower.

What am I to do?

He had found the Bifrost more than a decade ahead of the plan, and no plan that the duke had yet uttered laid out exactly what was to happen when it was found. That moment remained curiously undefined.

I must decide.

Christensen knew he could not carry the Bifrost home. He could bring it down out of the hellish tower so that it could be retrieved more safely by someone else, but he was not sure he should. *What if another Seygis Knight comes along?*

If only I had one of Gerveault's javelins with me. I could tell them what I've found. I could ask for advice. I could summon help.

The irony was not lost on the dying knight. He had worried so much about the unintended consequences of the Javelin project, but now he cursed not having the device.

A new idea occurred to him.

With his sword, he started etching words on the breastplate he had kept aside. As he wrote, his mind took flight. He imagined Nehring Ardgour after mistakenly conjuring up Skoll and Hati, after realizing he could neither send them back nor defeat them. It was easy to picture the Methueyn Knights making war first on Ardgour, then *with* him against Skoll, Hati, and the skolves. Sadly, it was easier still to picture the disastrous conclusion. They had lost the war. The demons and their wolfish allies had proved too powerful. The Methueyns and Deladieyrs had been depleted to the verge of extinction, and a vast, unpeopled wilderness had been Nehring Ardgour's legacy.

In the near distance a cloud began to form with a rapidity Christensen had never before seen, even at the height of summer. It began as a cumulus, then suddenly rose up and continued to grow, darkening as it climbed, coalescing into something more opaque and ominous by the minute. The developing storm spurred Christensen's imagination. He envisioned a desperate, grandiose plan. Gerveault had said that Ardgour must have had such a plan, but no one had been able to recreate it. Having now seen the torus and Ardgour's other works, Christensen's imagination soared higher. *I think I know what Ardgour had in mind.*

The blue, vertical, anvil-shaped cloud grew with shocking speed. Its height seemed infinite. White accents seethed along the low belly of the thick formation. Thunder rumbled within it. The wind picked up and the temperature dropped. The cloud began to rotate. Seeing it in all its threatening glory was spellbinding. As awful as it was, it was also unequivocally awesome. And there would be no hiding from its fury. There could be no escape.

As Christensen stared in fascination at the incredible thunderhead, he realized that while the Methueyn Knights had come up with a brave plan, it had not been brave enough.

I know what they should have done!

Formulating a new plan, an original idea, he looked back toward the tower.

I can do this.

Before he could take a single step back toward the tower, a bolt of lightning struck nearby. Thunder rolled behind it, close, deafening. Rain lashed down in sheets. Christensen looked over his shoulder at the midnight-black supercell. A blazing meteor roared out of the cloud, falling toward him.

Chapter Twenty

Thunder

"We have new orders," said Endicott, unnecessarily. Everyone had heard the exchange over the javelin. Even over the almost unimaginable distance that the strange dynamic device leapt across, they had also heard the stress in Koria's voice. "We will be moving out toward a new objective," Endicott announced.

Merrett crossed his arms and spat. "And your dice are going to tell us where. Is that it, Blouse?"

If they don't, we will have a real problem.

Endicott rummaged through his pack for the big bag of dice, the notebook, and the sand clock. They were far enough to the northwest of Heylor's anomalous calibration data that Endicott's data point should show whether they were closer to the cause of the anomaly or further away. Even a quick indication of direction might eliminate many of the potential locations in Christensen's notebook.

As soon as Endicott was ready, he began rolling the double handful of dice, only half listening to the chattering voices of his friends. It would have been better to ignore them altogether, but he preferred that distraction than thinking about the heraldic dreams he had begun to suffer.

"I don't know if I'm more excited or more scared at the idea that we might actually find the Bridge," said Lindseth.

"I don't know if I'm more excited or more scared that you might be an idiot," Merrett replied.

"Sir Christensen will need us." Marielle Engel said nothing to support this statement. They had heard well enough what his notebook had said and what his dreams had revealed.

"We could have helped him much more easily if he had coughed up the information sooner," Merrett growled.

Christensen's list of potential locations for the Methueyn Bridge had started out with those that Gerveault and Arthur Wolverton had agreed on, but the Deladieyr Knight had progressively revised the list by comparing the conjectures with notes from Sir Stirling's diary. Those notes had been found in Keith Euyn's study after the great man died but had somehow been overlooked until Sir Christensen had begun having heraldic dreams and had ripped through the great man's boxed-up possessions.

"We can assign blame and be angry all we want," Lindseth pointed out, "but this is still an amazing opportunity."

"Yes," Engel nodded, green eyes flashing. What she might really be thinking no one knew. Endicott suspected Engel was not much motivated by the idea of finding the Bridge and becoming a Methueyn Knight herself, but her true ambitions were impossible to discern. She seemed to feel no need to discuss them and certainly sought no validation for them. Endicott could only guess. *She loves the journey. And she wants above all to do the right thing. But only as she defines it.*

Merrett spat again. "It's an amazing opportunity to get killed doing something we were meant to do in a coordinated effort with a careful plan and overwhelming force. Instead, here we are, the four of us, in a panic, with no help anywhere nearby."

Merrett liked to appear blunt and straightforward, but Endicott did not entirely believe that these were the big man's true feelings.

At least that's not all he feels about our mission.

Lindseth started laughing.

"What?" Merrett asked.

"Someone will come along soon enough," Lindseth said brightly. "This is too important."

"So?"

"If we're all killed, at least our bodies will be found. They'll know what happened to us."

Merrett spat a third time. "Your mam will be so happy."

▽

"Where are they heading now?" Sir Hemdale demanded. His eyes bulged, which was—if not normal, at least unsurprising—but his hands were shaking, which was unheard of. The day had felt strange enough to Koria already. For hours she had noticed an electric feeling in the air, as if some extra potential hung there, waiting. The air had such a feeling of expectation about it that, looking at the fierce old knight, Koria almost expected to see his hair standing on end. Instead she noticed only his shaking hands.

That's not like him at all.

The big knight had not even waited to supervise the unloading of the Methueyn Treaty, he had been so agitated. The moment he was through the gates of the inner keep, he had leapt from his horse and charged down the stone corridors of Ardvaser in search of Kennyth Brice, Gerveault, and Koria. When he barged through the oak door of their small, sequestered planning room, Koria had thought he might take the door off its hinges.

Robert.

Sir Hemdale's entry reminded Koria of Robert tearing the door off the girls' floor of the Orchid after his first heraldic dream.

Hemdale has had one.

Koria knew how it felt. The effects of seeing a terrible future, feeling it as if it has already happened, could tear down anyone. From the smallest girl to the largest man, no one was immune. It was an unignorable, overwhelming trauma. And now, in these perilous days, the power of the locus was being felt more widely by those with the gift, and in a bewildering variety of ways. Reports were streaming in from all across Vercors. The weaker heralds did not experience such dreams, but apparently their ability to herald at all was compromised. There had also been reports of disturbing but incomprehensible dreams, and this was consistent with the records of historical loci. Koria herself had suffered weirdly disjointed visions every night and full heraldic dreams no less than five times. Bethyn had complained of nightmares, Christensen's journal spelled out what he had seen, and now Hemdale had arrived with shaking hands.

What has Robert been seeing? He never spoke of it over the javelin.

"They are heading southeast," Gerveault said. He pointed at a location on the map. "It has to be Arsenault."

Hemdale was closing and opening his eyes in an exaggerated, operatic fashion. *It's as if he is trying to change what he sees.* Koria knew that nothing he could do with his eyes would affect anything he had seen with his mind. She had been there. "How can we be sure about Arseneault?" the old knight said at last.

"Because," Bethyn said with an eye roll, "only Heylor's calibration data showed the anomaly. Robert is further north and west than anyone has been when performing the test. No anomaly in his case."

With a sarcastic flourish, she made a circle with the fingers of one hand and a circle with the other. With a street performer's relish, Bethyn moved her crude finger circles around each other until she created a narrow region of crossover. "The subset of potential locations that match our list and Christensen's leaves only one location along the vector toward Heylor, and that's Arsenault. See?" She smirked. "It's deductive logic."

Hemdale stared fiercely at her with his bulging, veiny eyes but said nothing. Koria could not be sure if he was just startled or angry enough to be on the verge of violently assaulting her caustic friend. Gerveault only shook his head at the mismatched pair, but Kennyth Brice shifted his position at the planning desk, perhaps anticipating the need to intervene in whatever was about to happen. Bethyn put both hands up in exasperation at Hemdale as the fierce old warrior continued to glare at her wordlessly. "Well?"

"You sound very sure," he growled at last. "In which case I should leave immediately."

"No, no, no," said Gerveault, almost shouting. "No, please."

Kennyth Brice's shook his head. "You cannot go, Sir Hemdale."

"I certainly can," replied Hemdale. "I am *free*. And they will need my help."

Koria was torn. Letting Hemdale go would certainly be a mistake considering what was happening at Ardvaser. It would probably be an even bigger mistake in relation to what might happen with the Methueyn Bridge. *He will see it and he will cross. No discussion, no analysis, no plan. Nothing could stop him from doing it.* What Hemdale did out there in the Wilderness could have world-transforming repercussions.

But against all that stood the undoubted fact that Hemdale's presence would make Robert safer. The most terrifying image from her heraldic dream flashed across her mind—the flaming meteor and the demon that rode it plunging toward Robert.

Go, Sir Hemdale. Do what you do.

"You cannot go," Kennyth Brice repeated. "The Methueyn Treaty is here, and the embassy from Armadale will arrive any day. Some of the other ambassadors are already with us. *You* must protect the treaty. *Only* you can."

Hemdale clenched his mighty fists, blue veins popping out along his forearms and hands, which no longer shook. Bethyn rolled her eyes again at this fierce display. At that moment, a low rumble shook the room. The wooden window shutter clattered.

"You are right," Hemdale said reluctantly. "I must stay."

Robert was on his own once more. Koria wrestled with her feelings and corrected herself. He was not literally alone. He had Jeyn and Bat with him. And as strong in their very different ways as the two men were, Marielle Engel was stronger still, and she was there too, with the gift that could enable a person to have powers like those of a Deladieyr Knight. It was a gift very much like the gift that wizards or dynamicists used to change the underlying energy states of the world, but it was subtly—uniquely—different.

Engel also had the gift of absolute certainty. Robert would be safe with her. A flash of light vibrated through the shutters, closely followed by a clap of thunder.

"—and I don't know what's keeping Sir Kaimari," Hemdale was saying as Koria returned her attention to the conversation.

"He has a long way to come, Sir Hemdale," Kennyth replied, trying to comfort the comfortless old man.

Hemdale looked at him almost scornfully. "He should have arrived weeks ago."

The room shook violently as thunder crashed even closer than before. Bethyn rushed to the shutters. She looked through a chink in the thick boards and gasped. Her hands flew as she tried to close and lock them. A gust of wind blew the shutter out of her hand, but Sir Hemdale grabbed it and thrust it into place, then locked it securely. Bethyn's eyes were big. She turned to Kennyth Brice. "That is the biggest damned storm I've ever seen, your grace. Maybe you should get everyone under cover."

▽

"You can still make it to the Ceremony of Rising if you leave in the next few days, Sir Kyre."

Eloise had been staring at the Vias of the Methueyn Knights for some time, the light through their stain glass images illuminating her face in rainbow colors. She turned to the priest who had spoken to her. The woman had dark hair and even darker eyes. She was the Bishop of Vercors, but she was unremarkable except for those eyes, the warmth of her smile, and the splendid ceremonial robes of the Steel Castle that she wore. Eloise barely kept a scowl off her face. She did not care for priests and their apparent need to tell her what to do. Eloise did not require assistance to know what she could do and when she should do it. *But I am unfailingly polite.* She smiled awkwardly in the attempt to live up to this patently false self-image. "I could," she managed to say in an almost pleasant tone.

The priest did not know when to leave well enough alone. "Wouldn't it be nice to have *two* new Deladieyr Knights?"

I bet that's what you say to all the girls.

Eloise shivered. There was a strange feeling in the air, as if something was about to happen. "Sure," she replied. "Are you planning to submit yourself to Rise?" Eloise had to admit that she might not always be polite.

"Oh no, Sir Kyre," the woman said, her smile even larger, laughing a little as she spoke. "I wish! I am no knight. Merely a humble priest who wishes to support the ascendancy of … worthier candidates. We are *so* in need of more Deladieyr Knights." She paused in what Eloise took to be a studied dramatic gesture. "I was thinking of you. Weren't you once considered a candidate?"

Eloise looked death at the smiling idiot. *When I was, like, three.* She bit her tongue and released her hard-eyed gaze. "That was long ago."

Light flashed weirdly through the stained glass, making the image of the second Via, the Middle Bridge to heaven, the hanging woman, flash staccato. *Lightning?* Thunder answered Eloise's question. It rattled the great, colorful windows of the Castle.

"Once a knight, always a knight," the priest said, not put off by Eloise's mood swings or the continuing grumble of thunder getting closer.

Eloise barely heard her. She had been thinking about Robert all those many miles north in the wilderness. As lightning illuminated the second Via again and again, she wondered if he would have any shelter from such a storm. "I will return to Ardvaser in a day or two." *I have a debt.*

Gregory's entropically braced leg was almost combat ready. In fact, the stupe was sparring with Eoyan and Arrayn even now. He had looked a little confused and hurt when Eloise had opted not to spar that morning, but she had other things on her mind, old memories that would not go away. For some reason she could not consciously explain to herself, she had decided to come and look again at the great stained-glass depictions of the three Vias and the eight apses of the Methueyn Knights. But it really was past time to go, past time to pay her debt.

The priest clapped her hands in suspiciously simple-minded delight. "Oh, that'll be in plenty of time. This storm will be long past by then."

▽

Heylor and Lynwen crept after the bishop, but they had barely made it a block down the street before the thunder and lightning were joined by a heavy, driving rain. It had taken some effort on Heylor's part not to jump up and say hello when Eloise had walked by them and entered the Steel Castle. Lynwen had held him back.

She's the hand on my shoulder, keeping me from skolving it all up.

They had visited Ailis Ellis, Lil Hilliard, and Deleske again, ostensibly to talk about the protestors but really to check on the position of the Eindarch Eye. No letter had come from Kennyth Brice yet, and Heylor was preparing for the theft. Lynwen was preparing to stop him, preferably by solving at least one of the cases in front of them. She would act as a gentle hand on his shoulder or a baton in his face, depending on how matters proceeded. There had been no reports of the cloaked man for a few days. They decided that the hanging man case stood a chance of being solvable while they waited for another appearance by the cloaked man, Kennyth's permission to borrow the Eye, or, if Heylor lost patience completely, its unsanctioned theft. One way or another, it would all come to a head soon.

The visit to the Steel Castle had lent support to Heylor's theory that the sequence of hangings about town had been neither murder nor suicide but some kind of perverse religious ceremony.

A secretive group is attempting their own Ceremony of Rising. And they are killing their own people.

The second Via had always seemed a bit shady to Heylor, and its depiction in the Castle had only strengthened his distrust of it. *That Middle Bridge to heaven looks more like the heavy rope to hell.*

Lynwen agreed on the need to expose and stop this new cult, if that's what it was.

"Keep an eye on her!" Lynwen yelled, trying to be heard over the rain. She said something else but Heylor could not decipher it over the deluge. Lightning flashed again.

Who called this storm in? What unlucky fool crossed Elysium and brought this on as punishment?

Heylor did not bother trying to voice his thoughts. The storm was becoming louder. Lightning flashed and flashed again, and the thunder rolled over them in waves, shaking the ground, ringing in their ears.

I wonder if this is what it was like that night four years back when Robert was out across the Line cooking skolves?

This was the worst storm that Heylor had ever been caught in, but from everything he had heard, that night between the towers four years ago had been worse. Even Eoyan March spoke about it in hushed tones.

He had lost sight of the priest. Despite the lightning flashes, visibility had shrunk to a few paces. *Lynwen!* He saw her just ahead but barely in sight. *Can't lose her.* Heylor knew that, no matter what she said to the contrary, she would tire of his moods, his impulsiveness, and his family soon enough, but he could not bear to lose her before he absolutely had to, before she had figured out that he was simply not a great man. The weird, electrical feeling he had experienced before the storm had only made him more antsy. Something was about to happen, and he did not want that something to be the loss of Lynwen. He reached forward and grasped her shoulder, then her waist, then switched to her hand.

Lynwen was yelling something at him as he pulled her into the shelter of an open porch. "We can't let her get away!" she cried over the still pounding rain. He could hear her now, under the shelter. Instead of answering, Heylor pulled her farther out of the storm, closer to the safe boundary of the stone wall. He put his arms around her waist and his cheek against her cheek and waited.

Sometimes when they kissed and petted before work, Heylor found himself in a quandary of indecision. What to do? Where to touch? What to kiss? There was so much he wanted to do with Lynwen, but only so much time. Here, on the edge of the storm, soaked and cold, he only wanted to do one thing. He just wanted to stay there with her, face to face, arms around each other. And never, ever move.

Gradually, the lightning began to flash less frequently and the thunder to rumble less palpably. The rain turned from lashing to whispering. Heylor did not know who started the touching first, and who the kissing, but at some point he and Lynwen crossed a line from blissful tranquility in a storm to ferocious canoodling in a shower. By now, his britches were heavy with water, and the soaking, leaden cloth made for an uncomfortable sensation, while his horrendous, pounding erection, thrusting against that constriction, made for a decidedly uncomfortable feeling. Even worse, the feeling reminded him of something else, something he did not wish to remember.

He broke away gently.

Lynwen smiled, her rapid breaths fogging in the frigid air.

"You really wanted to see where she went, didn't you?" Heylor asked.

"Yes. Don't you?"

Heylor could not help but smile. "I do, but you seem … unusually motivated over this priest."

Lynwen's big gray eyes flashed. "I am."

"Why?"

"I always wanted to be a constable, dear. You know I'm younger than you, right? I started in the constabulary a few months before you came to the New School." She leaned her whole body forward and kissed him playfully on the mouth before rocking back. "I believe in people, Heylor Style." She gently touched his cheek with her right hand. "I think we are capable of wonderful things. When we cooperate." She dropped her hand. "When we follow the rule of law."

She really *doesn't want me to steal the Eye. I'll have to do it when she's not watching and put it back before she knows I took it.*

"But what really makes me angry is when people in authority break the law," Lynwen said. Heylor thought she might grasp her baton now, but her hands stayed where they were. Her eyes were fixed on his. "And this priest," she gestured off into the drizzle, "a whole bishop, no less, may be abusing her authority and jeopardizing the institution she serves. We must know the truth. For the sake of the people who suffer for this craziness—"

"—by hanging themselves—or *being* hanged— in a desperate act they cannot hope to survive," Heylor interjected.

"Well, yes," Lynwen nodded. "But that's only a fanatical few. Many more will be hurt if the Steel Castle loses its way, if this perversion of the faith causes people to support stupid ideas and oppose good ones. We need change, and the Steel Castle is influential. They can either help the people work together to create change and build up the duchy or divide us with superstition and bring us down. And you and I can make the difference!"

Heylor glimpsed the scope of the problem for the first time. Goose bumps rose on his arms, but not from the cold. He had always known there was something special about the constable, and here was the proof. She believed in people, in what they could accomplish working together. She even seemed to believe in *him*. *That's only because she doesn't really know me or the things I've done yet.* Lynwen was special. *She is a knight of a different kind.*

"You know what's really strange, Heylor Style?" She smiled at him once more. "I noticed it first when we visited the medical dynamics research facility, then later at the Steel Castle."

"What?"

"The goose fever cure is being worked on in secret because the people are all worked up and suspicious. So at the research facility, the truth is hidden. But at the Steel Castle, the truth, at least as far as the liturgy is concerned, is known. It's proclaimed to everyone, but only the priests can speak it. In neither place are the truths truly *shared*. They are either hidden away or dictated, in both cases by an elite who want, or need, to control their truth."

▽

The buzz of grasshoppers seemed extra loud to Endicott. Since they had started walking again, after the long delay at Ardvaser while Bethyn and Koria performed their mathematical work, there had been a strange feeling in the air. He touched the hilt of Likelihood—Keith Euyn's old entropic blade—half expecting an electric shock. *Expectation.* Endicott chuckled to himself. In *The Lonely Wizard*, Likelihood had been called Expectation, but both names were about probability. *Today will in all likelihood be full of expectation.* He did not know what would happen, but it was going to be something awesome.

"Massive storm coming in from the east," Lindseth announced. He pointed to a black anvil on the horizon. "We had better look for shelter while we can."

"So you've cured the goose fever," Gregory said, nodding his head, visibly impressed. His movements made the bright chain mail he wore jingle. Eloise enjoyed the sound. She had brought her weapons but wore the New School tartan. It was their last day in town, and her last chance to dress in her old colors.

"What a difference it would have made to Keith Euyn if this cure had existed in his time," Gregory mused.

"It's not a cure," Ailis Ellis said. "It's a preventative."

Eloise respected the diminutive woman. She was short, but she spoke her mind. She had a good partner in Lil Hilliard too, and one of dubious attitude but decent skill in Deleske Lachlan. Ailis had also helped design security for the facility, an unusual sideline for a medical specialist. Eloise had been vastly impressed by the security measures at the laboratory. There had been some argument over Eloise and Gregory bringing their entropic swords and shields into the facility, which she had to admit made sense. Absent such exceptional weapons, the multiple sets of guards and doors that needed to be defeated to get into the place made it all but impregnable to anything short of an army with siege equipment and a lot of time. *Or a really good thief.*

The only really good thief she knew had been in her class at the New School, and oddly enough, Eloise had noticed him on the way, lurking at the end of the block, talking to his constable friend while almost ostentatiously casing the facility. *He isn't going to steal anything. Lynwen won't allow such stupidity.* Heylor was probably just posturing. Or trying to be funny. His cover story was that he was keeping an eye on the protestors. With someone as quirky as Heylor, the cover story was just as likely to be the *real* story and the outlandish, hinted, secret purpose the lie. Everyone in their class had learned the hard way to take people with signs seriously.

But no protestor is even going to find this place, let alone get in. She shook her head and smiled grimly. *Those stupes don't even know we are trying to help them.* Her pretty idiot of a husband would no doubt explain in his patient way that the people were just scared and did not know better, that it was better to say something, however stupid, than feel powerless or not care at all. Gregory was, all in all, just a little too much like Robert.

I still have to pull that other stupe's arse out of the fire. They were planning to leave for Ardvaser the next day. Eoyan was already off arranging the horses and supplies. Heylor's stories about Lil and Ailis's work had spurred Gregory's imagination, and though she was loath to admit it, Eloise's own curiosity. To stop a disease by using it against itself had a beautiful symmetry.

"This is just the beginning," Deleske added with uncharacteristic enthusiasm. "What you do out past the Line is all good, I suppose …"

Eloise supposed that Deleske did not *suppose* so at all.

"… but what dynamics can do for medicine is *amazing.*"

With this, Deleske's expression jumped from openly enthusiastic to smugly superior. "Our imaging opens the doorway to untold possibilities, endless discoveries. What we do is good for the entire world." He smirked. "Robert thinks he's such a hero. Sure, he made those shields …" Deleske pointed at Eloise and Gregory's shields, which had been stacked against the wall, and his eyes lingered on the bright, armored leg braces that Gregory still wore. "But all he's ever really done is kill people. He's reckless and violent. All he knows is violence, whereas we *save* lives and—Aaack!"

"You could save your own life right now by speaking about Robert a little more fairly."

Deleske did not reply. Eloise had him by the throat.

"Ghuhh … Ghuhh," he grunted as Eloise effortlessly pushed him up against the table where the Eindarch Eye rested. Deleske's left foot was tangled up in Eloise's scabbard, and his face was turning a dark, purplish red. His eyes desperately sought out Gregory, but Lord Justice evidently thought Eloise's admonishment was fair. He only frowned at Deleske as the wretched man choked. Deleske gaped at Ailis, but she only shrugged.

Lil Hilliard shook her head at him. "Sir Robert saved my life, Deleske." Her arms were almost as taut and veiny as Eloise's. She might have been almost as strong, even if she was more than a foot shorter. "None of us would be here without him." She crossed her arms. "It was Sir Robert who suggested we look deeper into the new grain in the first place. He is the one who persuaded Kennyth Brice to fund all this research."

Deleske's face was going from purple to black. "Ss—sorry," he managed to spit out.

Eloise released him and he collapsed onto the floor as Ailis reached out with startling swiftness to steady the Eindarch Eye in its cradle. "Got to protect what's important," she said with a wink. The heap on the floor did not join in the laughter that followed.

Gregory, still frowning at Deleske, resumed the discussion. "So these viruses, you can kill them—sorry, you can *prevent* them from infecting someone with your ..."

"Our vaccine," supplied Ailis.

Deleske had slowly, painfully, got to his feet and stumbled out of the room. No one had seemed to notice.

"What about battlefield infections? Gregory asked. "I almost died of one after the incident at the Bifrost. Can you also make a vaccine for those?"

Ailis and Lil exchanged a significant look. Lil uncrossed her arms. "I remember how sick you were, Sir Gregory," she said. Eloise remembered as well. She had almost lost her Gregory then. The memory was unsettling, even for someone as self-possessed as Eloise. *I am not the kind of woman who dwells on the past.*

Lil winced apologetically in Eloise's direction. "I did not know then what I do now, so I never asked what they thought that infection was. It could have been a virus. But it also could have been the type of infection caused by what we call a bacterium. Bacteria are much larger and act on the body quite differently."

"Bacteria," Gregory said, trying out the pronunciation. "Can you make a vaccine for those?"

"That question," Ailis said with heavy emphasis, "has been the topic of many discussions. Lil and Deleske here—oh, he seems to have gone somewhere to sulk—have used the Eindarch Eye to *see* how differently bacteria and viruses act. They have watched the disease progressions with their heraldry and confirmed that the bacteria are *very* different. Based on what we have learned so far about immune systems, vaccination is starting to look more like the exception than the rule for bacterial infections."

"So we're not sure what to do next," Lil added.

"Why don't you kill it?" Eloise asked, almost reaching for her sword.

Lil raised one eyebrow. For the life of her, Eloise had no idea why. "We *prevent*, Eloise, we don't kill, remember?"

"I *remember* that, Lil," Eloise shot back. "You vaccinate for the small little things. Why don't you kill the big ones?"

"Only you, Eloise," Gregory said, laughing.

What's so funny? Gregory was lucky Eloise was too busy to be angry with him just then. *Later.*

"Kill them?" Ailis's eyes looked moist. "Like in the old curatives? Some of those worked, but a lot of them didn't. Some did more harm than good."

"But these bacterium things are bigger, right?" Eloise said. "So you can watch them better and see what kind of compound or paste, or whatever, will work. This vaccine thing worked so well for you that it's put blinders on you. You're all wrapped up in your dynamics, forgetting what people used to know. We used to try to *cure* things. Kill them and let the angels sort them out."

"Brilliant," breathed Lil. "Bril—" The building shook with thunder.

CRRRRRRAAAK.

Gregory stopped chuckling and frowned, rather prettily, Eloise thought. "That's damned odd. The sky was clear when we came in."

His distractibility was starting to annoy Eloise. "Just ignore it, stupe."

"We could make a statistical study of cure frequencies, I suppose," Ailis said, pacing back and forth now.

"And try everything we can think of, including all the old customary treatments," added Lil, rapping the table with the knuckles of her strong hands.

"And you and Deleske could view the results in accelerated fashion using the Eindarch Eye," finished Ailis.

"We are going to make an anti-bacterial study," Lil crowed, which looked incongruent on her serious face. She smiled at Eloise. "And find ways to just *kill* the things."

CRRRRRRAAAK. CRRRRRRAAAK.

Again, thunder shook the building, this time even more violently than before. Ailis reached out and steadied the Eindarch Eye again.

Odd that stone should shake so. Eloise opened herself to the empyreal sky. "What the—" The sky made no sense. It was too energetic, too chaotic. She could see through the stone walls of the building that a massive storm had built up, but the wild electrical energy within it was unlike anything she had ever seen. She shrieked involuntarily. "Aaagh!" A jolt of electricity ran through her, but it was not, precisely, lightning.

I've felt this before. Eloise had felt a similar strange jolt on the terrible night when Robert reached into Elysium, when Keith Euyn slaughtered Rendell and Konrad, and then later, many times, when she lay in the infirmary while Robert fought Keith. *Someone's broken through to heaven.*

Only this time much more powerfully. Gregory was down on one knee, shaking his head. Lil was clutching the table to keep her balance with one hand while steadying the Eye with the other. Ailis Ellis's eyes were as large as saucers. "What on earth just happened?"

Two guards, one in chain mail and the other in full plate clanked into the doorway. "Is everyone okay in here, Miss Ellis? We heard screaming."

CRRRRRRAAAK. CRRRRRRAAAK.

Whatever Ailis might have said in reply was lost in the long, deafening reverberation.

The last thing Eloise saw before the building fell on her was Gregory lunging for his shield.

✝

Rain lashed Eloise's face. *What the hellish fuck happened to the roof?*

A chunk of time seemed to have been misplaced. Somewhere between the walls exploding, the stones of the ceiling raining down, and Eloise finding herself sprawled against one of the tables, lightning flashing behind her eyelids. *Who closed my eyes?*

And what the hell just happened?

CRRRRRRAAAK. CRRRRRRAAAK.

She ignored her own questions. She did not need to understand the mechanics of hundreds of tons of stone roof flying off, only that whatever could do such a thing was deadly serious and unimaginably dangerous. She did not need to understand how a storm of such dark and colossal proportions could materialize out of a blue sky so quickly. She did not, at the moment, need to guess why she had experienced such a strange sense of expectation the past two days, or why she had felt so alive with energy and so full of potential. She did not know why those good feelings rode on a carrier wave of dread. Eloise did not need those answers as she pushed herself upright in the lashing rain. *I am the kind of woman who knows when things have gotten cosmically bad.*

She scrambled around for her shield and found it pinned under several heavy shards of cracked stone. She did not remember afterwards how she found the strength to slide the massive rocks off and take her shield in hand. She drew her sword. It rang like a bell as it left the scabbard.

"Help me with Lil!" Ailis screamed over the wind, rain, and thunder. The short woman was by another table, struggling to shift a piece of the roof off her fallen friend. The rock hid Lil's face and neck so that Eloise could not tell if the muscular woman was conscious or not, or if her head had been caved in.

"No." Eloise's eyes scanned the dark, flashing sky. If she was going to help anyone, it would be Gregory, wherever he was, but instinct and the harsh lessons she had learned at three years of age told her she needed first to identify and deal with any ongoing threat.

There!

Whatever it was, it moved fast. It was faster than Marielle Engel, taller than Hemdale, and hidden inside some kind of moving, roiling shadow. The shadow was not a cloak, though it looked like one. It was not clothing at all. It was an expression of something … else … intruding on Eloise's perception. Somehow the creature was at once larger than a building yet shrunken down to the size of a person, albeit a large one. It was invisible to the eye, existing at right angles to sight, but too appalling not to be imaged as *something*. It did not speak. It made noises beyond hearing that sounded like screams or shouts. Whatever the creature was, was not knowable. It had no face, no armor, certainly no name. There was no rational knowledge or true understanding of it to be had.

It's Nimrheal!

A name people had made up to feel they knew something about a creature they could never understand. Such a naming might have been comforting when the creature was absent. But not now.

Nimrheal flowed over the rubble toward Ailis Ellis. She was still crouching over Lil and did not see death approaching. She did not see the black spear in the creature's equivalent of a long-fingered hand. She could not see that in the empyreal sky it was a black singularity into elsewhere.

Into hell.

Like an apparition, Gregory emerged on the other side of Ailis, shaking his head, blood flowing down his neck.

"Kill it!" Eloise screamed as she moved to intercept Nimrheal herself.

A crossbow bolt flew past her neck toward the demon but somehow failed to connect. Had the tall, cloaked figure flowed around it, or had the bolt unaccountably veered off to the side? It had happened too fast to see. All Eloise could be sure of was that the bolt hit a piece of rubble and clattered away into the rain. An arrow went by her in the opposite direction, lower this time, then seemed to dive into the debris on the floor and bounce crazily up. Gregory just managed to raise his shield and deflect it away.

For an instant, Eloise considered dynamics but discarded the notion just as quickly. She lacked the necessary precision in such tight quarters and, in any case, had no idea how to manage the sucking maelstrom that was Nimrheal in the empyreal sky. Lacking any other option, she lashed out with her unnamed entropic blade. The demon barely seemed to notice. Its unnaturally smooth flight continued through the rocky obstacle course the medical-dynamic facility had become. It looked like it had legs, but maybe not. Eloise did not care. She was trying to cut its head off.

The creature's black spear blocked her sword but did not damage the blade. The demon paused, as if startled, and turned its ill-defined, vaporous face toward her. In surprise? *It thinks it should have sheared my sword in two!*

"Ha!" Eloise screamed, whipping her sword around for another try, but Nimrheal's speed was uncanny. Before she even had her sword halfway back, the demon had straightened and, without resetting its position, thrust its monstrous black spear toward her heart.

BRRRAAAAAA.

If her shield had not been raised, Eloise would have been skewered. As it was, the blow knocked her backwards off her feet into the rubble. She had never been hit half so hard in her life, and she had sparred with Hemdale. From somewhere to her right, she heard Gregory calling her name, but she was in no condition to respond or even to look for him. She lay stunned, spread out over the assorted rocks and bricks like a storm-hurled tangle of seaweed. She tried to bring her shield up again, but her arm moved slowly. Luckily for her, Nimrheal had turned back to Ailis.

Eloise came to her senses just in time to see Gregory chop the head off the demon's black spear with Justice. The spearhead flew off into the rain and Nimrheal recoiled, but then thrust what was left of the spear at Ailis, whose eyes were wide with shock. Gregory rolled sideways, somehow not impaling himself on his own sword and wedged himself between the demon and Ailis.

BRRRAAAAA.

He barely caught the spear haft with the edge of his shield. The surface exploded, and he fell backward from the force of the blow, landing sprawled across Ailis.

Nimrheal stopped as if surprised again, took three quick steps back, and raised a hand to the sky. Lightning flashed.

CRRRRRRAAAK.

When Eloise's eyes cleared from the lightning, the afterimage was of a new, black spear in the demon's grasp. She scrambled to her feet but had to find her sword before she could do anything more. Another, more distant flash of lightning illuminated where it lay on her left. She lunged to pick it up.

BRRRAAAAA.

Eloise looked up as Gregory was hurled backwards as if hit by a speeding ice wagon, sword and shield flying out of his hands, ringing as they bounced in opposite directions off the remains of the walls and roof. The guard in plate armor who had been standing in the doorway just before the building exploded appeared out of the rubble a few feet from Ailis and Lil. Gregory must have just missed him as he flew across the room. The guard fired his crossbow, but Eloise did not see what became of the bolt. Then he drew a longsword from his hip. The blade had barely cleared the scabbard before Nimrheal's spear punctured the armored man's breastplate. It did not look to Eloise as if the armor did anything more to stop the spear than tissue paper would have. Without looking, the black-shrouded demon shook the armored man off its spear in Eloise's direction. She almost tripped on him as his torn body tumbled toward her.

Nimrheal did not pause again, and Eloise was too far away and too slow. It stabbed Lil through the stomach several times, like a woodpecker hammering a tree, then thrust the dripping weapon straight toward Ailis. She was still lying where she had been pushed by Gregory when he had saved her from Nimrheal's first assault. The spear shot forward … and missed her. She had disappeared.

What?

The demon appeared to be just as surprised. Its oil-dark cloak roiled around it, as if agitated by a gust of wind, but the creature held still, unmoving, as if frozen to the spot.

Where is Ailis?

She saw her at exactly the same time as Nimrheal's head swiveled in the same direction. The doctor was wrapped in the arms of Heylor Style a good thirty yards away.

How?

Then Eloise remembered Heylor Style's unique talent. It had stopped Keith Euyn when nothing else could, and now it had saved Ailis Ellis. Making a mental note to never again mock Heylor's trick, Eloise stepped toward Nimrheal.

The demon advanced toward her and Ailis.

CRRRRRRAAAK.

Lightning flashed again. Except for an ill-defined and eerie afterimage, Nimrheal was gone.

The Profits of Theft

"IF ONLY I HAD STYLE," HEYLOR SAID TO HIMSELF, A LITTLE DESPERATELY, AS HE DETACHED himself from Ailis Ellis and rushed through the debris field that had once been the secret medical dynamics facility. A minute ago he had been dividing his attention between the well-guarded building, the protestors as they encircled an unimportant decoy building, and the black, anvil-shaped thunderhead forming in the northern sky with abnormal rapidity. It was almost as if the storm had always been there but that Heylor's eyes had only just become capable of perceiving it. Or as if the empyreal sky were suddenly projecting itself onto the natural world. It was as if the storm was a mirage that had become real—material, weighty, and ominous.

It was certainly no mirage that had blown the stone building apart. Rocks, massive and damaging, had been hurled as far as the crowd of protestors, injuring many of them. An instant before the thunderclap of sound and flight of stone and brick, Heylor has seen something that made him yank Lynwen around the corner of the building where they stood. It had been a funnel cloud with some kind of fiery mass inside it reaching down like a gigantic hand to engulf the research building. As it struck, the ground convulsed and rocks and bricks tore past the edge of the building where Heylor and Lynwen sheltered. Screams from the protestors quickly followed. There had been lightning too, again and again, along with earsplitting thunder and pounding rain. A strange shrieking sound split the air, overriding the thunder and drowning the sound of heavy rain. It violently cut the air and seemed to make Heylor's teeth vibrate. Stunned and bewildered, he and Lynwen had needed a moment to collect themselves and venture out of their shelter to investigate whatever had happened.

BRRRAAAAA.

"That's Eloise's shield!" Heylor shouted over the downpour as he and Lynwen rounded the corner and sprinted toward what had been the research building and was now a mess of bricks and stone. He thought he saw a tall form—Eloise perhaps—fly backwards and unconsciously reached for Style, his sword, cursing when he remembered it was no longer there.

BRRRAAAAA.

This time, he saw Gregory take a hit on his shield so hard it hurled him backward twenty feet or more.

Nimrheal's nuts!

The profanity had barely echoed in Heylor's mind before he realized that the tall, black-shrouded figure that had delivered the blow might actually *be* Nimrheal and that Gregory might well be dead, dynamically engineered shield or no shield. He could see now that both of his tall friend's entropic weapons had been knocked among the bricks.

I need Style!

He would have reached across untold space in search of the lost sword Robert had made for him, but there was no time. Even in the instant in which he weighed the idea, a fully plate-armored guard had been torn apart like a rag doll.

When he saw Nimrheal turn and prepare to thrust his spear through Ailis Ellis, Heylor forgot about his sword and reached instead for Ailis, pulling her through space and into his arms.

Gotcha!

She plunged, unstabbed and alive, out of nothing and into him, limp but alive and unstabbed. *Huh. I don't even feel cold.*

This had nothing to do with the warmth of Ailis's body clinging to him. The probabilistic tunneling had been too easy.

I must be getting better at this.

His heart went cold when Nimrheal turned its roiling cowl toward him. He could not help but look for a face. There was none.

For a split second, Heylor felt himself looking deep into a darkness he could never have imagined. It was a null space that neither his eyes could penetrate nor his mind unravel. Then in another blinding flash of lightning, the demon seemed to evaporate. At once, the rain slowed, then stopped.

"Is it gone?" Lynwen asked, eyes wide with fear.

"Yes." He was glad she did not ask how he knew. It was nice to be trusted. "Here." He thrust Ailis into Lynwen's arms and began lurching through the detritus to find Gregory.

Eloise was faster. "Next time chop off Nimrheal's head, not its spear," she cried as she pulled the limp man out of a pile of rocks and crushed him to her. His face was covered in abrasions, and he complained feebly as Eloise manhandled him like a doll. Heylor smiled. His tall friend would be all right.

Are those tears on Eloise's face? Heylor decided to give her the benefit of the doubt. It must be rain that had soaked the unsentimental virago's face. He watched Gregory's mail-clad hand gently patting Eloise's broad back, then stepped gingerly around the two lovebirds. The last thing he needed to hear right now was whatever bizarre pillow talk those two might exchange instead of the things more normal people like him and Lynwen would have said in similar circumstances.

They're so weird.

Rummaging through the jumbled rock and brick, Heylor found the other guard who had been at the door of the lab, badly injured but still alive. He put him in the care of another, still ambulatory guard. He did not bother looking for the plate-armored man Nimrheal had skewered. No one got up from that kind of harpooning.

"We're leaving, stupe."

"Huh?" Heylor said, then cursed himself for responding to the name.

Eloise looked determined, which did not surprise Heylor, and scared, which did. Gregory, beside her, looked like a rat the barnyard dog had mangled for a week. He was breathing hard and cradling both arms. His shining shield was strapped to his back and had a huge dent in it, which shocked Heylor almost as much as the hint of fear in Eloise's eyes. "I said we're going." She frowned at him suddenly, all her fierceness to the fore again. "What do you intend—never mind." Her steely glare was replaced by weary disregard. "We have to get back to Ardvaser at once."

"What's the hurry?" Heylor called to their backs. They were already limping away and did not answer. Gregory's mail-clad arm rose floppily once, in what might have been a wave. "Well, thanks for all the help cleaning up!" Heylor yelled after them.

Some people are just insensitive. Heylor wondered how they could just walk away from all this carnage. Then he looked at all the destruction and wondered how they were walking at all.

Working together, he and Lynwen rescued three more guards who were trapped under rocks. Finally, mournfully, they arrived at the body of Lil Hilliard. The short, muscular dynamicist's head and shoulders had been pinned under a huge piece of wall, but thanks to some loose bricks, had not been crushed. She might have lived if the lower half of her body had also been covered instead of offering Nimrheal an easy, immobile target. She was deader than Keith Euyn's mother though. Her whole stomach had been turned into soup by the spear of Nimrheal.

"Lil?"

Heylor turned at the distraught tone. It was Deleske, his face as pale as a sheet, displaying the first uncynical emotions Heylor had ever seen in the man.

T

"Give it back."

"Give what back?" Heylor answered wearily. Lil's corpse was going to be hard to forget. It would be almost as indelibly burned into his memory as the dead faces of his eight. The only thing that might make it easier to bear was that Lil's death at least was not his fault.

If I'd had Style, maybe I could have saved her.

Maybe.

He thought about how easily Nimrheal had tossed Eloise and Gregory around and wondered what or who could hope to stop the thing.

But why did it disappear when I tunneled Ailis. Surely it could easily have killed us both?

"Don't be coy, Heylor Style," Lynwen said. "I know you took the Eye."

"Of course you know," he answered. "You know *me*. Of course I took it. There's no way I was going to leave the Eye out in the open in all that chaos. That it wasn't smashed was miracle number one. That some dazed protestor didn't make off with it was miracle number two." He shrugged. "Ailis won't be needing it for a while, that's for sure, so I'm just going to keep it safe."

"You have to let someone know you have it."

"Let's send Ailis a note in the morning. They won't be done digging bodies out of the wreckage until then." Heylor shivered. "And besides, I think Eloise knows I took it. She was giving me one of her looks."

"Fine."

"Fine? No batoning?"

"Not tonight."

See, we are so much more normal than Eloise and Gregory.

"Heylor Style!"

It was knights-damned Sackelly-belly-full-of-jelly, lurching along the wet cobbles toward them. The bearded man's face glowed red with anger, his expression taut with determination. Heylor wanted no part of the situation. He put a hand on Lynwen's back and rushed them across the Ring Road, narrowly missing being run over by a Vercors Ice Company wagon.

"Heylor! I'm going to—blah arrghh." The ice wagon collided with Heylor's old frenemy.

"Look at what you've done now!" Lynwen shouted. Totally unfairly, Heylor thought. They both rushed back toward the limp shape that had been Heylor's old schoolmate.

Or shapes. "Dear knights, he's been cut in half!" Lynwen shrieked as they drew closer.

Sackelly was alive, but his legs lay a good eight paces from the rest of him.

Legs?

They were a prosthetic.

That's why he lurches like that!

When did that *happen?*

Heylor picked up his old friend's legs. They were heavy wooden contraptions with hinges at the feet and cups near the hips, scratched and battered now from the impact but intact. "Uh," he said as he approached Sackelly, who was being helped to sit up by Lynwen. "Should I just stack these here to the side, or …?"

What do you do with fake legs at a time like this?

Lynwen just scowled at him, rather too much like Eloise had earlier.

No one even thanks me anymore. I did save Ailis, *and now I'm bringing someone their legs.*

Constable Lynwen was at her efficient, professional best. She got Sackelly cleaned up, dispersed the small crowd of rubbernecks that had gathered, and smoothed relations between the wagon driver, simultaneously scared and angry, and Sackelly, dazed and in shock. He had been crying, whether in pain or humiliation was not clear. There was snot all over his beard. Heylor stared at the pathetic sight, remembering Sackelly as a chubby, fresh-faced child, wondering if he was really the more pathetic one for running away from his oldest friend.

A sharp look from Lynwen brought him back to earth, and together they helped Sackelly-belly-full-of-jelly get his legs back on. The cups of the prosthetics smelled like old feet, a lot of old feet, concentrated into an extract over a long, long period of time. Heylor tried to keep that image off his face as they strapped the legs in place and helped the burly man to his feet.

"I'm sorry," he said to Sackelly, meaning it. "I should have stopped and spoken to you."

"You should have," Sackelly said, face reddening again. "You owe me that at least. And a lot more."

Heylor thought about this, remembering again.

I do. I do owe him.

"You're right. Do you want to—"

"Later," Sackelly said, hobbling away, taking his dignity with him. "We can settle it later."

T

"Well, this has just about been the worst day ever," Heylor said. It had been a dreadful day, but this was a lie. There had been far worse days. The terrible night had been one. The day Keith Euyn went crazy and killed Eleanor, the old duke, Davyn, Lord John Indulf, Jennyfer Gray, and a score of guardsmen was definitely another. And the day he himself had skolved up and killed his eight was the worst because it was his fault. Today, however, still qualified as *a* very bad day.

"You did well, dear," Lynwen said, putting her head on his shoulder. They were sitting on his bed, still in their wet clothes.

"I did?" Heylor could hardly believe it. He had assumed she was disappointed in him. He had always known she would be, eventually.

"You saved Ailis," she murmured from his shoulder. "That was more than anyone else managed against that thing."

"Nimrheal." The name had only been a word before today. Now it meant something, though he still did not understand what Nimrheal was. *Different from Skoll.* Skoll had reminded him of a bigger, more powerful, less humorous—though Heylor would have previously thought that impossible—and more murderous Sir Hemdale. As horrific and preternatural as Skoll had been, he could still be compared meaningfully to something Heylor understood, something real. Nimrheal did not seem like anything he could relate to in his mind or to any other thing anywhere at all. Nimrheal had moved, but Heylor could not swear through the swirling darkness that flowed over and around the creature that it walked or even had legs. *If what it moved with weren't legs, what were they?*

"And it gave up after you did what you did."

"I doubt it gave up because of me. Or gave up at all."

She lifted her head off his shoulder and looked him in the eyes. "And you might have finally begun to sort things out with Sackelly-jelly-belly. I've kept expecting him to ambush you in an alley somewhere."

Nice thought. As bad an image as an alleyway beating was, his memory of Lil lying dead in the rubble was much worse. She had always been such a strong woman. "It was still not a very good day," he said eventually.

"The day's not over yet," Lynwen said with a gleam in her eye.

Her expression belonged to the private, fun, *evil* Lynwen. The one who would lie to him, pull a baton on him, or kiss him. It was the gleam of *his* Lynwen. "What do you mean?" he asked, putting on his most innocent face.

"I mean it's time we got to it."

"Got to it?" A flash of something unexpected went through the young man. Trepidation?

"Yes, we know we are going to do it. We made our decision. We even went to the Steel Castle, so let's go."

Does she mean what I think she means? "Uh, okay." His pants were wet from the rain. He had always hated the feeling of wet ginch. *Maybe we can just dry off fir—*

"Why are you hesitating?" She grinned. "You've been scheming about it for so long, I'd have thought you would jump all over it when I finally said it was okay."

"I've been scheming?"

"Haven't you?"

Heylor nodded, excited and embarrassed. He had been thinking—okay, fantasizing— almost continuously about the day he and Lynwen would go beyond canoodling at last. Probably he had been thinking about it too much. *Way too much.*

"Just pull it out."

This was shocking. Heylor had been in the field with the boys and the girls. He was used to hearing coarse jokes and blunt talk. But from Lynwen? *Just pull it out?*

He could not tell which felt more urgent, the heat from his face or the erection against his damp pants.

"But my family are all home, Lynwen. They'll hear us!"

"What are you talking about?" she said, frowning. "Pull out the Eye and let's do this heraldry thing you've been scheming about so much."

"Oh." His red-hot face suddenly proved itself the victor over his retreating sexual excitement. "Well, I don't want to do that here," he said, trying to get some blood to his brain instead of the other two places it had gone to. "I was thinking about using it from the roof of the mathematics and physics building."

"Great, let's go, then." Lynwen said, bouncing off the bed. She turned to him and added with a straight face. "And maybe we'll do the other thing after."

T

"YOU CHANGED YOUR PANTS, HEYLOR!" SHELLEY ANNOUNCED TO THE WHOLE ROOM. "WHAT were you doing in there?"

Grandma was on the couch as usual, buried somewhere among cats, hammers, and old blankets. Shelley and Heylor's dad were cutting freshly washed carrots with rusty knives on their dirty, junk-covered table. His mom was doing something in the sink. "I just put on dry clothes so th—"

His sister's loud voice overrode his. "What's that bulge?"

"I—"

"I know what that is," said his father, pointing at Heylor.

"No, it's not what you—"

"Your dad does that all the time," said Heylor's mother when she turned around to view the cause of the hubbub. Her hands were on her hips.

"Oh, dear knights, I don't want to hear it." Heylor covered his reheated face with his hands. Lynwen laughed uproariously.

"Hand over the telescope, son," Herevor Style said, thrusting his hand out. "I want to see it."

Heylor almost fainted from the detonated embarrassment. *Thank the eight knights this is over.* "No," he said as sharply as he could manage with such a red face. He knew it might be some time before his complexion recovered.

"I want to see it too," pressed Shelley.

"We're sorry," said Lynwen, a laugh still in her voice, "but we were just on our way out."

"Where?" asked Shelley. "I know you're a constable, Lynwen, but it's dangerous out there. I hear they may close the New School tomorrow."

"Don't worry, I'll look after your brother."

"Someone has to."

"I really want to see it," Herevor repeated, hands waving rapidly in what he must have imagined was a commanding motion but that looked more like the flapping of a duck.

Thank the knights I don't herkie-jerk like that.

The Eindarch Eye, which had been tucked in an inside pocket of his jacket, suddenly disappeared and reappeared in his father's hands. Hot and cold rushes of air washed over the room.

"Ah," Herevor shook his head and frowned. "That wasn't too bad at all! I must be getting stronger. Hey, this is no telescope! This is the Eindarch Eye! It's—"

The Eindarch Eye popped out of existence and reappeared in Shelley's hands. More hot and cold waves swept through the room.

"It's cold in here," Grandma said. "Can't someone throw some wood on the fire?"

Heylor saw that the wheelbarrow, together with its occupying cat, still sat in the fireplace. "That's a great idea, Grandma," he said. "Why don't you do that Shelley, after you give me the Eye back?"

"What are you planning to do with it?" she demanded.

The Eindarch Eye popped into Heylor's right hand. More waves of hot and cold splashed across the house. A rogue wave caused a carrot to freeze and crack. "Never you mind."

The Eye suddenly appeared in Herevor's hands. Then Shelley's. Back to Heylor's, then Herevor's. The room was a maelstrom of freezing and steaming air.

"Stop it!" screamed mom as the room began to drip, frost, and smolder all at once from the chaotic, superimposing thermal error waves.

Yes. The Eye popped back into Heylor's hands, and a cat appeared in each of Shelley and Herevor's arms. Both felines began hissing and clawing for all they were worth. Heylor and Lynwen were out the door before the fur finished flying.

T

"You're going to be careful, right?" Lynwen asked for the umpteenth time.

"If I were careful, I wouldn't be doing this in the first place."

They were on the roof of the mathematics and physics building, looking down over the campus. Heylor had obtained a key from Professor Meredeth Callum on condition that she would observe the proceedings and safeguard the use of the Eye.

"Why haven't they gone home yet?" Meredeth asked. She was tall, though not quite as tall as Lynwen, and blond, though not as blond as Eloise. Heylor had always been attracted to her, but he also feared her. Anyone who knew as much math as Meredeth had to be frightening. Above all, he respected her expertise even if he had rarely managed to sit still during the lectures in which she tried to share her understanding of the deep relations between abstract equations and solid reality.

"Like you *have*?" asked Lynwen.

"Right," Meredeth said, straightening up and subtly changing, becoming the professor again instead of a frightened bystander. "It will be some time before we shut down properly. Maybe we shouldn't do this at all."

Heylor had seen Nimrheal. He thought shutting down might be a good idea. But in his mind, that had no bearing on his plan to use the Eye.

"And give up?" Lynwen replied.

"No one is giving up," Heylor said. He knew it was just nervous talk. "I'm ready to try something now, ladies,"

"Ready with my pen," announced Lynwen.

"Mine as well," added Meredeth Callum. They both had ink bottles, feather pens, and hardback notebooks. Dates and descriptions had been entered already. Whatever Heylor saw with the Eye would be evidence, and it needed to be properly recorded.

"Okay, then," Heylor muttered, opening himself to the empyreal sky. He knew he was no Koria, no Robert Endicott.

No Keith Euyn, that's for sure.

But I can do this, right?

Or maybe not. I only really do one thing well.

And skolve up the rest.

But I have to try.

I had better, after stealing this thing.

If heraldry was like an old man peeing in the night, which Heylor thought was one of Robert's funnier analogies, using the Eindarch Eye was like peeing with a four-man pumped firehose. His perception of the world exploded. The clouds in the sky flickered into different shapes, there and gone, the same and changing. A lone pigeon became a vast flight of birds that smudged across and around the buildings and through the squares. The few guardsmen and students still around detonated into confetti versions of themselves, fluttering here, there, and everywhere.

But there was no resolution, no heat map, no control, as there had been in the single-die experiment they had started with four years back or the multiple-dice calibrations Heylor had executed so many times out past the Line in the last year. He saw *everything* at once, and it made no sense. It also hurt, intensely, right above his eyes.

He exerted a little more control. The shapes of the clouds stabilized, the confetti explosions of people and birds became smudgy blurs, variations signaling nothing definite. Heylor realized that he had traded off time range for stability, which had in turn reduced the size of the outcome space. It had become less confusing but more inconsequential.

It's because I am only looking a few moments into the future. There is no space for variations. I'm seeing a thousand times more than I normally would, but it all signifies nothing. I must look ahead.

The problem was that Heylor was not a far herald. He had warned Lynwen, but he did not really know what it meant himself, other than that he was not one. After the Lonely Wizard's rampage, he had never wanted to be one. He had never practiced following one event through time for hours or days, never mind weeks or farther. It was said that the great far heralds like Keith Euyn or Finlay Endicott could see for years, maybe decades. They could close their eyes and the future would unfold back to them and be collected.

And somehow they come back with an interpretable understanding of what they see.

Heylor feared even to make an attempt at far heraldry. He had told Lynwen that it was impossible. But he did not really know that, and he had the Eye now. After all that had happened, it seemed better to take the initiative, to try to take control of something. To not wait on disaster, but get ahead of it. Seeking calm, telling himself it would be okay, he tried again. But the Eindarch Eye was a perceptual firehose. His mind shot ahead, a million images flooding into his brain. The lone pigeon he had been looking at exploded into an infinite bird, flying outwards in a cone of light and movement, passing from an inconsequential lack of variation into a different kind of inconsequentiality, one of unbounded, unassimilable variation, the possibilities of the bird's fate multiplying and multiplying, reaching a limit where the infinite came to mean nothing. Heylor lost the bird a moment later and was overwhelmed by an infinitely larger deluge of images. They were coming not just from his vicinity, but from everywhere. Colors, events, people, day and night, night and day, reverberating again and again, but always thunderheads, storms, lightning, then Camille Engel running, Nimrheal, Robert fighting, fire, Lynwen screaming, wheat waving in the wind, Gregory, Koria, Nimrheal, Robert carrying Bat, knights in black armor, Eloise hanging dead, Nimrheal again, Skoll with one arm, broken signs spreading in spirals, Nimrheal, always Nimrheal. Then armies, a vast stone structure in the air, Christensen hanging like a scarecrow, a noose, and a sword. All these images and more seemed to shoot into his overloading brain as he hit the locus.

If heraldry with the Eindarch Eye was like peeing with a firehose, heralding into the locus with the Eindarch Eye was like peeing with a firehose into a tornado.

"AAAAAAAAAAAAAAHHHHHHHHHHH!"

T

"You missed a little blood." It was Meredeth's voice.

"That's most of it." Lynwen this time. "What a mess," she added with a vast distaste.

Oh no. Heylor knew that is what someone would eventually, someday, say over his ruined body. His head pounded with intense, nauseating pain. "Am I bleeding from my mind?" he groaned, opening his eyes.

"No more than normal," said Lynwen. She was wiping her notebook with a handkerchief. It was spotted with blood.

"But … the mess. What happened?"

"You screamed," said Meredeth, "and passed out."

Heylor struggled up despite his reeling head, dizzy and staggering, and pointed at Lynwen's blood-spattered notebook, then at Meredeth's, which was similarly decorated. "What's all that, then?"

"A pigeon," Lynwen said. She looked at Meredeth. "It happened just when he screamed, didn't it?

"Yes," Meredeth replied. "Exactly at that moment. The bird flew straight into the chimney. It decapitated itself."

Heylor had to see this headless bird. He turned and almost fell from another bout of dizziness. The suicidal pigeon lay just behind him, and it really was missing its head. *Gross. Why would it knock its own head off like that?* But he knew nothing about the psychology of birds—*does anyone?*—so he let the question go. Something else bothered him more. He struggled over the fact that the blood was not his. The overwhelming assemblage of images had been so confounding, so painful, so emotionally traumatic, that he thought some kind of physical mark must have been left behind. *How am I supposed to get any sympathy now?*

In a jolt as sharp and unsettling as the lightning that had prefigured Nimrheal's arrival, Heylor remembered something more definite from the experiment. "We have to go. Now!" he shouted, hurling the Eindarch Eye to Meredeth. The professor barely managed to catch the precious instrument. She stared at Heylor, speechless and appalled.

Lynwen looked half amused and half afraid, and although she was famously open mouthed about some things, she had learned to deal with her fiancé's abrupt mood swings. "What are you on about, Heylor Style? We have to make our notes now."

"The cloaked man!" he blurted out, exasperated that they were reacting so slowly to the emergency only he could see. "He's after Camille. Right now. We have to stop him!"

Chapter Twenty-Three

Arsenault

"A GAIN?" MERRETT ASKED.

"Again," Endicott replied in a whisper, and not for the first time. They had been performing calibration tests twice a day every day since the storm. *Since Huygens changed. Since Nimrheal came back.*

The old calibration data no longer applied. Predicting dice rolls could no longer affect Endicott's temperature data at all. He had to switch to a backup method, something much harder. Instead of predicting a double handful of dice rolls, Endicott now forced eight dice to spin without throwing them. He could have made them levitate, but he was not well calibrated for that, and such an experiment would be too difficult to control. Before Huygens changed, the levitation trick had been too expensive and dangerous to attempt outside the hot pools. *Now, who knows? I will have to recalibrate everything I do now that it's so much easier.*

Having dynamics work so much better would have been good news if the cost had not been the reappearance of a murderous, seemingly unstoppable demon. Reports had come in to Ardvaser through the big, room-sized javelin kept in the mathematics and physics building basement, and then from Ardvaser to his portable javelin. Lil Hilliard was dead, the medical-dynamics research laboratory was destroyed, and an arts student Endicott had never met had also been murdered. Not long after that, an old lady died for, it was assumed, creating a new cross-stitch pattern. *Who will Nimrheal kill next?* But he knew. He had seen it.

Not Koria. It cannot be her.

That Koria was brilliant enough, creative enough, and driven enough to merit, from Nimrheal's perverse perspective, a violent, terrible death was a certainty. Endicott knew he could not stop her from being who she was, nor did he want to for one moment. *I did not marry a mouse.* Even if death was the price, he knew Koria would never accept a return to the dark ages when invention's only reward was mortal punishment. He also knew he could not abandon his mission and his comrades to return home and protect her. He could not be with her all the time anyway, even if she would allow him to tag after her everywhere. In any case his ability to fight off the demon was questionable at best.

The only thing to do is what we have planned all along, even if it has to come a decade early. Find the Bifrost. Bring the Bridge back and use it to figure out how to stop Nimrheal forever.

If Heylor's datapoint was correct, and they were now very close—perhaps within a few hundred yards of where Heylor performed his last, ill-fated calibration—then they could not be far from the Bridge either. Endicott brought his mind back down on the problem. He focused and took one slow breath. Then he cracked the sky and made the dice spin.

▽

"Have your calibrations shown that Huygens has continued to decline?" Endicott asked.

"No," came the voice of Koria through the javelin. "Huygens has been stable since the change."

"Well, that is strange data, then," Endicott said. "What should we do?"

There was a pause. Endicott could hear Gerveault's and Kennyth Brice's voices in the background conferring with Koria. Then Bethyn said something. He could not hear if an eye roll accompanied her comment. He laughed to himself, hoping it was so.

"Carry on as planned, Robert," came Koria's voice at last. "But be careful. The reports on Nimrheal are even worse than we thought."

Too bad Eloise and Gregory haven't made it there yet. Endicott wanted to hear their firsthand account of the battle. Quite a few others had witnessed their fight with Nimrheal, but his two old friends had left immediately afterwards. It had been javelined that they were on their way to Ardvaser, but they had not arrived yet. Endicott wanted that data, but he also felt some comfort knowing Eloise would soon be near his wife.

She has always been Koria's best knight.

"Weapons at the ready," Endicott said as soon as the javelin had been packed away once more. Merrett had his bow strung and an arrow in hand, and Lindseth's twin swords were on his hip ready to hand. Engel's sword was already in her hand. They would be noisier than before, but they were ready.

But am I?

It was a question Endicott used to ask himself quite often. Not so much lately. Since the embassy siege he more often asked, *what have I become?* Now, with Nimrheal back, he knew the time for preparation was over. He *had* to be ready. He still hated what had happened at the siege, but if—*when*—they met the demon, he would need everything he had. *I don't care what I have become or may still become, as long as we stop Nimrheal.*

I don't need to see Koria dead to know that.

Still, there was ready and then there was *ready*. Endicott took stock of their situation. They had backtracked south and east from their farthest position past the wheat line. They were still ridiculously distant from help, exposed and alone, but at least they were a few days closer now. They had ascended the rocky Roache Guyon Highlands and camped in a pine forest at the foot of the mountains. They were, in a cartographic sense, right on the position where Heylor's eight had met Skoll.

"I need to know something," growled Merrett.

"What?"

"If we run into Nimrheal, or Skoll or Hati, are you using *that?*" Merrett pointed at Likelihood, which was now strapped onto Endicott's hip rather than on the breakaway scabbard on his back. "Or that?" He pointed at Endicott's temple.

Good question. Force of arms had not worked well in the reports he had heard so far. He smiled tightly at the big man. "I'll use my head. Someone's got to."

Lindseth laughed, and even Engel smiled. Merrett did not. "Fine. Then you bring up the rear."

"Okay."

"Just don't get my bowstring wet, Blouse."

"No promises." Endicott took a breath. "Let's spiral out and see if we can't find out what happened to Heylor's eight." *Other than getting killed.* "There are people who need to know for certain," he added.

They discovered what had happened very quickly and all too clearly. Body parts of seven of Heylor's eight were scattered about under the pine trees as if they had exploded. Arms, legs, and hands littered the small clearing. There really was an arm in a tree, as Heylor had said. What had been done was a malicious, violent eruption of entropy. Seeing people he had known dead was upsetting enough for Endicott. Seeing their bodies so savagely and perversely desecrated took him several steps further. *Skoll did not have to kill them like this or leave them in pieces.* He looked at Ida's head and neck, the biggest part of her he could identify, and made a silent vow.

The sun was getting low before they had gathered up all the pieces of their comrades they could find and buried them.

"We aren't camping *here*," Endicott said, ignoring the late hour.

"Look at this," called Lindseth. "It's Style. We almost missed it."

It was a remarkable stroke of luck. An entropic weapon was rare and valuable indeed. It seemed obvious that they should bring it out of the wilderness and return it to Heylor. When he was ready, he would want his sword back. Endicott smiled as memories of Heylor dynamically tunneling objects into his pocket—stealing them—ran though his mind.

When he is ready.

"Where did you find it?" Endicott asked, making a decision.

▽

"There are two sets of tracks," said Engel early the next morning. She was in the lead and had entered the draw first. "One of them is in full armor." She gestured at one of the impressions. "That is from a sabaton."

Lindseth knelt to take a closer look. "Who would wear heavy armor like that out here?"

"What about the other one?" Merrett asked.

"Standard-issue leather boots," Engel replied. "Half our army wears them. But see here, the sabaton obscures the boot print. The knight walked second."

"Before or after the storm?" Merrett asked.

"Before," Engel replied, pointing at the smudged edges of the imprints. "We are lucky we can still see them."

Endicott wondered if one of those sets of tracks had been made by Christensen. He had never thought to ask what the Deladieyr Knight was wearing when he disappeared. *If one of them was him, which one was it?*

"We must be on the right track," observed Lindseth, standing up. They were on an ancient road up into the mountains, with Arsenault Castle ahead, out of sight among the peaks.

Endicott was tempted, very briefly, to herald. The heraldic dreams he was having every night were terrifying things to be avoided for sanity's sake, but looking just a little ahead was tempting. It might be possible even with the locus. Nimrheal's return was one powerful reason to break protocol, but the two sets of tracks they had found were a more exigent reason. Information of any kind could be invaluable, given what they were trying to do and the number of unknowns they faced. If they had not just found the remains of Heylor's eight, he might have done it. It had been reckless heralding that had doomed that team. Instead of taking the risk, he ordered weapons loosened and they marched on.

Moments later, Lindseth whispered, "What does it mean?" He did not turn to look at Endicott as he said this. His eyes remained fixed on the road ahead. But he was Lindseth, and even on high alert, he had questions.

"What?" Endicott whispered back. "Skoll attacking Heylor's group, Nimrheal returning, or the fact we are still following two sets of tracks up this road?"

"Nimrheal," Lindseth breathed. "What are we going to do about it?"

Endicott did not know how to respond. Engel and Merrett waited ahead, having taken a water break to keep the group tight. The roadway was hot. It wound through a box canyon that ascended a narrow valley. The sun was turning it hotter and hotter. It would have been an oven if not for the river off to the side and down a hundred feet. The water was moving fast and hard. Occasionally, residual spray drifted up, creating a cooler moment, but whenever boulders blocked the cut and the river, the road grew hot again.

"We recover the Methueyn Bridge, Lindseth," Endicott said at last. "And we do what we have said we would do. Use it to stop all of the demons, Nimrheal included." It had been discussed many times among insiders since the start of Lighthouse.

Lindseth smiled patiently. "Yes, but *how*? This plan, you have to admit, has a certain … vagueness to it, and it always assumed we would find the Bridge under more controlled circumstances. There was supposed to be an assessment period. But none of that is happening now. And even if we did have more time, Gerveault's lectures about the Bridge were rather conceptual. Wouldn't you agree, Marielle? Bat?"

Engel said nothing. "*All* the old man's lectures are conceptual," said Merrett. "I've heard enough of them to last me a lifetime."

"Not your area of responsibility?" Lindseth asked. "But we aren't leading an army up here. That may be coming, but right now it's just the four of us. What are the exact steps we plan to follow?"

"The exact steps are right in front of you, Jeyn. Up this damned, never-ending valley." Merrett scowled. "I made my peace with the situation the first time I complained. Why can't you do the same?"

"But—"

"Enough," said Endicott. "Jeyn's questions are fair." He smiled. "I just don't have any answers."

"But you're an *expert* at this, Robert," Lindseth protested.

Endicott sighed. "We are dealing with this a decade early, brother. We don't know what the Methueyns did at the end of the war. We can only guess. Koria has been working on it. Bethyn and Gerveault have been working on it. Others too. We simply don't know yet. If we'd had the extra ten years we expected to have, it might be different."

"Well, what about heraldry? You've been having the dreams every night. We've all seen you thrashing around and—"

"And I've almost smothered you in your sleep several times to stop the noise," Merrett interjected. "You've been … seriously agitated."

Engel frowned. "Leave him alone. He would tell us if what he dreamt was useful."

The silence from the two men was an acknowledgment that Engel was right. They knew Robert would use the dream material if he could.

"There's a problem you don't know about," Endicott said, feeling guilty for their trust. "It's a locus. You've heard us speaking of it over the javelin. We are at the center of some sort of pivotal event, though I think that's not quite accurate. I think there are actually several loci, and we are moving through them."

Lindseth blinked, then asked, reasonably enough. "How do you know there are several of these … loci?"

"It's a guess," Endicott admitted. "But even though all I see are flashes of jumbled images, and even though they vary a little each time I dream them, they changed materially once. It was immediately after that first intense storm. Something momentous and unprecedented happened that day, though whether by chance or design I cannot say. And when that change happened, the images changed, which means the locus changed."

"That makes even less sense than the shit you usually say," grumbled Merrett under his breath.

"But you can't interpret what you're seeing?" asked Lindseth.

Endicott felt his face flushing. "Only one sequence. One bit that I see does make sense." His eyes were wet now. "I see Nimrheal killing Koria." He rubbed at his eyes, refusing to let the tears come. "And there's only one way we're going to stop it."

He looked past Lindseth and Merrett to lock his burning eyes on Engel. "Marielle, if I am killed, swear that you will bring the Bridge back to Ardvaser. As quickly as you can."

"I will," she said, earnest but otherwise opaque.

Merrett spit sideways. "Well, it's good to know what you think the rest of our chances are, Blouse."

"You know I love you, Bat, but she's the best of us."

"That's for sure," Lindseth said, laughing.

"Hmmf," grunted the big man. Engel said nothing.

"There's just one other question on my mind now," said Lindseth after he had finished chuckling.

Merrett made a fist at him. "For knights' sake, Jeyn, enough! Haven't we had enough maudlin confessions and navel gazing already?"

"Let's have it," Endicott said.

Lindseth looked up the valley as he spoke. "It's just that, if Nimrheal is here already, how are you going to figure out what you need to do without it coming and killing you before you can act?"

$$\nabla$$

ENDICOTT HAD BEEN SENSING AN ELECTRIC QUALITY IN THE AIR FOR HOURS. IT WAS SIMILAR to what he had felt on the day of the massive storm. An expectation. And this time he felt it even more powerfully. The sensation was exciting and terrifying at the same time. Before the coming of Nimrheal, he would only have been excited, but now a feeling like this held dread too.

Was there now a risk that *any* action on their part might inadvertently summon the demon? Until a few days ago, Nimrheal had not been seen for centuries. No one knew exactly what rules governed the creature. Such old records as existed were being ransacked for clues, but they could not be trusted. Nimrheal could be operating by new rules for all they knew. How original did an idea have to be? What ancillary circumstances influenced whether the thing would come or not? How quickly could it return after each appearance? Could it be in two or more places at once? Was the act of upsetting the locus—tipping events off their whaleback of probability—something that, in itself, could summon the demon?

We have paralyzed ourselves out here past the wheat line by restricting heraldry because of Skoll and Hati. Now we could paralyze ourselves everywhere if we abandon any kind of enquiry for fear of Nimrheal. He did not know if the feeling in the air, that buzzing just below hearing, that sense of a vast potential on the verge of becoming actual, was caused by their potential proximity to the Bifrost or if it was a harbinger of Nimrheal.

How can we live like this, afraid to act, afraid to use our minds or ask a question, afraid to learn?

With that dilemma in mind, he risked the briefest possible look through the empyreal sky.

There was a physically palpable energy in the air. It was only just beyond the visual spectrum. Light waves, but something more. Something heavier and slower. Something deadly. The phenomenon reminded him of the greenstone he had examined at the old mine, transforming and shooting particles off into space and energy into elsewhere, deadly and unbound. There was not much of it at their current location, just a particle here or there, zipping about. Its source was ahead, at or somewhere beyond the castle they could now make out, looming ahead around a curve in the road.

Arsenault.

Endicott's most recent Huygens test had been even more anomalous than previous tests. Dynamics were materially easier to perform now, even in the short distance they had travelled since the morning redundancy check. The volatile energy he had been feeling—and had just *seen* in that brief peek through the empyreal medium—was connected to their proximity to the old castle. There was some lesson about the Bridge and the behavior of Huygens to be found in the contrary results of the calibration tests before and after the big storm. *But I don't understand what that lesson is.*

A distant rumbling made him look up at the sky. A black cloud was forming on the horizon. *Another storm?*

"You need to see this, Blouse," Merrett called from just ahead.

Rounding the turn of the narrow canyon, Endicott saw a wooden suspension bridge ahead. It crossed a deep, narrow gorge. The sounds of the river were loud now. *Is that what I heard, water not thunder?* A ruined castle lay just beyond. From the gorge, curtains of mist rose up around both structures. Just on their side of the bridge stood an armored scarecrow.

"Don't go near it!" Endicott commanded. He needed time to think. *We must go slowly now.*

"It's the fallen knight from *The Lonely Wizard*," shouted Lindseth over the din of the rushing water.

The Methueyn Knight who had been mounted on Nimrheal's spear.

"Draw weapons if you haven't," Endicott said and moved cautiously forward.

Merrett nocked one of his arrows. Lindseth drew both blades; Engel's was already out and shining against the darkening sky. Her family had preserved an old Deladieyr-class weapon from the days of Engevelen. It was not as good as the ones Endicott's family made, but it had a similar strange, liquid sheen and was incredibly strong and sharp, an astonishingly rare piece of kit. Cautiously, Endicott stepped closer to the ruined figure, his team fanning out around him. The pole had been planted deep in the rock of the canyon. The fact that the plate-armored figure had not fallen over in all these centuries already spoke to that, but that a polearm was needed to keep the figure upright spoke to the most relevant point. Whoever was in the armor was long dead. The bleached bones of the knight's jaw, visible through his helm even in the growing darkness, were a grim white testimony to this.

Is this all that's left when we die?

There was nothing majestic about death, about the shrinking of connective tissue, the rotting of flesh, or the bones that would crumble last. He had killed enough people to know that life, once gone, was gone. It could not be poured back in, nor did it survive elsewhere. When his mother's face was covered, they had refused to remove the blanket for him. He never saw her face again and could not remember it now. Hemdale had thought this a good thing. Was it? He remembered the dying Eleanor struggling for breath and wished that was not his last memory of her. Finding and gathering up Ida and the rest of Heylor's eight had done nothing to weaken Endicott's view that death could not be romanticized. There was no great story in it. It was only vastly … disappointing.

Keith Euyn's poem had indeed been etched into the dead knight's breastplate. Endicott read it to himself. The poem had been adapted for numerous uses, but its funereal form was the most touching. *The great man did one thing right.* Endicott could not think of a way to honor whoever had died on that path except to pause for a moment before continuing. As he gazed around, he saw that glass beads had been scattered throughout the spot.

"They went through here," Engel said, indicating scuff marks on stone, then pointing toward the tattered bridge.

Thunder rumbled. The sky darkened further. The thunderhead now looked like a vast black mushroom reaching into heaven. Its lower edge almost brushed the ground, but its upper reaches soared beyond imagination. Nimrheal had only just returned, but every thunderstorm had to be viewed with terror now. The cloud slowly rotated.

How can I not fear it? How can I not question it?

I must look. The danger was already so extreme that any information could be worthwhile. Endicott opened himself to the empyreal sky, but this time for more than just a quick peek. He did not herald fully, not quite, but he looked at where he was and what lay ahead.

The castle was surrounded by the river. It lay on a rocky island accessible by three suspension bridges. The one to the west, going toward Armadale, had been destroyed. Only a few crooked wooden posts remained. The north bridge led off toward a cliff face and just beyond that to a kind of hollow or bowl. In this bowl stood a colossal structure, a raised circular aqueduct the likes of which he had never seen before. He could feel through the sky that it was from here that the strange energy emanated. Huygens was weaker there.

So much weaker.

The third Via. The final bridge to heaven.

"We're in the near field!"

"The who?" Merrett shouted.

"The near field. Huygens is changing rapidly here." The big man looked blankly at Endicott, which was no surprise. The dynamicist's mind was working quickly, processing the latest information. Suddenly an intuition seized Endicott, and he released the empyreal sky. "I know what the Bifrost really is," he announced. No one heard him, for the heavens just then split.

CRRRRRRAAAK.

Lightning had struck on the far side of the bridge. Thunder rolled across the ancient structure like a shock wave, making each rotted wooden step bounce. Rain followed instantaneously, driving down in sheets so sudden and strong they almost drove Endicott into the earth.

"We have to cross the bridge now!" he roared out in order to be heard, scrambling not to slip on the suddenly slick stone of the old road. "We can take shelter in the castle!"

He moved forward, but Merrett's hand on his chest held him back until Engel, then Lindseth, moved ahead. They had to sheathe their weapons before they could step onto the bridge. It swayed wildly in the wind. If it had not been hung with steel cable, it would long ago have fallen into the gorge below. Endicott gave the bridge his full attention as he stepped out. There had been rope once too. A few bits remained, but they were all rotted like old, disproven folklore.

Only steel lasts.

The rain, thunder, and wind were so loud now that Endicott could barely hear the river rushing far below his feet. The bridge was so slick, rotted, and insecure that he dared not look anywhere but at his feet. He never saw the rushing ball of wind and fire falling from the sky toward them.

CRRRRRRAAAK.

The bridge jumped and buckled from the tremendous detonation, and Endicott would have been thrown off it if Merrett had not grabbed the collar of his tough leather jacket.

What just happened?

At the end of the bridge on the far side of the gorge stood a dark, roiling apparition. It did not move, yet it seemed to flow. Endicott could not say afterwards how tall it was, or even if it had arms or legs or hands. It certainly had no face, just an infinite darkness where that feature should have been. A huge black spear hung before it, perhaps held up by hands, perhaps not. An appalling, soul-rending sound poured off the dark, roiling demon. Was it a scream from Nimrheal or some awful report of injured reality that its presence made upon the world? The cloaked man, Keith Euyn, had been terrifying. Nimrheal made Keith seem like a clown.

Keith's insanity had never been explained, but Endicott had no doubt there had been some process of reasoning, however perverted, behind it. He could imagine no form of rationality behind Nimrheal's rage, if rage it was. Nimrheal was not *insane*. Reason and sanity were concepts that simply did not apply here.

Endicott's mind recoiled from whatever the demon was. In the empyreal sky, Nimrheal was a bottomless hole in reality. Grasping for some feeling of control, he tried to estimate the energy around the being, but quickly found that it was incalculable. For a fraction of a second, he was unmanned. His bladder loosened as the foul heraldic images of Koria being destroyed by this thing flashed in his mind. He had watched the scene many times before. It had killed her as he looked helplessly on. Again and again.

An electric jolt went through his mind as overwhelming fear instantly changed to rage.

"FUCK YOU, NIMRHEAL!" Endicott reached up toward the power of the awesome supercell with a hate that was both instinctive and learned. For an instant he grasped and held that power, then unleashed it on the roiling monstrosity.

CRRRRRRAAAK. CRRRRRRAAAK. CRRRRRRAAAK. CRRRRRRAAAK. CRRRRRRAAAK. CRRRRRRAAAK. CRRRRRRAAAK. CRRRRRRAAAK.

What he had done at the tower four years ago was nothing to what he did now. Vast sheets of electrons plowed across the rock where the demon stood, first in one direction and then in another. Huygens was so weak at this location, and Endicott so far beyond his earthbound mind, so deep in his loathing of the creature and his love for Koria, that turning the air of the entire plateau into plasma felt as easy as breathing.

"FUCKING DIE, FUCKER!"

CRRRRRRAAAK. CRRRRRRAAAK. CRRRRRRAAAK. CRRRRRRAAAK.

Something hit him. Hard. Then again. Harder.

"I said, stop, Blouse!" It was Merrett hitting him. "You're electrocuting us."

Endicott had not felt the residual shocks through the bridge, but he could see wild static discharges running off and along the metal cables.

"I HATE him, Bat!" Endicott roared, tears of fury streaming down his face.

"No shit! Get a grip before you kill us all." The big man blew rainwater out of his mouth. "Remember the embassy, Robert," he said in a different tone of voice.

That was the hardest slap of all.

Endicott came back to himself. He looked at the rocky plateau where Nimrheal had stood. *Did I get him?* For a moment, it seemed it must be so. Then Nimrheal flowed forth out of the shadows. It did not seem any different, except that it had moved at some point during his lightning attack.

How is it not dead? He asked the question, but instinctively—in his gut—he was not surprised.

Engel rushed across the remaining steps of the bridge, drew her sword, and reached the edge of the plateau. Lindseth was just behind her but was stuck on the last steps of the bridge. Endicott followed, opening himself to the empyreal sky once more, but he could not try anything dynamic with Engel so close. An arrow flew from Merrett's bow, a martial feat considering it had been shot off a suspended bridge, sure to hit the creature. From the empyreal sky, Endicott saw what happened. Just before reaching the demon, the arrow split into a flickering cone of arrows, each of which swerved around the creature, reforming on the other side and disappearing harmlessly into the storm. It was a probability manipulation beyond anything Endicott had ever seen.

What can we possibly do? Endicott's mind raced. He knew that part of the problem was simply the enormity of the energy around the demon. He could not model it as a dynamicist would. He could not create an accurate transform from such incalculable data, and so he could not force a specific outcome.

Exact shaping? It had never been tried in the field, but he had worked on it with Koria in the laboratory enough to know that, in theory, it would enable him to vastly exceed normal thermal limitations and still have an infinitesimally small application error. *Nimrheal should not be able to probabilistically dodge it.* But only within a very small area. The drawback was that, outside that very small area, the error field was horrific. Using exact shaping in the field had been expressly forbidden for that reason.

While Endicott weighed this risk, Marielle Engel demonstrated why she was such a bright hope. She moved like lightning, her sword whipping around at the demon, who backed slightly away and blocked her slashing blade with its spear. Behind her, Lindseth had almost enough room to join the fight, but Engel was *just* in his way, and moving too quickly for him to commit to action.

We have to get off this bridge! Engel's and Lindseth's fighting styles cry out for more space.

Marielle Engel's sword came around, evading the spear this time and coming down on the demon where a shoulder ought to have been. Nimrheal stumbled, then something that might have been a hand gripped Engel's blade. The other thing that could have been a hand shot straight forward and, with a sound like breaking boards, struck her in the chest. Engel flew backwards as if she had been kicked by one of Arrayn's draught horses. Lindseth flung his arms wide just in time to avoid impaling her with his swords as she hurtled into him. As they fell, Nimrheal flowed forward. Merrett fired another arrow in a desperate attempt to slow the creature's advance on his friends.

"Innovating!" Endicott yelled and executed three dipolar attacks in rapid succession. He knew the canned dynamic impulse would not stop Nimrheal. Like Merrett, he was only hoping for time.

Merrett's arrow had been transformed into another hail of useless probability projectiles that curved around the demon before collapsing behind it into a single arrow and disappearing uselessly into the storm. Endicott's triple burst of dipolar flashes made Nimrheal stutter and stop for a moment while the operator error rolled out in a sphere of buffeting hot and cold waves.

"Augh!" Merrett screamed as his bowstring snapped. The thermal effects had weakened the string too much. A scraping sound announced the big man's switch to his sword as Nimrheal began to move forward once more, but the delay had been enough. Lindseth, his jacket patterned now with alternating frost and scorch marks, twisted out from under Engel and got to his feet, both swords raised. "Help her, Bat!" he shouted and stepped into the demon's path.

Merrett reached ahead with his free hand and pulled Engel two paces back, off the plateau and onto the bridge. She tried to stand but fell. Merrett could only step in front of her and crouch, bow forgotten, sword drawn, waiting for the space he needed to step off the bridge without getting in Lindseth's way.

Lindseth was a consummate practitioner of two-blade combat. He was not as fast or as powerful as Engel, but he had a fluid command of his two weapons that bought him a moment against the demon. Endicott felt a brief flush of hope when he saw that Lindseth had driven Nimrheal far enough back from the bridgehead for Merrett to enter the fray. Nimrheal now faced two tough, immensely experienced opponents. But as tough as the two old comrades were, Endicott doubted they could do what Engel could not. She was alive, but still gathering her wits after the stunning blow Nimrheal had delivered, and despite Lindseth and Merrett's best efforts, there was still not enough room to move off the bridge.

Even if we do reach the plateau, what do we do then?

There was no choice. He had to risk exact shaping. He rushed to sort out a calculation as best he could in the circumstances, but there was no time, and worse, no safe way of executing it.

The problem was figuring out what would be effective against Nimrheal. The demon had easily survived the powerful, blanket lightning attacks, but the dipole had at least caught its attention and given it pause. Specificity must be the key. If so, exact shaping was worth trying—and probably the only approach that could have any chance of working He would have to try modeling the energy around the demon again.

It can be done up to a point, if I can just avoid the singularity.

In the meantime, Merrett struck with a windmill of overhand blows while Lindseth forced the demon to defend its midsection and lower limbs, if that's what they were, with his graceful, slashing, two-handed attack. The demon flowed like water, holding Lindseth at bay with its ebony spear like a staff and dodging Merrett's long sword with impossibly quick sidesteps. Before Merrett's blade could strike, Nimrheal lunged at the stocky man, striking him in the face with the haft of its spear. Merrett was knocked backwards, stumbling several paces back onto the bridge, blood gushing from his nose and mouth.

Alone, Lindseth pressed on desperately, fighting with a savagery that would have amazed anyone who only knew his affable peacetime demeanor. Endicott kept a hand on Engel, who was almost steady on her feet by now, looking around for her sword, still partly in a daze. She coughed and blood splattered out of her mouth, falling on the warped wood of the bridge.

We're losing. I have to act now!

But Endicott knew he could do nothing until Lindseth managed to disengage from Nimrheal, and meanwhile Merrett had rejoined the fray. He was bleeding heavily from his nose and mouth and his breathing came in gasps. *Broken nose?* Lindseth's mouth also gaped open, and he was slowing down. Abruptly, without any of the projection a natural creature would have made, Nimrheal slipped past Lindseth and caught Merrett with the butt end of his spear again, this time knocking him off his feet. Merrett fell flat on his back and slid onto the bridgehead, almost sliding off the bridge entirely, but somehow managed to keep hold of his sword. As the demon turned his spear to hurl it into the prone man, Lindseth stabbed at its side with his left-hand sword. The thrust only seemed to bite fractionally into the creature's shadowy, roiling cloak, but the momentary distraction allowed Merrett to regain his feet.

Perhaps too soon. As he tried to step forward, the heavyset man's knees buckled and he swayed, nearly falling again. Nimrheal whirled and seized Lindseth's left hand, which still struggled to drive the sword it held deeper into the demon's dark, swirling figure. Nimrheal twisted the sword and a wet cracking sound cut through the roar of the thunderstorm. The tall man collapsed to one knee, screaming in pain.

Lindseth!

Nimrheal released its spear, though Endicott did not see it fall. Quick as a shadow in flickering light, the demon grabbed Lindseth's other arm and twisted until it broke with another sickening pop. The tall man's last sword made a hollow clatter as it fell to the rocks.

Merrett tried again to step forward on shaky legs. It seemed to Endicott that Lindseth turned to stare at him then, his pain-filled eyes locking with the dynamicist's just as the demon found its black spear once more. Gripping the enormous weapon in both midnight-hued hands, or what should have been hands, Nimrheal viciously drove the spear through Lindseth's face and out through the back of his head.

Endicott could only watch, eyes still locked on those of his friend. He struggled to stop himself from retching. "Merrett! Step back now! Innovating!" he screamed. Then he unleashed his terrible shaping upon the empyreal sky.

It was wrong. He knew that. Everything he had done had been wrong. They had needed to escape the confines of the bridge to fight properly. He had failed to enable that. He had violated protocol by not announcing his lightning attack, and he had executed it with hate rather than mathematical precision. He had not kept a cool head. He had been subjective. But as he executed the forbidden act of exact shaping, he also doubted that much could have been done differently. They were overmatched.

It happened with excruciating slowness. Or so it seemed to Endicott. Merrett began to step back, sword raised and pointed at the demon. Engel had steadied herself on her feet and taken a position just in front of Endicott. Slowly, all the bright colors of the world seemed to descend on Nimrheal until the area immediately around the demon was a small sphere that shone with blinding white incandescence. The shock wave boomed in a depthless bass rumble like thunder from a slow-motion sheet of lightning, sweeping the rain off Endicott's face, hurling him and Merrett and Engel slowly backward, and buckling the bridge in an almost lethargic sequence of jerks and wrenches. As an intense wave of cold seared him, Endicott watched the advancing ring of instability grow out from the blinding sphere. Bright, sharp rings of fire and frost walked like the front of a wave toward Endicott and his friends. Along that wave front, the bridge burned and froze, fire reddening and then frost cracking the foot-thick wooden beams.

There shouldn't be this much of an error wave!

It was larger than he expected by a factor of at least five, maybe ten.

Merrett moved in slow motion, retreating from the artefact that seemed to race toward him. The wall of frost and fire reached the end of Merrett's sword. Then it stopped. A low whine rose from the end of the frost-tipped blade. The metal exploded. Merrett twisted his head aside as pieces of metal flew over his shoulder toward Engel's face. She clutched at her left eye with both hands. Merrett dropped his sword and turned to face Engel. His handsome features were crisscrossed with cuts. The bridge still shook from the blast.

A metallic snapping sound pierced the air as the bridge's iron support cables shattered. In the fraction of a second that passed before the whole structure began to crumble, Merrett lunged past Engel and grabbed Endicott's coat in a fierce grip. Wood, steel, swords, and three human bodies plunged toward the white waters far below, but all that Endicott could see was the broken form of Lindseth burning.

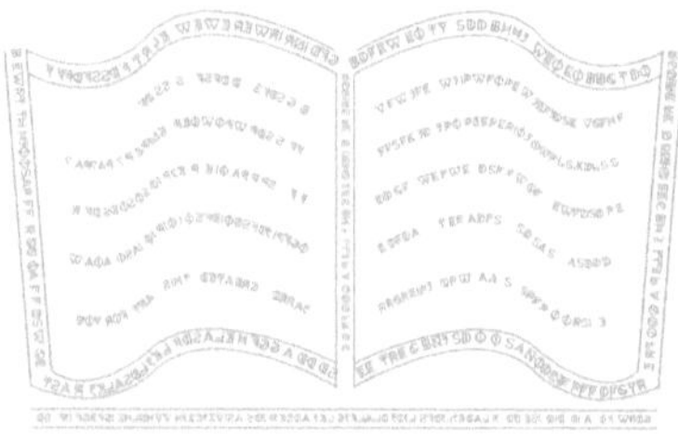

Chapter Twenty-Four

Arrivals

THERE ARE AN INFINITE NUMBER OF WORLDS. MOST ARE COMPRESSED AND UNTRAVELLABLE BY humans; some are beyond perception. We can only communicate with the ones most like our own. Elysium may be even less like our world than the hell of Nimrheal. Nimrheal at least seems to have a nearly physical form. Transformation into any of these domains is not survivable; our matter is unstable.

—Verinath, murdered by Nimrheal

"NOTHING?" BETHYN ASKED.

Koria answered with a blank expression. Robert had not responded to the last two scheduled javelin calls.

Bethyn's eyes wandered the room. "It could be broken," she suggested at last.

Koria did not bother replying. *Of course it could be broken.*

The silence went on, pregnant and tense.

"Well, fuck your stoicism, Koria," Bethyn sneered. "Try heralding him. You've always been able to find him if you tried hard enough, long enough. Knights know, you're the worst stalker I've ever seen, and that includes the cloaked man."

"The locus is still there. It's uninterpretable."

Bethyn rolled her eyes. Koria saw but did not care. Suddenly the brown-haired girl produced her usual sour smile. "How about a little deductive logic then?" She nodded pedantically. "This is your specialty, dear, so pay attention." Bethyn stared at Koria with big eyes.

"What?" Koria said when the expectant stare became irritating.

Bethyn's smile was almost sweet this time. "You don't need to interpret through the locus, Koria. You just need to see if Robert still shows up in the jumble of what you do see."

It was a clever idea. She had, in fact, seen Robert in her dreams again, but she did not fully trust these visions. "I love him *so* much, Bethyn. I might be projecting." A new idea gripped her. "*You* do it! Attempt a heraldic trance."

"In a locus?" Bethyn asked. Her expression was skeptical, but under this, Koria saw fear. Bethyn was a decent herald, but not a far one.

"Yes," Koria said. "I can watch over you."

"I don't think so," said Bethyn, sour again. "You know I love Robert too, so I might also project him into the heraldry." She got up and walked toward the heavy door. "But my love isn't as *perfect* as yours," she said acidly, "so it should all work out." She slammed the door behind her.

Bethyn. There was no predicting her moods and complex feelings. Koria also realized that her friend might have reason to feel hurt. And afraid. It had been easy, before, to dismiss the protestors who had ringed the New School from time to time. They were seldom well informed and often ridiculous. But they had also been manipulated by foreign powers and used against the duchy. More troubling, research from the medical-dynamics facility had found indications that the new grain *might* poison people, albeit a tiny percentage. To a very few, protesting the grain was not only correct, it was necessary. Koria did not like the protestors, but after living with the threat of Nimrheal for less than a week, she was starting to understand them better. Death from the heavens was a terrifying prospect. It threatened to reveal that the courage to learn new things was a kind of arrogance.

I am afraid, but I will fight.

Koria picked up another document. Verinath was an interesting writer, but she relied too much on logic and analogy. None of her conclusions were supported by proper testing. Still, it was interesting that she described Nimrheal as being *nearly* physical. Heylor had shown that Skoll was *definitively* physical. They still had the rotting arm to prove it. So, if Verinath's sources could be trusted, Nimrheal was similar to the other two demons, but *not* the same.

When are Eloise and Gregory going to arrive? She needed to hear their firsthand accounts.

The door swung open. "Armadale is here," Bethyn said. Her eyes were red, and her hair in disarray, bunched on one side.

"Okay," Koria said. "Thank you for telling me."

"No, you don't understand, Koria. *All* of Armadale is here."

Щ

Bethyn was exaggerating, but not by much. The Armadale embassy had brought two hundred soldiers. Standing high atop the cardinal tower with telescopes in hand, Koria and Bethyn were in an advantageous position to enjoy the spectacle. Sir Hemdale, in his dented armor, walked out to greet the ambassador. His massive Endicott sword was at his hip, and his hand was on its hilt. Gerveault and Arthur Wolverton walked on either side of the big knight, looking more like children than men next to him.

In the discussion that followed, Gerveault and Wolverton stood calmly enough, but Hemdale and the three plate-armored knights from Armadale who flanked their own ambassador did not appear so sanguine. "That's quite a lot of gesticulating, isn't it, Koria?" Bethyn was amused. One of the knights had tried to shove Hemdale but had instead almost fallen down. "What do you suppose they're arguing about?"

Koria did not have to think long. "How many of them to let in."

Bethyn's smile turned dark. "They should all be sent home."

"No," Koria said, "we want them here. We need to know what Armadale is up to." She did not say, "because we cannot tell by heraldry." Considering their last conversation, that would have been insensitive and might even have come across as a gibe. "Bethyn, I am sorry about putting pressure on you before. I—"

"No, it's fine," Bethyn interrupted. "I already looked. He's alive. Don't ask me more."

Koria hugged her friend, who went limp in her arms for a second or two before offering a cursory pat on the back. A moment later they had their telescopes to their eyes and were watching the drama again. Another knight from the castle had come out in full armor, though without her helm. *Sophia Haverland.* She was not tall, but her shining plate set off her dark Engevelen skin and hair to fine effect.

"It's escalating," murmured Bethyn.

Sophia had arrived about a week before to help ensure a quorum of the Council of Knights for the Ceremony of Rising. With Sir Kaimari unaccountably late and Sir Christensen having charged off alone to find the Bifrost, Haverland's presence was critical. *They still need at least one more Deladieyr.*

"Holy skolve shit, the bitch is back!" Bethyn exclaimed.

"What bitch?" Alone on a tower with Bethyn, Koria could indulge herself in the rare pleasure of coarse words.

"Look for yourself!" Bethyn pointed to three new horsemen who were passing through Armadale's lines.

It took Koria a moment to focus on them, but there was no doubt who they were. Eloise's size and long blond hair were strong indicators, but the shining shields that both she and Gregory bore before them were unequivocal. Gregory also wore bright chain mail and strangely reflective greaves. Eoyan March's goofy smile identified him just as surely. Koria could see his teeth all the way from the tower.

The three of them passed straight through the ranks of soldiers and through the first gate. Some waves were exchanged, but then Eloise spurred her horse and rode it around the small central group. Koria could hear Eloise's voice—the big woman was shouting—but could not make out the words. Koria trained her telescope on the ambassador. Yes, he was shouting as well. Eloise spurred her horse and drew her entropic sword, which flashed like lightning in daylight.

"Do you think she's going to start a war?" Bethyn said drily.

"Or end one." That was the kind of woman that Koria thought Eloise was. "Armadale does not always do what we expect," Koria mused, watching Eloise at work so far below. "Remember after the Battle of the Bifrost, when everyone thought we were going to war?" She remembered Robert and Christensen leaving to deliver the terrible news of the duchess's death to Kennyth Brice at the embassy siege. No one had expected that Armadale would back down after that. "And then they sued for peace."

Bethyn snorted, "Getting flattened will do that to you." Her voice took on a wistful tone. "Look at her go."

The shouting, gesticulating, and wild riding continued for a while longer. Finally, Gregory rode his horse up against Eloise's and nudged her away and on into the inner castle. Eoyan March followed them at a leisurely pace. Koria could see his lips move as he made some joke or other.

"Knights, I do hate her," Bethyn breathed.

"You do not."

"I don't." Bethyn collapsed her telescope. "Well, Ethelyn's going to get it tonight. I'll return your book." She winked at Koria. "I won't be needing it for a while."

Щ

In the end, it was decided that Armadale's ambassador could bring five attendants and whoever else they might have who was a candidate for the Ceremony of Rising. There was a bit of a game being played, because they immediately claimed that they had eight candidate knights, which was a ridiculous number, a clear ploy to get as many knights into the castle as they could. Even more strange was the absence of two Deladieyr Knights from Armadale, Sir Jormundheim and Sir Valcryst. It was their absence from the contingent that had caused Sir Hemdale to become so irate when the embassy arrived. Despite the fact that no explanation for the absences had been offered, it was decided that events would be allowed to proceed. The wall guards were doubled, and an additional encampment of soldiers of Vercors were stationed outside the walls to keep a close eye on the large contingent of Armadale denied entry to the castle. A feast was planned for that evening within the inner keep, and arrangements were also made so that the nearly two hundred other foreign soldiers left outside the wall could celebrate.

Koria sat at the duke's table. Eloise was also seated there, but farther down, on Kennyth Brice's right and as far from Armadale's ambassador as possible. Koria and Bethyn switched places with Lord and Lady Latimer so that she could speak with Eloise, who had been mysteriously unavailable before dinner. When Eloise arrived at the feast, she carried her sword and shield and an expression that said she was more likely to use them at dinner than her fork and knife. Lord Gregory Justice was a tall man, but he did not look it next to his wife. His amorphous greaves caused almost as much of a stir as his own sword and shield when he entered the room. Eoyan sauntered after the two, smiling his self-assured smile.

It's amazing Gregory is walking at all. The last time Koria had seen him, he had hobbled or needed to be carried. She could not help smiling. *If his wife had carried him into this dinner, there would have been no end of comments.*

Besides Armadale, both Kames and Harkness had small parties at the feast. Neither country had brought an army with them. In fact, neither had even brought a candidate for the ranks of the Deladieyr Knights. The word was that Sir Janice Nitrai had some problem to deal with back in Harkness, so she could only send her regrets and an envoy in her stead. Sir Leyzbeth Braynor of Kames was supposed to be coming but was still a few days out. She was also delayed by official duties but had been preceded by a small embassy.

That left Armadale's boisterous group. At the ducal table sat only the ambassador, Elias Vernon, cousin to the current king, Imre Vernon, and to the previous king, Albrecht Vernon, whom Sir Hemdale had executed nearly two decades previously, and a small blond boy who looked to be about eight years old. He was said to be Reingard Vernon, the only survivor of the embassy siege, the boy that Robert had carried out in his arms at the end of that terrible battle. Whenever Sir Hemdale looked his way, the lad flinched. Both Vernons had reason to fear the old knight. The display that Eloise had put on when she rode threatening circles around Elias's party must have made it clear that she also bore him a tremendous ill will. *I am starting to understand the reason that Armadale brought so many soldiers.*

Elias and Reingard might have been acting with a certain restraint for the sake of the occasion, but at the other table their knights were doing anything but. The loudest of that rowdy group were two rough-looking louts with "nine" blazoned in red on their surcoats. A somewhat sour young man sat between these two. He seemed quite popular, for the two ruffians were always laughing with him and slapping his back uproariously. More difficult to understand were the three red-haired women at the table. They were not the only women there, but they wore unusually fine cloaks, had hair the color of blood, and expressions sharp enough to draw some. Between whatever jokes were going around the table, these three women kept staring at Eloise. Was it a challenge? An invitation? The tallest of them even nodded to the Knight of Vercors. Eloise ignored them. Her eyes stayed on the two rough men, the Nines.

"There is something wrong with those men," she growled.

"There is something very right about those women," Bethyn said in a different kind of growl.

Eloise frowned thunderously. "Stay away from them, Bethyn. They aren't civilized like you are."

Bethyn colored at this as Eoyan March turned around to gaze at the three women. He was a man of happy, roguish looks, and his teeth were showing now. "They do look tasty. Uncle Eoyan can see why Bethyn is curious." He stood up. "Don't worry, *I* will wade into danger." He lowered his voice to a stage whisper and winked at Bethyn. "If they want to fraternize like civilized folk, I'll come get you. And by fraternize, I mean fu—"

"Eoyan!" Gregory interrupted, eyebrows clenching.

"Have *fun*, Lord Justice," Eoyan bowed. "I was about to say have *fun*. That must be why they came here, after all, not just to eat."

"Be careful it isn't *you* that gets eaten, stupe," Eloise sneered at his back. "And not in any way that's *fun*, you perv!" she called more loudly. Eoyan, well used to Eloise's scorn, sauntered toward the other table without reacting and was soon trading banter with the three women. In no time at all, they were all laughing like old friends. The tallest of the three women bounded up in response to something Eoyan had said. He pointed at a spot on his lower leg. The tall woman touched the spot. Eoyan tilted his head as if reconsidering some thought or memory and moved his finger higher on his leg. She followed it with her own, and the game continued, their fingers climbing toward Eoyan's groin. Everyone from Armadale seemed to find this hilarious. Their coarse guffaws echoed off the high stone ceiling of the feasting hall.

Koria remembered the last time she had heard such loud echoes in this room. It had been Heylor, covered in blood after appearing out of thin air and landing with a crash in the center of the duke's table. But the skinny young man had been as loud then by himself as Armadale's entire table was now. He had not, however, been laughing.

"Come on, stupe, let's go see that armorer now," Eloise said, pushing up from her chair. Gregory followed her without a word.

"What's this, Eloise?" Koria asked.

Eloise whirled on her, something fierce and primal flashing in her blue eyes. "What did you say? Look at what?" It was as if she was suddenly in another world.

Puzzled, Koria hesitated, but Bethyn scowled and jumped in. "She asked what you were on about, giant!"

Eloise froze, and her fierce expression evaporated as suddenly as it had appeared. "Oh," she said, snapping out of her trance and pushing her chair in. "I'll show you. Come on."

Koria, shaking her head, and Bethyn, still scowling, rose and followed Eloise and Gregory toward one of the arches leading out of the hall. As they left the room, Eloise gestured at Eoyan, who was still carrying on with the red-haired soldier. "Leave the stupe to do his work."

Moments later they passed out of the inner keep and turned down an alley within the outer castle walls. Koria counted eight separate forges. *The armorer's row.* It was not a place Koria frequented, swords and axes not being her interest. Every one of the forges was up and running despite the late hour. The air was filled with the sound of hammers banging, hand pumps pushing air, water sizzling, and rough voices calling back and forth. Smoke billowed everywhere, and the smell of hot metal and flaming coals was almost overpowering.

"What am I on about?" Eloise said, looking at both Bethyn and Koria in turn.

"We," said Gregory, "what are *we* on about."

"That's what I said, stupe!" growled Eloise. "Don't be so sensitive. We are preparing to leave. We've been provisioning since we got here. But we need to repair Gregory's shield first." She paused and glared at Koria. "And find out where Robert is."

"Gregory's shield is damaged!" exclaimed Bethyn. "I didn't think that was possible."

"It was Nimrheal, wasn't it?" Koria said. She had always known Gregory's shield was not invulnerable. Anything could be damaged, even destroyed, if enough power was applied, even the much stronger shield Eloise carried. But being possible did not make something likely. It would have required enormous, almost unimaginable force to damage the shield. *I'm surprised his arms weren't shattered.*

"It nearly broke both my arms," Gregory said as if reading her thoughts. He hefted up his shield to show the substantial dent just off the center of its face. "It must have thrown me twenty-five feet through the air."

Koria opened herself to the empyreal sky. There were a whole series of dislocations in the wonderful alloy that Robert had made. "I want to know everything you observed in your fight with Nimrheal."

"Sure," Eloise said. "We'll tell you everything. Stupe here," she pointed a thumb at Gregory, who listened unperturbed, "even made some notes right afterwards while I did all the work of saddling our horses. But first tell us where Robert is so we can finish the provisioning."

Koria almost asked Eloise why she was so focused on Robert but told herself that sometimes people kept secrets for good reason. *It could be argued that I trained her to stalk him.* Keeping Robert alive through that first year had become more than a hobby for the two girls. He had never realized how often he had been followed. "I don't know where he is, Eloise." She felt her eyes start to sting. "He is three check-ins overdue."

"Three," repeated Gregory, frowning. "So a day and a half or more." He knew the protocols for the Javelin mission. "Perhaps his javelin is damaged?"

All three women turned and stared at him at once. There had been a time when he would have blanched at this, but he had been married to Eloise for years. "It *could* be broken," he insisted.

"Where was he last?" Eloise shouted. Only the sounds of hammers on metal kept her volume and tone from attracting attention. With a look of monumental disgust, she bore her fierce blue eyes down on Koria. "How could you lose your stupe?"

Chapter Twenty-Five

The Three Vias of a Rising Knight

THE WEIGHT OF LIKELIHOOD WAS DROWNING ENDICOTT. IT WAS BELTED TO HIS HIP, and he was too busy being smashed against sharp rocks and tumbled around by angry water to even try unbuckling it. He did not know if he had killed Nimrheal—it seemed unlikely given how many times Koria had read the testimony of knights and wizards of the past who thought they had killed the demon—but he *knew* he had immolated Lindseth. Robert Endicott had fought and killed a great many people. All of them had been enemy combatants, most of them from Armadale, but their deaths weighed on the young man. He did not regret killing them. Not precisely. He had another feeling about it, one he had kept almost entirely to himself. Only one other person knew how he really felt. Koria. But Koria was not here, and now another, darker feeling weighed him down.

I have killed a friend.

Lindseth had been one of the finest people he knew. He had fought hard but hated no one, had been happy without being complacent, and had sought answers without the shackles of bias or the anger of insecurity. He had not been a quiet person. In fact, the lanky young man had asked more questions than anyone Endicott had ever met. But Lindseth had asked them softly, gently, carefully. Endicott had loved all those things about his friend. They had also been connected, deeply and intensely, through Syriol, Lindseth's beloved cousin, whose life Gregory and Endicott had once saved. Ever since Endicott had arrived at the New School, Lindseth had always been there, quietly cheerful, sanguine, philosophical. Now immolated by Endicott's own hand.

Endicott was wedged under a rocky shelf now, submerged and trapped. Rushing water would soon force its way into his lungs and end all his weighty thoughts. There was no escape.

He was abruptly yanked out and up by an irresistible force. From somewhere above, a hand grasped the collar of his leather jacket and hauled him, gasping and spluttering, onto a large, flat boulder just free of the current, where he lay coughing up water, dazed and disoriented. At first he thought it must have been Merrett. The big man had tried to keep a grip on him as they fell from the bridge, but the power of the racing water had been too strong even for Bat Merrett's grip. And Merrett, in any case, happened to be lying a few paces to Endicott's left, breathing hard and also trying to collect his wits, saved presumably by the same unknown hand. Endicott coughed up another lungful of water and looked up at his savior. Marielle Engel stood above him, gasping for breath, her right eye ruined by the chunk of metal that had flown into her skull as the bridge disintegrated.

It's a piece of Bat's sword, and it's there because of my recklessness, my crazy exact shaping innovation.

"I'm sorry," Endicott gasped.

"For love," she said puzzlingly and sat down.

That sounds familiar. He could not place the context. Maybe he would do so when he was not so fresh from nearly being drowned or as weighed down by other memories.

"I heard a voice, Robert. It called my name."

A voice? Engel's voice sounded exhausted for the first time Endicott had ever heard.

"What did you say?" Endicott asked when he had a little more breath in him and was able to raise his head to look at her.

Engel did not reply. She lay back on the sharp rocks and closed her one good eye.

"What happened to her?" Merrett asked a few moments later.

"Exhaustion," Endicott replied, though only after checking that she was still breathing. "Did she pull you out of the river too?"

Merrett nodded slowly, then began checking himself for injuries and missing equipment. "I've got nothing," he said when he had finished. Nothing but cuts on his face and arms and a broken nose. Even his backpack had fallen off. He looked ruefully at Endicott. "At least you've still got your pack."

"I do?" Endicott had not even noticed that he was still wearing his. *No wonder I couldn't seem to stay above water.* He spotted Engel's pack lying on some rocks not far away, though it looked crushed and empty. "She doesn't seem to be waking up," he said as Marielle Engel continued to lie still. He reached over and gently shook her. There was no reaction. He tried again. No response.

"Might be a while." He tried to keep the fear out of his voice.

All they could do was wait and in the meantime consolidate their remaining equipment into Endicott's backpack. When this was done, they managed to haul a still unresponsive Engel up a boulder-strewn line of weakness to the west side of the gorge, where they took stock. They had a few days of soggy hardtack, unappetizing fare to say the least, but with some nutritional value. They had one pair of even wetter extra socks, two waterskins, which were now full, a river-saturated blanket, and Endicott's water-damaged notebook. Their javelin had been smashed in the fall. The few pieces they had located were spread out before them.

"Can you fix it?" Merrett asked.

"Are you joking?"

"I saw you put together a cracked water reservoir with a hammer once."

"So you think if I hit this with a hammer, it would all pop back together again in working order?"

"Why not?"

"I didn't bring a hammer."

"Well, that was stupid of you, Blouse."

"What about Marielle?"

"I don't think you should hit her with a hammer."

"Too bad we don't have the shovel."

"She's not dead. You can't bury her."

Endicott tired of the game and started kicking the pieces of the javelin into the gorge. "To bury the pieces," he explained. "We need to make sure no one finds this."

"So they could hit it with a hammer?"

"Will you stop?" Endicott said, exasperated. He had never known Merrett to act quite so silly for quite so long. Taciturn was the word he normally used to describe the big, muscular man. Endicott took a good look at him. Bat was more deflated than Engel's pack had been. He looked smaller. Tired in spirit as much as in body

"We need to make a plan," Merrett said, crouching beside Engel, perhaps trying to rally himself. "What do you want to do, Captain?"

Endicott also crouched over Engel. The hunk of sword sticking out of her eye was too horrific to bear close examination. "In a perfect world, I would say that we find a way to the north plateau and go get the Bifrost. End of mission."

"If we try that, won't Nimrheal just come again?" Merrett asked, frowning at Engel's eye.

Would Nimrheal strike the same place twice? "Maybe. I don't know why it came last time." He sighed. "But we have only one sword between us, no way of contacting the duke or Gerveault for instructions when we do find the Bifrost, and Marielle to consider. I think we have to go back."

"What do you suppose this means?" Merrett gestured at Engel's sleeping form. "It can't be good that she's still unconscious."

Endicott sat down and looked at the big man. "It *might* be a good thing." Into Merrett's skeptical expression he added, "Remember the Three Vias?"

"What?"

"Those huge stained-glass windows in the Steel Castle in Vercors? All churches have them, though they're smaller at every other church. The three steps to Elysium, the bridges to heaven."

"Like the one you say is over there?" Merrett gestured vaguely in the direction of Arsenault Castle.

"Yes!" Endicott said, becoming excited now. "The last bridge has a physical component, well they all do, but the last one is an actual object. The journey to knighthood is a *metaphor*, that is what is important, Bat. Before becoming a Methueyn Knight, before crossing the last Via, the candidate must first Rise as a Deladieyr Knight. The Ceremony of Rising is also called the Middle Bridge to heaven. Do you know what happens there?"

"You hang."

"Yes. That has several purposes, Bat, and one is to demonstrate worthiness to the Council of Knights and everyone else. But the ceremony is just a structure people put around the deeper thing that is most important. The candidate must metaphorically *suffer.* They die and Rise, ready to become a knight, ready to join an angel in Elysium."

"I thought you hated the Steel Castle. How do you know all this?"

"I learned this in Statics as a child, same as you. Don't you remember?" Merrett shrugged, so Endicott forged on. "Everything in the first two Vias is about preparing. Preparing to become an adult, which must be about maturity, and then suffering, getting honed down to the one single idea that defines you. The middle bridge is a *traumatic* bridge, Bat, but when the candidate Rises from it—crosses it—they Rise more certain and powerful than before. *That* may be what is happening to Marielle right now. Passing through her suffering to wake in eight days—well, I hope sooner than that—more powerful than ever before. Angelic."

"You think so, Blouse?"

Endicott could not tell what Bat was feeling. The man was opaque to him. "I do. There must be ten old stories just like this. Remember Yeyncie Greene? She was the last one." Endicott had read a lot about the young girl after meeting Koria. "She Rose as a Deladieyr Knight and later crossed the Bridge as a Heydron after being beaten repeatedly by her father. She Rose after waking from a coma!"

"All right," Merrett said. "I'll carry her first."

▽

"HOW LONG IS THIS GOING TO TAKE?" THE BIG MAN DID NOT NORMALLY ASK QUESTIONS like this, but at the end of a long day of carrying Marielle Engel, the distance may have begun to feel personal to him.

"Probably the rest of our lives." Endicott broke off a piece of hardtack and passed it to Merrett. "Five or six days to the wheat line, two, two-and-a-half days to the Castlereagh Line, then maybe another day to Ardvaser."

"So four days," Merrett said.

"Four sounds good." Endicott did not dispute the dissociative mathematics. He looked over at Engel. He had used dynamics to dry off the soaked blanket, and they had propped her up and tucked her in with her head resting on Endicott's leather jacket. He was past caring whether Skoll or Hati might be attracted by his use of dynamics. *Protocol be damned.* "She looks like an angel, doesn't she?"

"In the moonlight, now that the moon is up."

"Ready then?"

"If you think you can carry her."

Engel was no Eloise Kyre, but she was not a small woman either. Endicott picked her up as gently as he could. There was no possibility of carrying her like a baby. He could not do that for any length of time with a hundred-and-fifty-pound load. She had to be carried over the shoulder. They rigged up the blanket around her chest so that her head would not bang against their backs as they walked. Neither man wanted to disturb that piece of metal in Engel's eye. In moonlight and silence, they walked on. They continued walking when the sun rose the next day, taking turns with their precious cargo whenever they needed to.

"She said she did it for love," Endicott mumbled as the day grew hot. "I used to do things for love."

"You still do." Merrett did not bother looking at him. His eyes stared straight in front of his feet. It was likely the only way he could keep going. "Shut up already, you're just tired."

"You know, I told myself I didn't love her because I couldn't ever really *know* her."

"Hmm."

"That was a lie, Bat. I love her now."

"Well, that's good. It's your turn to carry her." He stopped and gently lowered Engel. "You know what, though? She has one fat arse."

Engel's behind was not fat. It was sizable, but muscular. Not that this mattered. The mind goes to strange places to avoid pain and drudgery. Endicott's feet felt more like two hot coals than flesh and bone. He thought about taking his shoes off to have a look at them every time they stopped to nibble on a tiny piece of moldy hardtack or to sleep for an hour, but always thought better of it. *Best not to know.*

Much later and many miles farther, Endicott was reminded of his long, exhausting journey from the Line to the Battle of the Bifrost four years before. It had been very different then. He and Gregory had horses. They also had the guidance of Gael Guise. And good roads. There were no roads through the Ardgour wilderness, not now. The old Engevelen road system, which had existed long before Nehring Ardgour invaded, was overgrown, broken by rivers, and degraded by two centuries of erosion.

It had also been different then because Endicott had been out of his mind, only holding himself together through some strange equilibrium of love and need. He had found a simplicity in the insanity of his traumatic dreams, a mission that blotted out all others. He struggled with that now, not because he did not love Marielle Engel, but because he did not love himself as he used to. He was burdened by memories he did not have then, by terrible acts he had performed since.

Every step hurt. One after another into their hundreds, their thousands, into their tens of thousands. He accepted the pain. It was for Engel. As he marched through the night, the long misery sometimes brought some moments of giddy humor, at other times a vertiginous sense of separation from reality. Sometimes, returning to reality, even the smallest pleasant sensation was heavenly. The warm feeling of morning sunlight on his face was Elysium itself. He had not known until he felt those rays that the cold night was ending. The surprise arrival of daylight made him smile despite the weight on his shoulders.

"When do you suppose she's going to wake up and Rise?" Merrett suddenly asked.

"Soon, I hope." Endicott replied.

"What about her eye?"

"It will *heal*, Bat. Deladieyr Knights heal without medicine, and fast."

"I can't wait to see that."

"Me too."

Walking so far with such a burden and almost no food, and with a terrible psychic weight of worry, brings out elements of anyone's personality they would never normally expose. Merrett actually *conversed* at times. At one point they had to wade through a large, shallow pool in the moonlight. Beyond exhaustion, in a state where they lacked the will even to stop, the two men hoisted their friend together over their heads.

"Don't skolving drop her, Blouse!" Merrett warned when Endicott almost lost his grip on Engel as they struggled through a stretch of water up to their necks.

"*You* don't drop her."

"Maybe we could use her as a boat."

Endicott stumbled and almost went under. He coughed water from his mouth. "A boat would be nice right now."

"She can carry *us* for a change when she's done resting," Merrett grunted, his boot stuck on something.

"You? You're knights-damned heavy as a house, Bat. Nobody is carrying you anywhere."

"That's not true," Merrett said with affected soberness. "Looking after you school kids all these years has been a lot of work. I've lost weight."

Now Endicott's boot was stuck. It was soft mud that sucked at his feet as if it wanted to swallow him. "How—grrrh—did you manage it between our—knights-damned-mud—running around and Armadale, and Keith Euyn?"

"Lucky, I guess?"

"What, lucky you were assigned to us?" Endicott could not believe what he was hearing. "You didn't mind looking after us in the Orchid after all?"

"Hati's hell no, Blouse. I hated every minute of it. Still do." Merrett managed another sucking step through the muck. It was like wading through goose shit. "I was just lucky that, with all your stupidity, your rushing around half loaded, not listening to your professors—or my wise counsel—none of you ever died on me. That would have been tough on my chances for promotion."

"That at least makes sense." The mud was less troublesome and the water shallower. Endicott could see the shore not too far away, and not a moment too soon; his shoulders were shaking from the strain of holding Engel so high. "If we get out of this alive, let's agree never to work together again."

Merrett sighed long and loudly. "That hope is all that's keeping my feet going."

If we get out of this alive and Marielle is okay, I'll agree to anything.

They still had days of walking.

$$\nabla$$

"Maybe we'll Rise too after this," Endicott said, rubbing his toes through his rotting boot. He was seriously afraid now that if he took his feet out of the boots and his socks off his feet, his toes might fall off. "It's starting to feel a mite traumatic."

"This is the last of it." Merrett was carefully chewing the last finger-sized chunk of hardtack.

Endicott chewed on that news. "It wasn't very good anyway."

"That's a good thing."

"Why?"

"So we won't miss it now that there's none left."

"Mmm. I didn't realize you were an optimist, Bat."

"Maybe you could Rise, Blouse," Merrett said, swallowing the last tiny bit of the tack. "I always thought you would become a big-K knight."

"Really?"

"You just didn't let yourself."

If only it were that simple. He prepared the blanket again and, with Merrett's help, picked up the still form of Engel. His head swam, but he stood for a moment and the world stilled. "Well, I'm going to let myself carry Marielle out of here." Engel's weight began to seem less than it was, the burden easier.

What Merrett had said came very close to his secret, the thing he only discussed with Koria. Out so far in the wilderness, Endicott felt a new closeness to the big, unpredictable man. He knew it went both ways. They shared the knowledge that they would probably die, that their efforts to carry Marielle out were likely doomed. At any moment, skolves could find them, or Skoll or Hati. *Maybe I'll accidentally have an original thought and Nimrheal will come again.* He knew there would be no surviving that. The two men were as close as they would ever be, but Endicott would still not open up and discuss the last painful truth that he had learned the day Eleanor had died.

Not everything should be shared.

Day became night. They had meant to sleep for a half hour, but Endicott snapped awake, sure they had slept at least an hour, and got them moving again. He used heraldry to see in the moonless dark, not caring about Skoll and Hati.

Let them come.

He started walking. Full, ripe wheat heads brushed his legs as he trudged along. They had crossed the wheat line a few hours before but were still some distance from the Castlereagh Line. He knew if they did not come back from the wilderness soon, there was no point in ever returning. They would all be dead, events would move past them, or others more important than they would be dead. *Koria.* In the past, in fact as recently as the moment before the battle with Nimrheal, he would have been pleased to speak about how far the wheat had penetrated into the wilderness. The large new grain was one of the New School's proudest achievements, controversial though it was. It had pushed the skolves back as it advanced, but people had not yet followed. It was still too early for that. The area between the Castlereagh Line and the wheat line was still, in some sense, the most abandoned area in the world.

We are almost there, but who are we? What have we become?

Engel had spoken of love, as Endicott used to, but he remembered shouting hate into the wind as he attempted to obliterate the demon. *I do love.* Jon Indulf had said the same thing long ago. Strangely enough, the haughty young man had then found love with Jennyfer Gray. If Jon Indulf could find love, anyone could. Endicott knew it was right to hate Nimrheal. But he had shouted his hate, felt the hot, poisonous emotion before the demon had even acted. *That means the hate was within me.*

Endicott had opposed the protestors, but his most effective act had been, after much delay and debate, to speak with them. Even if a battle had followed, he had spoken, trying to find peace. *I did not hate them.* He had never hated anyone who spoke against him. Sometimes opposition was irritating, sometimes illuminating, but it did not merit the sick, angry feeling he had directed at the demon.

I hate myself.

Hatred felt sick. It was revolting. Hate felt like a delirium, an insanity. It was wrong. It took him away from who he was. He could not forget shouting at the demon. He could not forget how he had felt at the embassy siege.

Disappointed. That is when I started hating myself.

Engel was over his shoulder, and they had miles to go before they could get help for her, before she awoke, Risen.

I will not carry this woman with hate in my heart.

It was another thought that Merrett might have labelled maudlin, at least before this long return journey had started. And it might indeed have seemed trite or pretentious, probably like many of the things Endicott said, but it felt right. The truth can be uncomfortable, but out so far, beyond hungry and exhausted, he would not shy away from uncomfortable truths. He had never had any trouble speaking of his love before, but admitting to his own hate—and thus purging himself of it—was another thing. At the limit of extremity, there was no point in anything but the plainest truths or the most obvious lies.

Walking along, weighed down by his psychic burdens as much as his physical one, but determined to acknowledge only pure truth or honest lie, he thought about Lindseth.

I killed my friend.

It was an accident.

No, it had been deliberate. Yet he had not *wanted* to do it. He had had no choice, Nimrheal would have killed them all. He had been forced to use the exact shaping technique, but he had loved Jeyn Lindseth, and now he hated that he was not good enough or smart enough to have found a way that did not involve killing such a good man. It was disappointing, if such a small word could be used. It was the disappointment of falling into an infinitely deep well.

He thought about wise, gentle Lindseth. The man had been a soldier, but with a poet's sensitivity.

He knew I did what I had to do. That's why he looked me in the eye.

Jeyn Lindseth would not have been disappointed in his friend. Endicott knew that.

I wish I could have carried him out of there.

Before every mission, Jeyn's mother always asked Endicott to bring her son back safe to her. He would not do that this time. He could not bring Lindseth back at all.

But I can carry Marielle.

A realization clicked in his heart. Carrying Marielle so she could later Rise would be the act of suffering that would allow him to let go of his disappointment with himself. It was not, at first, a conscious thought, and it did not happen all it once. The emotional process had been building during the entire, painful journey. Understanding the journey as an act of contrition had coalesced as slowly as the accumulation of their thousands of steps, and it came together first in a deep, instinctive place, an unconscious, subliminal narrative in his soul. Only when the idea—the feeling—had fully formed did it click consciously. He understood in both his heart and his mind that protecting Engel the way he had not been able to protect Lindseth was sacred. Carrying this burden, this friend, was both an act of penance and of self-forgiveness. Even without all this, Endicott would have continued carrying Marielle. She was his teammate. They were supposed to look after each other. He knew she would become the greatest of the Deladieyr Knights.

I do love her. She raised me up out of the water, and I will carry her out of here like the person I used to be.

"Robert."

"What?"

"What do you mean, what?" Merrett growled.

"You just said my name."

Merrett scowled, but it was only half a scowl. His face looked droopy, and he did not seem to have the energy for his usual animosity. "I don't ever want to hear your name again. Didn't we agree on that?"

"We did," Endicott admitted. *Strange.* He was sure he had heard someone call his name.

"Great. Keep it to yourself."

"Okay."

Sometime later—probably a long time, but whatever time it was, it was sub-jectively very distant from the time before—Merrett decided to speak again. He had spent his entire turn carrying Marielle in a scowl-enforced silence. Now it was Endicott's time to carry her again. "You seem to be bearing up pretty good, considering."

"Considering wha—hey, there's the Line." The Castlereagh Line rose up ahead of them. They had been looking for it all day, but when Endicott saw it, he was surprised. And now, there it was, not more than a couple of miles away at most, though still only a blur. When they had hobbled a little closer, they were able to make out the tower farther down to their left. They angled toward it. The extra distance was worth it. They needed the garrison's help.

When they were four hundred yards out, the nested portcullises were raised, and eight soldiers rushed out, an officer following them.

"It's Sir Robert ..." one of the young men said, his voice trailing off. He tried to speak again, but only got out, "Oh, my knights."

Endicott was far beyond caring how bad he and Merrett looked. They were unshaven, mud-stained, reeking. Their boots were only holding on because the laces—which had snapped repeatedly—had been retied in shorter and shorter sections, their jackets were ruined, their hair greasy, their eyes red, and their reserves of strength totally used up. Endicott cared only about one thing.

"You obviously don't know Sir Robert very well, Private," came the voice of Emyr Wynn. "He never returns from across the Line with his equipment in good order." She stepped through her eight, mouth open to say something witty, happy, or buoyant, then got her first proper look at the trio. Her mouth tightened, and the sparkle left her dark eyes. "Daligh. Get a stretcher and blan-kets. Call the doctor here. Now! And get the kitchens fired up and some hot water in the troughs."

Endicott would not let any of the soldiers help him with Marielle Engel. When the stretcher arrived, he and Merrett laid her in it as gently as a baby. When she was tucked in, Endicott stumbled a few paces away to collect his thoughts and steady his hands. He wished he could fall asleep like the enchanted prince in some story and forget the long march out of the wilderness. Along with everything that had led up to it. He felt bone weary but doubted he could sleep more than fitfully, if at all. Every inch of his body throbbed with pain. And every corner of his soul. There might be sleep, but there would be no forgetting.

"She's dead," came the doctor's voice from behind him. "She's been dead for days. Stinks. Bloody stupid carrying her for that long when they aren't much better off than she is."

"Maybe they didn't realize," said one of the soldiers amid a rising hubbub.

Endicott looked sideways. Merrett was standing beside him, looking down at the dirt.

"Shut it!" shouted Emyr Wynn, then in a quieter tone. "Do you really think they didn't know?"

Chapter Twenty-Six

Style

"I NEED STYLE!" HEYLOR EXCLAIMED AS HE RACED DOWN THE STAIRWELL OF THE MATHematics and physics building. He tore along the steps, feet moving on the ragged physiologic ends of firing patterns, jumping some of the landings, willing gravity to allow him a faster flight. The torrent of images from the Eindarch Eye had been more like a chaotic punch to the mind than a coherent foretelling of the future, but he had *seen* the cloaked man following Camille and somehow known the image was not from a night in the future.

"Slow down, Style, or you're going to fall down and give yourself worse bruises than you had when Gael brought you to me." Lynwen was falling behind. She had a short sword on one hip and a baton on the other. They made it difficult to run at the best of times, and Heylor was nothing if not fast. And he had nothing on his hip. The sword he had proudly named Style was somewhere in the Ardgour Wilderness, lost.

I need something in my hand!

He had met two other cloaked men in the past. Neither of them had been vanquished without a sizable body count. Heylor almost ran past the ground floor door. If he had kept going, he would have encountered the secret guard troop who ensured the security of the huge javelin prototype that was kept in the basement. He almost collided with a runner who was rushing in from outside and heading down, probably with a message for the duke at Ardvaser. Despite the ground floor door being partly open, Heylor still jammed both hands on it. Stepping outside and entering the square, he cursed himself.

I should have borrowed a sword from one of the guards.

He would have turned around and done just that if he was the kind of person who made a habit of thinking twice, walking when he could run, or evaluating a situation carefully when he could jump in with both feet. He could pause and think only under great duress, after extensive training, or in one of his sour, self-critical moods.

This time something else prevented him from hesitating or turning back. It was a need in his heart, a hole in his reason, and a fuel for his muscles. He could not stop. Somewhere in the receding night behind him, he heard Lynwen open the heavy door behind him. "Behind the Lords' Commons!" he yelled over his shoulder and sprinted into the night. There could be no excuses this time.

In Aignen, Heylor had nearly destroyed both of the town's water tanks. He had taken the easy way out by succumbing to hypothermia while Robert saved the town. He had missed the battle of the Bisecting Alleys. Robert had fought it alone. He had run away from the Battle of the Bifrost, jumping in the river to avoid fighting, saved only because Robert had sent Jeyn Lindseth to fish him out, a decision that may have forced Robert into an act of self-damaging ruthlessness. When Keith Euyn had terrorized the Citadel, Heylor had only joined in at the last moment, leaving Robert to face the deadliest man of the modern world alone. In the wilderness, when Skoll came, he had left his eight to die.

I have been a coward.

The cloaked man had become a trigger for Heylor, a symbol of the greatest danger and malice. A cloaked man had killed Jeyk Johns, the guard at the Bifrost. A cloaked man had killed Davyn while Heylor had lain on the cold stone floor trying to gather the courage to get up. The very name made his heart race and his skin clammy. The name unmanned him. It stole his reason, his humanity, his heart. The cloaked man exposed the weak little boy that Heylor had always known he was.

But not today.

Heylor had always run away. Earlier today, he had seen a thing worse than any cloaked man, a demon from outside this world, a transcendental creature no one seemed capable of defeating. It was not that seeing Nimrheal had made the cloaked men seem smaller and less dangerous. The evil of humanity still had enough depths to terrorize anyone, certainly the flighty and sensitive young man that was Heylor. Seeing Nimrheal had crystallized something else, an awareness that cloaked *men* could be faced. They were human, and humans were responsible for them. Heylor knew he could never defeat an otherworldly entity like Nimrheal, but he had decided it was time to stop running away from his worldly responsibilities.

No cloaked human was going to terrorize his campus or his friends. For the first time in his life, Heylor used all his great speed to run toward something rather than away from it.

Tearing around a huge dark building, Heylor emerged into the lighted walkway to the Lords' Commons. He turned again, putting on a burst of speed and passing under the wide branches of a spruce tree, smelling sap and green needles. He turned another corner, saw the horses and carriages on the Ring Road to his right, and plunged into the shadows between two smaller buildings. There, ahead of him, a massive figure was raising a spear at someone. At Camille Engel. He reached for another burst of adrenaline and, shouting for all he was worth, flew the last few yards into a shuddering collision with the cloaked man.

The next thing he knew, he lay sprawled across the cobbles. "H-Heylor!" It was Camille, saying his name, pulling on his arm. "Get up."

Heylor scrambled to get his feet. A sharp pain shot through his scalp.

"Get back!" cried Camille "Ahhh!"

I've been stabbed.

Heylor felt the blood running down his face. The cloaked man was thrusting his spear wildly. There was no art to his technique, but it was fast and violent and potentially no less deadly for its lack of finesse. Heylor glanced quickly at Camille. She was holding her right shoulder.

The fucker has stabbed her too.

It was dark. Heylor could not see the face of whoever it was that was thrusting a spear at the two of them with more enthusiasm than skill. Between the dark cowl and the shadows, no glimpse of who the cloak hid could be obtained. But one thing was clear. Their adversary was a very loud breather.

He's enjoying himself.

Heylor pushed a half step in front of Camille, trying to protect her, and received a spear tip to his right hand for reward. The pain was sharp and brought nausea with it. "Fucking skolve! Stop that," he shouted at the cloaked man.

"Why are you doing this?" Camille desperately cried. Unlike her sister, she did not have exceptional strength, skill, or speed, and she was too early in her studies to be able to perform any useful dynamics. Heylor never even considered resorting to any himself. He was capable of powerful offensive dynamics, but he needed more space and time than he had now.

The cloaked man did not answer or stop. He stabbed at Camille again, but Heylor knocked the edge of the weapon aside with his left hand, taking another nasty cut.

"Fuck you!" Heylor cried, holding his bleeding hands out, trying to hold off the bloody spear. They were both going to die. He could leave, tunnel himself somewhere else as he had done before.

No.

Camille would die and, alive or not, Heylor knew that he would never truly live if he ran away again.

"Hhhah!" the cloaked man said, stabbing at him again, breathing harder than ever, frantically excited. Pain lanced from Heylor's left hand to his brain.

His mind went elsewhere. It flew up and out of the city, north, past Ardvaser Castle, past the Castlereagh Line, and the last standing wheat, farther north to a forest at the foot of a mountain range. His mind went to the small grove where Skoll had caught him, to the tangle of shrubbery and rotting wood where his sword had fallen when the demon had grabbed him by the throat.

Amazingly, it was still there.

CRRAAAK.

With a sound like thunder, Style appeared in Heylor's bleeding right hand. The spear hung in the air, whether because Heylor's mind was working at supernal speed or because the cloaked man had frozen in surprise did not matter. Ignoring the pain in his hand, Heylor struck and half the spear flew off to clatter against the wall of the building on his left.

"Don't move!" Heylor roared, Style ready to strike again.

The cloaked man threw what was left of his spear haft at Heylor, but instead hit Camille in the stomach. He turned to run.

THWACK.

His face had run straight into Lynwen's baton.

Cowls don't do much to cushion batons. The puddle of teeth on the pathway informed Heylor of this fact. The next thing he knew he was sitting not far from what had once been the cloaked man's smile, trying to arrange in his mind which jagged piece went with which and where in the cloaked man's jaw they had belonged. Heylor looked down and saw that his hands had been bandaged. He felt his forehead. His scalp wound had been sewn together, and a cloth was wrapped around his head. Someone had thrown a blanket over his shoulders. Camille was holding it down with her arm. She had finished giving her statement to the constabulary, and the toothless cloaked man—another student—had been taken away. A crowd of constables had shown up to light the alley with lanterns, make measurements, gather evidence, and count teeth.

"Mind if I steal the hero of the hour from you, Miss Engel?" It was his constable, free at last from her part of the proceedings. Lynwen started to take him by the hand, then reconsidered and grabbed his arm to pull him away from the lantern light and the other constables. "Are you cheating on me already, Heylor Style?"

He smiled. "Are you going to hit me with your baton now?"

"I'm thinking about it, but you may need your teeth."

"I love you."

Lynwen folded him into her arms. "Knights, you can run fast, Heylor." She squeezed him harder. "Don't do that again, okay?"

"You do scare me, but I don't really want to run from you, Lynwen."

He felt her lips near his ear. "Why don't we go do that thing we were talking about doing earlier?"

T

THEY DID NOT DO THAT THING. HEYLOR'S SCALP STARTED BLEEDING AGAIN, AND THEY DECIDED that his hands needed stitches too. He was not patched up properly until the early hours of the morning, and then the constabulary medic declared him unfit to work. He could not even carry Style, let alone wield it effectively, with his hands heavily bandaged. As they parted, he asked Lynwen to meet him at the Apprentice's Library in the afternoon instead of in the morning at his parents' house. Useless hands or not, he had something he had to get done in the morning, something that needed to be made right.

"Dad!" he called, walking into the kitchen where his father was eating oatmeal at the table. Pieces of telescopes and assorted tools lay all over the tabletop, along with what looked like pieces of a meat grinder. *He doesn't have the Eindarch Eye in pieces there, does he? And what on the knights' earth is the grinder for?* Then, recovering from the incongruity of the scene, Heylor remembered he had left the Eye with Meredeth Callum.

"Hmm?" said Herevor.

"Where did you get that top hat you were wearing the other day?"

It took longer than he expected, but a couple of hours later Heylor emerged from the high-end hatters' shop with a box under his arm. Later, he found the only distiller who seemed to be open and added two sealed glass jars to his goods. After concealing everything in a stout cloth bag, he went after his quarry. Despite the bag, he felt curiously unburdened.

Something was wrong in the city of Vercors, however. That was certain. Most shops were closed up tight, windows shuttered. Few people walked the streets. There seemed to be a low rumbling from somewhere. He walked the Ring Road, listening to the rumbling ebb and flow. When he stepped over an abandoned sign, he started to get an idea of what was going on. The sign read:

"Look at

What you

Have done!"

The return of Nimrheal had left a deep impression on Heylor, but his unauthorized use of the Eindarch Eye, the violent encounter with the locus it facilitated, and then the even more violent encounter with the cloaked man had made Nimrheal's reappearance seem like it had happened weeks ago rather than the day before. It must be very different for the people of the city.

The garbage has been picked up at least.

He knew he was on the right track.

A little farther down the street, Heylor saw the crowd of people ahead. Some had signs, some sticks, and some waved hats. Most waved fists. It was a mob. He crossed to the far side of the road and continued to approach. The mob roiled like a cloud. It reminded him of that day four years back when they had tried Syriol's surviving rapist in court. The crowd that day had seemed to almost boil, moving under the rules of some strange physics he did not understand.

Sergeant Kayne, Lynwen's superior officer, rushed by him with twenty other constables in tow. None of them were Lynwen. She also had the day off. Then he saw Tessa, the four-year-old girl from his last encounter with the protestors, and her mother. Tessa held a sign bearing the helpful message:

"You get

What you

Deserve."

Another sign, held by a well-dressed man, said:

"You change things
Saying you know best.
Why didn't you
See this coming?"

One more sign caught his attention. Carried by an ancient, stooped country woman, it said:

"You took the past.
Give us back
Our Knights."

I'm not changing any of these minds or hearts.

Heylor picked up his pace. He had resolved not to be a coward, but there was such a thing as idiotic bravery. He chuckled, thinking once more of the time Robert had lectured a crowd of Nimrheal cultists about accepting change. That had not worked out too well.

Only Robert would try that.

Once he had passed the mob, leaving behind what was already shaping up to be a pitched battle with the constabulary, Heylor recrossed the Ring Road again. Sackelly-belly-full-of-jelly was just ahead with his wagon and road crew, hobbling around like his legs were made of wood, picking up the garbage.

"Ho, Sackelly!" Heylor called, approaching.

Belly-full-of-jelly straightened up from throwing a pail full of night soil, rusty nails, and reddish clothing into the wagon so that he could relax his nostrils and frown at Heylor. "My old friend, Heylor Style. The big hero."

Heylor set down his bag and held his bandaged hands up for his old friend to see. "I've got the scars to prove it. Well, I will, when they heal."

"You were involved in all that ruckus last night?" Sackelly asked, leaning on the wagon. His two fellows joined him.

"I wouldn't have missed it." Heylor smiled at his bearded friend. "Hey, do you have a flat surface somewhere? I've got something for you."

Sackelly shook his head. "Yer bleeding, fool. Don't come any nearer to the garbage wagon." He looked down the road. "There's a bench down the way. Let's go there. The boys can get on without me for a bit."

When they were all set up at the bench. Heylor managed to get the two jars of water out of the bag despite his bandaged hands and lay the box a little to one side of them.

"You got a bit of a scratch on yer head too." Sackelly said, pointing at Heylor's scalp.

"You should see the other guy. My girlfriend got him good."

"That pretty constable? She looks like she can swing a big baton."

She certainly can.

"Watch this," Heylor instructed. He twisted the lids off the jars of water. *I learned my lesson on this.* Then he made a tiny innovation, borrowing energy from the air. Both mugs frosted. A succession of mist rings fluttered through the air.

Sackelly almost jumped off the bench, possibly would have if his legs were not, in fact, made of wood. "What the hey!"

"Try it," Heylor said, raising one of the jars to his lips and drinking. "It's cold."

Sackelly squinted suspiciously at him, a comical expression on his coarsely bearded face. "Are my lips going to freeze to the glass?"

"I'm not trying to trick you," Heylor said patiently. "I'm trying to make amends."

Still looking skeptical, Sackelly-belly-full-of-jelly took a cautious sip of the nearly frozen water. "Heydron! That's cold!" he almost dropped the jar. They both sipped a little more.

"So how is this supposed to make everything right between us, Heylor?" Sackelly said after taking a longer drink. "What you did wasn't very nice."

"I know," replied Heylor. "I'm sorry. Also for not apologizing years ago when I should have."

The bearded man's expression was opaque. "As if it would have done any good."

"Maybe, maybe not," said Heylor with a wry smile. "If I had done it, you might have felt better about it. I might've too. Instead, we're both stuck back at that moment when I did … what I did."

"So that's it, then?" Sackelly asked, finishing the drink.

Heylor slid the box toward him. Sackelly had lost both his legs somewhere in between their falling out and their reunion. There were years of hard, likely bitter events, unknown and unshared. What Heylor had done, the theft of Sackelly's hat—probably his only hat—all those years ago had seemed a small thing. Perhaps it meant nothing and had little to do with anything that had happened to his old friend afterwards, but Heylor knew that apologizing and sharing a glass of chilled water was certainly not all he could do now. "Nope. I thought we would catch up a little more when you aren't working and I've finished dealing with," he held up his bandaged hands, "the latest crises I've gotten myself into." He tapped the box. "This is a gift. Restitution for what I stole from you." *A chance for both of us to move on.*

Sackelly opened the box, unwrapped the tissue paper, and gently removed the leather sunhat from the box.

T

Lynwen found an uncharacteristically mellow-looking Heylor waiting for her at a table in one corner of the Apprentice's Library.

"Thanks for smashing that cloaked man's face," he said by way of greeting.

"For you dear, I did it with extra teeth." She widened her eyes and added, in a conspiratorial whisper, "Don't tell the posts I said that."

Heylor ordered scones, tea, and cream—his treat, he explained, because she had saved him the night before. Lynwen laughed, and he launched at once into the conversation that he most needed to have that day but also that he most dreaded. "I have something to tell you, Lynwen."

"Talk, apprentice constable," she said, thoughtfully chewing a mouthful of scone.

I'm not an apprentice constable.

Yes, I am.

Don't get distracted.

Get on with it.

Fine.

"Er, I don't want to bore you by talking about the same things I've been talking about since I returned from … up north, but I think I have to."

"Okay," she said.

"I mean, it really must seem trying to you that I can't just learn my lesson and move on, but I can't seem to."

He scratched his lacerated scalp with one bandaged hand, but Lynwen swatted his paw away before he could make his head bleed again.

"I've been counting, you know. This will be the twenty-ninth time I've brought some version of this up with you, dear. Twenty. Nine. *Th.* So, obviously, I need to find a way to move on, to change, even if there's a very good chance that when you know me … in full, you'll hate me, or at least just feel really tired of me and my endless stupidities. So I have to tell you one more time, and this time tell you everything."

"Hmmf." Lynwen raised her eyebrows. "Heylor Style, you know I have been a constable for almost five years now. That's a quarter of my life. I know what people are like. I see them all the time, though mostly when they're angry or frightened. I see them drunk, I see them despondent, I see them when their loved ones have died, and sometimes when they've killed their loved ones. In one way or another, I have seen people in every less than admirable state that human nature allows."

The young constable reached across the table, gently took Heylor's bandaged hands, and held his eyes with her hers. "I've seen them when they do the same dumb, wrong thing for the fiftieth, the hundredth time. I've heard them say they'll never drink another bottle, smoke another fag, raise a hand to their kids, wife, husband ever again. Then they do it again. And again." She smiled tightly. "Most people don't change much, and they don't change easy."

"So, okay, I'm not boring you, but you also don't believe I can change?"

Lynwen laughed softly. "You *never* bore me, Heylor Style. You're the most dynamic person I've ever met that never scared me to death."

"Oh." He remembered that Lynwen felt Robert Endicott was an enigma, barely human, terrifying, and that Koria Valcourt was unapproachable by the likes of her.

"Oh yes, dear. You have an awesome power to change things, but unlike some of your friends, you are still human. And," she squeezed his hands gently, "just because people rarely manage to change doesn't mean they shouldn't try."

"I want to marry you, Lynwen."

"Good."

"Right away, before Nimrheal comes back."

Life may be short.

"Always in such a hurry." But her eyes twinkled mischievously as she said this. She rubbed her fingers along the bandages that covered his hands. "You're not even out of your mittens yet."

Heylor took a deep, calming breath. His heart was racing. He knew he needed to tell her the whole story, expose himself fully. *She might not want to be with me afterward, but it's better if she knows now.* "You need to know the worst about me before we're married. There is a story I want to tell you. About what happened to my eight. You need to know why I killed them."

Chapter Twenty-Seven

Inventive Breakthrough, Part 3

We all stood on the edge of transformation. Cornell's fingers trembled on his stick of chalk. It seemed like no one breathed. Even the rough soldiers appeared to hold their breath. Despite the palpable tension in the air, I risked a glance up at Darday'l.

Standing on the retractable roof of the cardinal tower, she seemed to float on air. When I was with her last night, I had felt that I was floating. Several times. She had been wonderful. Soft, hard, giving, taking, strong, yielding … curious. I had known her in ways I had never known anyone before. It was not a question of her gender. It was because of who she was inside and what she was willing to share, what she was able to draw out of me. Did I view her now as a sex object? Well, I was not going to forget the sex anytime soon, but it was the intimacy that I would treasure. That was something that could not be objectified, a bridge between two souls that could not be laid down by force or empyreal power. The Methueyn Knights wrote on their treaty in their biggest letters, "You Are Free." I had never thought before that freedom was so crucial to intimacy, but I knew now that it was. The unburdening of pretensions, the freedom from affectations, these were the prerequisites to this exquisite but delicate phenomenon.

Even though I hoped Rodryck Cornell would snap, or at least snap his chalk instead of solving his equation, I smiled up at Darday'l. But what were the chances of a solution, really? Wasn't invention almost as delicate a thing as our intimacy? I thought Gil Harbinger was likely correct; no act of creativity was going to flower here under so many watchful, tense eyes. It would be like ordering up an orgasm.

"I have to go," Rodryck suddenly declared.

"What?" demanded Guard Captain Veygard through his beard, though I was sure he had heard well enough.

Cornell glared at the captain. Eydith glared at the bearded man to support her boss. Gil smothered a smile with his hand and looked away into a corner of the room to keep from laughing. The tables full of solemn scribes did not laugh either, but I could see a few of their feather pens begin to tremble. One of the younger guards clenched his fists, turned on his heels, and almost ran from the room. Mad howling flowed back through the doorway he had exited through. Lord and Lady Auvigne pretended they had heard and seen nothing. Probably it was only their amazing poise that kept the whole room from erupting. It had been a long week. Finally, the great mathematician gathered up his dignity and said in his crispest tones, "I said, I have to go. I have to take a break."

He had to go, all right. That kidney stone was flirting with his ureter, making him think he had to go all the time. Except that when he tried, he could not. He could not resolve that urge any easier than he could solve his transform. Or presumably have an orgasm, fifty watchful eyes or not.

"Come on, Luciena, it's our turn," said Gil on my left. I looked up at Darday'l and shrugged. Since she had requested that I stop interfering, I had not acted against the experiment, but the stone was cast, as they say. It would have to work itself out in its own time. I looked at the room as I left, wondering if voluble guffaws would break out as soon as we left it, but all I saw was Eydith staring intently at the chalkboard, Rodryck's stick of chalk still in her hand. With an eight of guardsmen, we followed the mathematician down several flights of stairs on his urgent quest for a privy.

"This is just for your ears, Luciena," whispered Harbinger. The smile on his mouth was entirely shadowed by the humungous round nose that overhung it. This proboscis was so big that no light from above could elude it to illuminate his lips or teeth below. "But I don't really think this equation matters at all."

The guards were between us and Cornell, so the mathematician heard none of this furtive whispering. It was an innuendo that had been going around the castle, and it was spreading wider and wider as the delay grew longer. The support of the townsfolk, once so enthusiastic as to border on the hysterical, was also starting to fracture. They weren't lining the road when he passed anymore or crowding close when he went to the market. Farmers no longer arrived at the front gate volunteering to help fight Nimrheal. There was lint on our mathematical hero now. The lint of delay, the hint of failure. Gil Harbinger, however, should have known better than to say what he just said.

"What are you saying?" I hissed. "It's only a whole new description of the world, a new domain to be discovered." I was angry. Yes, I had sabotaged Rodryck Cornell's work from the start. Yes, I had cried and cursed over the whole thing, lamenting the injustice of it. But I had acted for a noble cause. I did not want my Lord and Lady Auvigne anywhere near some Nimrheal-baiting experiment. If Rodryck wanted to be famous for creating something new, let him do it and die like a hero, alone, not take those I loved with him. But all this still did not make Harbinger right to declare mathematics irrelevant to the world. "And the transform could enable us to solve all kinds of new problems in differential mathematics. It might ev "

The Harbinger was laughing now, so I quit my rant. He had to stop and slap his skinny legs through his robe, he was laughing so hard. I thought about slapping his face. He was lucky the failing experiment had put me in such a good mood. "Why do you have to be such an old boot, Gil?"

He kept laughing. We had fallen well behind the guards and the hurrying mathematician. "You are just so cute, Lucy," he gasped between donkeyish chortling. "I do admire your enthusiasm." He straightened himself as we rounded a corner of the stairwell and caught sight of the guards some distance ahead. It would not do for the great Harbinger to be seen acting so childishly. He liked to save his foolishness for me. "You keep me young, though seriously, Luciena, you must know that all this math and science have nothing to do with us wizards." He spread his arms wide in an expansive, theatrical gesture. "We are beyond all that." He pointed to his temple. "It's not up here," he said, then patted his flabby chest, "it's here." He lowered his arms and smiled gently at me. "And you have a great heart, Lucy."

Eight knights, I don't want an intimate moment with this idiot! Sure, it would be a far different intimacy than I had shared with Darday'l, but he did seem to be speaking from his own heart, genuinely believing his advice could help me. Harbinger was a good wizard. He had excellent instincts, except perhaps for agreeing to this project. Underneath all his laziness and kibitzing, he might even be a good man. Probably was. But he had the classic handicap of the successful; he thought everything should stay the same. He had made his way to the top by doing things his way, so why shouldn't everyone else? He had gotten what he wanted, what he needed. The rest of world could just freeze in its tracks and go nowhere.

But how could I blame him for this attitude? For the old, change is almost always for the worse. That's aging for you. And he was old. Of course he wanted things to stay the same. The world almost never changed, and when it did the cost was blood. I am young and want the world to be better, though without cost to me. Between the two of us, we were bound to get nothing done. "Thanks, Gil," I said at last, hoping things weren't going to get awkward. "But I think I am going to use *everything* I've got and see how that goes." I couldn't help myself; I had to be honest.

Harbinger just pursed his lips and nodded, not much bothered, it seemed, that I didn't agree with him. No doubt he thought I would learn eventually. "Speaking of how things go," he said conversationally, "we better catch up with His Transformness Cornell."

Harbinger was right. We had fallen too far behind. I heard the big upper tower door close ahead of us around a corner. *He has left the Cardinal Tower altogether.*

Perhaps Cornell hoped that he could finally shake off his problem if he shook off his normal habits. On the first day, he had rejected the overcrowded baths closest to the observatory and had demanded use of a private privy three floors lower. He had a thing about privacy when he urinated, but I think he also disliked the guards. Maybe a soldier had made fun of his irrigation-gear when he was a boy, maybe he was just naturally high strung, or maybe he was one of those individuals who enjoy a moment for private thought while they do their private business. The prevailing theory around the feast hall was a combination of the first two notions. Only Darday'l and I knew it was I who had made his peeing a private hell. Until that kidney stone worked its way out of him, he wasn't going to be comfortable in any privy. But let's be honest, Cornell had problems long before I butted in and made things worse.

But where is he going now?

Harbinger opened the door, and we stepped out onto the sky bridge connecting the Cardinal Tower with the northwest tower. A breeze came up as we strode over the high, arching bridge. I opened myself to the empyreal sky and spotted Cornell a floor above us. *He's going to the crow's nest.* It was an observation post on the top of the tower a half floor above the final landing and had the best view in the fortress outside of the observatory itself. Below it, down a tight, circular stairwell, sat the loneliest privy in the castle.

Zzzziiippp.

Wow. The continuum was unusually vital. I saw a rare ray retrograde fly by. I released the empyreal sky with some reluctance. Maybe there would be more.

"We better hurry, Luciena," Harbinger said, a little worried. "There's a storm coming up."

For all his talk about hurrying, Harbinger was no stair climber. We failed to catch Rodryck before he found the crow's nest. When we finally emerged on the landing of the top floor, Harbinger puffing like a wind-broke horse and I vibrating with impatience, a guardsman held up his hand. "He's in there, lord and lady. He said he wants a few moments to himself."

"Quite a blow comin' in," exclaimed another guard looking out one of the big observation windows.

"About this mathematics ..." Harbinger said.

"Yes?" I asked, giving him permission to go on with his antinumeric theories. One of the guardsmen smiled at me and rolled his eyes.

"It's just this," Harbinger went on, an earnest expression on his reject-from-the-potato-bin face. "Maybe there *is* a use for all this math. Perhaps you will be proven right, Lucy, in time."

CRRRRRRAAAK.

The tower shook as the long tail of the thunder trailed slowly off.

"That was a mite big' un," the storm-watching guard said.

Acknowledging that mathematics might one day be useful was an unusual private admission from Harbinger, but I was pretty sure there was an admonition coming. "But?" I said, happy enough to play along until Cornell gave up on his attempts to urinate.

Harbinger smiled gently, trying to be intimate again. Knights, I hated it when he did that. "No buts. I just wanted to point out that not every-thing fits neatly into equations. Don't hold yourself back just because the math says otherwise than your heart."

I wasn't expecting aspirational, but he needed to understand some-thing. "Thank you, dear Harbinger, first of our order," I said sweetly. "I take your point in the spirit in which you mean it. However, you should know that is exactly why we need new ma-"

CRRRRRRAAAK. CRRRRRRAAAK. CRRRRRRAAAK.

Three shocks passed through my body, stronger than any electricity I had ever felt before.

The guards were shoulder to shoulder at the one big window. "Dear knights, it's a cyclone!"

I opened myself to the empyreal sky, and it was a cyclone there too. I could see the great anvil cloud reaching down like a twisting hand toward our tower. It existed in both domains. In the center of the cyclone, there suddenly appeared a black singularity.

"It's Nimrheal!" I screamed. Yes, I may have been a little panicked. I had never faced a transcendental being before.

The guards jumped, but Harbinger just nodded.

"He must have worked it out while relaxing over a piss!" shrieked the window watcher.

Perhaps the stone had finally passed. I had never considered that Rodryck Cornell might do his best thinking in the stall of the privy. But who doesn't? Suddenly it was obvious! He'd passed the stone and then, in a moment of supreme relief, broken the inventive barrier. I'd really fucked the whole thing up. What I had done might have *helped* Cornell solve his transform.

CRRRRRRAAAK.

The whole tower shook like it had been hit. One soldier ran off the landing the way we had come in, but the rest were hammering on the door to the crow's nest, demanding that Cornell open the door so they could protect him. They couldn't get the thick oaken door open any more than they were likely going to be able to stop Nimrheal.

"Step back" said Gil Harbinger, shocking me by not running away. *He promised he would be the first to run away!*

I covered my face, having a very clear idea of what was coming now that Gil wasn't fleeing. The doorway exploded outward, showering us with sawdust and small fragments of wood and ice. We were open to the sky now.

CRRRRRRAAAK.

I uncovered my face just in time to be blinded by the flash of lightning. I had already been deafened by the thunder. The whole tower shook once more. As the soldiers and Gil crowded around the gaping hole in the wall, perhaps considering how best to charge the demon, I considered what a disaster this was. Rodryck Cornell had carried no paper with him, no chalk. He had taken no scribes, sycophants, or assistant either. Eydith and all the rest were back in the observatory, waiting to pounce on the discovery when Cornell made it there. *How is he going to record his discovery before Nimrheal kills him? With his own shit?* His sacrifice would be for nothing.

Gil looked back at me. He had taken out the door in heroic fashion, but I could see he was scared now. His eyes were almost as big as the giant snout between and just below them. He did not want to go out there and face Nimrheal. He was too savvy to see that as a promising idea. But it was also too late for him to fake an injury, as I had once seen him do at the Battle of Meeting Rill against Armadale. He had not known I was watching then, but he could not take his eyes off me now. "Let's go, men," he said, waving his arms and stepping out into the wind and rain. "Stay there, Luciena!" he shouted over his shoulder.

That slowed me down for about two seconds, but only because it surprised me; it was good advice for once. The wind was horrific, blowing up my skirts as I stepped into the crow's nest. We were almost inside the great black cloud now, it was so low. It was as if heaven was reaching down to our little castle to snuff out our impertinent ideas. Cornell wasn't there. He was not mounted on Nimrheal's spear jammed into the crow's nest, spinning in the violent winds, which is where I would have mounted him if I were a demon. Hailstones hit me as I whirled around.

Where is he? There!

The soldiers were crowding around the narrow back stairwell that descended to the privy secreted there. There was a commotion going on, which made me flinch.

This is it!

It was not it. Nothing happened. The soldiers abruptly lost their tenseness and began to back out of the confines of the stairway. Gil came into sight, relief slackening his features. "He's fine. No Nimrheal."

A disheveled Rodryck Cornell followed, complaining as usual. "Can't I even take a shit in peace?"

This did not make any sense. The storm was unnatural, and I had *seen* the singularity. I could feel it still. Rays retrograde flew all around us.

CRRRRRRAAAK. CRRRRRRAAAK. CRRRRRRAAAK. CRRRRRRAAAK. CRRRRRRAAAK. CRRRRRRAAAK.

Reeling to maintain my balance against the multiple concussions, not to mention the wind, rain, and hail, I climbed up onto the crow's nest and looked across to the Cardinal Tower. It appeared as if it had been hit by a trebuchet. Thick black smoke was pouring out of the roof.

Eydith!

I remembered again the look on her face as she stared at the board, the stick of chalk in her hand.

It was difficult afterwards to decipher the new transform and its inverse because of all the blood on the chalkboard. Luckily, a few of the scribes had seen the solution before fleeing, and a brave or suicidal few had stayed to record what they could before Nimrheal began the slaughter. With the parts of the solution that were not drowned in blood, mashed by hail, washed by rain, or written in an illegible panic, the transform was reconstructed. After some debate between the scribes and Cornell, it was named the Lessingham Transform after Eydith. She was the one who had had the inventive breakthrough. She was the one that Nimrheal mounted on its spear.

The demon killed just about everyone who did not flee. Sir Hasconeyt had died only a few paces from Eydith and two soldiers. A few guards survived because they had been hidden by stones or chalkboards falling on them. A few others had just been lucky, becoming one of those rare individuals who could tell their grandchildren they had lived to watch the demon walk away.

Darday'l had not run. Her great maul was in pieces, and so was she. Seeing her like that, so was I. The night before we had become one soul. We had shared in a way and with a trust I had barely imagined was possible. What was left of her was scattered in an obscene display that was in every way the opposite of how we had been together. No person or creature should be able to do such things to another. Desperate to restore as much of her dignity as possible, I gathered her up.

The matter of life, once life is gone, is only a reproach to those who remain. The dead are nothing but meat, gross and rotting, lacking the spark that feeds love. Darday'l's magnificent connection to Elysium was gone. That was loss enough, but there had also been a light in her eyes that was all human, all woman, that I would miss even more. Seeing such an irredeemable diminishment of someone so great would never leave me. Darday'l, dead, did not care how broken she had been left, but I did. I gathered up the pieces and covered them. I did it for myself and my violated memories of that beautiful, honest, curious woman.

Lord and Lady Auvigne died together, also smashed by a power that did not belong on this earth. They would not smile upon me anymore, gift me with their generosity, or show me how to be a better person. It made no sense. Killing them was not rational; it served no purpose. They posed no threat to Nimrheal in the fight. Nor would they have understood the mathematics of Eydith's discovery. The demon had murdered them anyway.

It was wrong, it was perverse and evil, that such beings could come to our world and kill the best among us. That Nimrheal could kill the Auvignes so summarily, that it could take apart the shining, heavenly woman I had known, and loved, as Darday'l, was profoundly wicked. Simply entering this world was a violation of everything good. Heaven or hell may sit in judgment of our souls when we die, but they should not judge us while we live. We are supposed to be free. As I sat amid the wreckage and gazed at the two Auvignes lying side by side, I vowed to destroy the demon, come what may.

Chapter Twenty-Eight

On a Horse, Backwards

A*LL THE OTHER WORLDS ARE HELL.*

–Pessicaust

"E*NOUGH WITH THE BOOKS*, K*ORIA*," E*LOISE BELLOWED FROM THE DOORWAY*. "I*T'S TIME* we faced forward and took a risk. Long overdue, in fact. You must try heraldry again."

Koria put the book down. Eloise's opinions, like her moods, were subject to radical change, but the gigantic woman was not wrong about Pessicaust.

Pessicaust the pessimist.

There was so much Koria needed to know, so little time to learn it, and now— with Nimrheal back—so much risk in trying. Some of the original questions had been answered already. When would whatever the Methueyns and Ardgour had done to change Huygens fail? Well, it *had* failed. That answer was written in blood. Where is the key to that change, the Bifrost? Somewhere near Arsenault. Probably. The calibration data, combined with the list of potential locations, strongly suggested this. Robert and Marielle's disappearance supported it. But a precise location was still needed, and urgently.

Robert, as of the last heralding, appeared to be alive. But where exactly? And for how long would he stay that way? Would his report, if he ever made it back, provide them with the information they needed to act decisively?

The problem with putting the book down could be posed as another simple question: what was the alternative? Pessicaust, like every other writer of his period, had exceeded his data with his conclusions. His editorializing led no further than her own conclusions. *We do not know what Ardgour did, aside from a vague surmise. We do not know what the Methueyn Bridge actually was.* Ardgour had wanted it for a long period of time, had tried to steal it once, had attempted to replicate it with some physics of greenstone. But what *was* the Bridge and where did it come from? No one seemed to know. It had simply been used to, partially anyway, bridge Elysium and earth. If it was invented, no one had kept a record of who invented it or how. *That is the problem with religion. You can only accept it on faith and use it without question. Revere it beyond criticism.*

And even if she could set aside her frustration with the gaps and analytical failings of the historical record, she still faced the question of what to do. A question that was becoming more urgent with every passing minute. *The answer has to be in the data somewhere. And we have to find it if we are to survive.*

"Koria."

"What?" Her head jerked up. "Sorry, Eloise, I was thinking."

Her towering friend just frowned, and a cobweb of tiny wrinkles spread out from the sides of her big, crooked nose. "You're too deep in it, girl. I didn't say anything." She sat heavily down across the table from Koria. "Try your heraldry. I would do it, but I'm not as good as you, and … I'm pregnant."

Koria did not ask how Eloise knew she was pregnant. She had seen it herself the night before when she had looked for her old friend through the empyreal sky. Eloise was indeed pregnant, but very, very recently. It was still fragile, and Eloise knew what had happened to Koria's baby.

"Congratulations." Koria felt a small stab of jealousy. That would make three children for Eloise and Gregory, and Robert might never return. "Where did you find the time?"

Eloise smiled like the cat that caught the rat. "Oh, he wasn't running anywhere until I got what I wanted."

"Of course." Eloise was her own woman, Koria knew that all too well. She decided not to ask for details. She knew enough. She would set aside that sliver of jealousy too. Eloise was here, after all, when no one could have blamed her for staying on the Justice estate and looking after her daughters.

"I heralded this morning." Koria did not add that, as violent and confusing as the locus was, its impact was barely a fraction of what she had experienced when attempting to herald Elysium a few weeks before. What would be the point? From what she had seen, Eloise was going to have to be very cautious indeed for that pregnancy to reach full term.

"And?"

"Where are your stup—your men?"

Eloise smiled more softly now. "They are off beating on Gregory's shield. I don't think it's going to work out. There is no pounding out the dent from that metal. The armorer isn't sure he can heat it enough to soften it. The alloy is immensely resistant."

"If they do manage to get it hot enough, they'll only undo the entropic structure," Koria pointed out. "And only Robert is capable of restoring it."

"Or Deryn Endicott," said Eloise. "We should have asked him before we ran off, but ..."

You were in too much of a hurry to come help my husband. For some reasons I know and some I don't.

"So ... back to Robert."

"What did you see?"

At a party, telling people everything was the habit of a bore. With heraldry, telling everything could be deadly. Sometimes foreknowledge was a self-fulfilling prophecy, or it would make people act so differently that the heraldry was invalidated and the outcome something wholly unexpected and unprepared for. On the other hand, revealing too little could be worse than revealing nothing. It traumatized without being useful. Koria had to careful what she revealed.

"I saw a collage of images, some archetypal, some specific. Like everything to do with far heraldry right now, there was no consistent structure or narrative, no clear timeline. Causal coupling was uncertain, to say the least."

"Stop apologizing and start telling."

"Stop telling and start listening, El. Hearing this will save us a lot of wasted grumbling and questions later." Eloise was very unlikely to apologize, so Koria carried on without waiting for the miracle. "I saw a sword in an eye, a hilt in a hand, a horse backwards, Robert on a long march, a burning man, a noose, a one-armed giant, Robert up to his ears in water, Marielle in shadows, standing on a boulder, reaching down into clear, rushing waters, Heylor striking a priest, you surrounded by wheat, Hemdale turning and swinging his sword, Gerveault's javelin but no Gerveault, a second backwards horse behind the first, but only one casket, an empty book with a blank page, Kennyth Brice bleeding on stones."

Koria blew out a breath, trying to let go of the retelling and release some of the trauma of what she had seen. Many of the images were plainly portends of disaster, but of precisely what was unclear, while those that seemed to hint at something good were even less clear. When she had gone over the unabridged details with Gerveault and Kennyth Brice, they had offered plenty of theories and guesses, but as a totality the vision remained a puzzle. They had even put up all the bits and pieces on a board so they could pore over them like a mathematical problem, but they had gotten nowhere. They were still talking about it.

Eloise, however, was not saying anything. She was looking down at her hands. Finally, she reached up with her right hand and wiped her eyes. "Heydron, that's worse than a riddle." She said nothing further for a moment, then looked up at Koria. "Let's see those maps of the wilderness. If *I* was taking a long, brisk walk back from Arsenault, I would use the old roadways, which we know your big-in-to-planning husband has memorized. Which of those roadways might he choose, and which of *those* go through river systems or low ground that might flood?"

Щ

Koria went down to see her best knight off. It had not taken Eloise long to gather up Gregory and Eoyan. Their saddlebags had already been packed, and it was just the matter of Gregory's shield—finally declared irreparable—and the need for a plan to intercept Robert that had been holding them up. Bethyn came down with Koria, hoping for a report from Eoyan on the three attractive female knights he had been chatting up at the feast.

"Oh, they are a jolly group, Bethyn, up for anything," Eoyan said with his usual boy-eating-mud-pie grin. "Sir Astrid Kettel is the leader's name. She says that she and her two squires will join up with you and me anytime, anywhere, as long as Sir Eloise Kyre also joins in." He brandished his left hand, palm up, and brought his right palm down onto it. "Three on three, she says."

Sir Gregory's face hardened. "What the hell, Eoyan." He stared at his old companion. "You know, you're not as funny as you think you are. What did they really say?"

Eoyan's grin, if anything, went wider. "They *did* say that, my friend. I may have left out one part. They said, *or* the three of them and Eloise would be fine too. I left that proposition out because, well, it does nothing for me or my flank mate, Bethyn. But in either case, they really, really want Eloise."

Who doesn't? Koria noticed that Gregory's and Bethyn's faces had both turned red.

"That is ridiculous!" exclaimed Gregory, hefting his dented shield.

Eloise's expression was hard too, but not red at all. "It's not about you, stupe, so ease up and let those of us with calmer dispositions deal with this."

Koria tried not choking on that.

"Yes," agreed Bethyn. "You weren't invited to the orgy. This is between us girls."

"And me!" chipped in Eoyan.

"Nice!" Gregory mounted his horse. It danced about, infected with his irritation.

Eloise mounted as well and moved her horse next to her husband's. "Relax, dear, they are just trying to get me to some quiet place so they can murder me."

"Ohhhhh," said Gregory with colossal sarcasm, "well in that case, I'll just let it go. My best friend is missing, and everyone thinks it's the right time for jokes."

"He's so fun," observed Eoyan, spryly mounting up. "But that *is* what they said," he added in a stage whisper.

"We are going cross-country to East Tower Seven," Gregory said, looking down at Koria. "And leaving the horses there." His eyes slid to Eloise, who was looking firmly ahead. "You know the rest." Then his serious expression turned forty-five degrees in the direction of wry, and he added, "If you see any of Armadale's finest following us, send help, will you? I would hate for us to be murdered in some quiet place."

Eoyan's voice filtered back as he began trotting his horse. "When I get murdered, I want it to be noisy. In fact ..." His voice trailed off as he moved further away. In seconds, the three of them were through the inner gates and clattering at speed down the cobbles toward the outer gates. When the trio had disappeared from sight, Koria turned to Bethyn. "That was entertaining, but let's steer clear of those three women."

"I wonder why they're so interested in Eloise?" Bethyn mused. "Can it be the display she put on yesterday?"

Koria looked at her. "You've heard the *March of Sir Hemdale*, haven't you?"

"Yes, but—

"It fails to mention two key elements, Bethyn," Koria continued, gazing along the cobbles her friends had disappeared down. "First, *why* Hemdale went back to Armadale in the first place and, second, *who* he brought back with him."

"You mean it was about Eloise?" Bethyn asked. "I always thought Hemdale just got his big beak out of joint about something or other and decided to massacre the king and half his knights."

He does like to give that impression. But it's untrue, and it's unfair.

Koria did not have Gregory's obsession with being even-handed, but she had decided it was time to set the record straight. She also thought that they needed a break and that Bethyn would be interested in a story centering around Eloise. "You are letting what happened at the embassy siege color your thinking. Come on, let's go up to the observatory again and make sure that none of Armadale's encamped soldiers do decide to follow them. And while we're at it, I'll tell you why our big beautiful friend is even more special than you think."

The retractable roof of the observatory was wide open to the sky, but the only telescopes in use were in Koria and Bethyn's hands. The two women stood on the narrow walkway that formed a perimeter around the open ceiling of the top floor of the Cardinal Tower. Below them, the great hall of the observatory was being readied for Marielle Engel's Ceremony of Rising. Sir Hemdale strode back and forth, full of a weird energy. He was old now but still almost as strong as ever, and perhaps even more rough edged. But his demeanor today looked … happy.

"We can't get it up!" exclaimed a workman below as he and four others attempted to lift the enormous blade of the Methueyn Treaty.

Bethyn lowered her telescope and started laughing. Seeing that Eloise and her two men were safely off the road and cutting through fields of wheat toward East Tower Seven with no one in pursuit, Koria lowered her telescope and joined in the laughter.

"Well, I guess if you have a blade that big, getting it up could be a problem," Koria observed, sending Bethyn into fresh gales of laughter.

It was an obvious joke to make. The Methueyn Treaty *was* enormously long and hard. A heavy rope had been slung over an iron hook—painted to look invisible—with both ends of the rope ending in nooses. One noose was meant to capture the pommel of the great sword, while the other was meant for the candidate Deladieyr Knight's neck. Two metal cradles, built to resemble a sheath, would keep the sword from falling until the candidate's noosed neck could exert enough force to raise the sword. If the sword failed to leave its sheath and rise under the weight of the supplicant, that person would strangle. It had happened before, when the Council of Knights had failed to vet candidates properly, but not recently.

"How much does it weigh?" asked Bethyn, watching Sir Hemdale shoo the five workers out of the way and lift the sword by himself. He raised it by its blade, rotating the pommel higher and higher. Two other helpers scrambled to maneuver a ladder so they could hook the pommel.

"Over five hundred pounds."

Bethyn's right eyebrow went up. "Marielle does *not* weigh that much," she said in her driest voice. "It's impossible."

"*That*, my dear Bethyn, is the point."

Bethyn shrugged and sat on the low parapet to look down on the continuing work. "Pass me that wine bottle and a glass, would you, *my dear* Koria?" They had brought the wine because Bethyn had said it would not be much of a break without it. The brown-haired girl poured herself a dangerously full glass and said, "So what don't I know about Sir Eloise Kyre, gorgeous superwoman and ill-tempered maniac?"

Koria considered, for the second time that day, how best to tell a story properly without telling it all. *As if I know it all.* "Well," she said, making her decision, "Eloise's young father, Veritas, was a Royal Knight of Armadale. He was a little like his uncle Hemdale, though he technically wasn't a Deladieyr Knight. Veritas had not Risen yet because Armadale had been excluded from Ceremonies of Rising. Their king at the time thought he should control Armadale's Deladieyr Knights. Hemdale had been forcibly banished and was in Vercors because he had threatened the king over this. Eloise's mother, Aloysia, was a powerful wizard. The thinking at the time was that Eloise could end up being both, kind of like a Keith Euyn for her generation. The king then said certain things to suggest he wanted to ... take control of anyone with that kind of talent."

"Taking control of Eloise?" sneered Bethyn. She rolled her eyes. "What on earth was he thinking ..." Her voice trailed off. "I'm glad Hemdale killed him."

"Albrecht Vernon took a lot on himself, no doubt about that," replied Koria, watching Hemdale working to position the Methueyn Treaty below. "But not even Sir Hemdale in his prime could defeat an entire army of knights on his own. He asked the Endicott family to make him a sword, and after much effort, they did. His is the biggest and deadliest of the entropic weapons of the current age." She raised her eyebrows, "Almost twice as heavy as even Gregory's *Justice*, if you can believe it, and supposedly even harder."

Bethyn sputtered. "How would you even know that?"

"Right," said Koria. "Hemdale goes back to extricate his niece and her family, ends up killing everyone he meets, and only manages to come out with Eloise. They make a song about it, except the song rhymes better than it tells a true story."

"I think I'm very glad I didn't grow up in Armadale," observed Bethyn.

"No doubt. Coming back to your original question, that is what is so special about Eloise. There is a lot of bad blood between the entire Vernon family and Hemdale's on her account. That's why matters devolved so quickly when Eloise arrived and why those three attractive, red-haired knights might be trying to isolate and murder our friend." Koria looked down at Sir Hemdale, who was still working excitedly—perhaps too excitedly—on the arrangements for the Ceremony of Rising.

Bethyn downed the last of her wine and got up at once to pour herself another glass. "But Eloise never became a Deladieyr Knight," she said, passing Koria on her way to the bottle.

"No. But, hopefully, Hemdale will get his knight now."

"So what about Robert?" came Bethyn's voice from behind Koria.

Koria turned to meet her friend's stare. "What do you mean?"

"I *mean*," Bethyn said, "what is our next step? Eloise has conveniently removed herself from endangering this diplomatic situation to go look for him, but what are *we* going to do?"

"There are several experiments I was thinking of trying." Off in the distance, a rider was galloping toward the castle. A dust cloud rose behind the figure. Koria snapped open her telescope. *That looks like Gael Guise.*

Bethyn had not noticed the rider. She was too busy projecting her disgust onto Koria. "Experiment? That's what you want to do?"

"Yes," replied Koria, still watching Gael charge closer. "We have a great many problems to solve."

"What kind of woman are you, Koria?"

Koria was not offended. She knew Bethyn was just acting out her anxiety over what had happened to Robert's mission, not to mention her fear of Nimrheal's return. "Every woman is different, Bethyn. You know that as well as anyone. You also know that our list of problems is only getting longer. We need something other than a big heavy sword, and I happen to think that *knowledge* is what we need most."

"How about your stillborn baby?" Bethyn asked sourly.

"If this is your idea of catharsis, just stop it, Bethyn."

Bethyn did not stop. "Fuck your catharsis. You haven't even talked about it with Robert."

"And a whole lot of good talking about that over javelins would do him," Koria spat out.

Bethyn rolled her eyes before sneering, "You're just hiding behind your books."

This finally, really, really irritated Koria. She knew Bethyn, knew she could be a sour bitch, knew she was scared of more experiments, especially after what had happened last time. Especially since Nimrheal had come back. But knowing this did not take the sting from her friend's words, not this time. *As if things aren't hard enough without you making them harder!* She was irritated enough to fire back in kind. "More than you are by flirting with foreign killers and drinking all the wine?"

"I never flirted with them." Bethyn pursed her lips, put on her best fake smile, and slid a full glass in Koria's direction. "That was all the work of Uncle Eoyan."

Koria accepted the glass but only stared at it. "No one calls him uncle except himself."

They were still arguing when Gael Guise galloped through the inner gates. Moments later, the alarm bell began to ring, and they saw pages emerge from all corners of the castle, including the observatory below them, directing everyone to the main courtyard. Koria was still drinking wine—something she rarely did even at the best of times—when soldiers, cooks, armorers, housekeepers, valets, and foreign guests began to assemble far below in the courtyard of the massive fortress. The last to emerge were Kennyth Brice in full ducal regalia, Lord Latimer, looking equally lordly, Sir Hemdale in his dented armor, and Gerveault in his schoolmaster's robes. This unlikely quartet stood silently, watching the gates.

What are they looking for?

With a sinking feeling, Koria turned her attention from the castle back to the road. A group of riders were approaching, slowly this time. She trained her telescope on the group. It was difficult at first to see who the riders were because her hands were shaking so violently.

Robert and Bat Merrett rode side by side. Each weary-looking man held the reins of another horse that trailed behind them, these ones saddled but riderless. The saddles of the riderless horses were caparisoned in eight blue and yellow strips of cloth. A pair of boots had been fastened to the stirrups of both horses, facing backwards.

The backwards horses.

Behind these retrograde horses rode Emyr Wynn, Captain of East Tower Six, and another soldier. Bringing up the rear of the procession was a covered wagon pulled by a team of eight horses. With a cry, but not a word, Koria thrust her wine glass at Bethyn and ran.

To Rise, to Wake

ENDICOTT'S EYES BURNED FROM LACK OF SLEEP AND OVERABUNDANCE OF EMOTION AS he passed through the lines of soldiers camped outside Ardvaser. He kept his back straight and his tears to himself because the soldiers were from Armadale. They may have been watched by an even bigger contingent of the duchy's soldiers, but it would still not do for the enemy to see weakness. He wondered if Merrett also had to struggle to hide his feelings, but he did not ask. He knew the big man would not appreciate the question. Emyr Wynn had told Endicott that Armadale's embassy had brought two hundred fighters, but the sight of all of the foreign soldiers still surprised him.

Good thing Gael rode ahead.

He had guessed that the situation surrounding the Ceremony of Rising was likely to be somewhat… delicate. That is why he, with Merrett and Emyr Wynn, had devised a return appropriate to both the terrible outcome of his mission and the fragility of the diplomacy still in process. The plan also had to serve a purpose he did not need to think about to understand, honoring Jeyn Lindseth and Marielle Engel.

How do you go back and say your mission failed and your friends are dead?
Start with your friends.

Endicott understood Heylor's haunting screams better now. A similarly horrible thing had happened to the jittery young man just before he had so abruptly appeared in the feasting hall, coated in gore. Heylor had run afoul of Skoll. There was nothing he could have done.

Nothing.

Endicott had known at once, intellectually, that he was not at fault over his own failure. Carrying Marielle back had helped him come to know this emotionally.

What could I have done?

The question was retrograde, backward looking, emotionally driven, negative, and unproductive. At the start of the long march back, these negative thoughts and feelings had haunted him. But somewhere in that journey, carrying a person he considered better than himself, Endicott had at last shed the negative retrogradational element of the question. Now he asked it looking to the future.

Perhaps the fact that there was nothing that could be done is the sobering fact we all must come to understand if we are to move forward.

He knew he needed Koria, and needed her in countless ways. The cathartic power of his painful, self-destructive journey may have burned away his guilt, but it had not evaporated his pain. He needed his wife. He needed the half-space of love he shared with her. He also knew that if anyone could help him see what to do the next time he encountered Nimrheal, it would be her. One overriding thought burned in his mind.

I must prevent Nimrheal from killing anyone else that I love.

As he approached the fortress, his eyes sought the one he loved most.

"Steady up, Blouse," Merrett growled, low enough that only Endicott could hear. Endicott stopped looking around him. He bent his face forward and kept it there as they passed slowly under the first gates. Soldiers stood on the ramparts above and all along the cobbles on either side of the road. A soft murmuring rose up from the crowd, soldiers and others identifying Endicott and Merrett, speculating on the missing. The sounds of their horse's hooves became louder and lonelier. They passed into the castle proper. The whole staff and soldiery had been turned out. They lined the walls, the straight road, and the squares, no one speaking more than a whisper.

The echo of new sets of hooves sounded from somewhere ahead, getting louder and closer. A moment later, the titanic, brutal, armored form of Sir Hemdale rode up, Kennyth Brice beside him. They slowed as they approached Endicott and Merrett's column, and when both columns stopped, their horses were almost nose to nose. Kennyth Brice's face was closed and tight, Hemdale's red and raging. Kennyth smiled a fleeting smile. "Thank the knights you have returned, Sir Robert, my brother, and Bat Merrett, my faithful soldier."

"Who lies there interred?" growled Hemdale.

"Sir Marielle Engel," replied Endicott.

"She Rose before she died," supplied Merrett to the questioning looks on both Hemdale and Kennyth's faces.

Kennyth nodded slowly, seeming to take his time digesting what he was being told. Sir Hemdale's response was not so intellectual. "Yes! She Rose!" he cried with a spontaneous and frightening enthusiasm.

The duke's eyes flickered toward Hemdale for a split second before returning to the two young men before him. "And Jeyn Lindseth?"

"He purchased our return," said Endicott in as loud a voice as he could manage.

Sir Hemdale blinked slowly, the muscles in his face spasming, his mood abruptly shifting. Then he stood up in his stirrups and roared out in a deep basso profundo,

"Shout, shout.
Redoubt, redoubt
Redoubt Empyrean!
It's echoed, echoed
In the halls of Elysium!"

Every soldier there and most of the civilians knew the song. It had been adapted from *The Lonely Wizard*, the first part often used for marching, though chanted in higher notes for that purpose. At state funerals, the song was rolled out as if from a great horn and sung slowly and low, as Hemdale was doing now. Endicott recalled times in the past when he had heard it like this. He remembered it being sung for Eleanor and the old duke, for his grandpa, and part of it for himself once in a lonely tower. They were just words, but occasion made the music, and on this occasion, the song affected him as deeply as it ever had in those earlier times.

When the verse ended, Kennyth Brice and Hemdale slowly turned their horses and led Endicott's party toward the inner fortress. As they went, Hemdale sang the first verse again, but this time he did it with the accompaniment of those on the walls and the streets.

"Shout, shout
Redoubt, redoubt
Redoubt Empyrean!
It's echoed, echoed
In the halls of Elysium!"

Sometimes a groan went up as the wagon passed by, as death was made suddenly real. Some onlookers cried throughout the procession, their grief mixing with the verses of the song. Kennyth Brice led the next part in a tenor.

"Carried forth by friends, is the fallen knight,
Her hopes and dreams crushed by Nimrheal's might.
We will not let this be all that is left,
A lonely grave and a forgotten quest!"

While they sang, Endicott remembered Lindseth fighting and then burning. He remembered Engel pulling him from the water and the terrible sight of her eye pierced by steel. He remembered taking turns with Bat to carry her body for all those long days and nights to reach this moment of release. He looked over and saw that even Bat was singing with the crowd. Everyone joined Sir Hemdale to make the final verse the loudest of all.

"Raise voice and shout: Redoubt Empyrean!
Know that it's echoed in Elysium!
For we are here, showing that we revere.
Your strength, your cause, your soul surely endure."

Time seemed simultaneously to be moving slowly and quickly, as it did when he was in combat, as it had in his fight with Keith Euyn and at the embassy. It seemed to take hours to pass armorer's row, only to arrive too suddenly at the steps to the inner keep in what felt like less than a second. A great crowd stood on the steps, some in the colors of Armadale, others in the livery of other, less hostile foreign powers. A little to the side, Endicott spotted Koria at last. She was speaking with a dusty, sweat-stained Gael Guise. It looked urgent. Gael nodded briskly and started pushing through the crowd toward the stables. Koria watched her for a moment, then turned and held Endicott's eyes.

Something is not right.

Koria was partially screened by the crowd in front of her. He could see the dark skin of her face, the bright green of her eyes, but he could also see that his wife was not as she had been. He opened himself to the empyreal sky.

Heydron.

He knew at once that his daughter was gone. He found he was not breathing and told himself that he must.

I wasn't there. It was an echo of his childhood guilt. He had not been there when his mother had died and they covered her face. He was not there when Koria needed him.

He found he was not seeing and told himself to open his eyes. He found that he was crying and told himself that was okay, for the moment. When Koria began to slip through the crowd toward him, he stifled his tears.

Whatever I feel, she has felt something worse, and without me there. No questions. Don't let your first words bring her new pain!

"Where's Jeyn?"

Endicott looked down. Standing near the front leg of his horse was an old woman. She was shrunken, wrinkled, and homely. Her hips were thrust weirdly forward, and her upper back was strangely rounded, giving her the appearance of a walking question mark encased in the skin of an old apple. She moved her head slowly on a neck Endicott knew to be almost immobile, looking vainly upward with eyes full of cataracts. "Robert," she said, "where is Jeyn?"

Endicott swung his leg over his horse and stepped down. He knew that his news should not come from a height. He put his hands on the old woman's shoulders and spoke as softly and clearly as he could. "He is dead, Mrs. Lindseth. I—I could not bring him out."

A moment passed, and then he heard her old, quivering voice speak again. "Get up, Robert."

The young man did not know when he had fallen to his knees, but there he was, shorter now than Lindseth's mom, looking up at her. "I'm sorry," he said.

She put both hands on the sides of his head and kissed his forehead. "I know." She turned her head with great effort to look back at the steps of the keep and the armored knights assembled there. "Best you get up now, Robert. Come later and tell me how and why my boy died."

It took a monumental effort to stand up again. "I will."

"Leylah," whispered Merrett from his horse when Jeyn's mother had shuffled off. With movements scarcely faster than those of Lindseth's mother, Bat laboriously dismounted. A group of pages had approached from out of the crowd to take charge of their horses.

Koria stepped through this little bit of chaos and entered Endicott's arms. He held her and said nothing, thinking of the daughter they had lost—that Koria had lost without her husband to support her—and held his wife still tighter. "It's okay," he said to her after a time, which earned him a very strange look.

"Wait a moment here, Sir Robert, if you can," said Kennyth Brice, putting a gentle hand on Endicott's shoulder as he passed. He began to ascend the steps, then stopped and turned back. "Can you and Bat help carry Sir Engel in when it's time?"

"We carried her fat arse across half the Ardgour Wilderness," grunted Bat Merrett, though thankfully in a voice that did not carry as far as Sir Hemdale, who stood a little further away, keeping his baleful eyes on Armadale's embassy. "We'll carry her the rest of the way."

Kennyth's eyebrows registered something like shock at this, but he must have processed the gallows humor quickly, for he clapped both men on the shoulder and trotted up the stairs of the keep. When he reached the top, he turned and raised his voice to the crowd. "We have lost two brave and honorable soldiers of the duchy, Sir Marielle Engel and Lieutenant Jeyn Lindseth. Tonight eight urns will be lit for them here on the stairs of this keep, and a feast will be laid out for everyone to partake of."

The young duke spoke a few words more, but Endicott paid them little mind. He wanted to soak up the feeling of Koria in his arms. This small moment in Elysium ended when Merrett clapped him on the shoulder. "Come on, Blouse. It's time."

The casket containing Marielle's body was brought in by a special eight. Kennyth walked in front, Hemdale behind. Carrying the young woman were Endicott and Merrett, then Sir Sophia Haverland in shining plate armor opposite Arthur Wolverton, and finally Emyr Wynn and the soldier she had brought with her, Daligh. Endicott kept his face forward but could feel the eyes of the crowd on him, his fellow carriers, and the casket. From the corner of his eye, he saw two rough-looking knights from Armadale smile as he passed them. The letter nine was stitched on their surcoats, and this and something else he could not name gave Endicott a bad feeling as he went by. A red-haired woman stood not far from the two Armadale knights. Endicott could sense that she was watching him intently. Was she saying something to two other women who clustered near her?

▽

"Tell us again, from start to finish, everything that happened in your battle with Nimrheal, Sir Robert, if you please." Lord Latimer always acted part secretary, part interrogator in the after-experiment reviews. Endicott had already gone over the fight three times, and Bat had shared his perspective twice. Neither man had rested properly in six days if the walk up to Arsenault was included. Endicott's feet burned with pain, his back felt continuously on the verge of spasm, and he could barely stay awake. Still, he welcomed the questions. It was important that the data be fully and accurately shared.

He and Merrett sat in chairs that were supposed to be comfortable but today were not, facing a table at which sat Kennyth Brice's entire leadership team at Ardvaser: Koria, Gerveault, Hemdale, Lord Latimer, Sir Sophia Haverland, and Arthur Wolverton. In chairs at the far wall, taking notes, were Bethyn, Emyr Wynn, Corporal Rhysheart, several of the castle's senior guardsmen, and a group of Wolverton's military commanders. Rhysheart had come looking for news of Heylor Style's eight, and most particularly of his wife, Ida.

Setting aside his feelings about the pain Rhysheart must be feeling over Ida, Endicott went through the long report one more time, and a new round of more specific questions began. Gerveault was the first to speak. "How many lightning strikes did you hit Nimrheal with, Sir Robert?"

"Fifty to a hundred."

"How exactly? And why are you unable to provide a precise count?"

Robert shifted in his wooden chair, but there was no comfortable position for him. Whether or not his toes were still attached to his feet remained a mystery. He and Merrett had only been given time to splash water on their faces and hands after interring Marielle and stumbling to this meeting. He shifted again, wanting to stand but knowing that he would feel even worse if he did. *I must look like Heylor did back at the New School.*

"Nimrheal brought the storm, and I directed the lightning." He tried to shrug, but his trapezius spasmed and he got stuck, his shoulder almost in his ear. "The energy was there. Also, Huygens was weak there, incredibly weak. So weak that I felt Elysium was only the tiniest effort away."

Gerveault's eyebrows went up. "But you didn't break through?"

"I didn't have to."

Gerveault nodded to himself. "So why are you so unsure about how many strikes?"

Bat Merrett grabbed Endicott around the throat. *Oh, thank the knights, he's going to choke me to death.* The cheering prospect of a quick death vanished when

Endicott realized the big man was only pinching his spasming traps. "Because he was too busy screaming his hate at the thing," said Merrett as he continued to pulverize his smaller friend's neck.

"That is true," Endicott wheezed, half throttled. "It was a desperate and emotive moment."

"You still should have kept track …" Gerveault's voice trailed off.

Koria looked at the old dynamicist and jumped in with a question of her own. "Later, when you attempted the exact shaping, did you estimate the error wave?"

The spasm relaxed, but Merrett gave his neck one last shake. "Heuristically," Endicott said, finally getting enough air.

Koria's eyes widened, though Endicott could not fathom why. "Did your estimate show it would extend so powerfully to your position that it would destroy Merrett's sword?"

"No."

"I can't understand why the lightning didn't kill or drive off Nimrheal," said Arthur Wolverton.

"Perhaps," said Kennyth Brice, "it is simply not possible to do either. We have heard how arrows bend around the demon. Perhaps it dances between the lightning like the dice that Sir Robert can make spin."

"So we should give up?" grated Hemdale. "Heylor Style cut the arm off Skoll. Nimrheal can be beaten. A Methueyn Knight with an Endicott sword can cut any creature in half."

"There are no Methueyn Knights," interjected Gerveault.

"No, professor, you misspeak," said Hemdale with shining eyes. "It is unlike you. There *were* no Methueyn Knights. If Sir Robert is correct and the Bifrost waits on the far side of the Arsenault within this ring, then we should go and get it, cross over, and kill Nimrheal."

"As simple as that?" Gerveault asked in a flat tone.

"Yes! For once as simple as that. Robert, Sophia, and I will go. Immediately!" The big man stood up with a great creaking of old metal as if ready to march out of the room that instant. Before anyone in the room could groan at Hemdale's single-mindedness, Kennyth Brice reached out and grasped the old knight's arm. To the younger, quieter knight beside him, he said, "Do you agree, Sir Haverland?"

Sophia Haverland did not seem as eager to charge the battlements as her colleague. With Hemdale glaring at her, she took her time before she answered. "I would go with Sir Hemdale and Sir Robert. If we meet Nimrheal, I know what I will do. What I do not know is what will happen."

"Thank you, Sophia," Kennyth said, then returned his gaze to Hemdale, whose arm he still grasped. "Sir Robert can barely sit in a chair, let alone charge back into the wilderness. We had hoped to have a Ceremony of Rising, but instead we are having a wake, and our enemies are the guests at it. You and Sophia might be capable, Sir Hemdale, but neither of you must leave while the Armadale mission remains here and the Methueyn Treaty hangs in our observatory."

He let go of Hemdale and joined him on his feet. "The Aignen Legion is almost assembled at Byrste. Here is what we are going to do. Move the Legion to East Tower Six once it is ready, and past the Castlereagh Line after that. When we are ready. When we have a plan. Lady Koria, Bethyn Trail, Gerveault, and whoever else they need will continue to work on the gaps in our knowledge. Sir Robert and Bat Merrett will rest and recover." He looked around the table. "Has anyone sent a messenger to retrieve Sir Kyre and Sir Justice?"

"I asked Gael Guise to go," replied Koria.

Kennyth nodded. "Good thinking, Lady Koria. If anyone can actually catch them, it will be Gael. Let's get them back. They are needed." He glanced at Gerveault. "This would be a lot easier if we had a portable javelin in everyone's hands."

"I sent the second one to the Aignen Legion yesterday," Gerveault replied.

"Right." The duke nodded as if he already knew this. "How about Heylor Style? Is he ready to return to service?"

Lord Wolverton cleared his throat. "We have received word that he recently injured his hands capturing a cloaked man at the New School."

"Cloaked man?" asked Kennyth. "Not another wizard, surely?"

"A student," replied Wolverton with a thin smile. "However, the situation in Vercors is unsettled. The people are terrified of Nimrheal and have been protesting against your policies every day since his return."

Kennyth seemed to just catch himself from sighing. "That is unfortunate, but our problems must be solved here, not there."

Arthur Wolverton visibly flinched. "But they could burn down the ent—"

"Arthur," Kennyth said, "I know. It is a problem. Think about the instructions you want to send to the constabulary. What everyone here needs to understand—needs to *accept*—is that the situation has changed drastically. Horribly. There is no going back. There is only winning, and that requires our full commitment. Here. Now. Together."

Wolverton nodded. Kennyth Brice looked in turn at each person in the room, including the men and woman near the far wall, expecting their assent. When he had it, he continued. "Send word that Heylor Style is to come here as soon as he can use his hands again. You, Sir Hemdale and Sir Haverland, must keep an eye on our guests throughout the wake. We need to send them on their way as soon as possible. We do not need another complication."

Lord Latimer rubbed his jaw. "They're already a complication. We invited them. Sending them on their way will not be simple. Armadale believes very strongly that their candidates should be allowed to attempt the Ceremony of Rising. They won't leave until they've done so."

"The only way they are getting near the Treaty is if I use it to cut them down," vowed Hemdale, his eyes hard. "The Council of Knights will never approve the candidacy of those thugs."

Kennyth Brice pursed his lips. "Who is admitted to attempt the Ceremony is the prerogative of your order, Sir Hemdale, but try not to start another war until we have won this one." His eyes alighted briefly, pleadingly, on Sir Haverland. Her help could be crucial for keeping the peace.

As he left the meeting, Endicott could not help but notice how alone Sir Hemdale seemed. Sir Christensen had not returned, and neither Sir Kaimari nor Sir Braynor, now long overdue, had yet arrived. Only Sir Hemdale and Sophia Haverland were on hand to represent the once great order of Deladieyr Knights. It made Endicott feel at the same time both melancholy and relieved that he had not mentioned why he thought Nimrheal had returned.

▽

I wasn't there. Endicott thought it, but he knew he should not say it. Not being there did not allow him to make it about him. It still hurt; the absence remained present. His daughter was gone as if she had never been. She was now only a dream that Koria had carried for them both.

Nimrheal might be connected to whatever hell it came from by some dark singularity, but Endicott felt the loss of his daughter as a singularity in itself, immeasurable, indescribable, lying deep beyond words. "I love you," he said. For now, at least, in the few moments he had alone with Koria before the memorial, amid all the other feelings running through him, these seemed the only words that could reach across this void and bridge the distance between them.

▽

"THANKS FOR BURYING HER," SAID RHYSHEART AFTER THEY HAD DRUNK THEIR TOAST. "I always hoped that Ida might somehow have survived, even though it seemed more and more unlikely after so much time." He drank another gulp of wine, his eyes like fractured glass. "She was just so alive. Imagining her *not* was ..." His voice trailed off. It had gone somewhere else, like his youth.

Helping Rhysheart come to terms with Ida's death was important for Endicott. It was Ida and Rhysheart who had sung him and Gregory and Eoyan off when they were all trapped in the tower four years past. He would never forget that. But now he was exhausted. He had only had an hour with Koria before she had insisted he try to sleep a little more. He had dozed fitfully for another hour or so, then given up on the idea of sleeping properly and opened his eyes again, feeling not fully awake. But the second conversation with Koria was ... better. This time they had spoken concretely about what had happened to each of them, and it had felt transformative. It had put some life back into them and restored their connection.

Endicott was still a physical wreck. His feet hurt so badly that he had to wear sandals to the wake. His toes had not detached within his rotting socks as he had been imagining, but it did look like the nails would soon fall off. He no longer dreaded attending Engel and Lindseth's wake—his conscience felt unexpectedly free from the weight of the past—but it distressed him that there was so little he could say to comfort Rhysheart. He wondered what the young man would think about later. What would he remember? What would he see in his mind's eye when he said his goodbyes and shuffled off for the night?

You don't want to see what you love dead.

An old lesson came to mind. "Imagine her alive," he said to Rhysheart, and to himself. "Alive and singing in the tower when the lightning flashed and the thunder followed. Imagine her as she was in the special moments she shared only with you."

Rhysheart whispered, "I will."

"The thing about memory," Endicott continued, "is that we tend to remember only the really traumatic things. Those we remember clearly." Endicott knew that only too well. "The small, quieter moments fade and get forgotten." As he spoke, he remembered the long walk, carrying Marielle. Mostly it had been quiet, introspective. He remembered the other long journey he had made four years ago with Gregory. He remembered Lindseth's endless, gentle philosophizing, and he remembered sitting quietly with Koria in her room at the Orchid, rolling dice and taking temperatures. "Those uneventful times are important, perhaps the most important times. Try to reconstruct and reimagine them. Make those tranquil moments with Ida new again. Search for the silences you had in her company and the peace you felt then. Remember how she loved you and how you loved her."

Rhysheart nodded, tears streaming down his face.

"Stick to that."

Endicott had, unfortunately, seen Ida dead. In small, torn pieces. He wished he had not. After Rhysheart left him, Endicott reflected that some fights could not be won. Ida Yseult happened to have been in one of those. *Are the rest of us in one now?*

"Ho, Sir Robert Endicott, yes?" The plate-armored knight who interrupted these morbid thoughts was about Endicott's height. He was not wearing a helm, and his blond locks were on full display. Apparently plate armor was accepted dress at a wake in Armadale, but no one wore helmets unless they were planning to kill the other mourners.

It was one of the knights Endicott had glimpsed earlier in a surcoat with the number nine stitched on it. "You and your big friend carried this Sir Engel far, we hear. What—for four days? Five?"

Endicott was in no mood to play games. *He wants to know where we fought Nimrheal, but he has no idea.* As exhausted as he was, Endicott could see that quite clearly. "We carried her far enough."

"Far enough?" The blond knight turned to his companion, a somewhat taller man with hair like honey and scars that made his face look like it had merged with a thorn bush. "Do you hear that, Sir Steygur? Far enough, he says. A man of few words."

Steygur tucked his chin back in an evaluating gesture. The gesture made his Adam's apple bulge. "If he says it, Heykon, it must be so. He is Sir Robert Endicott, killer of Colborn Vig, destroyer of our old embassy. He is not a man to be trifled with." He smiled in a false way, a contemptuous way. "But you look a little tired today, my friend. I also hear you are not what you once were, even on your best days. That is unfortunate." He shook his head in a tutting motion. "We brought someone for you to play with." He thrust his long, scarred jaw toward another man standing not far away. This fellow was slight, with a sallow complexion, and wore no armor. "That is Heinrich Bitten." He lowered his voice conspiratorially. "He is something of a wizard."

"Sir Robert?"

The voice was tentative and high pitched, a child's voice. Endicott turned from Steygur and Heykon to look down at a boy of about eight years old. He had the thin blond hair of Armadale, but his expression lacked the malice Endicott was used to seeing in citizens of that country. "Reingard?" he guessed. He had carried a little boy out of the embassy. Reingard Vernon, the only survivor.

"You remember," the boy said evenly. He looked to the two armored men. "I must borrow Sir Robert from you, sir knights."

Steygur reached out and roughly grabbed Reingard's arm. "But we have other questions for Sir Robert." Without waiting for the boy to respond, he turned to Endicott again. "Did you see a man of Armadale in the wilderness? A knight like us. His name is Sir Penrod."

Enough of this shit. He innovated a low magnitude dipole around the two knights. They did not react, and it seemed to Endicott that the innovation broke up as it manifested close to them. They did not even seem to notice it.

Interesting. He remembered Keith Euyn's lightning bending around Sir Christensen during the fight in the throne room.

"Well?" Steygur asked again. Endicott ignored him.

Let's try something else.

He innovated a lesser dipole onto the skin of both knights to heat their bodies directly. There was an urn of fruit water ten paces away where he planned to deposit the heat energy. But there was a resistance. Endicott could feel it, almost like a strengthening of Huygens. With a small adjustment, he overcame the resistance and was able to execute the innovation. It was just hot enough to make both men jump and force Steygur to release the boy's arm. These two men were not ordinary knights. Dynamics had to be applied directly on them to be effective, and it was difficult execute, even with Huygens so low.

Endicott took Reingard's hand and led him away, ignoring the curses that followed him. The sound of a breastplate hitting the floor with a clang revealed something else: these knights did not fully understand dynamics, despite having a wizard as a friend. *I did not heat their armor.*

He stopped with Reingard under the shadow of the noose. The memorial was being held in several locations. Most of Ardvaser were feasting on the steps of the keep, but others were in the feasting hall, and a select group of special guests were in the observatory. In honor of Marielle and Jeyn, the great sword of the Methueyn Treaty hung suspended high above the floor, its cradles set aside, one end of the rope attached to a hook on the wall. Sir Hemdale stood below the Treaty, glowering at the guests from Armadale, presumably still tempted to use the twelve-foot blade as a weapon. Even from where Endicott was standing with Reingard, the three most prominent words of the Treaty were clearly visible: "You Are Free."

"Be careful of them, Sir Robert," said the boy.

Now there's some advice I didn't need. Heykon and Steygur were laughably obvious, only not in a funny way. They dripped malice, but there was something more disturbing about them than their hostility, something *off.*

"You've only just returned, so you don't know," Reingard whispered. "My people are up to something again."

Endicott took a moment to really look at the boy now. Reingard was frowning earnestly at him. *He's right. There is something I don't understand here.* Endicott was beyond exhausted, and his mind was moving at the pace of thick mud, but he could still see that. "Why are you telling me this, Reingard?"

"Because my people are liars," the child hissed, his unchildlike vehemence almost making Endicott take a step back. "They have no honor. Though that is almost all they speak of."

"Sometimes the quality we feel most insecure about is the thing we squeeze to death."

"Yes," said the boy more calmly, his voice soft again. "Honor for my people, faith for others." He looked squarely at Hemdale as he pronounced these last words. The old knight had been glaring at Elias Vernon, the Armadale ambassador. "I will vote against your *knights* when the Council meets," Hemdale suddenly announced in a voice barely less than a shout and with an inflection on the word "knights" that sounded like a curse.

Elias did not appear put off at all. He made an affected tutting sound. "You have not even properly interviewed our candidates yet. Your hatred for the country of your birth has made you prejudiced, Sir Hemdale. It is really quite sad." He smiled, spread his arms wide and half turned as if looking for something. "And where is your council, anyway? I see only you and Sir Haverland. That is no quorum."

Endicott turned back to Reingard. "Sir Hemdale does not lack faith or honor. He feels let down though. After many disappointments, this is the latest. Marielle Engel was supposed to Rise. Instead we have this wake."

"Yes, I see."

"Who has let *you* down, Reingard?"

"They want to use me, Sir Robert."

"How?"

"For their games," he said. "To embarrass Sir Hemdale, since he nearly killed me. They think your duchy is weak and they can take advantage of you." He laughed bitterly. It was an incongruous sound from a child. "That's what they said just before you crushed the embassy, you know. It's one of my earliest memories." He laughed again. This time the sound was haunting. "You could say my life started that day. The embassy was surrounded, but they only laughed and made insults. My father said we could push and push and push and Vercors would do nothing. That we could take what you had built because you are … simple. And weak because of that." He fixed Endicott with a cold stare. "And then you and your duke and Hemdale came and struck them all down."

Surely he must hate me. The weight of that day still hung on Endicott, but he had not lost a father there. He had done the killing. He felt profoundly sorry for the boy, but he could not apologize. His instincts told him, in any case, that an apology was not what the complicated young boy wanted. "How can I help you, Reingard?"

The boy's lips tightened. "Do you see all the people in this room from my country? Kill them all."

Chapter Thirty.
Cause of Death

I SQUIRMED. I COULD NOT GET COMFORTABLE IN MY PANTS. NOT A FUNNY SITUATION, being out in the wilderness for weeks at a time if your ginch gets wet. I don't know what it might be like for women, but I can tell you that nothing a guy keeps down there likes being damp. Even slightly moist is bad—no actually, *slightly* moist is even worse than *soaked*. When you are almost dry, but you are not, and no position you can get into feels right. And you know you will have to survive for days—maybe weeks—somewhere between feeling tickled down there and itchy. It can drive you mad.

"Knights alive, Heylor, what is going on with you?"

It was Ida Yseult, my corporal. She was immensely competent. Also a tall blond goddess. That she had noticed my twitching only made it worse. "Nothing!" I said with my usual suave charm. I jumped to my feel, shaking my legs out.

"Well, look," she said with an understanding expression, "if you've got to go stroke one off, do it now. We still have two or three minutes before we have to move out."

I waved my arm at her, dismissively I hoped, and stomped off into the woods.

Before I got out of earshot, I heard Sergeant Ildrys laugh at our witty repartee, and then add a quip of his to own. "Aren't we on water protocol this mission? He should do it in a stream, right?"

What you need to know about water protocol is that we have protocols for everything. This includes taking a piss or dropping a poo out in the woods. There are two main protocols for human elimination in the Ardgour Wilderness: shovel protocol and water protocol. You can probably figure out what shovel protocol is, but water protocol is the worst. In water protocol, you have to do your business in a creek or a river. Under water. Why? Good skolving question! Because we don't know what's harder for skolves to smell and track, buried waste or piss in a river.

Unfortunately, we had drawn water protocol for this mission, the main reason my ginch was damp in the first place.

I wasn't going to go *stroke one off* anywhere. I don't do that. In the woods. I just needed to get away somewhere private and air out my equipment. Dry things off. Heydron's tits, but it can get irritating being in the wilderness, even with your friends. In fact, being out with your friends can be the worst of all. I could not hate Ildrys or Ida. They were just having a little fun. My problem is that I lacked an appropriate outlet to vent my frustration … or my nuts. I just could not get comfortable, and the nagging irritation was driving me insane.

"Sir? Do you need anything, sir?"

I got my hands out of my junk, clutched at the drawstring of my pants, and whirled awkwardly to face the speaker. "No Candell, I'm skolving fine," I said, then winced at my tone. "Sorry, I'm a little … twitchy."

Candell Ankor was a dark-haired, muscular woman of about my age. Like all women in the army of Vercors, she was fit, and like all fit people, attractive. But what set Candell apart, what made her stand out for me was … nothing. She was absolutely ordinary, except that she was a part of my eight. And that her parts probably had some of the same issues as mine—she had been out here the same amount of time as me, under the same conditions. There was nothing about her to claim my affection, except that *everything* about her claimed my affection. Candell was one of my eight. As a member of my small team, I thought of her almost as another me.

"We're just about ready," she announced in a studiedly neutral tone.

I shook my legs again, turned and clapped her on the shoulder, unfortunately with the same hand that had just been down my pants. "Let's go."

We got back to camp. Everyone was set. Someone—Ida perhaps—had finished packing my gear for me. My pack sat there, all tight and quiet. I smiled and shook my head. Those skolving *bastards*, helping me out. "Who do you want on lead?" I asked Ildrys.

"Reyn is up," said my hirsute sergeant. Ildrys was built wide and hairy, like a wire brush. Despite all the hair on his body, his head was all stubble, clipped as short as a three-day beard.

"Reyn it is."

We left, making for the highlands, wet in the ginches and getting farther from dry clothes and a warm castle with every step.

T

"W E CAN'T HAVE A FIRE , H EYLOR ," SAID I DA .

"I *know* that, Yseult. I just want to hang my stuff to dry while I perform the calibration." I had to get into my pack to get the dice and notebook anyway, so hanging my spare ginch was not really a breach of protocol.

We had been walking all morning. Everything was tied down to avoid unnecessary noise. Even our weapons were tightly stowed. It would take a bit of time to get to them if any skolves detected us. Protocol is meant to keep you alive, but it can also work against you. Whether keeping quiet was really more important than being instantly battle ready was, like the water protocol, still being evaluated. We were still new in the wilderness. As leader of my eight, I had some discretion, but I had decided to go with the standard for the time being. It had worked out so far. But we had not been attacked so far.

It was time to roll the dice again.

"I don't understand why we have to keep doing this," groused Lockleyn. He was younger than Candell but equally competent and tough. Some say young comes dumb, but Lockleyn was not dumb, just impatient, and that I could sympathize with. Young also comes with fewer injuries and a freshness to the fight. Anyway, I tried to pair youngsters like Lockleyn with veterans like Ida or Ildrys to even things out.

Sure enough, Ida jumped in and set the lad straight. "This is almost the whole reason we're out here, Lock, so get with the program."

"But why?"

"Shut it and do your job, boy," barked Ildrys from the other side. "You're supposed to be guarding, not griping."

The answer to *why* was something none of them knew anyway. I was the only one in this group who knew that Huygens's current value was not absolutely consistent. It had been measured as far away as Neahon, where its value was close to that in Vercors, yet still slightly, just slightly, lower. The magnitude of the difference was only just above that of experimental error, but the repeatability of the data suggested that Huygens did in fact change over very large distances. The still vague theory being put forward was that the slowness and slightness of the change might point to the location of the Methueyn Bridge. Gerveault had gone a step further and proposed that, if something about the bridge was making Huygens larger, as was generally thought, and if Huygens slowly increased as we approached the bridge, then the change in Huygens could become rapidly greater as we got closer. The old dynamicist thought the field effect was wildly non-linear, so that a distinctive near-field effect would be felt at very close distances. I had once heard him say that what we had all been feeling was only a far-field asymptote to this near-field effect. Whatever that means.

As soon as my eight were in guard position, I started rolling a whole lot of dice, my spare ginch hanging on a stick behind me like a flag. The exercise—less the ginch flag—had become routine, and I finished quickly.

"What's the word, boss?" Ida asked as I stowed the dice and other items.

My notebook was tucked into the inside pocket of my jacket, but I knew what my numbers had told me. "No word. No change," I said. "But speaking of change, I'm just going to put this on now, so you can go back to watching—"

"For skolves," I added, as Ida started to give me a leering smile.

Before unhooking my ginch from its stick, I innovated a mild dipole just to give the vital article of clothing a little extra drying power. The risk of alerting skolves with such a tiny innovation was minimal—and worth a dry groin, as far as I was concerned. Dynamics did not interest Skoll or Hati, who were far more deadly foes this deep in the wilderness. Only heraldry could do that, or so we had always been told.

As we resumed our march, my warm, dry ginch felt good, and I told myself I really should have used dynamics sooner. Fear of the two demons, I decided, does get irrational at times. Superstitious, even.

On the other hand, I had to admit that a team had been lost without a trace about a year back. No one knew what had happened to them, but a dynamicist had been with them—no one I was close to—and everyone wondered if dynamics had had something to do with their disappearance. And now, a few weeks before I had set out with my eight, Guillaume's team had gone overdue with no word. By the time my mission left Ardvaser, hope of their return was fading, and I knew that if he and his team had not gotten back by now, they must be dead. Guillaume was also a dynamicist, though a fairly weak one. It was starting to look like a pattern.

But two events do *not* make a pattern, by the way. Talk about jumping into the grain bin with both feet. I hate sloppy thinking, and this was definitely that. Still, the prospect of an agonizing death at the hands, claws, paws, or whatever manual appendages demons have does affect one's thinking.

What does a demon look like anyway?

The images at the Steel Castles often put horns on them, which I've always liked, artistically speaking. Still, whenever I have closed my eyes and thought about what scares me most, I see images of those knights from Armadale as they were at the Battle of the Bifrost. Or Keith Euyn. The demons just did not mean anything tangible to me. Yes, they were a source of some superstition—and unnecessarily wet undergarments—but that was about it as far as I was concerned. I mean, why would such all-powerful creatures wreak such havoc in the Methueyn War but then go silent for all the years afterward? Why had they not taken over the world? They must be dead.

T

"You gonna have more kids with Rhysheart?" I asked Ida that night when we were camped.

"Assuming I see him again." Ida was a quick wit. "One more year and I get a plot in the new county." Long-term soldiers were being offered preferential treatment in the subdivision of land that would follow phase four of Lighthouse. It was a huge opportunity for anyone wishing to rise economically. The cost of a farm in Vercors was astronomical now, and to earn one through service, that meant something. I could imagine Ida and Rhysheart's blond kids running around, and Ida wearing an apron instead of a sword. Well, maybe it would be Rhysheart with the apron, but the idea was the same. The essence of my fantasy was a world in which my hard, blond corporal had a much softer look in her eye than she had to assume now in the wild.

"What about you, sergeant?" asked Lockleyn, looking at Ildrys. My hairy, stocky sergeant had just come back from pissing in a nearby creek.

"I don't know nothing about the future, Lock." He looked at me. "I've been looking after schoolboys like Lieutenant Style for so long, I'm not sure what I can do anymore."

"Has it been that bad?" I asked him, expecting a sarcastic comeback.

"Nope." He surprised me with that, but Ildrys liked to keep me just a little off balance. "Seen a lot of things." He closed his eyes. "I saw lightning in the sky and sang Redoubt Empyrean into the thunder." He opened his eyes and shook his head ruefully. "See, I'm all maudlin. But maybe I want to see something more before I'm done."

"You're seeing something more now, sarge," said Candell. She had been looking at the maps again. "We are *way* out. Do you realize how far past the wheat line we must be now? Might be nobody's been here for two hundred years or more."

Nobody but the Lonely Wizard. I didn't say it though. None of my eight had read the original edition, and I hated giving Keith Euyn's name more notoriety than it already had.

T

"NICE LITTLE RIVER, SCHOOLBOY," ILDRYS ANNOUNCED WATCHING THE WATER RUSH BY.

My eyes were on the bridge two hundred yards upstream. It looked intact through my telescope. I passed the instrument to him. "Water looks rough," I said. "Take a look at the bridge."

The water might not be dangerously rough, but it would certainly put an end to the hard-won comfort of my crotch. My ginch was still dry, and I had joyfully experienced my first decent nights' sleep in a week. Ildrys shrugged and handed the telescope to Ida, who took her time scanning the river, the bridge, the trees on the far side, and the mountains we were heading into. "Crossed worse," she said and handed the instrument to me.

I packed it carefully. "We're using it," I announced.

Ildrys scratched an old scar on his stubbly head. "What if we get tracked off it?"

I had made my decision, and once I made it, for some reason I just had to stick with it. "I'll herald it," I said, trading a bad idea for a worse one. To assuage their shocked looks, I added, "Hey, I'm the dynamicist here. It'll be quick and short." Imitating Ildrys's rough dialect, I added, "Nobody's gonna see nothin'."

"You sure?" asked Ida.

"Yup." I had made up my mind. No more wet ginch, and no more worrying about it for thoughtless and selfish Heylor Style. I ignored the evident disquiet of Ildrys and Ida and prepared to herald. Discretion is there to be used, you know. You remember the heraldry I did with the Eindarch Eye? This was nothing like that. I was heralding a bridge, a solid structure, a hard reality rooted in the firmament of probability like a … well, like a bridge made of stone. It didn't flicker enough to even flick a rock into the stream. I saw my eight cross it—that's seven plus me if you don't know that—Ildrys, Ida, Candell, Reyn, Lockleyn, Finbar, and Einin. *They* changed—they were living people—but they did not change much. Our tight protocols made sure of that. Finbar and Einin oscillated in position, switching places back and forth as they crossed the bridge, creating a vibrating standing wave of probability, bound as they were to the mission and each other. My eight were not as firm as stones, but within our little group, the cone of our shared path, we were our own harmonic. I smiled to see it, feeling for a moment some of that love Robert speaks of.

No skolves in my heraldry. No demons either. So we went.

Dry and happy, we marched for the highlands, entering the foothills and aiming for a big draw ahead and above us. Somewhere up there was the road to a castle called Arsenault. Our mission plan would not see us go all the way to the old castle, but we were definitely going in that direction. Every step took us higher and closer. We passed some thick, red pines and entered a small meadow surrounded by trees. "Let's calibrate here," I said. We were overdue, and it was nearly time to camp anyway. It was a good spot, and the only reason I had pushed so far without a break was the bridge crossing, now far behind us. If some skolve should wander by the bridge and pick up a scent, it would be better to be far away. I pulled out the dice, notebook, sand clock and thermometer—I told you about all that gear before—and started rolling the dice without further ado.

"N-Nimrheal's nuts, that's a l-little strange," I said as I tucked the notebook into my jacket and pondered the results.

Ildrys crossed his arms and rocked back on his heels. "What's that, schoolboy?"

The data was way off. Huygens wasn't just a *little* higher. It was up by an *enormous* factor, so high that hypothermia had almost prevented me from completing the experiment.

"It looks li—" The breath was knocked out of me as Candell's body crashed into me sideways, knocking me to the ground with her on top of my chest. As I struggled to breathe, I heard a clash of sword-on-sword and sword on something else. I rolled Candell off me and tried to help her up. It was pointless. Her head had been crushed like a nut, as if pressed in a jagged, uneven vise.

I tried not to vomit as I reached my feet. The rest of my eight were furiously, desperately engaging with what looked like a gigantic man. Lockleyn was slashing at the giant chest with his sword, but the eight-foot behemoth grabbed the sword like it was a toothpick, then Lockleyn's arm at the elbow and hurled the soldier away like a rag. He collided violently with an orange pine tree and collapsed in a heap at its base. He did not bounce back to his feet and rejoin the fight. He did not move at all.

I opened myself to the empyreal sky. The creature or demon was bleeding from Lockleyn's sword, but not nearly as badly as it should have. The empyreal sky warped around it, ultraviolet with energy, tethered to elsewhere, to hell, I suppose. I hate to say it, but it was impressive. Oddly, despite the thing's power, its clothes were unimpressive, to say the least. They looked like they had been made from old, worn-out tents or someone's rotting tapestry. The creature stunk worse than a hundred skolves too. Like meat that has been out in the sun for a week.

"KNEEL BEFORE ME. I AM SKOLL, YOUR GOD."

The voice nearly knocked me down, it was so deep. Each word was percussive and felt like a blow to the chest. Trying not to flinch, hoping the thing would not speak again, I prepared an innovation. At the point of execution, I noticed that skolves lined the meadow, watching. Why did they not seize their chance and attack too?

"Bake a cake, fucker!" I shouted and attempted to roast the demon. Why did I say, "Bake a cake?" That is a whole other story. I'll tell you later. There was a … resistance to my dynamics—something I'd never felt before—but I pushed harder and executed the innovation.

"AAAAAARRRRRGGGGGHHH!"

I had hurt the big bastard. His canvas tabard ignited, and he began to scream. Thermal operator errors rolled over us, but my eight, or as many of them as were still on their feet, were well trained and thoroughly determined. They knew what to do. They seized the opportunity and attacked. I drew Style but was too far away to be part of what followed. Reyn flew off over my head, leg bent backwards. Ida was picked up by her face and tossed into a thicket of bushes. The skolves did not move in on her even then. When I looked back, the demon was holding Ildrys up with one hand. They were eye to eye with each other, but Ildrys's sword was gone. He cried out in pain, then spat in the thing's face.

Skoll, for that was who the creature turned out to be, put both hands on my sergeant and began to shake him so hard and so violently that Ildrys became a blur in the air. He made a terrible rattling sound as his limbs shot back and forth. Then his arms flew off. One was caught on a branch fifteen feet up a tree. I never saw where the other landed. His legs went next. The left hit a skolve, which flinched and ran off. The right decorated another tree branch. I screamed and charged in, swinging the magnificent sword Robert made for me. I knew it could kill Skoll. The other swords had cut him. Style would cut him in two.

Skoll was covered in blackened, burning cuts now. Its putrid clothes were falling off. I could see it was hurt, that parts of it bubbled and other parts bled. My eight had spoken to it. Now came my turn.

Before I could swing my sword, Skoll moved like lightning, caught my arm and gave it one violent shake. Style flew helplessly off into a bush, while the demon picked me up by the neck and began to squeeze. I wanted to spit too. Ildrys might have been crying, but the old man had spit. I tried, but my neck was almost crushed.

I was desperate. Some of my eight were still alive, at least for the moment, but I was an instant away from being shaken apart like Ildrys. That's when my true nature surfaced, I suppose. I thought only of myself, or rather I did not *think* at all. It was instinctive.

I performed my famous trick and in an instant I was in the air above the duke's table in his feasting hall at Ardvaser. Kennyth Brice himself sat there in state, while I crashed down right in front of him, sending soup and silverware flying. Skoll's arm came with me. Its fingers were still gripping my neck, but the limb ended in a clean cut halfway through the bicep. I cried, "I killed them! I killed them! I killed them!" until I was hoarse and could cry no more.

But no one punished me.

T

"So Lynwen, I killed my eight because I didn't want to get my ginch wet again and have another uncomfortable walk."

The ridiculous triviality upon which so much death was heaped needed to be confessed. Heylor had reported his decision to cross the bridge and to use heraldry in the after-experiment review. Everyone in Lighthouse knew. But he had never, until now, privately to Lynwen, confessed the true motivation for his silly, selfish recklessness. *I never told them the real reason why I chose to use the bridge. Wet ginch avoidance.*

He had been looking down at his hands while he told the story. Now he looked at Lynwen and held her gaze, trying to read her eyes, to know her thoughts, ready to feel her scorn and endure her rejection, expecting both. She only blinked and said, "Yes, that makes a lot of sense."

"What do you mean?" He was aghast at her lack of reaction. "They're dead!" he must have raised his voice. Some of the other patrons of the Apprentice's Library turned to stare at him. He did not care. "I loved them!"

Lynwen reached across the table and very gently put the ends of her fingers on his bandaged hands. "I know you did. I would be appalled if you didn't." She looked off to some dark corner of the library. "Look, mittens, this is our life. It's a comedy of errors sometimes. I've made mistakes that I knew were mistakes as soon as I made them, sometimes before I made them. But your whole ginch-her-aldry-bridge thing may or may not have been a mistake. Who knows anything about Skoll? You said it yourself, nobody knows. Your protocols are just guesses, which is why you had discretion to break them."

"You don't think I'm a skolving coward?"

"I think you're human."

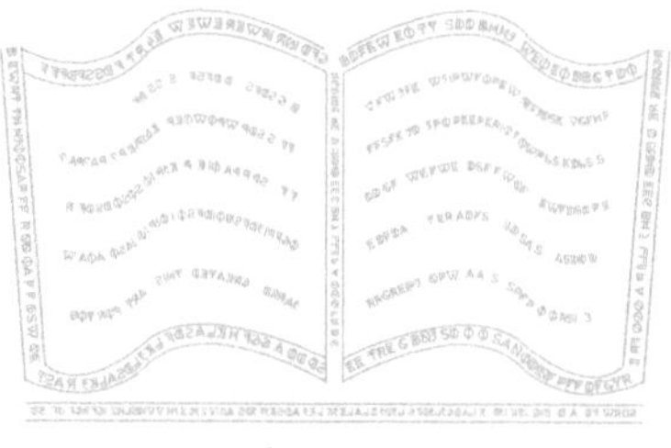

Chapter Thirty-One.
Trade-off

"STILL BURNING THE MIDNIGHT OIL?" SAID BETHYN. "I'M DONE." SHE HAD BEEN MAKING notes based on the latest residualizations of the calibration data as broken down by Meredeth Callum's team in Vercors. An empty wine glass was nestled between stacks of paper. "I was thinking of going back to the wake and seeing if Hemdale can be goaded into actually swinging that monstrosity he's got hanging up there." She laughed a little drunkenly. "*You are free*, indeed! Free that sword, Hemdale!"

"I would laugh too," said Koria, "but that wasn't even the worst thing said at the meeting. Take the Legion into the Ardgour Wilderness? That's all we need to do."

"These men are going to get us all killed."

"Well, themselves at least." It was a patter, a back and forth with wit and nervous relief its only goals, but there was too much truth in it for Koria not to feel a bitter taste on her tongue for being part of it. *I never have these kinds of conversations with anyone except Bethyn.*

"Your husband looked like he just about did the job on himself already. Did he really need to go to the wake after that?"

Koria broke the patter by taking Bethyn's last remark seriously. "Do you carry your friend so far and not see it through to the end?"

"Sorry," Bethyn said, making a surrendering gesture with her arms. "It seems like we are all stuck in our old patterns: you trying to figure it out and move the pieces where they have got to go, Robert carrying his moral burdens, Heylor making mistakes, running away, and feeling guilty about it, Hemdale full of awful intensity, marching us toward doom. How are we going to get a new outcome from old inputs?"

"We can't," Koria said. "We need to learn something genuinely new." Her eyes narrowed. "But perhaps we have and just don't know it yet. There are some things that were not mentioned in the AER."

"Oh? Are we going to have a little review of our own now? A run at what we know, with the added spice of a secret?" Despite her enthusiastic-sounding words, Bethyn slumped a little deeper in her chair. She might not be going anywhere just yet, but she also looked tired.

Everyone looks tired now. "Yes. The AER focused on Robert's data and his observations of Nimrheal, right? It focused on the fight with Nimrheal."

"Understandable. Plus most of them are men." Bethyn's eyes went wide as she pantomimed a strangling with both hands. "They want to know how to *kill* it!"

"They do." It was hard for her not to laugh at Bethyn. "Robert told us some of what he was thinking just before Nimrheal came, but not all of it. He never said exactly *why* he thought Nimrheal came."

"I think they've decided it doesn't matter," Bethyn replied. She made the strangling motion again, but only half-heartedly this time. "Just the fighting and the killing, please."

"Ah," Koria said with a little more energy. "But it *does* matter. Robert told me what it was, and he certainly thinks so. Gerveault knows it matters too, because I just told him. He had his suspicions already but purposely didn't bring them up at the meeting."

"A conspiracy." Bethyn yawned like conspiracies were boring. Perhaps they were, to her. "Where is the old coot now?"

"Working on other problems, talking with Kennyth, talking on the javelin. Gerveault is busy. It's up to us to make things happen."

"So tell me this secret."

"I need to begin with some background, starting with what Robert *did* say in the review. He said that Huygens was clearly lower—much lower—near Ardvaser. He thinks this is an effect of the Bifrost. Only the effect was in the exact opposite direction just days before, back when we assumed that Ardgour's apparatus still functioned and Nimrheal could not return."

"I'm with you so far, girl." Bethyn was curled deep on her chair now, legs under her like a cat.

"So the old theory was that Ardgour's machinery made Huygens stronger and that the Bifrost was somehow helping that. Ardgour did somehow manage to bring Skoll, Hati, and the other demons over, so he must have had some control over Huygens without the Bifrost."

"Using the greenstone element. That was the most accepted of all the made-up theories," agreed Bethyn.

"Well, Robert's theory differs. He thinks the Bifrost is the real key, that it strongly affects Huygens—"

Bethyn interrupted. "He said that, but I don't see how that's much different from Turreyn's theory that all Ardgour did was build a machine that altered the effect of the Methueyn Bridge."

"Let me walk you a step further, Bethyn," Koria said. "Through all recorded history, what is it that has enabled a Deladieyr Knight to merge with one of the eight angels of Elysium and become a Methueyn Knight?"

"A rhetorical question, but I'll answer it anyway. The Bifrost."

"That's right. It's all about the Bifrost. It always has been. Whatever Ardgour did was secondary."

"Which is why," Bethyn held up her hand and pinched her thumb close to her index finger, "Robert's theory is about *this* different from Turreyn's old theory."

"Yes, but it ends *very* differently. Robert thinks Ardgour's machines nullified the effects of the Bifrost more than flipped them. I know that sounds like a fine point, but hang on, there is one last thing that he didn't say in the meeting."

"Finally!" Declared Bethyn. "It's been a little boring up to now."

Koria sighed. "Really? Boring? Jeyn Lindseth and Marielle Engel probably died for this one last thing, so pay attention. The Bifrost is *why* we had Methueyn Knights. We know that from history. Robert's idea is that the Bifrost is why we had Nimrheal too, and why we have him again now that it operates as it used to in the old days. It's not just the bridge to heaven; it's also the bridge to hell." She sat down in the chair opposite Bethyn. "You don't get one without the other."

"Huh," said Bethyn.

"And one other thing," Koria added, "the one that he thinks brought Nimrheal. Robert got this idea that the Bifrost came from Elysium. The bridge to heaven is originally *from* heaven."

Bethyn squinted. "Interesting supposition. Any evidence for it?"

"Just logic. It follows."

Bethyn scowled. "What follows logically isn't always true. But I understand the reasoning." She replaced her scowl with a wicked smile as a new thought occurred. "Well, I can see why Robert didn't mention it to Sir Hemdale. I mean the part about the bridge working for Nimrheal as much as it works for the Methueyn Knights. If that crazy old man sees the Methueyn Bridge, he's crossing it, and nobody better get in the way."

Щ

Bethyn took the last thermometer reading, solved the multivariate equation, and spoke the results. "Huygens is definitely stable, at least over this past week."

"Just down an order of magnitude." Koria put her hands on her hips and stretched her back. It was even later than before. *Robert has got to be in bed by now.* She wondered if he would be able to sleep at all given the amount of pain he was in.

"Great," said Bethyn. "We done now? The time is running late, dear, and I'm sick of this dungeon."

She's right, we don't have enough time.

Koria wanted to be with her husband, to comfort him and be comforted, but she also wanted him to live. *He's going to call Nimrheal again.* She had to save him, and figuring things out was the only way to do that. Normally she would herald the problem into the next season, but with the loci, this was not possible. Experiments and readings were all she had left to save him with.

"Refill the cups and freshen the thermometers, Bethyn. I want to try one more thing."

They were in the dungeon. The observatory was sometimes used for experiments of this nature, but security issues concerning their guests and the ongoing wake for Lindseth and Engel put that out of the question. But the dungeon—the deepest basement—was safe, secure, and had plenty of room. They were in a huge square room, sixty feet wide and long, with ten-foot ceilings. It was all constructed in massive, homogeneous stone. The air temperature was always the same, barring dynamic interference, and it was a simple matter to place vessels in control positions. A large cabinet for experimental apparatus stood against the back wall, and a cistern in the adjoining room provided unlimited quantities of water. For this experiment, Koria and Bethyn placed a series of control cups in concentric circles. Two heavy stone vessels of water sat close together in the middle of the circle. The objective was to measure the error field very carefully. Their previous experiments had involved large-scale Huygens calibration testing, big sister tests to the field calibration procedure with dice, and were extremely accurate. But testing the error field was a different animal entirely. It was delicate, esoteric, and rarely done.

Like men and their single-minded stampede to fight, most dynamicists single-mindedly measured only the specific effects of an innovation on the target and the source of energy. The surrounding error field was usually ignored. The last time Koria had conducted such a test was with Robert when evaluating the risks of exact shaping dynamics. Exact shaping had the interesting property of producing a highly accurate effect inside a small core volume but with the trade-off of a much higher error field outside that volume. In the lab it had proven to be an efficient method of creating changes of higher magnitude, but it was also the innovation that had gone so spectacularly awry in Robert's fight with Nimrheal, where the error field had been even more volatile than expected, causing the death of Engel.

"I don't even know how to do this," declared Bethyn as she listlessly gathered up an armload of fresh cups from the cabinets at the back of the room. Her shoulders slumped with exhaustion. "Can't we finish up tomorrow?"

Koria never even considered the request. "We have to learn this *now*. Tomorrow we will have to figure something else out. We are out of time. We were out of time the day Nimrheal returned."

Bethyn rolled her eyes, though she was too tired and unmotivated to make it one of her better eye rolls. The amplitude of the movement was severely attenuated. "Fine, oh knight of the laboratory. Whatever you say."

They set to work laying out an azimuthally sectored grid that soon took up more than half the room, with the highest density of cups and thermometers placed near the two vessels of water. Each woman had an identical notebook with the cups' azimuthal sectors, radiuses, and pre-innovation temperatures recorded.

"The predicted temperature has to be adjusted for losses differently than we are used to," Koria explained. "The effect of exact shaping is to minimize losses within the area of effect, so we have to make an adjustment of affinity to infinity in the multivariate equation."

"Still sticking to Gerveault's models, are we?"

"As workarounds go ... it works," Koria replied. "Although we are going to have to perform the experiment twice to confirm our results. The second time will be without exact shaping."

Bethyn's arms flopped up in a lazy demonstration of exasperation. "Oh, of course. Unsurprising that you waited until now to mention that."

"It was obvious."

A quarter hour later, calculations complete, Koria and Bethyn stood at the far corner of the room. "Innovating," Koria said. An instant later the water in the first stone vessel was steaming and in the second frozen solid. Nothing exploded. The hot water was not even boiling. Waves of hot and freezing air rushed across the room. Repeating arcuate patterns of frost appeared at consistently increasing radii from the hot and cold vessels.

"Boring," said Bethyn, though she had known what the target temperatures were.

Koria was already moving, notebook open, to record the temperatures in each of the cups. "We don't need to detonate the cake to conduct a valid experiment." The old joke about Robert's incendiary baking experiment from their first year never seemed to get old.

As quickly as they could, they recorded the temperatures of all of the cups and made their calculations. Bethyn pursed her lips as she looked at the results. "Nothing blew up, but the error field is significantly higher than expected. We better do the second experiment, but the basic conclusions aren't going to change."

It was confusing, but it confirmed Robert's testimony. "But why?" Koria asked. "What does it mean?"

Both the hot and cold stone vessels reached the expected temperature with the updated Huygens value and exact shaping adjustment to the affinity term. Koria talked while she thought about this. "Even though Robert would have used the wrong value for Huygens—and he was aware it was lower—there is still a basic change in behavior here."

"Knights," Bethyn said with infinite disgust, "are you trying to tell me that the laws of physics have changed?"

"It seems so," Koria said. Goose bumps rose all over her as the inescapable conclusion became clear. "No, of course not. The laws of physics haven't changed, only our understanding of them."

"Really?" replied Bethyn in a perfectly flat tone that conveyed sarcasm better than any emphasis could have.

"Yes. There is a trade-off, an uncertainty principle. When Huygens is lower, the error floor is higher."

The heavy door into the dungeon abruptly flew open and Eloise strode into the room, sword at her hip and shield in hand. Sweat streaked her dusty face, forming brown rivulets against the blond framing of her hair. Her eyes were huge and wide. Her teeth gleamed. "Stop what you're doing right now, Koria!" she screamed, then added, staring at her friends' blank looks, "You can't do this kind of thing now."

Koria raised her eyebrows. "Because of Nimrheal? You think I'm going to stop because I'm scared? No!" *I've already lost something more precious to me than my life. I'm not losing another just for my own sake.*

Eloise sputtered, "Aaargh. You. Are. So. Stubborn." She drew her sword and looked up at the high ceiling of the room. "Just don't do it. Nimrheal is on its way right now!"

Bethyn closed her notebook and shook her head at the taller woman. "Nimrheal's not coming, Eloise. There's not even a storm."

"Are you both insane? You're in the deepest room in the basement! You can't hear the storm down here."

They did hear something then: a great clanging, clattering din. It was the sound of dozens of armored feet running with frightening, desperate urgency. It was exigent and powerful, echoing off the stone walls like a series of impossibly rapid explosions. The three women whirled to face the doorway and confront what might be coming through it. An instant later, Gregory and Eoyan charged into the room. They were both in the armor they had donned earlier in the day. Gregory slid uncontrollably across the floor, knocking over several of the cups but luckily not breaking the thermometers. Eoyan dived to avoid a similar collision, making a great mess of himself and his armament as he tried to avoid breaking anything. His efforts failed. Cups and thermometers went flying, rolling and breaking in an unending cacophony.

Bethyn's eyes had widened in fear when Eloise mentioned the storm, but Gregory and Eoyan's comic entrance—and Eloise's stare of death at the two men sprawling on the floor—triggered only raucous, involuntary laughter. "You see, El, everyth—"

The room exploded.

Chapter Thirty-Two

The Prophesy

"*In my dream.*" *She pointed one gnarled- shaking finger at her own head. "I dreamed him here. You will see him again. Twice more shall you see him.*"

The old lady cackled. "You will be blessed thusly, thrice. Finally, you shall pay the price. Rejoice! For when the third time finally arrives, he'll mount you up on that sword you so prize. You will become a sign for all to see, the cost of the Book of Nature perceived."

—Prophecy of a strange old lady, four years ago

"Is Ardvaser on fire?" Gregory asked. The entire five-towered structure glowed yellow in the dark sky.

"Those knights-damned bastards!" swore Eloise, instantly enraged. "They've started something."

Eoyan smirked at her as if something amusing were taking place. "Which bastards are those?"

"From Armadale. We aren't talking about your family right now, stupe."

"Ouch."

They drew closer to the fortress and rounded a turn in the road. From here they could make out the two military camps outside the castle walls. An unusual amount of light was coming from both the Vercors and Armadale encampments.

"Those bastards!" Eloise swore again, pointing at Armadale's tented camp ahead.

"I think it may be a celebration," said Gael Guise. "Listen, if you stop shouting, you can hear the dirge."

"Oh."

When Gael had caught up with them, she had told them that Marielle Engel and Jeyn Lindseth were dead and that Robert and Merrett had inexplicably carried Marielle's body all the way back from Arsenault. Eloise could hear the dirge now, lonely pipes calling out over darkened hills. It had been a shock to hear about the deaths. Soldiers were killed on Lighthouse from time to time. Skolve encounters were as rare as protocol could make them, but when they did happen, they sometimes destroyed entire teams. Still, Jeyn Lindseth had been an extraordinary fighter and Marielle Engel had been … something beyond. And it was not skolves that had done the damage this time. Engel and Lindseth had encountered something far, far worse than skolves. Eloise could not forget her own terrifying encounter with Nimrheal. Gregory's shield may have borne the dent, but the demon had left a more damaging impression on his and Eloise's minds. With a grunt, she heaved the memory aside and returned to the moment.

A memorial.

Gael had gotten the whole story of what happened at Arsenault from Robert and Bat while they traveled together from East Tower Six. Carrying Marielle so far had been dangerous as well as exhausting. Skolves could smell rotting flesh from enormous distances. It was miraculous that the two idiots had not been attacked, but Eloise was not surprised that Robert had taken such a risk to bring Engel back. He had always been willing to sacrifice himself for others, especially women.

He made one sacrifice he still doesn't know about.

I owe him for it.

They trotted past the watchful guardsmen of Vercors and then through Armadale's encampment, where Eloise's stately passage drew great attention despite the ongoing wake. Soldiers stared at her. Some pointed, a few waved, and a few shouted words that were lost in the night.

CRRRRRRAAAK.

In their focus on the burning torches and music coming out of the camp, they had missed the lightning in the distance. Storms at night can sneak up. Dark clouds are hard to see when there is no light.

CRRRRRRAAAK. CRRRRRRAAAK.

A brilliant double strike illuminated for a split second the monstrous, indigo supercell hovering directly above the castle.

CRRRRRRAAAK. CRRRRRRAAAK. CRRRRRRAAAK.

The vast, black, rotating anvil was shocking, illuminated out of the black night by three new sheets of lightning. For Eloise, seeing the awful storm so suddenly and so close was worse than being struck by lightning. She and Gregory had fought

Nimrheal once, and a storm like this had come with the demon then. Seeing this new supercell was like seeing the penumbra of Nimrheal.

"Heydron help us!" Gregory shouted, then spurred his horse into a gallop toward the gates of the fortress. He was already behind Eloise, who had reacted even more quickly.

CRRRRRRAAAK. CRRRRRRAAAK.

They charged through the first gate, not slowing for anyone. They twisted through the streets, narrowly avoiding collisions with soldiers, guests, and tradespeople, and stormed through the inner gates with no warning. Eloise's towering, instantly recognizable figure was the only thing that kept them from being peppered with arrows by the startled guards. Without pausing, Eloise rode her horse right up the steps of the keep and plunged among the feasting tables, where she finally had to dismount to avoid trampling the celebrants. She saw Gael Guise grab the reins of her horse, which was getting spooked by the partyers all around it. Singing, shouting, laughing—and mostly well drunk by now—the feasting crowd seemed oblivious both to the violent arrival of Eloise's heavily armed party on horseback and the impending disaster roiling above them.

CRRRRRRAAAK. CRRRRRRAAAK.

"Where is Robert Endicott?" Eloise roared to the first person she met on foot. If she had not already had her shield on one hand and her sword in the other, she might have lifted the lady—a tradesperson of some kind—off her feet to emphasize the urgency of the question. Eloise did not remember drawing the weapon. The startled woman pointed into the keep. Eloise whirled away from her and ran toward the door. She asked the same question of the guards there. They directed the frightening woman to the observatory.

"Does it have to be up on the highest possible floor?" Eoyan asked as he charged behind her and Gregory.

"Maybe you should sheathe your sword for the moment, Eloise," Gregory managed to gasp between gulps of breath. "You might kill the next person you run into."

Shut up and run, stupes! Eloise was too busy running to care, and when they hit the stairs, she continued to put distance between herself and the two men. She wondered for a moment what had happened to Gael, then remembered they had left her with their horses jammed between the meat and salad tables. *Eoyan's horse is probably drinking from the fruit urn right now.* She vaulted up three and four steps at a time, right hand on the hilt of her sword, which she had instinctively sheathed at some point.

"How. Is. She. So. Fast?" Eoyan gasped several flights of stairs below her.

Eloise emerged onto the observatory and thrust herself through the crowds of mourners there. Most of the embassy from Armadale seemed to be up here, including the red-haired Sir Astrid Kettel and the two knights who had made such a poor impression when Eloise had met them earlier, the ones who had worn tabards with the number nine stitched on them. The Methueyn Treaty was suspended by a thick rope in the center of the room.

CRRRRRRRRRAAAAAAAAAKKKKKKKKK.

BRAAAAAAHHH.

A flash of blinding light from the heavens struck the Treaty through the open roof. Everyone but Eloise and Sir Hemdale instinctively ducked at the flash and the deafening reverberation of thunder that instantly followed. The rope that held the great sword burst into flames. "Stand back!" roared Sir Hemdale, then rushed in as if ready to catch the blade in both hands if it fell. Eloise left him to his improbable task. She saw Lord Latimer staring appalled at the sight and hurled herself at him, grabbing him by the lapels of his gleaming formal coat. "Where is Robert Endicott?"

"He-he went to see Jeyn Lindseth's mother."

"At this hour?"

"No," Latimer's eyes were still on Hemdale, who stood expectantly below the sword and its burning rope. "Hours ago. He said he was going to sleep after that. He could barely stand."

Who called this storm, then? It was a relief to know Robert was safe, but there were others she cared about who might have brought the demon.

"Where's Gerveault?"

CRRRRRRRAAAK. CRRRRRRRAAAK.

"Who tries to catch a falling blade?" Latimer asked, his face flickering in the light of the burning rope.

"Gerveault, idiot! Where's Gerveault?"

Lord Latimer, normally the most composed of men, seemed stupefied. "Huh? Oh, he and Kennyth are closeted away in the duke's private meeting rooms."

Eloise turned and ran toward the door. The two odious Nines laughed as they watched the burning rope and Sir Hemdale standing directly underneath the great blade of the Treaty. Their countrywoman, Sir Astrid Kettel, lunged toward Eloise as she ran by. "Can I help you, Sir Kyre?" she asked.

Eloise almost drew on her out of instinct but managed to stay on task. "Stay where you are, bitch, or I'll help you fall down some stairs."

Eloise was out the door and approaching the stairs when she ran into Gregory and Eoyan as they reached the top landing, puffing like draught horses. "This way, stupes!"

Kennyth Brice's private meeting rooms were at the top of a different tower, so they had to descend back down to the inner keep, cross a wide hallway, turn a corner, cross another hallway, and start up a new stone stairwell. All this was done with swords and armor on while rushing past startled celebrants on the lower levels and guards on the others. Gregory and Eoyan fell behind again, though not as far this time. At every landing it seemed that lightning struck again.

Eight guards flanked the iron doors of the duke's meeting rooms. "Nimrheal's coming! Out of the way!" Eloise shouted and dived through the group of open-mouthed men. As they stared helplessly, she slammed the door open with one kick. It crashed against the opposite wall and bounced furiously back, but she caught it just before it connected with her bent nose. Then she took in the scene before her.

The whole room was covered in maps. There were maps with iron figurines on them, maps with strings, maps with colorful, painted lines. This was the duke's war room in Ardvaser, the place where he kept all his plans.

"What are you talking about, Sir Kyre?" Gerveault asked. He was leaning over a table pointing at something on a map. He and the duke appeared to be going over troop dispositions.

"Are you working on something original in here?" Eloise shouted, taking a single step inside the doorway. Gregory and Eoyan charged up and skidded to a halt behind her, crowding the entryway.

Kennyth Brice and Gerveault were open-mouthed with amazement, but then they looked up at the rattling shutters on the window. They had been too absorbed in their maps to notice the storm, but it registered now—with a vengeance. "Hati's hell, is this Nimrheal?" Kennyth asked, horror gripping him.

"Yes!" Eloise roared, at her wit's end now.

Gregory spoke up, "It has to be, your Grace. It came up suddenly out of nowhere, exactly like the one we saw in Vercors before Nimrheal destroyed the research facility. Its full power has not hit us yet."

"Well, Nimrheal is not coming for *us*," said Gerveault. His glance at the maps said it all. The work he and Kennyth were doing had been administrative, not creative.

Eloise stamped her foot in frustration. "That is *fucking* apparent!" she bellowed. Eloise whirled back in the direction she had come from, but there were two problems with that maneuver: first Gregory and Eoyan were in her way, and a more important second, she did not know where to go next. She tried to think. Eloise was not the kind of woman to waste time when Nimrheal was coming. "Koria. It has to be her. Where is she?"

†

CRRRRRRAAAK. CRRRRRRAAAK.

Endicott woke with a start. It was not the thunder that made him spring out of bed, his exhaustion, blistered feet, and stiffened muscles forgotten. It was the disjointed dream, more an epileptic assault of images than a cogent story, that told him that Eloise, Bethyn, and Koria were about to die. The thunder he heard as he woke only confirmed Nimrheal's arrival. He reached for Likelihood and thought about cups. In his dream the women had been surrounded by cups.

Where were *they?*

†

MOMENTS AFTER CONFRONTING KENNYTH BRICE AND GERVEAULT, ELOISE AND HER MEN were running back down the way they had come, legs moving as fast as they could while still retaining coordination, making an awful commotion. As they ran, they started picking up a train of guards, possibly at Kennyth Brice's orders. An alarm bell rang out, which added to the cacophony.

The sub-basement laboratory was as far away as it was possible to be from the Duke's Tower while remaining within the inner keep of Ardvaser. Eloise again put distance between herself and Gregory and Eoyan, and even more between them and the growing column of soldiers who pursued them. Finally, she hit the bottom step of the last basement stair and sprinted toward the closed door, shouldering into it like a battering ram. The heavy wood splintered, and she barged her way through into a room covered in cups. They were everywhere, all over the place, yet still in some kind of baffling, concentric pattern. If the cups had been candles, it could have been romantic or creepily occult, but since the cups were cups, it was … just weird. Koria and Bethyn were standing in the far corner of the room, each with a notebook in hand.

They have no idea.

After she shouted at them to stop, that Nimrheal was coming, the bookish fools kept insisting there was nothing to worry about. And to complete the farce, Gregory and Eoyan then skidded into their weird array of cups and made an embarrassing mess of themselves. Eloise only glared at her hapless companions. She was not the kind of woman who wasted time yelling at idiots when a fight was about to begin. But Bethyn was exactly that kind of woman. She burst into laughter. "You see, El, everyth—"

CRRRRRRAAAK.

BBBRRRROOOOM.

The room shook as a tremendous explosion was heard from somewhere above them. A growing number of guardsmen were crowding the door, finally catching up with the action. Eloise saw several heads turn from looking into the room to stare at something behind them in the hallway. Then the screaming began.

It's here.

Eloise drew her sword. It still had no name, but it sang sweetly. The sound was mirrored as Gregory drew Justice. She smiled at her husband as she set herself behind her entropic shield. He smiled back, though a little wanly. Gregory was good in a fight, but he did not crave the savage clarity of battle the way Eloise did.

"AAAAARRRHH!"

A soldier flew into the room, feet last, and crashed headfirst into the closest of the two large stone vessels at the center of the cups. Blood sprayed out from the impact as his head broke open. More screaming echoed from the hallway. A guard backed partway through the door but was abruptly yanked forward and out of sight. He did not come back.

Another soldier seemed to levitate backwards into the room, but then Eloise saw the spear that held him aloft, protruding from the center of his back. Nimrheal flowed after the spitted soldier and, one roiling motion later, another man was flung into the front wall. The demon was as ill-defined, amorphous, and hard to bring into focus as it had been the last time Eloise had fought the thing. Her eyes seemed to slide off it. No matter how hard she squinted at the creature, her brain received equivocal messages about size, position, movement, solidity. The dark cloak of shadow that rippled about it only added to the enigma. A sound rang out from Nimrheal like an incoherent scream and reverberated under Eloise's skin, ceaseless and punishing.

Eoyan hurled his spear with tremendous force. It flew on a dead-flat trajectory straight at the demon, but at the last second seemed to split into a cone of a dozen or more spears. Each of them swerved around the thing and coalesced again behind it. The reconstituted spear hit the stone wall and shattered.

"That was fascinating," Koria said in a voice probably meant only for herself. Then she shouted, "Innovating!"

Eloise never saw what Koria did next. She ignored the crack-crack-crack as every unspilled cup of water froze and percussive waves of alternating hot and frigid air shot around the room. Instead, she focused on leaping forward to cut the demon down and saw, as she did so, that Koria had indeed done something significant to Nimrheal. It no longer seemed to flow like smoke. Its ephemeral limbs, so ill-defined before, suddenly appeared solid. It was still a creature of horror, but now Eloise could focus on it and define it.

As she approached the demon, a crossbow bolt flew from the hallway and struck the thing's chest. It did not fall, but it did seem to pause for a moment, perhaps even stagger. Eloise struck in that instant, swinging high and wide with her entropic sword, but Nimrheal brought its spear up and caught the blow. Eloise's blade scored only a notch before being knocked violently back.

She did not see the blow that hit her in return. Afterward those who did told her the demon stepped inside her reach and hit her shield with one long hand-like extension of itself, collapsing her shield arm into her chest and sending her cartwheeling into the wall. "Eloise!" Gregory cried from somewhere out of sight. She tried to get up, but she seemed stuck in a sitting position, and her sword was out of her hand, lying a few paces away. Flames exploded around the demon, but faster than thought it hurled its spear at Koria. Eoyan, who had been running toward Eloise with Gregory, was hit side-on and hurled into Koria. Both went down.

"Do you see this, Eloise?" Gregory shouted.

"What?" Her head was swimming.

"I said, get up, Eloise. Please." Gregory was facing the demon, putting himself and his shield between her and Nimrheal.

CRRRRRRAAAK.

With a flash and a sound like thunder, a new spear appeared in Nimrheal's grasp, and with that, the creature's movements changed. It seemed to start flowing again, becoming by degrees harder to focus on. Eloise pressed her back against the wall and tried to push herself up.

BRRRAAAAA—CRRK

"Aaaaahhh!"

Gregory stared at her for a moment with a hopeless look in his eyes, then toppled over sideways. As he fell, Eloise saw that Nimrheal's spear had punctured his damaged shield and plunged through into his stomach. Six inches of the gleaming black tip stuck out of her husband's back.

No! NO!

CRRRRRRAAAK. CRRRRRRAAAK. CRRRRRRAAAK.

Three thunderous reports followed close on three blinding flashes of lighting. They came from Robert. He stood in the doorway directing his lightning at Nimrheal. When the afterimage cleared, the demon was gone. The spear in Gregory's belly remained.

✝

A haggard looking Robert Endicott crouched in front of Eloise. His skin was gray and his eyes red. His hands shook. "I owe you," she said to him.

"Come on, Eloise." The soothing voice belied his ravaged physical condition, "Let's get you out of here."

Gregory's body had been removed, but Eloise still saw it in her mind, it and the spear. A strange memory came from nowhere. Her lips moved, though she did not remember commanding them to speak. "The prophecy was wrong. He wasn't mounted on Justice."

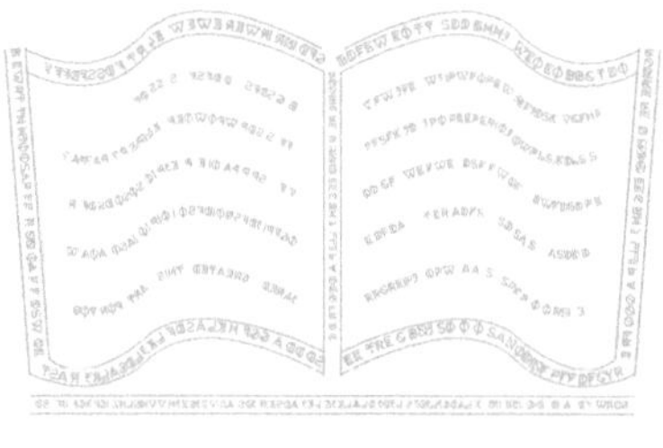

Chapter Thirty-Three

The Worst Guests

Skoll and Hati have not been seen since the war ended and Huygens changed. This is because they are afraid. Their connection to whatever orthogonal domain they came from has been weakened. In this new state, a sufficient number of Deladieyr Knights could hunt them down and kill them. Lamentably, we lack the necessary numbers. All of our best candidates are dead.

–From Orthogonal Consciousness, *by Veronica Brice. Written ten years after the end of the Methueyn War.*

Veronica may have had the right idea, thought Koria. Yet there were also the skolves to consider, hence the Lighthouse plan to systematically weaken both the skolves and the two demons. But the plan had been undone by events. They had needed to secure the Methueyn Bridge, and that had not happened. Huygens had reverted, and Skoll and Hati—less Skoll's arm—were probably back to their former glory. On top of everything else, Nimrheal had returned. And Gregory Justice had now been added to its list of victims.

Not just Gregory. Eloise had not been the same woman since the death of her husband. She had withdrawn into a shell that no one seemed able to penetrate. Robert had tried to speak to her, had even managed to have a long, private audience with her, but would only say afterwards that she had hardly seemed to hear him. The powerful, tall woman had refused to see any of the rest of her friends. No entreaty would bring her out of her shell, no provocation could bring forth the fire she had been so well known for.

At Gregory's funeral, she had said nothing, only staring off into the distance. She had not even visited Eoyan March, whose shoulder had been shattered by the spear thrown at Koria. Sometimes she could be seen wondering alone in the observatory, staring at the Methueyn Treaty and its new noose. The sword had fallen on the night Nimrheal attacked. Incredibly, Sir Hemdale had caught it, though he had been seriously injured in the process. No man, no matter how strong, stubborn, or full of righteousness can catch a five hundred pound falling sword and walk away unscathed.

I will visit Hemdale later and entreat him to visit his niece.

"It's too bad the Bridge failed so soon," Bethyn said. They were both seated in their usual workroom. "It's just too late. The demons are back. We have to deal with that." Bethyn had frozen during the fight with Nimrheal. She had never trained for combat, and it showed when combat came to her. It was lucky that she had managed to stay out of the way while the lightning and the spears had flown.

Yes, we do have to deal with it. "We had better hurry. Robert is almost ready to leave again."

Bethyn rolled her eyes again, which was really starting to annoy Koria. A lot of things were starting to annoy Koria. She was a subtle woman used to gaining a certain control over events through superior knowledge, but that strategy felt very compromised now. She was tempted to try far heraldry anyway, if only to be able to feel that she had taken the initiative, but that old tactic was arguably futile now as well as dangerous.

Heedless of her friend's darkening expression, Bethyn continued sneering. "Robert has to be stopped. The last thing we need is for your husband to charge off into the Ardgour Wilderness again and get himself killed."

Robert was only waiting for the Armadale mission to be escorted out of the duchy. Neither Sir Kaimari nor Sir Leyzbeth Braynor had arrived, and Sir Haverland had declared that none of Armadale's candidate knights could be accepted for Rising without a full quorum of the Council of Knights to rule for or against them. The discussion had quickly become acrimonious.

It was good that neither Hemdale nor Eloise had been present at that meeting.

"Well, there's no stopping him," said Koria, feeling more than a little helpless and even more angry. "He's virtually the only knight still on his feet. Haverland is going to return the Treaty to Vercors City and then do who knows what. The *You Are Free* in the Treaty cuts both ways."

"But Robert's just a little-k knight," Bethyn sputtered. "His days of fighting the Lonely Wizard are behind him."

Koria struggled to give her a neutral look and maintain her calm. *Bethyn does not know the whole story. And she does not know everything about Robert, whatever she thinks.*

"Maybe," Koria finally said. "So why don't we see if we can figure something out to help him?"

Yet again the two women went carefully over their recent experiment, the fight with Nimrheal, and everything they had observed about the strange nature of the demon.

"There seems to be a probabilistic uncertainty about it," Bethyn said. "Arrows miss it, spears miss it, sheets of lightning miss it. It is as if Nimrheal is both here and not here, simultaneously in our domain and orthogonal to it."

"In which case," Koria said, "Nimrheal is not like Skoll and Hati at all. Heylor came close to burning Skoll to the ground, and that was before he took its arm home with him."

Bethyn laughed at that. "Heylor Style. Who would have thought he would be so dangerous to transcendental monsters?" She shook her head in amused disbelief. "But you did do *something* to Nimrheal, Koria. You got the demon's attention at one point."

"That was an old trick," replied Koria, "from when Robert and I were preparing to fight the cloaked man four years ago. I attempted to suppress Nimrheal's own dynamics."

"Make sense, girl," Bethyn said dryly.

This time it was Koria's turn to laugh. "Oh, things need to make sense now?"

"We *are* dynamicists, dear."

"Fine," Koria said. "So normally when we suppress someone's dynamics, we camp out in the empyreal sky, and every time that person attempts to execute an innovation, we interfere with the probability. It's equivalent to making the cost go up. But Nimrheal is tethered to elsewhere by a dark singularity. It looks like the connection we see with the Deladieyr Knights sometimes. We've seen it in Robert in the past, in Marielle Engel too, and in Sir Hemdale." She smiled. "Well, I suppressed it. I couldn't sever the connection, but Nimrheal changed when I did it."

Bethyn grudgingly nodded. "And then, right after that, a crossbow bolt, which ought to have split and swerved around it, hit home. Followed by Robert blasting Nimrheal into the wall, which, okay, didn't kill him but did send him packing."

"Luckily for all of us."

"Right, but can Robert do what you did? Suppress another person's—or creature's—dynamics?"

Koria remembered Robert making such an attempt during the fight with Keith Euyn. But Davyn Daly had still died. "We need to come up with other solutions. A different transform maybe. We've always said that the right transform can solve any problem. Let's prove that's true."

"Oh, we're going to do some original thinking, are we? And then maybe die." Bethyn rolled her eyes. "That sounds smart. You know, I *was* here two nights ago when Nimrheal showed up uninvited and killed Gregory. Maybe we should try something else and live a little longer."

This was too much for even Koria's equanimity. "As slaves to the past? Afraid to even fucking *think?*" She pushed her chair back and stood up. "Not me, Bethyn. I won't live like that. Nimrheal has already killed too many of our friends. You know who's next."

"Knights, Koria, we need to die just because your husband can't leave things well enough alone?"

Koria slammed her hand down on the table. "No. Knights damn you, Bethyn! Who cried and ran like a maniac four years ago thinking a hair on your uncaring head might have been hurt? Who *loves* you?"

Bethyn's hands went up in surrender. "I was just teasing. Calm down. Things have gotten really bad when no one can even take a joke anymore."

"Really?" Koria said. She suddenly became aware that she was crying. Gregory's death had been a terrible blow, but it was even worse for Robert, who had been like a brother to him, and worse still, of course, for Eloise, who looked like she might never recover. Meanwhile, the constant threat of Nimrheal lent a feeling of terror to the idea of trying *anything* new. In Vercors City, Nimrheal had appeared again, murdering a professor of agriculture working on a refinement of the new grain. No one who was creative or curious felt safe, and a lot of people were looking for someone to blame.

"Yes," Bethyn said in an unusual sarcasm-free tone. "Nobody gets me. I was just trying to be funny. But seriously, truthfully, I'm scared shitless too." She shook her head and looked carefully at Koria. "And yeah, we have to do *something.*"

Koria sat down, wiping her eyes. "So you're willing to take a chance and get creative with me?" She smiled. "That's really quite brave and noble of you."

Bethyn scowled, more herself again. "No, not really. Nimrheal just came for us. What's the probability we'll come up with something murder-worthy again so soon?"

"Or that Nimrheal will strike the same place twice?" Koria said, chuckling. "Just when I was starting to think of you as a hero. So you don't think we'll come up with anything new?"

"Stay there, Koria." Bethyn got up and cautiously peered between the window shutters. Satisfied, she swung them wide open so Koria could see the cloudless sky. "One of us can watch at the window. First sign of anything and we stop." She put her head out the window and craned her neck around. "But I don't think Nimrheal will come today even if we do discover something. I think the new idea has to be really good to be dangerous. Otherwise Nimrheal would come every time some farmer noticed something new about the texture of her cowpads. But it doesn't happen. So even if we come up with something new it might not be … interesting enough to summon Nimrheal."

Maybe.

"But there's something else too," Bethyn added. "If there is one rule we are sure about, it's that Nimrheal only comes once for the same invention, right?"

"Right," agreed Koria.

Bethyn smiled at her friend. "Don't you see? A lot of new ideas have been forgotten. No matter how hard we try to keep track of things, discoveries can get lost when their creators are killed. We might reinvent something that has already been paid for. That would be … a kind of immunity, right?"

"That sounds better," Koria said. "I'll take first watch at the window."

"Yah. Watch close."

Despite her smiles and reassurances, Koria needed some relief. Worry over Robert was consuming her. And though she tried not to think about her daughter, the pain was still there, like the black storms of Nimrheal, hanging over her mind. Perhaps it would be there forever. Perhaps it should be. *How many more will we lose?*

Bethyn's turn at being creative started out with some similarities to the story of Luciena that Koria was rereading. Just as in Luciena's story, creativity does not come on demand, and Bethyn was not by nature a patient woman. There was pacing, cursing, a lot of whispering to herself, and much noisy flipping through books. Followed by more cursing. After some drumming of hands on the table, then some forehead banging, and finally a long spell of staring darkly off into space, Bethyn asked, "You said that Nimrheal's connection to hell was a singularity?"

Koria checked the window before answering. Clear skies. "Very much so. Robert had an almost impossible time modeling it during his initial encounter."

Bethyn smiled like a big, mean cat. "Well, that's it, then. We're using the wrong transform. Lessingham is good for continuous functions. Radial too. But we need to change our transform to something from a discontinuous family."

Щ

"Your husband will die.
YOU will die.
Come and see me now.
Stables.
Come alone.
~~HURRY.~~
—A friend."

Koria passed the note to Bethyn. It had been delivered barely a moment ago by a page who said she had gotten it from another page.

"Come alone!" Bethyn slapped the message down on the table with the pages of notes they had made on the demon-killing discontinuous transform they hoped to create. The new mathematics that might make it possible had been developed just a year earlier by Meredeth Callum and a group of her senior students. It was a discontinuous transform with piecewise, constant values that had proved useful in isolating signals through the javelin prototype that Gerveault had been working on at the time. It also had an orthogonal basis, which made it fast to calculate. So far, it seemed feasible. They had been making steady progress in turning the strange mathematics into something useable in the field. They were almost there, at least in theory. Then the note arrived.

"What kind of street-performer villain writes *come alone?*" Bethyn added. "And says, hurry! Then claims to be *a friend*. Not a very friendly kind of message." She rolled her eyes for the twelfth time that day. Koria was counting.

"This is a joke," Bethyn pronounced, handing back the note.

Only a very good friend would try such a macabre joke.

"Let's go." Koria stood up and started walking toward the door.

"We're going?" Bethyn asked, still sitting, clearly startled that Koria was taking the note seriously.

Koria opened the door. "Doesn't it sound like something Eoyan March would write?"

"Kind of," replied Bethyn, pushing her chair back. "Although his note would say something about what you should wear to his little clandestine meeting. Come naked, come wearing silk, come lubricated, come—what?" She cut herself off when she saw Koria's dark look, for once reading her friend's mood accurately.

Koria marched them along quickly, only stopping long enough to collect four guardsmen to accompany them. They crossed the inner keep to the guest stables under the outer gate. "Swords drawn," Koria instructed the guards as they came up on the large building of stone and wood. "But stay here." Her position as advisor to Kennyth Brice, her title as Lady of Engevelen, her striking dark hair and skin, but above all her naturally commanding presence made the guards' obedience absolute.

Koria approached a small side door and opened herself to the empyreal sky. She pushed the creaking door and stepped into the dimly lit space, smelling the familiar aroma of horse, hay, and leather. A nickering sound rolled out from somewhere deeper within the building. No threats revealed themselves. Yet.

In front of one of the stalls, a groom, dressed in the livery of Vercors, was silhouetted in the light from the door. "Lady Valcourt? May I help you?" There was no accent of Armadale hiding in his voice, and no secret nervousness or heightened heartbeat in the empyreal sky. Koria looked sharply at the young man, remembering him.

"Kyle, I think. Please take us to our three guests."

Kyle immediately led the two ladies down the lengthy line of stalls, past horses' noses, bales of hay, bags of grain, and hanging saddles, toward the sound of the nickering horse. Koria had looked deeper into the sky and saw the three women who waited ahead, ostensibly grooming their mounts. There were no other soldiers or knights of Armadale in the stables.

"Lady Koria, Lady Bethyn, thank you for joining us," said Sir Astrid Kettel. She was the tallest of the three women, though there was a strong resemblance among them, and not just in their red hair. They were all freckled and had large, prominent noses. None of the women were as big as Eloise, and none of their noses as impressive as hers, but the women carried themselves in a physically assured way that reminded Koria of her remarkable friend.

Koria watched Astrid brush her horse for a moment before replying. "Your note implied some urgency."

Astrid gestured toward the other two women with her brush. "These are my squires. Eindride Kettel is my younger sister, and the one beside her is Egil Stenner."

Koria exchanged a glance with Bethyn, who only shrugged. Her red face spoke more clearly. "What is it that you want?" Koria asked.

"We want to defect from Armadale."

"All three of you?"

The two squires nodded, but only Astrid replied. "Yes. We have been preparing since we arrived here, but no one will speak with us privately."

Bethyn shifted. "So that's why you wanted to get together with Eloise so badly?"

"She won't see us." Astrid sighed. "Especially not now. We tried to send a message through her man Eoyan, but he didn't seem to understand."

"He thought you wanted to have sex," Bethyn replied.

"Certainly, sex too, if it's on offer." Astrid smiled coolly before continuing. "But the main thing is to get free of our country before it's too late."

Koria had been watching the three women in the empyreal sky. Everything they said appeared to be true. Her face reddened, though for different reasons than Bethyn's. "So my husband is not about to die? I am not about to die? This is just about you wanting to leave Armadale?"

Astrid handed her brush to Eindride and gave Koria a direct look. "Oh no, your husband is about to die all right. Your duke too. Our countrymen are planning murder."

"Guards!" Koria shouted, her heart racing, but her mind working. A moment later, the four soldiers rushed through the big front doors of the stable and skidded to a halt before the women.

"There is treachery being planned by our guests from Armadale," Koria instructed. "Not these three." In the past she would have known through heraldry exactly where her husband was, but the locus made that impossible. *I need to be as comprehensive and as quick as possible.* She looked at the guards one at a time as she spoke her next words. "Send a runner to the outer encampment, ring the alarm bell, and inform Lord Wolverton. While he gets organized, assemble three eights on the steps of the keep. One job for each of you. Now go!"

"Kyle!" she shouted. The groom had been listening not far off, pretending to oil a saddle. He jumped at the sound of her voice. "I need you to do something very particular for me." She gave him his instructions in a whisper, then turned back to the three tall women. "We have a moment now to let those orders work in our favor. Why don't you tell us as quickly as possible what is going on?" *When we act, it must be decisively.*

"Pass me my sword belt, would you?" Astrid said to Egil. "Thank you." She belted it on before she answered. "Our king has broken the Methueyn Treaty. He has created his own line of knights, the Order of Seygis. They have come to steal the Treaty, kill the duke, murder Robert Endicott, and most importantly, steal the location of the Methueyn Bridge, which they think is on a map in the duke's private apartments."

"That just sounds like typical Armadale politics," sneered Bethyn, her attitude peeking out from under her infatuation with the three women.

"Ha! Maybe," Astrid allowed. Her squires were checking their own sword belts. "But these Seygis Knights have no honor. They poisoned Sir Jormundheim and Sir Valcryst rather than fight them. They ambushed and murdered Sir Kaimari as he attempted to cross Armadale." She locked eyes with Koria. "They ate his body. They are cannibals."

Koria remembered a legend concerning Sir Seygis, the ninth knight, the cannibal knight. He had nearly destroyed both the Deladieyr and Methueyn orders back before the first fall of Engevelen. After he was accused of cannibalism and put down like a mad dog, the rules for the Council of Knights were changed forever. He was the reason the vetting process was treated so seriously. *And the reason some have speculated that there might be many more than eight angels in Elysium.*

Stifling her horror and disgust, Koria said, "They may find that killing Robert Endicott is more difficult than they think."

The alarm bell started to ring.

"But Lady Koria, they brought a wizard-savant with them."

"A what?"

"A wizard only good at one thing, but at that thing, unbeatable."

"What thing?" Whatever it was, it felt to Koria that the other shoe had just dropped.

"Suppressing other wizards."

Koria started running.

Chapter Thirty-Four

Siege of the Embassy

I feel sorry for the feckless, the fearful, and the lost who go through their lives misunderstanding such issues. Such people should avoid taking actions of consequence, for surely they will only feel regret whether they fail or succeed. When I act, I act with purpose and with no internal conflict. When I kill, I feel no remorse.

–The Lonely Wizard

"RISE, GREGORY," ENDICOTT SAID AS THEY PUT HIS FRIEND INTO THE GROUND. KORIA STOOD beside him, holding his hand. Eloise stood on his other side, and he held her hand as well, but it was limp. Later, he told Eloise a secret. It was something he thought she needed to know, that perhaps would help her, but the colossal woman seemed not to hear him.

Gregory Justice would never have become a Deladieyr Knight, could never have survived the Ceremony of Rising that candidates were required to take. Gregory knew his own mind, but he lacked that nearly sociopathic certainty the Deladieyr Knights all seemed to have—that Hemdale said they *must* have. And their special talent as well. All Deladieyr Knights were born with it, with a gift to naturally bend the empyreal sky to augment their own strength. Gregory did not have that. His dynamics were mediocre, his mathematical skills average at best, his personal fortune unimpressive among the nobility. Gregory was good at a great many things, but great at none of them. *Then why do I feel that a great man has left us?*

The question was no insult. Endicott knew that Gregory had truly been a great man, yet he struggled to say *how*. He felt that if he could figure this out, he would be honoring his friend properly.

After sharing an overdue, elegiac, and absolutely necessary hour of love with Koria, he walked up the stairs to the observatory. He wanted to see the Methueyn Treaty, but when he stepped onto the landing at the top of the last flight of stairs, he saw that Eloise was there already. She stood staring at the great metal blade and the writing upon it. Endicott approached cautiously, saying nothing.

His feet were healing quickly, and his preparations were almost complete. *I am leaving soon, but not before I know.* Standing beside Eloise, under the shadow of the monolithic sword, he said, "Gregory was a great man." Eloise did not look at him. She only stared up at the sword and its rope. Endicott followed her gaze to the cursive script etched in the steel of the blade. He contemplated once again the largest words cut into the metal, the ones most in need of explanation. "You Are Free."

A thought suddenly burned whole into his consciousness. "I think I understand a piece of it now," he announced carefully. "I don't think being a knight is all about feats of strength and violence. I'm not sure we need to lose what makes us each who we are." Endicott tried to read Eloise's face, but she was giving nothing away. "Gregory was worth as much as any god or angel I ever met." He understood something else too, something he had already discussed with Koria. It was something that had become clear while carrying Marielle Engel, but it was personal, more about him than Gregory, so he did not speak it. This was a time to think about his friend, the third he had lost in one horrible week.

"Gregory was great because he stood up to Nimrheal despite not being able to hang from a five-hundred-pound sword." Endicott would have loved to see Marielle hang from the sword and Rise, but he would much rather that she was simply alive. He would rather Lindseth was alive and Gregory was alive. None of them had Risen, and his words, though aimed at Gregory, applied as well to all three of the dead.

Endicott had been half dead himself by the time they made it to Ardvaser. His mind had been overwhelmed then, but now he felt he was thinking more clearly and could mourn properly. Perhaps he could even achieve an honorable catharsis. "Gregory was great because he was a calm second thought when I was lost, a port in a storm, an arm in a fight, a friend against any enemy, and a gentleman always. He was right but not righteous, moral but did not seek control. He never let his weaknesses affect his resolve. I wish I was more like him."

He looked to the side to see if Eloise had reacted and might speak, but she had walked quietly away. He put his hand on the hilt of his sword, Keith Euyn's sword, and left. As he walked down the many flights of stairs and started up the stairs in the Duke's Tower toward Kennyth Brice's private apartments, he thought again about the other thing he had learned, the thing he had only discussed with Koria.

▽

THAT YOU NEVER KNOW WHEN A FIGHT WILL END, ONLY WHEN IT STARTS, IS AN OLD MAXIM, a warning about the lack of control in a conflict and the unpredictability of war. Standing in the burning rubble of Armadale's embassy estate, Endicott wondered if he had even controlled the start of that conflict.

Did it start with the Battle of the Bifrost? Or was it when Colborn Vig murdered Conor? Had it all begun when the greatest man of the age had a dream so appalling that his sanity could not bear the weight of it? Did it start when Kennyth Brice lost his famously cool temper and charged the wall? Or when Hemdale returned, or when that idiot of an ambassador made a joke about Eleanor? Was the war inevitable only when Eleanor stopped breathing? Was it already inevitable when my mother died?

Endicott suddenly came to himself. Such questions counted for nothing in the current, urgent moment. He raised Eloise's sword against the plate-armored soldier advancing on him and cut the man in half down to his stomach. Kicking the body off his entropic blade, he sent it slamming into the broken stones, scattering viscera and shit over a broad swath of rubble.

All vain speculations banished now, Endicott launched himself forward, moving with supernal alacrity to intercept another knight who was raising his blade to strike down Kennyth Brice. Endicott hit the man at incredible speed. The kinetic energy of the impact made his shield ring as if he had punched the man with a gigantic bell, its momentum flinging the knight off into the clouds of dark smoke that now enveloped the embassy compound. The soldier could not even have registered the blow before he hit the air and plunged into whatever horrors the smoke hid. A part of Endicott's mind registered the strange fact that, even considering how quickly he had struck the man, the law of conservation of momentum did not appear to be operating normally. Unless his own mass had unaccountably increased.

More soldiers appeared through the billowing, acrid smoke, but in fighting Keith Euyn, Endicott had learned something about power and action. From that lonely wizard, he had learned something about accepting the cruel reality of his own wizardry. Desperate to protect Kennyth Brice, ruthless in his loyalty, he broke through to Elysium and called its lightning down without compunction. In eight rapid flashes, he cooked every mother's son of them, every complex, sentient, feeling being that emerged from the smoke. He was so angry he barely shivered, so beyond reason that he never thought twice about the risks involved in breaking the extradimensional barrier.

Hemdale appeared beside him, glowing ethereally in the empyreal sky, then Sir Christensen, too, though less clearly. With Kennyth Brice, they strode forward killing everyone they saw who was not one of them. There was no thought involved, no hesitation, and no mercy. All the thinking had occurred earlier when the decision to attack the embassy had been made and would occur again and again, painfully, once the battle was over and for long afterward, but now, in the urgency and rage of the moment, there was no thought, no morality.

At last the four men came upon Ambassador Dyre Vernon. Hemdale unhesitatingly decapitated him and then raised his sword against a small figure huddled in fear on the floor, concealed by a blanket. Endicott saw in the empyreal sky that it was a child wrapped up, perhaps against the smoke or the fearful sight of inevitable death approaching. Endicott's sword flashed out at the speed of instinct and intercepted Hemdale's. For a moment the two men contended.

"That is a child!" Endicott roared, stepping into the path of the bigger, angrier man.

With a cry, Hemdale staggered back, lowering his massive weapon. Endicott sheathed his sword and gathered up the tiny form. Whether boy or girl, it could not have been older than four. Endicott held the shivering bundle tight to his chest and walked carefully out of the rubble. *No child should see this.*

But Endicott could not escape the sight of what he had done. Some of the fried bodies strewn across the compound had exploded inside their armor. He hid the child from the horror but opened his own eyes wider. When you set someone on fire and see the charred corpse, the bubbling skin, can you ever forget? When you expose the insides of men and women so that their viscera are opened up to the blank sky, can you forget? When you smash another human being like a brick or tear them in half, should you forget? He could not. He would not. *A child should not see this, but I did it, so I must.*

People said afterwards that Robert Endicott lost his strength as a knight that day.

$$\nabla$$

He knew something was wrong when he reached the top landing of the Duke's Tower and found no guards there. Looking to the left, he saw a crumpled shape and two feet sticking out from under a tapestry at the end of the hall. Endicott drew Likelihood and opened himself to the empyreal sky.

He rushed to the tapestry and pulled the body of a guard out from under the heavy cloth. The man was dead. His throat had been slashed with more savagery than care. Moving quickly, Robert picked the man up and carried him to the stairwell. With a heave, he threw the man over the edge to fall between flights and explode silently far below.

An unmissable alarm signal having been sent, he did not waste time looking for the other bodies he knew must be hidden elsewhere on the landing. Instead he crossed the hallway toward the duke's apartments, hearing a muffled thumping sound as he got closer. Through the empyreal sky, he could see Kennyth Brice's predicament and knew he needed to hurry. The big, heavy door was closed, but his heraldry told him it was not barred on the inside. *Strange.*

Before pushing the door open, Endicott took a moment to examine the stone floor carefully, swiftly making the calculations he would need to use it as a heat sink. Then he pushed gingerly on the hardwood.

The thumping sound became louder. As Endicott had already seen in the empyreal sky, there were five men in the ducal apartments who should not have been there. Four of them stood on the far side of the room at another door, the door that led to Kennyth Brice's bedchambers. Two of them, in full plate armor, held a rug up to the door, while a third man in chain mail smashed against it with a heavy, long-handled battle axe. A fourth, unarmored man watched. "Not long now," the watcher said in a nasally voice, chuckling. It was Heinrich Bitten, the wizard. The fifth man wore the chain of an ambassador. Elias Vernon. He was poring over the maps laid out on the duke's tables but started and looked up as Endicott stepped through the main door.

Endicott innovated immediately. He meant to burn all four of those at the door to ashes, sparing only the ambassador for more exemplary punishment. But something went awry. Only the man swinging the axe ignited, though the expected drumbeat of hot and frigid air washed over the room, fluttering papers and hair.

"AAAAHHH!" the burning man screamed through scorching lips. He dropped his axe at the same time that the two men holding the rug dropped their burden. Shooting flames into the air, the axe man staggered about in a panicked, ragged circle. When he collided with the map table, threatening the papers there, the ambassador pursed his lips and said, "Put him down, please, Sir Steygur." All four non-burning men were staring at Endicott.

"Impressive, Sir Robert, but you won't be able to do that twice," Elias Vernon said in an oily, professional voice.

Why not? Endicott wanted to ask. He needed to know what had interfered with his thermal innovation, but he did not ask. He preferred to draw events out as long as possible.

Sir Heykon, the thick-bodied knight that Endicott had met at Marielle and Lindseth's wake, answered the unspoken question as Sir Steygur, the scarred one, drew his sword and slashed the burning man's neck, producing a spray of blood and a messy corpse that still took three more steps before careening into a wall and going down. "We brought our own wizard with us, Sir Robert."

"I've always wanted to kill a dynamicist," said Heinrich Bitten in a cold voice.

"I've fought other wizards before," replied Endicott just as coldly. "Perhaps you've heard of Keith Euyn." His nonchalance was affected, a further play for time. He could see they had almost made it through the duke's door. Behind it, Kennyth Brice's face could be glimpsed now that the rug had fallen away, watching the scene through a large gash in the wood.

Endicott took a step forward. Elias Vernon stepped back, but the wizard stayed where he was by the door. Heykon waggled his finger at Endicott while Steygur calmly cleaned the blood from his sword. "But you have never contended with Heinrich, have you?" Heykon smiled, now patronizingly. "He only does one thing, Sir Robert, but he does it very, very well. He cannot see a minute into the future. He cannot even light a campfire." The smug smile widened. "But he can smother any other wizard's work."

"I see" said Endicott, keeping his expression blank. "That may not be relevant at the moment. Your ambassador is hiding in the corner there, and Heinrich doesn't seem to want any part of my steel. So it will be me against the two of you. A very fair fight." Endicott did not believe his own words. He could see that there was a strong, dark power around the two knights and a heaviness in the empyreal sky. *Someone better find that guard's body soon!*

Sir Steygur stepped to his right to stand by Heykon, a cold look of disdain on his face. "We are more than enough, I think." He puffed himself up, standing a little taller. "We are Seygis Knights."

Endicott knew the reputation of Sir Seygis too well, the ninth knight, but he only shrugged. "Who? Never heard of the kid."

"Get on with it, for Seygis's sake," came the sharp, peremptory voice of the ambassador, now backed into shadow as far from the impending mayhem as he could squeeze himself.

Endicott's jibe had infuriated Steygur. His scars turned purple, and he did not seem to hear his ambassador's words. "We are every bit as good as your *precious* Deladieyr Knights, boy. Better in fact. We aren't held back."

"Unlike you, Robert *Endicott*." Heykon sneered the family name, eager to get in his own insults. "You've been weakened by a soft conscience and your childish regrets. Everyone knows it. You're a shadow of the man who fought Colborn Vig and Keith Euyn, only good now for carrying the dead."

Endicott could not maintain his pose of nonchalance through that. His blood heated. "Any one of my dead friends is worth ten of you."

"Join them, then!" shouted Steygur. He shook his sword and took his first step forward. "You're going to die today. And you're going to lose your precious duke too."

▽

"You are so tired, Robert," said Koria, straddling his chest and peering into his eyes. He had woken from about an hour of pseudo sleep. Nothing about his physical being felt right, but waking to the sight—and warm weight—of his wife crouching over him was infinitely better than the sights and weights he had grown used to over the last weeks. Her gentle voice was pure relief, no matter the words. "You've lost so much," she said.

"So have you."

"Yes." She would not deny it any longer. They had finally spoken of the daughter they had lost, trying to find meaning in the tragedy, finally sharing the pain. Koria put her face right up to her husband's and drilled her eyes into his. "But even though you look three-quarters ready for Elysium, you also look better than you have since the day Eleanor died. Since the embassy."

"Thank you. I guess," he replied. When she had pulled back enough that he no longer had to cross his eyes to see her properly, he continued. "I forgave myself, carrying Marielle. It made me feel I've finally paid the price for what I did."

Koria was the most intelligent woman Endicott had ever met. She knew he was speaking about his horror at what he, Sir Christensen, Kennyth, and Hemdale had done at the embassy. "I was angry and disappointed with myself, but I never *regretted* it, you know," he said. "Keith was right. When you do what you must—when you *must*—it cannot be regretted. But he was wrong when he said that we should not feel sad, that we should not feel remorse. No one should be happy or feel nothing after killing other people."

"Is that why you have never shown what you can do since then?"

"Yes," he smiled just a little, "though I really could not do much. Until, perhaps, now."

"But you didn't want to be a Deladieyr Knight after that?"

"Oh, knights, no. Too much certainty and not enough remorse felt wrong to me. Hemdale's … blankness, his lack of any reaction, after the debacle at the embassy made me feel sick. I did not want any part of that."

"And now?" She slid downwards and laid her head on his chest.

"Marielle made a good point about not *aspiring*. I'll just be myself." He ran his fingers through her hair. "But I am in accord with myself, finally. She died, and in, I don't know, *allowing* me to carry her, she lifted me from the waters, saved me from drowning. It's as if she brought me into balance again."

They lay silent for a long while. After a time, Robert opened his eyes to find his wife's green eyes on him again.

"But I never understood how you managed at the embassy in the first place," she said.

"What do you mean?"

"You were exhausted, Robert." Koria turned her head to the side but still watched his eyes. "After the Battle of the Bifrost and then Keith Euyn, I didn't think you could fight a puppy, let alone level a fortified estate."

Robert kissed her lips, then laid his head back. "You're right. So damn smart." He waited a moment until she looked at him directly again. "I guess I never said what triggered me then."

"Which was?"

"I had just lost Eleanor. She was so … good. I loved her, Koria."

"I know." Her green eyes were wet now.

"Well, I wasn't going to let Eleanor lose her son that day."

▽

"I'LL COME HELP YOU, ROBERT!" THE DUKE SHOUTED THROUGH THE GASH IN THE DOOR.

"Stay there!" Endicott shouted back. "That's what they want. Don't give it to them." Kennyth Brice was a statesman, not a warrior. *If Kennyth is to live, I must succeed. If Koria is to live, I must kill these men.* He unleashed eleven separate thermal dipole operators in staggered succession, testing the wizard, who had now backed up against the door Kennyth Brice sheltered behind.

The sallow wizard flinched, but no one from Armadale died. Elias Vernon jumped, his face suddenly looking scalded. *A little got through.* The dipole innovations did not lower Endicott's temperature noticeably. They were simple operations he was skilled and experienced enough to innovate easily and now, with the lower value of Huygens, almost effortlessly.

"Hold him off, idiot!" Vernon squealed. The skin of his forehead had begun to show a scattering of angry bubbles.

For an instant, Endicott considered breaking the extradimensional barrier as a further test of Heinrich's dampening skills, then decided the risks to himself and Kenneth Brice were too great. At that moment, perhaps sensing his distraction, Steygur and Heykon attacked. Somewhere in the keep a bell began ringing a deep-pitched alarm.

Endicott stepped around Heykon, neutralizing Steygur's ability to strike for the moment. Heavy and strong, Heykon was clearly happy enough to kill Endicott himself. He wound himself up for a tremendous blow, but his leaner, quicker opponent used Likelihood to slice straight through Heykon's heavy sword, two thirds of which broke off and flew out the open doorway, disappearing into the gloom of the landing. Wasting no time, Endicott followed up with a cut that his heavier opponent could not quite evade. Likelihood sliced through the bottom of Heykon's nose, sending a spray of blood and snot flying into the air.

"Gahhh!" Heykon clutched his nose and stumbled back, temporarily out of Endicott's reach.

"How on earth?" asked Steygur, eyes widening in amazement. Or was it terror now?

Endicott did not answer. He was concentrating as deeply as the moment would allow. He could not far herald due to the locus, but millisecond certainty was still available to him. It was a trick from *The Lonely Wizard* that Endicott had learned to manage. Sometimes. It required heralding about two hundred milliseconds into the future, just far enough to anticipate an opponent's action but not far enough to decouple prediction from outcome. When done properly, it was still slightly uncertain, but not enough to compromise the practitioner. Could it be something the narrow talents of Heinrich would be unable to nullify?

In all the other battles in which he had needed his utmost strength or speed, Endicott had been out of his mind with rage, desperate to act, triggered by threat and the childhood trauma such moments always seemed to educe. He was still angry and righteous, and his childhood trauma had not magically disappeared, but he had also come to accept his feelings, and himself, better. Carrying Marielle had relieved the burden of compunction. He did not like killing, but he would do it. He had to. If he failed, Nimrheal would kill Koria and Eleanor would lose her son. The decision to kill Steygur had been made. There was no reason to answer the doomed knight's question.

Footsteps sounded behind him, but he knew they were not friends. More soldiers from Armadale had been busy on a lower floor, up to some other mischief, Endicott supposed. Perhaps the alarm bell had sent them running to join the ambassador. He stepped to the side, and one of the two arrows his millisecond heraldry had detected missed and hit Elias Vernon in the hip.

"Aayeehhh!" the ambassador screamed.

The other arrow hit Endicott in the back. He staggered and felt a short, sharp instant of pain. He ignored it and turned in time to slice off the mailed arm of the first of Armadale's bowmen. The arrow that had hit Endicott fell slowly to the ground, but the arm of the guardsman flew sideways and hit the wall with a wet thud. A line of shattered rings from the man's mailed sleeve tinkled as they scattered across the room. His bow flew even further, hitting the wall higher up and clattering as it fell to the floor. Endicott stepped through, farther away from Steygur, who had frozen in surprise, and split the skull of the other man-at-arms to the teeth. This man's bow made only a soft sound as it hit the thick rug at his feet.

Ignoring the fates of the two bowmen, Endicott pivoted again to face Steygur and Heykon before they could make their next move.

"You said he was weak!" shrieked Vernon, staring like a madman, slumped now against the far wall, dividing his panicked attention between the arrow sticking out of his hip and the unfolding confrontation. Unsure of the damage he had taken from the one arrow that had hit him, Endicott took a chance and broke through to Elysium. He wanted the lightning he had unleashed against Nimrheal in the basement, but this time he seemed to hit a wall in the empyreal domain. His temperature dropped sharply too, and he knew he could not afford another attempt. The only sign that his interference was taxing the strength of Armadale's wizard was the flinch that ran through him a second time.

Heykon had now retrieved the axe from the dead grasp of the man Endicott had burned. His eyes were huge, but not with the fear that Steygur had momentarily shown and that Vernon radiated without pause. Heykon was in a state of rage. His nose streaming blood, and breathing through his mouth in loud, rattling gasps, his dark energy swelled in the empyreal sky.

"He *is* weak!" Heykon bellowed. He pointed with the axe in his hands. "See, he is shivering. *Mighty* Robert Endicott is frightened of us."

Heykon charged, swinging his axe in wide but impossibly rapid arcs. Steygur also advanced, though more cautiously, perhaps worried that he might accidently be struck by his comrade's weapon.

There was nothing for Endicott to do but abandon himself to the fight, to his millisecond heraldry, to the desperate need to win at any cost. Heykon's battle axe had two blades and a vicious center spike. When he closed to striking distance, the plate-armored man switched from broad swings to jabs with the spike. He did not want to lose his axe to Likelihood as he had lost his sword. Endicott took a step backwards, managing only to notch the spike, then feinted and moved suddenly to Heykon's flank, slashing at his leg.

Heykon batted Endicott's attack aside with a rushed, glancing axe blow, but Endicott had already taken another step, enabling him to swing overhead at Steygur. The tall, scarred knight was quick enough to turn the strike but at the cost of a long shallow cut out of his sword. As Steygur stared aghast for a moment at the damage, Endicott took advantage of his distraction to move on the wizard, who was still huddled by the inner door, seemingly fascinated by the unfolding violence.

Both Seygis Knights cried out, suddenly understanding Endicott's intention. He wished to kill the wizard first, then them. They rushed toward him.

Time fell away.

"Robert!" It was Kennyth's voice. "I'm coming out!"

Kennyth's voice brought the awareness of time back into focus. Endicott suddenly became conscious of sweat falling in a steady stream from his forehead. It fell like water from a pump. He was on one knee. Blood trickled slowly down his sword hand, and the wound in his back stung with every breath.

How long have we been fighting?

"Stay there, Kennyth," Endicott panted. "For Eleanor's sake."

"Yes!" said Heykon between his own grotesque gasps for breath. His nose streamed blood and more blood soaked his lips. When he spoke, he gurgled nasally. One blade from his axe had been sheared off, and the spike was now a nub. "You should come out, sweet duke."

Thank you. Heykon's sneers would keep Kennyth from succumbing to the irrational.

"It's just like when we took down Kaimari, yes?" Heykon spat out when Kennyth failed to open the door.

"Yea, brother," Steygur said. His sword had a dozen gashes out of it, and he favored his left leg. "We will eat Robert too."

Endicott struggled to his feet as Steygur and Heykon, both grinning now, advanced on him cautiously despite their grim boast, perhaps still hoping Kennyth Brice would emerge first. He heard heavy footsteps behind him and saw Steygur and Heykon's eyes suddenly widen. Heinrich, panicking, backed sideways across the duke's doorway, then shrieked, "Aaagh," as the point of a thin blade jabbed through the gash in the door and plunged into the wizard's back.

The young dynamicist instantly innovated, breaking through to Elysium and applying the extra effort he had learned was required to affect the Seygis Knights.

CCRRRK.

WOOSH.

Heykon froze solid from toe to head. Simultaneously, Steygur ignited from the neck up. Endicott charged between the two men and slashed broadly with Likelihood, shearing Heinrich in two parts at the belly.

"Thank you," he gasped to Kennyth Brice as the duke opened the half-broken door, a bloody dagger in his shaking hand. The duke dropped the knife and hugged his young champion. "Thank *you*, brother," he said, his normally smooth voice quavering.

▽

ENDICOTT WAS NOT PRECISELY UNCONSCIOUS, BUT HE LET AWARENESS SLIP FROM HIM AS HIS breathing slowed. When he opened his eyes, he was seated in a chair, leaning forward. Koria was dressing the wound in his back, her gentle touch unmistakable.

"You sent Hemdale," he said to her. It had been Hemdale who had distracted Heykon, Steygur, and Heinrich. The enormous man's intimidating arrival had made Heinrich forget the gash in the door, and in his frightened attempt to move farther into the shadows, expose his back to Kennyth's dagger.

Koria dabbed at Endicott's back. "This needs stitches," she said to someone beside her, then came around to stand in front of her husband. "Well, you didn't expect me to run up and cut everyone in half, did you?" She nodded her head to the right. "There are better tools for that."

Endicott followed the direction of Koria's nod and saw Hemdale, wearing only a ginch and holding his massive sword, standing with Kennyth Brice and addressing a seated Elias Vernon. Heykon and Steygur were nowhere to be seen, presumably lying among the dead bodies covered by blankets that were now strewn about the room.

"I take it that all of Armadale's embassy was somehow involved by the time this was over."

Koria stepped forward so Endicott could rest his face against her stomach while another sewed the stitches into his back. "Not all of them," she replied. Sir Astrid and her squires warned us, then helped in the fight."

"Really?" he asked, astonished but very happy to stay where he was.

"Oh yes. They fought alongside our guardsmen in another battle at the after-experiment review room against Vernon's other men. There was also a short … disagreement outside the walls. We have a large number of prisoners now."

"There's going to be full-scale war this time for sure, isn't there?"

Koria's stomach tightened. "It looks like it," came her voice from above.

"But I am an ambassador!" shouted Elias from the other side of the room.

Koria stepped back so Robert could see what the shouting was about.

"You are a treacherous, murderous dog," Sir Hemdale shouted back, apparently not put off at all to be standing in his ginch before a growing assembly of gaping onlookers. He was a hairy, scarred, muscular slab of a man, not attractive so much as scary, not so much perfectly proportioned as built for purpose. That purpose, killing.

Endicott made out Gerveault, Lord Latimer, Sir Sophia Haverland, and Bethyn among the crowd. "In fact, you are not even a dog," Hemdale's voice rose louder. "A dog does not lie. A dog does not steal or murder. A dog does not *betray*."

Elias Vernon was seated in a simple, wooden chair, his face and neck spotted with bubbles from his burns, his expensive pants cut away to reveal the more acute damage that the arrow had done to his hip. He was being worked on by a doctor, but he raised his hands forbiddingly. "I am under orders from my king. I had no choice!"

"But *you are free*, Vernon!" Hemdale shouted. "You *always* have a choice. And right now," he intoned more quietly, "your choice is to take what's coming to you either on your feet or on your arse."

The angry red cuts that spanned the line of Hemdale's inner arms showed in ghastly relief as he gestured in his usual dramatic manner. Those injuries, Endicott knew, had not been received in the battle, but when the ancient warrior had caught the great falling blade of the Methueyn Treaty on the night Nimrheal had come. The massive weight of the sword had cut right through his metal vambraces, only stopped at last by his empyreal-toughened skin.

Elias Vernon's head swiveled toward Kennyth Brice. "Can't you restrain this maniac?"

"The time for restraint has passed," replied Kennyth. His controlled, mellifluous voice had returned. Without another word, he motioned sharply with his head for the doctor to move away, then indicated that Vernon should stand.

"I refuse!" the ambassador cried, raising his shaking hands off the chair's armrests. "I-I don't even have pants. How can I stand up?"

Kennyth Brice took two steps back.

Sir Hemdale raised his great Endicott sword and brought it down on the ambassador.

Chapter Thirty-five

The Middle Bridge to Heaven

"MAYBE YOU SHOULD GO SEE INGRID AND EGYL," EOYAN MARCH SAID FROM HIS BED in the infirmary. His goofy grin was strangely absent, his face instead contorted by pain from a shattered shoulder. Behind this pain, and in his subdued voice, grief for a fallen comrade was unmissable. "Someone is going to have to explain to them what happened to their father."

Eloise did not respond. She had ignored all his attempts at small talk, and now his first serious suggestion—that she should go home to see her daughters and speak to Gregory's parents—would be no more successful in overcoming her sullen silence. She knew those things needed to be done, but she was in no state of mind to hear this. She had put off her family duties too long. Going home *now* was not going to help the girls.

She had not even listened to Eoyan's long soliloquies about what a good man Gregory Justice had been. She knew what her husband was. She knew he had a lord's arrogance in him that he had struggled, mostly successfully, to suppress. She knew he had made a religion of being fair, of making the metaphor of his family name and the name of his sword literal. She knew how proud Gregory had been to fight beside Robert out across the Castlereagh Line four years ago, and then survive the now legendary journey back to fight again in the Battle of the Bifrost. Eloise knew Gregory had not cared about ego-serving and self-justification. He had cared about justice and fairness, and about his friends. She was not the kind of woman who misjudged people, especially not the ones she loved.

"He knew you loved him!" Eoyan shouted at her as she left the room.

Eloise knew Gregory had loved her and that he had done so since the first time they met. How could he not? She had not entered her self-imposed prison of silence because she had failed to tell Gregory what her own feelings were. Eloise had shown him physically and emotionally—abundantly—how she felt, without reservation or inhibition. She did not feel bad for calling him "stupe," for kicking his dice or his thermometer. Eloise was not the kind of woman who looked backward. She did not give any thought to the small insults and injustices she had dealt her husband. Gregory had been a great man, great in his compassion and forgiveness, unsurpassed in his rationality. He had known she respected him as much as she loved him. She had no regrets about how she had treated him. She only wanted him back. She would readily have admitted that if she had talked to anyone.

Eloise walked along the corridors of the keep and crossed over to the stairwell that led up to the observatory. She felt a great, bottomless hole in her being where his love for her had been. Where she kept her image of him. As deep as her grief remained, Eloise was not the kind of woman who moped about feeling sorry for herself.

Knights, I miss him!

Gregory should not have died for her. Too many others already had. His death was another debt she could never repay. That he had died to save her made her really, really angry at him, at all the others. At herself.

She wanted them *all* back, but Gregory most. She wanted to pay off the debt and die for him, for them.

She trudged up the stairs on her way to hang herself.

✝

The observatory was usually empty now that Armadale's diplomatic mission was gone. The mission itself had been virtually wiped out. Of those the ambassador had brought into the keep with him, only the boy, Reingard Vernon, together with Astrid Kettel and her squires, had survived. Astrid and her squires were now citizens of Vercors. The soldiers camped outside Ardvaser's walls had surrendered and were being held prisoner, except for the three highest ranking ones. They had been sent back to Armadale with young Reingard, under heavy escort. Reingard alone seemed happy. Virtually everyone from his country who had attended the wake and planned the treachery were dead.

Robert and Bat Merrett had left the castle together, bound once more for Arsenault and the Bridge Robert felt sure was there. Hemdale had wanted to go with them, but he and Sophia Haverland had been asked to reinforce the Aignen

Legion against Skoll and Hati as it entered the Ardgour Wilderness. Gerveault would be there too, but more vigorous forces than an old and fading dynamicist were needed to face the potentially army-breaking power of the demons. And so, for the moment, the great open-roofed hall of the observatory was empty except for two guards. They alone protected the twelve-foot blade of the Methueyn Treaty.

Obtaining a ladder from the observatory storeroom and dismissing the guards was not a problem for Eloise. Towering over them, she told the men to go, and they did, with alacrity. Climbing the ladder and sticking her head through the noose of heavy, new rope was also easy. Eloise Kyre was a brave and determined young woman. She dropped a note onto the floor beneath her giving Koria guardianship of her and Gregory's children. Her mind had turned gray and cold, and she knew she was no longer good for her children, was no good for her unborn baby. The world was no longer good for her daughters, not the way it was now, with Nimrheal back again. Eloise knew that things had reached a breaking point, a moment of profound, noxious transformation. Eloise Kyre leapt off the ladder and began to choke.

†

"Do you see this, Eloise?" She looked up at the colossal form of her great uncle. His armor was gone. For the longest time, pieces of the plate and chain had hung from his long limbs, broken, dented, cracked, like ripped clothes but made of metal, ruined in the brittle ways that only hard things can be. Now, finally, the last pieces had fallen away. Blood streamed down his face, his arms, off the ends of his fingers, but he held the sword up to show her the hilt. "Do you *see* it?"

†

Eloise was only three years old, but she had heard her parents whispering for months about the need to flee Armadale. The king wanted to steal Eloise, or perhaps her mother, Aloysia, or perhaps he wanted to imprison all three of them. Eloise did not discriminate between the possible threats. As soon as she understood the whisperings, she insisted they fight. Her father, Veritas, kissed her forehead and said everything would be okay. With a strained smile, he asked her to stop sharpening her dollies into knives and spears. But the very next night she heard them whispering again. It went on for weeks.

"Hemdale will come," Aloysia would say late at night when they thought Eloise was asleep. They did not realize that she was not the kind of little girl who would sleep through danger or not recognize when her parents were trying to hide their fear. She did not understand why they would deny their fear or delay their actions. She had no comprehension or sympathy for the rationalizations her parents made, for their unreasoning hope that flight would be unnecessary.

"Let's fight *now!*" Eloise demanded at breakfast six weeks into the whisperings, brandishing a fork whose tines she had bent for maximum raking damage. "Or run. One of the two. Why wait?"

"Wow," Veritas said, examining her martial take on cutlery. He looked over Eloise's head at his wife. "I can't believe you did that, El. You really are special."

Eloise sputtered, "Of course I am. Now let's go cut up those fuckers." She did not know who the fuckers were, but that is what her mom had called them in the whispering of the previous night.

"Go to your room, El!" Aloysia said, pointing to it. "We don't use those words here."

"*You* do," Eloise grumbled as, with ostentatiously slow movements, she grudgingly left the table.

When, a few days later, her Uncle Hemdale crashed through the door in the middle of the night, Eloise was ready. She bounded out of her little bed with her repurposed fork in one hand and her fight bag in the other. Her father had told her he never went into battle without a packed bag, and her mother had always emphasized the wisdom of careful preparation. So Eloise was prepared. She had known for weeks that it was past time to get on with it, whatever it was going to be. Now she was amazed and disappointed that her mom and dad were not ready. They rushed about their little house, gathering necessaries, while Eloise stared at her big, scary uncle.

He was dressed in black armor and had no bag, bottle, or dolls on him anywhere, but he had the biggest sword that Eloise had ever seen. Her daddy was as tall as Uncle Hemdale, maybe taller, her mommy not much shorter, but none of them had a sword half so big. He held it in front of him, and it shone strangely too, like dense, silvery water or shiny, liquid glass. It hummed as it cut the air whenever Uncle Hemdale moved it. "You like this, Eloise?" he asked. "It was ma—"

He was cut off by a loud, violent knocking on the door.

"Hide her eyes," Hemdale said. "It's best she does not see this."

Eloise's parents ran up to block Eloise's view, but the little girl peered around them to see. Hemdale had raised his sword in one hand as if to strike. As she watched through her daddy's legs, he opened the door with the other. Eloise wondered how her uncle could pull off a swipe with a sword so long inside their tiny house, but she was looking forward to seeing this. On the other side of the door was a woman in armor like her uncle's. She was not tall at all, but she looked confident. Uncle Hemdale lowered his gargantuan weapon. "Chamyle, you came," he said, his rough voice sounding almost happy for once.

Chamyle took off her helm. Long, braided blond hair spilled out like golden ropes. "Hello, little one," she said, peering at Eloise.

"I'm almost as big as you!" Eloise piped back.

The knight smiled. "I'm Sir Valcryst. Maybe I'll see you again." Looking back at Hemdale, she said, "I'll head out to the correction line and see if I can put a stop to this, but they may also be coming by the south road. Jormundheim is joining us too, but he may be held up."

The night was a long nightmare of running that Eloise, dying on the rope, could not remember all of. She was only three when it had all happened, and what remained was a curious, traumatic mix of vivid, vague, and simply missing. She could only piece together that her father had died first, holding off a group of men in a moonlit field. She never saw him go down, but she knew that he had stayed behind to buy time and had never managed to rejoin them. Later, her mother disappeared doing the same. Balls of fire and sheets of lightning coursed across the sky throughout the journey. Columns of soldiers exploded, smoke blotted out the moon, and at some point Aloysia was suddenly covered in frost and shivering like a leaf. Then she was gone too.

"It's best you don't see," Hemdale whispered, covering her eyes as he ran through fields. Three times, he threw her under a hedge while he fought groups of men in the chaotic dark. "It's best you don't see," he said again and again as he ran through fields or carried the little girl across streams. "Don't see what you love dead," he huffed, perhaps speaking to himself as well. Eloise never saw and barely remembered, but as she hung by her neck, she grew confident at last that Hemdale *had* seen and *did* remember their faces and their sacrifices.

Finally, Hemdale's armor lost the long war of attrition. Utterly destroyed, it hung off him with no greater tensile strength than the blood that streamed off the dozens of wounds he had taken that night. Even her Uncle Hemdale could eventually be spent. As terrific as the sword he carried was at slicing through hardened plate armor and sending limbs flying, even it needed to be swung extraordinarily hard to do so. When the double troop of horsemen rode out to cut them off, Hemdale took a knee and faced his niece. He lifted the hilt of the great sword to show it to Eloise and changed his words from "It's best you don't see" to "Do you see this, Eloise?"

"Do you see it?" he repeated. "This sword was made by Meycal Endicott. It is the hardest steel in the world, the strongest ever forged, made into the biggest sword of its kind ever contemplated. Making it was a huge risk for Meycal and his dad. Nothing even close to it had been done before. But you know what made them take the decision to try?"

Eloise shook her head and Hemdale smiled, though his was not a pretty smile as when other people smiled. "Meycal has a little boy named Robert. He's just your age."

"So?" Eloise asked, lower lip trembling.

"So?" Hemdale mirrored Eloise's question. "Meycal's wife had just died, so Robert only had a father. And Meycal, that little boy's father, is dead now too. He died making this for me. For you."

"But why?"

Hemdale looked back at the troop of knights as they marched closer. There were at least forty of them. "Meycal and his father think you're important. They thought you were worth the risk of making this steel."

Eloise's eyes blurred. *I want my mommy.* "Am I worth it?" Even at three, she only spoke the relevant words.

"It's called Sacrifice, Eloise," Hemdale said, standing up. He looked back at her. "That's the name of the sword, and it's also the thing about sacrifice. It's worth it, but real sacrifice always hurts. Not everyone or everything can be saved. If they could be, there would not be sacrifice. Now stay here."

Eloise did not stay there. She was not the kind of little girl who missed a fight. And with her parents both gone, some part of her felt tremendous guilt that they were gone, guilt that they had died for her, had disappeared without being able to say goodbye. Now this new guilt, that a boy had lost his father because of her, was piled on top of all that. Hemdale was all she had left, all she knew. She would not bear that guilt as well. Eloise would not allow him to go down without her.

It's time to cut the fuckers up.

Three knights and one rich man broke off from the group. The rich man wore purple robes and a crown, but no armor.

"Give it up, Sir Hemdale," said the portly, absurd-looking, robed fellow. "Despite what you've done, we'll let you walk if you leave us the girl. Go no—AAAUGGH!"

Eloise had thrown her bent and mangled fork and hit him in the cheek just below his left eye.

The three knights rode their horses straight at Hemdale then, and a flash of light shot through Eloise as her nose broke and she was knocked off her feet by one of the gigantic beasts. She did not see what happened next, but there was a great sound of horses charging, a cloud of blinding dust, and a deafening racket of metal on metal.

"Up you come, little one." Sir Chamyle was helping Eloise gently to her feet. Hemdale and another big man in black armor were standing over the ruined corpses of the three knights who had escorted the silly man with the crown. The forty or so other knights sat on their horses, neither advancing nor retreating.

Hemdale stepped forward and decapitated the purple-robed fucker. His crown rolled in the dirt.

✝

ELOISE REMEMBERED IT ALL, UNDERSTOOD IT MORE CLEARLY NOW THAN SHE EVER HAD. But she still choked on the rope. They should have left sooner. They all could have lived! Robert's father could have survived, and no remnants of her horrifying memories would have existed to torture her as she died. Something was pushing up on her legs, but she was still asphyxiating. Her time had come. Then she remembered something Robert had whispered into her ears while they mourned together for Gregory. It was a small thing, barely heard, but a small thing that still, surprisingly, mattered.

✝

"I know why you think you owe me, Eloise." Robert said, eyes gentle, voice soft. Eloise did not reply. She barely registered that he had spoken. "But my father made Sir Hemdale's sword so that he could rescue your family. Yes, I figured it out a few years ago." He smiled at her. "It was not an accident. He was not careless, as I was told during the twenty-four-hour test. It was a calculated risk he willingly took and that … didn't work out. For him."

Eloise still did not respond, but this did not deter Robert from continuing. "I never knew my father, but I respect his decision." Robert started chuckling softly. "And besides, I only know *you*, Eloise. I respect him theoretically—at a remove—but I *love* you completely, fully, deeply." He smiled again. "You owe me nothing."

After a moment, he added, "Your parents loved you too."

"Now Rise."

†

Had Robert actually said all that? Certainly he had once more declared his love for her, but had he told her that her parents loved her? Had he told her to Rise? Eloise was no longer sure what Robert had said, but she knew the words were true. They resonated within her now, releasing in one stroke all her horror, guilt, and frustration. She felt unburdened for the first time since that night when she had been a little girl.

Then she stopped choking and started to float to the ground.

"Eloise."

She opened her eyes. Koria was underneath her, pushing on her legs, but Eloise had suddenly become very heavy and, despite her friend's best efforts, had continued to sink. Koria was almost on her knees. Eloise looked over her shoulder and saw the great blade of the Methueyn Treaty. It was floating in the air.

Eloise Kyre was not the kind of woman to allow sacrifices to be made in vain.

Chapter Thirty-Six

Retrograde Journey

"*Robert.*"

Time travel is impossible. The past may be viewed, but not acted on, perceived but not affected. Mistakes once made cannot be unmade, harsh words cannot be unsaid nor cruel actions rescinded. Things that have been destroyed cannot be restored. Lives already lost cannot be saved. The retrograde wave of heraldry sees the past but goes in one direction only, and slowly, like a turtle. The wave moves forward, but it always shows the past.

If the past cannot be changed, what can? We can also view the future, although only as probabilities of what may be. The past's solidity—its certainty—allows it to be known but never changed. The future can only be guessed. It may be vexing, sometimes alarming, occasionally horrific, uncertain always. The trade-off against the future's uncertainty is hope. We can always hope to change an uncertain future. Its very uncertainty is the doorway through which hope may enter. Any potential alteration of the future can only happen in one continuum: the present. Hope for a better future always depends on the present, on what we are doing right now. In every passing moment.

It probably bodes poorly that this present seems like a step in reverse.

Endicott could not shake the feeling that he had done all this before, that it was familiar, that he was, in fact, living in the past. He was on another long journey with Bat Merrett, going out where they had been before, on a more direct but still similar path, and with a similar feeling of exigency. He felt this paramnesia as they galloped to the Castlereagh Line with Gael Guise, as they washed in rain barrels there, and as they resupplied. He felt it as they switched horses and galloped north toward the wheat line, and as he thought of Eoyan March, injured and left behind … again. Gael Guise's presence only intensified the sensation. She reminded Endicott of the long journey he had taken with her and Gregory four years before when Eoyan had first been hurt. Gregory was dead now, but that only made this seeming journey into the past feel worse and more threadbare than it had originally been.

Taking horses into the wilderness was new, at least for Endicott. It was normally avoided due to the risk of attracting skolves. They were chancing it on this trip because, even as they charged across the wild, Sir Hemdale, Gerveault, and Sir Sophia Haverland were a day ahead of them, leading army elements to the northeast. At each of the towers along the Line, urine was being dumped and other provocations made. Dynamicists of lesser powers and experience were also heralding all along the Line. Everything that could be done to draw the skolves away, to confuse and scatter them, was being done. The precautions were also meant for Skoll and Hati. The dice were being loaded to give Robert Endicott and Bat Merrett the best possible odds of reaching Arsenault and retrieving the Methueyn Bridge.

Kennyth Brice had again called Endicott his brother for saving his life and, in recognition of this, had granted the young man the honor of being the one to retrieve the Bifrost. He had also, privately, given Endicott the right to decide what to do with the Bifrost if a quick decision had to be made. Whatever happened, Armadale could not be allowed to obtain the Bridge. Their true mission at Arsenault had been to discover its location. Brice had whispered something else into Endicott's ear, and Gerveault had later done the same: "It must be you and not Sir Hemdale, love him as we do."

Despite these new wrinkles, the journey still felt overwhelmingly familiar. If he had survived Nimrheal, Jeyn Lindseth would have spoken at great length about how their retrograde journey was a metaphor. For something. He would have waxed philosophical about their return to Arsenault, about this journey into the ruins of a destroyed civilization.

"Perhaps he would have said that a future of wheat is consuming the past," Endicott said out loud.

Merrett scowled at him. "What now?"

"I was thinking how much I miss Jeyn and Gregory. Marielle too," Endicott replied.

"I note," interjected Gael Guise, "that you have not said you would miss Bat being here."

Endicott smiled, "Well, Bat *is* here, and being his usual charming self." They rode on a while longer, Endicott noting that it was now the old wheat that brushed against his legs and his horse's belly. "I wonder," he mused, "if we were to somehow resurrect the County of Ardgour, or better yet the storied Old Engevelen that preceded it, if we brought them back, would we think they were so great?"

The big man shook his head. "What are you on about, Blouse?"

"You both heard the last reports over the javelin as well as I did," Endicott replied, shaking his head. "Mobs are rioting in Vercors City. They say they want the old ways back. They want Engevelen *now*. They want its greatness and certainties restored and the dangerous, uncertain, decadent present tossed aside." Endicott pointed at a crumbling pile of boulders not far from their path through the grass and scrub. "I just wonder if they would be so happy if they got their wish. The glowing golden age of the past might seem rather dark and leaden if it suddenly materialized in the present."

Gael played with a stalk of grass in her mouth. "Agreed. Nimrheal was around back then, only I bet you couldn't fight him as good as you can now because of what you know about mathematics. Look at what you were telling me that Koria and Bethyn just figured out. No one had that math back then."

Merrett spat out, "Math!" and then spat literally into a bush. "They had Methueyn Knights back then. That's what people want, not numbers and formulas."

Gael stood in her stirrups and spat her stalk of grass at Merrett. "And what did the Methueyn Knights do for anyone? Nothing. They couldn't beat Nimrheal."

"Neither have we," Merrett retorted.

As in so many arguments, Endicott reflected, there was more than one good point to be made.

But I don't want to score points. I want Nimrheal gone. And Koria to live.

They rode for days. Endicott's back, somehow not ruined by an arrow that had struck it dead center from a distance of barely more than an arm's length, had healed almost completely by the time Gael finally called a halt to riding.

"The horses are done, gentlemen," she said. She pointed past them at the foothills and the mountains beyond. "You're almost there anyway. We can camp now and chat all night like I know Bat here likes to do, or we can part company now, and you can keep going on foot for a few more hours."

"We're going on," said Endicott.

Gael nodded. "I thought so." After the two men had collected all their supplies and packed them tightly and quietly in backpacks, their old scout collected the horses' reins in one lead and announced. "It's been a harvest, gentlemen."

As she walked away, horses in tow, she called cheerfully over her shoulder. "I bet I'm home before you get to the river."

▽

"Those were the worst knights-damned orders I've ever been given," groused Bat. The comment surprised Endicott. It was a complaint, but it was also an implied question. The big man rarely asked questions, but there he was, staring at Endicott, clearly expecting an answer. They had finally made camp when the moon set. Endicott could have used heraldry to keep going but decided it would be too risky. The time was not right to spend their strength recklessly. That would come. In the meantime, they had a chance to recover from the long ride and the shorter but more arduous hike. A good time for questions from the usually incurious. And for the usually curious to ask a question back.

"What was so bad about the orders? That they sent you back out with me?"

"No. Well, that is always a mystery, them putting you in charge." Merrett shook his head. "I mean the orders that weren't really orders. Telling us to go out and evaluate what we see, use the javelin if we can, do whatever we think we should. If we have to. What the hell is all that?"

"Oh," Endicott said, understanding now. "They are afraid of summoning Nimrheal."

"Huh."

"Yes." Endicott looked off into the darkening sky. "No one knows when some smart comment or question is going to lead to another smart question, a bright new idea, and then storm, lightning, Nimrheal, mass death. So it's vague orders and hope against hope. Until Nimrheal is no longer a threat."

"That's stupid."

"You only say that because you're in no real danger of an original thought, big man."

"Yah." A little later, Merrett spoke again. "Is this what used to happen in the old days before the Methueyn War? Everyone afraid to speak and think?"

Endicott was surprised again. "Probably." Then he checked himself and amended his answer. "Honestly, Bat, I don't know. I'm not sure anyone does. I suspect that only the really brave or the truly reckless took the risk of trying new ideas. Everyone else was probably beat down." *No wonder people are* still *protesting new things.* Of everyone who had seen Nimrheal this time, only Koria and Bethyn had dared to continue working on something new. Their plan of using a discontinuous transform against the demon was brilliant. It was an idea that Endicott did not intend to waste.

He stared at the big lumpy shadow that was his old comrade. Yes, apart from Koria and Bethyn, almost everyone else seemed traumatized. Even broken.

But not you either, Bat.

Almost everyone else was shutting up and hoping for the best except for Bethyn, Koria, and a strangely, newly curious Bat Merrett. "I think you must really miss Jeyn asking all the questions, Bat. It's almost like you've become him now that he's gone. Could it be that you were never really annoyed with him?"

"That'll be one of those mysteries you never solve, Blouse."

Endicott thought he knew the answer already. Not even in this strangely curious frame of mind would Merrett talk about his real feelings. Whatever the stolid soldier's true feelings were, Endicott was convinced the big man was, unconsciously or not, filling the gap left by their dead friend.

An old thought occurred to him. "You know, I've been thinking ever since we left Ardvaser that we have done all this before. It feels to me as if we are traveling back in time somehow and just repeating what we've already done."

Merrett only grunted.

"The biggest problem with everything in our first year at the New School was our ignorance. We d—"

"That's still *your* biggest problem," said Merrett.

Endicott smiled, unsurprised at the shot. "That is just where I was going. We did not know who the cloaked man—men—were, and we failed to act decisively against Armadale because we did not know we needed to. We acted on guesses. Now here we are charging off again to face an incomprehensible threat with only a location and an untested transform on our side."

"Yup."

What else was there to say? What else was there to do but what they were doing? Endicott looked at Likelihood in its scabbard beside him and knew sharp steel was not going to be enough. *We need to change the pattern.* He sat there wondering how to make a difference, how to make any change at all. He was committed to trying, but he did not know how.

For the third time, Merrett surprised Endicott with a question. "Are you tempted, Blouse?"

"Tempted by what? This isn't going to be an Uncle Eoyan moment, is it?"

"I'd hurt you, Blouse, so don't get your hopes up," Merrett growled. In a different tone, he added, "I wondered if you were tempted to cross the Methueyn Bridge yourself and become Heydron."

"I'm not even a Deladieyr, Bat."

Merrett snorted. "You carried Marielle for five days."

"So did you."

"I'm twice your size." He spat, the loogie flying off into the dark. "And you healed faster than me. I was still barely able to walk before we got going on this latest mad journey. Then you took an arrow to the back and fought off two of those Nines."

"I don't care about knights," Endicott said, glad that Merrett could not see his face.

"Right," said Merrett. Endicott hoped that would be the end of it, but Bat would not let it go. "And you've been jumping around most days, asking me 'what?' as if I'd been calling your name. I think you've been hearing a voice, Blouse. Maybe that's how we win. We follow that voice, find the Bridge, and you cross it."

"Look," Endicott said. "I'll tell you what I care about. I care about people not being murdered just because they write a new poem. I care that some curious physicist trying to understand how the world works doesn't have their own world end. Or how about Bethyn? She'd be dead now if Nimrheal had its way. Anyone anywhere whose mind is free is at risk, but every person at the New School must feel that threat doubly. Lil's dead. And for what? For trying to help people, to end, once and for all, the goose fever. How many women, men, and children did she save from having their brains cooked? I want to protect people like Lil. Most of all, I don't want my wife murdered by Nimrheal. And I sure don't want her to be any less than she can be to appease a monster that doesn't belong in this world. Or a rampaging mob of her fellow citizens. That is my whole mind, Bat. Stop Nimrheal. Protect the freedom to think and invent. Protect my wife. Protect her genius, her beauty, her grace, that ineffable gift she has for figuring things out."

"Robert."

"What?"

"I didn't say anything, Blouse," came Bat's voice. "That wasn't me."

The big man stopped and rustled about in the dark, finding a more comfortable position on his back, Endicott guessed. "But I was just thinking that, if you're right that the past is repeating itself, maybe it *is* more likely that your genius wife is going to save the day rather than either you or me."

Do It Yourself

"WHERE IS THE DUKE?" THE SIGN READ. IT WAS CARRIED BY A MERCHANT IN SHINING shoes and immaculate dress. Beside him stood an old lady in what could best be described as a grain sack and twine. She had her own sign. In a suspiciously similar hand, it said:

"YOU BROUGHT
NIMRHEAL.
NOW BRING
THE KNIGHTS."

"I'm not sure we should walk into that," Lynwen said, peering around the corner, pressed up against Heylor, who was crouching in front of her, peering around it too. The sensation felt delightfully familiar to the young man. If that proximity was all there was to it, he would happily have repeated the slyly intimate contact all day, every day, but unfortunately, there was the matter of the two mobs whose collision they were about to witness.

The larger of the two groups seemed to feel that the current power structure was failing to protect the people of the Duchy of Vercors. They wondered where their shiny, plate-armored protectors were. They asked, "Where are the Methueyn Knights?"

Heylor could have helped them. He had kept in touch with events at Ardvaser through daily javelin reports in the basement of the mathematics and physics building. He knew that Marielle Engel, Jeyn Lindseth, and Sir Gregory Justice were all dead, that Sir Eloise Kyre was in mourning, that Sir Robert Endicott had left for the Ardgour Wilderness again, that Sir Hemdale and Sir Haverland had led the Aignen Legion north. There were no available knights of any order left in the duchy. *But I'm not going down there and telling them that.*

The smaller mob just wanted to burn down the New School. They did not bother explaining why. Perhaps they thought the reason was self-evident. Their only sign was more a statement of faith than an argument. It read simply:

"Burn them all.

Let Nimrheal

Sort them out."

Heylor had studied wave phenomena enough to see that the two positions were not mutually exclusive. That the mobs might combine in some awful and destructive superposition to bring a wave of fire over the New School was a distinct possibility. The constables and reserve soldiers lined up to contain the protestors seemed puny in numbers compared to the mighty surge they would face if the two groups merged.

"Maybe I should get going for Ardvaser as the duke ordered," said Heylor, leaning back and putting a reassuringly thick brick wall between him and the Ring Road where the mobs were converging.

Lynwen was breathing hard, scared or excited, probably both. Her big gray eyes seemed to shine. "It can't be worse up there than here. All you'll face are Skoll, Hati, and thousands of skolves. Down here we've got angry, irrational people."

"That's worse."

"Yes," she agreed, "but least you can reason with people … sometimes." Lynwen tilted her head to better hear some roared-out slogan coming from across the street. "I still can't quite believe that you have managed to avoid doing what Kennyth Brice commanded. It sounds like he really wants you at Ardvaser."

Heylor held up both bandaged hands. "He said I could wait until they're *halfway* healed."

"Which they are," she said. "And have been for a while."

"Which only you and I know," Heylor pointed out.

"You have to go."

Heylor could have stood and stared at Lynwen and her serious, sad, loving expression all day, every day. He could have followed her orbit anywhere. He would gladly orbit *her*, but everyone wanted him somewhere else. It was the story of Heylor Style's life that he was always restless, never happy except when he was moving, never in the moment, always a moment ahead, and yet now he wanted all of time to stand still and leave him with her, endlessly investigating together, endlessly recovering from some injury, endlessly falling in love. He almost said, "Come with me," but he had said it too many times before. He wanted to stay, but he had to go. At last he admitted that their time was up. "Let's do this one final thing first."

Ⴒ

"We cannot go in there, Heylor." Vice-Constable Edwyn Perry had not changed. If anything, he looked more like himself, as if the years had boiled him down to his essence. Live long enough and everyone becomes who they truly are. His long neck had grown longer. He looked like a caricature now, all neck and hanging head and been-a-constable-too-long-platitudes.

"The duke will kill me if anything happens to you," Perry continued, pointing down from the roof at the mob gathering at the border of the New School campus. Beside Perry stood the harder-than-rocks Constable Kayne and smarter-than-everyone Professor Meredeth Callum. Meredeth held the Eindarch Eye in one hand and a letter in the other.

"We have to," said Heylor under his breath, though recognizing that the vice-constable was making sense. He usually did. Still, Heylor Style was not one to be thwarted. He dreamt every night about the hangings. They were the stuff of his new favorite nightmare, this one apparently locus-induced and surpassing even his nightmares about meeting Skoll again or seeing the New School burn. His sleeping mind was now filled with hangings and riots. Sometimes he saw Lynwen hanging there, sometimes his father. His sister once. *We won't need cloaked men if we all start killing ourselves.* The hangings did not make sense to Heylor, not really. They were more, much more than just products of the actual hangings he and Lynwen had investigated. He had a theory about what they meant, but theory did not equal truth. He put his hands on his hips and scanned the streets below.

Meredeth Callum and Lynwen joined him. Ring Road was blocked just north of their position, the two mobs having coalesced into one, their anger too similar, in effect if not in cause, to fail to merge into a superposition of frustration and potential violence. A stream of students from the Military School had added themselves to the thin line of constables and reservists that formed a still dangerously thin shield along the arc of the road to protect the campus from impending assault. The normal hum of business, the movement of shoppers, merchants, farmers, tradespeople, and ice wagons, was silent. The mob had created a vacuum, a shadow zone in which no one who was not either part of the mob or the opposing civil authority would willingly enter.

With one exception. Three blocks to the south, a solitary garbage wagon collected refuse, slowly working its way toward the mob, either oblivious to the brewing crisis or indifferent.

I hope they have the sense to stop before they get too close.

"Show me which building it is, Constable," Meredeth asked Lynwen.

Lynwen pointed to a shop on the near side of the road, right at the edge of the mob. "The latest hanging man is supposedly there, professor."

"No back door?"

"Barred according to Kayne. Not even a lock to pick. The front and side doors have locks, but there's the mob to deal with there."

That was unwelcome news. Sergeant Kayne was not a man to accept the dictates of a weak door. If he could not jimmy it, no one could, not without a battering ram.

Meredeth turned to Heylor. Her expression was a new one for the young man. She looked apologetic. "I'm sorry, Heylor. I cannot in good conscience allow the Eindarch Eye to go there."

"I know," Heylor said, thinking.

What would Robert do?

"Perhaps we should discuss this message from Koria Valcourt," Meredeth was saying. It had come in, marked highest priority, over the room-sized javelin they kept under guard in the basement of the mathematics and physics building. In the message, Koria personally asked Heylor to return to Ardvaser immediately. The professor tried to hand the message to Heylor, but his mind was elsewhere. In frustration, she spoke again. "I don't know why she says that the duke's feasting table has been cleared, but the rest of the letter sounds *very* urgent. More urgent than anything I've ever seen from her. Maybe you should look at it again, Heylor."

Where was the soup he could use to hide his antics this time? Heylor never forgot the day Robert had devised the plan to throw Lord Jon Indulf's brooch into some soup to save Heylor from a beating. Things had not worked out quite as planned that time, but Heylor had always loved the misdirection Robert had used. He was dimly aware that Meredeth Callum was still trying to hand him the message. He took it and absently stuffed it into his pocket.

"We are going into the soup," he said at last, "and no one is even going to notice."

Meredeth frowned. "I don't follow."

"See that garbage wagon?" Heylor pointed to the crew still working its way north.

"The one with the suicidal crew that doesn't know when to stop?" Vice-Constable Edwyn Perry was shaking his head. "They are either stubborn or plain stupid."

Heylor smiled. "Both, actually. That's my friend Sackelly-belly-full-of-jelly down there."

Perry scratched his long neck. "No one looks particularly fat down there. Why—"

"It's a nickname from childhood," explained Lynwen.

Heylor's smile grew larger. "We are going to catch them before they get too close and switch clothes with my old friend's crew. Then we will get into the merchant's shop under cover of the garbage wagon."

"What is it with you New School kids and going undercover?" Perry asked rhetorically.

No one pays attention to the fat man going up to the buffet. Or the garbage man collecting the trash.

T

"WHY DO THEY HAVE TO SHIT ALL OVER MY ROAD?" SACKELLY ASKED WITH ALL THE SINcerity of the person who had to clean it up. "Protest away, I say. You New School types need people to keep an eye on you. But why do they always take a dump right there?"

Sackelly may have viewed Heylor with a certain suspicion when he and Lynwen intercepted him and his crew, but that had not stopped him from giving the order for the wagon to pull off the Ring Road and out of sight where Kayne, Meredeth Callum, and the vice-constable waited. He had looked more than just suspicious when he saw them, but Heylor managed to calm him down long enough for the plan to be explained. At that point, Sackelly's misgivings were replaced by the satisfying prospect of taking revenge on the protestors who had befouled his professional territory. His enthusiasm reminded Heylor of the days of their childhood friendship before he had stolen Sackelly's hat on a whim.

Sometimes going back in time was not so bad.

In moments, Heylor, Lynwen, and Perry emerged dressed as Sackelly and his crew. Their hats were pulled low and Lynwen's cuffs were rolled up, but to a casual onlooker the garbage wagon and its crew had returned from a break. As they worked their way up the street, Heylor found plenty to do. Some of the signs had fallen apart, and no mob ever cleaned up after itself. One broken sign read, ironically enough:

> "If it ain't broke,
> Don't fix it.
> If it ain't known,
> Leave it alone."

Well, I intend to find out. It was past time for the rash of hangings around the city to be dealt with. It was that mystery, together with his injured hands and disinclination to leave Lynwen, that had kept Heylor in Vercors against repeated requests that he return to Ardvaser.

Heylor kept the Eindarch Eye well hidden in Sackelly's loose-fitting jacket. He had managed to obtain Meredeth's grudging permission to take it this close to the mob as much through sheer enthusiasm as on the merits of his audacious plan. The mob paid them little attention as they rolled the wagon closer and closer, picking up rags, busted signs, and a continually surprising amount of feces. The old donkey pulled the wagon without much regard for the litter or the breakdown of society manifesting around it. With every step, Heylor wondered if someone in the roiling cloud of angry humanity would notice the sword belted at his waist or Lynwen's baton secreted in her over-large jacket, but the mob remained as incurious about the garbage crew as they wanted people to be about everything else.

At least they're not total *hypocrites.*

But *partial* hypocrites they certainly were. Heylor saw stitching-machined clothing everywhere. He also noted that no one in the mob was starving. Some were downright plump. *How quickly they forget that the new grain has brought food stocks into steady surplus for the first time.* The new grain was unequivocally responsible for these people's good health. Until a time well within living memory, the history of Vercors—and that of most of the known world—had been one of recurrent famine. But when the invention of better equipment and bigger kernels of grain made it easier to farm, food production had finally shot ahead of need permanently. *Why is no one saying thank you for that?*

At last they pulled up to the large wholesaler's shop Heylor had pointed out to Meredeth from the rooftop. They pulled the wagon as far away from the New School side of the road as they could and as discreetly as possible, as if hunting for garbage in alleys around the shop. Behind the wagon, the three imposters crowded the locked side door.

"I can cut it with Style," Heylor hissed as Edwyn Perry barged into his line of sight and began trying to pick the lock.

Perry looked back it him flatly. "Per regulations," he declared, "let's keep the damage to private property to a minimum, shall we?"

"You do realize they are destroying all the public benches on that side of the road, don't you?" From the wagon Heylor had seen a group of protestors hurling the broken pieces of a bench at the line of constables. Backing, boards, and nails had flown everywhere, demonstrating that benches made haphazard missiles at best.

"I got it," announced Perry in a triumphant whisper as if he, not Ailis Ellis and Lil Hilliard, had just cured goose fever. But the door opened, which is all they needed at that moment, and without any noise to draw attention from the mob, so it really was a good thing Perry knew how to pick a lock. The mob was not to be trusted, and none of them wanted to be exposed to its volatile temperament a moment longer.

They slipped into the shop and made their way quickly to the storeroom. The shop owner had given them a good description of how to reach the root cellar, where he had been horrified to find a body hanging earlier that morning. He had reported the situation immediately but refused to go back to his shop, and by the time Lynwen and Heylor were called in, he had fled town altogether, taking his keys with him. As far as Heylor was concerned, this was a typical example of the constabulary's inefficiency, but he had kept his thoughts to himself. Luckily, into the imperfect situation had come an unexpected level of cooperation from Edwyn Perry and from Meredeth, who had become guardian of the Eindarch Eye after Nimrheal's destruction of the research facility. As Heylor guessed, they were eager to help him solve the mystery if only so that he would finally obey the duke and head back to Ardvaser.

The cellar was a good eight feet under the earth. Edwyn led Lynwen and Heylor down the narrow, rickety stairs and opened a thick, insulated door. The long-necked man passed into the room and halted mid-step almost as soon as he was inside. "How could that damned merchant fail to mention this?" he exclaimed.

Lynwen stiffened and stopped just behind Perry, half blocking the doorway. She turned to Heylor and grabbed at his arm. "Deep breath," she said in an odd tone. "Just take a deep breath," she added in a weirder, more warbly voice.

"Does it stink already?" Heylor said crudely, starting to push past despite her clutching fingers. "Don't worry, I'm a veteran now. This is my third hanger, you know."

"Wait, kid!" Perry hissed, looking back.

Heylor ignored both of them and crossed the threshold. "Oh, look, vomit. Big deal," he said, then froze as he looked up from the vomit toward the ceiling. Hanging by her neck, twisting slowly on the end of a heavy rope, was a little girl. She could not have been older than five years old. Maybe less. Maybe four—

Tessa!

She was so small that whoever hanged her had only needed to weigh her down with a stout chair.

The Eindarch Eye almost fell and smashed when Heylor hauled it out of his jacket. His hands were shaking so badly that the precious device slipped, bounced from one hand to the other, and was only saved by his talent for transporting objects without any need for hands. As the Eye plunged toward the stone floor, it disappeared. After a deep, slow breath, Heylor pulled the Eye out of his jacket again. The vice-constable gave Heylor a steely glare.

Not far from the pathetic hanging form of the little girl, a broken sign lay face down on the floor. Perry took a knee and turned it over. It read:

"You get

What you

Deserve."

That was too much. Heylor almost dropped the Eindarch Eye for a second time. If he had been Hemdale, he would probably have crushed the device in an explosion of rage. If he had been Robert Endicott, he might have broken through to heaven and burned the travesty away. If he were Koria Valcourt, he would have prevented the tragedy from ever happening through some subtle machination.

If he were Eloise Kyre, he would have found and slain everyone involved. But he was only Heylor Style and he could only scream.

T

HEYLOR BECAME AWARE THAT HE WAS TALKING. IT FELT LIKE HE HAD BEEN DOING SO FOR a long time, but he could not recall the sequence of events that had brought him to this point. His throat hurt, and it seemed to him that he must have been repeating himself. "That was the little girl, Lynwen. The one I talked to. I know her. I know her." Heylor mumbled more of the same while Perry examined the room and Lynwen hugged his shaking shoulders. She knew not to say anything. There was nothing to say when children were hanged from ropes.

I know her. I know her. I know her …

Eventually, Heylor's thinking coalesced around a more productive idea. *I will know what happened here. What happened to Tessa. I will solve this.*

Heylor opened the Eye and entered the empyreal sky.

The room vibrated. He walked backward to the door, Perry, also in reverse, following him to the doorway where he paused with a look of horror sweeping retrograde across his face. Lynwen backed toward the door, clutched at Heylor's arm, let go, stiffened, and backed out the door.

Much later, a man in an apron reversed his way into the room. A yellow, chunky puddle gathered itself and flew in an arc toward his mouth. He too walked backwards and disappeared.

Heylor poured energy into the Eye, pushing its focal limit to pick up the lessening stream of the turtle wave, finding the retrograde rays that travelled more slowly than the others. Time regressed, but the girl hung there still. Time regressed further, and still she hung.

A crowd of backward walkers slowly gathered. The last to enter was Tessa's mother. The sign flew from the floor into her hands. Tessa's mother and another woman—someone familiar—clutched at each other, though the causal relationship between their movements was confusing; Heylor had little experience at retrograde heraldry outside the classroom. Tessa's legs started thrashing, and the two women seemed to grapple. Others in the crowd moved uneasily. A few individuals that Heylor had not seen before entered the room in reverse, turned, put their hands to their faces, and looked up at Tessa as she spasmed on the end of the rope.

The crowd moved in unsettling ways, but not one person tried to take the little girl's neck out of the noose. The tiny figure's spasms increased, then stopped. Tessa's arms went out to her sides as if in triumph. Moments later, a chair moved under Tessa's feet, and she stepped backwards onto it, took the noose off her neck, and stepped off the chair, which was hauled away.

The image was losing stability, but Heylor pushed harder, watching a scene unfold that he could never forget, a nightmare beyond comprehension. Tessa had hanged herself, and her mother and all those other people who had gathered there had let her do it. They had let her die.

A headache was building rapidly. Heylor began to shake, and the image degraded further. Who was that other, that familiar woman?

T

"It was the Bishop of Vercors," Heylor croaked in a hoarse whisper, still shaking. He was on both knees now. "She was the leader." The pain in his head was intense. He closed his eyes. "Tessa's mother was also there."

Lynwen was still holding Heylor's shoulders, but Edwyn Perry crouched in front of the young man. "Which one of them hung the girl?" he asked.

Heylor laughed piteously. "None of them. She hung herself," he gasped. With trembling hands, he fumbled the Eye back into his jacket. "But they let her. They helped her. Brought a chair for her to stand on. Tied the rope down. Watched her struggle, waited until she stopped. Left her there."

"No," breathed Lynwen. "No mother would do that."

Edwyn Perry stood up, looking a little wobbly himself. "Don't look for an explanation. Don't doubt the evidence." He seemed to be talking to himself. His voice was barely audible. He repeated himself twice in the same eerie whisper. "I—" he raised his voice. "I will gather whoever isn't needed to hold off this riot and interview the bishop at once." He looked directly at Heylor. "I'm sorry about this, kid. Sorry you had to see it for us." He turned toward the door, then turned back to the young man, who remained kneeling. "Maybe it's time for you to go back to the wilderness. There are fewer monsters there." The vice-constable hurried away as if some of those monsters were on his heels.

It took some time before Heylor rose to his feet again and accompanied Lynwen back into the shop and out the now unbarred back door. There they found Meredeth Callum and Kayne waiting. Perry had rushed off without saying anything to them, and Heylor, too, kept silent as Lynwen painstakingly relayed what he told her he had seen. He was busy committing it all to paper. A written statement was going to be necessary for what followed.

"Do you think she'll admit to her complicity?" asked Meredeth. The professor had not gone below to look at Tessa, who still hung there, but Kayne had.

Constable Kayne crossed his arms. "Our bishop? She might."

"It's not normal," said Lynwen.

"That's why she might," Kayne said, veins throbbing on his neck, hands, and forehead. "No person in their right mind hangs a child. I don't care that the little girl put the noose around her own neck, they still killed her. That kind of lunatic may think they did something noble or good."

"And if she doesn't confess?" Meredeth asked.

Lynwen looked at Heylor. "Then there will be an investigation. Heylor's statement will help us find other participants, but alone it won't be enough to bring the bishop to court. It could ta—"

"I'm no Lonely Wizard, you know," interrupted Heylor bitterly. Keith Euyn's words had been enough to convict Syriol's rapist back in their first year.

And I'm not waiting.

He stood up and made for the stairs. "Meet me at the Steel Castle," he said over his shoulder. He charged across the shop toward the root cellar stairs again, his heart pounding as loudly in his ears as his feet did against the wooden floor.

"Just what exactly does that mean?" Kayne shouted after him. He got no response.

The young man bounded down the straits into the cellar and strode past the medical investigators still taking measurements and making notes. Ignoring their protests, he stepped over the puddle of vomit and walked to the chair the rope was tied to, trying not to walk through the blood and fluids that had drained out of Tessa.

"Heylor!" He turned toward the voice. It was Lynwen's. She and the others had belatedly followed him down. "You catch her," she said, "I'll cut the rope."

Heylor was gratified that Lynwen had decided to help him. "Use Style." Heylor stood below Tessa, hands on her tiny legs, while Lynwen took his sword. A moment later, the little girl fell into his arms. The medical investigators, Kayne, and Meredeth Callum all stared at him. "Can someone please remove the noose?" Heylor asked.

Frowning, Kayne stepped forward and, as gently as his big, veiny hands allowed, removed the thick rope. "Now what?" he said.

"Stand back," Heylor instructed.

Lynwen tried to hand Heylor his sword. He shook his head. He did not trust himself to hold both the little girl and Style. "Keep it for now."

Then he enacted his trick …

T

… AND AT ONCE APPEARED, STILL CARRYING TESSA'S BODY, ON THE GREAT HANGING BRIDGE in the Steel Castle. A gasp went up, echoing loudly from the stone walls, the vaulted central spire, and the eight apses. As people followed others' eyes to the pitiable figures on the pulpit, more gasps arose from the worshippers. Heylor had not arrived in the midst of some liturgy during a service, but there had still been hundreds of the faithful praying or meditating in the vast room. Now they were all staring up at the bridge, slack-mouthed and silent.

"Where is the bishop?" Heylor cried, his voice reverberating like a cannon shot. Some of the parishioners fell to their knees while a few pointed mutely toward the far corner of the great hall. Heylor turned toward the closed door just visible in the shadows there, but before he could take a step, the bishop emerged from behind the door along with Vice-Constable Edwyn Perry and three other constables.

"What have you done?" the bishop gasped.

Heylor walked rapidly toward her now, shouting. "I have brought the little girl you murdered." He started down the stairs, walking faster and faster, almost running.

"I don't know who that is," said the bishop, but her rich voice trembled. Its smooth assurance when she led the liturgy was gone.

Heylor jogged down the far side of the bridge, his footsteps echoing loudly off the stone walls. "You do," he shouted, "You do know her!" He charged the last few yards separating himself from the priest and thrust his tiny burden toward her. "Her name is Tessa," he roared. "You watched her hang! And then you walked away." He thrust the tiny girl at the bishop again, making her flinch. "Are you still going to deny her?"

"No," came the whispered response.

Heylor was frowning at the priest with such intensity that his eyes had nearly closed. "Why did you let her die?"

"I didn't *know!*" the bishop wailed, falling on her knees. "I thought she would live. She said she was the new Yeyncie Greene!"

T

THE BISHOP HAD FOLDED AT THE SIGHT OF TESSA, THOUGH THE DETAILS OF THE STORY hardly mattered to Heylor. He did not care if it had been the little girl or her mother, someone else, or the bishop who had pushed the notion that Yeyncie Greene, most famous of the Methueyn Knights, might come again when all other attempts by the bishop's secret group to raise a new knight had failed. It did not matter that the death of the little girl may have destroyed the group—the cult—that they may have seen that their belief was madness when the little girl died. It did not matter that everyone was so terribly sorry. None of them had tried to take Tessa down or remove her from the noose.

It did not matter if, now they were caught, they were all spinning a new narrative about their motivations. It did not matter if they had been terrorized by their own locus-induced dreams into a desperate irrationality. It did not matter if they felt they had to do something or if they regretted it now. Whatever they felt, sorrow or not, did not matter. Whatever they said, however badly everyone thought they needed the Methueyn Knights to return, whatever yarns they spun to justify themselves, did not matter.

They had still let a misguided little girl hang herself. They had let Tessa die.

And not just her. For all their talk of faith and heaven and angels, the cult had let three people hang themselves. Heylor had realized something when he confronted the bishop and had looked from her to the bridge floating in air. Tessa was only the most egregious victim of the desperate search for a miracle that had led the cult into a profound moral failing. The hangings were not a sign of faith. They were a proof of failure. For all their stone edifices and treaties written in steel on great unwieldy swords, these people were cowards. The fear of a changing, uncertain world, and later of Nimrheal, was what drove them—not faith. They were cowards grasping at any magical solution to a world that frightened them.

Heylor Style understood this because he had also been a coward. Like the bishop, like Tessa's mother, he had been afraid and small. And now, thinking about this, he realized with a sudden, awful clarity that his greatest act of cowardice had not been running away from Skoll, as he had thought and told Lynwen. It was his silence about Keith Euyn's dying words, those strange words that he alone had heard. Breathing blood, the old man had spat out with his last, sputtering breaths, "I saw the Bridge, only it is not a bridge. It hangs in the air. It is a circle in the sky, floating on the mountain. Skolves gather on the margins, worshipping. Skoll and Hati come and Vercors City burns. The New School burns."

Heylor had kept the old wizard's dying declaration to himself partly because he hated the old man for killing Davyn and Eleanor and wanted nothing more to do with him, even the memory of him. He was small and disregarded, and he wanted this great man's last words to fall on deaf ears. But he had also kept silent because the words made no sense to him. He had kept the words to himself, he now realized, because he had been afraid to consider them properly, afraid of the perils and terrors the words might draw him into if they were revealed to others.

But now he knew that Keith had seen where the Bridge was. Robert's latest after-experiment review—sent over the javelin to select insiders, including one Heylor Style, who Kennyth wanted back at Ardvaser so urgently—confirmed that Keith had spoken the truth, however cryptically. Heylor realized that he, too, knew where it was. He had been within a day's march of the place when Skoll had killed his eight.

Heylor Style had been a coward, perhaps still was a coward, but he knew that the root problem could only be solved at the Bridge, the *real* Bridge. He did not wish to face Skoll or Nimrheal again. He did not want to face such limitless, otherworldly power, and he did not want to die. But a little girl had hanged herself because those around her had all been cowards.

This shit has got to end.

At home, dressed again as he had been when he first returned from the wild, Heylor sheathed Style and kissed Lynwen. It was time to return to Ardvaser.

Chapter Thirty-Eight

Inventive Breakthrough, Part 4

My name is Gil Harbinger. I am the current Harbinger Wizard of Engevelen. Luciena Fortis, the original author of this journal, which I will now continue and complete, was my protégé. It was my pleasant task to instruct and mentor that most promising of young wizards over these last few years. Of all the things I have done in my long life, the task of adding this final chapter to her journal is the one I am most proud of.

†

Ardvaser Castle had, in a moment, changed. Lord and Lady Auvigne were dead as were most of the mathematicians, scribes, and guards who had worked on the new mathematical transform: the *Lessingham Transform*, named after Eydith Lessingham, chief assistant to Rodryck Cornell. It is a magnificent transform. It does all kinds of wonderful things, such as ...

Well, truthfully, I don't know what in Nimrheal's hell it actually does. Is it just language? Is that all that math is? Some kind of compact script? A way for mathematicians to imagine they can actually *do* things? Is it only a delusion to believe we understand something fundamental about the world, that we exercise some kind of control? I really have no idea. I'm a wizard, you see, not a mathematician. What I know the Lessingham transform *did* was somehow to call down Nimrheal, who then put a hole the width of a wagon through the walls of the cardinal tower, and by killing those it killed, instantly plunged this country of Engevelen into turmoil.

No one was left in charge. That is the cause of the present turmoil, the cause of everything that has changed. With a vacuum at the top, half the surviving guards have abandoned their posts. The other half still patrols the walls but with an uncertain conviction. Unless and until a new prince or princess is chosen, I suppose they will be lost. But who is left to do the choosing?

I have thought about heading back to South ~~H~~arkness. I belong there, even if I am Engevelen's harbinger. I hate to admit this, even to myself, but what good is a harbinger wizard when the doom has already come? I should go home.

"Look at this, Gil."

It was Luciena, my protégé. She was pointing excitedly at the chalkboard. ~~H~~er enthusiasm almost brought a tear to my lazy, jaded eyes. Luciena had been alternately in a manic rage or a sullen depression in the days after the tragedy. The loss of her adoptive parents and her lover Sir Darday'l had destroyed her, or so it seemed. But here she was, pointing at the Lessingham transform on the chalkboard and smiling. It was like sunrise on a chilly morning to see the joy on her face. Some part of me basked in the rays of that happiness like a marmot on the rocks. That one smile changed everything. I had to pretend I had something in my eye to hide the tears that blurred my vision when I saw the girl smile again.

If you are thinking of later denouncing me for being in love with Luciena, rest easy, because I *do* love her. It was not a feeling such as I had for my wife, Emreyta, dead now these twenty-five years. Those days of passion are behind me. I loved her ... the way I loved her. Anyone who could love anything at all loved Lucy. There was nothing wrong with my feelings, but I kept them to myself as a man should with a protégé.

Note to self: remove this admission later. Maybe.

"What have you got there, Luciena?" I asked, rubbing at my glistening eyes.

She steadied the chalkboard. The old observatory was a shambles. Most of the boards were shattered, though some had been roughly glued back together in the first days after Nimrheal came in the effort to understand what Eydith had done. Cornell opined that it was the orthogonality proof that had brought the demon, but what that meant was a mystery to me. Eydith had solved the transform, solved the inverse, and shown how to determine the Lessingham coefficients. Any or all of that had been her death warrant, signed in hell, detonated here in the tower. The chalkboard that Luciena was pointing at so excitedly was only upright because someone had hammered its stand back into one precarious, haphazard piece.

There were plenty of other minor hazards strewn about. Broken boards, shattered benches, and crushed or cracked stones lay everywhere in a great, heterogeneous mess. Almost every single one of the hundreds of long, slim sticks of chalk the mathematicians like to use were broken into stubby bits, jammed into every nook and cranny of a room that was *all* nooks and crannies now. I saw a piece of someone's helmet somewhere, and I would not be surprised if a sword or two still stuck out of the rubble, waiting for someone to trip over it or fall on it.

"This transform can be related to objects in space, Gil. I think I could use it to make a model for just about anything."

I gave her a skeptical look, not because I know anything at all about the math, but because skepticism is the first and last refuge of the experienced. Yes, it was a bluff.

She pointed a finger at me. "You're right, Gil, it would help if the object—thing—was periodic and continuous." I smiled to myself. She had fallen for my bluff. "But I expect we don't need to adhere literally to the rules on this," she continued, growing even more excited. "No, not at all."

I gave her a grudging nod—also a bluff as I still had no idea what she meant—and she continued playing with broken bits of chalk and shattered boards. I was happy enough to let her play at math as if it meant something other than nothing ... or death.

Time passed. Luciena continued working. I stayed there, watching her, thinking of the children that Emreyta and I never had.

"What are you doing?" Rodryck Cornell shouted as he hobbled unathletically through the debris. Luciena did not even bother looking at the great mathematician, but I did. Cornell's face was mottled, an inflamed red mixed with an infirmary white. His eyes were bloodshot, and it looked as if he had pulled out some of the hair on his head. Certainly, what he had up top was thin enough. It also stuck out like a horsehair brush. Eydith's absence was hurting him in more ways than one. Perhaps he had loved something other than himself after all.

Cornell stumbled on a broken shield, skidded on some shattered chalk, and waved his arms wildly as he careened into a recently righted and dubiously repaired table. He was so comical that I did not follow through on the impulse to threaten him if he should so much as touch a thread on my Luciena in this distraught state. "What *is* that?" Cornell asked when he had recovered his balance. His voice was softer this time, though perhaps only because he was out of breath after his near fall.

Luciena looked over her shoulder at him but kept one hand on the nub of chalk she had been writing with. "I was thinking about the thermal equation," she said. "Maybe it can be solved in Lessingham space."

"It had crossed my mind to try," Cornell admitted, "but start with a thin rod."

They got to talking and scratching away on the patchwork chalkboard with more bits of chalk. Luciena had always thought she could use mathematics in her wizardry as a way of going beyond the imagination that the rest of us used. She claimed that a mathematical model could be more precise—if the math was sufficiently correct—than the heuristics and instincts that wizards relied on. It gave us a lot of laughs. Most of us anyway. I shielded her from most of the mockery, cautioned her sometimes, but I had to admit privately that there was a certain appeal to the purposefulness of her concept.

Really, no one should have laughed, especially us wizards. If Luciena was correct, she could radically lower the uncertainty of what we did. Precision was to be desired. We wizards do not like to admit that we are not well liked. We tend to destroy things. We lack a deft touch. Most of us. If we were not so very good at getting things done, if we were not so very powerful, I suspect we would be shunned for the collateral damage we inflict too casually. Luciena wanted to change that.

As I see it, there are two fundamental problems with math. The first is that it is just so damned difficult. It's hard work, and I do not like that. Instinct is so much easier, but it is for the lazy. Let's face it, if you have the talent, why not be lazy?

I might rewrite this part later when I'm feeling better. Too much grief makes me too honest, and too much honesty makes me look bad.

The other problem with mathematics was obvious in the evidence that was all around me. It could bring Nimrheal. Mathematicians were few and far between—fewer now after this latest debacle—and the best of them were culled like wild barley. Mathematics was dangerous, particularly for the masters.

"Amazing," exclaimed Rodryck. "As simple as that." His voice, normally full of arrogance or pretense, held genuine awe. It was the first time I had ever heard him speak with simple sincerity.

"Yup," said Luciena, tossing her nub of chalk off into the air. "Easy to solve in the transform space" She laughed, and added, "Once we have a transform space."

BRRRAAAAA.

I may have jumped. So close on the heels of the storm that brought Nimrheal, I think I could be forgiven for flinching at the sound of thunder. I could see the sky through the giant hole in the tower wall as well as through the open roof. It was purple, bordering on black. But there is an old saying, "Nimrheal never strikes in the same place twice."

"Let's go in before the rain comes," I said to Luciena and Rodryck. Looking at the awful, roiling cloud, I thought it might even hail. I didn't want any part of that, not sitting under a gaping hole to the sky.

Luciena thrust her journal into my hands. "No!" she exclaimed. "We have to write it down before the rain washes the chalk away."

Between the blood, the exploded chalkboards, the rain and the hail—oh, and all the dead people—it had been very difficult to piece together the Lessingham transform after the last storm. A lot of the work had been washed away. "Okay, Lucy. This one time," I said, and started writing. Nimrheal's hell, she was *my* protégé, and here I was writing notes for her!

CRRRRRRAAAK. CRRRRRRAAAK. CRRRRRRAAAK.

NO!

Nimrheal does not strike in the same place twice.

CRRRRRRAAAK. CRRRRRRAAAK. CRRRRRRAAAK. CRRRRRRAAAK.

No. The motto is wrong. Nimrheal does not strike for the same idea *twice.*

"Run!" I shouted to Luciena, trying to be heard over the booming thunder. The tower shook so hard that the rickety chalkboard she had been working on collapsed like a house of cards. The wind and thunder were so loud I did not even hear the patchwork chalkboard fall. I could see Lucy's lips moving but could not hear her.

"—the book! Keep it—"

I stuffed her journal into my robes and looked up just in time to see the cyclone reach down through the roof of the observatory and deposit a figure like a black flame right onto the table Cornell had bumped into earlier. The flabby mathematician was hit by something. An arm maybe. It was difficult to resolve detail with the wind, the pounding hail, and the boiling shadow that was the demon. Then I saw a spear in the thing's excuse for hands. It thrust the weapon at Luciena. I was sure she would be impaled on the spot.

Lucy disappeared.

Then reappeared behind the demon, shouting something full of hate and rage—Luciena could always rage powerfully—and I saw lightning fall out of the sky, rise out of the stone ... and miss the demon, whose location stuttered to the far side of the tower, near the vast hole in the wall.

If you cannot hit the demon, take out everything around it. I pushed through the final barrier and took Nimrheal's side of the tower apart in a heaven-fueled entropic acceleration. Huge blocks of stone fell away with a reverberating crash. The entire tower shuddered as the error waves from my spell shattered stone, froze wood, pulverized furniture. For a moment, I thought I had gone too far, that the entire tower might collapse instead of only the side where Nimrheal was. I thought I had killed us all. Stone showered everywhere and it seemed that the floor tilted. I was hit in the hip by something hard and fell down, stunned. My left leg did not seem to work.

I heard Lucy scream again and looked up. She was leaping in the air, fire shooting from her hands, toward the black cloud that was Nimrheal. I had failed to kill it, and so did Luciena's latest attempt. The fire parted around the front of the demon and coalesced behind it. Again, Nimrheal thrust for my Lucy, and again she tunneled herself behind it.

But this time Nimrheal was ready for her trick. Almost at the instant Luciena reappeared behind it, the demon flipped around. In one blink, it went from facing one way to facing the other. There was no in-between, no turning. There was only Nimrheal facing one way and then Nimrheal facing the other. The same, unfortunately, was true of the creature's spear. One moment the spear was facing toward Luciena's old position, and the next, it went through her face.

LUCY!

I came to my senses sometime later, covered in my own urine and shit. My eyes were crusted. I could not stand. Hailstones must have awakened me. I tried to roll onto my arse, but a flash of pain from my hip made me lose time again. When next I opened my eyes, the storm had passed. This time I managed to roll over and sit up. I looked around for Luciena. Some part of me wanted that awful memory of Luciena to be false. I fantasized that she was alive. I dreamed that the demon had killed Cornell instead. That would be okay. That is what the mathematician and everyone else probably wanted anyway.

Lucy?

I rolled around in my soiled robes until, among the debris and melting hailstones, I found her. Luciena's face was gone. Nimrheal had not only killed her, it had tried to obliterate her identity by destroying that beautiful face. I crawled to her and, as gently as I could, pulled the spear out, trying not to look, trying not to see what I loved dead.

Servants came. Soldiers too. I hardly saw them. I refused to answer their questions. I was locked in mortal combat with my own mind. I had a terrible memory to forget, and for my sanity's sake, I needed to forget it immediately. I told myself again and again that Luciena was beautiful and alive. I knew she was not, but I needed to see her so in my mind. I needed to reconstruct her and keep the happy, vibrant image of her smiling face at the forefront of my memory. I could not afford to remember what Nimrheal had done to her. I needed to visualize who she had been. I patted my robes. The journal was there. I would keep that for her, and I would publish it, unedited, just as it was, with the one additional chapter you are reading now. Everyone should know her and see her, not as another victim of the demon, but as the brilliant young woman she had been.

"He didn't even want me," lamented Cornell, lying in a stained and unpoised heap. He had survived. That only made sense. He had, in fact, been lying not far from me in the rubble. I had probably rolled over him as I looked for my Lucy. The mathematician was mumbling to himself. I realized with some disgust that Cornell was distraught at being spared a second time. For Rodryck, it was all about him, and because it was all about him, he had learned nothing.

Nimrheal only takes the best of us. Those that are left are made less. Terrorized, traumatized, afraid, ignorant. Robbed by the loss of our betters. Wishing it had been us instead.

†

It would not surprise me if many years from now the deaths of the Auvignes are described as an event of historical significance. I doubt anyone will care about the Lessingham transform. It is only mathematics and will have a dubious utility in the future, especially given our proven inability to sidestep Nimrheal and avoid the cost of true creativity. Even if the transform could have some use, it will never be used. The slow, bloody process of learning will stultify its development.

The Auvigne's sponsorship of this project, and their deaths, will have been in vain. Nimrheal is undefeatable, as I have always maintained. The Auvigne's sponsorship of such a brave but unlikely adventure was unsurprising to those who truly knew all the players involved. They loved Lucy, who had ever been a curious girl, and they genuinely wanted to change the world for the better. Now we have lost a Prince and Princess of Engevelen, our true leaders. That is a blow. It may even be that the loss of the Auvignes proves so traumatic to our little country that their passing is someday identified as the cause of the fall of our nation in its ongoing battles with Novgoreyl and Armadale.

I understand that sentiment. I was here through it all. But as I sit and complete the final words of the journal of my extraordinary young friend, I think that the loss of Luciena is the greatest of all the prices we have paid. She was a woman of unique curiosity and passion. She was sweet, lovable, volatile, brilliant, intrepid and—most of the time— principled. Lucy was the most dynamic person I have ever met, and I do not believe that the world can change for the better without her. You may not agree. You never met Lucy. But perhaps, when enough time has passed, you will understand how rare true invention is and how valuable the truly dynamic are.

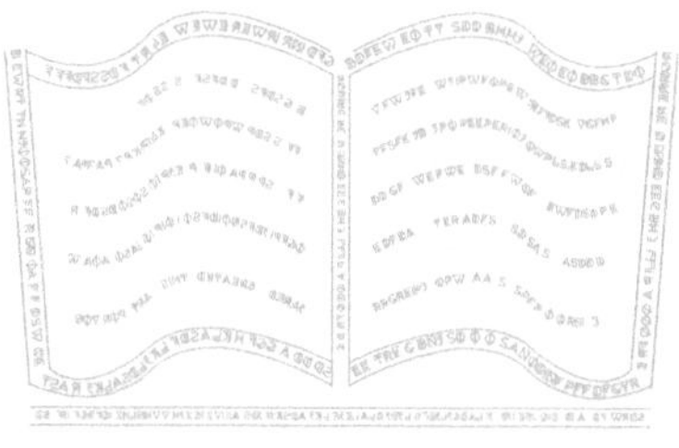

Chapter Thirty-Nine.
Futility

I HAVE AN IDEA; IT IS NEARLY FORMED- ALMOST READY. I HAVE BEEN DEVELOPING THIS IDEA since matters began to go wrong, but I have not quite arrived at it. Even these ruined heraldic dreams—nonsensical flashes—have begun to point to a destination for this journey toward the complete idea. I am on an asymptote of the solution, on the cusp, the border, a single onionskin layer away. Now my idea is about to be born. When it is, Nimrheal may come again. We must both be ready.

—Excerpt from a javelin message to Robert Endicott from Koria Valcourt.

"NO, NOT AT ALL," CAME THE PRECISE TONES OF GERVEAULT OVER THE JAVELIN. "THERE have been a vast number of skolves shadowing us, but they have not attacked."

Kennyth Brice shifted in his seat beside Koria. Lord Latimer sat farther down the long table, and Bethyn farther yet. They were in the Javelin room. This older, prototypical version of the device took up most of the free space in the room. Only Robert and Gerveault had the newer, portable units. Their production on such a small scale was still very time consuming. The day would come when the portable units were everywhere. If, that is, Nimrheal did not kill everyone involved first. And if Skoll and Hati did not destroy the whole Duchy of Vercors. "Highly unusual, wouldn't you agree?" Kennyth asked. "Skolves always attack once they detect you."

They always *had*. Except in *The Lonely Wizard* when they had grown afraid of the wizard, when they thought of him as a god.

"It's Skoll and Hati," Koria said. The two demons were ubiquitous in her loci-ruined heraldic dreams. "They have asserted control over the skolves again now that Huygens is restored at its lower value."

"That conforms with Heylor's reports," added Bethyn.

"Agreed," came Gerveault's voice, "though I have not seen either demon yet, just traces of their effects in the empyreal sky."

Kennyth put a finger on the map laid out in front of him. A marker showed the current location of the Aignen Legion, which was closing on Arsenault now. It had set out a few days before Robert and Bat in order to draw the skolves and the demons away from that far more vulnerable duo. But there were other enemies in the field too. The duke had also marked another position to the east. "How about Armadale's force? Have they encountered the demons yet?"

Gerveault's voice sounded resigned as it came over the big device. "We have not wanted to risk our scouts. And unless we do so, we have no way of knowing."

Koria hazarded a guess. "They haven't. You would have seen the destruction. It would be too widespread. I'm confident Astrid Kettel's report was accurate."

Almost as soon as she defected, Astrid had revealed that Armadale's army was already marching secretly into the wilderness. The expedition had begun even before the embassy arrived at Ardvaser, its aim nothing less than an alliance with Skoll and Hati.

"It's a huge gamble for Armadale," Koria said, "though it will be worth the risk if they succeed. But I think Astrid is right. They won't achieve the alliance, at least not the kind they seek."

"Why not?" asked Lord Latimer. "How can you and Astrid feel so sure?"

"Skoll asked Heylor to kneel and acknowledge him as a god, that's true, but then he just killed the rest. He would have killed Heylor, too, if he had not … escaped. That's not an alliance-building attitude." Perhaps if Armadale could find the correct, suppliant demeanor, Skoll and Hati would help instead of killing them, and from what Koria had seen of the royal family, the Vernons were not very brave. Yet she was certain that, while they might cower in private, they were unlikely to do so in front of their knights. "I doubt Skoll and Hati view human beings as anything other than potential slaves. They won't negotiate."

A rough, loud voice blared over the javelin. It was Hemdale. "So what are Skoll and Hati waiting for?"

Щ

THE MEETING BROKE UP WITH HEMDALE'S QUESTION UNANSWERED, BUT LATER THAT EVENING, Kennyth asked a much smaller group—just Koria and Bethyn—the same question. "Oh, and thank you for taking my hint," he added before Koria could say anything. Earlier, she had looked like she wanted to answer Sir Hemdale, but the duke had stared at her with widening eyes and raised eyebrows, which Koria had correctly interpreted as a plea for discretion.

Sitting now in the duke's private apartments, feet resting on new carpet, eyes scanning the restored furniture and the repaired door to the inner chambers, Koria wondered at the power of a duke. *He can have his castle repaired easily enough, but his subjects require handling with tact. And those who are not his subjects—Deladieyr Knights, for example—require even more careful handling. As a Deladieyr, Hemdale is perfectly free to do as he pleases. He owes the duke no fealty at all.*

In fact, as Koria knew, Kennyth Brice had not been totally forthcoming either to Hemdale or even to his inner circle. He had preemptively moved an army into the Ardgour Wilderness, but he had not told anyone the ultimate objective of the march.

Koria now gave the duke the same answer she would have given Hemdale. "Skoll and Hati may be waiting to see what our army and Armadale's will do if and when they encounter one another. That's one possibility. Or they may be waiting for us to recover the Bridge. I think that's much more likely."

Kennyth blinked. "Because they still fear it?"

"Possibly," Koria allowed. It had been one of Gerveault's theories that the two demons feared the Bridge, that its effect on the Huygens modulus had long been anathema to them in the very near field. But that, Koria knew, was in the past. For two hundred and fifty years, Nimrheal had been absent and Skoll and Hati had hid. For two hundred and fifty years, Huygens had been high, especially in the near field where it would have been so exceedingly high that the demons would have been fantastically weak. That had changed. Huygens was low again. Was the Bridge still something the demons should fear? A bridge to heaven *might* weaken the two demons. Robert's idea that the Methueyn Bridge went to both heaven and hell seemed to contradict Gerveault's explanation.

Bethyn sighed theatrically and brought up the point that Koria was turning to in her head. "Or the other possibility, they are just waiting for us to get it free from the apparatus Ardgour wrapped the bridge in, whatever that was."

Greenstone.

This was another in a lengthy list of theories as to why Skoll and Hati had failed to interact with the Bridge over the past quarter millennium. Ardgour's apparatus was perhaps also anathema to them. Koria thought this was closest to being true. The apparatus had acted on the Bridge to tighten Huygens. It—and the Bridge—had denied empyreal power to the demons.

Does it still hurt them? The demons are just watching for a reason.

The brown-haired girl rolled her eyes. Apparently, sighing alone was not enough. "In any case, Skoll and Hati aren't allowing us free movement for no reason. We should assume they are allowing our army to march because it pleases them to do so. Perhaps they are waiting so they can destroy us utterly, when we are so far from support that, when they strike, they kill everyone."

"Armadale's command isn't leading, though," Koria added. "They don't know where the Bridge is. They're just shadowing our soldiers until they are led to it."

"It's a double trap for us, then" Bethyn said. "Twice the risk and ... I'm not sure what the reward is."

"So how do we win?" asked Kennyth. He looked a little lonely without Gerveault. The old dynamicist had been by his parents' side, their counselor and confidant, all of Kennyth's life, and after their deaths, the old professor had assumed the same role at Kennyth's side. Now the duke had bid Gerveault dress for war despite his age and go with Sir Hemdale and Sir Haverland to catch up with the Aignen Legion. The young duke had also sent Robert into the wilderness, someone he had always seemed to look out for. And he had done so right after Robert had saved his life again. Kennyth might be lonely, but he was not without his own strength. *Or his own plan.* Koria knew Kennyth was not as directionless as he seemed.

"That is indeed the question," she said. "Why don't you tell us what winning looks like for you?"

"I don't want to say." Kennyth frowned and looked away, perhaps fearing that his answer seemed weak. Then he added, unhelpfully, "I want things to go back to how they used to be."

Bethyn jumped on that. "Like two *weeks* ago used to be, or two *centuries* ago used to be?"

"With or without Nimrheal?" Koria added. "With or without Skoll and Hati? With or without Methueyn Knights? Because I think it's all one or all the other.

Two weeks ago has *none* of the above, two centuries ago *all* of the above. I don't think there can be any in-between."

Щ

"I CAN'T BELIEVE HE DIDN'T ANSWER YOUR QUESTION," COMPLAINED BETHYN AFTER THE two women returned to their workroom.

"But he did."

"That was *not* an answer. Saying that he would hold the Legion a day's march from Arsenault was not an answer." Bethyn slapped her hand down on the table with that special laziness she had that made it sound like a rope hitting wood. "When did our duke, Kennyth Brice, turn into a weasel?"

It was obvious to Koria. She guessed it might be obvious to Bethyn as well but that her friend enjoyed pretending not to understand so she could continue to complain. "He is taking the opportunity of what you call the double trap our army is in to preserve the initiative for someone else. He's giving Robert a chance to get to the Bridge first."

"And then?" Bethyn looked genuinely perplexed now. "Is Robert supposed to cross?"

Koria just stared at her friend. Robert had fought the two Nines to a draw despite the wizard they had brought with them. This had caused some of those in the know to revise their view that Robert Endicott could not cross the Methueyn Bridge without having first undergone the Ceremony of Rising.

"And even if he did," Bethyn went on, "can he beat Skoll and Hati by himself? It doesn't seem to me that Kennyth Brice answered those questions at all."

"Because nothing makes sense?" Koria asked. "You'll have to think a little harder, girl."

Bethyn's face turned red. "Knights, you piss me off sometimes, Koria." She raised her voice to a shout, "Robert will never beat either demon alone. Eight Methueyn Knights couldn't do it, and neither can he. Oh, he'll try, all right, but your husband is going to die."

"Yes."

Koria's stark response only seemed to enrage Bethyn further. "And even if he could win against them, he isn't beating Nimrheal, new transform or not."

"Why not?"

"Because Nimrheal is something totally different!" Bethyn shot back, roaring now. "We don't even know what the fucking thing is."

Koria nodded. "That's right."

Bethyn's rage went up yet another, even more unlikely, notch. "Then why are you so calm!" she shrieked, spittle flying.

Koria smiled tightly. "When my daughter died, I realized most of this. I didn't entirely accept it, but it has been floating around in my head since then. You and I have spoken about it many times, you know, one way or another." She looked away for a moment as if composing her thoughts, then turned to Bethyn again.

Koria was no longer smiling. "Through this entire time, some part of my mind has remained lying in that hot water, still pregnant, still approaching Elysium, a breath away from breaking through, a breath away from my daughter's last heartbeat. But no matter what we do, no matter how many daughters die, no matter how many friends are killed, we are not going to get to heaven. We lack the means or the knowledge to acquire the means. We aren't prepared. We aren't ready. It is futile. If we go on as we have been going, we will all die."

Bethyn's rage had evaporated the instant Koria said the word "daughter." Tears had taken its place. "So we lie down and die, then?"

"No. I have a plan."

"What?"

"First, we get Heylor Style here." Koria tapped a finger with precision against the table. "Now. Today. Then we get our strongest knight back into the field."

Щ

A nother , and this time peremptory , message having been sent to H eylor over the javelin, and with Bethyn and a troop of guards waiting at the duke's feasting table to protect the requested point of materialization, Koria went in search of Eloise. Her improbably tall friend, she realized, had not been herself since well before Gregory's death. Koria had detected a change ripening for some time before that tragedy. She had even tried to find out what the issue was, but Eloise had been typically prickly about revealing anything. After Gregory's death, Kennyth had ordered Eloise moved off the duty roster, and she should long ago have gone home to her children, but she had not even acknowledged the opportunity. For reasons known only to herself, she had moped about the castle, barely interacting with anything or anyone, refusing to go home to her daughters, refusing even to discuss the idea.

Koria had lacked the time to deal with Eloise properly. She had tried now and then, whenever she had a moment. Robert had tried before he left. Hemdale had tried. They had all tried, but Eloise was her own woman, and she was not going to manage her grief on anyone else's schedule. *In all honesty, I failed her. I've failed to find the time for her.*

But there simply had not been enough time. Nimrheal was not waiting, nor were Skoll and Hati going to wait forever. It reminded Koria of their fraught first year at the New School. There had been no time then either.

When she found the observatory guards lounging in the lobby of the Cardinal Tower, Koria knew something was seriously amiss. Racing up the stairs, she lamented her lack of fitness. Youth still lent some speed to her steps, some endurance to her muscles, but she was a woman of the mind, and in a sprint up so many flights of stairs, it showed. When she at last reached the final stair and crossed the threshold of the observatory level, she was hit by an odd feeling of repetition. Eloise had charged up the same steps to save Robert from Nimrheal, but it had turned out to be Koria that needed saving. Eloise at a full run had been an unstoppable giant, a goddess of speed and power. Koria knew she was a different creature entirely. Then she saw her friend hanging by the neck.

Eloise's face was blue, and her legs twitched in a ghastly dance, but the dance was already winding down as a panting Koria rushed toward her dying friend. The scene was an appalling parody of the Ceremony of Rising. The tip of the great sword of the Methueyn Treaty just touched the stone floor, but Eloise's spasming feet hung five feet above that cold surface. Koria almost slid on the polished flagstones as she scrambled desperately to get under her friend and grasp her legs. She pushed up to take the weight off Eloise's neck. "Help!" she screamed. *Where are those guards?* They had started up the stairs behind her.

Eloise was too far off the ground. Koria could not even reach her friend's knees. As she pushed up, Eloise's legs only buckled and spun around. Koria looked for something to help. A stepladder stood just a few feet away. Could she leave Eloise dangling for long enough to drag it over, or would that only make matters worse?

Suddenly, Koria was staggered by a great weight and pushed down to a crouching position by a mass she could not resist, then knocked to her knees.

What?

Looking up past Eloise's big feet, she saw a triumphant, beaming face. Her friend's eyes were open, blazing blue, ignited by light from the open roof. Her arms were spread wide, and she smiled, ascendant now, graceful as an eagle. The sword hung balanced behind her, its five hundred pounds of steel floating free. Eloise had Risen.

The moment stretched on as if time had been suspended. Koria gazed up at her transfigured friend. The woman hanging there was still Eloise, but it was as if she had let go of something of herself and yet had become greater, not less, for its absence. The true Eloise had emerged, and she was stupendous. The guards had finally reached the landing, only to be stopped in their tracks, astonished, awestruck. For all that a Ceremony of Rising had been scheduled weeks ago by Sir Hemdale, no one had really known what to expect. To the guards, Eloise must have appeared a goddess. Her first words, after they had sorted out how to remove the noose and secure the treaty were pure Eloise, however. "Stop kneeling, stupes. Have you never seen a woman before?"

Щ

While Eloise worked on her kit, Koria wrote a message for Robert. It would be sent by javelin either at the appointed transmission time or when Robert reached the river and called them. Bethyn would have to deliver it, though. Koria had other plans.

A few day's water. A rope, backpack, and a cloak. A notebook. Koria almost chuckled at herself and tossed the notebook aside. She thought again and kept it. Then she added her bag of dice and a thermometer.

There was a knock on the door. "Lady Koria?" a guard asked when she opened. "Heylor Style has arrived. He is in the feasting room."

"Good," she said. "Will you get him a backpack, waterskin, and cloak?" When the man nodded, she added. "And please send a message to the duke asking him to join us in the feasting room urgently."

A half hour later, Koria joined Kennyth Brice, Eloise, Bethyn, and Heylor in the feasting room and announced, without any preamble, "I have a plan—"

Of which I will tell you only a portion.

"I'm going after Robert and Bat," Eloise said before Koria could continue. She was dressed in a chainmail skirt. Her entropic sword was on her hip, her shield was on her left arm, and her pack was on the table beside her. Koria had known that as soon as Eloise learned about Astrid Kettel's defection, the attempt on Kennyth Brice's life, the Nines' desire to find the Bifrost, the looming war between the duchy and Armadale, and two armies marching into the wilderness, her Risen friend would want to join Robert. The reaction had been exactly according to Koria's plan.

"Yes, you are," agreed Koria. "I am too."

Eloise scowled "You? You can't even march a day across the wilderness."

"I'm not going to," Koria replied with a wide grin that was quite unlike her. She pointed at Heylor. "He's going to take us both to Arsenault without any long journeying."

Bethyn crossed her arms and looked suspiciously at Heylor. "Can you do that?"

Heylor hesitated only a moment. "I think so," he hedged. "I tunneled Ailis. Then a little girl." He looked up at Eloise and his lips curled back. "Nobody Eloise's size, but … Nimrheal's nuts, you *are* big. Ah … not that I'm saying you're *too* big Eloise. You're just perfect."

"Of course I am, stupe."

"Right," Heylor pressed on. "I didn't mean that to come out creepy. I don't think I can *carry* you. Maybe a hug? Skolve it, I'm getting married, you know." He winced, then continued more confidently, "Sure. Yah. Faster than your favorite horse. That's me."

"And then what?" asked Kennyth Brice, somehow still patient.

Koria looked him in the eye, trying as hard as she could to transfer her confidence to him. "We will catch up with Robert and support him in retrieving the Methueyn Bridge."

"That's good." Eloise nodded. "I like this plan. Where's my uncle?"

"Sir Hemdale is busy protecting the army," Kennyth said. "Skoll, Hati, and a large force of skolves are in close proximity. An army from Armadale too."

Eloise smiled fiercely. "Before this is over, everyone is going to fight."

Koria hoped not. Eloise's big arm went around her shoulders. "This is going to be like the old days, Koria. You and I off to save the boys." She squeezed Koria again. Her grip felt like a vise. "And when Nimrheal comes," Eloise said in a very different voice, cold and serious now, "I am going to kill it."

Koria shuddered, thinking about her true plan. Killing Nimrheal was not on the agenda. Reacting to the terror of her ongoing heraldic dreams was not on the list either. Fighting any of the demons was the last thing she wanted to do. Koria's plan—the plan she had concentrated so hard on not quite finishing for fear of drawing Nimrheal—had emerged from a rigorous application of logic, an unbiased consideration of information. It came from Esthauer, Pessicaust, Huygens, Verinath, and Luciena Fortis. It came from reading about the hundreds of unsuccessful attempts to kill or stop Nimrheal in the past. Her plan was all about knowledge.

"Koria."

"You know," Eloise whispered in Koria's ear, "I keep hearing my name. Perhaps I'll cross that bridge while we are at it. Then we'll see how much Nimrheal likes what happens next."

Chapter Forty

The Retrograde Knight

WITH THE RIGHT TRANSFORMATION AND THE RIGHT DOMAIN- *I WOULD NOT NEED ELYSIUM- we would not need the Methueyn Knights.*

–Robert Endicott

"KORIA!" ENDICOTT STARTED AWAKE, THE DISJOINTED, WOULD-BE HERALDIC DREAM SNAPping him out of equilibrium. In the past, such things had always cohered into some sort of narrative, but in the unending loci of the present, the dreams were only staccato flashes of possibility, potential facts without reference or meaning.

"Finally," grunted Merrett. He was already on his feet, tying off his backpack. It was still mostly dark. Dawn had not yet come. "You've been doing that all night, Blouse."

"Feels more like getting kicked by a horse than tickled by a dream," Endicott said, blinking the sleep out of his eyes.

Merrett snorted. "I may have literally kicked you a few times." While Endicott dug around for some hardtack, the big man scanned the small clearing. Black was turning indigo; dawn was coming. "Did you learn anything?"

"Nothing that made any sense." He had dreamed of fighting Hemdale, of Koria being murdered by more of those odious Nines, the Seygis Knights. "That's not right," he amended. "One thing did. Whatever is going to happen, I think it is all going to happen today."

"We best get to it, then, Blouse."

The sun rose. The world had not ended yet, though there was a strange darkness on the far eastern horizon. As they moved at a run uphill toward Arsenault, the darkness resolved into nascent storm clouds that seemed to line up in an arc, rising with the sun.

"Nimrheal?" Merrett asked.

"Some storms are just storms."

No one trusted the weather anymore, so the two young men kept a close watch on the growing storm front as they worked their way up the old road, continuing to retrace their former path. Endicott tried to shake off the dread from his heraldic dream. It had been a fractured, turbulent set of images, soaked in violence, colored by fear. *Is it just the locus? Or is my anxiety the cause of such darkness?* The continuing set of loci were there for a reason—several reasons or there would not be such a succession of them—so he doubted that the ominous collage of images he had seen was solely a function of his anxious mindset. All the same, they had lost Gregory, his best friend. They had lost Lindseth, their old comrade-in-arms. Marielle Engel, the green-eyed rising star that everyone had thought would be the answer to the crisis, was gone too. And Nimrheal had come to within a hair of murdering Bethyn and Eloise. And Koria. Those horrible deaths and hairsbreadth escapes only deepened Endicott's conflated hypotheses about his torturous dreams: the images his sleeping mind received backwards from the future were the disturbed products of both the loci and his own anxiety.

Long before they came again to the dead sentinel from *The Lonely Wizard*, it was clear that the brunt of the storm would miss them and trouble somewhere to the southeast instead. The javelin meeting was able to go ahead as scheduled, but the message from Koria that Bethyn read out to Endicott was cryptic. He knew he needed a bigger picture of what was going on. There was little he could do with Koria's note, and he guessed she was holding things back for fear of summoning Nimrheal. She would do what she would do regardless. *Please be okay. Be okay. Be okay.*

Koria's plan might be entirely in her own hands, but Robert still needed to find out more about how the world around him was shaping up. He knew from the other parts of the report that, not far away, an army from Armadale was facing off against the Aignen Legion and perhaps Skoll and Hati as well, but the few words from Bethyn heard through a metal box could not tell him what was really going on. To their left, to the northwest, surged the river, its jagged path cut into bedrock and a high set of cliffs. To their right was another broken wall of rock, beyond which lay the lowlands they had spent the last day and more climbing up from. The road had originally been laid in a kind of box canyon, which did not make for good viewing, even though the two young men had climbed far above the flats of the past. *How can I get a better understanding of the larger situation?*

The river and its cliffs were out of the question, but the southeast wall was not so high and steep as to make a better view unattainable. Endicott eventually found a line of weakness to follow off the road and onto a narrow scree field that led up to the rough, crumbling southeast ridge. Working along the ridge, past scraggly spruce trees and precariously perched boulders, he finally achieved an unobstructed view of the vast plain below.

"Get up here, Bat!" he called. It took some time for the big man, huffing and grumbling all the way, to join him. By then, Endicott had a telescope to his eye. "See there," he said, handing the instrument to Bat and pointing downward with some satisfaction and more than a little horror. "It's beginning."

Bat took the telescope while Endicott switched to the empyreal sky. The Aignen Legion was camped on a tilted flat just on the edge of the highlands. Another army—Armadale's—had camped to the southeast on somewhat lower ground. Both armies faced north, which was strange.

Why?

He looked harder. A dark light pulsed there in the empyreal sky. *Skoll and Hati? And their skolves?* He could not see them through the telescope, but Endicott realized that the demons' singularities might look, from so far away, like a dark pulsing light in the empyrean. In any event, the movements of the soldiers drew all his attention. As the storm moved close, the Aignen Legion began to wheel clockwise, rotating its formations toward the other army. At the same time, someone began adjusting potentialities along the storm front.

Gerveault.

Lightning began to fall, striking at the army of Armadale.

"The old man's still got it," whispered Bat over the distant thunder.

A sheet of blue-white lightning shot across a curiously specific rear line of Armadale's force before shifting abruptly to the front line, where Armadale's steel-clad knights were ranged. It looked no less ferocious in the empyreal sky than through the lens of the telescope. It would be worse still down there where the electrons burned through flesh.

"Yes, he does," Endicott finally replied.

After the fight at the Citadel, no one had been sure how much of Gerveault's former power remained. Keith Euyn had been the more powerful of the two men that day, and some had hinted afterward that Gerveault was only good for inventing and advising now. The carnage below said otherwise.

"He waited until the storm front had come almost too close," Endicott added. *Specific preparation.* "And only then decided to end the standoff."

Merrett handed back the telescope. "Let's go do *our* job, then."

He was right. It was time. But as the two men descended from their viewpoint and resumed the march toward Arsenault, Endicott was still thinking about all the knights and soldiers dying down below while he and his companion worked their way up the canyon. The old Nimrheal-mounted knight, still planted there on his spear, did nothing to distract him from such dark thoughts as they finally passed it by.

▽

This is where they died. Koria did not speak the thought. Heylor's ashen face was not, she knew, caused by any difficulty in dynamically tunneling Eloise and her all the way to the highlands. In fact, Koria could feel that Huygens was weaker already up here. Heylor had brought them across quite easily, an enormous contrast to his hypothermic state so many weeks ago when he had first appeared on Kennyth Brice's feasting table, frostbitten and shaking. His jittery movements today were not due to hypothermia. He looked different in other ways too. Older, stronger, more confident—perhaps even healed—but he was still Heylor Style. He could not walk through the graveyard of his eight and be unaffected.

"Someone cleaned it up," the skinny young man said in wonder.

"They weren't very careful about it," observed Eloise in a hard voice. Rising had not made her any less judgmental. "Robert should have left them as they lay." Her husband had reported his burials in the after-experiment review—he could not have failed to honor the remains of old friends—but that did not mollify Eloise. She was the kind of woman who knew when to be practical. "And look at all the *new* tracks too."

Koria could not see the spoor that had given rise to Eloise's irritation. She was not trained for it, but she knew why Robert and Bat Merrett had not cared about leaving tracks. "They're in a hurry," she observed. *As if everyone isn't.* A moment before, she had opened herself to the empyreal sky and detected a battle beginning to the east. *Not Nimrheal, I think.* Giant thunderclouds roiled there, but not the life-ending, infinite anvil supercell that always seemed to attend Nimrheal.

Eloise gave Koria a pointed look. "Well, we aren't going to catch them if you don't start moving your arse, Koria." Eloise had already groused about Koria's inexperience in the wilderness and overall lack of fitness when the plan had been explained. Koria knew her friend was simply being … practical and that her lack of charity was impersonal. Eloise was just being Eloise. But Koria also knew the big woman did not know everything.

▽

"I don't need my arse to catch Robert," Koria said with the knowing look Eloise recognized so well from their days at the New School. "I'm going to use a different muscle."

She did not point at her head as a less subtle person might have, but Eloise supplied the image in her own mind. *She's up to something. And she's keeping it from me.* Eloise was not the kind of woman who took kindly to being excluded from a secret, but she also knew that Koria was a woman of foresight and subtlety. She decided to be magnanimous this time. She would wait—a little while—for her friend to reveal what she had in mind.

"Heylor," Koria said, pulling his attention away from the mounds of dirt covering the remains of his eight, "you have to know where you are tunneling to, correct?"

The young man looked back at Koria with an expression bordering somewhere between what Eloise would have called suspicious and guilty and answered in a hedging tone, almost as if he was arguing with himself. "Y-yes."

"Or see it?" Koria persisted.

"Y-yes."

Despite Heylor's weird hesitation, Koria had the answer she wanted. She smiled reassuringly. "Then I want you to tunnel us forward by stages, jumping each time as far as the line of sight allows." She pulled a small telescope from her bag and handed it him. "Use this."

Turning to Eloise, she gave her a knowing look and said, "My arse will be quite fine."

"Humph," grunted Eloise, knowing Koria had more in her bag than a telescope and a new travel concept.

▽

Hemdale enjoyed killing the Nines that came against him, though he had no strong feelings about how far a limb flew when he hacked one off or how much the Seygis Knights flopped about when he caved in their helm or breastplate. He did not care if they died slowly in agonizing pain or expired quickly, or if they were surprised or sad that their lives were over. He did not care how they experienced or interpreted their end. He only cared that he had ended them. According to Robert, they had eaten Sir Kaimari, and according to Astrid Kettel, they had poisoned his old friends Sir Jormundheim and Sir Valcryst. He enjoyed killing the Nines because they needed to be killed. They deserved to die and for no one to care after that. *That is true vengeance.*

"Hemdale."

It was the voice again. It had called before. He had heard it first when he executed Armadale's ambassador, and several times after that. This time it was different, as if conveying an implied command, an irresistible feeling that he should go to Arsenault. Immediately. He had ignored the voice up until now, dismissing it as trick of the mind. He could not do that now.

"AAAAAHHH!" screamed another knight, a Nine by the etching on his shining breastplate, as he charged Hemdale. The man was connected elsewhere in the empyreal sky by a shadowy hole, a boiling vacuum of dark energy. Hemdale ducked under his opponent's wide, telegraphed swing, then spun and cut sideways through the knight's bascinet, cleaving the top of the helm and a thin slice of his scalp underneath. Fragments of helm, hair, and skin flew off in a wild spray of blood, but the Nine did not fall. He spun off on an arc, momentum taking him five or more strides before he whirled, a bloody mess, to face Hemdale again.

"GRRRRRRAAAAAHHHHH!" It was Hemdale who shouted this time, though he had no need for words. His cry was the essence of impending violence. It was the stopper being pulled off the bottle before the havoc it contained was unleashed. He cut through the Nine's sword on his next swing, sending a chunk of it spinning off into the fray, one more piece of chaos in the battle, then followed up with a diagonal downstroke through the man's hip, shearing straight through his armor. Hemdale's entropic sword only stopped when it reached the air between the Seygis Knight's legs. The Nine fell sideways, but before he could hit the blood-soaked earth, Hemdale came over the top and cleaved what remained of his skull in half. He pounded the remains twice more before the dead man was fully down and, not fully satisfied, kicked a piece of the man's head—with an ear still attached—into a pile of pine needles and broken branches. It was easy work killing men, and the Seygis Knights, though more powerful than most, were not so difficult on this day. They all seemed to overestimate themselves, and none that he had encountered so far were nearly as strong as he was.

None of them have Risen. They do not understand what the Ceremony of Rising really is.

It was not a thing that could be explained. It was a transformation that could not be taught, only experienced. Hemdale blinked blood out of his eyes and mused for a moment on the shortcomings of his enemies.

They lack the balance and grace of those who have Risen.

"Hemdale!" Sophia Haverland called. Her shield was gone, her sword ruined from being swung harder than common metal could withstand. She did not have an Endicott sword, and at the moment faced two Knights of Armadale with only a hilt and six inches of jagged blade.

Hemdale tossed Sacrifice to Sophia and charged the knight closest to her. The man hit him hard on his pauldron, breaking the metal but failing to cut flesh. Hemdale took the man down hard, mounted him, and began smashing his helm into the ground. When he had finished pulping the knight's head into a raw stew, he stood up to see if Haverland still needed his help.

She did not. Her opponent had been skewered through the chest by Hemdale's massive blade and lay unmoving a few paces away. Sophia held Sacrifice high as she watched the nearby soldiers run away. Nodding his pleasure at the sight, Hemdale took the sword back into his own hands.

He surveyed the larger battlefield. They had won. Armadale was withdrawing wholesale to the east. Gerveault's first move had been to kill their wizards with an opening barrage of lightning strikes. After that, the old dynamicist had raked the front lines of Armadale's finest knights with sheets of lightning and fire, immolating whole ranks of them. Then Hemdale and Haverland had charged, killing whatever surviving Nines they could find. Archers and crossbowmen had opened up on Armadale's ranks with armor-piercing arrowheads from Deryn Endicott's forge, and the regular soldiers soon decided they had more than had enough. He looked again at the fleeing mass of men. *No more Seygis Knights? Unless some of them had abandoned the battle and sneaked off to Arsenault.*

Hemdale turned to look up at the mountains in the northwest. *If I heard a voice, a voice of command, might they too? Might they have heard that ninth angel?*

Hemdale wanted to be the one to retrieve the Bifrost. From boyhood, he had dreamt of crossing it, and when he became a man, he had searched fruitlessly for it. After Armadale's king, Albrecht Vernon, had banished him for opposing the king's plan to take personal command of the Deladieyr order, Hemdale had wanted to find the Methueyn Bridge even more. He had never been a man to doubt himself, but he knew that he alone could not change the world. He needed help from Elysium. Losing his nephew and his niece-by-marriage—and nearly losing Eloise—had only made that clearer. The world needed Methueyn Knights. Hemdale wanted to become one so he could wreak vengeance on the Albrecht Vernons of the world.

So he could save himself from seeing what he loved dead.

Hearing the voice call his name had almost been enough to make Hemdale abandon duty and go. It was his right to choose his path. He was free. But Hemdale also cared about Gerveault, and about the women and men of the Aignen Legion. He knew he could not allow Armadale's force to prevail. But looking up at the heights, he knew something else as well. *I cannot allow any of the Nines to cross the Bridge.*

"Where are Skoll and Hati?" Sir Haverland asked, standing beside him. When Hemdale failed to answer, she asked a different question. "Why do you suppose they let us come so far in the first place? The distractions up and down the wheat line might have accounted for our first few days of movement, but this … makes no sense. They should attack now, while we are weakest."

"I think that was their original plan," said Gerveault, still hoarse from the battle. There was mud on the old man's face, in his thinning hair, on his hands, and he was panting. "Let our two armies wear out their strength on each other. Perhaps they hoped we would ourselves destroy most of those capable of crossing the

Bifrost." The dynamicist looked up toward the mountain behind which Arsenault sheltered. "I saw them watching—could not miss them in the empyreal sky—but they suddenly left. Something else caught their attention."

$$\nabla$$

"I DON'T SEE ROBERT," SAID HEYLOR, LOOKING THROUGH THE TELESCOPE.

They had tunneled in jumps up the road, bound more by sightlines than distance, by the turnings in the road than the magnification of the focal lens. Contrary to Koria's prediction of not needing her arse, they had been forced to run some of the shorter sections between jumps. Eloise had pushed Koria up some of the steeper slopes, one big hand planted on the middle of the green-eyed-girl's back. A part of Heylor wondered if Eloise would end up having to carry Koria if they didn't find better sightlines, but then the road straightened into a long box canyon. Dynamic jumps made an enormous difference then, and at a cost Heylor had been able to manage so far. In fact, his ability to tunnel seemed to be getting better and better the closer they got to the ruined castle. The air felt electric, almost like it had when he had seen Nimrheal. He kept looking for the thunderclouds, but they had passed away to the south, and the storm had been nothing like the cataclysm accompanying Nimrheal's appearance at the New School.

Every time that buzzing feeling of potentiality made Heylor look for a thunderstorm, every time he flinched, thinking Nimrheal was about to materialize, he regretted coming. And every time he considered his own reactions—the fear, the regret, the feelings of powerlessness—he was glad that he had. Their last big jump took them to the dead knight from *The Lonely Wizard*, a sight Heylor had never imagined to be real, let alone something he would see. Koria immediately ordered them to stop and evaluate.

The ruins of an old bridge hung down into the gorge about four hundred yards past the dead knight. Its posts were intact on their side but charred and cracked on the other. Its rope was reduced to a frizzy mess where it could be found at all, like a rotted hairball from a gigantic cat. The metal cables were still attached to the near-side posts, but Heylor, hanging precariously over the gorge, could see that the thick wooden steps were missing and only one of the metal cables even made it as far as the churning water. The old castle of Arsenault, sitting forlornly on the far side of the plateau, was no more than a couple of hundred yards further on. Heylor could see it quite well with the telescope. He could also see another bridge on the north side of the castle, its appearance softened by mist from the river. What Heylor could not seem to find anywhere was his friend Robert.

"He could be in the gorge somewhere," Koria said, taking the telescope back. "Trying to find a way across now that the bridge is down." At one time, Heylor would have thought it ridiculous that they could be so close to Robert and Bat and still miss them. But his time in the wilderness, experiencing firsthand the mishaps and follies of actual operations, had taught him not to laugh off Koria's suggestion. It was easy to become lost, and hard to be found.

"They should have brought me with them instead of running off alone," said Eloise.

Heylor saw Koria give Eloise a dark look.

What does Eloise think she could have done to help? Jump the gorge?

No way.

Maybe.

Nope. Not even her.

That river is scary.

The roaring of the water below was loud in Heylor's ears. There was no spray on his face yet, but he could see water glistening in the sunlight a few hundred yards ahead near the castle.

"I have a plan," announced Koria. For some reason, Eloise shot a darkly suspicious look of her own at her smaller friend.

What am I missing here?

▽

"What are we missing here, Bat?"

Endicott and Bat Merrett had dropped down into the gorge by the same route they had carried Marielle out two weeks earlier. Even that line of weakness had been difficult to locate despite the fact that they had been there before. Finding a way across the river looked impossible. They could not reach the remains of the old bridge—the walls of the gorge were too steep—and it would not have done them any good even if they could have. The posts on the far side of the ravine had been destroyed. There was not enough left of them to anchor a rope. Their attempts to find a tree to put across the gorge had also failed. The pines in these highlands were scrubby and short. There was no question of jumping, and swimming was almost as ridiculous an idea.

"I could try freezing the river," Endicott mused.

Merrett shook his head in pure disdain. "I've seen you explode a cake too many times, Blouse. Now you're going freeze a whole river, and a fast-moving torrent at that?" He kicked a rock into the clear, cold water. "How many tries do you think you're gonna get before you kill yourself. Or worse, me?"

Endicott imagined how he might do it. Freeze the water to a depth of three feet upstream and displace the heat downstream. *The error wave would be bad.* He had an image of the entire gorge filled with super-heated steam. That could boil both of them in an instant. Then he imagined the water starting to flow over his ice plug. That could kill both of them too.

"Yes, Bat, it does seem to pose some challenges."

"It's downright crazy if you ask me!" Bat shouted over the tumult of the waters.

Endicott chuckled. He was not put off yet. He thought of his grandpa, that quiet, thoughtful man. Finlay had been all calm all the time: all thought, few words. Endicott thought back to the great mystery of his father's death. It had never been a secret after all. Finlay had told him about it, without hesitation, though in his usual laconic style, when Endicott had finally asked. That his grandson had already guessed the truth did not matter. Finlay's son had simply accepted the potential outcome of making Hemdale's sword, painful as he had known it would be. Endicott expected the same from this mission. There was going to be pain. *But we can accept our fate with grace.*

"Well, this is a difficult situation," he said to Merrett, smiling now. "You didn't think it was going to be easy, did you?"

"Fuck you, Blouse."

This poor attempt at humor, if that is what it was, only brought the humor out in Endicott. "It's all just physics, Bat," he said. "The water is moving, very fast, and there's a *lot* of it. That's just scale and thermodynamics." He looked up and down the line of the river. "But we're hemmed in by this gorge. That will funnel the error wave, which will already be bigger than it has ever been, thanks to Huygens being so low." An old memory shot into his mind. "And yes, we haven't tried anything like this before. We don't know what the downstream consequences might be. Remember back at Aignen when Heylor tried to make a hot water tank for the town?"

"Oh, I skolving remember it all right," Bat sneered. "Heylor Style and his antics are the last thing we need right now."

POP

With this odd, almost comical little explosion, Heylor materialized next to Bat. "Need some help?"

▽

"KORIA THOUGHT OF IT," HEYLOR EXPLAINED FROM THE BROKEN ROOF OF ARSENAULT castle. "She guessed we might be able to spot you two from up here." The jittery young man was wearing Style on his hip, which was a relief to Endicott. Leaving the entropic sword in the bushes where Lindseth had found it had been a painful choice at the time. Heylor had retrieved it when he was ready, when he had forgiven himself for what happened when he had left the sword—and his eight—behind. Seeing Heylor whole once more, and strangely confident, made Endicott smile.

"Koria Valcourt is a woman *made* of plans," said Eloise, also looking better than she had the last time that Endicott had seen her. She had crushed Endicott in one of her vise-tight, uncomfortably intimate hugs when he, Bat, and Heylor had appeared next to her and Koria. There was no resisting it, and Endicott knew better than to try. He had been so relieved to see Eloise full of life again that he did not care what she did. *Just live, Eloise.*

Underneath her ferocious hug, he sensed that Eloise was still in pain over the death of Gregory but that she had turned her agony into something else. She was more alive, fiercer, more dangerous than ever. Endicott did not have to look through the empyreal sky to see that Eloise had Risen. She blazed in that fiery domain that underwrote this reality.

But, oddly, so did Koria. Elysium was not a place in the sky like the sun. It was a place that was not a place, located in a direction and at a distance that meant nothing in Endicott's world. It was orthogonal. Koria Valcourt shone, connected to heaven along an infinitely long, yet infinitesimally short bridge of luminous power. In his soul, she had always shone so. From the moment he had first met her, there had been something about her he had loved, a thing that resonated with him, that made *him* resonate. She had always been his goddess. That she now shone like one in the empyreal sky just seemed natural.

Her hug had been shorter and less fierce than Eloise's, but it had been *her* authentic touch, and he had felt an unlikely peace in and from it despite the peril they shared. "Let's hear the plan, then," he said.

$$\triangledown$$

KORIA POINTED OVER THE GORGE, OVER THE RIVER, PAST THE PLATEAU, TOWARD THE SHEER bowl set into the mountain. She pointed at the great ring that seemed to float in the air, the place at the epicenter of the Huygens near-field effect, the cause of the loci they had all suffered under for months now, the source of the buzzing potentiality in the air. The colossal torus was beautiful and terrifying, its size almost beyond even Koria's ability to fully comprehend.

Pffft.

She did not draw attention to the energized particles that zipped by the castle at astronomical speeds. It was not time yet to talk of such things. "Heylor dynamically tunnels us as close as he safely can to the torus. And then we see."

$$\triangledown$$

"THEY'RE COMING FAST!" SHOUTED HEYLOR, LOOKING BACKWARDS, STILL RUNNING. "I DON'T know how they cleared the river!" He tripped over a pile of skolve bones, and his feet and hands shot antically away from the glass beads that seemed to be scattered everywhere. Koria had spotted the two singularities in the empyreal sky to their southeast just as Heylor was vacillating over how close to the torus he would be able to tunnel everyone. She knew what the singularities were and why they were hurtling toward them. *Skoll and Hati. Panicking, maybe?* Pointing them out had certainly caused Heylor to come to a decision quickly. The two demons had been some distance away, but Koria knew they would not be distant for long. That prediction had unfortunately turned out to be true. Despite Heylor's probabilistic tunneling, the demons were not far behind.

Pffft.

"Greenstone," Robert whispered. It was only just loud enough for Koria to hear over the cacophony that was Heylor Style flailing and scrambling in the marbles.

"Get up, you idiot!" Bat said, pulling the skinny man roughly to his feet. Koria knew that Bat could not see the demons yet. He had no ability to visualize the empyreal sky, but he accepted the fact that Skoll and Hati were coming. The great broken torus hung just ahead now, its shadow darkening the ground at their feet. It had been beautiful from afar, but close up its ruin spoke to a different and darker beauty. Enormous boulders littered the path, pieces of the structure that had broken away over the years. Koria had seen little of the Ardgour Wilderness. She had heard Robert's descriptions of the ruined castles and structures he had encountered, had listened to his retelling of Jeyn Lindseth's many philosophical musings on the abandoned county, but the stories could do no justice to the reality of experiencing firsthand what had been lost. Looking up at a pockmarked and cracked section of the outer ring, Koria took the awesome wreck before her as a renewed warning.

Pffft. Pffft.

A ringing sound echoed off the sheer walls of the bowl. Eloise had drawn her sword and stopped. She looked back toward Arsenault and the two transcendental beings that were rapidly approaching. "No," Koria called to her, "keep going."

"Because you have a plan, Koria?" Eloise hissed. "It's about time you revealed it."

Not yet.

"Soon," she shouted. She doubted that Eloise would like the idea she had been harboring, the plan she had been consciously *not* developing fully, the stratagem she had purposely kept nascent for fear of Nimrheal. *The demon may not be the only one to react with violence.*

She looked at her husband as he ran beside her. He was hanging back, keeping guard, protecting her. He was more than capable of pulling ahead, of reaching the finish line first and taking the Bifrost, but she knew he would not. *He* knew that neither running nor fighting had ever interested his wife. *Perhaps my idea will not surprise him at all.* But Robert also blazed in the empyreal sky. He had something to lose too.

As they passed under the perimeter of the great suspended aqueduct, the glass beads lessened, then disappeared. There were no more skolve bones either. Koria instantly assessed it as an important new line, a border different from, yet somehow the same as, the Castlereagh Line and, later, the wheat line. *Will Sköll and Hati stop there?* That would conform to the general theory, though the proximity of this line to Ardgour's apparatus and the Bifrost had been an unknown. No one had known about the bones or the beads then, and there were other questions too. Even if the apparatus was anathema before, when Huygens was high, would it remain so now? Koria would not speak of this, at least not yet. What was the point? If the theory was wrong, they were about to lose, almost certainly about to die. She did her best to continue running.

When they had reached about halfway between the perimeter of the torus and the central structure—perhaps far enough, though Koria could only guess at the right distance—she said, "Stay here, Bat, and watch our back trail. Skoll and Hati shouldn't cross the bone line."

The big man was a sweaty mess. Rivulets ran down his face, and his hair was matted. He could jog easily for miles, but he was not built for sprinting. Too out of breath to say anything, or perhaps seeing no need to, he only nodded and dropped back. Heylor, Eloise, Koria, and Robert kept on, slower now, more careful as they picked their way through the chaotic ruins of the crumbling aqueduct.

Pffft. Pffft.

"What's that?" gasped Heylor from twenty strides ahead. He slowed from a run to a jog, then to a walk, and stopped. "Oh, dear knights, no." Eloise stopped too, though they did not speak. Catching up, Koria and Robert saw what had caused Heylor to stop.

It was Sir Christensen. He was mounted on a black spear. Its dark blade protruded from his face. *Nimrheal can come even here.* It was an unfortunate complication for Koria's plan.

"I can't believe it," sputtered Heylor. "Christensen never hurt anyone. He was the nice—"

Koria brushed past and kept going, trying not to listen to Heylor's lament. There was no time to mourn the Deladieyr Knight. They were in the kairotic moment, at the center of the event or events that had spawned the loci. Behind the tragic figure of Christensen they made out a ridge, and just beyond that, a line of rocky graves. Six of them. Six signs that Nimrheal could operate this close to the Methueyn Bridge. Beyond the graves stood a central tower, the place to which all the spokes in the sky connected.

Pffft. Pffft.

Pffft. Pffft.

"You're too late," said the man in plate armor. He had been crouched behind a wagon- sized boulder, a piece of the toroid, fallen at some point in the past quarter millennium. His helm was off, and his long, thin blond hair was whirling around by the wind. Or perhaps it was the particles streaming by. His breastplate had the number nine embossed on it, and a two-handed sword was still in its scabbard on his hip. "My colleagues have already gone in to retrieve the Bridge." He smiled beatifically. "I expect they will kill and eat you when they come back."

Pffft. Pffft.

Pffft. Pffft.

Eloise took a step toward the Seygis Knight, but Koria whispered, "Wait," and although Eloise scowled, she obeyed.

"What makes you think your friends are coming back?" Koria asked the Nine.

"Your sign doesn't scare us!" he sneered.

"Sign?" Robert asked.

The knight drew his two-handed, five-foot-long blade. "Yes! The si—"

"So there's a message," Koria interrupted, having heard enough. "Good. Go ahead now, Eloise." *This Nine is irrelevant.* Her mind was already moving on, taking in the central tower, searching for the alleged message. Eloise raised her sword.

"No need for that," said the Nine, taking a step backwards. "I surrender," he said with a smirk, going down on his left knee.

Eloise's eyes caught Koria's. She had been told what the Nines had done to Hemdale's friend, Sir Kaimari, and about the poisoning of Sir Valcryst and Jormundheim, whom she had known from childhood. Koria nodded her head and Eloise charged the kneeling knight, swinging her sword in a flat arc. "I said I surrender!" he shouted, jumping backwards and bringing his sword up.

Pffft.

Eloise did not hesitate. She stepped into him and swung again. He caught her blade on his and, for a moment, held her off with two trembling hands, looking in desperation to Robert and then to Koria.

"You are being executed," Koria said evenly. It was all the explanation she was going to give to a poisoner and cannibal.

He pushed back on Eloise's sword to gain some distance and drew his sword back. "What ar—"

WHUMP!

The Nine ignited from inside his armor. His blond hair burned white. The air in his lungs ignited, smothering his screams, but his armor screeched from the thermal strain, the metal lending its horrific accompaniment to the man's dying groans. Koria was buffeted from a percussive set of hot and cold thermal waves. The stink of burning meat assaulted her next, but she had no time to be disgusted or to acknowledge the nausea it produced, no desire to remember the Battle of the Bifrost where she had first smelled the odor of roasted human flesh. She tried to breathe through her mouth and think only about the message the Nine had mentioned.

"He was mine, Robert!" Eloise shouted as Koria searched for the message,

Robert held up his hands in a conciliating gesture, "He didn't deserve you."

"Well … that's right," she replied grudgingly, "but next time, ask."

Pffft. Pffft.

"Try his friends if you're so bloodthirsty," suggested a horrified, shaking Heylor. He turned unbelieving eyes to Robert and said, "We should have taken him prisoner."

Robert was unmoved. He had fought Seygis Knights before. He had executed Knights of Armadale summarily too. "We aren't required to play their games." From the flatness of his voice, Koria did not think he was going to debate this decision later, as he had after the Battle of the Bifrost.

Eloise only answered Heylor's statement with a look of contempt.

"He was only surrendering until his friends came down with the Bifrost to kill us," Koria explained from her position beside the graves. As soon as the knight had ignited, she had started searching. "But he was wrong. His friends aren't coming back." She soon found what she was looking for: an old breastplate with recent markings etched on it. She read them out.

"Bifrost is in the tower.

Surrounded by poison.

Beware.

I did not cross."

~C

"Poison?" Heylor asked. "Is that what I keep seeing?"

"They are particles from greenstone," Robert said. "I've seen them before, though never as richly concentrated."

"It's part of how Ardgour changed the effect of the Bifrost," Koria added. "But it is not an insurmountable problem." She looked at Heylor, who was still having trouble with what had happened and said, "If you look up in the tower, you will see the three other Nines. None of them is nearly as strong as Christensen was. One of them has already collapsed on the lower stairs. One more got a floor higher but has almost stopped moving, and the last one is on her knees vomiting just outside the door leading to what has to be the Bifrost. It looks like a crystal, perhaps about the size of a human hand, though it is difficult for me to see clearly with all the breakdown around it. When it's time, you will use your gift to bring it here."

"I will?" said Heylor.

"When it's time?" asked Eloise.

Pffft. Pffft.

Koria looked at her friend, trying to read her expression. As often happened, she could not. The tall woman was so transparent in so many ways, yet perfectly opaque in others. *It is time to take the biggest chance of all.* Koria looked up at the sky. There were no storm clouds. Breathing out a sigh of relief, she said, "After we've decided what we are going to do with it."

▽

THAT WAS THE NUB OF KORIA'S SECRET PLAN. THE GREEN-EYED GIRL HAD ALWAYS LOVED her secrets and her subtle manipulations, and it always annoyed Eloise when she was kept on the outside of them. "Finally," she grunted. "Let's get on with it before we all die of this poison."

Pffft. Pffft.

"I think we can back off a little," Koria said, perhaps thinking about the damage those small particles must be doing to them, "now that we know where the Bridge is and can retrieve it any time we want."

"Robert!" Bat Merrett called, jogging up to them, telescope in one hand. "Hemdale is here. Well, almost. I just spotted him climbing the near bank of the river, but Skoll and Hati are between him and us."

"Skoll is here?" asked Heylor, face white.

"Yah," said Merrett laconically. "The reeking eight-foot-tall demon with one arm that I just saw could only be Skoll."

"What are they doing?" asked Koria.

"Let's go kill them!" demanded Eloise at the same moment.

Merrett frowned at Eloise and answered Koria. "They're marching back and forth. Down by the last of the bones. Watching, I suppose."

"I hate repeating myself," said Eloise, "but I think we should go and kill them. Right now."

"We can't," Koria replied. "Not yet. They're too powerful." She gave Eloise a look that she probably thought was stern. "I know we outnumber them, El, but if we step past the line of the bones now, we will all die."

Pffft.

Suddenly it made sense to Eloise, both the voice she had been hearing and Koria's determination to wait. She smiled. "Good plan, Koria. We lure them here, cross the Bridge, and *then* kill them."

Koria closed her eyes and blew out a breath. Opening her eyes again, she said, "No, Eloise. That's not the plan."

"Well, what the hell is it, then?"

"Go tunnel Hemdale past Skoll and Hati, Heylor, before he tries fighting both of them on his own," Robert said.

"And take a closer look at Skoll and Hati while you do that," added Koria.

Heylor and Bat ran off to do as Robert and Koria had asked.

Eloise did not miss Koria mouthing "Thank you" to Robert. Did he know what her plan was?

Though she said nothing, Eloise's frustration must have been obvious, since Koria now asked, "Do you trust me, Eloise? Can you trust me enough to wait just a few more minutes?"

Eloise *did* trust Koria. Most of the time, her small friend's plans were clever and effective. Very different from the ones Eloise would make—if Eloise ever made a plan—but always effective. So far, anyway. Still, Koria's words reminded her too much of her parents' hesitations on that tragic night long ago when waiting and planning had cost them their lives.

"Nothing good comes of waiting when something cries out to be done, Koria."

"Yes, if you know exactly what it is you should do, Eloise."

"Don't we?"

Pffft.

Robert started laughing. It was a strange sound to come at such a time from a man Eloise knew to have a long history of second-guessing himself. Perhaps he had finally changed.

"We don't," Robert said. "We never seem to know enough." He looked up at her and smiled. "Let's wait and hear Koria out. Besides, it can't be a disadvantage to have Sir Hemdale with us."

A great crashing sound echoed through the ruins behind them. Eloise whirled around, but there was too much rubble to make out what had caused it. A moment later, Sir Hemdale stumbled out of the rubble, Heylor beside him looking like a little boy next to the plate-armored, colossus and shaking more than usual. Hemdale was completely drenched—perhaps he had swum the river—but his eyes sparkled with excitement.

"Skoll threw a boulder at me!" exclaimed Heylor, wide-eyed either with fear or relief, or both.

"Doesn't matter," said Hemdale dismissively. "He missed."

"But he *remembers*," Heylor replied, still shaking.

Robert looked back toward the bone line. "Where is Bat?"

"He has taken cover, watching" said Hemdale. "You should know, as I have just informed Merrett, that a group of Seygis Knights may have left the battlefield to come this way before me," he added.

Heylor pointed a trembling hand at the burned-up knight, lying just visible in the rubble, halfway between them and the tower. "The other three are up there," he said in a small voice. "Dead." He seemed to hesitate, looking toward the tower. "Dead-*ish*, anyway."

Pffft.

"Good," was all Hemdale said to this.

"They aren't the only ones," said Robert. He told Hemdale about Christensen's grotesquely mounted body, which the grizzled old warrior had not yet seen, and about the message that brave knight had managed to scratch onto the old breast-plate before he died.

Hemdale had to see this for himself. When he came back from looking at Christensen, he went on to his next idea without comment. "We must cross the Bridge now. My brother has bought us our passage."

These words were music to Eloise's ears. Yet Koria had asked her to wait. *Robert* had asked her. For them, Eloise would wait. Then she would cross the Bifrost, grab her angel—whatever that meant—and *then* kill the demons.

"Eloise."

"Wait, uncle," she said. "Koria has something to tell us." She glared meaningfully at her friend. "Tell us. It's now or never."

"Very well," replied Koria. "You have all heard your names being called," she said. "I have been hearing mine too. Like you, again and again."

She paused. "I could cross with you now. There is an angel waiting for me too. Darday'l, in my case. Just as I know Robert keeps hearing Heydron, and Eloise Michael, I think, while Hemdale hears Volsang. We can all cross and join our angels."

"I haven't heard any voice," piped Heylor in a tiny voice that no one responded to.

"Let's do it, then," roared Hemdale.

"Wait," said Robert with a calmness that contrasted so sharply with the older knight's almost frantic tone that the other man, who was already turning as if to charge into the night at once, suddenly went still. Few people could make Hemdale stop and think, but it appeared that Robert was one of them. Perhaps Hemdale felt he owed Robert too.

Pffft.

Robert turned to his wife. It was if he knew what she was thinking. It was an invitation to proceed.

"We could cross together," Koria said again, then added, "just like the old Methueyn Knights did."

"Together!" Hemdale shouted, fiercely elated again, itching to move.

It sounded pretty good to Eloise too, but a part of her hesitated.

"We can be just like them," Koria continued. "We can fight as they did in the old days. And die like them."

"Why do you doubt us?" asked Eloise. "We have the new transform. You and Robert can use it on them. Even without that, Heylor took Skoll's *arm* off. *Heylor.* He's no warrior."

"Hey," whined Heylor.

Eloise ignored him. "They can be beaten!"

"Perhaps," responded Koria. She turned to Heylor, who was gazing at his shoes, deflated. "Did Skoll look the same today as when you took off his arm?"

"No," he replied, unconsciously looking over his shoulder toward the bone line. "He is way more powerful in the empyreal sky now. Heavier. His connection wasn't really a singularity before. And he stinks even more."

Pffft.

"How much more powerful?" Robert asked. "Twice? Five times? Ten?"

"Ten," Heylor said. "A hundred? It's a singularity."

Koria nodded. "That's what I thought. The Skoll that Heylor maimed is not the Skoll that's here today. We—together—might have won then, but we won't now."

"Knights damn it, how can you be so sure?" Hemdale growled.

"*Think*," Koria implored him. "Why have Skoll and Hati hidden away since the Methueyn War? Why did they come out only when Ardgour's apparatus started to fail?"

"It makes sense," Heylor interjected. "Keith's last words were all about this place and Skoll and Hati destroying Vercors. He thought they would come back and that they would win!"

This revelation was beyond belief. *That stupe knew all along!* "And you're just mentioning this now?" Eloise asked.

"Y-yes," Heylor replied, blanching. "I didn't believe it. I didn't think it meant anything."

"It didn't," Hemdale spat. "Keith Euyn was insane."

Robert sighed, "He seemed to be, but that doesn't mean everything in his dream was wrong. A few weeks ago, we saw a tower that had been blown down like dandelion spores in a storm. Later we saw another castle ruined as if a fist from heaven had smashed it open. That was Skoll and Hati back in the days when they were at their full power. As they now are again."

Eloise remembered the castle that she and Eoyan had explored with Gregory: Site 127, with its ruined portcullis. "Why haven't they fought us already if they're so powerful?" she asked, frustrated that matters were not simpler. "Why hasn't this turned into a fight already?"

"We stole the initiative," replied Robert. "We distracted them with the Aignen Legion, the urine dumps. Even Armadale's army helped. And the rest of us got here in ways they didn't expect. But our advantage won't last. Right now, we are standing in the only place where they won't come. The only place skolves won't come. And we have very little time to make the right decision."

"We won't get another chance either," Koria added. "But Skoll and Hati aren't even what is important here." Her eyes went to the central tower and then to Eloise. "As bad as they are, as difficult to kill as they might be, they are not the real problem. They never have been, any more than Armadale or the Nines have been. Nimrheal is the problem, and Nimrheal is very different from Skoll and Hati. The Bifrost cannot hold that thing off. And I don't think we can kill it either. I don't think it *can* be killed."

"How do you know that?"

Koria pointed at Robert. "He hit Nimrheal with enough electrons to burn down a forest. Once only a few miles from here and again in Ardvaser, but it wasn't killed. For centuries, others have tried to kill it, and some thought they had succeeded. They were *all* wrong. Nimrheal can't be killed because it isn't *alive*, not like we are, not in any sense we can understand. It is nothing like us. Where it comes from, where the angels of Elysium come from, is beyond our comprehension."

Koria looked at her husband. "We lost our daughter finding out how far over our heads we are." Then she looked at Hemdale. "I doubt we can kill Skoll and Hati now, the way they are, with Huygens as it is. But even if we do, Nimrheal will still be here and we will just go back to the way things used to be two hundred years ago, back to the dark ages. Nothing new. Nothing learned. No new inventions. No new poems, no new songs."

Pffft.

"So what in Hati's hell do you fucking propose we do, Koria?" Eloise was so frustrated she could hardly speak coherently. Her teeth grated as she spat out the question, and she could hear her heart pounding in her ears. "We have to do something. Let's hear your plan. Now! No more waiting."

Koria's eyebrows went up like a shrug. "We *destroy* the Methueyn Bridge. Heylor tunnels it here and then we smash it to pieces. If I am right, Nimrheal will be gone forever."

There was a stunned silence not unlike the aftermath of an unintentional shattering of antique, irreplaceable porcelain when, gazing down at the brittle, fragile pieces, no one dares to speak or move. But this silence was for a prospect much more terrible. Eloise was as stunned as everyone else, but for a different reason. Koria's plan was not subtle or complicated; it was *obvious*.

And it was unthinkable. There was only one Methueyn Bridge. No one alive today even knew how it worked. If they agreed to Koria's proposal, the Methueyn order would be lost forever. Elysium too.

"Are you serious?" asked Heylor in a timid voice. He was the person most likely to drop a precious ceramic cup, so perhaps it made sense that he should speak first. "I-I mean, what happens to Huygens then, to our dynamics?"

"I'm *sure* Nimrheal will be gone," replied Koria. Her eyes moved rapidly over the others, pausing on Hemdale, whose face looked like cracked granite, made fleeting contact with Robert's, then Eloise's eyes, and then went back to Heylor. "Huygens will be similar to how we have always known it, possibly a little lower, but not much. I doubt you will find tunneling people easy and safe afterward."

Pffft.

"But what about all the people who go to church? What will they do?" Heylor said in the same attenuated voice.

What kind of stupid question is that?

Eloise's first reaction to Heylor's question was almost instinctive, but then she remembered the liturgy at the Steel Castle, the appeal to the word of Elysium. That odd, random detail said a lot. She whispered, "It will destroy the Steel Castle."

Robert frowned. "No, but they will have to change. And drastically. Their liturgy is wrong anyway."

Robert had never cared for the Steel Castle, but his dismissive comment was too much for Eloise. "How would you know, stupe? You never go."

"Why do you speak blasphemy, nephew?" rumbled Hemdale.

"I don't," Robert replied, perhaps to both questions. "You said it yourself, Hemdale, the Methueyn Knights are about *ideas*, not answers. The ideas will still be there. Ideas never die."

Heylor wore a frown of his own now, as if retreating into a new, unusual silence. For her part, Eloise was not sure how much she cared that their actions would affect church services, or even if they ended up being branded as heretics, but the hypothetical consequences to the Steel Castle pointed to an underlying lack of certainty in Koria's plan. She searched her friend's face and asked, "You're sure about Nimrheal?"

Koria did not hesitate. "I'm sure that it's our only chance of stopping the thing."

"No…" breathed Hemdale, his normal granitic expression sliding into something else, something more desperate. "What about the old ways? The Methueyn Knights' whole purpose was to fight Nimrheal. They—we—can do it."

"In ten thousand years that has never worked. Nimrheal is beyond us, beyond anything we can do or anything we can become. Repeating the methods of past failures will never lead to new success." Koria said this flatly, as if simply repeating the thesis of an abstract argument. Bethyn would have rolled her eyes, but Eloise knew Koria was too wise to bait Sir Hemdale at such a moment.

"We aren't destroying it!" shouted Hemdale, his hard, scarred face completing its transformation to volcanic fury. "We should fight!"

"That's all we need," replied Koria calmly. "A return to the old days, to the fight everyone is expecting, except that people die in fights, and the old days were not as good as our romantic legends make them out to have been." She looked imploringly at Robert and raised her voice. "We don't need more steel, more force, more sharp blades and shattered hearts. We don't need extinct knights and absent angels to fight the same fights they fought—and lost—two hundred years ago. We don't need to become some kind of retrograde knights trying to bring back a failed past. We need a new solution."

Pffft.

"What do *you* think of Koria's plan, Sir Robert?" Hemdale's voice trembled. His hands were clenched white, his face a livid red. The ancient warrior's eyes blazed with barely suppressed fury.

Endicott's brows went slowly up, and his mouth showed the merest turn toward a wry smile. "It's what I had been planning to do anyway. Koria is right. The old ways won't work. They never did. We have to *change* the problem to *solve* the problem, even if that means taking on the burden of uncertainty." He spoke with no pretense, anger or caution, apparently unconcerned at how close to exploding Hemdale clearly was. At last he broke eye contact with the colossal knight and gazed up at the sky. "Taking on that burden means destroying the Bifrost."

Endicott seemed to be waiting. No one spoke. Only Hemdale's rasping breaths broke the silence until the younger knight looked at him again and said, "I was almost sure Nimrheal would come if I so much as said that aloud. But it didn't come when Koria proposed the idea … I don't think it will come now."

Pffft.

"Yeah," Heylor exclaimed, almost jumping up and down. "Why isn't Nimrheal here already? This idea is huge!"

Koria shook her head. "In all our research, we found only one inviolable rule about Nimrheal. It only comes once for any new idea. Sir Christensen saw the Bifrost but did not take it. Perhaps he thought of the idea first and paid for it. For us."

"You said yourself," she added, turning to Hemdale, "that he bought our passage."

"Your plan is insane," Hemdale sputtered. He shook his head as if arguing with himself, eyes bulging, face purple now, seemingly teetering on the precipice of some dangerous action yet unable to commit himself to it.

"We should do it," Heylor said abruptly. "People are hanging themselves in Vercors City, trying to bring back some magical solution from heaven. *That's* insane. They let a four-year-old girl hang herself. The *bishop* let it happen. Damn the Steel Castle and their liturgy."

"I'm not going to let this happen!" roared Hemdale, internal argument apparently over, drawing Sacrifice.

Pffft.

Moving more quickly than Eloise would have thought possible, Robert stepped in front of him, Likelihood in his hand.

Hemdale pulled his sword back as if to strike. Spittle spraying, he shouted, "Stay out of my way, nephew!"

"As at the embassy, Sir Hemdale?" Robert replied, not moving. "You would have killed that little boy. You were sure of yourself then too!"

Robert's words hit the old knight like a blow. He staggered but did not lower his sword. "This is completely different!"

"How? Because it's what *you* want?" Robert asked. "Take a moment and *think*! Don't blindly follow the same old idea you've followed your whole life." He smiled. It was gorgeous. Eloise saw him blaze in the empyreal sky. "Look around. We stand in the ruins of the yesterday, ruins left by people who made the same choice in the past that you want to make again today. We must—at last—do something new," he said, imploring Hemdale, "something unexpected, or nothing new is ever going to happen again." Then he sheathed Likelihood and calmly spread his arms, blazing still more brightly. "I swore to stop Nimrheal. I cannot think of a single other thing we can do that has the faintest chance of doing that."

"MOVE!" bellowed Hemdale.

Robert gestured to his wife. "Nimrheal will kill her if we don't do this. Then he will kill the next one who invents something. And on it will go forever. We can stop all that. What are the old fever dreams of dusty yesterday worth compared to protecting people now and for endless years to come? Are you going to throw countless future lives away to gratify your own passions? Are you going to strike me down just so you can act the great, indomitable knight?

"I must, and I will!" Tears flowed down the old man's face. He looked over his shoulder at Eloise. It was a plea.

Eloise knew the moment had come. If they had ten or fifteen more years, as the Lighthouse plan had originally stipulated, perhaps they would have known enough to make a different choice. Perhaps. But they did not. Eloise knew she had to take a stand. She nodded to herself, understanding. Yes, Koria's idea was deeply, painfully uncertain, as truly new ideas must be. That is why they tended to be avoided, as night after night her parents had avoided acknowledging that the time had come to abandon their country and leave their home. Until it had been too late. She thought of her own children, whom she had not seen in over a month, and the kind of world she wanted for them. She thought of those she needed to save. Eloise had lived her life struggling with the guilt of her parents' deaths and her frustration that they had not been brave enough to face reality. She did not want Ingrid and Egyl to suffer the same feelings about their mother's inability to face the truth.

I must choose here and now. I must be brave.

If Koria was right, the choice was a tradeoff between having heaven *with* Nimrheal or having neither. She looked at the great blade in her uncle's hands. *Only the deepest truths are written in steel.* She took three steps and stood beside Robert. "Show us what kind of knight you are, uncle," she said.

"We will be cut off from Elysium forever!" Hemdale cried, still holding Sacrifice aloft. "There will be no word from heaven. People won't know what to believe."

Eloise suddenly appreciated Robert's new equanimity, even his flashes of humor, which had earlier seemed out of place, for she suddenly found herself chuckling. "I don't know what heaven has to say other than my name." She remembered hanging on the rope back in the observatory. That wiped away her smile but reminded herself of something important. *Rising is an inward journey.* "Only a stupe thinks that certainty can come from somewhere else. Since when have you needed help knowing what to believe? You're plenty pig-headed all on your own."

"This is not about me," he replied mournfully.

"Right now it is." Eloise pointed to the massive sword in Hemdale's shaking, white-knuckled grip. "Do you see that, Uncle? That's Sacrifice. It was made for us. Now we must make a sacrifice of our own."

▽

WHILE THEY WAITED FOR BAT MERRETT TO REJOIN THEM, KORIA ASKED ELOISE WHAT had persuaded her there was no other way.

"*I am free.* That's what it says in the Treaty." Eloise shrugged. "And I never wanted to be a Methueyn Knight. Joining with some angel … it seems … wrong. It doesn't fit somehow." She smiled fiercely and added, "Eloise Kyre isn't the kind of woman who needs heaven in order to do what's right."

Koria could not help but be amused. Perhaps it was unsurprising that Eloise would make this choice, the only choice that could guarantee Nimrheal would never return. That creature had killed her Gregory, after all. And Eloise was her own woman. That had always been abundantly obvious. That Robert was going along with the plan—that he had independently had the same idea—was even less surprising. He shared Eleanor's dream: a world that could change and grow and progress. Still, for most, what they were about to do would come as a shock, an outrage. They would be condemned, perhaps despised, abominated. They were taking it upon themselves to choose for *everyone*, and not everyone was going to like it. Most will have expected a fight, a war, a continuation of the way things had been. *I don't know what the future will be, but at least it will not be held hostage by the past.*

Pffft.

As soon as Bat joined them, Koria laid out how the plan would be executed. "No one knows for sure what will happen when we smash the Bifrost, so Bat, you need to hit it from behind cover. *Completely* behind cover. The rest of us, except you, Heylor, will move off a little way."

"Are you afraid that you'll cross the Bridge if you get too close?" Heylor asked.

"Perhaps." Koria did not think that they could involuntarily cross and join with their angels, but she did not really know how the process of crossing worked, so she was taking no chances.

Bat scowled and said, "So you go off and hide over there while Heylor and I risk blowing ourselves up. Your plan isn't exactly inspiring confidence."

"I'll do it," offered Sir Hemdale.

"No," said Koria, not wanting Hemdale anywhere near the Bifrost. *Who knows what he might do if the Bifrost comes within his reach?* The big man's agreement was clearly still reluctant and fragile. "Bat will do it."

Merrett shook his head. "Great. I can't believe we're even calling this a plan."

The comment was transparently pro forma. Koria knew he would do as he was asked. A few minutes later, everyone had found their positions. Hemdale and Eloise both drew their swords. Irrationally, Koria thought. Heylor's eyes were huge again. He was gulping big, rapid breaths and looking back and forth between Koria, Robert, and the tower. "Now?" he asked.

"When you are ready," Robert supplied reassuringly.

"What stinks?" Eloise asked.

That was when the enormous rock hit Heylor in the face and Koria realized she had been wrong about something very, very important.

Chapter Forty-One

The Last Knight

WHEN THE ROCK SMASHED INTO HEYLOR'S FACE AND THE JITTERY MAN DISAPPEARED into the debris, Endicott also realized immediately that one of Koria's key assumptions had been wrong. *Skoll and Hati can cross the bone line now.*

Pffft.

Even as he opened himself to the empyreal sky, his mind formulated an explanation. He saw that Nehring Ardgour's greenstone apparatus and the Bifrost, working as a unit, had been anathema to the demons for two hundred and fifty years. Skoll and Hati had learned they could not approach closer because of the near-field Huygens effect and, possibly too, the breakdown energy from the greenstone. But when Huygens reverted to its old value and the apparatus failed, it had become possible for the demons to approach. Skoll and Hati had stopped at the bone line because that was what they had always done. They had not known, until just now, that conditions had changed and they could cross it. *While we argued, they figured it out. Or grew frustrated enough to overcome a quarter millennium of conditioning and try.*

"KNEEL AND BE SPARED!" intoned the demon, raising two arms in a grotesque benediction. Hati, Endicott realized. Almost amused, he ignored the melodramatic instruction and took a careful look at his foes. They were, indeed, very different from Nimrheal: solid, stable in form, fully invested in down-to-earth reality. And huge. They looked like two colossal men dressed in rags and rotting carpets. Rock cracked beneath their feet, tortured by heavy steps. Lightning played around their forms, arcing off their skin and their weapons. Hati carried an enormous axe, while Skoll had an incongruously small-looking sword shoved through a rough piece of rope tied around his waist.

Not exactly skilled in the arts of sewing.

It was a strange thought, seemingly banal, even inconsequential, but certain implications followed quickly. *They are not geniuses. They wear tatters and old tapestries because they can't make clothes of their own. They clearly want to be dressed but lack the skill to make even simple garments.* He thought about the rock that had hit Heylor. *A rock? They are all about brute strength because they are powerful, but they have no knowledge or skill of their own. Without their connection to the empyreal sky, they are less than us. No wonder they couldn't get anything done when Huygens changed. All they had was strength, and not enough of it back then.*

But they were enormously strong now. Endicott could see the black singularities they were tied into, infinite wells of power from elsewhere. The energy they drew was staggering. If the empyreal sky had sound, it would have roared. There was sound enough coming from them in the real world, from their percussive voices, to their thunderous steps, to their effect on the very air. Electrons danced around them, arcing out of the charged atmosphere, hissing as they struck the two demons.

It's coming from the greenstone. Hurting them? Yes.

Skoll and Hati constantly flinched and growled at the violent discharges. But they were too powerful now to be stopped by the greenstone alone. Perhaps too powerful to be stopped by anything.

Pffft.

We need to execute Koria's plan. Even that may not work, but it's the only chance we have.

"Robert."

He ignored the voice of Heydron and turned toward the tower. At the same moment, Koria struck, hammering Skoll with the discontinuous transform she and Bethyn had discovered, the Callum transform. It was a version of the same procedure Heylor had tried, more instinctively, when he and his eight had first encountered Skoll, but with a more appropriate basis function.

"AAAARGH!"

Out of the corner of his eye, Endicott saw the flash, then almost lost his footing as the sharp, explosive sound and percussive error waves of hot and cold hit him. He kept running but sensed that Skoll was not a heap of ashes, had somehow resisted Koria's dynamics. He risked a glance behind him. The demon's clothes, such as they had been, were gone, burned away, and its skin was red and bubbling. It was screaming, but it was not dying.

Skoll turned toward Koria, still roaring. She hit the demon again, this time using the Callum transform to smother its connection to elsewhere through the empyreal sky. It was the same innovation she had once tried against Nimrheal, but now tailored specifically for the discontinuous nature of Skoll's connection.

Skoll stumbled this time, its singularity diminished significantly. Then it screamed again and resumed its slow march toward Koria.

Run, Koria!

But Koria did not run. In fact, she ignored Skoll, who was closing on her. Koria's focus had shifted elsewhere.

Endicott looked around for Eloise, but she, Merrett, and Hemdale were all engrossed in close combat with Hati. With a discordant flash in the empyreal sky, Endicott saw Koria hit the demon with the same powerful innovation. Hati stumbled onto one knee, but then, with a growl, regained its footing and swung its axe in a whistling arc at Eloise. None of the others were in any position to break off and help Koria, even if they had known she was in danger.

Endicott skidded to a stop, his feet sliding on a band of frosted rock and almost flying out from under him. Climbing the tower and smashing the Bifrost would have to wait.

Pffft.

He had to do something, but it had to be something different. Instead of running away from Skoll, Koria had weakened both demons, but in a moment Skoll would reach her, and that would be the end. Blue-white lightning fizzed and sparked over the demon as it limped toward Endicott's beloved.

The power of the greenstone was amazing. When he had first looked through the sky at it, Endicott had been amazed. It was a pure source like nothing he had ever seen or imagined. It continuously transformed, discharging as it did so, and those discharges shot off everywhere, but disproportionately, into the demons. Desperate, he innovated a stream of dipoles, then drew Likelihood and charged toward Skoll. The minor, irritating thermal innovations could do little damage— he did not mean them to—but they angered the demon. It turned, distracted and enraged, then saw Endicott and abandoned Koria for the moment, intent on punishing the knight and his dazzling blade.

Committed to action now, Endicott said nothing as he closed with the colossal figure. There were no further questions to be asked, no negotiations to be made. He did not care what the demon might offer. Skoll did not belong in this world.

The first clash of swords told Endicott that Skoll carried a blade of similar excellence to Likelihood, perhaps an old Methueyn blade taken from a fallen knight, hundreds of years before. A wearer of rotted tapestry could never have made such a weapon or even conceived of it. It looked undersized in the giant demon's hands, but the initial exchange of blows confirmed that Skoll was much, much stronger than Endicott. The young man was as strong and as fast now as he had ever been. In combat, time travelled as slowly as ever for him, and thanks to Marielle Engel, he had forgiven himself and had no doubts about his purpose. But even after being hammered by Koria's Callum transform, Skoll was still stronger and faster.

Two things saved Endicott from being sliced into pieces in the opening seconds of the fight. One came from Koria, who peppered the demon with thermal and electrical innovations that harried and distracted the creature. The second was Endicott's own millisecond certainty. He found the correct heraldic lead time, a few hundred milliseconds, to give him an advantage in reaction time but without decoupling him from firm reality. This split-second jump on Skoll enabled him to side-step, block, or slide away from the demon's unsubtle but ceaseless overhand blows.

Suddenly Skoll flinched as a new and stronger wave of thermal dipoles hit it. Steam billowed off its titanic form in complex patterns, and Endicott lunged into the billows and hit the demon in the left abdomen. Sparks of static electricity leapt and flashed from Likelihood as it speared into the creature, only stopping on the edge of a massive rib.

"AARRGH!"

Go home. Endicott drew Likelihood back as the demon made a grab for the blade. Skoll's skin was incredibly hard. The same thrust would have punctured heavy gauge plate armor, but had barely made it to a rib. As strong as Endicott currently was, he knew it would take someone much stronger to do real damage to the demon.

Or something stronger than a sword.

He jumped just in time to keep his legs from being hacked off at the knees and struck back as hard as he could at the demon's neck. The creature blocked the blow with ease. Stray electrical discharges rolled up Endicott's sword, making him freeze in an involuntary muscle contraction. Skoll raised his sword to strike again.

WHUMP!

A flash of light blinded the young man and he fell backwards, knocked off his already precarious footing by the force of whatever Koria had done. He was hammered by a staccato series of painfully hot and bitingly cold waves. *Exact shaping?*

Shaking his head to clear his vision and trying to stand up at the same time, Endicott looked off to the side in time to see Sir Hemdale's left forearm hacked off by Hati. He missed hearing the knight's scream due to the buzzing in his own ears, but he saw the old man's face and the open-mouthed expression of incredulity on it. Eloise and Merrett charged the demon as Hemdale stumbled away.

We are losing.

It was no surprise. Koria had predicted defeat. Huygens was too low, and the demons, as a consequence, were too strong. But accepting this reality only drove Endicott to a new height of desperate resolve. *Where is Skoll now?*

On his feet at last, Endicott saw that the demon was at least not about to cut him in two. It had moved away and was throwing rocks at Koria now. A head-sized chunk of granite connected with her right hip and knocked her into the rubble. Skoll lurched slowly toward her prone body. closer to her now than Endicott was to either the demon or to Koria.

NOOO!

Trying to calm his frantically pounding heart, Endicott thought fast.

Whatever the risk, I must try something new. Now.

Likelihood threw off static electricity as he sheathed it. The breakdown of the constantly transforming greenstone was still all around them, thick and pervasive. Energized particles and flashes of light buzzed through the ruins, cutting destructive paths through the air. He thought about how the energy had killed three Seygis Knights before they could climb even a few flights of stairs. It was deadly at close range. That poison, together with the change in Huygens, had been enough to keep the demons away for hundreds of years. A flash of inspiration seized him. He remembered the experiment he had done in the lab with the greenstone when he had directed its breakdown, the procedure he had been tempted to try again when he visited the old mine.

I have an enormous, pure source of the material right here. I may be able to accelerate the breakdown, make an engine out of the greenstone, channel the particles.

Such a reckless act of dynamics would have been lethal under the regime of the old, higher Huygens modulus. It might be lethal still, but there was no time for additional theorizing and calibrating. There was only this instant and nothing more. It was all about probability, and Endicott had always had a wizard's instinct for such things.

CRRRRRRAAAK. CRRRRRRAAAK. CRRRRRRAAAK.

Ignoring the turmoil of lightning and thunder, Endicott reached into the sky and heedlessly wrested the change he needed out of the greenstone in the tower.

BZZZZZZZZAAAAAAAAACCCCH!

A blinding cone of light shot from the tower and punched a hole through Skoll's chest.

CRRRRRRAAAK. CRRRRRRAAAK. CRRRRRRAAAK. CRRRRRRAAAK. CRRRRRRAAAK. CRRRRRRAAAK.

An instant later, Endicott found himself writhing on the uneven, broken rocks. *Error wave?* If so, it was a very different kind from any operator artefact he had ever experienced. He was ice-cold, certainly, but the main problem was his muscles, which were locked in spasm from, he guessed, an electrical overload to his nervous system.

CRRRRRRAAAK. CRRRRRRAAAK.

What have I done now?

He unclenched his teeth and struggled to look up, hoping the thunder he heard was only the result of the strange electrical error wave he had produced, not a harbinger of Nimrheal.

CRRRRRRAAAK. CRRRRRRAAAK. CRRRRRRAAAK.

His hopes were dashed. An anvil of inky, black, roiling air rose above him, rising from the top of the torus to the top of the sky. Nimrheal was coming.

Fighting to unlock his spasming muscles, Endicott pushed himself to his feet. He looked around desperately for Koria and saw her sprawled beside a half ton chunk of rock. He ran to help her stand, but her legs collapsed under her. She could only manage a sitting position. Skoll lay smoking only a few steps away, a hole the size of a watermelon gaping in its massive chest.

"Nimrheal!" Koria shouted over the howling winds and the relentless barrage of lightning. "It's coming!"

CRRRRRRAAAK. CRRRRRRAAAK. CRRRRRRAAAK.

Fuck.

Endicott reluctantly let go of his wife's hand and gathered himself for another, final effort. The fight with Hati was going even worse for his friends than before. He made out Hemdale crawling toward the tower, nearing its open door, leaving a trail of blood from the stump of his left arm behind him. He still held his great entropic sword in his remaining hand, but the big knight looked to be permanently out of the fight. Bat Merrett lay on the rubble, clutching his side. His sword was nowhere to be seen. Hati stood directly above him, axe raised high.

BRAAAAAAAH.

Eloise appeared out of the wind and a sudden wall of rain just in time to get her shield between Merrett and the demon's blade.

"D-duck!" Endicott roared and innovated again.

BZZZZZZZZAAAAAAAACCCCH!

Hati's head evaporated in the beam of charged particles and light that shot out from the tower.

CRRRRRRAAAK. CRRRRRRAAAK. CRRRRRRAAAK.

Again Endicott found himself writhing on the ground, gripped in the vise-like, agonizing artefact of his innovation. He shivered and spasmed violently, beyond all self-control.

Nimrheal is almost here.

"Get up, Robert!"

It was Koria—she was standing crookedly now, looking down at him, her expression a strange meld of pity and panic—but still he could not make his muscles do what he told them to.

"Robert!" she cried a second time, and his muscles unlocked. He rolled to his knees, struggled to rise but failed. He could feel empyreal discharges emanating from somewhere nearby as Koria continued trying to get him to his feet. He could not see what was happening, but he could hear the soul-piercing, terrible screaming that he had come to know as the sonic signature of Nimrheal.

BRAAAAAAAAH.

His vision cleared. Nimrheal had arrived and was facing off against Eloise. It appeared to have just struck at her, but somehow she was still standing. Koria hit it with the Callum transform, but the demon only roiled and blurred more than ever.

It's the proximity to the Bifrost. Huygens was so low here in the near field now that the Bifrost had returned to its normative mode that Nimrheal was almost impossible to cut off from its empowering connection to hell. Or was it possible that Nimrheal simply could not be fought the same way twice?

BRAAAAAAAH.

Eloise used her shield to block the demon a second time. Risen, she had a power of her own, Endicott saw. She was even managing to keep her feet against the massive power of Nimrheal's repeated assaults.

"Fuck you, fucker!" Eloise shrieked as she unleashed her own answering torrent of blows, forcing the demon to take several steps backward. The big woman's fury was transcendent as she unleashed herself utterly on the demon that had killed Gregory. Endicott had to forcibly break himself from staring at the spectacle to assess the situation.

Where is Hemdale?

Looking desperately through the empyreal sky for the indomitable old warrior, he found him at last on the second flight of stairs in the tower, working his way upwards. Endicott did not know what Hemdale might do if he managed to reach the top, but there was nothing he could do to help or hinder the ancient knight. He got unsteadily to his feet, still fighting off the last of the spasms. "T-try d-dipoles," he said to Koria as he drew his sword with a trembling hand. He did not think he would survive a third attempt at using the greenstone. He doubted Nimrheal could be destroyed that way in any case.

It's down to Likelihood now.

Sir Hemdale rose to his feet when he reached the room with the Bifrost. He ignored the dead Nines as he passed them, he ignored his bleeding arm, the smell of ozone in the air, the strange metallic stink that pervaded the tower, and he ignored the great greenstone torus even as it shot poison through his body and made lightning dance along the keen edge of Sacrifice. He was dying, but it did not matter.

The Methueyn Bridge lay at his feet at last. His lifelong quest was complete.

"Hemdale."

The voice again. *What does it want from me?*

Gazing at the crystal, he finally beheld what he had dreamt of all his life. A bridge appeared to him, floating in the sky. He saw an image with his mind, a face he could not ken, heard words he did not understand. The words did not matter, the idea alone did. He knew he could cross and be reborn, transfigured.

"I always wanted the power to make a difference," he gasped, standing on the very edge of the Bridge.

▽

Even the rage and ferocity of Eloise Kyre had its limits. She had fought the demon to a standstill, but her breath was coming in great, heaving gasps now, and Nimrheal still floated and swirled with unnatural speed and grace. Blood flowed down her face from a spear thrust that had almost gone through her head. She had deflected it just far enough to avoid being killed on the spot, but now her left arm hung limp and her shield was gone.

Endicott sprinted to cover the distance as Nimrheal raised its spear to strike at Eloise again for what would surely be the last time. Likelihood sliced the demon's black metal spear, and what should have been an arm—in two. Nimrheal turned, a cloak of black vapor, there and absent, the shape of a man with one arm and then the shape of nothing with two arms. As indefinable as it was, it seemed to hesitate and study its broken spear for a moment. Endicott thought it looked at him then. Eloise stood up, sword ready again, standing firm beside her comrade. The demon flickered, its position impossible to fix. It seemed to bifurcate, materializing two steps to the left, then back where it had been.

CRRRRRRAAAK.

A new spear appeared in the demon's smoky, vibrating appendage.

"I always said you shouldn't fight without me," Eloise said, an incongruous, fierce smile on her face. "We'll take him together. For Gregory."

"T-that sounds … g-good," Endicott said, knowing that their fight would not end well. "F-for Gregory."

BRRROOOOOOMMMM!

The central tower exploded in a flash of blue light, throwing a thick cloud of tumbling rocks high into the air.

"Look out!" Eloise called as the glowing pieces rained down all around them.

▽

"What the fuck was that?" Eloise asked. The rocks had stopped crashing down and the dust was clearing rapidly, washed away by rain. The lightning, too, had stopped.

Koria stumbled over, limping badly. Her hip moved in grotesque jerks. Through teeth gritted in pain, she said, "That was the Bifrost. Hemdale must have smashed it with his sword."

"Well, that wouldn't have worked out so well for me, would it?" groaned Merrett from where he still lay helplessly on the ground. "Half the tower's gone."

So was Nimrheal.

And so, it turned out, was Hemdale. No one approached the broken tower or its deadly greenstone afterward, but extensive searches were made in the empyreal sky. There were no traces to be found of the crystal that was the Bifrost, or of Sir Hemdale and his sword.

▽

Heylor, surprisingly, was found alive, though unconscious, near the body of Sir Christensen. He had lost most of his teeth and broken his nose and the orbital bone of his left eye. He claimed, though a series of nervous grunts and rapid pantomime gestures, that he had seen the stone that Skoll had thrown at the last second and had been tunneling away from it just as he was hit. Otherwise, he boasted, his skull would have crushed. Whatever the truth of this, neither he, Koria, nor Merrett, who had several broken ribs, would be able to travel for some time.

Endicott recovered his pack and used the javelin to contact Ardvaser and request that the Aignen Legion send help as soon as it could, but the legion was engaged in widespread battles with skolves, and it was uncertain if, or how soon, help would arrive. It was apparent in using the javelin that the Huygens modulus was strong again. It felt only a little different from the days before Nimrheal had returned.

"We could have used that to ask for advice when we were deciding on the *plan*," Merrett said in a wheezy voice. Speaking and breathing hurt him, and now that the adrenaline from battle was spent, he could only manage a whisper, but his usual sarcasm came through clearly enough.

Endicott looked at Koria, then at Eloise. He remembered what Eloise had said earlier about what kind of woman she was.

He started laughing. "It was our decision to make."

"Yes," said Koria, but she was not laughing. It would be harder for her to forget all the horrific things that had happened.

Endicott's laughter faded away. "It was Hemdale's, actually. In the end. He stuck to his word."

Eloise nodded, blues eyes flashing. "The last Methueyn Knight."

And not so backward looking after all.

Selected people and places

† *WITHIN THE STORY* BREAKTHROUGH

Luciena Fortis, a seventeen-year-old wizard

Lady Auvigne, hostess and Princess of Engevelen

Lord Auvigne, host and Prince of Engevelen

Sir Darday'l, a Methueyn Knight

Sir Hasconeyt, a Deladieyr Knight

Gil Harbinger, Harbinger Wizard of Engevelen

Rodryck Cornell, a mathematician

Eydith, Rodryck's assistant

† *AT ARDVASER CASTLE OR ON THE CASTLEREAGH LINE*

Lord Kennyth Brice, the Duke of Vercors

Gerveault Heys, Senior Professor of Dynamics

Lord Arthur Wolverton, military commander

Sir Robert Endicott, Knight of Vercors

Koria Valcourt, Lady of Engevelen

Sir Eloise Kyre, Knight of Vercors

Sir Gregory Justice, Knight of Vercors

Bethyn Trail, a researcher at Ardvaser

Jeyn Lindseth, a lieutenant assigned to assist Robert

Bat Merrett, a lieutenant assigned to assist Robert

Eoyan March, a lieutenant assigned to assist Eloise

Eirnyn Quinn, a sergeant

Ildrys, a sergeant in Heylor's eight

Rhysheart, a corporal

Ida Yseult, a corporal in Heylor's eight

Emyr Wynn, a captain at the Castlereagh Line

Gael Guise, a sergeant at the Castlereagh Line

Lord Latimer, an agent for the duke

Vyrnus Hedt, a dynamics researcher

† Vercors - The Capitol City of the Duchy of Vercors

Eleanor Brice, former Duchess of Vercors, deceased

Heylor Style, a dynamicist, leader of an eight

Lynwen, a constable assigned to Heylor Style

Elyze Astarte, a senior herald at Rawles Trading Company

Arrayn Endicott, one of Robert's many uncles

Deryn Endicott, another of Robert's many uncles

Aunt Ellys, one of Roberts many aunts

Eryka Lyon, Chief Constable of Vercors

Edwyn Perry, Vice-Constable of Vercors

Syriol Lindseth, a young woman, cousin to Jeyn Lindseth

Kayne, a sergeant constable

† At the New School

Lady Gwenyfer, administrator of the Duchess's Program, deceased

Keith Euyn, Professor Emeritus of Dynamics, deceased, and inspiration for the story *The Lonely Wizard*

Meredeth Callum, Senior Professor of Mathematics

Annabelle Currik, Senior Professor of Physics

Davyn Daly, a student, deceased

Deleske Lachlan, a researcher

Camille Engel, a student

Shelley Style, a student

Lord Jon Indulf, a student, deceased

Jennyfer Gray, an arts student, deceased

Lil Hilliard, a dynamics researcher

Ailis Ellis, a medical researcher

Konrad Folke, a dynamics researcher, deceased

Rendell, a dynamics researcher, deceased

† Bron - a small farming town within the Duchy of Vercors

Meycal Endicott, Robert's long-dead father

Finlay Endicott, Robert's grandfather, deceased

Grandma, Robert's grandmother

✝ DELADIEYR KNIGHTS

Sir Racheyl Stirling, also known as Sir Ameleyn Forteys in *The Lonely Wizard*, deceased

Sir Hemdale, formerly a citizen of Armadale

Sir Christensen

Marielle Engel, a candidate

Sir Kaimari, from Neahon across the sea

Sir Sophia Haverland

Sir Leysbeth Braynor

Sir Janice Nitrai

Sir Jormundheim

Sir Chamyle Valcryst

✝ FROM ARMADALE

Albrecht Vernon, King of Armadale at the time of *The March of Sir Hemdale*

Imre Vernon, current King of Armadale

Dyre Vernon, Ambassador of Armadale at the time of the embassy siege

Reingard Vernon, young son of Dyre Vernon

Elias Vernon, current Ambassador of Armadale

Heinrich Bitten, a wizard

Sir Astrid Kettel, Royal Knight of Armadale

Eindride Kettel, Astrid's squire

Egil Stenner, Astrid's other squire

Veritas Kyre, Eloise's father

Aloysia Kyre, Eloise's mother

✝ Methueyn Knights

Urieyn, Angel of Music. Symbol, a blazing sun. First day of the week, Ursday

Sendeyl, Angel of Endurance. Symbol, a broken sandal. Second day of the week, Senday

Michael, Angel of War, usually male. Symbol, a great sword. Third day of the week, Michsday

Heydron, Angel of Protection, usually female. Symbol, a shield. Fourth day of the week Heyday

Darday'l, Angel of Knowledge. Symbol, a scroll hung on a maul. Fifth day of the week, Darday.

Volsang, Angel of Righteous Vengeance. Symbol, an axe. Sixth day of the week, Volsday

Hervor, Angel of Warning. Symbol, a bursting horn. Seventh day of the week, Hersday

Leylah, Angel of Night, usually female. Symbol, a crescent moon. Eighth day of the week, Leyday

✝ Seygis Knights

Sir Seygis, the heretical Ninth Knight. Symbol, a man in black plate armor or the number nine

Sir Penrod

Sir Heykon

Sir Steygur

† Transcendental beings

Nimrheal, a demon who punishes creativity. Absent since the end of the Methueyn War

Skoll, a demon who first appeared during the Methueyn War

Hati, a demon who first appeared in the Methueyn War

Acknowledgements

Thank you to my test readers George Fairs, Lori Hunt, Dr. Greg Arkos, Cheryl Kendall, Lyda Mclallen, Graham Hack, and Leah Bray. Thank you, Eric Street, for the gonzo inspiration. Shawn Crawford, psychology professor at Mount Royal University, was a very helpful resource. Thankfully, he never seemed to tire of my questions regarding the causes and effects of trauma.

John McAllister, my editor, also showed great patience and editorial acumen. He never tired of talking about commas, proper nouns, and capitalization. Not many are willing to do that, especially for fantasy novels where the author can arbitrarily and perniciously decide what noun is proper and what is not. Jared Shapiro is the person responsible for the creative typesetting of the novel, and Jeff Brown designed the equally interesting and unique cover. Nimrheal would surely slay both Jared and Jeff. It is imperative that I thank Lyda Mclallen a second time. She is my marketing advisor, but in truth, she coordinated just about everything that needed to be done to get this book into your hands.

And thank you, reader. I am selfishly glad you took the time to read my book. Having no one read your book is like having no one to tell a joke to. It is like talking to yourself. It's okay with me if some parts of the book were upsetting to read. Some parts were upsetting to write. If you want to argue about something in the book, so much the better. Reading, having some contrary thought, getting into a civilized argument, those are all good things. All those things get us out of the echo chambers of our own minds.

About The Author

After having the last rights read to him at the age of twenty-five, Lee Hunt came to appreciate the power of catharsis. He was born on a farm with only one working lung but has gone on to become an Ironman triathlete, sport rock climber, professional geophysicist, and writer.

As a Scientist, Lee has published close to fifty papers, articles, or expanded abstracts, has been awarded numerous technical awards, and was even sent on a national speaking tour. He enjoys discussing the amorality of science and is useful at parties in explaining the physics of whether fracture stimulation might be a risk to the fuzzy, cuddly things of nature. After 28 years trying to understand the earth as a geophysicist, Lee turned to writing fiction. He now spends time hiking, cycling, floundering in a lake, clinging desperately to a wall, or at his desk trying to write an entertaining story.